THE SECRET GARDEN

A LITTLE PRINCESS

LITTLE LORD FAUNTLEROY

Frances Hodgson Burnett

octopus

Frances Hodgson Burnett was born in England in 1849 and emigrated to America in 1865 where the family struggled against poverty until Frances began to get her stories published at the age of nineteen. Her first full-length novel (published 1877) about Manchester was a great success and brought her fame and wealth.

Little Lord Fauntleroy was her first and most famous book for children (published in 1886) and Cedric was modelled on her own son. Cedric's clothes set the fashion for the Fauntleroy suit for fifty years. Mrs. Hodgson Burnett wrote many novels and books for children, the best known being *A Little Princess* (published 1905), the rewritten version of her earlier story *Sarah Crewe*, and *The Secret Garden* (published in 1911).

She died in 1924 on Long Island.

This edition first published in Great Britain in 1978 by
Octopus Books Limited
59 Grosvenor Street London W.1.

© 1978 illustrations Octopus Books Limited
ISBN 0 7064 0781 4
Printed in Czechoslovakia

Illustrated by Gareth Floyd

THE SECRET GARDEN

A LITTLE PRINCESS

LITTLE LORD FAUNTLEROY

Frances Hodgson Burnett

THE SECRET GARDEN

THE SECRET GARDEN

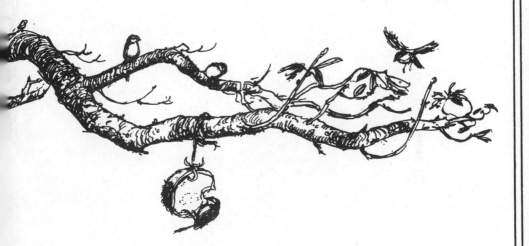

Frances Hodgson Burnett

Contents

List of Illustrations

1 There is No One Left

When Mary Lennox was sent to Misselthwaite Manor to live with her uncle, everybody said she was the most disagreeable-looking child ever seen. It was true, too. She had a little thin face and a little thin body, thin light hair and a sour expression. Her hair was yellow, and her face was yellow because she had been born in India and had always been ill in one way or another. Her father had held a position under the English Government and had always been busy and ill himself, and her mother had been a great beauty who cared only to go to parties and amuse herself with gay people. She had not wanted a little girl at all, and when Mary was born she handed her over to the care of an Ayah, who was made understand that if she wished to please the Memsahib she must keep the child out of sight as much as possible. So when she was a sickly, fretful, ugly little baby she was kept out of the way, and when she became a sickly, fretful, toddling thing she was kept out of the way also. She never remembered seeing familiarly anything but the dark faces of her Ayah and the other native servants, and as they always obeyed her and gave her her own way in everything, because the Memsahib would be angry if she was disturbed by her crying, by the time she was six years old she was as tyrannical and selfish a little pig as ever lived. The young English governess who came to teach her to read and write disliked her so much that she gave up her place in three months, and when other governesses came to try to fill it they always went away in a shorter time than the first one. So if Mary had not chosen really to want to know how to read books, she would never have learned her letters at all.

One frightfully hot morning, when she was about nine years old, she awakened feeling very cross, and she became crosser still when she saw that the servant who stood by her bedside was not her Ayah.

'Why did you come?' she said to the strange woman. 'I will not let you stay. Send my Ayah to me.'

The woman looked frightened, but she only stammered that the Ayah could not come, and when Mary threw herself into a passion and beat and kicked her, she looked only more frightened and repeated that it was not possible for the Ayah to come to Missie Sahib.

There was something mysterious in the air that morning. Nothing was done in its regular order and several of the native servants seemed missing, while those whom Mary saw slunk or hurried about with ashy and scared faces. But no one would tell her anything, and her Ayah did not come. She was actually left alone as the morning went on, and at last wandered out into the garden and began to play by herself under a tree near the veranda. She pretended that she was making a flower-bed, and she stuck big scarlet hibiscus blossoms into little heaps of earth, all the time growing more and more angry and muttering to herself the things she would say and the names she would call Saidie when she returned.

'Pig! Pig! Daughter of Pigs!' she said, because to call a native a pig is the worst insult of all.

She was grinding her teeth and saying this over and over again when she heard her mother come out on the veranda with someone. She was with a fair young man, and they stood talking together in low strange voices. Mary knew the fair young man who looked like a boy. She had heard that he was a very young officer who had just come from England. The child stared at him, but she stared most at her mother. She always did this when she had a chance to see her, because the Memsahib – Mary used to call her that oftener than anything else – was such a tall, slim, pretty person and wore such lovely clothes. Her hair was like curly silk and she had a delicate little nose which seemed to be disdaining things, and she had large laughing eyes. All her clothes were thin and floating, and Mary said they were 'full of lace'. They looked fuller of lace than ever this morning, but her eyes were not laughing at all. They were large and scared and lifted imploringly to the fair boy officer's face.

'Is it so very bad? Oh, is it?' Mary heard her say.

'Awfully,' the young man answered in a trembling voice. 'Awfully, Mrs. Lennox. 'You ought to have gone to the hills two weeks ago.'

The Memsahib wrung her hands.

'Oh, I know I ought!' she cried. 'I only stayed to go to that silly dinner-party. What a fool I was!'

At that moment such a loud sound of wailing broke out from the servants' quarters that she clutched the young man's arm, and Mary stood shivering from head to foot. The wailing grew wilder and wilder.

'What is it? What is it?' Mrs. Lennox gasped.

'Someone has died,' answered the boy officer. 'You did not say it had broken out among your servants.'

'I did not know!' the Memsahib cried. 'Come with me! Come with me!' and she turned and ran into the house.

After that, appalling things happened, and the mysteriousness of the morning was explained to Mary. The cholera had broken out in its most fatal form and people were dying like flies. The Ayah had been taken ill in the night, and it was because she had just died that the servants had wailed in the huts. Before the next day three other servants were dead and others had run away in terror. There was panic on every side, and dying people in all the bungalows.

During the confusion and bewilderment of the second day Mary hid herself in the nursery and was forgotten by everyone. Nobody thought of her, nobody wanted her, and strange things happened of which she knew nothing. Mary alternately cried and slept through the hours. She only knew that people were ill and that she heard mysterious and frightening sounds. Once she crept into the dining-room and found it empty, though a partly finished meal was on the table and chairs and plates looked as if they had been hastily pushed back when the diners rose suddenly for some reason. The child ate some fruit and biscuits, and being thirsty she drank a glass of wine which stood nearly filled. It was sweet, and she did not know how strong it was. Very soon it made her intensely drowsy, and she went back to her nursery and shut herself in again, frightened by cries she heard in the huts and by the hurrying sound of feet. The wine made her so sleepy that she could scarcely keep her eyes open, and she lay down on her bed and knew nothing more for a long time.

Many things happened during the hours in which she slept so heavily, but she was not disturbed by the wails and the sound of things being carried in and out of the bungalow.

When she awakened she lay and stared at the wall. The house was perfectly still. She had never known it to be so silent before. She heard neither voices nor footsteps, and wondered if everybody had got well of the cholera and all the trouble was over. She wondered also who would take care of her now her Ayah was dead. There would be a new Ayah, and perhaps she would know some new stories. Mary had been rather tired of the old ones. She did not cry because her nurse had died. She was not an affectionate child and had never cared much for anyone. The noise and hurrying about and wailing over the cholera had frightened her, and she had been angry because no one seemed to remember that she was alive. Everyone was too panic-stricken to think of a little girl no one was fond of. When people had the cholera it seemed that they remembered nothing but themselves. But if everyone had got well again, surely someone would remember and come to look for her.

But no one came, and as she lay waiting the house seemed to grow more and more silent. She heard something rustling on the matting, and when she looked down she saw a little snake gliding along and watching her with eyes like jewels. She was not frightened, because he was a harmless little thing who would not hurt her, and he seemed in a hurry to get out of the room. He slipped under the door as she watched him.

'How queer and quiet it is', she said. 'It sounds as if there was no one in the bungalow but me and the snake.'

Almost the next minute she heard footsteps in the compound, and then on the veranda. They were men's footsteps, and the men entered the bungalow and talked in low voices. No one went to meet or speak to them, and they seemed to open doors and look into rooms.

'What desolation!' she heard one voice say, 'That pretty, pretty woman! I suppose the child, too. I heard there was a child, though no one ever saw her.'

Mary was standing in the middle of the nursery when they opened the door a few minutes later. She looked an ugly, cross little thing and was frowning because she was beginning to be hungry and feel disgracefully neglected. The first man who came in was a large officer she had once seen talking to her father. He looked tired and troubled, but when he saw her he was so startled that he almost jumped back.

'Barney!' he cried out. 'There is a child here! A child alone! In a place like this! Mercy on us, who is she?'

'I am Mary Lennox,' the little girl said, drawing herself up stiffly. She thought the man was very rude to call her father's bungalow 'A place like this!' 'I fell asleep when everyone had the cholera and I have only just wakened up. Why does nobody come?'

'It is the child no one ever saw!' exclaimed the man, turning to his companions. 'She has actually been forgotten!'

'Why was I forgotten?' Mary said, stamping her foot. 'why does nobody come?'

The young man whose name was Barney looked at her very sadly. Mary even thought she saw him wink his eyes as if to wink tears away.

'Poor little kid!' he said. 'There is nobody left to come.'

It was in that strange and sudden way that Mary found out that she had neither father nor mother left; that they had died and been carried away in the night, and that the few native servants who had not died also had left the house as quickly as they could get out of it, none of them even remembering that there was a Missie Sahib. That was why the place was so quiet. It was true that there was no one in the bungalow but herself and the little rustling snake.

2 Mistress Mary Quite Contrary

Mary had liked to look at her mother from a distance, and she had thought her very pretty, but as she knew very little of her, she could scarcely have been expected to love her or to miss her very much when she was gone. She did not miss her at all, in fact, and as she was a self-absorbed child she gave her entire thought to herself, as she had always done. If she had been older she would no doubt have been very anxious at being left alone in the world, but she was very young, and as she had always been taken care of, she supposed she always would be. What she thought was that she would like to know if she was going to nice people, who would be polite to her and give her her own way as her Ayah and the other native servants had done.

She knew that she was not going to stay at the English clergyman's house where she was taken at first. She did not want to stay. The English clergyman was poor and he had five children all nearly the same age and they wore shabby clothes and were always quarrelling and snatching toys from each other. Mary hated their untidy bungalow and was so disagreeable to them that after the first day or two nobody would play with her. By the second day they had given her a nickname which made her furious.

It was Basil who thought of it first. Basil was a little boy with impudent blue eyes and a turned-up nose, and Mary hated him. She was playing by herself under a tree, just as she had been playing the day the cholera broke out. She was making heaps of earth and paths for a garden and Basil came and stood near to watch her. Presently he got rather interested and suddenly made a suggestion.

'Why don't you put a heap of stones there and pretend it is a rockery?' he said. 'There in the middle,' and he leaned over her to point.

'Go away!' cried Mary. 'I don't want boys. Go away!'

For a moment Basil looked angry, and then he began to tease. He was always teasing his sisters. He danced round and round her and made faces and sang and laughed.

> Mistress Mary, quite contrary,
> How does your garden grow?
> With silver bells, and cockle shells,
> And marigolds all in a row.

He sang it until the other children heard and laughed, too; and the crosser Mary got, the more they sang 'Mistress Mary Quite Contrary'; and after that as long as she stayed with them they called her 'Mistress Mary Quite Contrary' when they spoke of her to each other, and often when they spoke to her.

'You are going to be sent home,' Basil said to her, 'at the end of the week. And we're glad of it.'

'I am glad of it, too,' answered Mary. 'Where is home?'

'She doesn't know where home is!' said Basil, with seven-year-old scorn. 'It's England, of course. Our grandmamma lives there, and our sister Mabel was sent to her last year. You are not going to your grandmamma. You have none. You are going to your uncle. His name is Mr Archibald Craven.'

'I don't know anything about him,' snapped Mary.

'I know you don't,' Basil answered. 'You don't know anything. Girls never do. I heard Father and Mother talking about him. He lives in a great, big, desolate old house in the country, and no one goes near him. He's so cross he won't let them, and they wouldn't come if he would let them. He's a hunchback and he's horrid.'

'I don't believe you,' said Mary; and she turned her back and stuck her fingers in her ears, because she would not listen any more.

But she thought over it a great deal afterward; and when Mrs. Crawford told her that night that she was going to sail away to England in a few days and going to her uncle, Mr. Archibald Craven, who lived at Misselthwaite Manor, she looked so stony and stubbornly uninterested that they did not know what to think about her. They tried to be kind to her, but she only turned her face away when Mrs. Crawford attempted to kiss her, and held herself stiffly when Mr. Crawford patted her shoulder.

'She is such a plain child,' Mrs. Crawford said pityingly afterward. 'And her mother was such a pretty creature. She had a very pretty manner, too, and Mary has the most unattractive ways I ever saw in a child. The children call her "Mistress Mary Quite Contrary", and though it's naughty of them, one can't help understanding it.'

'Perhaps if her mother had carried her pretty face and her pretty manners oftener into the nursery, Mary might have learned some pretty ways, too. It is very sad, now the poor beautiful thing is gone, to remember that many people never even knew that she had a child at all.'

'I believe she scarcely ever looked at her,' sighed Mrs. Crawford. 'When her Ayah was dead there was no one to give a thought to the little thing. Think of the servants running away and leaving her all alone in that deserted bungalow. Colonel McGrew said he nearly jumped out of his skin when he opened the door and found her standing by herself in the middle of the room.'

Mary made the long voyage to England under the care of an officer's wife, who was taking her children to leave them in a boarding-school. She was very much absorbed in her own little boy and girl, and was rather glad to hand the child over to the woman Mr. Archibald Craven sent to meet her in London. The woman was his housekeeper at Misselthwaite Manor, and her name was Mrs. Medlock. She was a stout woman, with very red cheeks and sharp black eyes. She wore a very purple dress, a black silk mantle with jet fringes on it, and a black bonnet with purple velvet flowers which stuck up and trembled when she moved her head. Mary did not like her at all, but as she very seldom liked people, there was nothing remarkable in that; besides which it was very evident Mrs. Medlock did not think much of her.

'My word! she's a plain little piece of goods!' she said. 'And we'd heard that her mother was a beauty. She hasn't handed much of it down, has she, ma'am?'

'Perhaps she will improve as she grows older,' the officer's wife said good-naturedly. 'If she were not so sallow and had a nicer expression, her features are rather good. Children alter so much.'

'She'll have to alter a good deal,' answered Mrs. Medlock. 'And there's nothing likely to improve children at Misselthwaite – if you ask me!'

They thought Mary was not listening because she was standing a little apart from them at the window of the private hotel they had gone to. She was watching the passing buses and cabs and people, but she heard quite well and was made very curious about her uncle and the place he lived in. What sort of a place was it, and what would he be like? What was a hunchback? She had never seen one. Perhaps there were none in India.

Since she had been living in other people's houses and had had no Ayah, she had begun to feel lonely and to think queer thoughts which were new to her. She had begun to wonder why she had never seemed to belong to anyone even when her father and mother had been alive. Other children seemed to belong to their fathers and mothers, but she had never seemed to really be anyone's little girl. She had had servants, and food and clothes, but no one had taken any notice of her. She did not know that this was because she was a disagreeable child; but then, of course, she did not know she was disagreeable. She often thought that other people were, but she did not know that she was so herself.

She thought Mrs. Medlock the most disagreeable person she had ever seen, with her common, highly coloured face and her common fine bonnet. When the next day they set out on their journey to Yorkshire, she walked through the station to the railway carriage with her head up and trying to keep as far away from her as she could, because she did not want to seem to belong to her. It would have made her very angry to think people imagined she was her little girl.

But Mrs. Medlock was not in the least disturbed by her and her thoughts. She was the kind of woman who would 'stand no nonsense from young ones'. At least, that is what she would have said if she had been asked. She had not wanted to go to London just when her sister Maria's daughter was going to be married, but she had a comfortable, well-paid place as housekeeper at Misselthwaite Manor, and the only way in which she could keep it was to do at once what Mr. Archibald Craven told her to do. She never dared even to ask a question.

'Captain Lennox and his wife died of the cholera,' Mr. Craven had said in his short, cold way, 'Captain Lennox was my wife's brother and I am their daughter's guardian. The child is to be brought here. You must go to London and bring her yourself.'

So she packed her small trunk and made the journey.

Mary sat in her corner of the railway carriage and looked plain and fretful. She had nothing to read or to look at, and she had folded her thin little black-gloved hands in her lap. Her black dress made her look yellower than ever, and her limp light hair straggled from under her black crêpe hat.

'A more marred-looking young one I never saw in my life,' Mrs. Medlock thought. (Marred is a Yorkshire word and means spoiled and pettish.) She had never seen a child who sat so still without doing anything; and at last she got tired of watching her and began to talk in a brisk, hard voice.

'I suppose I may as well tell you something about where you are going to,' she said. 'Do you know anything about your uncle?'

'No,' said Mary.

'Never heard your father and mother talk about him?'

'No,' said Mary, frowning. She frowned because she remembered that her father and mother had never talked to her about anything in particular. Certainly they had never told her things.

'Humph,' muttered Mrs. Medlock, staring at her queer, unresponsive little face. She did not say any more for a few moments, and then she began again.

'I suppose you might as well be told something – to prepare you. You are going to a queer place.'

Mary said nothing at all, and Mrs. Medlock looked rather discomfited by her apparent indifference, but after taking a breath, she went on.

'Not but that it's a grand big place in a gloomy way, and Mr. Craven's proud of it in his way – and that's gloomy enough, too. The house is six hundred years old, and it's on the edge of the moor, and there's near a hundred rooms in it, though most of them's shut up and locked. And there's pictures and fine old furniture and things that's been there for ages, and there's a big park round it and gardens and trees with branches trailing to the ground – some of them.' She paused and took another breath. 'But there's nothing else,' she ended suddenly.

Mary had begun to listen in spite of herself. It all sounded so unlike India, and anything new rather attracted her. But she did not intend to look as if she were interested. That was one of her unhappy, disagreeable ways. So she sat still.

'Well,' said Mrs. Medlock. 'What do you think of it?'

'Nothing,' she answered. 'I know nothing about such places.'

That made Mrs. Medlock laugh a short sort of laugh.

'Eh!' she said. 'But you are like an old woman. Don't you care?'

'It doesn't matter,' said Mary, 'whether I care nor not.'

'You are right enough there,' said Mrs. Medlock. 'It doesn't. What you're to be kept at Misselthwaite Manor for I don't know, unless because it's the easiest way. *He's* not going to trouble himself about you, that's sure and certain. He never troubles himself about no one.'

She stopped herself as if she had just remembered something in time.

'He's got a crooked back,' she said. 'That's set him wrong. He was a sour young man and got no good of all his money and big place till he was married.'

Mary's eyes turned towards her, in spite of her intention not to seem to care. She had never thought of the hunchback's being married, and she was a trifle surprised. Mrs. Medlock saw this, and as she was a talkative woman, she continued with more interest. This was one way of passing some of the time, at any rate.

'She was a sweet, pretty thing, and he'd have walked the world over to get her a blade o' grass she wanted. Nobody thought she'd marry him, but she did, and people said she married him for his money. But she didn't – she didn't,' positively. 'When she died——'

Mary gave a little involuntary jump.

'Oh! did she die?' she exclaimed, quite without meaning to. She had just remembered a French fairy story she had once read called *Riquet à la Houppe*. It had been about a poor hunchback and a beautiful princess, and it had made her suddenly sorry for Mr. Archibald Craven.

'Yes, she died,' Mrs. Medlock answered. 'And it made him queerer than ever. He cares about nobody. He won't see people. Most of the time he goes away, and when he is at Misselthwaite he shuts himself up in the West Wing and won't let anyone but Pitcher see him. Pitcher's an old fellow, but he took care of him when he was a child and he knows his ways.'

It sounded like something in a book, and it did not make Mary feel cheerful. A house with a hundred rooms, nearly all shut up and with their doors locked – a house on the edge of a moor – whatsoever a moor was – sounded dreary. A man with a crooked back who shut himself up also! She stared out of the window with her lips pinched together, and it seemed quite natural that the rain should have begun to pour down in grey slanting lines and splash and stream down the window-panes. If the pretty wife had been alive, she might have made things cheerful by being something like her own mother and by running in and out and going to parties as she had done in frocks 'full of lace'. But she was not there any more.

'You needn't expect to see him, because ten to one you won't,' said Mrs. Medlock. 'and you mustn't expect that there will be people to talk to you. You'll have to play about and look after yourself. You'll be told what rooms you can go into and what rooms you're to keep out of. There's gardens enough. But when you're in the house don't go wandering and poking about. Mr. Craven won't have it.'

'I shall not want to go poking about,' said sour little Mary; and just as suddenly as she had begun to be rather sorry for Mr. Archibald Craven, she began to cease to be sorry and to think he was unpleasant enough to deserve all that had happened to him.

And she turned her face towards the streaming panes of the window of the railway carriage and gazed out at the grey rain-storm which looked as if it would go on for ever and ever. She watched it so long and steadily that the greyness grew heavier and heavier before her eyes and she fell asleep.

3 Across the Moor

She slept a long time, and when she awakened Mrs. Medlock had
bought a lunch-basket at one of the stations, and they had some
chicken and cold beef and bread-and-butter and some hot tea. The
rain seemed to be streaming down more heavily than ever, and
everybody in the station wore wet and glistening waterproofs. The
guard lighted the lamps in the carriage, and Mrs. Medlock cheered up
very much over her tea and chicken and beef. She ate a great deal, and
afterwards fell asleep herself, and Mary sat and stared at her and
watched her fine bonnet slip on one side until she herself fell asleep
once more in the corner of the carriage, lulled by the splashing of the
rain against the windows. It was quite dark when she awakened again.
The train had stopped at a station and Mrs. Medlock was shaking her.

'You have had a sleep!' she said. 'It's time to open your eyes!
We're at Thwaite Station, and we've got a long drive before us.'

Mary stood up and tried to keep her eyes open while Mrs.
Medlock collected her parcels. The little girl did not offer to help her,
because in India native servants always picked up or carried things,
and it seemed quite proper that other people should wait on one.

The station was a small one, and nobody but themselves seemed to
be getting out of the train. The station-master spoke to Mrs. Medlock
in a rough, good-natured way, pronouncing his words in a queer broad
fashion which Mary found out afterwards was Yorkshire.

'I see tha's got back,' he said. 'An' tha's browt th' young 'un with
thee.'

'Aye, that's her,' answered Mrs. Medlock, speaking with a
Yorkshire accent herself and jerking her head over her shoulder
towards Mary. 'How's thy missus?'

'Well enow. Th' carriage is waitin' outside for thee.'

A brougham stood on the road before the little outside platform. Mary saw that it was a smart carriage and that it was a smart footman who helped her in. His long waterproof coat and the waterproof covering of his hat were shining and dripping with rain as everything was, the burly station-master included.

When he shut the door, mounted the box with the coachman, and they drove off, the little girl found herself seated in a comfortably cushioned corner, but she was not inclined to go to sleep again. She sat and looked out of the window, curious to see something of the road over which she was being driven to the queer place Mrs. Medlock had spoken of. She was not at all a timid child, and she was not exactly frightened, but she felt that there was no knowing what might happen in a house with a hundred rooms nearly all shut up – a house standing on the edge of a moor.

'What is a moor?' she said suddenly to Mrs. Medlock.

'Look out of the window in about ten minutes and you'll see,' the woman answered. 'We've got to drive five miles across Missel Moor before we get to the Manor. You won't see much because it's a dark night, but you can see something.'

Mary asked no more questions, but waited in the darkness of her corner, keeping her eyes on the window. The carriage lamps cast rays of light a little distance ahead of them, and she caught glimpses of the things they passed. After they had left the station they had driven through a tiny village and she had seen whitewashed cottages and the lights of a public house. Then they had passed a church and a vicarage and a little shop window or so in a cottage with toys and sweets and odd things set out for sale. Then they were on the high road, and she saw hedges and trees. After that there seemed nothing different for a long time – or at least it seemed a long time to her.

At last the horses began to go more slowly, as if they were climbing up-hill, and presently there seemed to be no more hedges and no more trees. She could see nothing, in fact, but a dense darkness on either side. She leaned forward and pressed her face against the window just as the carriage gave a big jolt.

'Eh! We're on the moor now sure enough,' said Mrs. Medlock.

The carriage lamps shed a yellow light on a rough-looking road which seemed to be cut through bushes and low-growing things which ended in the great expanse of dark apparently spread out before and around them. A wind was rising and making a singular, wild, low, rushing sound.

'It's – it's not the sea, is it?' said Mary, looking round at her companion.

'No, not it,' answered Mrs. Medlock. 'Nor it isn't fields nor mountains, it's just miles and miles and miles of wild land that nothing grows on but heather and gorse and broom, and nothing lives on but wild ponies and sheep.'

'I feel as if it might be the sea, if there were water on it,' said Mary. 'It sounds like the sea just now.'

'That's the wind blowing through the bushes,' Mrs. Medlock said. 'It's a wild, dreary enough place to my mind, though there's plenty that likes it – particularly when the heather's in bloom.'

On and on they drove through the darkness, and though the rain stopped, the wind rushed by and whistled and made strange sounds. The road went up and down, and several times the carriage passed over a little bridge beneath which water rushed very fast with a great deal of noise. Mary felt as if the drive would never come to an end, and that the wide, bleak moor was a wide expanse of black ocean through which she was passing on a strip of dry land.

'I don't like it,' she said to herself. 'I don't like it,' and she pinched her thin lips more tightly together.

The horses were climbing up a hilly piece of road when she first caught sight of a light. Mrs. Medlock saw it as soon as she did, and drew a long sigh of relief.

'Eh, I am glad to see that bit o' light twinkling,' she exclaimed. 'It's the light in the lodge windows. We shall get a good cup of tea after a bit, at all events.'

It was 'after a bit', as she said, for when the carriage passed through the park gates there was still two miles of avenue to drive through, and the trees (which nearly met overhead) made it seem as if they were driving through a long dark vault.

They drove out of the vault into a clear space and stopped before

'*A very small, odd little black figure*'

an immensely long but low-built house, which seemed to ramble round a stone court. At first Mary thought that there were no lights at all in the windows, but as she got out of the carriage she saw that one room in a corner upstairs showed a dull glow.

The entrance door was a huge one made of massive, curiously shaped panels of oak studded with big iron nails and bound with great iron bars. It opened into an enormous hall, which was so dimly lighted that the faces in the portraits on the walls and the figures in the suits of armour made Mary feel that she did not want to look at them. As she stood on the stone floor she looked a very small, odd little black figure, and she felt as small and lost and odd as she looked.

A neat, thin old man stood near the manservant who opened the door for them.

'You are to take her to her room,' he said in a husky voice. 'He doesn't want to see her. He's going to London in the morning.'

'Very well, Mr. Pitcher,' Mrs. Medlock answered. 'So long as I know what's expected of me, I can manage.'

'What's expected of you, Mrs. Medlock,' Mr. Pitcher said, 'is that you make sure that he's not disturbed and that he doesn't see what he doesn't want to see.'

And when Mary Lennox was led up a broad staircase and down a long corridor and up a short flight of steps and through another corridor and another, until a door opened in a wall and she found herself in a room with a fire in it and a supper on a table.

Mrs. Medlock said unceremoniously:

'Well, here you are! This room and the next are where you'll live – and you must keep to them. Don't you forget that!'

It was in this way Mistress Mary arrived at Misselthwaite Manor, and she had perhaps never felt quite so contrary in all her life.

4 Martha

When she opened her eyes in the morning it was because a young housemaid had come into her room to light the fire and was kneeling on the hearth-rug raking out the cinders noisily. Mary lay and watched her for a few moments and then began to look about the room. She had never seen a room at all like it, and thought it curious and gloomy. The walls were covered with tapestry with a forest scene embroidered on it. There were fantastically dressed people under the trees, and in the distance there was a glimpse of the turrets of a castle. There were hunters and horses and dogs and ladies. Mary felt as if she were in the forest with them. Out of a deep window she could see a great climbing stretch of land which seemed to have no trees on it, and to look rather like an endless, dull, purplish sea.

'What is that?' she said, pointing out of the window.

Martha, the young housemaid, who had just risen to her feet, looked, and pointed also.

'That there?' she said.

'Yes.'

'That's th' moor,' with a good-natured grin. 'Does tha' like it?'

'No,' answered Mary. 'I hate it.'

'That's because tha'rt not used to it,' Martha said going back to her hearth. 'Tha' thinks it's too big an' bare now. But tha' will like it.'

'Do you?' inquired Mary.

'Aye, that I do,' answered Martha, cheerfully polishing away at the grate. 'I just love it. It's none bare. It's covered wi' growin' things as smells sweet. It's fair lovely in spring an' summer when th' gorse an' broom an' heather's in flower. It smells o' honey an' there's such a lot o' fresh air – an' th' sky looks so high an' th' bees an' skylarks makes such a noise hummin' an' singing'. Eh! I wouldn't live away from th' moor for anythin'.'

Mary listened to her with a grave, puzzled expression. The native servants she had been used to in India were not in the least like this. They were obsequious and servile and did not presume to talk to their masters as if they were their equals. They made salaams and called them 'protector of the poor' and names of that sort. Indian servants were commanded to do things, not asked. It was not the custom to say 'Please' and 'Thank you', and Mary had always slapped her Ayah in the face when she was angry. She wondered a little what this girl would do if one slapped her in the face. She was a round, rosy, good-natured looking creature, but she had a sturdy way which made Mistress Mary wonder if she might not even slap back – if the person who slapped her was only a little child.

'You are a strange servant,' she said from her pillows, rather haughtily.

Martha sat up on her heels, with her blacking-brush in her hand, and laughed, without seeming the least out of temper.

'Eh! I know that,' she said. 'If there was a grand missus at Misselthwaite I should never have been even one of th' under-housemaids. I might have been let to be scullery-maid, but I'd never have been let upstairs. I'm too common an' I talk too much Yorkshire. But this is a funny house for all it's so grand. Seems like there's neither master nor mistress except Mr. Pitcher and Mrs. Medlock. Mr. Craven, he won't be troubled about anythin' when he's here, an' he's nearly always away. Mrs. Medlock gave me th' place out o' kindness. She told me she could never have done it if Misselthwaite had been like other big houses.'

'Are you going to be my servant?' Mary asked, still in her imperious little Indian way.

Martha began to rub her grate again.

'I'm Mrs. Medlock's servant,' she said stoutly. 'And she's Mr. Craven's – but I'm to do the housemaid's work up here an' wait on you a bit. But you don't need much waitin' on.'

'Who is going to dress me?' demanded Mary.

Martha sat up on her heels again and stared. She spoke in broad

Yorkshire in her amazement.

'Canna' tha' dress thysen?' she said.

'What do you mean? I don't understand your language,' said Mary.

'Eh! I forgot,' Martha said. 'Mrs. Medlock told me I'd have to be careful or you wouldn't know what I was sayin'. I mean can't you put on your own clothes?'

'No,' answered Mary, quite indignantly. 'I never did in my life. My Ayah dressed me, of course.'

'Well,' said Martha, evidently not in the least aware that she was impudent, 'it's time tha' should learn. Tha' cannot begin younger. It'll do thee good to wait on thysen a bit. My mother always said she couldn't see why grand people's children didn't turn out fair fools – what with nurses an' bein' washed an' dressed an' took out to walk as if they was puppies!'

'It is different in India,' said Mistress Mary disdainfully. She could scarcely stand this.

But Martha was not at all crushed.

'Eh! I can see it's different,' she answered almost sympathetically. 'I dare say it's because there's such a lot o' blacks there instead o' respectable white people. When I heard you was comin' from India I thought you was a black too.'

Mary sat up in bed, furious.

'What!' she said. 'What! You thought I was a native. You – you daughter of a pig!'

Martha stared and looked hot.

'Who are you callin' names?' she said. 'You needn't be so vexed. That's not th' way for a young lady to talk. I've nothin' against th' blacks. When you read about 'em in tracts they're always very religious. You always read as a black's a man an' a brother. I've never seen a black, an' I was fair pleased to think I was goin' to see one close. When I come in to light your fire this mornin' I crep' up to your bed an' pulled th' cover back careful to look at you. An there you was,' disappointedly, 'no more black than me – for all you're so yeller.'

Mary did not even try to control her rage and humiliation.

'You thought I was a native! You dared! You don't know anything about natives! They are not people – they're servants who must salaam to you. You know nothing about India. You know nothing about anything!'

She was in such a rage and felt so hopeless before the girl's simple stare, and somehow she suddenly felt so horribly lonely and far away from everything she understood and which understood her, that she threw herself face downward on the pillows and burst into passionate sobbing. She sobbed so unrestrainedly that good-natured Yorkshire Martha was a little frightened and quite sorry for her. She went to the bed and bent over her.

'Eh! you mustn't cry like that there!' she begged. 'You mustn't for sure. I didn't know you'd be vexed. I don't know anythin' about anythin' – just like you said. I beg your pardon, miss. Do stop cryin'.'

There was something comforting and really friendly in her queer Yorkshire speech and sturdy way which had a good effect on Mary. She gradually ceased crying and became quiet. Martha looked relieved.

'It's time for thee to get up now,' she said. 'Mrs. Medlock said I was to carry tha' breakfast an' tea an' dinner into th' room next to this. It's been made into a nursery for thee. I'll help thee on with thy clothes if tha'll get out of bed. If th' buttons are at th' back tha' cannot button them up tha'self.'

When Mary at last decided to get up, the clothes Martha took from the wardrobe were not the ones she had worn when she arrived the night before with Mrs. Medlock.

'Those are not mine,' she said. 'Mine are black.'

She looked the thick white wool coat and dress over, and added with cool approval:

'Those are nicer than mine.'

'These are th' ones tha' must put on,' Martha answered. 'Mr. Craven ordered Mrs. Medlock to get 'em in London. He said, "I won't have a child dressed in black wanderin' about like a lost soul," he said. "I'd make the place sadder than it is. Put colour on her." Mother she said she knew what he meant. Mother always knows what a body means. She doesn't hold with black hersel'.'

'I hate black things,' said Mary.

The dressing process was one which taught them both something. Martha had 'buttoned up' her little sisters and brothers, but she had never seen a child who stood still and waited for another person to do things for her as if she had neither hands nor feet of her own.

'Why doesn't tha' put on tha' own shoes?' she said when Mary quietly held out her foot.

'My Ayah did it,' answered Mary, staring. 'It was the custom.'

She said that very often – 'It was the custom.' The native servants were always saying it. If one told them to do a thing their ancestors had not done for a thousand years they gazed at one mildly and said, 'It is not the custom' and one knew that was the end of the matter.

It had not been the custom that Mistress Mary should do anything but stand and allow herself to be dressed like a doll, but before she was ready for breakfast she began to suspect that her life at Misselthwaite Manor would end by teaching her a number of things quite new to her – things such as putting on her own shoes and stockings, and picking up things she let fall. If Martha had been a well-trained fine young lady's-maid she would have been more subservient and respectful and would have known that it was her business to brush hair, and button boots, and pick things up and lay them away. She was, however, only an untrained Yorkshire rustic who had been brought up in a moorland cottage with a swarm of little brothers and sisters who had never dreamed of doing anything but waiting on themselves and on the younger ones who were either babies in arms or just learning to totter about and tumble over things.

If Mary Lennox had been a child who was ready to be amused she would perhaps have laughed at Martha's readiness to talk, but Mary only listened to her coldly and wondered at her freedom of manner. At first she was nor at all interested, but gradually, as the girl rattled on in her good-tempered, homely way, Mary began to notice what she was saying.

'Eh! you should see 'em all,' she said. 'There's twelve of us an' my father only gets sixteen shilling a week. I can tell you my mother's put to it to get porridge for 'em all. They tumble about on th' moor an' play there all day, an' mother says th' air of th' moor fattens 'em. She says she believes they eat th' grass same as th' wild ponies do. Our Dickon, he's twelve years old and he's got a young pony he calls his own.'

'Where did he get it?' asked Mary.

'He found it on th' moor with its mother when it was a little one, an' he began to make friends with it an' give it bits o' bread an' pluck young grass for it. And it got to like him so it follows him about an' it lets him get on its back. Dickon's a kind lad an' animals like him.'

Mary had never possessed an animal pet of her own and had always thought she should like one. So she began to feel a slight interest in Dickon, and as she had never been interested in anyone but herself, it was the dawning of a healthy sentiment. When she went into the room which had been made into a nursery for her, she found that it was rather like the one she had slept in. It was not a child's room, but a grown-up person's room, with gloomy old pictures on the walls and heavy old oak chairs. A table in the centre was set with a good, substantial breakfast. But she had always had a very small appetite, and she looked with something more than indifference at the first plate Martha set before her.

'I don't want it,' she said.

'Tha' doesn't want thy porridge!' Martha exclaimed incredulously.

'No.'

'Tha' doesn't know how good it is. Put a bit o' treacle on it or a bit o' sugar.'

'I don't want it,' repeated Mary.

'Eh!' said Martha. 'I can't abide to see good victuals go to waste. If our children was at this table they'd clean it bare in five minutes.'

'Why?' asked Mary coldly.

'Why!' echoed Martha. 'Because they scarce ever had their stomachs full in their lives. They're as hungry as young hawks an' foxes.'

'I don't know what it is to be hungry,' said Mary, with the indifference of ignorance.

Martha looked indignant.

'Well, it would do thee good to try it. I can see that plain enough,' she said outspokenly. 'I've no patience with folks as sits an' just stares at good bread an' meat. My word! don't I wish Dickon and Phil an'

Jane an' th' rest of 'em had what's here under their pinafores.'

'Why don't you take it to them?' suggested Mary.

'It's not mine,' answered Martha stoutly. 'An' this isn't my day out. I get my day out once a month same as the rest. Then I go home an' clean up for mother an' give her a day's rest.'

Mary drank some tea and ate a little toast and some marmalade.

'You wrap up warm an' run out an' play you,' said Martha. 'It'll do you good and give you some stomach for your meat.'

Mary went to the window. There were gardens and paths and big trees, but everything looked dull and wintry.

'Out? Why should I go out on a day like this?'

'Well, if tha' doesn't go out tha'lt have to stay in, an' what has tha' got to do?'

Mary glanced about her. There was nothing to do. When Mrs. Medlock had prepared the nursery she had not thought of amusement. Perhaps it would be better to go and see what the gardens were like.

'Who will go with me?' she inquired.

Martha stared.

'You'll go by yourself,' she answered. 'You'll have to learn to play like other children does when they haven't got sisters and brothers. Our Dickon goes off on th' moor by himself an' plays for hours. That's how he made friends with th' pony. He's got sheep on th' moor that knows him, an' birds as comes an' eats out of his hand. However little there is to eat, he always saves a bit o' his bread to coax his pets.'

It was really this mention of Dickon which made Mary decide to go out, though she was not aware of it. There would be birds outside, though there would not be ponies or sheep. They would be different from the birds in India, and it might amuse her to look at them.

Martha found her coat and hat for her and a pair of stout little boots and she showed her her way downstairs.

'If tha' goes round that way tha'll come to th' gardens,' she said, pointing to a gate in a wall of shrubbery. 'There's lots o' flowers in summer-time, but there's nothin' bloomin' now.' She seemed to hesitate a second before she added, 'One of th' gardens is locked up. No one has been in it for ten years.'

'Why?' asked Mary in spite of herself. Here was another locked door that added to the hundred in the strange house.

'Mr. Craven had it shut when his wife died so sudden. He won't let no one go inside. It was her garden. He locked th' door an' dug a hole and buried th' key. There's Mrs. Medlock's bell ringing – I must run.'

After she was gone Mary turned down the walk which led to the door in the shrubbery. She could not help thinking about the garden which no one had been into for ten years. She wondered what it would look like and whether there were any flowers still alive in it. When she had passed through the shrubbery gate she found herself in great gardens, with wide lawns and winding walks with clipped borders. There were trees, and flower-beds, and evergreens clipped into strange shapes, and a large pool with an old grey fountain in its midst. But the flower-beds were bare and wintry and the fountain was not playing. This was not the garden which was shut up. How could a garden be shut up? You could always walk into a garden.

She was just thinking this, when she saw that, at the end of the path she was following, there seemed to be a long wall, with ivy growing over it. She was not familiar enough with England to know that she was coming upon the kitchen-gardens where the vegetables and fruit were growing. She went towards the wall and found that there was a green door in the ivy, and that it stood open. This was not the closed garden evidently, and she could go into it.

She went through the door and found that it was a garden with walls all around it and that it was only one of several walled gardens which seemed to open into one another. She saw another open green door, revealing bushes and pathways between beds containing winter vegetables. Fruit-trees were trained flat against the wall, and over some of the beds there were glass frames. The place was bare and ugly enough, Mary thought, as she stood and stared about her. It might be nicer in summer, when things were green, but there was nothing pretty about it now.

Presently an old man with a spade over his shoulder walked through the door leading from the second garden. He looked startled when he saw Mary, and then touched his cap. He had a surly old face, and did not seem at all pleased to see her – but then she was displeased with his garden and wore her 'quite contrary' expression, and certainly did not seem at all pleased to see him.

'What is this place?' she asked.

'One o' th' kitchen-gardens,' he answered.

'What is that?' said Mary, pointing through the other green door.

'Another of 'em,' shortly. 'There's another on t'other side o' th' wall an' there's th' orchard t'other side o' that.'

'Can I go in them?' asked Mary.

'If tha' likes. But there's nowt to see.'

· Mary made no response. She went down the path and through the second green door. There she found more walls and winter vegetables and glass frames, but in the second wall there was another green door and it was not open. Perhaps it led into the garden which no one had seen for ten years. As she was not at all a timid child and always did what she wanted to do, Mary went to the green door and turned the handle. She hoped the door would not open, because she wanted to be sure she had found the mysterious garden – but it did open quite easily and she walked through it and found herself in an orchard. There were walls all around it also and trees trained against them, and there were bare fruit-trees growing in the winter-browned grass – but there was no green door to be seen anywhere. Mary looked for it, and yet when she entered the upper end of the garden she had noticed that the wall did not seem to end with the orchard, but to extend beyond it as if it enclosed a place at the other side. She could see the tops of trees above the wall, and when she stood still she saw a bird with a bright red breast sitting on the topmost branch of one of them, and suddenly he burst into his winter song – almost as if he had caught sight of her and was calling to her.

She stopped and listened to him, and somehow his cheerful, friendly little whistle gave her a pleased feeling – even a disagreeable little girl may be lonely, and the big closed house and big bare moor and big bare gardens had made this one feel as if there was no one left in the world but herself. If she had been an affectionate child, who had been used to being loved, she would have broken her heart, but even though she was 'Mistress Mary Quite Contrary' she was desolate, and the bright-breasted little bird brought a look into her sour little face which was almost a smile. She listened to him until he flew away. He was not like an Indian bird, and she liked him and wondered if she should ever see him again. Perhaps he lived in the mysterious garden and knew all about it.

Perhaps it was because she had nothing whatever to do that she thought so much of the desired garden. She was curious about it, and wanted to see what it was like. Why had Mr. Archibald Craven buried the key? If he had liked his wife so much why did he hate her garden? She wondered if she should ever see him but she knew that if she did she should not like him, and he would not like her, and that she should only stand and stare at him and say nothing, though she should be wanting dreadfully to ask him why he had done such a queer thing.

'People never like me and I never like people,' she thought. 'And I never can talk as the Crawford children could. They were always talking and laughing and making noises.'

She thought of the robin and of the way he seemed to sing his song at her, and as she remembered the tree-top he perched on she stopped rather suddenly on the path.

'I believe that tree was in the secret garden – I feel sure it was,' she said. 'There was a wall round the place and there was no door.'

She walked back into the first kitchen-garden she had entered and found the old man digging there. She went and stood beside him and watched him a few moments in her cold little way. He took no notice of her, and so at last she spoke to him.

'I have been into the other gardens,' she said.

'There was nothin' to prevent thee,' he answered crustily.

'I went into the orchard.'

'There was no dog at th' door to bite thee,' he answered.

'There was no door there into the other garden,' said Mary.

'What garden?' he said in a rough voice, stopping his digging for a moment.

'The one on the other side of the wall,' answered Mistress Mary. 'There were trees there – I saw the tops of them. A bird with a red breast was sitting on one of them, and he sang.'

To her surprise the surly old weather-beaten face actually changed its expression. A slow smile spread over it and the gardener looked quite different. It made her think that it was curious how much nicer a person looked when he smiled. She had not thought of it before.

He turned about to the orchard side of his garden and began to whistle – a low, soft whistle. She could not understand how such a surly man could make such a coaxing sound.

Almost the next moment a wonderful thing happened. She heard a soft little rushing flight through the air – and it was the bird with the red breast flying to them, and he actually alighted on the big clod of earth quite near to the gardener's foot.

'Here he is,' chuckled the old man, and then he spoke to the bird as if he were speaking to a child.

'Where has tha' been, tha' cheeky little beggar?' he said. 'I've not seen thee before today. Has tha' begun tha' courtin' this early in th' season? Tha'rt too for'ard.'

The bird put his tiny head on one side and looked up at him with his soft bright eye, which was like a black dewdrop. He seemed quite familiar and not the least afraid. He hopped about and pecked the earth briskly, looking for seeds and insects. It actually gave Mary a queer feeling in her heart, because he was so pretty and cheerful and seemed so like a person. He had a tiny plump body and a delicate beak, and slender delicate legs.

'Will he always come when you call him?' she asked almost in a whisper.

'Aye, that he will. I've knowed him ever since he was a fledgling. He come out of th' nest in th' other garden, an' when first he flew over th' wall he was too weak to fly back for a few days an' we got friendly. When he went over th' wall again th' rest of th' brood was gone an' he was lonely an' he come back to me.'

'What kind of a bird is he?' Mary asked.

'Doesn't tha' know? He's a robin redbreast, an' they're th' friendliest, curiousest birds alive. They're almost as friendly as dogs – if you know how to get on with 'em. Watch him peckin' about there an' lookin' round at us now an' again. He knows we're talkin' about him.'

It was the queerest thing in the world to see the old fellow. He looked at the plump little scarlet-waistcoated bird as if he were both proud and fond of him.

'He's a conceited one,' he chuckled. 'He likes to hear folk talk about him. An' curious – bless me, there never was his like for curiosity an' meddlin'. He's always comin' to see what I'm plantin'. He knows all th' things Mester Craven never troubles hissel' to find out. He's th' head gardener, he is.'

The robin hopped about, busily pecking the soil, and now and then stopped and looked at them a little. Mary thought his black dewdrop eyes gazed at her with great curiosity. It really seemed as if he were finding out all about her. The queer feeling in her heart increased.

'Where did the rest of the brood fly to?' she asked.

'There's no knowin'. The old ones turn 'em out o' their nest an' make 'em fly an' they're scattered before you know it. This one was a knowin' one an' he knew he was lonely.'

Mistress Mary went a step nearer to the robin and looked at him very hard.

'I'm lonely,' she said.

She had not known before that this was one of the things which made her feel sour and cross. She seemed to find it out when the robin looked at her and she looked at the robin.

The old gardener pushed his cap back on his bald head and stared at her a minute.

'Art tha' th' little wench from India?' he asked.

Mary nodded.

'Then no wonder tha'rt lonely. Tha'lt be lonelier before tha's done,' he said.

He began to dig again, driving his spade deep into the rich black garden soil, while the robin hopped about, very busily employed.

'What is your name?' Mary inquired.

He stood up to answer her.

'Ben Weatherstaff,' he answered, and then he added with a surly chuckle, 'I'm lonely mysel' except when he's with me,' and he jerked his thumb towards the robin. 'He's th' only friend I've got.'

'I have no friends at all,' said Mary. 'I never had. My Ayah didn't like me and I never played with anyone.'

It is a Yorkshire habit to say what you think with blunt frankness, and old Ben Weatherstaff was a Yorkshire moor man.

'Tha' an' me are a good bit alike,' he said. 'We was wove out of th' same cloth. We're neither of us good-lookin' an' we're both of us as sour as we look. We've got the same nasty tempers, both of us, I'll warrant.'

This was plain speaking, and Mary Lennox had never heard the truth about herself in her life. Native servants always salaamed and submitted to you, whatever you did. She had never thought much about her looks, but she wondered if she was as unattractive as Ben Weatherstaff, and she also wondered if she looked as sour as he had looked before the robin came. She actually began to wonder also if she was 'nasty-tempered'. She felt uncomfortable.

Suddenly a clear rippling little sound broke out near her and she turned round. She was standing a few feet from a young apple-tree, and the robin had flown on to one of its branches and had burst out into a scrap of a song. Ben Weatherstaff laughed outright.

'What did he do that for?' asked Mary.

'He's made up his mind to make friends with thee,' replied Ben. 'Dang me if he hasn't took a fancy to thee.'

'To me?' said Mary, and she moved towards the little tree softly and looked up.

'Would you make friends with?' she said to the robin, just as if she were speaking to a person. 'Would you?' And she did not say it either in her hard little voice or in her imperious Indian voice, but in a tone so soft and eager and coaxing that Ben Weatherstaff was as surprised as she had been when she heard him whistle.

'Why,' he cried out, 'tha' said that as nice an' human as if tha' was a real child instead of a sharp old woman. Tha' said it almost like Dickon talks to his wild things on th' moor.'

'Do you know Dickon?' Mary asked, turning round rather in a hurry.

'Everybody knows him. Dickon's wanderin' about everywhere. Th' very blackberries an' heather-bells knows him. I warrant th' foxes shows him where their cubs lies an' th' skylarks doesn't hide their nests from him.'

Mary would have liked to ask some more questions. She was

almost as curious about Dickon as she was about the deserted garden. But just as that moment the robin, who had ended his song, gave a little shake of his wings, spread them, and flew away. He had made his visit and had other things to do.

'He has flown over the wall!' Mary cried out, watching him. 'He has flown into the orchard – he has flown across the other wall – into the garden where there is no door!'

'He lives there,' said old Ben. 'he came out o' th' egg there. If he's courtin', he's makin' up to some young madam of a robin that lives among th' old rose-trees there.'

'Rose-trees,' said Mary. 'Are there rose-trees?'

Ben Weatherstaff took up his spade again and began to dig.

'There was ten year' ago,' he mumbled.

'I should like to see them,' said Mary. 'Where is the green door? There must be a door somewhere.'

Ben drove his spade deep and looked as uncompanionable as he had looked when she first saw him.

'There was ten year' ago, but there isn't now,' he said.

'No door!' cried Mary. 'There must be.'

'None as anyone can find, an' none as is anyone's business. Don't be a meddlesome wench an' poke your nose where it's no cause to go. Here, I must go on with my work. Get you gone an' play you. I've no more time.'

And he actually stopped digging, threw his spade over his shoulder, and walked off, without even glancing at her or saying good-bye.

5 The Cry in the Corridor

At first each day which passed by for Mary Lennox was exactly like the others. Every morning she awoke in her tapestried room and found Martha kneeling upon the hearth building her fire; every morning she ate her breakfast in the nursery which had nothing amusing in it; and after each breakfast she gazed out of the window across to the huge moor, which seemed to spread out on all sides and climb up to the sky, and after she had stared for a while she realized that if she did not go out she would have to stay in and do nothing – and so she went out. She did not know that this was the best thing she could have done, and she did not know that, when she began to walk quickly or even run along the paths and down the avenue, she was stirring her slow blood and making herself stronger by fighting with the wind which swept down from the moor. She ran only to make herself warm, and she hated the wind which rushed at her face and roared and held her back as if it were some giant she could not see. But the big breaths of rough fresh air blown over the heather filled her lungs with something which was good for her whole thin body and whipped some red colour into her cheeks and brightened her dull eyes when she did not know anything about it.

But after a few days spent almost entirely out of doors, she wakened one morning knowing what it was to be hungry, and when she sat down to her breakfast she did not glance disdainfully at her porridge and push it away, but took up her spoon and began to eat it and went on eating it until her bowl was empty.

'Tha' got on well enough with that this mornin', didn't tha'?' said Martha.

'It tastes nice today,' said Mary, feeling a little surprised herself.

'It's th' air of th' moor that's givin' thee stomach for tha' victuals,' answered Martha. 'It's lucky for thee that tha's got victuals as well as an appetite. There's been twelve in our cottage as had th' stomach an' nothing to put in it. You go on playin' you out o' doors every day an' you'll get some flesh on your bones an' you won't be so yeller.'

'I don't play,' said Mary. 'I have nothing to play with.'

'Nothin' to play with!' exclaimed Martha. 'Our children plays with sticks and stones. They just runs about an' shouts an' looks at things.

Mary did not shout, but she looked at things. There was nothing else to do. She walked round and round the gardens and wandered about the paths in the park. Sometimes she looked for Ben Weatherstaff, but though several times she saw him at work he was too busy to look at her or was too surly. Once when she was walking towards him he picked up his spade and turned away, as if he did it on purpose.

One place she went to oftener than to any other. It was the long walk outside the gardens with the walls round them. There were bare flower-beds on either side of it and against the walls ivy grew thickly. There was one part of the wall where the creeping dark green leaves were more bushy than elsewhere. It seemed as if for a long time that part had been neglected. The rest if it had been clipped and made to look neat, but at this lower end of the walk it had not been trimmed at all.

A few days after she had talked to Ben Weatherstaff, Mary stopped to notice this and wondered why it was so. She had just paused and was looking up at a long spray of ivy swinging in the wind, when she saw a gleam of scarlet and heard a brilliant chirp, and there, on the top of the wall, perched Ben Weatherstaff's robin redbreast, tilting forward to look at her with his small head on one side.

'Oh!' she cried out, 'is it you – is it you?' And it did not seem at all queer to her that she spoke to him as if she was sure that he would understand and answer her.

He did answer. He twittered and chirped and hopped along the wall, as if he were telling her all sorts of things. It seemed to Mistress Mary as if she understood him, too, though he was not speaking in words. It was as if he said:

'Good morning! Isn't the wind nice? Isn't the sun nice? Isn't everything nice? Let us both chirp and hop and twitter. Come on! Come on!'

Mary began to laugh, and as he hopped and took little flights along the wall she ran after him. Poor little thin, sallow, ugly Mary – she actually looked almost pretty for a moment.

'I like you! I like you!' she cried out, pattering down the walk; and she chirped and tried to whistle, which last she did not know how to do in the least. But the robin seemed to be quite satisfied and chirped and whistled back at her. At last he spread his wings and made a darting flight to the top of a tree, where he perched and sang loudly.

That reminded Mary of the first time she had seen him. He had been swinging on a tree-top then and she had been standing in the orchard. Now she was on the other side of the orchard and standing in the path outside a wall – much lower down – and there was the same tree inside.

'It's in the garden no one can go into,' she said to herself. 'It's the garden without a door. He lives in there. How I wish I could see what it is like!'

She ran up the walk to the green door she had entered the first morning. Then she ran down the path through the other door and then into the orchard, and when she stood and looked up there was the tree on the other side of the wall, and there was the robin just finishing his song and beginning to preen his feathers with his beak.

'It is the garden,' she said. 'I am sure it is.'

She walked round and looked closely at that side of the orchard wall, but she only found what she had found before – that there was no door in it. Then she ran through the kitchen-gardens again and out into the walk outside the long ivy-covered wall, and she walked to the end of it and looked at it, but there was no door; and then she walked to the other end, looking again, but there was no door.

'It's very queer,' she said. 'Ben Weatherstaff said there was no door and there is no door. But there must have been one ten years ago, because Mr. Craven buried the key.'

This gave her so much to think of that she began to be quite interested and feel that she was not sorry that she had come to

Misselthwaite Manor. In India she had always felt hot and too languid to care much about anything. The fact was that the fresh wind from the moor had begun to blow the cobwebs out of her young brain and to waken her up a little.

She stayed out of doors nearly all day, and when she sat down to her supper at night she felt hungry and drowsy and comfortable. She did not feel cross when Martha chattered away. She felt as if she rather liked to hear her, and at last she thought she would ask her a question. She asked it after she had finished her supper and had sat down on the hearth-rug before the fire.

'Why did Mr. Craven hate the garden?' she said.

She had made Martha stay with her and Martha had not objected at all. She was very young, and used to a crowded cottage full of brothers and sisters, and she found it dull in the great servants' hall downstairs, where the footman and upper-housemaids made fun of her Yorkshire speech and looked upon her as a common little thing, and sat and whispered among themselves. Martha liked to talk, and the strange child who had lived in India, and been waited upon by 'blacks', was novelty enough to attract her.

She sat down on the hearth herself without waiting to be asked.

'Art tha' thinkin' about that garden yet?' she said. 'I knew tha' would. That was just the way with me when I first heard about it.'

'Why did he hate it?' Mary persisted.

Martha tucked her feet under her and made herself quite comfortable.

'Listen to th' wind wutherin' round the house,' she said. 'You could bare stand up on the moor if you was out on it tonight.'

Mary did not know what 'wutherin' ' meant until she listened, and then she understood. It must mean that hollow, shuddering sort of roar which rushed round and round the house, as if the giant no one could see were buffeting it and beating at the walls and windows to try to break in. But one knew he could not get in, and somehow it made one feel very safe and warm inside a room with a red coal fire.

'But why did he hate it so?' she asked, after she had listened. She intended to know if Martha did.

Then Martha gave up her store of knowledge.

'Mind,' she said, 'Mrs. Medlock said it's not to be talked about. There's lots o' things in this place that's not to be talked over. That's Mr. Craven's orders. His troubles are none servants' business, he says. But for th' garden he wouldn't be like he is. It was Mrs. Craven's garden that she had made when first they were married an' she just loved it, an' they used to 'tend the flowers themselves. An' none o' th' gardeners was ever let to go in. Him an' her used to go in an' shut th' door an' stay there hours an' hours, readin' an' talkin'. An' she was just a bit of a girl an' there was an old tree with a branch bent like a seat on it. An' she made roses grow over it an' she used to sit there. But one day when she was sittin' there th' branch broke an' she fell on th' ground an' was hurt so bad that next day she died. Th' doctors thought he'd go out o' his mind an' die, too. That's why he hates it. No one's never gone in since, an' he won't let anyone talk about it.'

Mary did not ask any more questions. She looked at the fire and listened to the wind 'wutherin' '. It seemed to be 'wutherin' ' louder than ever.

At that moment a very good thing was happening to her. Four good things had happened to her, in fact, since she came to Misselthwaite Manor. She had felt as if she had understood a robin and that he had understood her; she had run in the wind until her blood had grown warm; she had been healthily hungry for the first time in her life; and she had found out what it was to be sorry for someone. She was getting on.

But as she was listening to the wind she began to listen to something else. She did not know what it was, because at first she could scarcely distinguish it from the wind itself. It was a curious sound – it seemed almost as if a child were crying somewhere. Sometimes the wind sounded rather like a child crying, but presently Mistress Mary felt quite sure that this sound was inside the house, not outside it. It was far away, but it was inside. She turned round and looked at Martha.

'Do you hear anyone crying?' she said.

Martha suddenly looked confused.

'No,' she answered. 'It's th' wind. Sometimes it sounds as if someone was lost on th' moor an' wailin'. It's got all sorts o' sounds.'

'But listen,' said Mary. 'It's in the house – down one of those long corridors.'

And at that moment a door must have been opened somewhere downstairs; for a great rushing draught blew along the passage and the door of the room they sat in was blown open with a crash, and as they both jumped to their feet the light was blown out and the crying sound was swept down the far corridor, so that it was to be heard more plainly than ever.

'There!' said Mary. 'I told you so!' It is someone crying – and it isn't a grown-up person.'

Martha ran and shut the door and turned the key, but before she did it they both heard the sound of a door in some far passage shutting with a bang, and then everything was quiet, for even the wind ceased 'wutherin'' for a few moments.

'It was th' wind,' said Martha stubbornly. 'An' if it wasn't, it was little Betty Butterworth, th' scullery-maid. She's had th' toothache all day.'

But something troubled and awkward in her manner made Mistress Mary stare very hard at her. She did not believe she was speaking the truth.

6 'There was someone crying – there was!'

The next day the rain poured down in torrents again, and when Mary looked out of her window the moor was almost hidden by grey mist and cloud. There could be no going out today.

'What do you do in your cottage when it rains like this?' she asked Martha.

'Try to keep from under each other's feet mostly,' Martha answered. 'Eh! there does seem a lot of us then. Mother's a good-tempered woman, but she gets fair moithered. The biggest ones goes out in th' cow-shed and plays there. Dickon he doesn't mind th' wet. He goes out just th' same as if th' sun was shinin'. He says he sees things on rainy days as doesn't show when it's fair weather. He once found a little fox cub half drowned in its hole and he brought it home in th' bosom of his shirt to keep it warm. Its mother had been killed near by an' th' hole was swum out an' th' rest o' th' litter was dead. He's got it at home now. He found a half-drowned young crow another time an' he brought it home, too, an' tamed it. It's named Soot, because it's so black an' it hops an' flies about with him everywhere.'

The time had come when Mary had forgotten to resent Martha's familiar talk. She had even begun to find it interesting and to be sorry when she stopped or went away. The stories she had been told by her Ayah when she lived in India had been quite unlike those Martha had to tell about the moorland cottage which held fourteen people who lived in four little rooms and never had quite enough to eat. The children seemed to tumble about and amuse themselves like a litter of rough, good-natured collie puppies. Mary was most attracted by the mother and Dickon. When Martha told stories of what 'mother' said or did they always sounded comfortable.

'If I had a raven or a fox cub I could play with it,' said Mary. 'But I have nothing.'

Martha looked perplexed.

'Can tha' knit?' she asked.

'No,' answered Mary.

'Can tha' sew?'

'No.'

'Can tha' read?'

'Yes.'

'Then why doesn't tha' read somethin' or learn a bit o' spellin'? Tha'st old enough to be learnin' thy book a good bit now.'

'I haven't any books,' said Mary. 'Those I had were left in India.'

'That's a pity,' said Martha. 'If Mrs. Medlock'd let thee go int' th' library, there's thousands o' books there.'

Mary did not ask where the library was, because she was suddenly inspired by a new idea. She made up her mind to go and find it herself. She was not troubled about Mrs. Medlock. Mrs. Medlock seemed always to be in her comfortable housekeeper's sitting-room downstairs. In this queer place one scarcely ever saw anyone at all. In fact, there was no one to see but the servants, and when their master was away they lived a luxurious life below stairs, where there was a huge kitchen hung about with shining brass and pewter, and a large servants' hall where there were four or five abundant meals eaten every day, and where a great deal of lively romping went on when Mrs. Medlock was out of the way.

Mary's meals were served regularly, and Martha waited on her, but no one troubled themselves about her in the least. Mrs. Medlock came and looked at her every day or two, but no one inquired what she did or told her what to do. She supposed that perhaps this was the English way of treating children. In India she had always been attended by her Ayah, who had followed her about and waited on her, hand and foot. She had often been tired of her company. Now she was followed by nobody and was learning to dress herself, because Martha looked as though she thought she was silly and stupid when she wanted to have things handed to her and put on.

'Hasn't tha' got good sense?' she said once, when Mary had stood waiting for her to put on her gloves for her. 'Our Susan Anne is twice as sharp as thee an' she's only four year' old. Sometimes tha' looks fair soft in th' head.'

Mary had worn her contrary scowl for an hour after that, but it made her think several entirely new things.

She stood at the window for about ten minutes this morning after Martha had swept up the hearth for the last time and gone downstairs. She was thinking over the new idea which had come to her when she heard of the library. She did not care very much about the library itself, because she had read very few books; but to hear of it brought back to her mind the hundred rooms with closed doors. She wondered if they were all really locked and what she would find if she could get into any of them. Were there a hundred really? Why shouldn't she go and see how many doors she could count? It would be something to do on this morning when she could not go out. She had never been taught to ask permission to do things, and she knew nothing at all about authority, so she would not have thought it necessary to ask Mrs. Medlock if she might walk about the house, even if she had seen her.

She opened the door of the room and went into the corridor, and then she began her wanderings. It was a long corridor and it branched into other corridors and it led her up short flights of steps which mounted to others again. There were doors and doors, and there were pictures on the walls. Sometimes they were pictures of dark, curious landscapes, but oftenest they were portraits of men and women in queer, grand costumes made of satin and velvet. She found herself in one long gallery whose walls were covered with those portraits. She had never thought there could be so many in any house. She walked slowly down this place and stared at the faces, which also seemed to stare at her. She felt as if they were wondering what a little girl from India was doing in their house. Some were pictures of children – little girls in thick satin frocks which reached to their feet and stood out about them, and boys with puffed sleeves and lace collars and long hair, or with big ruffs around their necks. She always stopped to look at the children, and wonder what their names were, and where they had gone, and why they wore such odd clothes. There was a stiff, plain little girl rather like herself. She wore a green brocade dress and held a green parrot on her finger. Her eyes had a sharp, curious look.

'Where do you live now?' said Mary aloud to her. 'I wish you were here.'

Surely no other little girl ever spent such a queer morning. It seemed as if there was no one in all the huge, rambling house but her own small self, wandering about upstairs and down, through narrow passages and wide ones, where it seemed to her that no one but herself had ever walked. Since so many rooms had been built, people must have lived in them, but it all seemed so empty that she could not quite believe it true.

It was not until she climbed to the second floor that she thought of turning the handle of a door. All the doors were shut, as Mrs. Medlock had said they were, but at last she put her hand on the handle of one of them and turned it. She was almost frightened for a moment when she felt that it turned without difficulty and that when she pushed upon the door itself it slowly and heavily opened. It was a massive door and opened into a big bedroom. There were embroidered hangings on the wall, and inlaid furniture such as she had seen in India stood about the room. A broad window with leaded panes looked out upon the moor; and over the mantel was another portrait of the stiff, plain little girl who seemed to stare at her more curiously than ever.

'Perhaps she slept here once,' said Mary. 'She stares at me so that she makes me feel queer.'

After that she opened more doors and more. She saw so many rooms that she became quite tired and began to think that there must be a hundred, though she had not counted them. In all of them there were old pictures or old tapestries with strange scenes worked on them. There were curious pieces of furniture and curious ornaments in nearly all of them.

In one room, which looked like a lady's sitting-room, the hangings were all embroidered velvet, and in a cabinet were about a hundred little elephants made of ivory. They were of different sizes, and some had their mahouts or palanquins on their backs. Some were much bigger than the others and some were so tiny that they seemed only babies. Mary had seen carved ivory in India and she knew all about the elephants. She opened the door of the cabinet and stood on a footstool and played with these for quite a long time. When she got tired she set the elephants in order and shut the door of the cabinet.

In all her wanderings through the long corridors and the empty rooms she had seen nothing alive; but in this room she saw something. Just after she had closed the cabinet door she heard a tiny rustling sound. It made her jump and look around at the sofa by the fireplace, from which it seemed to come. In the corner of the sofa there was a cushion, and in the velvet which covered it there was a hole, and out of the hole peeped a tiny head with a pair of frightened eyes in it.

Mary crept softly across the room to look. The bright eyes belonged to a little grey mouse, and the mouse had eaten a hole into the cushion and made a comfortable nest there. Six baby mice were cuddled up asleep near her. If there was no one else alive in the hundred rooms there were seven mice who did not look lonely at all.

'If they wouldn't be so frightened I would take them back with me,' said Mary.

She had wandered about long enough to feel too tired to wander any further, and she turned back. Two or three times she lost her way by turning down the wrong corridor and was obliged to ramble up and down until she found the right one; but at last she reached her own floor again, though she was some distance from her own room and did not know exactly where she was.

'I believe I have taken a wrong turning again,' she said, standing still at what seemed the end of a short passage with tapestry on the wall. 'I don't know which way to go. How still everything is!'

It was while she was standing here and just after she had said this that the stillness was broken by a sound. It was another cry, but not quite like the one she had heard last night; it was a short one, a fretful, childish whine muffled by passing through walls.

'It's nearer than it was,' said Mary, her heart beating rather faster. 'And it *is* crying.'

She put her hand accidentally upon the tapestry near her, and then sprang back, feeling quite startled. The tapestry was the covering of a door which fell open and showed her that there was another part of the corridor behind it, and Mrs. Medlock was coming up it with her bunch of keys in her hand and a very cross look on her face.

"*What are you doing here?*"

'What are you doing here?' she said, and she took Mary by the arm and pulled her away. 'What did I tell you?'

'I turned round the wrong corner,' explained Mary, 'I didn't know which way to go and I heard someone crying.'

She quite hated Mrs. Medlock at the moment, but she hated her more the next.

'You didn't hear anything of the sort,' said the housekeeper. 'You come along back to your own nursery or I'll box your ears.'

And she took her by the arm and half pushed, half pulled her up one passage and down another, until she pushed her in at the door of her own room.

'Now,' she said, 'you stay where you're told to stay or you'll find yourself locked up. The master had better get you a governess, same as he said he would. You're one that needs someone to look sharp after you. I've got enough to do.'

She went out of the room and slammed the door after her, and Mary went and sat on the hearth-rug, pale with rage. She did not cry, but ground her teeth.

'There *was* someone crying – there *was* – there *was*!' she said to herself.

She had heard it twice now, and some time she would find out. She had found out a great deal this morning. She felt as if she had been on a long journey, and at any rate she had had something to amuse her all the time, and she had played with the ivory elephants and had seen the grey mouse and its babies in their nest in the velvet cushion.

7 The Key of the Garden

Two days after this, when Mary opened her eyes she sat upright in bed immediately, and called to Martha.

'Look at the moor! Look at the moor!'

The rain-storm had ended and the grey mist and clouds had been swept away in the night by the wind. The wind itself had ceased and a brilliant, deep blue sky arched high over the moorland. Never, never had Mary dreamed of a sky so blue. In India skies were hot and blazing; this was of a deep, cool blue, which almost seemed to sparkle like the waters of some lovely, bottomless lake, and here and there, high, high in the arched blueness, floated small clouds of snow-white fleece. The far-reaching world of the moor itself looked softly blue instead of gloomy purple-black or awful dreary grey.

'Aye,' said Martha, with a cheerful grin. 'Th' storm's over for a bit. It does like this at this time o' th' year. It goes off in a night like it was pretendin' it had never been here an' never meant to come again. That's because th' springtime's on its way. It's a long way off yet, but it's comin'.'

'I thought perhaps it always rained or looked dark in England,' Mary said.

'Eh! no!' said Martha sitting up on her heels among her black-lead brushes. 'Nowt o' th' soart!'

'What does that mean?' asked Mary seriously. In India the natives spoke different dialects which only a few people understood, so she was not surprised when Martha used words she did not know.

Martha laughed as she had done the first morning.

'There now,' she said. 'I've talked broad Yorkshire again like Mrs. Medlock said I mustn't. "Nowt o' the soart" means "nothin' of the sort",' slowly and carefully, 'but it takes so long to say it. Yorkshire's th' sunniest place on earth when it is sunny. I told thee tha'd like th' moor after a bit. Just you wait till you see th' gold-coloured gorse blossoms an' th' blossoms o' th' broom, an' th' heather flowerin', all purple bells, an' hundreds o' butterflies flutterin' an' bees hummin' an' skylarks soarin' up an' singin'. You'll want to get out on it at sunrise an' live out on it all day like Dickon does.'

'Could I ever go there?' asked Mary wistfully, looking through her window at the far-off blue. It was so new and big and wonderful and such a heavenly colour.

'I don't know,' answered Martha. 'tha's never used tha' legs since tha' was born, it seems to me. Tha' couldn't walk five mile. It's five mile to our cottage.'

'I should like to see your cottage.'

Martha stared at her a moment curiously before she took up her polishing brush and began to rub the grate again. She was thinking that the small plain face did not look quite as sour at this moment as it had done the first morning she saw it. It looked just a trifle like little Susan Ann's when she wanted something very much.

'I'll ask my mother about it,' she said. 'She's one o' them that nearly always sees a way to do things. It's my day out today an' I'm goin' home. Eh! I am glad. Mrs. Medlock thinks a lot o' mother. Perhaps she could talk to her.'

'I like your mother,' said Mary.

'I should think tha' did,' agreed Martha, polishing away.

'I've never seen her,' said Mary.

'No, tha' hasn't,' replied Martha.

She sat up on her heels again and rubbed the end of her nose with the back of her hands, as if puzzled for a moment, but she ended quite positively.

'Well, she's that sensible an' hard workin' an' good-natured an' clean that no one could help likin' her, whether they'd seen her or not. When I'm going home to her on my day out I just jump for joy when I'm crossin' th' moor.'

'I like Dickon,' added Mary. 'And I've never seen him.'

'Well,' said Martha stoutly. 'I've told thee that th' very birds like him an' th' rabbits an' wild sheep an' ponies, an' th' foxes themselves. I wonder,' staring at her reflectively, 'what Dickon would think of thee?'

'He wouldn't like me,' said Mary in her stiff, cold little way. 'No one does.'

Martha looked reflective again.

'How does tha' like thysel'?' she inquired, really quite as if she were curious to know.

Mary hesitated a moment and thought it over.

'Not at all – really,' she answered. 'But I never thought of that before.'

Martha grinned a little as if at some homely recollection.

'Mother said that to me once,' she said. 'She was at her wash-tub an' I was in a bad temper an' talkin' ill of folk an' she turns round on me an' says: "Tha' young vixon, tha'! There tha' stands sayin' tha' doesn't like this one an' tha' doesn't like that one. How does tha' like thysel'?" It made me laugh an' it brought me to my senses in a minute.'

She went away in high spirits as soon as she had given Mary her breakfast. She was going to walk five miles across the moor to the cottage, and she was going to help her mother with the washing and do the week's baking and enjoy herself thoroughly.

Mary felt lonelier than ever when she knew she was no longer in the house. She went out into the garden as quickly as possible, and the first thing she did was to run round and round the fountain flower garden ten times. She counted the times carefully and when she had finished she felt in better spirits. The sunshine made the whole place look different. The high, deep, blue sky arched over Misselthwaite, as well as over the moor, and she kept lifting her face and looking up into it, trying to imagine what it would be like to lie down on one of the little snow-white clouds and float about. She went into the first kitchen-garden and found Ben Weatherstaff working there with two other gardeners. The change in the weather seemed to have done him good. He spoke to her of his own accord.

'Springtime's coming,' he said. 'Cannot tha' smell it?'

Mary sniffed and thought she could.

'I smell something nice and fresh and damp,' she said.

'That's th' good rich earth,' he answered, digging away. 'It's in a good humour makin' ready to grow things. It's glad when plantin' time comes. It's dull in th' winter when it's got nowt to do. In th' flower gardens out there things will be stirrin' down below in th' dark. Th' sun's warmin' 'em. You'll see bits o' green spikes stickin' out o' th' black earth after a bit.'

'What will they be?' asked Mary.

'Crocuses an' snowdrops an' daffydowndillys. Has tha' never seen them?'

'No. Everything is hot, and wet, and green after the rains in India,' said Mary. 'And I think things grow up in a night.'

'These won't grow up in a night,' said Weatherstaff. 'Tha'll have to wait for 'em. They'll poke up a bit higher here, and push out a spike more there, an' uncurl a leaf this day an' another that. You watch 'em.'

'I am going to,' answered Mary.

Very soon she heard the soft rustling flight of wings again and she knew at once that the robin had come again. He was very pert and lively, and hopped about so close to her feet, and put his head on one side and looked at her so shyly that she asked Ben Weatherstaff a question.

'Do you think he remembers me?' she said.

'Remembers thee!' said Weatherstaff indignantly. 'He knows every cabbage stump in th' gardens, let alone th' people. He's never seen a little wench here before, an' he's bent on findin' out all about thee. Tha's no need to try to hide anything from *him*.'

'Are things stirring down below in the dark in that garden where he lives?' Mary inquired.

'What garden?' grunted Weatherstaff, becoming surly again.

'The one where the old rose-trees are.' She could not help asking, because she wanted so much to know. 'Are all the flowers dead, or do some of them come again in the summer? Are there ever any roses?'

'Ask him,' said Ben Weatherstaff, hunching his shoulders towards the robin. 'He's the only one as knows. No one else has seen inside it for ten year'.'

Ten years was a long time, Mary thought. She had been born ten years ago.

She walked away, slowly thinking. She had begun to like the

garden just as she had begun to like the robin and Dickon and Martha's mother. She was beginning to like Martha, too. That seemed a good many people to like – when you were not used to liking. She thought of the robin as one of the people. She went to her walk outside the long, ivy-covered wall over which she could see the tree-tops; and the second time she walked up and down the most interesting and exciting thing happened to her, and it was all through Ben Weatherstaff's robin.

She heard a chirp and a twitter, and when she looked at the bare flower-bed at her left side there he was hopping about and pretending to peck things out of the earth to persuade her that he had not followed her. But she knew he had followed her, and the surprise so filled her with delight that she almost trembled a little.

'You do remember me!' she cried. 'You do! You are prettier than anything else in the world!'

She chirped, and talked, and coaxed and he hopped and flirted his tail and twittered. It was as if he were talking. His red waistcoat was like satin, and he puffed his tiny breast out and was so fine and so grand and so pretty that it was really as if he were showing her how important and like a human person a robin could be. Mistress Mary forgot that she had ever been contrary in her life when he allowed her to draw closer and closer to him, and bend down and talk and try to make something like robin sounds.

Oh! to think that he should actually let her come as near to him as that! He knew nothing in the world would make her put out her hand towards him or startle him in the least tiniest way. He knew it because he was a real person – only nicer than any other person in the world. She was so happy that she scarcely dared to breathe.

The flower-bed was not quite bare. It was bare of flowers because the perennial plants had been cut down for their winter rest, but there were tall shrubs and low ones which grew together at the back of the bed, and as the robin hopped about under them she saw him hop over a small pile of freshly turned-up earth. He stopped on it to look for a worm. The earth had been turned up because a dog had been trying to dig up a mole and he had scratched quite a deep hole.

Mary looked at it, not really knowing why the hole was there, and as she looked she saw something almost buried in the newly turned soil. It was something like a ring of rusty iron or brass, and when the robin flew up into a tree near by she put out her hand and picked the ring up. It was more than a ring, however; it was an old key which looked as if it had been buried a long time.

Mistress Mary stood up and looked at it with an almost frightened face as it hung from her finger.

'Perhaps it has been buried for ten years,' she said in a whisper. 'Perhaps it is the key to the garden!'

8 The Robin Who Showed the Way

She looked at the key quite a long time. She turned it over and over, and thought about it. As I have said before, she was not a child who had been trained to ask permission or consult her elders about things. All she thought about the key was that if it was the key to the closed garden, and she could find out where the door was, she could perhaps open it and see what was inside the walls, and what had happened to the old rose-trees. It was because it had been shut up so long that she wanted to see it. It seemed as if it must be different from other places and that something strange must have happened to it during ten years. Besides that, if she liked it she could go into it every day and shut the door behind her, and she could make up some play of her own and play it quite alone, because nobody would ever know where she was, but would think the door was still locked and the key buried in the earth. The thought of that pleased her very much.

Living, as it were, all by herself in a house with a hundred mysteriously closed rooms and having nothing whatever to do to amuse herself, set her inactive brain to work and was actually awakening her imagination. There is no doubt that the fresh, strong, pure air from the moor had a great deal to do with it. Just as it had given her an appetite, and fighting with the wind had stirred her blood, so the same things had stirred her mind. In India she had always been too hot and languid and weak to care much about anything, but in this place she was beginning to care and to want to do new things. Already she felt less 'contrary', though she did not know why.

She put the key in her pocket and walked up and down her walk. No one but herself ever seemed to come there, so she could walk slowly and look at the wall, or, rather, at the ivy growing on it. The ivy was the baffling thing. Howsoever carefully she looked, she could see nothing but thickly growing, glossy, dark green leaves. She was very much disappointed. Something of her contrariness came back to her as she paced the wall and looked over it at the tree-tops inside. It seemed so silly, she said to herself, to be near it and not be able to get in. She took the key in her pocket when she went back to the house, and she made up her mind that she would always carry it with her when she went out, so that if she ever should find the hidden door she would be ready.

Mrs. Medlock had allowed Martha to sleep all night at the cottage, but she was back at her work in the morning with cheeks redder than ever and in the best of spirits.

'I got up at four o'clock,' she said. 'Eh! it was pretty on th' moor with th' birds gettin' up an' th' rabbits scamperin' about an' th' sun risin'. I didn't walk all th' way. A man gave me a ride in his cart an' I can tell you I did enjoy myself.'

She was full of stories of the delights of her day out. Her mother had been glad to see her, and they had got the baking and washing all out of the way. She had even made each of the children a dough-cake with a bit of brown sugar in it.

'I had 'em all pipin' hot when they came in from playin' on th' moor. An' th' cottage all smelt o' nice, clean, hot bakin' an' there was a good fire, an' they just shouted for joy. Our Dickon, he said our cottage was good enough for a king to live in.'

In the evening they had all sat round the fire, and Martha and her mother had sewed patches on torn clothes and mended stockings, and Martha had told them about the little girl who had come from India and who had been waited on all her life by what Martha called 'blacks' until she didn't know how to put on her own stockings.

'Eh! they did like to hear about you,' said Martha. 'They wanted to know all about th' blacks an' about th' ship you came in. I couldn't tell 'em enough.'

Mary reflected a little.

'I'll tell you a great deal more before your next day out,' she said, 'so that you will have more to talk about. I dare say they would like to hear about riding on elephants and camels, and about the officers going to hunt tigers.'

'My word!' cried delighted Martha. 'it would set 'em clean off their heads. Would tha' really do that, Miss? It would be the same as a wild beast show like we heard they had in York once.'

'India is quite different from Yorkshire,' Mary said slowly, as she thought the matter over. 'I never thought of that. Did Dickon and your mother like to hear you talk about me?'

'Why, our Dickon's eyes nearly started out o' his head, they got that round,' answered Martha. 'But Mother, she was put out about your seemin' to be all by yourself like. She said: "Hasn't Mr. Craven got no governess for her, nor no nurse?" and I said: "No, he hasn't, though Mrs. Medlock says he will when he thinks of it, but she says he mayn't think of it for two or three years."'

'I don't want a governess,' said Mary sharply.

'But Mother says you ought to be learnin' your book by this time an' you ought to have a woman to look after you, an' she says: "Now, Martha, you just think how you'd feel yourself, in a big place like that, wanderin' about alone, an' no mother. You do your best to cheer her up,' she says, an' I said I would.'

Mary gave her a long, steady look.

'You do cheer me up,' she said. 'I like to hear you talk.'

Presently Martha went out of the room and came back with something held in her hands under her apron.

'What does tha' think,' she said, with a cheerful grin. 'I've brought thee a present.'

'A present!' exclaimed Mistress Mary. How could a cottage full of fourteen hungry people give anyone a present!

'A man was drivin' across the moor peddlin',' Martha explained. 'An' he stopped his cart at our door. He had pots an' pans an' odds an' ends, but Mother had no money to buy anythin'. Just as he was goin' away our 'Lizbeth Ellen called out: "Mother, he's got skippin'-ropes with red an' blue handles." An' Mother, she calls out quite sudden: "Here, stop, mister! How much are they?" An' he says "Tuppence," an' Mother she began fumblin' in her pocket, an' she says to me: "Martha, tha's brought thee thy wages like a good lass, an' I've got four places to put every penny, but I'm just goin' to take tuppence out of it to buy that child a skippin'-rope," an' she bought one, an' here it is.'

She brought it out from under her apron and exhibited it quite proudly. It was a strong, slender rope with a striped red and blue handle at each end, but Mary Lennox had never seen a skipping-rope before. She gazed at it with a mystified expression.

'What is it for?' she asked curiously.

'For!' cried out Martha. 'Does tha' mean that they've not got skippin'-ropes in India, for all they've got elephants and tigers and camels? No wonder most of 'em's black. This is what it's for; just watch me.'

And she ran into the middle of the room and, taking a handle in each hand, began to skip, and skip, and skip, while Mary turned in her chair to stare at her, and the queer faces in the old portraits seemed to stare at her, too, and wonder what on earth this common little cottager had the impudence to be doing under their very noses. But Martha did not even see them. The interest and curiosity in Mistress Mary's face delighted her, and she went on skipping and counted as she skipped until she had reached a hundred.

'I could skip longer than that,' she said when she stopped. 'I've skipped as much as five hundred when I was twelve, but I wasn't as fat then as I am now, an' I was in practice.'

Mary got up from her chair beginning to feel excited herself.

'It looks nice,' she said. 'Your mother is a kind woman. Do you think I could ever skip like that?'

'You just try it,' urged Martha, handing her the skipping-rope. 'You can't skip a hundred at first, but if you practise you'll mount up. That's what Mother said. She says: "Nothin' will do her more good than skippin'-rope. It's th' sensiblest toy a child can have. Let her play out in th' fresh air skippin' an it'll stretch her legs an' arms an' give her some strength in 'em"'

It was plain that there was not a great deal of strength in Mistress Mary's arms and legs when she first began to skip. She was not very clever at it, but she liked it so much that she did not want to stop.

'Put on tha' things and run an' skip out o' doors,' said Martha. 'Mother said I must tell you to keep out o' doors as much as you could, even when it rains a bit, so as tha' wrap up warm.'

Mary put on her coat and hat and took her skipping-rope over her arm. She opened the door to go out, and then suddenly thought of something and turned back rather slowly.

'Martha,' she said, 'they were your wages. It was your twopence really. Thank you.' She said it stiffly because she was not used to thanking people or noticing that they did things for her. 'Thank you,' she said, and held out her hand because she did not know what else to do.

Martha gave her hand a clumsy little shake, as if she was not accustomed to this sort of thing either. Then she laughed.

'Eh! tha' art a queer, old-womanish thing,' she said. 'If tha'd been our 'Lizabeth Ellen tha'd have given me a kiss.'

Mary looked stiffer than ever.

'Do you want me to kiss you?'

Martha laughed again.

'Nay, not me,' she answered. 'If tha' was different, p'raps tha'd want to thysel'.' But tha' isn't. Run off outside an' play with thy rope.'

Mistress Mary felt a little awkward as she went out of the room. Yorkshire people seemed strange, and Martha was always rather a puzzle to her. At first she had disliked her very much, but now she did not.

The skipping-rope was a wonderful thing. She counted and skipped, and skipped and counted, until her cheeks were quite red, and she was more interested than she had ever been since she was born. The sun was shining and a little wind was blowing – not a rough wind, but one which came in delightful little gusts and brought a fresh scent of newly turned earth with it. She skipped round the fountain garden, and up one walk and down another. She skipped at last into the kitchen-garden and saw Ben Weatherstaff digging and talking to his robin, which was hopping about him. She skipped down the walk towards him and he lifted his head and looked at her with a curious expression. She had wondered if he would notice her. She really wanted him to see her skip.

'Well!' he exclaimed. 'Upon my word! P'raps tha' art a young 'un, after all, an' p'raps tha's got child's blood in thy veins instead of sour buttermilk. Tha's skipped red into thy cheeks as sure as my name's Ben Weatherstaff. I wouldn't have believed tha' could do it.'

'I never skipped before,' Mary said. 'I'm just beginning. I can only go up to twenty.'

'Tha' keep on,' said Ben. 'Tha' shapes well enough at it for a young 'un that's lived with heathen. Just see how he's watchin' thee,' jerking his head towards the robin. 'He followed after thee yesterday. He'll be at it again today. He'll be bound to find out what th' skippin'-rope is. He's never seen one. Eh!' shaking his head at the bird, 'tha' curiosity will be th' death of thee some time if tha' doesn't look sharp.'

Mary skipped round all the gardens and round the orchard, resting every few minutes. At length she went to her own special walk and made up her mind to try if she could skip the whole length of it. It was a good long skip, and she began slowly, but before she had gone half-way down the path she was so hot and breathless that she was obliged to stop. She did not mind much, because she had already counted up to thirty. She stopped with a little laugh of pleasure, and there, lo and behold, was the robin swaying on a long branch of ivy. He had followed her, and he greeted her with a chirp. As Mary had skipped towards him she felt something heavy in her pocket strike against her at each jump, and when she saw the robin she laughed again.

'You showed me where the key was yesterday,' she said. 'You ought to show me the door today; but I don't believe you know!'

The robin flew from his swinging spray of ivy on to the top of the wall and he opened his beak and sang a loud, lovely trill, merely to show off. Nothing in the world is quite as adorably lovely as a robin when he shows off – and they are nearly always doing it.

Mary Lennox had heard a great deal about Magic in her Ayah's stories, and she always said what happened almost at that moment was Magic.

One of the nice little gusts of wind rushed down the walk, and it was a stronger one than the rest. It was strong enough to wave the branches of the trees, and it was more than strong enough to sway the trailing sprays of untrimmed ivy hanging from the wall. Mary had stepped close to the robin, and suddenly the gust of wind swung aside some loose ivy trails, and more suddenly still she jumped towards it and caught it in her hand. This she did because she had seen something under it – a round knob which had been covered by the leaves hanging over it. It was the knob of a door.

She put her hands under the leaves and began to pull and push them aside. Thick as the ivy hung, it nearly all was a loose and swinging curtain, though some had crept over wood and iron. Mary's heart began to thump and her hands to shake a little in her delight and excitement. The robin kept singing and twittering away and tilting his head on one side, as if he were as excited as she was. What was this under her hands which was square and made of iron and which her fingers found a hole in?

It was the lock of the door which had been closed ten years, and she put her hand in her pocket, drew out the key, and found it fitted the keyhole. She put the key in and turned it. It took two hands to do it, but it did turn.

And then she took a long breath and looked behind her up the long walk to see if anyone was coming. No one was coming. No one ever did come, it seemed, and she took another long breath, because she could not help it, and she held back the swinging curtain of ivy and pushed back the door which opened slowly – slowly.

Then she slipped through it, and shut it behind her, and stood with her back against it, looking about her and breathing quite fast with excitement, and wonder, and delight.

She was standing *inside* the secret garden.

9 The Strangest House Anyone Ever Lived In

It was the sweetest, most mysterious-looking place anyone could imagine. The high walls which shut it in were covered with the leafless stems of climbing roses, which were so thick that they were matted together. Mary Lennox knew they were roses because she had seen a great many roses in India. All the ground was covered with grass of a wintry brown, and out of it grew clumps of bushes which were surely rose-bushes if they were alive. There were numbers of standard roses which had so spread their branches that they were like little trees. There were other trees in the garden, and one of the things which made the place look strangest and loveliest was that climbing roses had run all over them and swung down long tendrils which made light swaying curtains, and here and there they had caught at each other or at a far-reaching branch and had crept from one tree to another and made lovely bridges of themselves. There were neither leaves nor roses on them now, and Mary did not know whether they were dead or alive, but their thin grey or brown branches and sprays looked like a sort of hazy mantle spreading over everything, walls, and trees, and even brown grass, where they had fallen from their fastenings and run along the ground. It was this hazy tangle from tree to tree which made it look so mysterious. Mary had thought it must be different from other gardens which had not been left all by themselves so long; and, indeed, it was different from any other place she had ever seen in her life.

'How still it is!' she whispered. 'How still!'

Then she waited for a moment and listened at the stillness. The robin, who had flown to his tree-top, was still as all the rest. He did not even flutter his wings; he sat without stirring, and looked at Mary.

'No wonder it is still,' she whispered again. 'I am the first person who has spoken in here for ten years.'

She moved away from the door, stepping as softly as if she were afraid of awakening someone. She was glad that there was grass under her feet and that her steps made no sounds. She walked under one of the fairy-like arches between the trees and looked up at the sprays and tendrils which formed them.

'I wonder if they are all quite dead,' she said. 'Is it all a quite dead garden? I wish it wasn't.'

If she had been Ben Weatherstaff she could have told whether the wood was alive by looking at it, but she could only see that there were only grey or brown sprays and branches, and none showed any signs of even a tiny leaf-bud anywhere.

But she was *inside* the wonderful garden, and she could come through the door under the ivy any time, and she felt as if she had found a world all her own.

The sun was shining inside the four walls and the high arch of blue sky over this particular piece of Misselthwaite seemed even more brilliant and soft than it was over the moor. The robin flew down from his tree-top and hopped about or flew after her from one bush to another. He chirped a good deal and had a very busy air, as if he were showing her things. Everything was strange and silent, and she seemed to be hundreds of miles away from anyone, but somehow she did not feel lonely at all. All that troubled her was her wish that she knew whether all the roses were dead, or if perhaps some of them had lived and might put out leaves and buds as the weather got warmer. She did not want it to be a quite dead garden. If it were a quite alive garden, how wonderful it would be, and what thousands of roses would grow on every side?

Her skipping-rope had hung over her arm when she came in, and after she had walked about for a while she thought she would skip round the whole garden, stopping when she wanted to look at things. There seemed to have been grass paths here and there, and in one or two corners there were alcoves of evergreen with stone seats or all moss-covered flower-urns in them.

As she came near the second of these alcoves she stopped skipping. There had once been a flower-bed in it, and she thought she saw something sticking out of the black earth – some sharp little pale green points. She remembered what Ben Weatherstaff had said, and she knelt down to look at them.

'Yes, they are tiny growing things and they *might* be crocuses or snowdrops or daffodils,' she whispered.

She bent very close to them and sniffed the fresh scent of the damp earth. She liked it very much.

'Perhaps there are some other ones coming up in other places,' she said. 'I will go all over the garden and look.'

She did not skip, but walked. She went slowly and kept her eyes on the ground. She looked in the old border-beds and among the grass, and after she had gone round, trying to miss nothing, she had found ever so many more sharp, pale green points, and she had become quite excited again.

'It isn't a quite dead garden,' she cried out softly to herself. 'Even if the roses are dead, there are other things alive.'

She did not know anything about gardening, but the grass seemed so thick in some of the places where the green points were pushing their way through that she thought they did not seem to have room enough to grow. She searched about until she found a rather sharp piece of wood and knelt down and dug and weeded out the weeds and grass until she made nice little clear places around them.

'Now they look as if they could breathe,' she said, after she had finished with the first ones. 'I am going to do ever so many more. I'll do all I can see. If I haven't time today I can come tomorrow.'

She went from place to place, and dug and weeded, and enjoyed herself so immensely that she was led on from bed to bed and into the grass under the trees. The exercise made her so warm that she first threw her coat off, and then her hat, and without knowing it she was smiling down on to the grass and the pale green points all the time.

The robin was tremendously busy. He was very much pleased to see gardening begun on his own estate. He had often wondered at Ben Weatherstaff. Where gardening is done all sorts of delightful things to eat are turned up with the soil. Now here was this new kind of creature who was not have Ben's size and yet had the sense to come into his garden and begin at once.

Mistress Mary worked in her garden until it was time to go to her midday dinner. In fact she was rather late in remembering, and when she put on her coat and hat and picked up her skipping-rope, she could not believe that she had been working two or three hours. She had been actually happy all the time; and dozens and dozens of the tiny, pale green points were to be seen in cleared places, looking twice as cheerful as they had looked before when the grass and weeds had been smothering them.

'I shall come back this afternoon,' she said, looking all round at her new kingdom, and speaking to the trees and rose-bushes as if they heard her.

Then she ran lightly across the grass, pushed open the slow old door, and slipped through it under the ivy. She had such red cheeks and such bright eyes and ate such a dinner that Martha was delighted.

'Two pieces o' meat an' two helps o' rice-puddin'!' she said. 'Eh! Mother will be pleased when I tell her what th' skippin'-rope's done for thee.'

In the course of her digging with her pointed stick, Mistress Mary had found herself digging up a sort of white root rather like an onion. She had put it back in its place and patted the earth carefully down on it, and just now she wondered if Martha could tell her what it was.

'Martha,' she said, 'what are those white roots that look like onions?'

'They're bulbs,' answered Martha. 'Lots o' spring flowers grow from 'em. Th' very little ones are snowdrops an' crocuses an' th' big ones are narcissusis an' jonquils an' daffydowndillys. Th' biggest of all is lilies an' purple flags. Eh! they are nice. Dickon's got a whole lot of 'em planted in our bit o' garden.'

'Does Dickon know all about them?' asked Mary, a new idea taking possession of her.

'Our Dickon can make a flower grow out of a brick wall. Mother says he just whispers things out o' th' ground.'

'Do bulbs live a long time? Would they live years and years if no one helped them?' inquired Mary anxiously.

'They're things as helps themselves,' said Martha. 'That's why poor folk can afford to have 'em. If you don't trouble 'em, most of 'em'll work away underground for a lifetime an' spread out an' have little 'uns. There's a place in th' park woods here where there's snowdrops by thousands. They're the prettiest sight in Yorkshire when th' spring comes. No one knows when they was first planted.'

'I wish the spring was here now,' said Mary. 'I want to see all the things that grow in England.'

She had finished her dinner and gone to her favourite seat on the hearth-rug.

'I wish – I wish I had a little spade,' she said.

'Whatever does tha' want a spade for?' asked Martha laughing. 'Art tha' goin' to take to diggin'? I must tell Mother that, too.'

Mary looked at the fire and pondered a little. She must be careful if she meant to keep her secret kingdom. She wasn't doing any harm, but if Mr. Craven found out about the open door, he would be fearfully angry and get a new key and lock it up for ever more. She really could not bear that.

'This is such a big, lonely place,' she said slowly, as if she were turning matters over in her mind. 'The house is lonely, and the park is lonely, and the gardens are lonely. So many places seem shut up. I never did many things in India, but there were more people to look at – natives and soldiers marching by – and sometimes bands playing, and my Ayah told me stories. There is no one to talk to here except you and Ben Weatherstaff. And you have to do your work and Ben Weatherstaff won't speak to me often. I thought if I had a little spade I could dig somewhere as he does, and I might make a little garden if he would give me some seeds.'

Martha's face lighted up.

'There now!' she exclaimed, 'if that wasn't one of the things Mother said. She says: "There's such a lot o' room in that big place, why don't they give her a bit for herself, even if she doesn't plant nothin' but parsley an' radishes? She'd dig an' rake away an' be right down happy over it." Them was the very words she said.'

'Were they?' said Mary. 'How many things she knows, doesn't she?'

'Eh!' said Martha. 'It's like she says: "A woman as brings up twelve children learns something besides her A. B. C. Children's as good as 'rithmetic to set you findin' out things.'''

'How much would a spade cost – a little one?' Mary asked.

'Well,' was Martha's reflective answer, 'at Thwaite village there's a shop or so an' I saw little garden sets with a spade an' a rake an' a fork all tied together for two shillings. An' they was stout enough to work with, too.'

'I've got more than that in my purse,' said Mary. 'Mrs. Morrison gave me five shillings, and Mrs. Medlock gave me some money from Mr. Craven.

'Did he remember thee that much?' exclaimed Martha.

'Mrs. Medlock said I was to have a shilling a week to spend. She gives me one every Saturday. I didn't know what to spend it on.'

'My word! that's riches,' said Martha. 'Tha' can buy anything in the world tha' wants. The rent of our cottage is only one an' threepence, an' it's like pulling eye-teeth to get it. Now I've just thought of somethin',' putting her hands on her hips.

'What?' said Mary eagerly.

'In the shop at Thwaite they sell packages o' flower-seeds for a penny each, and our Dickon, he knows which is th' prettiest ones an' how to make 'em grow. He walks over to Thwaite many a day for th' fun of it. Does tha' know how to print letters?' suddenly.

'I know how to write,' Mary answered.

Martha shook her head.

'Our Dickon can only read printin'. If tha' could print we could write a letter to him an' ask him to go an' buy th' garden tools an' th' seeds at th' same time.'

'Oh! you're a good girl!' Mary cried. 'You are, really. I didn't know you were so nice. I know I can print letters if I try. Let's ask Mrs. Medlock for a pen and ink and some paper.'

'I've got some of my own,' said Martha. 'I bought 'em so I could print a bit of a letter to Mother of a Sunday. I'll go and get it.'

She ran out of the room, and Mary stood by the fire and twisted her thin little hands together with sheer pleasure.

'If I have a spade,' she whispered, 'I can make the earth nice and soft and dig up weeds. If I have seeds and can make flowers grow, the garden won't be dead at all – it will come alive.'

She did not go out again that afternoon because when Martha returned with her pen and ink and paper she was obliged to clear the table and carry the plates and dishes downstairs, and when she got into the kitchen Mrs. Medlock was there, and told her to do something, so Mary waited for what seemed to her a long time before she came back. Then it was a serious piece of work to write to Dickon. Mary had been taught very little because her governess had disliked her too much to stay with her. She could not spell particularly well, but she found that she could print letters when she tried. This was the letter Martha dictated to her:

MY DEAR DICKON,—This comes hoping to find you well as it leaves me at present. Miss Mary has plenty of money and will you go to Thwaite and buy her some flower seeds and a set of garden tools to make a flower-bed. Pick the prettiest ones and easy to grow because she has never done it before and lived in India which is different. Give my love to mother and every one of you. Miss Mary is going to tell me a lot more so that on my next day out you can hear about elephants and camels and gentlemen going hunting lions and tigers.

Your loving sister,
MARTHA PHOEBE SOWERBY

'We'll put the money in th' envelope an' I'll get th' butcher's boy to take it in his cart. He's a great friend o' Dickon's,' said Martha.

'How shall I get the things when Dickon buys them?' asked Mary.

'He'll bring 'em to you himself. He'll like to walk over this way.'

'Oh!' exclaimed Mary, 'then I shall see him! I never thought I should see Dickon.'

'Does tha' want to see him?' asked Martha suddenly, she had looked so pleased.

'Yes, I do. I never saw a boy foxes and crows loved. I want to see him very much.'

Martha gave a little start, as if she suddenly remembered something.

'Now to think,' she broke out, 'to think o' me forgettin' that there;

an' I thought I was goin' to tell you first thing this mornin'. I asked Mother – and she said she'd ask Mrs. Medlock her own self.'

'Do you mean——' Mary began.

'What I said Tuesday. Ask her if you might be driven over to our cottage some day and have a bit o' Mother's hot oat cake, an' butter, an' a glass o' milk.'

It seemed as if all the interesting things were happening in one day. To think of going over the moor in the daylight and when the sky was blue! To think of going into the cottage which held twelve children!

'Does she think Mrs. Medlock would let me go?' she asked, quite anxiously.

'Aye, she thinks she would. She knows what a tidy woman Mother is and how clean she keeps the cottage.'

'If I went I should see your mother as well as Dickon,' said Mary, thinking it over and liking the idea very much. 'She doesn't seem to be like the mothers in India.'

Her work in the garden and the excitement of the afternoon ended by making her feel quiet and thoughtful. Martha stayed with her until tea-time, but they sat in comfortable quiet and talked very little. But just before Martha went downstairs for the tea-tray, Mary asked a question.

'Martha,' she said, 'has the scullery-maid had the toothache again today?'

Martha certainly started slightly.

'What makes thee ask that?' she said.

'Because when I waited so long for you to come back I opened the door and walked down the corridor to see if you were coming. And I heard that far-off crying again, just as we heard it the other night. There isn't a wind today, so you see it couldn't have been the wind.'

'Eh!' said Martha restlessly. 'Tha' mustn't go walkin' about in corridors an' listenin'. Mr. Craven would be that there angry there's no knowin' what he'd do.'

'I wasn't listening,' said Mary. 'I was just waiting for you – and I heard it. That's three times.'

'My word! There's Mrs. Medlock's bell,' said Martha, and she almost ran out of the room.

'It's the strangest house anyone ever lived in,' said Mary drowsily, as she dropped her head on the cushion seat of the arm-chair near her. Fresh air, and digging, and skipping-rope had made her feel so comfortably tired that she fell sleep.

10 Dickon

The sun shone down for nearly a week on the secret garden. The Secret Garden was what Mary called it when she was thinking of it. She liked the name, and she liked still more the feeling that when its beautiful old walls shut her in, no one knew where she was. It seemed almost like being shut out of the world in some fairy place. The few books she had read and liked had been fairy-story books, and she had read of secret gardens in some of the stories. Sometimes people went to sleep in them for a hundred years, which she had thought must be rather stupid. She had no intention of going to sleep, and, in fact, she was becoming wider awake every day which passed at Misselthwaite. She was beginning to like to be out of doors; she no longer hated the wind, but enjoyed it. She could run faster, and longer, and she could skip up to a hundred. The bulbs in the secret garden must have been much astonished. Such nice clear spaces were made round them that they had all the breathing space they wanted, and really, if Mistress Mary had known it, they began to cheer up under the dark earth and work tremendously. The sun could get at them, and warm them, and when the rain came down it could reach them at once, so they began to feel very much alive.

Mary was an odd, determined little person, and, now she had something interesting to be determined about, she was very much absorbed indeed. She worked and dug and pulled up weeds steadily, only becoming more pleased with her work every hour instead of tiring of it. It seemed to her like a fascinating sort of play. She found many more of the sprouting pale green points than she had ever hoped to find. They seemed to be starting up everywhere, and each day she was sure she found tiny new ones, some so tiny that they barely peeped above the earth. There were so many that she remembered what Martha had said about the 'snowdrops by the thousands', and about bulbs spreading and making new ones. These had been left to themselves for ten years and perhaps they had spread, like the snowdrops, into thousands. She wondered how long it would be before they showed that they were flowers. Sometimes she stopped digging to look at the garden and try to imagine what it would be like when it was covered with thousands of lovely things in bloom.

During that week of sunshine, she became more intimate with Ben Weatherstaff. She surprised him several times by seeming to start up beside him as if she sprang out of the earth. The truth was that she was afraid that he would pick up his tools and go away if he saw her coming, so she always walked towards him as silently as possible. But, in fact, he did not object to her as strongly as he had at first. Perhaps he was secretly rather flattered by her evident desire for his elderly company. Then, also, she was more civil than she had been. He did not know that when she first saw him she spoke to him as she would have spoken to a native, and had not known that a cross, sturdy old Yorkshireman was not accustomed to salaam to his masters, and be merely commanded by them to do things.

'Tha'rt like th' robin,' he said to her one morning when he lifted his head and saw her standing by him. 'I never knows when I shall see thee or which side tha'll come from.'

'He's friends with me now!' said Mary.

'That's like him,' snapped Ben Weatherstaff. 'Makin' up to th' women-folk just for vanity an' flightiness. There's nothin' he wouldn't do for th' sake o' showin' off an' flirtin' his tail-feathers. He's as full o' pride as an egg's full o' meat.'

He very seldom talked much and sometimes did not even answer Mary's questions except by a grunt, but this morning he said more than usual. He stood up and rested one hobnailed boot on the top of his spade while he looked her over.

'How long has tha' been here?' he jerked out.

'I think it's about a month,' she answered.

'Tha's beginnin' to do Misselthwaite credit,' he said. 'Tha's a bit fatter than tha' was an' tha's not quite so yeller. Tha' looked like a young plucked crow when tha' first came into this garden. Thinks I to myself I never set eyes on an uglier, sourer-faced young 'un.'

Mary was not vain, and as she had never thought much of her looks, she was not greatly disturbed.

'I know I'm fatter,' she said. 'My stockings are getting tighter. They used to make wrinkles. There's the robin, Ben Weatherstaff.'

There, indeed, was the robin, and she thought he looked nicer than ever. His red waistcoat was as glossy as satin and flirted his wings and tail and tilted his head and hopped about with all sorts of lively graces. He seemed determined to make Ben Weatherstaff admire him. But Ben was sarcastic.

'Aye, there tha' art!' he said. 'Tha' can put up with me for a bit sometimes when tha's got no one better. Tha's been reddening' up thy waistcoat an' polishin' thy feathers this two weeks. I know what tha's up to. Tha's courtin' some bold young madam somewhere, tellin' thy lies to her about bein' th' finest cock robin on Missel Moor an' ready to fight all th' rest of 'em.'

'Oh! look at him!' exclaimed Mary.

The robin was evidently in a fascinating, bold mood. He hopped closer and closer and looked at Ben Weatherstaff more and more engagingly. He flew on to the nearest currant-bush and tilted his head and sang a little song right at him.

'Tha' thinks tha'll get over me by doin' that,' said Ben, wrinkling his face up in such a way that Mary felt sure he was trying not to look pleased. 'Tha' thinks no one can stand out against thee – that's what tha' thinks.'

The robin spread his wings – Mary could scarcely believe her eyes. He flew right up to the handle of Ben Weatherstaff's spade and alighted on the top of it. Then the old man's face wrinkled itself slowly into a new expression. He stood still as if he were afraid to breathe – as if he would not have stirred for the world, lest his robin should start away. He spoke quite in a whisper.

'Well, I'm danged!' he said as softly as if he were saying something quite different. 'Tha' does know how to get at a chap – tha' does! Tha's fair unearthly, tha's so knowin'.'

And he stood without stirring –almost without drawing his breath

"'There's the robin, Ben Weatherstaff'"

– until the robin gave another flirt to his wings and flew away. Then he stood looking at the handle of the spade as if there might be Magic in it, and then he began to dig again and said nothing for several minutes.

But because he kept breaking into a slow grin now and then, Mary was not afraid to talk to him.

'Have you a garden of your own?' she asked.

'No. I'm a bachelor an' lodge with Martha at th' gate.'

'If you had one,' said Mary, 'what would you plant?'

'Cabbages an' taters' an' onions.'

'But if you wanted to make a flower-garden,' persisted Mary, 'what would you plant?'

'Bulbs an' sweet-smellin' things – but mostly roses.'

Mary's face lighted up.

'Do you like roses?' she said.

Ben Weatherstaff rooted up a weed and threw it aside before he answered.

'Well, yes, I do. I was learned that by a young lady I was gardener to. She had a lot in a place she was fond of, an' she loved 'em like they was children – or robins. I've seen her bend over an' kiss 'em.' He dragged out another weed and scowled at it. 'That were as much as ten year' ago.'

'Where is she now?' asked Mary, much interested.

'Heaven,' he answered, and drove his spade deeply into the soil, ''cording to what parson says.'

'What happened to the roses?' Mary asked again, more interested than ever.

'They was left to themselves.'

Mary was becoming quite excited.

'Did they quite die? Do roses quite die when they are left to themselves?' she ventured.

'Well, I'd got to like 'em – an' I liked her – 'an she liked 'em,' Ben Weatherstaff admitted reluctantly. 'Once or twice a year I'd go an' work at 'em a bit – prune 'em an' dig about th' roots. They run wild, but they was in rich soil, so some of 'em lived.'

'When they have no leaves and look grey and brown and dry, how can you tell whether they are dead or alive?' inquired Mary.

'Wait till th' spring gets at 'em – wait till th' sun shines on th' rain an' th' rain falls on the sunshine an' then tha'll find out.'

'How – how?' cried Mary, forgetting to be careful.

'Look along th' twigs an' branches an' if tha' sees a bit of a brown lump swelling here an' there, watch it after th' warm rain an' see what happens.' He stopped suddenly and looked curiously at her eager face. 'Why does tha' care so much about roses an' such, all of a sudden?' he demanded.

Mistress Mary felt her face grow red. She was almost afraid to afraid to answer.

'I – I want to play that – that I have a garden of my own,' she stammered. 'I – there is nothing for me to do. I have nothing – and no one.'

'Well,' said Ben Weatherstaff slowly, as he watched her, 'that's true. Tha' hasn't.'

He said it in such an odd way that Mary wondered if he was actually a little sorry for her. She had never felt sorry for herself; she had only felt tired and cross, because she disliked people and things so much. But now the world seemed to be changing and getting nicer. If no one found out about the secret garden, she should enjoy herself always.

She stayed with him for ten or fifteen minutes longer and asked him as many questions as she dared. He answered every one of them in his queer, grunting way, and he did not seem really cross and did not pick up his spade and leave her. He said something about roses just as she was going away, and it reminded her of the ones he had said he had been fond of.

'Do you go and see those other roses now?' she asked.

'Not been this year. My rheumatics has made me too stiff in th' joints.'

He said it in his grumbling voice, and then quite suddenly he seemed to get angry with her, though she did not see why he should.

'Now look here!' he said sharply. 'Don't tha' ask so many questions. Tha'rt th' worst wench for askin' questions I've ever come across. Get thee gone an' play thee. I've done talkin' for today.'

And he said it so crossly that she knew there was not the least use in staying another minute. She went skipping slowly down the outside walk, thinking him over and saying to herself that, queer as it was, here was another person whom she liked, in spite of his crossness. She liked old Ben Weatherstaff, Yes, she did like him. She always wanted to try to make him talk to her. Also she began to believe that he knew everything in the world about flowers.

There was a laurel-hedged walk which curved round the secret garden and ended at a gate which opened into a wood in the park. She thought she would skip round this walk and look into the wood and see if there were any rabbits hopping about. She enjoyed the skipping very much, and when she reached the little gate she opened it and went through because she heard a low, peculiar whistling sound and wanted to find out what it was.

It was a very strange thing indeed. She quite caught her breath as she stopped to look at it. A boy was sitting under a tree, with his back against it, playing on a rough wooden pipe. He was a funny-looking boy about twelve. He looked very clean and his nose turned up and his cheeks were as red as poppies, and never had Mistress Mary seen such round and such blue eyes in any boy's face. And on the trunk of the tree he leaned against, a brown squirrel was clinging and watching him, and from behind a bush near by a cock pheasant was delicately stretching his neck to peep out, and quite near him were two rabbits sitting up and sniffing with tremulous noses – and actually it appeared as if they were all drawing near to watch him and listen to the strange, low, little call his pipe seemed to make.

When he saw Mary he held up his hand and spoke to her in a voice almost as low as and rather like his piping.

'Don't tha' move,' he said. 'It'd flight 'em.'

Mary remained motionless. He stopped playing his pipe and began to rise from the ground. He moved so slowly that it scarcely seemed as though he were moving at all, but at last he stood on his feet and then the squirrel scampered back up into the branches of his tree, the pheasant withdrew his head, and the rabbits dropped on all fours and began to hop away, though not at all as if they were frightened.

'I'm Dickon,' the boy said. 'I know tha'rt Miss Mary.'

Then Mary realized that somehow she had known at first that

he was Dickon. Who else could have been charming rabbits and pheasants as the natives charm snakes in India? He had a wide, red, curving mouth and his smile spread all over his face.

'I got up slow,' he explained, 'because if tha' makes a quick move it startles 'em. A body 'as to move gentle an' speak low when wild things is about.'

He did not speak to her as if they had never seen each other before, but as if he knew her quite well. Mary knew nothing about boys, and she spoke to him a little stiffly because she felt rather shy.

'Did you get Martha's letter?' she asked.

He nodded his curly, rust-coloured head.

'That's why I come.'

He stooped to pick up something which had been lying on the ground beside him when he piped.

'I've got th' garden tools. There's a little spade an' rake an' a fork an' hoe. Eh! they are good 'uns. There's a trowel, too. An' th' woman in th' shop threw in a packet o' white poppy an' one o' blue larkspur when I bought th' other seeds.'

'Will you show the seeds to me?' Mary said.

She wished she could talk as he did. His speech was so quick and easy. It sounded as if he liked her and was not the least afraid she would not like him, though he was only a common moor boy, in patched clothes and with a funny face and a rough, rusty-red head. As she came closer to him she noticed that there was a clean fresh scent of heather and grass and leaves about him, almost as if he were made of them. She liked it very much, and when she looked into his funny face with the red cheeks and round blue eyes she forgot that she had felt shy.

'Let us sit down on this log and look at them,' she said.

They sat down and he took a clumsy little brown-paper package out of his coat pocket. He untied the string and inside there were ever so many neater and small packages, with a picture of a flower on each one.

'There's a lot o' mignonette an' poppies,' he said. 'Mignonette's th' sweetest smellin' thing as grows an' it'll grow wherever you cast it, same as poppies will. Them as'll come up an' bloom if you just whistle to 'em, them's th' nicest of all.'

He stopped and turned his head quickly, his poppy-cheeked face lighting up.

'Where's that robin as is callin' us?' he said.

The chirp came from a thick holly bush, bright with scarlet berries, and Mary thought she knew whose it was.

'Is it really calling us?' she asked.

'Aye,' said Dickon, as if it was the most natural thing in the world, 'he's callin' someone he's friends with. That's same as sayin' "Here I am. Look at me. I want a bit of a chat." There he is in the bush. Whose is he?'

'He's Ben Weatherstaff's, but I think he knows me a little,' answered Mary.

'Aye, he knows thee,' said Dickon in his low voice again. 'An' he likes thee. He's took thee on. He'll tell me all about thee in a minute.'

He moved quite close to the bush with the slow movement Mary had noticed before and then he made a sound almost like the robin's own twitter. The robin listened a few seconds, intently, and then answered quite as if he were replying to a question.

'Aye, he's a friend o' yours,' chuckled Dickon.

'Do you think he is?' cried Mary eagerly. She did so want to know. 'Do you think he really likes me?'

'He wouldn't come near thee if he didn't,' answered Dickon. 'birds is rare choosers an' a robin can flout a body worse than a man. See, he's making up to thee now. "Cannot tha' see a chap?" he's sayin'.'

And it really seemed as if it must be true. He so sidled and twittered and tilted as he hopped on his bush.

'Do you understand everything birds say?' said Mary.

Dickon's grin spread until he seemed all wide, red, curving mouth, and he rubbed his rough head.

'I think I do, and they think I do,' he said. 'I've lived on th' moor with 'em so long. I've watched 'em break shell and come out an' fledge an' learn to fly an' begin to sing, till I think I'm one of 'em. Sometimes I think p'raps I'm a bird, or a fox, or a rabbit, or a squirrel, or even a beetle, an' I don't know it.'

He laughed and came back to the log and began to talk about the flower seeds again. He told her what they looked like when they were flowers; he told her how to plant them, and watch them, and feed and water them.

'See here,' he said suddenly, turning round to look at her. 'I'll plant them for thee myself. Where is tha' garden?'

Mary's thin hands clutched each other as they lay on her lap. She did not know what to say, so for a whole minute she said nothing. She had never thought of this. She felt miserable. And she felt as if she went red and then pale.

'Tha's got a bit o' garden, hasn't tha?' Dickon said.

It was true that she had turned red and then pale. Dickon saw her do it, and as she still said nothing, he began to be puzzled.

'Wouldn't they give thee a bit?' he asked. 'Hasn't tha' got any yet?'

She held her hands even tighter and turned her eyes towards him.

'I don't know anything about boys,' she said slowly. 'Could you keep a secret, if I told you one? It's a great secret, I don't what I should do if anyone found it out. I believe I should die!' She said the last sentence quite fiercely.

Dickon looked more puzzled than ever and even rubbed his hand over his rough head again, but he answered good-humouredly.

'I'm keepin' secrets all th' time,' he said. 'If I couldn't keep secrets from th' other lads, secrets about foxes' cubs, an' birds' nests, an' wild things' holes, there'd be naught safe on th' moor. Aye, I can keep secrets.'

Mistress Mary did not mean to put out her hand and clutch his sleeve, but she did it.

'I've stolen a garden,' she said very fast. 'It isn't mine. It isn't anybody's. Nobody wants it, nobody cares for it, nobody ever goes into it. Perhaps everything is dead in it already; I don't know.'

She began to feel hot and as contrary as she had ever felt in her life.

'I don't care, I don't care! Nobody has any right to take it from me when I care about it and they don't. They're letting it die, all shut in by itself,' she ended passionately, and she threw her arms over her face and burst out crying – poor little Mistress Mary.

Dickon's curious blue eyes grew rounder and rounder.

'Eh-h-h!' he said, drawing his exclamation out slowly, and the way he did it meant both wonder and sympathy.

'I've nothing to do,' said Mary. 'Nothing belongs to me. I found it myself and I got into it myself. I was only just like the robin, and they wouldn't take it from the robin.'

'Where is it?' asked Dickon in a dropped voice.

Mistress Mary got up from the log at once. She knew she felt contrary again, and obstinate, and she did not care at all. She was imperious and Indian, and at the same time hot and sorrowful.

'Come with me and I'll show you,' she said.

She led him round the laurel path and to the walk where the ivy grew so thickly. Dickon followed her with a queer, almost pitying, look on his face. He felt as if he were being led to look at some strange bird's nest and must move softly. When she stepped to the wall and lifted the hanging ivy he started. There was a door and Mary pushed it slowly open and they passed in together, and then Mary stood and waved her hand round defiantly.

'It's this,' she said. 'It's a secret garden, and I'm the only one in the world who wants it to be alive.'

Dickon looked round and round about it, and round and round again.

'Eh!' he almost whispered, 'it is a queer, pretty place. 'It's like as if a body was in a dream.'

11 The Nest of the Missel Thrush

For two or three minutes he stood looking round him, while Mary watched him, and then he began to walk about softly, even more lightly than Mary had walked the first time she had found herself inside the four walls. His eyes seemed to be taking in everything – the grey trees with the grey creepers climbing over them and hanging from their branches, the tangle on the wall and among the grass, the evergreen alcoves with the stone seats and tall flower urns standing in them.

'I never thought I'd see this place,' he said at last in a whisper.

'Did you know about it?' asked Mary.

She had spoken aloud and he made a sign to her.

'We must talk low,' he said, 'or someone'll hear us an' wonder what's to do in here.'

'Oh! I forgot!' said Mary, feeling frightened and putting her hand quickly against her mouth. 'Did you know about the garden?' she asked again when she had recovered herself.

Dickon nodded.

'Martha told me there was one as no one ever went inside,' he answered. 'Us used to wonder what it was like.'

He stopped and looked round at the lovely grey tangle about him, and his round eyes looked queerly happy.

'Eh! The nests as'll be here come springtime,' he said. 'It'd be th' safest nestin' place in England. No one ever comin' near an' tangles o' trees an' roses to build in. I wonder all th' birds on th' moor don't build here.'

Mistress Mary put her hand on his arm again without knowing it.

'Will there be roses?' she whispered. 'Can you tell? I thought perhaps they were all dead.'

'Eh! Not them − not all of 'em!' he answered. 'Look here!'

He stepped over to the nearest tree − an old, old one with grey lichen all over its bark, but upholding a curtain of tangled sprays and branches. He took a thick knife out of his pocket and opened one of its blades.

'There's lots o' dead wood as ought to be cut out,' he said. 'An' there's a lot o' old wood, but it made some new last year. This here's a new bit,' and he touched a shoot which looked brownish-green instead of hard, dry grey.

Mary touched it herself in an eager, reverent way.

'That one?' she said. 'Is that one quite alive − quite?'

Dickon curved his wide, smiling mouth.

'It's as wick as you or me,' he said; and Mary remembered that Martha had told her that 'wick' meant 'alive' or 'lively'.

'I'm glad it's wick!' she cried out in her whisper. 'I want them all to be wick. Let us go round the garden and count how many wick ones there are.'

She quite panted with eagerness, and Dickon was as eager as she was. They went from tree to tree and from bush to bush. Dickon carried his knife in his hand and showed her things which she thought wonderful.

'They're run wild,' he said, 'but th' strongest ones has fair thrived on it. The delicatest ones has died out, but the others has growed an' growed, an' spread an' spread, till they's a wonder. See here!' and he pulled down a thick, grey, dry-looking branch!' 'A body might think this was dead wood, but I don't believe it is − down to th' root. I'll cut it low down an' see.'

He knelt and with his knife cut the lifeless-looking branch through, not far above the earth.

'There!' he said exultantly. 'I told thee so.' There's green in that wood yet. Look at it.'

Mary was down on her knees before he spoke, gazing with all her might.

'When it looks a bit greenish an' juicy like that, it's wick,' he explained. 'When th' inside is dry an' breaks easy, like this here piece

I've cut off, it's done for. There's a big root here as all this live wood sprung out of, an' if th' old wood's cut off an' it's dug round, an' took care of there'll be' – he stopped and lifted his face to look up at the climbing and hanging sprays about him – 'there'll be a fountain o' roses here this summer.'

They went from bush to bush and from tree to tree. He was very strong and clever with his knife and knew how to cut the dry and dead wood away, and could tell when an unpromising bough or twig had still green life in it. In the course of half an hour, Mary thought she could tell too, and when he cut through a lifeless-looking branch she would cry out joyfully under her breath when she caught sight of the least shade of moist green. The spade, and hoe, and fork were very useful. He showed her how to use the fork while he dug about the roots with the spade and stirred the earth and let the air in.

They were working industriously round one of the biggest standard roses when he caught sight of something which made him utter an exclamation of surprise.

'Why!' he cried, pointing to the grass a few feet away. 'Who did that?'

It was one of Mary's own little clearings round the pale-green points.

'I did it,' said Mary.

'Why, I thought tha' didn't know nothin' about gardenin',' he exclaimed.

'I don't,' she answered, 'but they were so little and the grass was so thick and strong, and they looked as if they had no room to breathe. So I made a place for them. I don't even know what they are.'

Dickon went and knelt down by them, smiling his wide smile.

'Tha' was right,' he said. 'A gardener couldn't have told thee better. They'll grow now like Jack's bean-stalk. They're crocuses an' snowdrops, an' these here is narcissuses,' turning to another patch, 'an' here's daffydowndillys. Eh! They will be a sight.'

He ran from one clearing to another.

'Tha' has done a lot o' work for such a little wench,' he said looking her over.

'I'm growing fatter,' said Mary, 'and I'm growing stronger. I used always to be tired. When I dig I'm not tired at all. I like to smell the earth when its turned up.'

'It's rare good for thee,' he said, nodding his head wisely. 'There's naught as nice as th' smell o' good clean earth, except th' smell o' fresh growin' things when th' rain falls on 'em. I get out on th' moor many a day when it's rainin' an' I lie under a bush an' listen to th' soft swish o' drops on th' heather an' I just sniff an' sniff. My nose end fair quivers like a rabbit's, Mother says.'

'Do you never catch cold?' inquired Mary, gazing at him wonderingly. She had never seen such a funny boy, or such a nice one.

'Not me,' he said, grinning. 'I never ketched cold since I was born. I wasn't brought up nesh enough. I've chased about th' moor in all weathers, same as th' rabbits does. Mother says I've sniffed too much fresh air for twelve year' to ever get to sniffin' with cold. I'm as tough as a whitethorn knobstick.'

He was working all the time he was talking and Mary was following him and helping him with her fork or the trowel.

'There's a lot of work to do here!' he said once, looking about quite exultantly.

'Will you come again and help me to do it?' Mary begged. 'I'm sure I can help, too. I can dig and pull up weeds, and do whatever you tell me. Oh! do come, Dickon!'

'I'll come every day if tha' wants me, rain or shine,' he answered stoutly. 'It's th' best fun I ever had in my life – shut in here an' wakening' up a garden.'

'If you will come,' said Mary, 'if you will help me to make it alive I'll – I don't know what I'll do,' she ended helplessly. What could you do for a boy like that?

'I'll tell thee what tha'll do,' said Dickon, with his happy grin. 'Tha'll get fat an' tha'll get as hungry as a young fox an' tha'll learn how to talk to th' robin same as I do. Eh! We'll have a lot o' fun.'

He began to walk about, looking up in the trees and at the walls and bushes with a thoughtful expression.

'I wouldn't want to make it look like a gardener's garden, all clipped an' spick an' span, would you?' he said. 'It's nicer like this with things runnin' wild, an' swingin' an' catchin' hold of each other.'

'Don't let us make it tidy,' said Mary anxiously. 'it wouldn't seem like a secret garden if it was tidy.'

Dickon stood rubbing his rusty-red head with a rather puzzled look.

'It's a secret garden sure enough,' he said, 'but seems like someone besides th' robin must have been in it since it was shut up ten year' ago.'

'But the door was locked and the key was buried,' said Mary. 'No one could get in.'

'That's true,' he answered. 'It's a queer place. Seems to me as if there'd been a bit o' prunin' done here an' there, later than ten year' ago.'

'But how could it have been done?' said Mary.

He was examining a branch of a standard rose and he shook his head.

'Aye! How could it!' he murmured. 'With th' door locked an' th' key buried.'

Mistress Mary always felt that however many years she lived she should never forget that first morning when her garden began to grow. Of course, it did seem to begin to grow for her that morning. When Dickon began to clear places to plant seeds, she remembered what Basil had sung at her when he wanted to tease her.

'Are there any flowers that look like bells?' she inquired.

'Lilies o' th' valley does,' he answered, digging away with the trowel, 'an' there's Canterbury bells, an' campanulas.'

'Let us plant some,' said Mary.

'There's lilies o' th' valley here already; I saw 'em. They'll have growed too close an' we'll have to separate 'em, but there's plenty. Th' other ones take two years to bloom from seed, but I can bring you some bits o' plants from our cottage garden. Why does tha want 'em?'

Then Mary told him about Basil and his brothers and sisters in India and of how she had hated them, and of their calling her 'Mistress Mary Quite Contrary'.

'They used to dance round and sing at me. They sang:

Mistress Mary, quite contrary,
    How does your garden grow?
With silver bells and cockle shells,
    And marigolds all in a row.

I just remembered it and it made me wonder if there were really flowers like silver bells.'

She frowned a little and gave her trowel a rather spiteful dig into the earth.

'I wasn't as contrary as they were.'

But Dickon laughed.

'Eh!' he said, and as he crumpled the rich black soil she saw he was sniffing up the scent of it, 'there doesn't seem to be no need for no one to be contrary when there's flowers an' such like, an' such lots o' friendly wild things runnin' about makin' homes for themselves, or buildin' nests an' singin' an' whistling, does there?'

Mary, kneeling by him holding the seeds, looked at him and stopped frowning.

'Dickon,' she said. 'You are as nice as Martha said you were. I like you, and you make the fifth person. I never thought I should like five people.'

Dickon sat up on his heels as Martha did when she was polishing the grate. He did look funny and delightful, Mary thought, with his round blue eyes and red cheeks and happy-looking turned-up nose.

'Only five folks as tha' likes?' he said. 'Who is th' other four?'

'Your mother and Martha,' Mary checked them off on her fingers, 'and the robin and Ben Weatherstaff.'

Dickon laughed, so that he was obliged to stifle the sound by putting his arm over his mouth.

'I know tha' thinks I'm a queer lad,' he said, 'but I think tha' art th' queerest little lass I ever saw.'

Then Mary did a strange thing. She leaned forward and asked him a question she had never dreamed of asking anyone before. And she tried to ask it in Yorkshire because that was his language, and in India a native was always pleased if you knew his speech.

'Does tha' like me?' she said.

'Eh!' he answered heartily, 'that I does. I likes thee wonderful, an' so does th' robin, I do believe!'

'That's two, then,' said Mary. 'That's two for me.'

And then they began to work harder than ever and more joyful. Mary was startled and sorry when she heard the big clock in the courtyard strike the hour of her midday dinner.

'I shall have to go,' she said mournfully. 'And you will have to go too, won't you?'

Dickon grinned.

'My dinner's easy to carry about with me,' he said. 'Mother always lets me put a bit o' somethin' in my pocket.'

He picked up his coat from the grass and brought out of a pocket a lumpy little bundle tied up in a quite clean, coarse, blue and white handkerchief. It held two thick pieces of bread with a slice of something laid between them.

'It's oftenest naught but bread,' he said, 'but I've got a fine slice o' fat bacon with it today.'

Mary thought it looked a queer dinner, but he seemed ready to enjoy it.

'Run on an' get thy victuals,' he said. 'I'll be done with mine first. I'll get some more work done before I start back home.'

He sat down with his back against a tree.

'I'll call th' robin up,' he said, 'and give him th' rind o' th' bacon to peck at. They likes a bit o' fat wonderful.'

Mary could scarcely bear to leave him. Suddenly it seemed as if he might be a sort of wood fairy who might be gone when she came into the garden again. He seemed too good to be true. She went slowly half-way to the door in the wall and then she stopped and went back.

'Whatever happens, you – never would tell?' she said.

His poppy-coloured cheeks were distended with his first big bite of bread and bacon, but he managed to smile encouragingly.

'If tha' was a missel thrush an' showed me where thy nest was, does tha' think I'd tell anyone? Not me,' he said. 'Tha' art as safe as a missel thrush.'

And she was quite sure she was.

12 Might I have a bit of earth?'

Mary ran so fast that she was rather out of breath when she reached her room. Her hair was ruffled on her forehead and her cheeks were bright pink. Her dinner was waiting on the table, and Martha was waiting near it.

'Tha's a bit late,' she said. 'Where has tha' been?'

'I've seen Dickon!' said Mary. 'I've seen Dickon!'

'I knew he'd come,' said Martha exultantly. 'How does tha' like him?'

'I think – I think he's beautiful!' said Mary in a determined voice.

Martha looked rather taken aback, but she looked pleased, too.

'Well,' she said, 'he's th' best lad as ever was born, but us never thought he was handsome. His nose turns up too much.'

'I like it to turn up,' said Mary.

'An' his eyes is so round,' said Martha, a trifle doubtful. 'Though they're a nice colour.'

'I like the- round,' said Mary. 'And they are exactly the colour of the sky over the moor.'

Martha beamed with satisfaction.

'Mother says he made 'em that colour with always lookin' up at th' birds an' th' clouds. But he has got a big mouth, hasn't he, now?'

'I love his big mouth,' said Mary obstinately. 'I wish mine were just like it.'

Martha chuckled delightedly.

'It'd look rare an' funny in thy bit of a face,' she said. 'But I knowed it would be that way when tha' saw him. How did tha' like th' seeds an' th' garden tools?'

'How did you know he brought them?' asked Mary.

'Eh! I never thought of his not bringin' 'em. He'd be sure to bring 'em if they was in Yorkshire. He's such a trusty lad.'

Mary was afraid that she might begin to ask difficult questions, but she did not. She was very much interested in the seeds and gardening tools, and there was only one moment when Mary was frightened. This was when she began to ask where the flowers were to be planted.

'Who did tha' ask about it?' she inquired.

'I haven't asked anybody yet,' said Mary, hesitatingly.

'Well, I wouldn't ask th' head gardener. He's too grand, Mr. Roach is.'

'I've never seen him,' said Mary. 'I've only seen under-gardeners and Ben Weatherstaff.'

'If I was you, I'd ask Ben Weatherstaff,' advised Martha. 'He's not half as bad as he looks, for all he's so crabbed. Mr. Craven lets him do what he likes, because he was here when Mrs. Craven was alive, an' he used to make her laugh. She liked him. Perhaps he'd find you a corner somewhere out o' the way.'

'If it was out of the way and no one wanted it, no one *could* mind my having it, could they?' Mary said anxiously.

'There wouldn't be no reason,' answered Martha. 'You wouldn't do no harm.'

Mary ate her dinner as quickly as she could, and when she rose from the table she was going to run to her room to put on her hat again, but Martha stopped her.

'I've got somethin' to tell you,' she said. 'I thought I'd let you eat your dinner first. Mr. Craven came back this mornin' and I think he wants to see you.'

Mary turned quite pale.

'Oh! she said. 'Why? Why? He didn't want to see me when I came. I heard Pitcher say he didn't.'

'Well,' explained Martha. 'Mrs. Medlock says it's because o' Mother. She was walkin' to Thwaite village an' she met him. She'd never spoke to him before, but Mrs. Craven had been to our cottage two or three times. He'd forgot, but Mother hadn't, an' she made bold to stop him. I don't know what she said to him about you, but she said somethin' as put him in th' mind to see you before he goes away again, tomorrow.'

'Oh!' cried Mary, 'is he going away tomorrow? I'm so glad!'

'He's goin' for a long time. He mayn't come back till autumn or winter. He's goin' to travel in foreign places. He's always doin' it.'

'Oh! I'm so glad – so glad!' said Mary thankfully.

If he did not come back until winter, or even autumn, there would be time to watch the secret garden come alive. Even if he found out then and took it away from her, she would have had that much at least.

'When do you think he will want to see——'

She did not finish the sentence, because the door opened, and Mrs. Medlock walked in. She had on her best black dress and cap, and her collar was fastened with a large brooch with a picture of a man's face on it. It was a coloured photograph of Mr. Medlock, who had died years ago, and she always wore it when she was dressed up. She looked nervous and excited.

'Your hair's rough,' she said quickly. 'Go and brush it. Martha, help to slip on her best dress. Mr. Craven sent me to bring her to him in his study.'

All the pink left Mary's cheeks. Her heart began to thump and she felt herself changing into a stiff, plain, silent child again. She did not even answer Mrs. Medlock, but turned and walked into her bedroom, followed by Martha. She said nothing while her dress was changed, and her hair brushed, and after she was quite tidy she followed Mrs. Medlock down the corridors, in silence. What was there for her to say? She was obliged to go and see Mr. Craven, and he would not like her, and she would not like him. She knew what he would think of her.

She was taken to a part of the house she had not been into before. At last Mrs. Medlock knocked at a door, and when someone said, 'Come in,' they entered the room together. A man was sitting in an arm-chair before the fire, and Mrs. Medlock spoke to him.

'This is Miss Mary, sir,' she said.

'You can go and leave her here. I will ring for you when I want you to take her away,' said Mr. Craven.

When she went out and closed the door, Mary could only stand waiting, a plain little thing, twisting her thin hands together. She could see that the man in the chair was not so much a hunchback as a man with high, rather crooked shoulders, and he had black hair streaked with white. He turned his head over his high shoulders and spoke to her.

'Come here!' he said.

Mary went to him.

He was not ugly. His face would have been handsome if it had not been so miserable. He looked as if the sight of her worried and fretted him and as if he did not know what in the world to do with her.

'Are you well?' he asked.

'Yes,' answered Mary.

'Do they take good care of you?'

'Yes.'

He rubbed his forehead fretfully as he looked her over.

'You are very thin,' he said.

'I am getting fatter,' Mary answered, in what she knew was her stiffest way.

What an unhappy face he had! His black eyes seemed as if they scarcely saw her, as if they were seeing something else, and he could hardly keep his thoughts upon her.

'I forgot you,' he said. 'How could I remember you? I intended to send you a governess or nurse or someone of that sort, but I forgot.'

'Please,' began Mary. 'Please——' and then the lump in her throat choked her.

'What do you want to say?' he inquired.

'I am – I am too big for a nurse,' said Mary. 'And please – please don't make me have a governess yet.'

He rubbed his forehead again and stared at her.

'That was what the Sowerby woman said,' he muttered absent-mindedly.

Then Mary gathered a scrap of courage.

'Is she – is she Martha's mother?' she stammered.

'Yes, I think so,' he replied.

'She knows about children,' said Mary. 'She has twelve. She knows.'

He seemed to rouse himself.

'What do you want to do?'

'I want to play out of doors,' Mary answered, hoping that her voice did not tremble. 'I never liked it in India. It makes me hungry here, and I am getting fatter.'

He was watching her.

'Mrs. Sowerby said it would do you good. Perhaps it will,' he said. 'She thought you had better get stronger before you had a governess.'

'It makes me feel strong when I play and the wind comes over the moor,' argued Mary.

'Where do you play?' he asked next.

'Everywhere,' gasped Mary. 'Martha's mother sent me a skipping-rope. I skip and run – and I look about to see if things are beginning to stick up out of the earth. I don't do any harm.'

'Don't look so frightened,' he said in a worried voice. 'You could not do any harm, a child like you! You may do what you like.'

Mary put her hand up to her throat because she was afraid he might see the excited lump which she felt jump into it. She came a step nearer to him.

'May I?' she said tremulously.

Her anxious little face seemed to worry him more than ever.

'Don't look so frightened,' he exclaimed. 'Of course you may. I am your guardian, though I am a poor one for any child. I cannot give you time or attention. I am too ill, and wretched and distracted; but I wish you to be happy and comfortable. I don't know anything about children, but Mrs. Medlock is to see that you have all you need. I sent for you today because Mrs. Sowerby said I ought to see you. Her daughter had talked about you. She thought you needed fresh air and freedom and running about.'

'She knows all about children,' Mary said again in spite of herself.

'She ought to,' said Mr. Craven. 'I thought her rather bold to stop me on the moor, but she said Mrs. Craven had been kind to her.' 'She is a respectable woman. Now I have seen you I think she said sensible things. Play out of doors as much as you like. It's a big place, and you may go where you like and amuse yourself as you like. Is there anything you want?' As if a sudden thought had struck him. 'Do you want toys, books, dolls?'

'Might I,' quavered Mary, 'might I have a bit of earth?'

In her eagerness she did not realize how queer the words would sound and that they were not the ones she had meant to say. Mr. Craven looked quite startled.

'Earth!' he repeated. 'What do you mean?'

'To plant seeds in   to make things grow – to see them come alive,' Mary faltered.

He gazed at her a moment and then passed his hands quickly over his eyes.

'Do you – care about gardens so much?' he said slowly.

'I didn't know about them in India,' said Mary. 'I was always ill and tired, and it was so hot. I sometimes made little beds in the sand and stuck flowers in them. But here it is different.'

Mr Craven got up and began to walk slowly across the room.

'A bit of earth,' he said to himself and Mary thought that somehow she must have reminded him of something. When he stopped and spoke to her his dark eyes looked almost soft and kind.

'You can have as much earth as you want,' he said. 'You remind me of someone else who loved the earth and things that grow. When you see a bit of earth you want,' with something like a smile, 'take it, child, and make it come alive.'

'May I take it from anywhere – if it's not wanted?'

'Anywhere,' he answered. 'There! You must go now, I am tired.' He touched the bell to call Mrs. Medlock. 'Good-bye. I shall be away all summer.'

Mrs. Medlock came so quickly that Mary thought she must have been waiting in the corridor.

'Mrs. Medlock,' Mr Craven said to her, 'now I have seen the child I understand what Mrs. Sowerby meant. She must be less delicate before she begins lessons. Give her simple, healthy food. Let her run wild in the garden. Don't look after her too much. She needs liberty and fresh air and romping about. Mrs. Sowerby is to come and see her now and then, and she may sometimes go to the cottage.'

Mrs. Medlock looked pleased. She was relieved to hear that she need not 'look after' Mary too much. She had felt her a tiresome charge, and had, indeed, seen as little of her as she dared. In addition to this, she was fond of Martha's mother.

'Thank you, sir,' she said. 'Susan Sowerby and me went to school together, and she's as sensible and good-hearted a woman as you'd find in a day's walk. I never had any children myself and she's had twelve, and there never was healthier or better ones. Miss Mary can get no harm from them. I'd always take Susan Sowerby's advice about children myself. She's what you might call healthy-minded – if you understand me.'

'I understand,' Mr. Craven answered. 'Take Miss Mary away now and send Pitcher to me.'

When Mrs. Medlock left her at the end of her own corridor Mary flew back to her room. She found Martha waiting there. Martha had, in fact, hurried back after she had removed the dinner service.

'I can have my garden!' cried Mary. 'I may have it where I like! I am not going to have a governess for a long time! Your mother is coming to see me and I may go to your cottage. He says a little girl like me could not do any harm and I may do what I like – anywhere!'

'Eh!' said Martha, delighted, 'that was nice of him, wasn't it?'

'Martha,' said Mary solemnly, 'he is really a nice man, only his face is so miserable and his forehead is all drawn together.'

She ran as quickly as she could to the garden. She had been away so much longer than she had thought she should, and she knew Dickon would have to set out early on his five-mile walk. When she slipped through the door under the ivy, she saw he was not working where she had left him. The gardening tools were laid together under a tree. She ran to them, looking all round the place, but there was no Dickon to be seen. He had gone away and the secret garden was empty – except for the robin, who had just flown across the wall and sat on a standard rose-bush watching her.

'He's gone,' she said woefully. 'Oh! Was he – was he – was he only a wood fairy?'

Something white fastened to the standard rose-bush caught her eye. It was a piece of paper – in fact, it was a piece of the letter she had printed for Martha to send to Dickon. It was fastened on the bush with a long thorn, and in a minute she knew Dickon had left it there. There were some roughly printed letters on it and a sort of picture. At first she could not tell what it was. Then she saw it was meant for a nest with a bird sitting on it. Underneath were the printed letters, and they said:

'I will cum bak.'

13 'I am Colin'

Mary took the picture back to the house when she went to her supper and she showed it to Martha.

'Eh!' said Martha with great pride. 'I never knew our Dickon was as clever as that. That there's a picture of a missel thrush on her nest, as large as life an' twice as natural.'

Then Mary knew Dickon had meant the picture to be a message. He had meant that she might be sure he would keep her secret. Her garden was her nest and she was like a missel thrush. Oh, how she did like that queer, common boy!

She hoped he would come back the very next day, and she fell asleep looking forward to the morning.

But you never know what the weather will do in Yorkshire, particularly in the springtime. She was awakened in the night by the sound of rain beating with heavy drops against her window. It was pouring down in torrents and the wind was 'wuthering' round the corners and in the chimneys of the huge old house. Mary sat up in bed and felt miserable and angry.

'The rain is as contrary as I ever was,' she said. 'It came because it knew I did not want it.'

She threw herself back on her pillow and buried her face. She did not cry, but she lay and hated the sound of the heavily beating rain, she hated the wind and its 'wuthering'. She could not go to sleep again. The mournful sound kept her awake, because she felt mournful herself. If she had felt happy it would probably have lulled her to sleep. How it 'wuthered' and how the big raindrops poured down and beat against the pane!

'It sounds just like a person lost on the moor and wandering on and on crying,' she said.

*

She had been lying awake, turning from side to side for about an hour, when suddenly something made her sit up in bed and turn her head towards the door listening. She listened and she listened.

'It isn't the wind now,' she said in a loud whisper. 'That isn't the wind. It is different. It is that crying I heard before.'

The door of her room was ajar and the sound came down the corridor, a far-off faint sound of fretful crying. She listened for a few minutes and each minute she became more and more sure. She felt as if she must find out what it was. It seemed even stranger than the secret garden and the buried key. Perhaps the fact that she was in a rebellious mood made her bold. She put her foot out of bed and stood on the floor.

'I am going to find out what it is,' she said. 'Everybody is in bed and I don't care about Mrs. Medlock – I don't care!'

There was a candle by her bedside and she took it up and went softly out of the room. The corridor looked very long and dark, but she was too excited to mind that. She thought she remembered the corners she must turn to find the short corridor with the door covered with tapestry – the one Mrs. Medlock had come through the day she lost herself. The sound had come up that passage. So she went on with her dim light, almost feeling her way, her heart beating so loud that she fancied she could hear it. The far-off, faint crying went on and led her. Sometimes it stopped for a moment or so and then began again. Was this the right corner to turn? She stopped and thought. Yes, it was. Down this passage and then to the left, and then up two broad steps, and then to the right again. Yes, there was the tapestry door.

She pushed it open very gently and closed it behind her, and she stood in the corridor and could hear the crying quite plainly, though it was not loud. It was on the other side of the wall at her left and a few yards farther on there was a door. She could see a glimmer of light coming from beneath it. The Someone was crying in that room, and it

'*Mary stood near the door with her candle in her hand*'

was quite a young Someone.

So she walked to the door and pushed it open, and there she was standing in the room!

It was a big room with ancient, handsome furniture in it. There was a low fire glowing faintly on the hearth and a night-light burning by the side of a carved, four-poster bed hung with brocade, and on the bed was lying a boy, crying pitifully.

Mary wondered if she was in a real place or if she had fallen asleep again and was dreaming without knowing it.

The boy had a sharp, delicate face, the colour of ivory, and he seemed to have eyes too big for it. He had also a lot of hair which tumbled over his forehead in heavy locks and made his thin face seem smaller. He looked like a boy who had been ill, but he was crying more as if he were tired and cross than as if he were in pain.

Mary stood near the door with her candle in her hand, holding her breath. Then she crept across the room, and as she drew nearer the light attracted the boy's attention and he turned his head on his pillow and stared at her, his grey eyes opening so wide that they seemed immense.

'Who are you?' he said at last in a half-frightened whisper. 'Are you a ghost?'

'No, I am not,' Mary answered, her own whisper sounding half-frightened. 'Are you one?'

He stared and stared and stared. Mary could not help noticing what strange eyes he had. They were agate-grey and they looked too big for his face because they had black lashes all round them.

'No,' he replied, after waiting a moment or so. 'I am Colin.'

'Who is Colin?' she faltered.

'I am Colin Craven. Who are you?'

'I am Mary Lennox. Mr. Craven is my uncle.'

'He is my father,' said the boy.

'Your father!' gasped Mary. 'No one ever told me he had a boy! Why didn't they?'

'Come here,' he said, still keeping his strange eyes fixed on her with an anxious expression.

She came close to the bed and he put out his hand and touched her.

'You are real, aren't you?' he said. 'I have such real dreams very often. You might be one of them.'

Mary had slipped on a woollen wrapper before she left her room and she put a piece of it between his fingers.

'Rub that and see how thick and warm it is,' she said. 'I will pinch you a little if you like, to show you how real I am. For a minute I thought you might be a dream, too.'

'Where did you come from?' he asked.

'From my own room. The wind wuthered so I couldn't go to sleep and I heard someone crying and wanted to find out who it was. What were you crying for?'

'Because I couldn't go to sleep either, and my head ached. Tell me your name again.'

'Mary Lennox. Did no one ever tell you I had come to live here?'

He was still fingering the fold of her wrapper, but he began to look a little more as if he believed in her reality.

'No,' he answered. 'They daren't.'

'Why?' asked Mary.

'Because I should have been afraid you would see me. I won't let people see me and talk me over.'

'Why?' Mary asked again, feeling more mystified every moment.

'Because I am like this always, ill and having to lie down. My father won't let people talk me over, either. The servants are not allowed to speak about me. If I live I may be a hunchback, but I shan't live. My father hates to think I may be like him.'

'Oh, what a queer house this is!' Mary said. 'What a queer house! Everything is a kind of secret. Rooms are locked up and gardens are locked up – and you! Have you been locked up?'

'No. I stay in this room because I don't want to be moved out of it. It tires me too much.'

'Does your father come and see you?' Mary ventured.

'Sometimes. Generally when I am asleep. He doesn't want to see me.'

'Why?' Mary could not help asking again.

A sort of angry shadow passed over the boy's face.

'My mother died when I was born and it makes him wretched to look at me. He thinks I don't know, but I've heard people talking. He almost hates me.'

'He hates the garden because she died,' said Mary, half speaking to herself.

'What garden?' the boy asked.

'Oh! Just – just a garden she used to like,' Mary stammered. 'Have you been here always?'

'Nearly always. Sometimes I have been taken to places at the seaside, but I won't stay because people stare at me. I used to wear an iron thing to keep my back straight, but a grand doctor came from London to see me and said it was stupid. He told them to take it off and keep me out in the fresh air. I hate fresh air and I don't want to go out.'

'I didn't when first I came here,' said Mary. 'Why do you keep looking at me like that?'

'Because of the dreams that are so real,' he answered rather fretfully. 'Sometimes when I open my eyes I don't believe I'm awake.'

'We're both awake,' said Mary. She glanced round the room with its high ceiling and shadowy corners and dim firelight. 'It looks quite like a dream, and it's the middle of the night, and everybody in the house is asleep – everybody but us. We are wide awake.'

'I don't want it to be a dream,' the boy said restlessly.

Mary thought of something all at once.

'If you don't like people to see you,' she began, 'do you want me to go away?'

He still held the fold of her wrapper and he gave it a little pull.

'No,' he said. 'I should be sure you were a dream if you went. If you are real, sit down on that big footstool and talk. I want to hear about you.'

Mary put down her candle on the table near the bed and sat down on the cushioned stool. She did not want to go away at all. She wanted to stay in the mysterious, hidden-away room and talk to the mysterious boy.

'What do you want me to tell you?' she said.

He wanted to know how long she had been at Misselthwaite; he wanted to know which corridor her room was on; he wanted to know what she had been doing; if she disliked the moor as he disliked it;

where she had lived before she came to Yorkshire. She answered all these questions and many more, and he lay back on his pillow and listened. He made her tell him a great deal about India and about her voyage across the ocean. She found out that because he had been an invalid he had not learned things as other children had. One of his nurses had taught him to read when he was quite little and he was always reading and looking at pictures in splendid books.

Though his father rarely saw him when he was awake, he was given all sorts of wonderful things to amuse himself with. He never seemed to have been amused, however. He could have anything he asked for and was never made to do anything he did not like to do.

'Everyone is obliged to do what pleases me,' he said indifferently. 'It makes me ill to be angry. No one believes I shall live to grow up.'

He said it as if he was so accustomed to the idea that it had ceased to matter to him at all. He seemed to like the sound of Mary's voice. As she went on talking he listened in a drowsy, interested way. Once or twice she wondered if he were not gradually falling into a doze. But at last he asked a question which opened up a new subject.

'How old are you?' he asked.

'I am ten,' answered Mary forgetting herself for the moment, 'and so are you.'

'How do you know that?' he demanded in a surprised voice.

'Because when you were born the garden door was locked and the key was buried. And it has been locked for ten years.'

Colin half sat up, turning towards her, leaning on his elbows.

'What garden door was locked? Who did it? Where was the key buried?' he exclaimed, as if he were suddenly very much interested.

'It – it was the garden Mr. Craven hates,' said Mary nervously. 'He locked the door. No one – no one knew where he buried the key.'

'What sort of a garden is it?' Colin persisted eagerly.

'No one has been allowed to go into it for ten years,' was Mary's careful answer.

But it was too late to be careful. He was too much like herself. He, too, had nothing to think about, and the idea of a hidden garden attracted him as it had attracted her. He asked question after question.

Where was it? Had she never looked for the door? Had she never asked the gardeners?

'They won't talk about it,' said Mary. 'I think they have been told not to answer questions.'

'I would make them,' said Colin.

'Could you?' Mary faltered, beginning to feel frightened. If he could make people answer questions, who knew what might happen?

'Everyone is obliged to please me. I told you that,' he said. 'If I were to live, this place would some time belong to me. They all know that. I would make them tell me.'

Mary had not known that she had been spoiled, but she could see quite plainly that this mysterious boy had been. He thought that the whole world belonged to him. How peculiar he was and how coolly he spoke of not living.

'Do you think you won't live?' she asked, partly because she was curious and partly in hope of making him forget the garden.

'I suppose I shall,' he answered as indifferently as he had spoken before. 'Ever since I remember anything I have heard people say I shan't. At first they thought I was too little to understand, and now they think I don't hear. But I do. My doctor is my father's cousin. He is quite poor and if I die he will have all Misselthwaite when my father is dead. I should think he wouldn't want me to live.'

'Do you want to live?' inquired Mary.

'No,' he answered, in a cross, tired fashion. 'But I don't want to die. When I feel ill I lie here and think about it until I cry and cry.'

'I have heard you crying three times,' Mary said, 'but I did not know who it was. Were you crying about that?' She did so want him to forget the garden.

'I dare say,' he answered. 'Let us talk about something else. Talk about that garden. Don't you want to see it?'

'Yes,' answered Mary in quite a low voice.

'I do,' he went on persistently. 'I don't think I ever really wanted to see anything before, but I want to see that garden. I want the key dug up. I want the door unlocked. I would let them take me there in my chair. That would be getting fresh air. I am going to make them open the door.'

He had become quite excited and his strange eyes began to shine like stars and looked more immense than ever.

'They have to please me,' he said. 'I will make them take me there and I will let you go, too.'

Mary's hands clutched each other. Everything would be spoiled – everything. Dickon would never come back. She would never again feel like a missel thrush with a safe-hidden nest.

'Oh, don't – don't – don't – don't do that!' she cried out.

He stared as if he thought she had gone crazy!

'Why?' he exclaimed. 'you said you wanted to see it.'

'I do,' she answered, almost with a sob in her throat, 'but if you make them open the door and take you in like that it will never be a secret again.'

He leaned still farther forward.

'A secret,' he said. 'What do you mean?' Tell me.'

Mary's words almost tumbled over one another.

'You see – you see,' she panted, 'if no one knows but ourselves – if there was a door, hidden somewhere under the ivy – if there was – and we could find it; and if we could slip through it together and shut it behind us, and no one knew anyone was inside and we called it our garden and pretended that – that we were missel thrushes and it was our nest, and if we played there almost every day and dug and planted seeds and made it all come alive——'

'Is it dead?' he interrupted her.

'It soon will be if no one cares for it,' she went on. 'The bulbs will live but the roses——'

He stopped her again as excited as she was herself.

'What are bulbs?' he put in quickly.

'They are daffodils and lilies and snowdrops. They are working in the earth now – pushing up pale-green points because the spring is coming.'

'Is the spring coming?' he said. 'What is it like? You don't see it in rooms if you are ill.'

'It is the sun shining on the rain and the rain falling on the sunshine, and things pushing up and working under the earth,' said Mary. 'If the garden was a secret and we could get into it we could watch the things grow bigger every day, and see how many roses are alive. Don't you see? Oh, don't you see how much nicer it would be if it was a secret?'

He dropped back on his pillow and lay there with an odd expression on his face.

'I never had a secret,' he said, 'except that one about not living to grow up. They don't know I know that, so it is a sort of secret. But I like this kind better.'

'If you won't make them take you to the garden,' pleaded Mary, 'perhaps – I feel almost sure I can find out how to get in some time. And then – if the doctor wants you to go out in your chair, and if you can always do what you want to do, perhaps – perhaps we might find some boy who would push you, and we could go alone and it would always be a secret garden.'

'I should – like – that,' he said very slowly, his eyes looking dreamy. 'I should like that. I should not mind fresh air in a secret garden.'

Mary began to recover her breath and feel safer, because the idea of keeping the secret seemed to please him. She felt almost sure that if she kept on talking and could make him see the garden in his mind as she had seen it, he would like it so much that he could not bear to think that everybody might tramp into it when they chose.

'I'll tell you what I *think* it would be like, if you could go into it,' she said. 'It has been shut up so long things have grown into a tangle perhaps.'

He lay quite still and listened while she went on talking about the roses which *might* have clambered from tree to tree and hung down – about the many birds which *might* have built their nests there because it was so safe. And then she told him about the robin and Ben Weatherstaff, and there was so much to tell about the robin and it was so easy and safe to talk about it that she ceased to feel afraid. The robin pleased him so much that he smiled until he looked almost beautiful, and at first Mary had thought that he was even plainer than herself, with his big eyes and heavy locks of hair.

'I did not know birds could be like that,' he said. 'But if you stay in a room you never see things. What a lot of things you know. I feel as if you had been inside that garden.'

She did not know what to say, so she did not say anything. He evidently did not expect an answer and the next moment he gave her a surprise.

'I am going to let you look at something,' he said. 'Do you see that rose-coloured silk curtain hanging on the wall over the mantelpiece?'

Mary had not noticed it before, but she looked up and saw it. It was a curtain of soft silk hanging over what seemed to be some picture.

'Yes,' she answered.

'There is a cord hanging from it,' said Colin. 'Go and pull it.'

Mary got up, much mystified, and found the cord. When she pulled it the silk curtain ran back on rings and when it ran back it uncovered a picture. It was the picture of a girl with a laughing face. She had bright hair tied up with a blue ribbon and her gay, lovely eyes were exactly like Colin's unhappy ones, agate-grey and looking twice as big as they really were, because of the black lashes all round them.

'She is my mother,' said Colin complainingly. 'I don't see why she died. Sometimes I hate her for doing it.'

'How queer!' said Mary.

'If she had lived I believe I should not have been ill always,' he grumbled. 'I dare say I should have lived, too. And my father would not have hated to look at me. I dare say I should have had a strong back. Draw the curtain again.'

Mary did as she was told and returned to her footstool.

'She is much prettier than you,' she said, 'but her eyes are just like yours – at least they are the same shape and colour. Why is the curtain drawn over her?'

He moved uncomfortably.

'I made them do it,' he said. 'Sometimes I don't like to see her looking at me. She smiles too much when I am ill and miserable. Besides, she is mine, and I don't want everyone to see her.'

There were a few moments of silence and then Mary spoke.

'What would Mrs. Medlock do if she found out that I had been here?' she inquired.

'She would do as I told her to do,' he answered. 'And I should tell her that I wanted you to come here and talk to me every day. I am glad you came.'

'So am I,' said Mary. 'I will come as often as I can, but' – she hesitated – 'I shall have to look every day for the garden door.'

'Yes, you must,' said Colin, 'and you can tell me about it afterwards.'

He lay thinking a few minutes, as he had done before, and then he spoke again.

'I think you shall be a secret, too,' he said. 'I will not tell them until they find out. I can always send the nurse out of the room and say that I want to be by myself. Do you know Martha?'

'Yes, I know her very well,' said Mary. 'She waits on me.'

He nodded his head towards the outer corridor.

'She is the one who is asleep in the other room. The nurse went away yesterday to stay all night with her sister and she always makes Martha attend to me when she wants to go out. Martha shall tell you when to come here.'

Then Mary understood Martha's troubled look when she had asked questions about the crying.

'Martha knew about you all the time?' she said.

'Yes; she often attends to me. The nurse likes to get away from me and then Martha comes.'

'I have been here a long time,' said Mary. 'Shall I go away now? Your eyes look sleepy.'

'I wish I could go to sleep before you leave me,' he said rather shyly.

'Shut your eyes,' said Mary, drawing her footstool closer, 'and I will do what my Ayah used to do in India. I will pat your hand and stroke it and sing something quite low.'

'I should like that perhaps,' he said drowsily.

Somehow she was sorry for him and did not want him to lie awake, so she leaned against the bed and began to stroke and pat his hand and sing a very low little chanting song in Hindustani.

'That is nice,' he said more drowsily still, and she went on chanting and stroking, but when she looked at him again his black lashes were lying close against his cheeks, for his eyes were shut and he was fast asleep. She got up softly, took her candle, and crept away without making a sound.

14 A Young Rajah

The moor was hidden in mist when the morning came, and the rain had not stopped pouring down. There could be no going out of doors. Martha was so busy that Mary had no opportunity of talking to her, but in the afternoon she asked her to come and sit with her in the nursery. She came, bringing the stocking she was always knitting when she was doing nothing else.

'What's the matter with thee?' she asked as soon as they sat down. 'Tha' looks as if tha'd somethin' to say.'

'I have. I have found out what the crying was,' said Mary.

Martha let her knitting drop on her knee and gazed at her with startled eyes.

'Tha' hasn't!' she exclaimed. 'Never!'

'I heard it in the night,' Mary went on. 'And I got up and went to see where it came from. It was Colin. I found him.'

Martha's face became red with fright.

'Eh! Miss Mary!' she said, half crying. 'Tha' shouldn't have done it – tha' shouldn't. Tha'll get me in trouble. I never told thee nothin' about him – but tha'll get me in trouble. I shall lose my place and what'll Mother do!'

'You won't lose your place,' said Mary. 'He was glad I came. We talked and talked and he said he was glad I came.'

'Was he?' cried Martha. 'Art tha' sure? Tha' doesn't know what he's like when anything vexes him. He's a big lad to cry like a baby, but when he's in a passion he'll fair scream just to frighten us. He knows us daren't call our souls our own.'

'He wasn't vexed,' said Mary. 'I asked him if I should go away and he made me stay. He asked me questions and I sat on a big footstool and talked to him about India and about the robin and gardens. He wouldn't let me go. He let me see his mother's picture. Before I left him I sang him to sleep.'

Martha fairly gasped with amazement.

'I can scarcely believe thee!' she protested. 'It's as if tha'd walked straight into a lion's den. If he'd been like he is most times he'd have throwed himself into one of his tantrums and roused th' house. He won't let strangers look at him.'

'He let me look at him. I looked at him all the time and he looked at me. We stared!' said Mary.

'I don't know what to do!' cried agitated Martha. 'If Mrs. Medlock finds out, she'll think I broke orders and told thee and I shall be packed back to Mother.'

'He's not going to tell Mrs. Medlock anything about it yet. It's to be a sort of secret just at first,' said Mary firmly. 'And he says everybody is obliged to do as he pleases.'

'Aye, that's true enough – th' bad lad!' sighed Martha, wiping her forehead with her apron.

'He says Mrs. Medlock must. And he wants me to to come and talk to him every day. And you are to tell me when he wants me.'

'Me!' said Martha; 'I shall lose my place – I shall for sure!'

'You can't if you are doing what he wants you to do and everybody is ordered to obey him,' Mary argued.

'Does tha' mean to say,' cried Martha with wide-open eyes, 'that he was nice to thee?'

'I think he almost liked me,' Mary answered.

'Then tha' must have bewitched him!' decided Martha, drawing a long breath.

'Do you mean Magic?' inquired Mary. 'I've heard about Magic in India, but I can't make it. I just went into his room and I was so surprised to see him I stood and stared. And then he turned round and stared at me. And he thought I was a ghost or a dream and I thought perhaps he was. And it was so queer being there alone together in the middle of the night and not knowing about each other. And we began to ask each other questions. And when I asked him if I must go away he said I must not.'

'Th' world's comin' to an end!' gasped Martha.

'What is the matter with him?' asked Mary.

'Nobody knows for sure and certain,' said Martha. 'Mr. Craven went off his head like when he was born. Th' doctors thought he'd have to be put in a 'sylum. It was because Mrs. Craven died like I told you. He wouldn't set eyes on th' baby. He just raved and said it'd be another hunchback like him and it'd better die.'

'Is Colin a hunchback?' Mary asked. 'He didn't look like one.'

'He isn't yet,' said Martha. 'But he began all wrong. Mother said that there was enough trouble raging in th' house to set any child wrong. They was afraid his back was weak an' they've always been takin' care of it – keepin' him lyin' down and not lettin' him walk. Once they made him wear a brace, but he fretted so he was downright ill. Then a big doctor came to see him an' made them take it off. He talk'd to th' doctor quite rough – in a polite way. He said there'd been too much medicine and too much lettin' him have his own way.'

'I think he's a very spoiled boy,' said Mary.

'He's th' worst young nowt as ever was!' said Martha. 'I won't say as he hasn't been ill a good bit. He's had coughs an' colds that's nearly killed him two or three times. Once he had rheumatic fever an' once he had typhoid. Eh! Mrs. Medlock did get a fright then. He'd been out of his head an' she was talkin' to th' nurse, thinkin' he didn't know nothin', an' she said: "He'll die this time sure enough, an' best thing for him an' for everybody." An' she looked at him, an' there he was with his big eyes open, starin' at her as sensible as she was herself. She didn't know what'd happen, but he just stared at her an' says: "You give me some water an' stop talkin'."'

'Do you think he will die?' asked Mary.

'Mother says there's no reason why any child should live that gets no fresh air an' doesn't do nothin' but lie on his back an' read picture-books an' take medicine. He's weak and hates th' trouble o' bein' taken out o' doors, an' he gets cold so easy he says it makes him ill.'

Mary sat and looked at the fire.

'I wonder,' she said slowly, 'if it would not do him good to go out into a garden and watch things growing. It did me good.'

'One of th' worst fits he ever had,' said Martha, 'was one time they took him out where the roses is by the fountain. He'd been readin' in a paper about people gettin' somethin' he called "rose cold", an' he began to sneeze an' said he'd got it, an' then a new gardener as didn't know th' rules passed by an' looked at him curious. He threw himself into a passion an' he said he'd looked at him because he was going to be a hunchback. He cried himself into a fever an' was ill all night.'

'If he ever gets angry at me, I'll never go and see him again,' said Mary.

'He'll have thee if he wants thee,' said Martha. 'Tha' may as well know that at th' start.'

Very soon afterwards a bell rang, and she rolled up her knitting.

'I dare say th' nurse wants me to stay with him a bit,' she said. 'I hope he's in a good temper.'

She was out of the room about ten minutes and then she came back with a puzzled expression.

'Well, tha' has bewitched him,' she said. 'He's up on his sofa with his picture-books. He's told the nurse to stay away until six o'clock. I'm to wait in the next room. Th' minute she was gone he called me to him an' says: "I want Mary Lennox to come and talk to me, and remember you're not to tell anyone." You'd better go as quick as you can.'

Mary was quite willing to go quickly. She did not want to see Colin as much as she wanted to see Dickon, but she wanted to see him very much.

There was a bright fire on the hearth when she entered his room, and in the daylight she saw it was a very beautiful room indeed. There were rich colours in the rugs and hangings and pictures and books on the walls, which made it look glowing and comfortable even in spite of the grey sky and falling rain. Colin looked rather like a picture himself. He was wrapped in a velvet dressing-gown and sat against a big brocaded cushion. He had a red spot on each cheek.

'Come in,' he said. 'I've been thinking about you all the morning.'

'I've been thinking about you, too,' answered Mary. 'You don't know how frightened Martha is. She says Mrs. Medlock will think she told me about you and then she will be sent away.'

He frowned.

'Go and tell her to come here,' he said. 'She is in the next room.'

Mary went and brought her back. Poor Martha was shaking in her shoes. Colin was still frowning.

'Have you to do what I please or have you not?' he demanded.

'I have to do what you please, sir,' Martha faltered, turning quite red.

'Has Medlock to do what I please?'

'Everybody has, sir,' said Martha.

'Well, then, if I order you to bring Miss Mary to me, how can Medlock send you away if she finds it out?'

'Please don't let her, sir,' pleaded Martha.

'I'll send *her* away if she dares to say a word about such a thing,' said Master Craven grandly. 'She wouldn't like that, I can tell you.'

'Thank you, sir,' bobbing a curtsy. 'I want to do my duty, sir.'

'What I want is your duty,' said Colin, more grandly still. 'I'll take care of you. Now go away.'

When the door closed behind Martha, Colin found Mistress Mary gazing at him as if he had set her wondering.

'Why do you look at me like that?' he asked her. 'What are you thinking about?'

'I am thinking about two things.'

'What are they? Sit down and tell me.'

'This is the first one,' said Mary, seating herself on the big stool. 'Once in India I saw a boy who was a rajah. He had rubies and emeralds and diamonds stuck all over him. He spoke to his people just as you spoke to Martha. Everybody had to do everything he told them – in a minute. I think they would have been killed if they hadn't.'

'I shall make you tell me about rajahs presently,' he said, 'but first tell me what the second thing was.'

'I was thinking,' said Mary, 'how different you are from Dickon.'

'Who is Dickon?' he said. 'What a queer name!'

She might as well tell him, she thought. She could talk about Dickon without mentioning the secret garden. She had liked to hear Martha talk about him. Besides, she longed to talk about him. It would seem to bring him nearer.

'He is Martha's brother. He is twelve years old,' she explained.

'He is not like anyone else in the world. He can charm foxes and squirrels and birds just as the natives in India charm snakes. He plays a very soft tune on a pipe and they come and listen.'

There were some big books on a table at his side, and he dragged one suddenly towards him.

'There is a picture of a snake-charmer in this,' he exclaimed. 'Come and look at it.'

The book was a beautiful one with superb coloured illustrations, and he turned to one of them.

'Can he do that?' he asked eagerly.

'He played on his pipe and they listened,' Mary explained. 'But he doesn't call it Magic. He says it's because he lives on the moor so much and he knows their ways. He says he feels sometimes as if he was a bird or a rabbit himself, he likes them so. I think he asked the robin questions. It seemed as if they talked to each other in soft chirps.'

Colin lay on his cushion and his eyes grew larger and larger and the spots on his cheeks burned.

'Tell me some more about him,' he said.

'He knows all about eggs and nests,' Mary went on. 'And he knows where foxes and badgers and otters live. He keeps them secret so that other boys won't find their holes and frighten them. He knows about everything that grows or lives on the moor.'

'Does he like the moor?' said Colin. 'How can he when it's such a great, bare, dreary place?'

'It's the most beautiful place,' protested Mary. 'Thousands of lovely things grow on it, and there are thousands of little creatures all busy building nests and making holes and burrows and chippering or singing or squeaking to each other. They are so busy and having such fun under the earth or in the trees or heather. It's their world.'

'How do you know all that?' said Colin, turning on his elbow to look at her.

'I have never been there once, really,' said Mary, suddenly remembering. 'I only drove over it in the dark. I thought it was hideous. Martha told me about it first, and then Dickon. When Dickon talks about it you feel as if you saw things and heard them, and as if you were standing in the heather with the sun shining and the gorse smelling like honey – and all full of bees and butterflies.'

'You never see anything if you are ill,' said Colin restlessly. He looked like a person listening to a new sound in the distance and wondering what it was.

'You can't if you stay in a room,' said Mary.

'I couldn't go on the moor,' he said in a resentful tone.

Mary was silent for a minute, and then she said something bold.

'You might – some time.'

He moved as if he were startled.

'Go on the moor! How could I? I am going to die.'

'How do you know?' said Mary unsympathetically. She didn't like the way he had of talking about dying. She did not feel very sympathetic. She felt rather as if he almost boasted about it.

'Oh, I've heard it ever since I remember,' he answered crossly. 'They are always whispering about it and thinking I don't notice. They wish I would, too.'

Mistress Mary felt quite contrary. She pinched her lips together.

'If they wished I would,' she said, 'I wouldn't. Who wishes you would.'

'The servants – and, of course, Dr. Craven, because he would get Misselthwaite and be rich instead of poor. He daren't say so, but he always looks cheerful when I am worse. When I had typhoid fever his face got quite fat. I think my father wishes it, too.'

'I don't believe he does,' said Mary quite obstinately.

That made Colin turn and look at her again.

'Don't you?' he said.

And then he lay back on his cushion and was still, as if he were thinking. And there was quite a long silence. Perhaps they were both of them thinking strange things children do not usually think of.

'I like the grand doctor from London, because he made them take the iron thing off,' said Mary at last. 'Did he say you were going to die?'

'No.'

'What did he say?'

'He didn't whisper,' Colin answered. 'Perhaps he knew I hated whispering. I heard him say one thing quite aloud. He said: "The lad might live if he would make up his mind to it. Put him in the humour."

It sounded as if he was in a temper.'

'I'll tell you who would put you in the humour, perhaps,' said Mary, reflecting. She felt as if she would like this thing to be settled one way or the other. 'I believe Dickon would. He's always talking about live things. He never talks about dead things or things that are ill. He's always looking up in the sky to watch birds flying – or looking down at the earth to see something growing. He has such round blue eyes and they are so wide open with looking about. And he laughs such a big laugh with his wide mouth – and his cheeks are as red – as red as cherries.'

She pulled her stool nearer to the sofa and her expression quite changed at the remembrance of the wide, curving mouth and wide open eyes.

'See here,' she said. 'Don't let us talk about dying; I don't like it. Let us talk about living. Let us talk and talk about Dickon. And then we will look at your pictures.'

It was the best thing she could have said. To talk about Dickon meant to talk about the moor and about the cottage and the fourteen people who lived in it on sixteen shillings a week – and the children who got fat on the moor grass like the wild ponies. And about Dickon's mother – and the skipping-rope – and the moor with the sun on it – and about pale green points sticking up out of the black sod. And it was all so alive that Mary talked more than she had ever talked before – and Colin both talked and listened as he had never done either before. And they both began to laugh over nothing as children will when they are happy together. And they laughed so that in the end they were making as much noise as if they had been two ordinary, healthy, natural, two-year-old creatures – instead of a hard, little, unloving girl and a sickly boy who believed that he was going to die.

They enjoyed themselves so much that they forgot the pictures and they forgot about the time. They had been laughing quite loudly over Ben Weatherstaff and his robin, and Colin was actually sitting up as if he had forgotten about his weak back when he suddenly remembered something.

'Do you know there is one thing we have never once thought of?' he said. 'We are cousins.'

It seemed so queer that they had talked so much and never remembered this simple thing that they laughed more than ever, because they had got into the humour to laugh at anything. And in the midst of the fun the door opened and in walked Dr. Craven and Mrs. Medlock.

Dr. Craven started in actual alarm and Mrs. Medlock almost fell back because he had accidentally bumped against her.

'Good Lord!' exclaimed poor Mrs. Medlock, with her eyes almost starting out of her head. 'Good Lord!'

'What is this?' said Dr. Craven, coming forward. 'What does it mean?'

Then Mary was reminded of the boy rajah again. Colin answered as if neither the doctor's alarm nor Mrs. Medlock's terror were of the slightest consequence. He was as little disturbed or frightened as if an elderly cat and dog had walked into the room.

'This is my cousin, Mary Lennox,' he said. 'I asked her to come and talk to me. I like her. She must come and talk to me whenever I send for her.'

Dr. Craven turned reproachfully to Mrs. Medlock.

'Oh, sir,' she panted. 'I don't know how it's happened. There's not a servant on the place that'd dare to talk – they all have their orders.'

'Nobody told her anything,' said Colin. 'She heard me crying and found me herself. I am glad she came. Don't be silly, Medlock.'

Mary saw that Dr. Craven did not look pleased, but it was quite plain that he dare not oppose his patient. He sat down by Colin and felt his pulse.

'I am afraid there has been too much excitement. Excitement is not good for you, my boy,' he said.

'I should be excited if she kept away,' answered Colin, his eyes beginning to look dangerously sparkling. 'I am better. She makes me better. The nurse must bring up her tea with mine. We will have tea together.'

Mrs. Medlock and Dr. Craven looked at each other in a troubled way, but there was evidently nothing to be done.

'He does look rather better, sir,' ventured Mrs. Medlock. 'But' – thinking the matter over – 'he looked better this morning before she came into the room.'

'She came into the room last night. She stayed with me a long time. She sang a Hindustani song to me and it made me go to sleep,' said Colin. 'I was better when I wakened up. I wanted my breakfast. I want my tea now. Tell nurse, Medlock.'

Dr. Craven did not stay very long. He talked to the nurse for a few minutes when she came into the room and said a few words of warning to Colin. He must not talk too much; he must not forget that he was ill; he must not forget that he was very easily tired. Mary thought that there seemed to be a number of uncomfortable things he was not to forget.

Colin looked fretful and kept his strange, black-lashed eyes fixed on Dr. Craven's face.

'I *want* to forget it,' he said at last. 'She makes me forget it. That is why I want her.'

Dr. Craven did not look happy when he left the room. He gave a puzzled glance at the little girl sitting on the large stool. She had become a stiff, silent child again as soon as he entered, and he could not see what the attraction was. The boy actually did look brighter, however – and he sighed rather heavily as he went down the corridor.

'They are always wanting me to eat things when I don't want to,' said Colin, as the nurse brought in the tea and put it on the table by the sofa. 'Now, if you'll eat I will. Those muffins look so nice and hot. Tell me about rajahs.'

15 Nest Building

After another week of rain, the high arch of blue sky appeared again and the sun which poured down was quite hot. Though there had been no chance to see either the secret garden or Dickon, Mistress Mary had enjoyed herself very much. The week had not seemed long. She had spent hours of every day with Colin in his room, talking about rajahs or gardens or Dickon and the cottage on the moor. They had looked at the splendid books and pictures, and sometimes Mary had read things to Colin, and sometimes he had read a little to her. When he was amused and interested she thought he scarcely looked like an invalid at all, except that his face was so colourless and he was always on the sofa.

'You are a sly young one to listen and get out of your bed to go following things up like you did that night,' Mrs. Medlock said once. 'But there's no saying it's not been a sort of blessing to the lot of us. He's not had a tantrum or a whining fit since you made friends. The nurse was just going to give up the case because she was so sick of him, but she says she doesn't mind staying now you've gone on duty with her,' laughing a little.

In her talks with Colin, Mary had tried to be very cautious about the secret garden. There were certain things she wanted to find out from him, but she felt that she must find them out without asking him direct questions. In the first place, as she began to like to be with him, she wanted to discover whether he was the kind of boy you could tell a secret to. He was not in the least like Dickon, but he was evidently so pleased with the idea of a garden no one knew anything about that she thought perhaps he could be trusted. But she had not known him long enough to be sure. The second thing she wanted to find out was this: If he could be trusted – if he really could – wouldn't it be possible to take him to the garden without having anyone find it out? The grand doctor had said that he must have fresh air, and Colin had said that he would not mind fresh air in a secret garden. Perhaps if he had a great deal of fresh air and knew Dickon and the robin and saw things growing, he might not think so much about dying. Mary had seen herself in the glass sometimes lately when she had realized that she looked quite a different creature from the child she had seen when she arrived from India. This child looked nicer. Even Martha had seen a change in her.

'Th' air from th' moor has done thee good already,' she had said. 'Tha'rt not nigh so yeller and tha'rt not nigh so scrawny. Even tha' hair doesn't slamp down on tha' head so flat. It's got some life in it so as it sticks out a bit.'

'It's like me,' said Mary. 'It's growing stronger and fatter. I'm sure there's more of it.'

'It looks it, for sure,' said Martha, ruffling it up a little round her face. 'Tha'rt not half so ugly when it's that way an' there's a bit o' red in tha' cheeks.'

If gardens and fresh air had been good for her, perhaps they would be good for Colin. But then, if he hated people to look at him, perhaps he would not like to see Dickon.

'Why does it make you angry when you are looked at?' she inquired one day.

'I always hated it,' he answered, 'even when I was very little. Then when they took me to the seaside and I used to lie in my carriage, everybody used to stare and ladies would stop and talk to my nurse and then they would begin to whisper, and I knew when they were saying I shouldn't live to grow up. Then sometimes the ladies would pat my cheeks and say "Poor child!" Once when a lady did that I screamed out loud and bit her hand. She was so frightened she ran away.'

'She thought you had gone mad like a dog,' said Mary, not at all admiringly.

'I don't care what she thought,' said Colin, frowning.

'I wonder why you didn't scream and bite me when I came into your room?' said Mary. Then she began to smile slowly.

'I thought you were a ghost or a dream,' he said. 'You can't bite a ghost or a dream, and if you scream they don't care.'

'Would you hate it if – if a boy looked at you?' Mary asked uncertainly.

He lay back on his cushion and paused thoughtfully.

'There's one boy,' he said quite slowly, as if he were thinking over every word, 'there's one boy I believe I shouldn't mind. It's that boy who knows where the foxes live – Dickon.'

'I'm sure you wouldn't mind him,' said Mary.

'The birds don't and other animals,' he said, still thinking it over, 'perhaps that's why I shouldn't. He's a sort of animal-charmer and I am a boy animal.'

Then he laughed and she laughed too; in fact, it ended in their both laughing a great deal and finding the idea of a boy animal hiding in his hole very funny indeed.

What Mary felt afterwards was that she need not fear about Dickon.

*

On that first morning when the sky was blue again, Mary wakened very early. The sun was pouring in slanting rays through the blinds and there was something so joyous in the sight of it that she jumped out of bed and ran to the window. She drew up the blinds and opened the window itself, and a great waft of fresh, scented air blew in upon her. The moor was blue and the whole world looked as if something Magic had happened to it. There were tender little fluting sounds here and there and everywhere, as if scores of birds were beginning to tune up for a concert. Mary put her hand out of the window and held it in the sun.

'It's warm – warm!' she said. 'It will make the green points push up and up and up, and it will make the bulbs and roots work and struggle with all their might under the earth.'

She kneeled down and leaned out of the window as far as she could, breathing big breaths and sniffing the air until she laughed because she remembered what Dickon's mother had said about the end of his nose quivering like a rabbit's.

'It must be very early,' she said. 'The little clouds are all pink and

I've never seen the sky look like this. No one is up. I don't even hear the stable-boys.'

A sudden thought made her scramble to her feet.

'I can't wait! I am going to see the garden!'

She had learnt to dress herself by this time, and she put on her clothes in five minutes. She knew a small side door which she could unbolt herself, and she flew downstairs in her stocking feet and put on her shoes in the hall. She unchained and unbolted and unlocked, and when the door was open she sprang across the step with one bound, and there she was standing on the grass, which seemed to have turned green, and with the sun pouring down on her and warm, sweet wafts about her and the fluting and twittering and singing coming from every bush and tree. She clasped her hands for pure joy and looked up in the sky, and it was so blue and pink and pearly and white and flooded with springtime light that she felt as if she must flute and sing aloud herself, and knew that thrushes and robins and skylarks could not possibly help it. She ran around the shrubs and paths towards the secret garden.

'It is all different already,' she said. 'The grass is greener and things are sticking up everywhere and things are uncurling and green buds of leaves are showing. This afternoon I am sure Dickon will come.'

The long warm rain had done strange things to the herbaceous beds which bordered the walk by the lower wall. There were things sprouting and pushing out from the roots of clumps of plants and there were actually here and there glimpses of royal purple and yellow unfurling among the stems of crocuses. Six months before Mistress Mary would not have seen how the world was waking up, but now she missed nothing.

When she had reached the place where the door hid itself under the ivy, she was startled by a curious loud sound. It was the caw-caw of a crow, and it came from the top of the wall, and when she looked up, there sat a big, glossy-plumaged, blue-black bird, looking down at her very wisely indeed. She had never seen a crow so close before, and he made her a little nervous, but the next moment he spread his wings and flapped away across the garden. She hoped he was not going to stay inside, and she pushed the door open wondering if he would. When she got fairly into the garden she saw that he probably did intend to stay, because he had alighted on a dwarf apple-tree, and under the apple-tree was lying a little reddish animal with a bushy tail, and both of them were watching the stooping body and rust-red head of Dickon, who was kneeling on the grass working hard.

Mary flew across the grass to him.

'Oh, Dickon! Dickon!' she cried out. 'How could you get here so early! How could you! The sun has only just got up!'

He got up himself, laughing and glowing, and tousled; his eyes like a bit of the sky.

'Eh!' he said. 'I was up long before him. How could I have stayed abed! Th' world's all fair begun again this mornin', it has. An' it's workin' an' hummin' an' hummin' an' scratchin' an' pipin' an' nest-buildin' an' breathin' out scents, till you've got to be out on it 'stead o' lyin' on your back. When th' sun did jump up, th' moor went mad for joy, an' I was in the midst of th' heather, an' I run like mad myself, shoutin' an' singin'. An' I come straight here. I couldn't have stayed away. Why, th' garden was lyin' here waitin'!'

Mary put her hands on her chest, panting, as if she had been running herself.

'Oh, Dickon! Dickon!' she said. 'I'm so happy I can scarcely breathe!'

Seeing him talking to a stranger, the little bushy-tailed animal rose from its place under the tree and came to him, and the rook, cawing once, flew down from its branch and settled quietly on his shoulder.

'This is th' little fox cub,' he said, rubbing the little reddish animal's head. 'It's named Captain. An' this here's Soot. Soot, he flew across th' moor with me, an' Captain he run same as if th' hounds had been after him. They both felt same as I did.'

Neither of the creatures looked as if they were the least afraid of Mary. When Dickon began to walk about, Soot stayed on his shoulder and Captain trotted quietly close to his side.

'See here!' said Dickon. 'See how these has pushed up, an' these an' these! An' eh! look at these here!'

He threw himself upon his knees and Mary went down beside

him. They had come upon a whole clump of crocuses burst into purple and orange and gold. Mary bent her face down and kissed and kissed them.

'You never kiss a person in that way,' she said when she lifted her head. 'Flowers are so different.'

He looked puzzled, but smiled.

'Eh!' he said, 'I've kissed Mother many a time that way when I come in from th' moor after a day's roamin' an' she stood there at th' door in th' sun, lookin' so glad an' comfortable.'

They ran from one part of the garden to another and found so many wonders that they were obliged to remind themselves that they must whisper or speak low. He showed her swelling leaf-buds on rose branches which had seemed dead. He showed her ten thousand new green points pushing through the mould. They put their eager young noses close to the earth and sniffed its warmed springtime breathing; they dug and pulled and laughed low with rapture until Mistress Mary's hair was as tumbled as Dickon's and her cheeks were almost as poppy red as his.

There was every joy on earth in the secret garden that morning, and in the midst of them came a delight more delightful than all, because it was more wonderful. Swiftly something flew across the wall and darted through the trees to a close-grown corner, a little flare of red-breasted bird with something hanging from its beak. Dickon stood quite still and put his hand on Mary almost as if they had suddenly found themselves laughing in a church.

'We munnot stir,' he whispered in broad Yorkshire. 'We munnot scarce breathe. I knowed he was mate-huntin' when I seed him last. It's Ben Weatherstaff's robin. He's buildin' his nest. He'll stay if us don't flight him.'

They settled down softly upon the grass and sat there without moving.

'Us mustn't seem as if us was watchin' him too close,' said Dickon. 'He'd be out with us for good if he got th' notion us was interferin' now. He'll be a good bit different till all this is over. He's settin' up housekeepin'. He'll be shyer an' readier to take things ill. He's got no time for visitin' an' gossipin'. Us must keep still a bit an' try to look as if us was grass an' trees an' bushes. Then when he's got used to seein' us I'll chirp a bit an' he'll know us'll not be in his way.'

Mistress Mary was not at all sure that she knew, as Dickon seemed to, how to try to look like grass and trees and bushes. But he had said the queer thing as if it were the simplest and most natural thing in the world, and she felt it must be quite easy to him, and, indeed, she watched him for a few minutes carefully, wondering if it was possible for him to turn quietly green and put out branches and leaves. But he only sat wonderfully still, and when he spoke dropped his voice to such a softness that it was curious that she could hear him, but she could.

'It's part o' th' springtime, this nest-buildin' is,' he said. 'I warrant it's been goin' on in th' same way every year since th' world was begun. They've got their way o' thinkin' and doin' things, an' a body had better not meddle. You can lose a friend in springtime easier than any other season if you're too curious.'

'If we talk about him I can't help looking at him,' Mary said as softly as possible. 'We must talk of something else. There is something I want to tell you.'

'He'll like it better if us talks o' somethin' else,' said Dickon. 'What is it tha's got to tell me?'

'Well – do you know about Colin?' she whispered.

He turned his head to look at her.

'What does tha' know about him?' he asked.

'I've seen him. I have been to talk to him every day this week. He wants me to come. He says I'm making him forget about being ill and dying,' answered Mary.

Dickon looked actually relieved as soon as the surprise died away from his round face.

'I am glad o' that,' he exclaimed. 'I'm right down glad. It makes me easier. I knowed I must say nothin' about him an' I don't like havin' to hide things.'

'Don't you like hiding the garden?' said Mary.

'I'll never tell about it,' he answered. 'But I says to Mother: "Mother," I says, "I got a secret to keep. It's not a bad 'un, tha' knows that. It's no worse than hidin' where a bird's nest is. Tha' doesn't mind it, does tha'?"'

Mary always wanted to hear about Mother.

'What did she say?' she asked, not at all afraid to hear.

Dickon grinned sweet-temperedly.

'It was just like her, what she said,' he answered. 'She give my head a bit of a rub an' laughed an' she says: "Eh, lad, tha' can have all th' secrets tha' likes. I've knowed thee twelve year'."'

'How did you know about Colin?' asked Mary.

'Everybody as knowed about Mester Craven knowed there was a little lad as was like to be a cripple, an' they knowed Mester Craven didn't like him to be talked about. Folks is sorry for Mester Craven because Mrs. Craven was such a pretty young lady an' they was so fond of each other. Mrs. Medlock stops in our cottage whenever she goes to Thwaite an' she doesn't mind talkin' to Mother before us children, because she knows us has been brought up to be trusty. How did tha' find out about him? Martha was in fine trouble th' last time she came home. She said tha'd heard him frettin' an' tha' was askin' questions an' she didn't know what to say.'

Mary told him her story about the midnight wuthering of the wind which had wakened her and about the faint, far-off sounds of the complaining voice which had led her down the dark corridors with her candle and had ended with her opening of the door of the dimly lighted room with the carven four-poster bed in the corner. When she described the small, ivory-white face and the strange black-rimmed eyes, Dickon shook his head.

'Them's just like his mother's eyes, only hers was always laughin', they say,' he said. 'They say as Mr. Craven can't bear to see him when he's awake, an' it's because his eyes is so like his mother's an' yet looks so different in his miserable bit of a face.'

'Do you think he wants him to die?' whispered Mary.

'No, but he wishes he'd never been born. Mother, she says that's th' worst thing on earth for a child. Them as is not wanted scarce ever thrives. Mester Craven, he'd buy anythin' as money could buy for th' poor lad, but he'd like to forget he's on earth. For one thing, he's afraid he'll look at him some day and find he's growed hunchback.'

'Colin's so afraid of it himself that he won't sit up,' said Mary. 'He says he's always thinking that if he should feel a lump coming he should go crazy and scream himself to death.'

'Eh! he oughtn't to lie there thinkin' things like that,' said Dickon. 'No lad could get well as thought them sort o' things.'

The fox was lying on the grass close by him looking up to ask for a pat now and then, and Dickon bent down and rubbed his neck softly and thought a few minutes in silence. Presently he lifted his head and looked round the garden.

'When first we got in here,' he said, 'it seemed like everything was grey. Look round now and tell me if tha' doesn't see a difference.'

Mary looked and caught her breath a little.

'Why!' she cried, 'the grey wall is changing. It is as if a green mist were creeping over it. It's almost like a green gauze veil.'

'Aye,' said Dickon. 'An' it'll be greener and greener till th' grey's all gone. Can tha' guess what I was thinkin'?'

'I know it was something nice,' said Mary eagerly. 'I believe it was something about Colin.'

'I was thinkin' that if he was out here he wouldn't be watchin' for lumps to grow on his back; he'd be watchin' for buds to break on th' rose-bushes, an' he'd likely be healthier,' explained Dickon. 'I was wonderin' if us could ever get him in th' humour to come out here an' lie under th' trees in his carriage.'

'I've been wondering that myself. I've thought of it almost every time I've talked to him,' said Mary. 'I've wondered if he could keep a secret and I've wondered if we could bring him here without anyone seeing us. I thought perhaps you could push his carriage. The doctor said he must have fresh air, and if he wants us to take him out, no one dare disobey him. He won't go out for other people, and perhaps they will be glad if he will go out with us. He could order the gardeners to keep away so they wouldn't find out.'

Dickon was thinking very hard as he scratched Captain's back.

'It'd be good for him, I'll warrant,' he said. 'Us'd not be thinkin' he'd better never been born. Us'd be just two children watchin' a garden grow, an' he'd be another. Two lads an' a little lass just lookin' on at th' springtime. I warrant it'd be better than doctor's stuff.'

'He's been lying in his room so long and he's always been so afraid of his back that it has made him queer,' said Mary. 'He knows a good many things out of books, but he doesn't know anything else. He says he has been too ill to notice things, and he hates going out of doors and hates gardens and gardeners. But he likes to hear about this garden because it is a secret. I daren't tell him much, but he said he wanted to see it.'

'Us'll have him out here some time for sure,' said Dickon. 'I could push his carriage well enough. Has tha' noticed how th' robin an' his mate has been workin' while we've been sittin' here? Look at him perched on that branch wonderin' where it'd be best to put that twig he's got in his beak.'

He made one of his low, whistling calls, and the robin turned his head and looked at him inquiringly, still holding his twig. Dickon spoke to him as Ben Weatherstaff did, but Dickon's tone was one of friendly advice.

'Wheres'ever tha' puts it,' he said, 'it'll be all right. Tha' knew how to build tha' nest before tha' came out o' th' egg. Get on with thee, lad. Tha'st got no time to lose.'

'Oh! I do like to hear you talk to him!' Mary said, laughing delightedly. 'Ben Weatherstaff scolds him and makes fun of him, but he hops about and looks as if he understood every word, and I know he likes it. Ben Weatherstaff says he is so conceited he would rather have stones thrown at him than not be noticed.'

Dickon laughed too, and went on talking.

'Tha' knows us won't trouble thee,' he said to the robin. 'Us is near bein' wild things ourselves. Us is nest-buildin' too, bless thee. Look out tha' doesn't tell on us.'

And though the robin did not answer, because his beak was occupied, Mary knew that when he flew away with his twig to his own corner of the garden, the darkness of his dew-bright eye meant that he would not tell their secret for the world.

16 'I won't!' said Mary

They found a great deal to do that morning, and Mary was late in returning to the house and was also in such a hurry to get back to her work that she quite forgot Colin until the last moment.

'Tell Colin that I can't come and see him yet,' she said to Martha. 'I'm very busy in the garden.'

Martha looked rather frightened.

'Eh! Miss Mary,' she said, 'it may put him all out of humour when I tell him that.'

But Mary was not as afraid of him as other people were, and she was not a self-sacrificing person.

'I can't stay,' she answered. 'Dickon's waiting for me'; and she ran away.

The afternoon was even lovelier and busier than the morning had been. Already nearly all the weeds were cleared out of the garden and most of the roses and trees had been pruned or dug about. Dickon had brought a spade of his own, and he had taught Mary to use all her tools so that by this time it was plain that though the lovely wild place was not likely to become a 'gardener's garden', it would be a wilderness of growing things before the springtime was over.

'There'll be apple-blossoms an' cherry-blossoms overhead,' Dickon said, working away with all his might. 'An' there'll be peach an' plum trees in bloom against th' walls, an' th' grass'll be a carpet o' flowers.'

The little fox and the rook were as happy and busy as they were, and the robin and his mate flew backwards and forwards like tiny streaks of lightning. Sometimes the rook flapped his black wings and soared away over the tree-tops in the park. Each time he came back and perched near Dickon and cawed several times as if he were relating his adventures, and Dickon talked to him just as he had talked to the robin. Once when Dickon was so busy that he did not answer him at first, Soot flew on to his shoulder and gently tweaked his ear with his large beak. When Mary wanted to rest a little, Dickon sat down with her under a tree, and once he took his pipe out of his pocket and played the soft, strange little notes, and two squirrels appeared on the wall and looked and listened.

'Tha's a good bit stronger than tha' was,' Dickon said, looking at her as she was digging. 'Tha's beginnin' to look different, for sure.'

Mary was glowing with exercise and good spirits.

'I'm getting fatter and fatter every day,' she said quite exultantly. 'Mrs. Medlock will have to get me some bigger dresses. Martha says my hair is growing thicker. It isn't so flat and stringy.'

The sun was beginning to set and sending deep gold-coloured rays slanting under the trees when they parted.

'It'll be fine tomorrow,' said Dickon. 'I'll be at work by sunrise.'

'So will I,' said Mary.

*

She ran back to the house as quickly as her feet would carry her. She wanted to tell Colin about Dickon's fox cub and the rook and about what the springtime had been doing. She felt sure he would like to hear. So it was not very pleasant when she opened the door of her room to see Martha standing waiting for her with a doleful face.

'What is the matter?' she asked. 'What did Colin say when you told him I couldn't come?'

'Eh!' said Martha, 'I wish tha'd gone. He was nigh goin' into one o' his tantrums. There's been a nice to do all afternoon to keep him quiet. He would watch the clock all th' time.'

Mary's lips pinched themselves together. She was no more used to considering other people than Colin was, and she saw no reason why an ill-tempered boy should interfere with the thing she liked best. She knew nothing about the pitifulness of people who had been ill and nervous and who did not know that they could control their tempers

'"Tha's a good bit stronger than tha' was," Dickon said'

and need not make other people ill and nervous, too. When she had had a headache in India, she had done her best to see that everybody else also had a headache or something quite as bad. And she felt she was quite right; but, of course, now she felt that Colin was quite wrong.

He was not on his sofa when she went into his room. He was lying flat on his back in bed, and he did not turn his head towards her as she came in. This was a bad beginning, and Mary marched up to him with her stiff manner.

'Why didn't you get up?' she said.

'I did get up this morning when I thought you were coming,' he answered, without looking at her. 'I made them put me back in bed this afternoon. My back ached and my head ached and I was tired. Why didn't you come?'

'I was working in the garden with Dickon,' said Mary.

Colin frowned and condescended to look at her.

'I won't let that boy come here if you go and stay with him instead of coming to talk to me,' he said.

Mary flew into a fine passion. She could fly into a passion without making a noise. She just grew sour and obstinate and did not care what happened.

'If you send Dickon away, I'll never come into this room again,' she retorted.

'You'll have to if I want you,' said Colin.

'I won't!' said Mary.

'I'll make you,' said Colin. 'They shall drag you in.'

'Shall they, Mr. Rajah!' said Mary fiercely. 'They may drag me in, but they can't make me talk when they get me here. I'll sit and clench my teeth and never tell you one thing. I won't even look at you. I'll stare at the floor!'

They were a nice agreeable pair as they glared at each other. If they had been two little street boys they would have sprung at each other and had a rough-and-tumble fight. As it was, they did the next thing to it.

'You are a selfish thing!' cried Colin.

'What are you?' said Mary. 'Selfish people always say that.

Anyone is selfish who doesn't do what they want. You're more selfish than I am. You're the most selfish boy I ever saw.'

'I'm not!' snapped Colin. 'I'm not as selfish as your fine Dickon is! He keeps you playing in the dirt when he knows I am all by myself. He's selfish, if you like!'

Mary's eyes flashed fire.

'He's nicer than any other boy that ever lived!' she said. 'He's – he's like an angel!' It might sound rather silly to say that, but she did not care.

'A nice angel!' Colin sneered ferociously. 'He's a common cottage boy off the moor!'

'He's better than a common rajah!' retorted Mary. 'He's a thousand times better!'

Because she was the stronger of the two, she was beginning to get the better of him. The truth was that he had never had a fight with anyone like himself in his life, and, upon the whole, it was rather good for him, though neither he nor Mary knew anything about that. He turned his head on his pillow and shut his eyes and a big tear was squeezed out and ran down his cheek. He was beginning to feel pathetic and sorry for himself – not for anyone else.

'I'm not as selfish as you, because I'm always ill, and I'm sure there is a lump coming on my back,' he said. 'And I am going to die besides.'

'You're not!' contradicted Mary unsympathetically.

He opened his eyes quite wide with indignation. He had never heard such a thing said before. He was at once furious and slightly pleased, if a person could be both at the same time.

'I'm not?' he cried. 'I am! You know I am! Everybody says so.'

'I don't believe it!' said Mary sourly. 'You just say that to make people sorry. I believe you're proud of it. I don't believe it! If you were a nice boy it might be true – but you're too nasty!'

In spite of his invalid back, Colin sat up in bed in quite a healthy rage.

'Get out of the room!' he shouted, and he caught hold of his pillow and threw it at her. He was not strong enough to throw it far, and it only fell at her feet, but Mary's face looked as pinched as a nut-cracker.

'I'm going,' she said. 'And I won't come back!'

She walked to the door, and when she reached it she turned round and spoke again.

'I was going to tell you all sorts of nice things,' she said. 'Dickon brought his fox and his rook and I was going to tell you all about them. Now I won't tell you a single thing!'

She marched out of the door and closed it behind her, and there to her great astonishment she found the trained nurse standing as if she had been listening and, more amazing still – she was laughing. She was a big, handsome young woman, who ought not to have been a trained nurse at all, as she could not bear invalids, and she was always making excuses to leave Colin to Martha or anyone else who would take her place. Mary had never liked her, and she simply stood and gazed up at her as she stood giggling into her handkerchief.

'What are you laughing at?' she asked her.

'At you two young ones,' said the nurse. 'It's the best thing that could happen to the sickly, pampered thing to have someone to stand up to him that's as spoiled as himself'; and she laughed into her handkerchief again. 'If he'd had a young vixen of a sister to fight with, it would have been the saving of him.'

'Is he going to die?'

'I don't know and I don't care,' said the nurse. 'Hysterics and temper are half what ails him.'

'What are hysterics?' asked Mary.

'You'll find out if you work him into a tantrum after this – but at any rate, you've given him something to have hysterics about, and I am glad of it.'

Mary went back to her room not feeling at all as she had felt when she had come in from the garden. She was cross and disappointed, but not at all sorry for Colin. She had looked forward to telling him a great many things, and she had meant to try to make up her mind whether it would be safe to trust him with the great secret. She had been beginning to think it would be, but now she had changed her mind entirely. She would never tell him and he could stay in his room and never get any fresh air and die if he liked! It would serve him right! She felt so sour and unrelenting that for a few minutes she almost forgot about Dickon and the green veil creeping over the world and the soft wind blowing down from the moor.

Martha was waiting for her, and the trouble in her face had been temporarily replaced by interest and curiosity. There was a wooden box on the table and its cover had been removed and revealed that it was full of neat packages.

'Mr. Craven sent it to you,' said Martha. 'It looks as if it had picture-books in it.'

Mary remembered what he had asked her the day she had gone to his room. 'Do you want anything – dolls – toys – books?' She opened the package wondering if he had sent a doll, and also wondering what she should do with it if he had. But he had not sent one. There were several beautiful books such as Colin had, and two of them were about gardens and were full of pictures. There were two or three games and there was a beautiful little writing-case with a gold monogram on it and a gold pen and ink-stand.

Everything was so nice that her pleasure began to crowd her anger out of her mind. She had not expected him to remember her at all, and her hard little heart grew quite warm.

'I can write better than I can print,' she said, 'and the first thing I shall write with that pen will be a letter to tell him I am much obliged.

If she had been friends with Colin she would have run to show him her presents at once, and they would have looked at the pictures and read some of the gardening books and perhaps tried playing the games, and he would have enjoyed himself so much he would never once have thought he was going to die or have put his hand on his spine to see if there was a lump coming. He had a way of doing that which she could not bear. It gave her an uncomfortable, frightened feeling because he always looked so frightened himself. He said that if he felt even quite a little lump some day he should know his hunch had begun to grow. Something he had heard Mrs. Medlock whispering to the nurse had given him the idea, and he had thought over it in secret until it was quite firmly fixed in his mind. Mrs. Medlock had said his father's back had begun to show its crookedness in that way when he was a child. He had never told anyone but Mary that most of his 'tantrums', as they called them, grew out of his hysterical hidden fear. Mary had been sorry for him when he had told her.

'He always began to think about it when he was cross or tired,' she said to herself. 'And he has been cross today. Perhaps – perhaps he has been thinking about it all the afternoon.'

She stood still, looking down at the carpet and thinking.

'I said I would never go back again—' she hesitated, knitting her brows – 'but perhaps, just perhaps, I will go and see – if he wants me – in the morning. Perhaps he'll try to throw his pillow at me again, but – I think – I'll go.'

17 A Tantrum

She had got up very early in the morning and had worked hard in the garden, and she was tired and sleepy, so as soon as Martha had brought her supper and she had eaten it, she was glad to go to bed. As she laid her head on the pillow, she murmured to herself:

'I'll go out before breakfast and work with Dickon and then afterwards – I believe – I'll go to see him.'

She thought it was the middle of the night when she was awakened by such dreadful sounds that she jumped out of bed in an instant. What was it – what was it? The next minute she felt quite sure she knew. Doors were opened and shut and there were hurrying feet in the corridors and someone was crying and screaming at the same time, screaming and crying in a horrible way.

'It's Colin,' she said. 'He's having one of those tantrums the nurse calls hysterics. How awful it sounds.'

As she listened to the sobbing screams she did not wonder that people were so frightened that they gave him his own way in everything rather than hear them. She put her hands over her ears and felt sick and shivering.

'I don't know what to do. I don't know what to do,' she kept saying. 'I can't bear it.'

Once she wondered if he would stop if she dared go to him, and then she remembered how he had driven her out of the room and thought that perhaps the sight of her might make him worse. Even when she pressed her hands more tightly over her ears she could not keep the awful sounds out. She hated them so and was so terrified by them that suddenly they began to make her angry, and she felt as if she should like to fly into a tantrum herself and frighten him as he was frightening her. She was not used to anyone's temper but her own. She took her hands from her ears and sprang up and stamped her foot.

'He ought to be stopped! Somebody ought to make him stop! Somebody ought to beat him!' she cried out.

Just then she heard feet almost running down the corridor, and her door opened and the nurse came in. She was not laughing now by any means. She even looked rather pale.

'He's working himself into hysterics,' she said in a great hurry. 'He'll do himself harm. No one can do anything with him. You come and try, like a good child. He likes you.'

'He turned me out of the room this morning,' said Mary, stamping her foot in excitement.

The stamp rather pleased the nurse. The truth was that she had been afraid she might find Mary crying and hiding her head under the bed-clothes.

'That's right,' she said. 'You're in the right humour. You go and scold him. Give him something new to think of. Do go, child as quick as ever you can.'

It was not until afterwards that Mary realized that the thing had been funny as well as dreadful – that it was funny that all the grown-up people were so frightened that they came to a little girl just because they guessed she was almost as bad as Colin himself.

She flew along the corridor, and the nearer she got to the screams the higher her temper mounted. She felt quite wicked by the time she reached the door. She slapped it open with her hand and ran across the room to the four-poster bed.

'You stop!' she almost shouted. 'You stop!' I hate you! Everybody hates you! I wish everybody would run out of the house and let you scream yourself to death! You *will* scream yourself to death in a minute, and I wish you would!'

A nice, sympathetic child could neither have thought nor said such things, but it just happened that the shock of hearing them was the best possible thing for this hysterical boy whom no one had ever dared to restrain or contradict.

He had been lying on his face beating his pillow with his hands, and he actually almost jumped around, he turned so quickly at the sound of the furious little voice. His face looked dreadful, white and red, and swollen, and he was gasping and choking; but savage little Mary did not care an atom.

'If you scream another scream,' she said, 'I'll scream, too – and I can scream louder than you can, and I'll frighten you, I'll frighten you!'

He actually had stopped screaming because she had startled him so. The scream which had been coming almost choked him. The tears were streaming down his face and he shook all over.

'I can't stop!' he gasped, and sobbed. 'I can't – I can't!'

'You can!' shouted Mary. 'Half that ails you is hysterics and temper – just hysterics – hysterics – hysterics!' and she stamped each time she said it.

'I felt the lump – I felt it,' choked out Colin. 'I knew I should. I shall have a hunch on my back and then I shall die,' and he began to writhe again and turned on his face and sobbed and wailed, but he didn't scream.

'You didn't feel a lump!' contradicted Mary fiercely. 'If you did it was only a hysterical lump. Hysterics makes lumps. There's nothing the matter with your horrid back – nothing but hysterics! Turn over and let me look at it.'

She liked the word 'hysterics', and felt somehow as if it had an effect on him. He was probably like herself and had never heard it before.

'Nurse,' she commanded, 'come here and show me his back this minute!'

The nurse, Mrs. Medlock, and Martha had been standing huddled together near the door staring at her, their mouths half open. All three had gasped with fright more than once. The nurse came forward as if she were half afraid. Colin was heaving with great breathless sobs.

'Perhaps he – he won't let me,' she hesitated, in a low voice.

Colin heard her, however, and he gasped out between two sobs: 'Sh-show her! She-she'll see then!'

It was a poor, thin back to look at when it was bared. Every rib could be counted and every joint of the spine, though Mistress Mary did not count them as she bent over and examined them with a solemn, savage little face. She looked so sour and old-fashioned that the nurse turned her head aside to hide the twitching of her mouth. There was just a minute's silence, for even Colin tried to hold his breath while Mary looked up and down his spine and down and up, as intently as if she had been the great doctor from London.

'There's not a single lump there!' she said at last. 'There's not a lump as big as a pin – except backbone lumps, and you can only feel them because you're thin. I've got backbone lumps myself, and they used to stick out as much as yours do, until I began to get fatter, and I am not fat enough to hide them. There's not a lump as big as a pin. If you ever say there is again, I shall laugh!'

No one but Colin himself knew what effect those crossly spoken childish words had on him. If he had ever had anyone to talk to about his secret terrors – if he had ever dared to let himself ask questions – if he had had childish companions and had not lain on his back in the huge closed house, breathing an atmosphere heavy with the fears of people who were most of them ignorant and tired of him, he would have found out that most of his fright and illness was created by himself. But he had lain and thought of himself and his aches and weariness for hours and days and months and years. And now that an angry, unsympathetic little girl insisted obstinately that he was not at all as he thought he was, he actually felt as if she might be speaking the truth.

'I didn't know,' ventured the nurse, 'that he thought he had a lump on his spine. His back is weak because he won't try to sit up. I could have told him there was no lump there.' Colin gulped and turned his face a little to look at her.

'C-could you?' he said pathetically.

'Yes, sir.'

'There!' said Mary, and she gulped, too.

Colin turned on his face again, and but for his long-drawn broken breaths, which were the dying down of his storm of sobbing, he lay still for a minute, though great tears streamed down his face and wet the pillow. Actually the tears meant that a curious great relief had come to him. Presently he turned and looked at the nurse again, and strangely enough he was not like a rajah at all as he spoke to her.

'Do you think – I could – live to grow up?' he said.

The nurse was neither clever nor soft-hearted, but she could repeat some of the London doctor's words.

'You probably will if you will do what you are told to do, and not give way to your temper, and stay out a great deal in the fresh air.'

Colin's tantrum had passed and he was weak and worn out with crying, and this perhaps made him feel gentle. He put out his hand a little towards Mary, and I am glad to say that, her own tantrum having passed, she was softened too, and met him half-way with her hands, so that it was a sort of making up.

'I'll – I'll go out with you, Mary,' he said. 'I shan't hate fresh air if we can find——' He remembered just in time to stop himself from saying 'if we can find the secret garden,' and he ended: 'I shall like to go out with you if Dickon will come and push my chair. I do so want to see Dickon and the fox and the crow.'

The nurse remade the tumbled bed and shook and straightened the pillows. Then she made Colin a cup of beef-tea and gave a cup to Mary, who really was very glad to get it after her excitement. Mrs. Medlock and Martha gladly slipped away, and after everything was neat and calm and in order, the nurse looked as if she would very gladly slip away also. She was a healthy young woman who resented being robbed of her sleep, and she yawned quite openly as she looked at Mary, who had pushed her big footstool close to the four-poster bed and was holding Colin's hand.

'You must go back and get your sleep out,' she said. 'He'll drop off after a while – if he's not too upset. Then I'll lie down myself in the next room.'

'Would you like me to sing you that song I learned from my Ayah?' Mary whispered to Colin.

His hand pulled hers gently and he turned his tired eyes on her appealingly.

'Oh, yes!' he answered. 'It's such a soft song. I shall go to sleep in a minute.'

'I will put him to sleep,' Mary said to the yawning nurse. 'You can go if you like.'

'Well,' said the nurse, with an attempt at reluctance. 'If he doesn't go to sleep in half an hour you must call me.'

'Very well,' answered Mary.

The nurse was out of the room in a minute, and as soon as she was gone Colin pulled Mary's hand again.

'I almost told,' he said: 'but I stopped myself in time. I won't talk and I'll go to sleep, but you said you had a whole lot of nice things to tell me. Have you – do you think you have found out anything at all about the way into the secret garden?'

Mary looked at his poor little tired face and swollen eyes and her heart relented.

'Ye-es,' she answered, 'I think I have. And if you will go to sleep I will tell you tomorrow.'

His hand quite trembled.

'Oh, Mary!' he said 'Oh, Mary! If I could go into it I think I should live to grow up! Do you suppose that instead of singing the Ayah song – you could just tell me softly as you did that first day what you imagine it looks like inside? I am sure it will make me go to sleep.'

'Yes,' answered Mary. 'Shut your eyes.'

He closed his eyes and lay quite still and she held his hand and began to speak very slowly and in a very low voice.

'I think it has been left alone so long – that it has grown all into a lovely tangle. I think the roses have climbed and climbed and climbed until they hang from the branches and walls and creep over the ground – almost like a strange grey mist. Some of them have died, but many – are alive, and when the summer comes there will be curtains and fountains of roses. I think the ground is full of daffodils and snowdrops and lilies and iris working their way out of the dark. Now the spring has begun – perhaps – perhaps——'

The soft drone of her voice was making him stiller and stiller, and she saw it and went on.

'Perhaps they are coming up through the grass – perhaps there are clusters of purple crocuses and gold ones – even now. Perhaps the leaves are beginning to break out and uncurl – and perhaps – the grey is changing and a green gauze veil is creeping – and creeping over – everything. And the birds are coming to look at it – because it is – so safe and still. And perhaps – perhaps – perhaps –' very softly and slowly indeed, 'the robin has found a mate – and is building a nest.'

And Colin was asleep.

18 'Tha' munnot waste no Time'

Of course, Mary did not waken early the next morning. She slept late because she was tired, and when Martha brought her breakfast she told her that though Colin was quite quiet, he was ill and feverish, as he always was after he had worn himself out with a fit of crying. Mary ate her breakfast slowly as she listened.

'He says he wishes tha' would please go and see him as soon as tha' can,' Martha said. 'It's queer what a fancy he's took to thee. Tha' did give it him last night for sure – didn't tha'? Nobody else would have dared to do it. Eh! poor lad! He's been spoiled till salt won't save him. Mother says as th' two worst things as can happen to a child is never to have his own way – or always to have it. She doesn't know which is th' worst. Tha' was in a fine temper tha'self, too. But he says to me when I went into his room: "Please ask Miss Mary if she'll please come an' talk to me?" Think o' him saying please! Will you go, Miss?'

'I'll run and see Dickon first,' said Mary. 'No, I'll go and see Colin first and tell him – I know what I'll tell him,' with a sudden inspiration.

She had her hat on when she appeared in Colin's room, and for a second he looked disappointed. He was in bed, and his face was pitifully white and there were dark circles round his eyes.

'I'm glad you came,' he said. 'My head aches and I ache all over because I'm so tired. Are you going somewhere?'

Mary went and leaned against his bed.

'I won't be long,' she said. 'I'm going to Dickon, but I'll come back. Colin, it's – it's something about the secret garden.'

His whole face brightened and a little colour came into it.

'Oh! is it?' he cried out. 'I dreamed about it all night. I heard you say something about grey changing into green, and I dreamed I was standing in a place all filled with trembling little green leaves – and there were birds on nests everywhere and they looked so soft and still. I'll lie and think about it until you come back. ,

In five minutes Mary was with Dickon in their garden. The fox and the crow were with him again, and this time he had brought two tame squirrels.

'I came over on the pony this mornin',' he said. 'Eh! he is a good little chap – Jump is! I brought these two in my pockets. This here one he's called Nut an' this here other one's called Shell.'

When he said 'Nut' one squirrel leaped on to his right shoulder, and when he said 'Shell' the other one leaped on to his left shoulder.

When they sat down on the grass with Captain curled at their feet, Soot solemnly listening on a tree and Nut and Shell nosing about close to them, it seemed to Mary that it would be scarcely bearable to leave such delightfulness, but when she began to tell her story somehow the look in Dickon's funny face gradually changed her mind. She could see he felt sorrier for Colin than she did. He looked up at the sky and all about him.

'Just listen to them birds – th' world seems full of 'em – all whistlin' an' pipin', he said. 'Look at 'em dartin' about, an' hearken at 'em callin' to each other. Come springtime seems like as if all th' world's callin'. The leaves is uncurlin' so you can see 'em – an', my word, th' nice smells there is about!' sniffing with his happy turned-up nose. 'An' that poor lad lyin' shut up an' seein' so little that he gets to thinkin' o' things as sets him screamin'. Eh! my! we mun get him out here – we mun get him watchin' an' listenin' an' sniffin' up th' air an' get him just soaked through wi' sunshine. An' we munnot lose no time about it.'

When he was very much interested he often spoke quite broad Yorkshire, though at other times he tried to modify his dialect so that Mary could better understand. But she loved his broad Yorkshire, and had, in fact, been trying to learn to speak it herself. So she spoke a little now.

'Aye, that we mun,' she said (which meant 'Yes, indeed, we must'). 'I'll tell thee what us'll do first,' she proceeded, and Dickon grinned, because when the little wench tried to twist her tongue into speaking Yorkshire it amused him very much. 'He's took a graidely fancy to thee. He wants to see thee and he wants to see Soot an' Captain. When I go back to the house to talk to him I'll ax him if tha' canna come an' see him tomorrow mornin' – an' bring tha' creatures wi' thee – an' then – in a bit, when there's more leaves out an' happen a bud or two, we'll get him to come out an' tha' shall push him in his chair an' we'll bring him here an' show him everything.'

When she stopped she was quite proud of herself. She had never made a long speech in Yorkshire before, and she had remembered very well.

'Tha' mun talk a bit o' Yorkshire like that to Mester Colin,' Dickon chuckled. 'Tha'll make him laugh an' there's nowt as good for ill folk as laughin' is. Mother says she believes as half a hour's good laugh every mornin' 'ud cure a chap as was making ready for typhus fever.'

'I'm going to talk Yorkshire to him this very day,' said Mary, chuckling herself.

The garden had reached the time when every day and every night it seemed as if Magicians were passing through it drawing loveliness out of the earth and the boughs with wands. It was hard to go and leave it all, particularly as Nut had actually crept on to her dress and Shell had scrambled down the trunk of the apple-tree they sat under and stayed there looking at her with inquiring eyes. But she went back to the house and when she sat down close to Colin's bed he began to sniff as Dickon did, though not in such an experienced way.

'You smell like flowers and – and fresh things,' he cried out quite joyously. 'What is it you smell of? It's cool and warm and sweet all at the same time.'

'It's th' wind from th' moor,' said Mary. 'It comes o' sittin' on the' grass under a tree wi' Dickon an' wi' Captain an' Soot an' Nut an' Shell. It's th' springtime an' out o' doors an' sunshine as smells so graidely.'

She said it as broadly as she could, and you do not know how broadly Yorkshire sounds until you have heard someone speak it. Colin began to laugh.

'What are you doing?' he said. 'I never heard you talk like that before. How funny it sounds.'

'I'm givin' thee a bit o' Yorkshire,' answered Mary triumphantly. 'I canna talk as graidely as Dickon an' Martha can, but tha' sees I can shape a bit. Doesn't tha' understand a bit o' Yorkshire when tha' hears it? An' tha' a Yorkshire lad thysel' bred an' born! Eh! I wonder tha'rt not ashamed o' thy face.'

And then she began to laugh too, and they both laughed until they could not stop themselves, and they laughed until the room echoed and Mrs. Medlock opening the door to come in drew back into the corridor and stood listening, amazed.

'Well, upon my word!' she said, speaking rather broad Yorkshire herself because there was no one to hear her, and she was so astonished. 'Whoever heard th' like! Whoever on earth would ha' thought it!'

There was so much talk about. It seemed as if Colin could never hear enough of Dickon and Captain and Soot and Nut and Shell and the pony whose name was Jump. Mary had run round into the wood with Dickon to see Jump. He was a tiny little shaggy moor pony with thick locks hanging over his eyes and with a pretty face and a nuzzling velvet nose. He was rather thin with living on moor grass, but he was as tough and wiry as if the muscle in his legs had been made of steel springs. He had lifted his head and whinnied softly the moment he saw Dickon, and he had trotted up to him and put his head across his shoulder, and then Dickon had talked into his ear and Jump had talked back in odd little whinnies and puffs and snorts. Dickon had made him give Mary his small front hoof and kiss her on her cheek with his velvet muzzle.

'Does he really understand everything Dickon says?' Colin asked.

'It seems as if he does,' answered Mary. 'Dickon says anything will understand if you're friends with it for sure, but you have to be friends for sure.'

Colin lay quiet a little while, and his strange grey eyes seemed to be staring at the wall, but Mary saw he was thinking.

'I wish I was friends with things,' he said at last, 'but I'm not. I never had anything to be friends with, and I can't bear people.'

'Can't you bear me?' asked Mary.

'Yes, I can,' he answered. 'It's very funny, but I even like you.'

'Ben Weatherstaff said I was like him,' said Mary. 'He said he'd warrant we'd both got the same nasty tempers. I think you are like him, too. We are all three alike – you and I and Ben Weatherstaff. He said we were neither of us much to look at, and we were as sour as we looked. But I don't feel as sour as I used to before I knew the robin and Dickon.'

'Did you feel as if you hated people?'

'Yes,' answered Mary, without any affectation. 'I should have detested you if I had seen you before I saw the robin and Dickon.'

Colin put out his thin hand and touched her.

'Mary,' he said, 'I wish I hadn't said what I did about sending Dickon away. I hated you when you said he was like an angel and I laughed at you, but – but perhaps he is.'

'Well, it was rather funny to say it,' she admitted frankly, 'because his nose does turn up and he has a big mouth and his clothes have patches all over them and he talks broad Yorkshire, but – but if an angel did come to Yorkshire and live on the moor – if there was a Yorkshire angel – I believe he'd understand the green things and know how to make them grow and he would know how to talk to the wild creatures as Dickon does, and they'd know he was friends for sure.'

'I shouldn't mind Dickon looking at me,' said Colin; 'I want to see him.'

'I'm glad you said that,' answered Mary, 'because – because——'

Quite suddenly it came into her mind that this was the minute to tell him. Colin knew something new was coming.

'Because what?' he cried eagerly.

Mary was so anxious that she got up from her stool and came to him and caught hold of both his hands.

'Can I trust you? I trusted Dickon because birds trusted him. Can I trust you – for sure – *for sure*?' she implored.

Her face was so solemn that he almost whispered his answer.

'Yes – yes!'

'Well, Dickon will come to see you tomorrow morning and he'll bring his creatures with him.'

'Oh! Oh!' Colin cried out in delight.

'But that's not all,' Mary went on, almost pale with solemn excitement. 'The rest is better. There is a door into the garden. I found it. It is under the ivy on the wall.'

'If he had been a strong, healthy boy, Colin would probably have shouted, 'Hooray! Hooray! Hooray!' but he was weak and rather hysterical; his eyes grew bigger and bigger and he gasped for breath.

'Oh! Mary!' he cried out, with a half sob. 'Shall I see it? Shall I get into it? Shall I *live* to get into it?' and he clutched her hands and dragged her towards him.

'Of course you'll see it!' snapped Mary indignantly. 'Of course you'll live to get into it! Don't be silly!'

And she was so un-hysterical and natural and childish that she brought him to his senses and he began to laugh at himself, and a few minutes afterwards she was sitting on her stool again telling him not what she imagined the secret garden to be like, but what it really was, and Colin's aches and tiredness were forgotten and he was listening enraptured.

'It is just what you thought it would be,' he said at last. 'It sounds just as if you had really seen it. You know I said that when you told me first.'

Mary hesitated about two minutes and then boldly spoke the truth.

'I had seen it – and I had been in,' she said. 'I found the key and got in weeks ago. But I daren't tell you – I daren't because I was so afraid I couldn't trust you – *for sure!*'

19 'It has come!'

Of course, Dr. Craven had been sent for the morning after Colin had had his tantrum. He was always sent for at once when such a thing occurred, and he always found, when he arrived, a white, shaken boy lying on his bed, sulky and still so hysterical that he was ready to break into fresh sobbing at the least word. In fact, Dr. Craven dreaded and detested the difficulties of these visits. On this occasion he was away from Misselthwaite Manor until afternoon.

'How is he?' he asked Mrs. Medlock rather irritably when he arrived. 'He will break a blood-vessel in one of those fits some day. The boy is half insane with hysteria and self-indulgence.'

'Well, sir,' answered Mrs. Medlock, 'you'll scarcely believe your eyes when you see him. That plain, sour-faced child that's almost as bad as himself has just bewitched him. How she's done it there's no telling. The Lord knows, she's nothing to look at and you scarcely ever hear her speak, but she did what none of us dare do. She just flew at him like a little cat last night, and stamped her feet and ordered him to stop screaming, and somehow she startled him so that he actually did stop, and this afternoon – well, just come up and see, sir. It's past crediting.'

The scene which Dr. Craven beheld when he entered his patient's room was indeed rather astonishing to him. As Mrs. Medlock opened the door he heard laughing and chattering. Colin was on his sofa in his dressing–gown and he was sitting up quite straight looking at a picture in one of the garden books and talking to the plain child who at that moment could scarcely be called plain at all because her face was so glowing with enjoyment.

'Those long spires of blue ones – we'll have a lot of those,' Colin was announcing. 'They're called Del-phin-iums.'

'Dickon says they're larkspurs made big and grand,' cried Mistress Mary. 'There are clumps there already.'

Then they saw Dr. Craven and stopped. Mary became quite still and Colin looked fretful.

'I am sorry to hear you were ill last night, my boy,' Dr. Craven said, a trifle nervously. He was rather a nervous man.

'I'm better now – much better,' Colin answered, rather like a rajah. 'I'm going out in my chair in a day or two if it is fine. I want some fresh air.'

Dr. Craven sat down by him and felt his pulse and looked at him curiously.

'It must be a very fine day,' he said, 'and you must be very careful not to tire yourself.'

'Fresh air won't tire me,' said the young rajah.

As there had been occasions when this same young gentleman had shrieked aloud with rage and had insisted that fresh air would give him cold and kill him, it is not to be wondered at that his doctor felt somewhat startled.

'I thought you did not like fresh air,' he said.

'I don't when I am by myself,' replied the rajah; 'but my cousin is going out with me.'

'And the nurse, of course?' suggested Dr. Craven.

'No, I will not have the nurse,' so magnificently that Mary could not help remembering how the young native prince had looked with his diamonds and emeralds and pearls stuck all over him and the great rubies on the small dark hand he had waved to command his servants to approach with salaams and receive his orders.

'My cousin knows how to take care of me. I am always better when she is with me. She made me better last night. A very strong boy I know will push my carriage.'

Dr. Craven felt rather alarmed. If this tiresome, hysterical boy should chance to get well, he himself would lose all chance of inheriting Misselthwaite; but he was not an unscrupulous man, though he was a weak one, and he did not intend to let him run into actual danger.

'He must be a strong boy and a steady boy,' he said. 'And I must know something about him. Who is he? What is his name?'

'It's Dickon,' Mary spoke up suddenly. She felt somehow that everyone who knew the moor must know Dickon. And she was right, too. She saw that in a moment Dr. Craven's serious face relaxed into a relieved smile.

'Oh, Dickon,' he said. 'If it is Dickon you will be safe enough. He's as strong as a moor pony, is Dickon.'

'And he's trusty,' said Mary. 'He's th' trustiest lad i' Yorkshire.' She had been talking Yorkshire to Colin and she forgot herself.

'Did Dickon teach you that?' asked Dr. Craven, laughing outright.

'I'm learning it as if it was French,' said Mary, rather coldly. 'It's like a native dialect in India. Very clever people try to learn them. I like it and so does Colin.'

'Well, well,' he said. 'If it amuses you perhaps it won't do you any harm. Did you take your bromide last night, Colin?'

'No,' Colin answered. 'I wouldn't take it at first, and after Mary made me quiet she talked me to sleep – in a low voice – about the spring creeping into a garden.'

'That sounds soothing,' said Dr. Craven, more perplexed than ever and glancing sideways at Mistress Mary sitting on her stool and looking down silently at the carpet. 'You are evidently better, but you must remember——'

'I don't want to remember,' interrupted the rajah, appearing again. 'When I lie by myself and remember I begin to have pains everywhere, and I think of things that make me begin to scream because I hate them so. If there was a doctor anywhere who could make you forget you were ill instead of remembering it, I would have him brought here.' And he waved a thin hand which ought really to have been covered with royal signet rings made of rubies. 'It is because my cousin makes me forget that she makes me better.'

Dr. Craven had never made such a short stay after a 'tantrum'; usually he was obliged to remain a very long time and do a great many things. This afternoon he did not give any medicine or leave any new orders, and he was spared any disagreeable scenes. When he went downstairs he looked very thoughtful, and when he talked to Mrs.

Medlock in the library she felt that he was a much puzzled man.

'Well, sir,' she ventured, 'could you have believed it?'

'It is certainly a new state of affairs,' said the doctor. 'And there's no denying it is better than the old one.'

'I believe Susan Sowerby's right – I do that,' said Mrs. Medlock. 'I stopped in her cottage on my way to Thwaite yesterday, and had a bit of talk with her. And she says to me: "Well, Sarah Ann, she mayn't be a good child, an' she mayn't be a pretty one, but she's a child, an' children needs children." We went to school together, Susan Sowerby and me.'

'She's the best sick nurse I know,' said Dr. Craven. 'When I find her in a cottage I know the chances are that I shall save my patient.'

Mrs. Medlock smiled. She was fond of Susan Sowerby.

'She's got a way with her, has Susan,' she went on quite volubly. 'I've been thinking all morning of one thing she said yesterday. She says: "Once when I was givin' th' children a bit of a preach after they'd been fightin' I ses to 'em all, 'When I was at school my jography told as th' world was shaped like a orange an' I found out before I was ten that th' whole orange doesn't belong to nobody. No one owns more than his bit of a quarter an' there's times it seems like there's not enow quarters to go round. But don't you – none o' you – think as you own th' whole orange or you'll find out you're mistaken, an' you won't find it out without hard knocks.' What children learns from children," she says, "is that there's no sense in grabbin' at th' whole orange – peel an' all. If you do, you'll likely not get even th' pips, an' them's too bitter to eat."'

'She's a shrewd woman,' said Dr. Craven, putting on his coat.

'Well, she's got a way of saying things,' ended Mrs. Medlock, much pleased. 'Sometimes I've said to her, "Eh, Susan, if you was a different woman an' didn't talk such broad Yorkshire I've seen the times when I should have said you was clever."'

*

That night Colin slept without once awakening, and when he opened his eyes in the morning he lay still and smiled without knowing it – smiled because he felt so curiously comfortable. It was actually nice to be awake, and he turned over and stretched his limbs luxuriously. He felt as if tight strings which had held him had loosened themselves and let him go. He did not know that Dr. Craven would have said that his nerves had relaxed and rested themselves. Instead of lying and staring at the wall and wishing he had not awakened, his mind was full of the plans he and Mary had made yesterday, of pictures of the garden and of Dickon and his wild creatures. It was so nice to have things to think about. And he had not been awake more than ten minutes when he heard feet running along the corridor and Mary was at the door. The next minute she was in the room and had run across to his bed, bringing with her a waft of fresh air full of the scent of the morning.

'You've been out! You've been out! There's that nice smell of leaves!' he cried.

She had been running and her hair was loose and blown, and she was bright with the air and pink-cheeked, though he could not see it.

'It's so beautiful!' she said a little breathless with her speed. 'You never saw anything so beautiful! It has *come*! I thought it had come that other morning, but it was only coming. It is here now! It has come, the Spring! Dickon says so!'

'Has it?' cried Colin, and though he really knew nothing about it, he felt his heart beat. He actually sat up in bed.

'Open the window!' he added, laughing half with joyful excitement and half at his own fancy. 'Perhaps we may hear golden trumpets!'

And though he laughed, Mary was at the window in a moment and in a moment more it was opened wide and freshness and softness and scents and birds' songs were pouring through.

'That's fresh air,' she said. 'Lie on your back and draw in long breaths of it. That's what Dickon does when he's lying on the moor. He says he feels it in his veins and it makes him strong and he feels as if he could live for ever and ever. Breathe it and breathe it.'

She was only repeating what Dickon had told her, but she caught Colin's fancy.

' "For ever and ever!" Does it make him feel like that?' he said, and he did as she told him, drawing in long deep breaths over and over again, until he felt that something quite new and delightful was happening to him.

Mary was at his bedside again.

'Things are crowding up out of the earth,' she ran on in a hurry. 'And there are flowers uncurling and buds on everything and the green veil has covered nearly all the grey and the birds are in such a hurry about their nests for fear they may be too late, that some of them are even fighting for places in the secret garden. And the rose-bushes look as wick as wick can be, and there are primroses in the lanes and woods, and the seeds we planted are up, and Dickon has brought the fox and the crow and the squirrels and a new-born lamb.'

And then she paused for breath. The new-born lamb Dickon had found three days before lying by its dead mother among the gorse bushes on the moor. It was not the first motherless lamb he had found and he knew what to do with it. He had taken it to the cottage wrapped in his jacket and he had let it lie near the fire and had fed it with warm milk. It was a soft thing, with a darling silly baby face and legs rather long for its body, Dickon had carried it over the moor in his arms, and its feeding-bottle was in his pocket with a squirrel, and when Mary had sat under a tree with its limp warmness huddled on her lap, she had felt as if she were too full of strange joy to speak. A lamb – a lamb! a living lamb who lay on your lap like a baby!

She was describing it with great joy and Colin was listening and drawing in long breaths of air when the nurse entered. She started a little at the sight of the open window. She had sat stifling in the room many a warm day because her patient was sure that open windows gave people cold.

'Are you sure you are not chilly, Master Colin?' she inquired.

'No,' was the answer. 'I am breathing long breaths of fresh air. It makes you strong. I am going to get up to the sofa for breakfast and my cousin will have breakfast with me.'

The nurse went away, concealing a smile, to give the order for two breakfasts. She found the servants' hall a more amusing place than the invalid's chamber, and just now everybody wanted to hear the news from upstairs. There was a great deal of joking about the unpopular young recluse who, as the cook said, 'had found his master, and good for him.' The servants' hall had been very tired of the tantrums, and the butler, who was a man with a family, had more than once expressed his opinion that the invalid would be all the better 'for a good hiding'.

When Colin was on his sofa and the breakfast for two was put upon the table, he made an announcement to the nurse in his most rajah-like manner.

'A boy, and a fox, and a crow, and two squirrels, and a new-born lamb, are coming to see me this morning. I want them brought upstairs as soon as they come,' he said. 'You are not to begin playing with the animals in the servants' hall and keep them there. I want them here.'

The nurse gave a light gasp and tried to conceal it with a cough.

'Yes, sir,' she answered.

'I'll tell you what you can do,' added Colin, waving his hand. 'You can tell Martha to bring them here. The boy is Martha's brother. His name is Dickon and he is an animal charmer.'

'I hope the animals won't bite, Master Colin,' said the nurse.

'I told you he was a charmer,' said Colin austerely. 'Charmers' animals never bite.'

'There are snake-charmers in India,' said Mary; 'and they can put their snakes' heads in their mouths.'

'Goodness!' shuddered the nurse.

They ate their breakfast with the morning air pouring in upon them. Colin's breakfast was a very good one, and Mary watched him with serious interest.

'You will begin to get fatter just as I did,' she said. 'I never wanted my breakfast when I was in India, and now I always want it.'

'I wanted mine this morning,' said Colin. 'Perhaps it was the fresh air. When do you think Dickon will come?'

He was not long in coming. In about ten minutes Mary held up her hand.

'Listen' she said. 'Did you hear a caw?'

Colin listened and heard it, the oddest sound in the world to hear inside a house, a hoarse 'caw-caw'.

'Yes,' he answered.

'That's Soot,' said Mary. 'Listen again! Do you hear a bleat – a tiny one?'

'Oh, yes!' cried Colin, quite flushing.

'That's the new-born lamb,' said Mary. 'He's coming.'

Dickon's moorland boots were thick and clumsy, and though he tried to walk quietly they made a clumping sound as he walked through the long corridors. Mary and Colin heard him marching – marching, until he passed through the tapestry door on to the soft carpet of Colin's own passage.

'If you please, sir,' announced Martha, opening the door, 'if you please, sir, here's Dickon an' his creatures.'

Dickon came in smiling his nicest wide smile. The new-born lamb was in his arms and the little red fox trotted by his side. Nut sat on his left shoulder and Soot on his right, and Shell's head and paws peeped out of his coat pocket.

Colin slowly sat up and stared and stared – as he had stared when he first saw Mary; but this was a stare of wonder and delight. The truth was that in spite of all he had heard he had not in the least understood what this boy would be like and that his fox and his crow and his squirrels and his lamb were so near to him and his friendliness that they seemed almost to be part of himself. Colin had never talked to a boy in his life, and he was so overwhelmed by his own pleasure and curiosity that he did not even think of speaking.

But Dickon did not feel the least shy or awkward. He had not felt embarrassed because the crow had not known his language and had only stared and had not spoken to him the first time they met. Creatures were always like that until they found out about you. He walked over to Colin's sofa and put the new-born lamb quietly on his lap, and immediately the little creature turned to the warm velvet dressing-gown and began to nuzzle and nuzzle into its folds and butt its tight-curled head with soft impatience against his side. Of course, no boy could have helped speaking then.

'What is it doing?' cried Colin. 'What does it want?'

'It wants its mother,' said Dickon, smiling more and more. 'I brought it to thee a bit hungry because I knowed tha'd like to see it feed.'

He knelt down by the sofa and took a feeding-bottle from his pocket.

Come on, little 'un,' he said, turning the small, woolly, white head with a gentle brown hand. 'This is what tha's after. Tha'll get more out o' this than tha' will out o' silk velvet coats. There now,' and he pushed the rubber tip of the bottle into the nuzzling mouth and the lamb began to suck it with ravenous ecstasy.

After that there was no wondering what to say. By the time the lamb fell asleep questions poured forth, and Dickon answered them all. He told them how he had found the lamb just as the sun was rising three mornings ago. He had been standing on the moor listening to a skylark and watching him swing higher and higher into the blue, until he was only a speck in the heights of blue.

'I'd almost lost him but for his song an' I was wonderin' how a chap could hear it when it seemed as if he'd get out o' th' world in a minute – an' just then I heard somethin' else far off among th' gorse bushes. It was a weak bleatin', an' I knowed it was a new lamb as was hungry an' I knowed it wouldn't be hungry, if it hadn't lost its mother somehow, so I set off searchin'. Eh! I did have a look for it. I went in an' out among th' gorse bushes an' round an' round an' I always seemed to take th' wrong turnin'. But at last I seed a bit o' white by a rock on top o' th' moor an' I climbed up an' found th' little 'un half dead wi' cold an' clemmin'.'

While he talked, Soot flew solemnly in and out of the open window and cawed remarks about the scenery, while Nut and Shell made excursions into the big trees outside and ran up and down trunks and explored branches. Captain curled up near Dickon, who sat on the hearth-rug from preference.

They looked at the pictures in the gardening books and Dickon knew all the flowers by their country names and knew exactly which ones were already growing in the secret garden.

'I couldna' say that there name,' he said, pointing to one under which was written 'Aquilegia,' 'but us calls that a columbine, an' that there one it's a snapdragon and they both grow wild in hedges, but these is garden ones an' they're bigger and grander. There's some big clumps o' columbine in th' garden. They'll look like a bed o' blue an' white butterflies flutterin' when they're out.'

'"I'm going to see them," cried Colin'

'I'm going to see them,' cried Colin. 'I am going to see them!'

'Aye, that tha' mun,' said Mary quite seriously. 'An' tha' munnot lose no time about it.'

20 'I shall live for ever – and ever – and ever!'

But they were obliged to wait more than a week because first there
came some very windy days and then Colin was threatened with a cold,
which two things happening one after the other would no doubt have
thrown him into a rage, but that there was so much careful and
mysterious planning to do and almost every day Dickon came in, if
only for a few minutes, to talk about what was happening on the moor
and in the lanes and hedges and on the borders of streams. The things
he had to tell about otters' and badgers' and water-rats' houses, not to
mention birds' nests and field-mice and their burrows, were enough
to make you almost tremble with excitement, when you heard all the
intimate details from an animal charmer and realized with what
thrilling eagerness and anxiety the whole busy underworld was
working.

'They're same as us,' said Dickon, 'only they have to build their
homes every year. An' it keeps 'em so busy they fair scuffle to get 'em
done.'

The most absorbing thing, however, was the preparations to be
made before Colin could be transported with sufficient secrecy to the
garden. No one must see the chair-carriage and Dickon and Mary after
they turned a certain corner of the shrubbery and entered upon the
walk outside the ivied walls. As each day passed, Colin had become
more and more fixed in his feeling that the mystery surrounding the
garden was one of its greatest charms. Nothing must spoil that. No one
must ever suspect that they had a secret. People must think that he was
simply going out with Mary and Dickon because he liked them and did
not object to their looking at him. They had long and quite delightful
talks about their route. They would go up this path and down that one

and cross the other and go round among the fountain flower-beds as if they were looking at the 'bedding-out plants' the head gardener, Mr. Roach, had been having arranged. That would seem such a rational thing to do that no one would think it at all mysterious. They would turn into the shrubbery walks and lose themselves until they came to the long walls. It was almost as seriously and elaborately thought out as the plans of march made by great generals in time of war.

Rumours of the new and curious things which were occurring in the invalid's apartments had, of course, filtered through the servants' hall into the stableyards and out among the gardeners, but, not-withstanding this, Mr. Roach was startled one day when he received orders from Master Colin's room to the effect that he must report himself in the apartment no outsider had ever seen, as the invalid himself desired to speak to him.

'Well, well,' he said to himself, as he hurriedly changed his coat, 'what's to do now? His Royal Highness that wasn't to be looked at calling up a man he's never set eyes on.'

Mr. Roach was not without curiosity. He had never caught even a glimpse of the boy and had heard a dozen exaggerated stories about his uncanny looks and ways and his insane tempers. The thing he had heard oftenest was that he might die at any moment and there had been numerous fanciful descriptions of a humped back and helpless limbs, given by people who had never seen him.

'Things are changing in this house, Mr. Roach,' said Mrs. Medlock, as she led him up the back staircase to the corridor on to which opened the hitherto mysterious chamber.

'Let's hope they're changing for the better, Mrs. Medlock,' he answered.

'They couldn't well change for the worse,' she continued; 'and queer as it all is, there's them as finds their duties made a lot easier to stand up under. Don't you be surprised, Mr. Roach, if you find yourself in the middle of a menagerie and Martha Sowerby's Dickon more at home than you or me could ever be.'

There really was a sort of Magic about Dickon as Mary always privately believed. When Mr. Roach heard his name he smiled quite leniently.

'He'd be at home in Buckingham Palace or at the bottom of a coal mine,' he said. 'And yet it's not impudence, either. He's just fine, is that lad.'

It was perhaps well he had been prepared or he might have been startled. When the bedroom door was opened a large crow, which seemed quite at home perched on the high back of a carven chair, announced the entrance of a visitor by saying 'Caw-caw' quite loudly. In spite of Mrs. Medlock's warning, Mr. Roach only just escaped being sufficiently undignified to jump backwards.

The young rajah was neither in bed nor on his sofa. He was sitting in an arm-chair and a young lamb was standing by him shaking its tail in feeding-lamb fashion as Dickon knelt giving it milk from its bottle. A squirrel was perched on Dickon's bent back attentively nibbling a nut. The little girl from India was sitting on a big footstool looking on.

'Here is Mr. Roach, Master Colin,' said Mrs. Medlock.

The young rajah turned and looked his servitor over – at least that was what the head gardener felt happened.

'Oh, you are Roach, are you?' he said. 'I sent for you to give you some very important orders.'

'Very good, sir,' answered Roach, wondering if he was to receive instructions to fell all the oaks in the park or to transform the orchards into water-gardens.

'I am going out in my chair this afternoon,' said Colin. 'If the fresh air agrees with me I may go out every day. When I go, none of the gardeners are to be anywhere near the Long Walk by the garden walls. No one is to be there. I shall go out about two o'clock and everyone must keep away until I send word that they may go back to their work.'

'Very good, sir,' replied Mr. Roach, much relieved to hear that the oaks might remain and that the orchards were safe.

'Mary,' said Colin, turning to her, 'what is that thing you say in India when you have finished talking and want people to go?'

'You say, "You have my permission to go," ' answered Mary.

The rajah waved his hand.

'You have my permission to go, Roach,' he said. 'But remember, this is very important.'

'Caw-caw!' remarked the crow hoarsely, but not impolitely.

'Very good, sir. Thank you, sir,' said Mr. Roach, and Mrs. Medlock took him out of the room.

Outside in the corridor, being a rather good-natured man, he smiled until he almost laughed.

'My word!' he said, 'he's got a fine, lordly way with him, hasn't he? You'd think he was a whole Royal Family rolled into one – Prince Consort and all.'

'Eh!' protested Mrs. Medlock, 'we've had to let him trample all over every one of us ever since he had feet, and he thinks that's what folks was born for.'

'Perhaps he'll grow out of it, if he lives,' suggested Mr. Roach.

'Well, there's one thing pretty sure,' said Mrs. Medlock. 'If he does live and that Indian child stays here, I'll warrant she teaches him that the whole orange does not belong to him, as Susan Sowerby says. And he'll be likely to find out the size of his own quarter.'

Inside the room Colin was leaning back on his cushions.

'It's all safe now,' he said. 'And this afternoon I shall see it – this afternoon I shall be in it!'

Dickon went back to the garden with his creatures, and Mary stayed with Colin. She did not think he looked tired, but he was very quiet before their lunch came, and he was quiet while they were eating it. She wondered why, and asked him about it.

'What big eyes you've got, Colin,' she said. 'When you are thinking they get as big as saucers. What are you thinking about now?'

'I can't help thinking about what it will look like,' he answered.

'The garden?' asked Mary.

'The springtime,' he said. 'I was thinking that I've really never seen it before. I scarcely ever went out, and when I did go I never looked at it. I didn't even think about it.'

'I never saw it in India, because there wasn't any,' said Mary.

Shut in and morbid as his life had been, Colin had more imagination than she had, and at least he had spent a good deal of time looking at wonderful books and pictures.

'That morning when you ran in and said "It's come! It's come!" you made me feel quite queer. It sounded as if things were coming with a great procession and big bursts and wafts of music. I've a picture like it in one of my books – crowds of lovely people and children with garlands and branches with blossoms on them, everyone laughing and dancing and crowding and playing on pipes. That was why I said, "Perhaps we shall hear golden trumpets," and told you to throw open the window.'

'How funny!' said Mary. 'That's really just what it feels like. And if all the flowers and leaves and green things and birds, and wild creatures danced past at once, what a crowd it would be! I'm sure they'd dance and sing and flute and that would be the wafts of music.'

They both laughed, but it was not because the idea was laughable, but because they both so liked it.

A little later the nurse made Colin ready. She noticed that instead of lying like a log while his clothes were put on, he sat up and made some efforts to help himself, and he talked and laughed with Mary all the time.

'This is one of his good days, sir,' she said to Dr. Craven, who dropped in to inspect him. 'He's in such good spirits that it makes him stronger.'

'I'll call in again later in the afternoon, after he has come in,' said Dr. Craven. 'I must see how the going out agrees with him. I wish,' in a very low voice, 'that he would let you go with him.'

'I'd rather give up the case this moment, sir, than even stay here while it's suggested,' answered the nurse with sudden firmness.

'I hadn't really decided to suggest it,' said the doctor, with his slight nervousness. 'We'll try the experiment. Dickon's a lad I'd trust with a new-born child.'

The strongest footman in the house carried Colin downstairs and put him in his wheeled-chair, near which Dickon waited outside. After the manservant had arranged his rugs and cushions, the rajah waved his hand to him and to the nurse.

'You have my permission to go,' he said, and they both disappeared quickly, and it must be confessed, giggled, when they were safely inside the house.

Dickon began to push the wheeled-chair slowly and steadily. Mistress Mary walked beside it and Colin leaned back and lifted his face to the sky. The arch of it looked very high and the small snowy clouds seemed like white birds floating on outspread wings below its crystal blueness. The wind swept in soft big breaths down from the moor and was strange with a wild clear-scented sweetness. Colin kept lifting his thin chest to draw it in, and his big eyes looked as if it were they which were listening – listening, instead of his ears.

'There are so many sounds of singing and humming and calling out,' he said. 'What is that scent the puffs of wind bring?'

'It's gorse on th' moor that's openin' out,' answered Dickon. 'Eh! th' bees are at it wonderful today.'

Not a human creature was to be caught sight of in the paths they took. In fact every gardener or gardener's lad had been witched away. But they wound in and out among the shrubbery and out and round the fountain beds, following their carefully planned route for the mere mysterious pleasure of it. But when at last they turned into the Long Walk by the ivied walls, the excited sense of an approaching thrill made them, for some curious reason they could not have explained, begin to speak in whispers.

'This is it,' breathed Mary. 'This is where I used to walk up and down and wonder and wonder.'

'Is it?' cried Colin, and his eyes began to search the ivy with eager curiousness. 'But I can seen nothing,' he whispered. 'There is no door.'

'That's what I thought,' said Mary.

Then there was a lovely, breathless silence and the chair wheeled on.

'That is the garden where Ben Weatherstaff works,' said Mary.

'Is it?' said Colin.

A few yards more and Mary whispered again.

'This is where the robin flew over the wall,' she said.

'Is it?' cried Colin. 'Oh! I wish he'd come again!'

'And that,' said Mary with solemn delight, pointing under a big lilac bush, 'is where he perched on the little heap of earth and showed me the key.'

Then Colin sat up.

'Where? Where? There?' he cried, and his eyes were as big as the wolf's in Red Riding Hood, when Red Riding Hood felt called upon to remark on them. Dickon stood still and the wheeled-chair stopped.

'And this,' said Mary, stepping on to the bed close to the ivy, 'is where I went to talk to him when he chirped at me from the top of the wall. And this is the ivy the wind blew back,' and she took hold of the hanging green curtain.

Oh! is it—' gasped Colin.

'And here is the handle, and here is the door. Dickon, push him in – push him in quickly!'

And Dickon did it with one strong, steady, splendid push.

But Colin had actually dropped back against his cushions, even though he gasped with delight, and he had covered his eyes with his hands and held them there, shutting out everything until they were inside and the chair stopped as if by magic and the door was closed. Not till then did he take them away and look round and round and round as Dickon and Mary had done. And over walls and earth and trees and swinging sprays and tendrils the fair green veil of tender little leaves had crept, and in the grass under the trees and the grey urns in the alcoves and here and there everywhere, were touches or splashes of gold and purple and white and the trees were showing pink and snow above his head, and there were fluttering of wings and faint sweet pipes and humming and scents and scents. And the sun fell warm upon his face like a hand with a lovely touch. And in wonder Mary and Dickon stood and stared at him. He looked so strange and different because a pink glow of colour had actually crept all over him – ivory face and neck and hands and all.

'I shall get well! I shall get well!' he cried out. 'Mary! Dickon! I shall get well! And I shall live for ever and ever and ever!'

21 Ben Weatherstaff

One of the strange things about living in the world is that it is only now and then one is quite sure one is going to live for ever and ever and ever. One knows it sometimes when one gets up at the tender, solemn dawn-time and goes out and stands alone and throws one's head far back and looks up and up and watches the pale sky slowly changing and flushing and marvellous unknown things happening until the East almost makes one cry out and one's heart stands still at the strange, unchanging majesty of the rising of the sun – which has been happening every morning for thousands and thousands and thousands of years. One knows it then for a moment or so. And one knows it sometimes when one stands by oneself in a wood at sunset and the mysterious deep gold stillness slanting through and under the branches seems to be saying slowly again and again something one cannot quite hear, however much one tries. Then sometimes the immense quiet of the dark-blue at night with millions of stars waiting and watching makes one sure; and sometimes a sound of far-off music makes it true; and sometimes a look in someone's eyes.

And it was like that with Colin when he first saw and heard and felt the springtime inside the four high walls of a hidden garden. That afternoon the whole world seemed to devote itself to being perfect and radiantly beautiful and kind to one boy. Perhaps out of pure heavenly goodness the spring came and crowded everything it possibly could into that one place. More than once Dickon paused in what he was doing and stood still with a sort of growing wonder in his eyes, shaking his head softly.

'Eh! It is graidely,' he said. 'I'm twelve goin' on thirteen an' there's a lot o' afternoons in thirteen years; but seems to me like I never seed one as graidely as this 'ere.'

'Aye, it is a graidely one,' said Mary, and she sighed for mere joy. 'I'll warrant its th' graidliest one as ever was in this world.'

'Does tha' think,' said Colin, with dreamy carefulness, 'as happen it was made loike this 'ere all o' purpose for me?'

'My word!' cried Mary admiringly, 'that there is a bit o' good Yorkshire. Tha'rt shapin' first rate – that – tha' art.'

And delight reigned.

They drew the chair under the plum-tree, which was snow-white with blossoms and musical with bees. It was like a king's canopy, a fairy king's. There were flowering cherry-trees near and apple-trees whose buds were pink and white, and here and there one had burst open wide. Between the blossoming branches of the canopy bits of blue sky looked down like wonderful eyes.

Mary and Dickon worked a little here and there and Colin watched them. They brought him things to look at – buds which were opening, buds which were tight closed, bits of twig whose leaves were just showing green, the feather of a woodpecker which had dropped on the grass, the empty shell of some bird early hatched. Dickon pushed the chair slowly round and round the garden, stopping every other moment to let him look at wonders springing out of the earth of trailing down from trees. It was like being taken in state round the country of a magic king and queen and shown all the mysterious riches it contained.

'I wonder if we shall see the robin?' said Colin.

'Tha'll see him often enow after a bit,' answered Dickon. 'When th' eggs hatches out th' little chap he'll be kep' so busy it'll make his head swim. Tha'll see him flyin' backward an' for'ard carryin' worms nigh as big as himsel' an' that much noise goin' on in th' nest when he gets there as fair flusters him so as he scarce knows which big mouth to drop th' first piece in. An' gapin' beaks an' squawks on every side. Mother says as when she sees th' work a robin has to keep them gapin' beaks filled, she feels like she was a lady with nothin' to do. She says she's seen th' little chaps when it seemed like th' sweat must be droppin' off 'em, though folk can't see it.'

This made them giggle so delightedly that they were obliged to

cover their mouths with their hands, remembering that they must not
be heard. Colin had been instructed as to the law of whispers and low
voices several days before. He liked the mysteriousness of it and did his
best, but in the midst of excited enjoyment it is rather difficult never to
laugh above a whisper.

Every moment of the afternoon was full of new things and every
hour the sunshine grew more golden. The wheeled-chair had been
drawn back under the canopy and Dickon had sat down on the grass
and had just drawn out his pipe when Colin saw something he had not
had time to notice before.

'That's a very old tree over there, isn't it?' he said.

Dickon looked across the grass at the tree and Mary looked and
there was a brief moment of stillness.

'Yes,' answered Dickon, after it, and his low voice had a very
gentle sound.

Mary gazed at the tree and thought.

'The branches are quite grey and there's not a single leaf
anywhere,' Colin went on. 'It's quite dead, isn't it?'

'Aye,' admitted Dickon. 'But them roses as has climbed all over it
will near hide every bit o' th' dead wood when they're full o' leaves an'
flowers. It won't look dead then. It'll be th' prettiest of all.'

Mary still gazed at the tree and thought.

'It looks as if a big branch had been broken off,' said Colin. 'I
wonder how it was done.'

'It's been done many a year,' answered Dickon. 'Eh!' with a
sudden relieved start and laying his hand on Colin, 'Look at that robin!
There he is! He's been foragin' for his mate.'

Colin was almost too late, but he just caught sight of him, the flash
of red-breasted bird with something in his beak. He darted through
the greenness and into the close-grown corner and out of sight. Colin
leaned back on his cushion again, laughing a little.

'He's taking her tea to her. Perhaps it's five o'clock. I think I'd like
some tea myself.'

And so they were safe.

'It was Magic which sent the robin,' said Mary secretly to Dickon
afterwards. 'I know it was Magic.' For both she and Dickon had been

afraid Colin might ask something about the tree whose branch had broken off ten years ago, and they had talked it over together and Dickon had stood and rubbed his head in a troubled way.

'We mun look as if it wasn't no different from th' other trees,' he had said. 'We couldn't never tell him how it broke, poor lad. If he says anything about it we mun – we mun try to look cheerful.'

'Aye that we mun,' had answered Mary.

But she had not felt as if she looked cheerful when she gazed at the tree. She wondered and wondered in those few moments if there was any reality in that other thing Dickon had said. He had gone on rubbing his rust-red hair in a puzzled way, but a nice comforted look had begun to grow in his blue eyes.

'Mrs. Craven was a very lovely young lady,' he had gone on rather hesitatingly. 'An' Mother she thinks maybe she's about Misselthwaite many a time lookin' after Mester Colin, same as all mothers do when they're took out o' th' world. They have to come back, tha' sees. Happen she's been in the garden an' happen it was her set us to work, an' told us to bring him here.'

Mary had thought he meant something about Magic. She was a great believer in Magic. Secretly she quite believed that Dickon worked Magic, of course, good Magic, on everything near him and that was why people liked him so much and wild creatures knew he was their friend. She wondered, indeed, if it were not possible that his gift had brought the robin just at the right moment when Colin asked that dangerous question. She felt that his Magic was working all the afternoon and making Colin look an entirely different boy. It did not seem possible that he could be the crazy creature who had screamed and beaten and bitten his pillow. Even his ivory whiteness seemed to change. The faint glow of colour which had shown on his face and neck and hands when he first got inside the garden really never quite died away. He looked as if he were made of flesh instead of ivory or wax.

They saw the robin carry food to his mate two or three times, and it was so suggestive of afternoon tea that Colin felt they must have some.

'Go and make one of the manservants bring some in a basket to the rhododendron walk,' he said. 'And then you and Dickon can bring it here.'

It was an agreeable idea; easily carried out, and when the white cloth was spread upon the grass, with hot tea and buttered toast and crumpets, a delightfully hungry meal was eaten, and several birds on domestic errands paused to inquire what was going on and were led into investigating crumbs with great activity. Nut and Shell whisked up trees with pieces of cake, and Soot took the entire half of a buttered crumpet into a corner and pecked at and examined and turned it over and made hoarse remarks about it until he decided to swallow it all joyfully in one gulp.

The afternoon was dragging towards its mellow hour. The sun was deepening the gold of its lances, the bees were going home and the birds were flying past less often. Dickon and Mary were sitting on the grass, the tea-basket was repacked ready to be taken back to the house, and Colin was lying against his cushions with his heavy locks pushed back from his forehead and his face looking quite a natural colour.

'I don't want this afternoon to go,' he said; 'but I shall come back tomorrow, and the day after, and the day after, and the day after.'

'You'll get plenty of fresh air, won't you?' said Mary.

'I'm going to get nothing else,' he answered. 'I've seen the spring now and I'm going to see the summer. I'm going to see everything grow here. I'm going to grow here myself.'

'That tha' will,' said Dickon. 'Us'll have thee walkin' about here an' diggin' same as other folk afore long.'

Colin flushed tremendously.

'Walk!' he said. 'Dig! Shall I?'

Dickon's glance at him was delicately cautious. Neither he nor Mary had ever asked if anything was the matter with his legs.

'For sure tha will,' he said stoutly. 'Tha' – tha's got legs o' thine own, same as other folks!'

Mary was rather frightened until she heard Colin's answer.

'Nothing really ails them,' he said, 'but they are so thin and weak. They shake so that I'm afraid to try to stand on them.'

Both Mary and Dickon drew a relieved breath.

'When tha' stops bein' afraid tha'lt stand on 'em,' Dickon said with renewed cheer. 'An' tha'lt stop bein' afraid in a bit.'

'I shall?' said Colin, and he lay still, as if he were wondering about things.

They were really very quiet for a little while. The sun was dropping lower. It was that hour when everything stills itself, and they really had had a busy and exciting afternoon. Colin looked as if he were resting luxuriously. Even the creatures had ceased moving about and had drawn together and were resting near them. Soot had perched on a low branch and drawn up one leg and dropped the grey film drowsily over his eyes. Mary privately thought he looked as if he might snore in a minute.

In the midst of this stillness it was rather startling when Colin half lifted his head and exclaimed in a loud, suddenly alarmed whisper:

'Who is that man?'

Dickon and Mary scrambled to their feet.

'Man?' they both cried in low, quick voices.

Colin pointed to the high wall.

'Look!' he whispered excitedly. 'Just look!'

Mary and Dickon wheeled about and looked. There was Ben Weatherstaff's indignant face glaring at them over the wall from the top of a ladder! He actually shook his fist at Mary.

'If I wasn't a bachelder, an' tha' was a wench o' mine,' he cried, 'I'd give thee a hidin'!'

He mounted another step threateningly, as if it were his energetic intention to jump down and deal with her; but as she came towards him he evidently thought better of it and stood on the top step of his ladder shaking his fist down at her.

'I never thowt much o' thee!' he harangued, 'I couldna' abide thee th' first time I set eyes on thee. A scrawny, buttermilk-faced young besom, allus askin' questions an' pokin' tha' nose where it wasna' wanted. I never knowed how tha' got so thick wi' me. If it hadna' been for th' robin – drat him——'

'Ben Weatherstaff,' called out Mary, finding her breath. She stood below him and called up to him with a sort of gasp. 'Ben Weatherstaff, it was the robin who showed me the way!'

Then it did seem as if Ben really would scramble down on her side of the wall, he was so outraged.

'Tha' young bad 'un!' he called down to her. 'Layin' tha' badness on a robin – not but what he's impidint enow for anythin'. Him showin' thee th' way! Him! Eh! tha' young nowt' – she could see his next words burst out because he was overpowered by curiosity – 'however i' this world did tha' get in?'

'It was the robin who showed me the way,' she protested obstinately. 'He didn't know he was doing it, but he did. And I can't tell you from here, while you're shaking your fist at me.'

He stopped shaking his fist very suddenly at that very moment and his jaw actually dropped as he stared over her head at something he saw coming over the grass towards him.

At the first sound of his torrent of words Colin had been so surprised that he had only sat up and listened as if he were spellbound. But in the midst of it he had recovered himself and beckoned imperiously to Dickon.

'Wheel me over there!' he commanded. 'Wheel me quite close and stop right in front of him!'

And this if you please, this is what Ben Weatherstaff beheld and which made his jaw drop. A wheeled-chair with luxurious cushions and robes which came towards him looking rather like some sort of state coach because a young rajah leaned back in it with royal command in his great, black-rimmed eyes and a thin white hand extended haughtily towards him. And it stopped right under Ben Weatherstaff's nose. It was really no wonder his mouth dropped open.

'Do you know who I am?' demanded the rajah.

How Ben Weatherstaff stared! His red old eyes fixed themselves on what was before him as if he were seeing a ghost. He gazed and gazed and gulped a lump down his throat and did not say a word.

'Do you know who I am?' demanded Colin still more imperiously. 'Answer!'

Ben Weatherstaff put his gnarled hand up and passed it over his eyes and over his forehead and then he did answer in a queer, shaky voice.

'Who tha' art?' he said. 'Aye, that I do – wi' tha' mother's eyes starin' at me out o' tha' face. Lord knows how tha' come here. But tha'rt th' poor cripple.'

Colin forgot that he had ever had a back. His face flushed scarlet and he sat bolt upright.

'I'm not a cripple!' he cried out furiously. 'I'm not!'

'He's not!' cried Mary, almost shouting up the wall in her fierce indignation. 'He's not got a lump as big as a pin! I looked and there was none there – not one!'

Ben Weatherstaff passed his hand over his forehead again and gazed as if he could never gaze enough. His hand shook and his mouth shook and his voice shook. He was an ignorant old man and a tactless old man and he could only remember the things he had heard.

'Tha' – tha' hasn't got a crooked back?' he said hoarsely.

'No!' shouted Colin.

'Tha' – tha' hasn't got crooked legs?' quavered Ben more hoarsely yet.

It was too much. The strength which Colin usually threw into his tantrums rushed through him now in a new way. Never yet had he been accused of crooked legs – even in whispers – and the perfectly simple belief in their existence which was revealed by Ben Weatherstaff's voice was more than rajah flesh and blood could endure. His anger and insulted pride made him forget everything but this one moment, and filled him with power he had never known before, an almost unnatural strength.

'Come here!' he shouted to Dickon, and he actually began to tear the coverings off his lower limbs and disentangle himself. 'Come here! Come here! This minute!'

Dickon was by his side in a second. Mary caught her breath in a short gasp and felt herself turn pale.

'He can do it! He can do it! He can do it! He can!' she gabbled over to herself under her breath as fast as she could.

There was a brief, fierce scramble, the rugs were tossed on to the ground, Dickon held Colin's arm, the thin legs were out, the thin feet were on the grass. Colin was standing upright – upright – as straight as an arrow and looking strangely tall – his head thrown back and his strange eyes flashing lightning.

'Look at me!' he flung up at Ben Weatherstaff. 'Just look at me – you! Just look at me!'

'He's as straight as I am,' cried Dickon. 'He's as straight as any lad i' Yorkshire!'

What Ben Weatherstaff did Mary thought queer beyond measure. He choked and gulped and suddenly tears ran down his weather-wrinkled cheeks as he struck his old hands together.

'Eh!' he burst forth, 'th' lies folk tells! Tha'rt as thin as a lath an' as white as a wraith, but there's not a knob on thee. Tha'lt make a mon yet. God bless thee!'

Dickon held Colin's arms strongly, but the boy had not begun to falter. He stood straighter and straighter and looked Ben Weatherstaff in the face.

'I'm your master,' he said, 'when my father is away. And you are to obey me. This is my garden. Don't dare to say a word about it! You get down from that ladder and go out to the Long Walk and Miss Mary will meet you and bring you here. I want to talk to you. We did not want you, but now you will have to be in the secret. Be quick!'

Ben Weatherstaff's crabbed old face was still wet with that one queer rush of tears. It seemed as if he could not take his eyes from thin, straight Colin standing on his feet with his head thrown back.

'Eh! lad,' he almost whispered. 'Eh! my lad!' And then remembering himself he suddenly touched his hat gardener fashion and said, 'Yes, sir! Yes, sir!' and obediently disappeared as he descended the ladder.

22 When the Sun went down

When his head was out of sight, Colin turned to Mary.

'Go and meet him,' he said, and Mary flew across the grass to the door under the ivy.

Dickon was watching him with sharp eyes. There were scarlet spots on his cheeks and he looked amazing, but he showed no signs of falling.

'I can stand,' he said, and his head was still held up and he said it quite grandly.

'I told thee tha' could as soon as tha' stopped bein' afraid,' answered Dickon. 'An' tha's stopped.'

'Yes, I've stopped,' said Colin.

Then suddenly he remembered something Mary had said.

'Are you making Magic?' he asked sharply.

Dickon's curly mouth spread in a cheerful grin.

'Tha's doin' Magic thysel',' he said. 'It's same Magic as made these 'ere work out o' th' earth,' and he touched with his thick boot a clump of crocuses in the grass.

Colin looked down at them.

'Aye,' he said slowly, 'there couldna' be bigger Magic than that there — there couldna' be.'

He drew himself up straighter than ever.

'I'm going to walk to that tree,' he said, pointing to one a few feet away from him. 'I'm going to be standing when Weatherstaff comes here. I can rest against the tree if I like. When I want to sit down I will sit down, but not before. Bring a rug from the chair.'

He walked to the tree, and though Dickon held his arm he was wonderfully steady. When he stood against the tree trunk it was not too plain that he supported himself against it, and he still held himself so straight that he looked tall.

When Ben Weatherstaff came through the door in the wall he saw him standing there and he heard Mary muttering something under her breath.

'What art sayin'?' he asked rather testily, because he did not want his attention distracted from the long, thin, straight boy figure and proud face.

But she did not tell him. What she was saying was this:

'You can do it! You can do it! I told you you could! You can do it! You can do it! You *can*!'

She was saying it to Colin because she wanted to make Magic and keep him on his feet looking like that. She could not bear that he should give in before Ben Weatherstaff. He did not give in. She was uplifted by a sudden feeling that he looked quite beautiful in spite of this thinness. He fixed his eyes on Ben Weatherstaff in his funny, imperious way.

'Look at me!' he commanded. 'Look at me all over! Am I a hunchback? Have I got crooked legs?'

Ben Weatherstaff had not quite got over his emotion, but he had recovered a little and answered almost in his usual way.

'Not tha',' he said. 'Nowt o' th' sort. What's tha' been doin' with thysel' – hidin' out o' sight an' lettin' folk think tha' was cripple an' half-witted?'

'Half-witted!' said Colin angrily. 'Who thought that?'

'Lots o' fools,' said Ben. 'Th' world's full o' jackasses brayin' an' they never bray nowt but lies. What did tha' shut thysel' up for?'

'Everyone thought I was going to die,' said Colin shortly. 'I'm not!'

And he said it with such decision Ben Weatherstaff looked him over, up and down, down and up.

'Tha' die!' he said with dry exultation. 'Nowt o' th' sort. Tha's got too much pluck in thee. When I seed thee put tha' legs on th' ground in such a hurry I knowed tha' was all right. Sit thee down on th' rug a bit, young Mester, an' give me thy orders.'

There was a queer mixture of crabbed tenderness and shrewd

understanding in his manner. Mary had poured out speech as rapidly as she could as they had come down the Long Walk. The chief thing to be remembered, she had told him, was that Colin was getting well – getting well. The garden was doing it. No one must let him remember about having humps and dying.

The rajah condescended to seat himself on a rug under the tree.

'What work do you do in the gardens, Weatherstaff?' he inquired.

'Anythin' I'm told to do,' answered old Ben. 'I'm kep' on by favour – because she liked me.'

'She?' said Colin.

'Tha' mother,' answered Ben Weatherstaff.

'My mother?' said Colin, and he looked about him quietly. 'This was her garden, wasn't it?'

'Aye, it was that!' and Ben Weatherstaff looked about him too. 'She were main fond of it.'

'It is my garden now. I am fond of it. I shall come here every day,' announced Colin. 'But it is to be a secret. My orders are that no one is to know that we come here. Dickon and my cousin have worked and made it come alive. I shall send for you sometimes to help – but you must come when no one can see you.'

Ben Weatherstaff's face twisted itself in a dry old smile.

'I've come here before when no one saw me,' he said.

'What!' exclaimed Colin. 'When?'

'Th' last time I was here,' rubbing his chin and looking round, 'was about two year' ago.'

'But no one has been in it for ten years!' cried Colin. 'There was no door!'

'I'm no one,' said old Ben dryly. 'An' I didn't come through th' door, I come over th' wall. Th' rheumatics held me back th' last two year'.'

'Tha' come an' did a bit o' prunin'!' cried Dickon. 'I couldn't make out how it had been done.'

'She was fond of it – she was!' said Ben Weatherstaff slowly. 'An' she was such a pretty young thing. She says to me once, "Ben," says she laughin', "if ever I'm ill or if I go away you must take care of my roses." When she did go away th' orders was no one was ever to come nigh. But I come,' with grumpy obstinacy. 'Over th' wall I come – until th' rheumatics stopped me – an' I did a bit of work once a year. She'd gave her order first.'

'It wouldn't have been as wick as it is if tha' hadn't done it,' said Dickon. 'I did wonder.'

'I'm glad you did it, Weatherstaff,' said Colin. 'You'll know how to keep the secret.'

'Aye, I'll know, sir,' answered Ben. 'An' it'll be easier for a man wi' rheumatics to come in at th' door.'

On the grass near the tree Mary had dropped her trowel. Colin stretched out his hand and took it up. An odd expression came into his face and he began to scratch at the earth. His thin hand was weak enough, but presently as they watched him – Mary with quite breathless interest – he drove the end of the trowel into the soil and turned some over.

'You can do it! You can do it!' said Mary to herself. 'I tell you, you can!'

Dickon's round eyes were full of eager curiousness, but he said not a word. Ben Weatherstaff looked on with interested face.

Colin persevered. After he had turned a few trowelfuls of soil he spoke exultantly to Dickon in his best Yorkshire.

'Tha' said as tha'd have me walkin' about here same as other folk – an' tha' said tha'd have me diggin'. I thowt tha' was just leein' to please me. This is only th' first day an' I've walked – an' here I am diggin'.'

Ben Weatherstaff's mouth fell open again when he heard him, but he ended by chuckling.

'Eh!' he said, 'that sounds as if tha'd got wits enow. Tha'rt a Yorkshire lad for sure. An' tha'rt diggin', too. How'd tha' like to plant a bit o' somethin? I can get thee a rose in a pot.'

'Go and get it!' said Colin, digging excitedly. 'Quick! Quick!'

It was done quickly enough indeed. Ben Weatherstaff went his way forgetting rheumatics. Dickon took his spade and dug the hole deeper and wider than a new digger with thin hands could make it. Mary slipped out to run and bring back a watering-can. When Dickon had deepened the hole, Colin went on turning the soft earth over and over. He looked up at the sky, flushed and glowing with the strangely new exercise, slight as it was.

'I want to do it before the sun goes quite – quite down,' he said.

Mary thought that perhaps the sun held back a few minutes just on purpose. Ben Weatherstaff brought the rose in its pot from the greenhouse. He hobbled over the grass as fast as he could. He had begun to be excited, too. He knelt down by the hole and broke the pot from the mould.

'Here, lad,' he said, handing the plant to Colin. 'Set it in the earth thysel' same as th' king does when he goes to a new place.'

The thin white hands shook a little and Colin's flush grew deeper as he set the rose in the mould and held it while old Ben made firm the earth. It was filled in and pressed down and made steady. Mary was leaning forward on her hands and knees. Soot had flown down and marched forward to see what was being done. Nut and Shell chattered about it from a cherry-tree.

'It's planted!' said Colin at last. 'And the sun is only slipping over the edge. Help me up, Dickon. I want to be standing when it goes. That's part of the Magic.'

And Dickon helped him, and the Magic – or whatever it was – so gave him strength that when the sun did slip over the edge and end the strange, lovely afternoon for them, there he actually stood on his two feet – laughing.

23 Magic

Dr. Craven had been waiting some time at the house when they returned to it. He had indeed begun to wonder if it might not be wise to send someone out to explore the garden paths. When Colin was brought back to his room, the poor man looked him over seriously.

'You should not have stayed so long,' he said. 'You must not over-exert yourself.'

'I am not tired at all,' said Colin. 'It has made me well. Tomorrow I am going out in the morning as well as in the afternoon.'

'I am not sure that I can allow it,' answered Dr. Craven. 'I am afraid it would not be wise.'

'It would not be wise to try to stop me,' said Colin quite seriously. 'I am going.'

Even Mary had found out that one of Colin's chief peculiarities was that he did not know in the least what a rude little brute he was with his way of ordering people about. He had lived on a sort of desert island all his life and as he had been the king of it he had made his own manners and had had no one to compare himself with. Mary had indeed been rather like him herself, and since she had been at Misselthwaite had gradually discovered that her own manners had not been of the kind which is usual or popular. Having made this discovery, she naturally thought it of enough interest to communicate to Colin. So she sat and looked at him curiously for a few minutes after Dr. Craven had gone. She wanted to make him ask her why she was doing it, and of course she did.

'What are you looking at me for?' he said.

'I'm thinking that I am rather sorry for Dr. Craven.'

'So am I,' said Colin calmly, but not without an air of some satisfaction. 'He won't get Misselthwaite at all now I'm not going to die.'

'I'm sorry for him because of that, of course,' said Mary, 'but I was thinking just then that it must have been very horrid to have to be polite for ten years to a boy who was always rude. I would never have done it.'

'Am I rude?' Colin inquired undisturbedly.

'If you had been his own boy and he had been a slapping sort of man,' said Mary, 'he would have slapped you.'

'But he daren't,' said Colin.

'No, he daren't,' answered Mistress Mary, thinking the thing out quite without prejudice. 'Nobody ever dared to do anything you didn't like – because you were going to die and things like that. You were such a poor thing.'

'But,' announced Colin stubbornly, 'I am not going to be a poor thing. I won't let people think I'm one. I stood on my feet this afternoon.'

'It is always having your own way that has made you so queer,' Mary went on, thinking aloud.

Colin turned his head, frowning.

'Am I queer?' he demanded.

'Yes,' answered Mary, 'very. But you needn't be cross,' she added impartially, 'because so am I queer – and so is Ben Weatherstaff. But I am not as queer as I was before I began to like people and before I found the garden.'

'I don't want to be queer,' said Colin. 'I am not going to be,' and he frowned again with determination.

He was a very proud boy. He lay thinking for a while and then Mary saw his beautiful smile begin and gradually change his whole face.

'I shall stop being queer,' he said, 'if I go every day to the garden. There is Magic in there – good Magic, you know, Mary, I am sure there is.'

'So am I,' said Mary.

'Even if it isn't real Magic,' Colin said, 'we can pretend it is. *Something* is there – *something*!'

'It's Magic,' said Mary, 'but not black. It's as white as snow.'

They always called it Magic, and indeed it seemed like it in the months that followed – the wonderful months – the radiant months – the amazing ones. Oh! the things which happened in that garden! If you have never had a garden, you cannot understand, and if you have had a garden, you will know that it would take a whole book to describe all that came to pass there. At first it seemed that green things would never cease pushing their way through the earth, in the grass, in the beds, even in the crevices of the walls. Then the green things began to show buds, and the buds began to unfurl and show colour, every shade of blue, every shade of purple, every tint and hue of crimson. In its happy days flowers had been tucked away into every inch and hole and corner. Ben Weatherstaff had seen it done and had himself scraped out mortar from between the bricks of the wall and made pockets of earth for lovely clinging things to grow on. Iris and white lilies rose out of the grass in sheaves, and the green alcoves filled themselves with amazing armies of the blue and white flower lances of tall delphiniums or columbines or campanulas.

'She was main fond o' them – she was,' Ben Weatherstaff said. 'She liked them things as was allus pointin' up to th' blue sky, she used to tell. Not as she was one o' them as looked down on th' earth – not her. She just loved it, but she said as th' blue sky allus looked so joyful.'

The seeds Dickon and Mary had planted grew as if fairies had tended them. Satiny poppies of all tints danced in the breeze by the score, gaily defying flowers which had lived in the garden for years, and which it might be confessed seemed rather to wonder how such new people had got there. And the roses – the roses! Rising out of the grass, tangled round the sun-dial, wreathing the tree-trunks, and hanging from their branches, climbing up the walls and spreading over them with long garlands falling in cascades – they came alive day by day, hour by hour. Fair, fresh leaves, and buds – and buds – tiny at first, but swelling and working Magic until they burst and uncurled into cups of scent delicately spilling themselves over their brims and filling the garden air.

Colin saw it all, watching each change as it took place. Every morning he was brought out and every hour of each day, when it didn't rain, he spent in the garden. Even grey days pleased him. He would lie on the grass 'watching things growing,' he said. If you watched long enough, he declared, you could see buds unsheathe themselves. Also you could make the acquaintance of strange, busy insect things running about on various unknown but evidently serious errands, sometimes carrying tiny scraps of straw or feather or food, or climbing blades of grass as if they were trees from whose tops one could look out to explore the country. A mole throwing up its mound at the end of its burrow and making its way out at last with the long-nailed paws, which looked so like elfish hands, had absorbed him one whole morning. Ants' ways, beetles' ways, bees' ways, frogs' ways, birds' ways, plants' ways, gave him a new world to explore, and when Dickon revealed them all and added foxes' ways, otters' ways, ferrets' ways, squirrels' ways, and trouts' and water-rats' and badgers' ways, there was no end to the things to talk about and think over.

And this was not the half of the Magic. The fact that he had really once stood on his feet had set Colin thinking tremendously, and when Mary told him of the spell she had worked, he was excited and approved of it greatly. He talked of it constantly.

'Of course, there must be lots of Magic in the world,' he said wisely one day, 'but people don't know what it is like or how to make it. Perhaps the beginning is just to say nice things are going to happen until you make them happen. I am going to try an experiment.'

The next morning when they went to the secret garden, he sent at once for Ben Weatherstaff. Ben came as quickly as he could, and found the rajah standing on his feet under a tree and looking very grand, but also very beautifully smiling.

'Good morning, Ben Weatherstaff,' he said. 'I want you and Dickon and Miss Mary to stand in a row and listen to me because I am to tell you something very important.'

'Aye, aye, sir!' answered Ben Weatherstaff, touching his forehead. (One of the long-concealed charms of Ben Weatherstaff was that in his boyhood he had once run away to sea and had made voyages. So he could reply like a sailor.)

'I am going to try a scientific experiment,' explained the rajah. 'When I grow up I am going to make great scientific discoveries and I am going to begin now with this experiment.'

'Aye, aye, sir!' said Ben Weatherstaff promptly, though this was the first time he had heard of great scientific discoveries.

It was the first time Mary had heard of them, either, but even at this stage she had begun to realize that, queer as he was, Colin had read about a great many singular things and was somehow a very convincing sort of boy. When he held up his head and fixed his strange eyes on you, it seemed as if you believed him almost in spite of yourself, though he was only ten years old – going on eleven. At this moment he was especially convincing because he suddenly felt the fascination of actually making a sort of speech like a grown-up person.

'The great scientific discoveries I am going to make,' he went on, 'will be about Magic. Magic is a great thing, and scarcely anyone knows anything about it except a few people in old books – and Mary a little, because she was born in India, where there are fakirs. I believe Dickon knows some Magic, but perhaps he doesn't know he knows it. He charms animals and people. I would never have let him come to see me if had not been an animal-charmer – which is a boy-charmer, too, because a boy is an animal. I am sure there is Magic in everything, only we have not sense enough to get hold of it and make it do things for us – like electricity and horses and steam.'

This sounded so imposing that Ben Weatherstaff became quite excited and really could not keep still.

'Aye, aye, sir,' he said, and he began to stand up quite straight.

'When Mary found this garden it looked quite dead,' the orator proceeded. 'Then something began pushing things up out of the soil and making things out of nothing. One day things weren't there and another they were. I had never watched things before, and it made me feel very curious. Scientific people are always curious, and I am going to be scientific. I keep saying to myself: "What is it? What is it?" It's something. It can't be nothing! I don't know its name, so I call it Magic. I have never seen the sun rise, but Mary and Dickon have, and from what they tell me I am sure that is Magic, too. Something pushes it up and draws it. Sometimes since I've been in the garden I've looked up through the trees at the sky and I have had a strange feeling of being happy as if something were pushing and drawing in my chest and making me breathe fast. Magic is always pushing and drawing and making things out of nothing. Everything is made out of Magic, leaves and trees, flowers and birds, badgers and foxes and squirrels and people. So it must be all around us. In this garden – in all the places. The Magic in this garden has made me stand up and know I am going to live to be a man. I am going to make the scientific experiment of trying to get some and put it in myself and make it push and draw me and make me strong. I don't know how to do it, but I think that if you keep thinking about it and calling it, perhaps it will come. Perhaps that is the first baby way to get it. When I was going to try to stand that first time, Mary kept saying to herself as fast as she could, "You can do it! You can do it!" and I did. I had to try myself at the same time, of course, but her Magic helped me – and so did Dickon's. Every morning and evening and as often in the day-time as I can remember I am going to say, "Magic is in me! Magic is making me well! I am going to be as strong as Dickon, as strong as Dickon!" And you must all do it, too. That is my experiment. Will you help, Ben Weatherstaff?'

'Aye, aye sir!' said Ben Weatherstaff. 'Aye, aye!'

'If you keep doing it every day as regularly as soldiers go through drill, we shall see what will happen and find out if the experiment succeeds. You learn things by saying them over and over and thinking about them until they stay in your mind for ever, and I think it will be the same with Magic. If you keep calling it to come to you and help you, it will get to be part of you and it will stay and do things.'

'I once heard an officer in India tell my mother that there were fakirs who said words over and over thousands of times,' said Mary.

'I've heard Jem Fettleworth's wife say th' same thing over thousands o' times – callin' Jem a drunken brute,' said Ben Weatherstaff dryly. 'Summat allus comes o' that, sure enough. He gave her a good hidin' an' went to th' Blue Lion an' got as drunk as a lord.'

Colin drew his brows together and thought a few minutes. Then he cheered up.

'Well,' he said, 'you see something did come of it. She used the wrong Magic until she made him beat her. If she'd used the right Magic and had said something nice, perhaps he wouldn't have got as drunk as a lord and perhaps – perhaps he might have brought her a new bonnet.'

Ben Weatherstaff chuckled and there was shrewd admiration in his little old eyes.

'Tha'rt a clever lad as well as a straight-legged one, Mester Colin,' he said. 'Next time I see Bess Fettleworth I'll give her a bit of a hint o' what Magic will do for her. She'd be rare an' pleased if th' sinetifik 'speriment worked – an' so 'ud Jem.'

Dickon had stood listening to the lecture, his round eyes shining with curious delight. Nut and Shell were on his shoulders, and he held a long-eared, white rabbit in his arm and stroked and stroked it softly while it laid its ears along its back and enjoyed itself.

'Do you think the experiment will work?' Colin asked him, wondering what he was thinking. He so often wondered what Dickon was thinking when he saw him looking at him or at one of his 'creatures' with his happy, wide smile.

He smiled now, and his smile was wider than usual.

'Aye,' he answered, 'that I do. It'll work same as th' seeds do when th' sun shines on 'em. It'll work for sure. Shall us begin it now?'

Colin was delighted and so was Mary. Fired by recollections of fakirs and devotees in illustrations, Colin suggested that they should all sit cross-legged under the tree, which made a canopy.

'It will be like sitting in a sort of temple,' said Colin. 'I'm rather tired and I want to sit down.'

'Eh!' said Dickon, 'tha' mustn't begin by sayin' tha'rt tired. Tha' might spoil th' Magic.'

Colin turned and looked at him – into his innocent, round eyes.

'That's true,' he said slowly. 'I must only think of the Magic.'

It all seemed most majestic and mysterious when they sat down in their circle. Ben Weatherstaff felt as if he had somehow been led into appearing at a prayer-meeting. Ordinarily he was very fixed in being what he called 'agen' prayer-meetin's', but this being the rajah's affair, he did not resent it, and was, indeed, inclined to be gratified at being called upon to assist. Mistress Mary felt solemnly enraptured. Dickon held his rabbit in his arm, and perhaps he made some charmer's signal no one heard, for when he sat down, cross-legged like the rest, the crow, the fox, the squirrels, and the lamb slowly drew near and made part of the circle, settling each into a place of rest as if of their own desire.

'The "creatures" have come,' said Colin gravely. 'They want to help us.'

Colin really looked quite beautiful, Mary thought. He held his head high as if he felt like a sort of priest, and his strange eyes had a wonderful look in them. The light shone on him through the tree canopy.

'Now we will begin,' he said. 'Shall we sway backwards and forwards, Mary, as if we were dervishes?'

'I canna' do no swayin' back'ard and for'ard,' said Ben Weatherstaff. 'I've got th' rheumatics.'

'The Magic will take them away,' said Colin in a High Priest tone, 'but we won't stay until it has done it. We will only chant.'

'I canna' do no chantin',' said Ben Weatherstaff, a trifle testily. 'They turned me out o' th' church choir th' only time I ever tried it.'

No one smiled. They were all too much in earnest. Colin's face was not even crossed by a shadow. He was thinking only of the Magic.

'Then I will chant,' he said. And he began, looking like a strange boy spirit. 'The sun is shining – the sun is shining. That is the Magic. The flowers are growing – the roots are stirring. That is the Magic. Being alive is the Magic – being strong is the Magic. The Magic is in me – the Magic is in me. It is in me – it is in me. It's in every one of us. It's in Ben Weatherstaff's back. Magic! Magic! Come and help!' He said it a great many times – not a thousand times, but quite a goodly number. Mary listened entranced. She felt as if it were at once queer and beautiful and she wanted him to go on and on. Ben Weatherstaff began to feel soothed into a sort of dream which was quite agreeable. The humming of the bees in the blossoms mingled with the chanting voice and drowsily melted into a doze. Dickon sat cross-legged with his rabbit asleep on his arm and a hand resting on the lamb's back. Soot had pushed away a squirrel and huddled close to him on his shoulder; the grey film dropped over his eyes. At last Colin stopped.

'Now I am going to walk round the garden,' he announced.

Ben Weatherstaff's head had just dropped forward and he lifted it with a jerk.

'You have been asleep,' said Colin.

'Nowt o' th' sort,' mumbled Ben. 'Th' sermon was good enow – but I'm bound to get out afore th' collection.'

He was not quite awake yet.

'You're not in church,' said Colin.

'Not me,' said Ben, straightening himself. 'Who said I were? I heard every bit of it. You said th' Magic was in my back. Th' doctor calls it rheumatics.'

The rajah waved his hand.

'That was the wrong Magic,' he said. 'You will get better. You have my permission to go to your work. But come back tomorrow.'

'I'd like to see thee walk round the garden,' grunted Ben.

It was not an unfriendly grunt, but it was a grunt. In fact, being a stubborn old party and not having entire faith in Magic, he made up his mind that if he were sent away he would climb his ladder and look over the wall so that he might be ready to hobble back if there were any stumbling.

The rajah did not object to his staying, and so the procession was formed. It really did look like a procession. Colin was at its head with Dickon on one side and Mary on the other. Ben Weatherstaff walked behind, and the 'creatures' trailed after them, the lamb and the fox cub keeping close to Dickon, the white rabbit hopping along or stopping to nibble and Soot following with the solemnity of a person who felt himself in charge.

It was a procession which moved slowly, but with dignity. Every few yards it stopped to rest. Colin leaned on Dickon's arm and privately Ben Weatherstaff kept a sharp look-out, but now and then Colin took his hand from its support and walked a few steps alone. His head was held up all the time and he looked very grand.

'The Magic is in me!' he kept saying. 'The Magic is making me strong! I can feel it! I can feel it!'

It seemed very certain that something was upholding and uplifting him. He sat on the seats in the alcoves and once or twice he sat down on the grass and several times he paused in the path and leaned on Dickon, but he would not give up until he had gone all round the

"'I did it! The Magic worked!'"

garden. When he returned to the canopy tree his cheeks were flushed and he looked triumphant.

'I did it! The Magic worked!' he cried. 'That is my first scientific discovery.'

'What will Dr. Craven say?' broke out Mary.

'He won't say anything,' Colin answered, 'because he will not be told. This is to be the biggest secret of all. No one is to know anything about it until I have grown so strong that I can walk and run like any other boy. I shall come here every day in my chair and I shall be taken back in it. I won't have people whispering and asking questions and I won't let my father hear about it until the experiment has quite succeeded. Then some time when he comes back to Misselthwaite I shall just walk into his study and say: "Here I am: I am like any other boy. I am quite well and I shall live to be a man. It has been done by a scientific experiment."'

'He will think he is in a dream,' cried Mary. 'He won't believe his eyes.'

Colin flushed triumphantly. He had made himself believe that he was going to get well, which was really more than half the battle, if he had been aware of it. And the thought which stimulated him more than any other was this imagining what his father would look like when he saw that he had a son who was as straight and strong as other fathers' sons. One of his darkest miseries in the unhealthy, morbid past days had been his hatred of being a sickly, weak-backed boy, whose father was afraid to look at him.

'He'll be obliged to believe them,' he said. 'One of the things I am going to do, after the Magic works and before I begin to make scientific discoveries, is to be an athlete.'

'We shall have thee takin' to boxin' in a week or so,' said Ben Weatherstaff. 'Tha'lt end wi' winnin' th' Belt an' bein' champion prize-fighter of all England.'

Colin fixed his eyes on him sternly.

'Weatherstaff,' he said, 'that is disrespectful. You must not take liberties because you are in the secret. However much the Magic works, I shall not be a prize-fighter. I shall be a Scientific Discoverer.'

'Ax pardon – ax pardon sir,' answered Ben, touching his forehead in salute. 'I ought to have seed it wasn't a jokin' matter,' but his eyes twinkled and secretly he was immensely pleased. He really did not mind being snubbed, since the snubbing meant that the lad was gaining strength and spirit.

24 'Let them laugh'

The secret garden was not the only one Dickon worked in. Round the cottage on the moor there was a piece of ground enclosed by a low wall of rough stones. Early in the morning and late in the fading twilight and on all the days Colin and Mary did not see him, Dickon worked there planting or tending potatoes and cabbages, turnips and carrots and herbs for his mother. In the company of his 'creatures' he did wonders there and was never tired of doing them, it seemed. While he dug or weeded he whistled or sang bits of Yorkshire moor songs or talked to Soot or Captain or the brothers and sisters he had taught to help him.

'We'd never get on as comfortable as we do,' Mrs. Sowerby said, 'if it wasn't for Dickon's garden. Anything'll grow for him. His 'taters and cabbages is twice th' size of anyone else's an' they've got a flavour with 'em as nobody's has.'

When she found a moment to spare she liked to go out and talk to him. After supper there was still a long clear twilight to work in, and that was her quiet time. She could sit upon the low rough wall and look on and hear stories of the day. She loved this time. There were not only vegetables in this garden. Dickon had bought penny packages of flower seeds now and then and sown bright, sweet-scented things among gooseberry bushes and even cabbages and he grew borders of mignonette and pinks and pansies and things, whose seeds he could save year after year or whose roots would bloom each spring and spread in time into fine clumps. The low wall was one of the prettiest things in Yorkshire because he had tucked moorland foxglove and ferns and rock-cress and hedgerow flowers into every crevice until only here and there glimpses of the stones were to be seen.

'All a chap's got to do to make 'em thrive, Mother,' he would say, 'is to be friends with 'em for sure. They're just like th' "creatures". If they're thirsty give 'em a drink, and if they're hungry give 'em a bit o' food. They want to live same as we do. If they died I should feel as if I'd been a bad lad and somehow treated them heartless.'

It was in these twilight hours that Mrs. Sowerby heard of all that happened at Misselthwaite Manor. At first she was only told that 'Mester Colin' had taken a fancy to going out into the grounds with Miss Mary and that it was doing him good. But it was not long before it was agreed between the two children that Dickon's mother might 'come into the secret'. Somehow it was not doubted that she was 'safe for sure'.

So one beautiful, still evening, Dickon told the whole story, with all the thrilling details of the buried key and the robin and the grey haze which had seemed like deadness and the secret Mistress Mary had planned never to reveal. The coming of Dickon and how it had been told to him, the doubt of Mester Colin and the final drama of his introduction to the hidden domain, combined with the incident of Ben Weatherstaff's angry face peering over the wall and Mester Colin's sudden indignant strength, made Mrs. Sowerby's nice-looking face quite change colour several times.

'My word!' she said. 'It was a good thing that little lass came to th' Manor. It's been th' makin' o' her an' th' savin' o' him. Standin' on his feet! An' us all thinkin' he was a poor, half-witted lad with not a straight bone in him.'

She asked a great many questions and her blue eyes were full of deep thinking.

'What do they make of it at th' Manor – him being so well an' cheerful an' never complainin'?' she inquired.

'They don't know what to make of it,' answered Dickon. 'Every day as comes round his face looks different. It's fillin' out and doesn't look so sharp an' th' waxy colour is goin'. But he has to do his bit o' complainin',' with a highly entertained grin.

'What for, i' Mercy's name?' asked Mrs. Sowerby.

Dickon chuckled.

'He does it to keep them from guessin' what's happened. If the doctor knew he'd found out he could stand on his feet, he'd likely write and tell Mester Craven. Mester Colin's savin' th' secret to tell himself. He's goin' to practise his Magic on his legs every day till his father comes back an' then he's goin' to march into his room an' show him he's as straight as other lads. But him an' Miss thinks it's best plan to do a bit o' groanin' and frettin' now an' then to throw off th' scent.'

Mrs. Sowerby was laughing a low, comfortable laugh long before he had finished his last sentence.

'Eh!' she said, 'that pair's enjoyin' theirselves, I'll warrant. They'll get a good bit o' play actin' out of it, an' there's nothin' children likes as much as play actin'. Let's hear what they do, Dickon, lad.'

Dickon stopped weeding and sat up on his heels to tell her. His eyes were twinkling with fun.

'Mester Colin is carried down to his chair every time he goes out,' he explained. 'An' he flies out at John th' footman, for not carryin' him careful enough. He makes himself as helpless-lookin' as he can an' never lifts his head until we're out o' sight o' th' house. An' he grunts an' frets a good bit when he's bein' settled into his chair. Him an' Miss Mary's both got to enjoyin' it, an' when he groans an' complains she'll say: "Poor Colin! Does it hurt you so much? Are you so weak as that, poor Colin?" – but th' trouble is that sometimes they can scarce keep from burstin' out laughin'. When we get safe into the garden they laugh till they've no breath left to laugh with. An' they have to stuff their faces into Mester Colin's cushions to keep the gardeners from hearin', if any of 'em's about.'

'Th' more they laugh th' better for 'em!' said Mrs. Sowerby, still laughing herself. 'Good, healthy child laughin's better than pills any day o' th' year. That pair'll plump up for sure.'

'They are plumpin' up,' said Dickon. 'They're that hungry they don't know how to get enough to eat without makin' talk. Mester Colin says if he keeps sendin' for more food, they won't believe he's an invalid at all. Miss Mary says she'll let him eat her share, but he says that if she goes hungry she'll get thin an' they mun both get fat at once.'

Mrs. Sowerby laughed so heartily at the revelation of this difficulty that she quite rocked backwards and forwards in her blue cloak, and Dickon laughed with her.

'I'll tell thee what, lad,' Mrs. Sowerby said when she could speak. 'I've thought of a way to help 'em. When tha' goes to 'em in th' mornin's tha' shall take a pail o' good new milk an' I'll bake 'em a crusty cottage loaf or some buns wi' currants in 'em, same as you children like. Nothin's so good as fresh milk an' bread. Then they could take off th' edge o' their hunger while they were in their garden an' th' fine food they get indoors 'ud polish off th' corners.'

'Eh! Mother!' said Dickon admiringly, 'what a wonder tha' art! Tha' always sees a way out o' things. They was quite in a pother yesterday. They didn't see how they was to manage without orderin' up more food – they felt that empty inside.'

'They're two young 'uns growin' fast, and health's comin' back to both of 'em. Children like that feels like young wolves an' food's flesh an' blood to 'em,' said Mrs. Sowerby. Then she smiled Dickon's own curving smile. 'Eh! but they're enjoyin' theirselves for sure,' she said.

She was quite right, the comfortable, wonderful mother creature – and she had never been more so than when she said their 'play actin'' would be their joy. Colin and Mary found it one of their most thrilling sources of entertainment. The idea of protecting themselves from suspicion had been unconsciously suggested to them first by the puzzled nurse and then by Dr. Craven himself.

'Your appetite is improving very much, Master Colin,' the nurse had said one day. 'You used to eat nothing, and so many things disagreed with you.'

'Nothing disagrees with me now,' replied Colin, and then seeing the nurse looking at him curiously, he suddenly remembered that perhaps he ought not to appear too well just yet. 'At least, things don't so often disagree with me. It's the fresh air.'

'Perhaps it is,' said the nurse, still looking at him with a mystified expression. 'But I must talk to Dr. Craven about it.'

'How she stared at you!' said Mary when she went away. 'As if she thought there must be something to find out.'

'I won't have her finding out things,' said Colin. 'No one must begin to find out yet.'

When Dr. Craven came that morning he seemed puzzled, too. He asked a number of questions, to Colin's great annoyance.

'You stay out in the garden a great deal,' he suggested. 'Where do you go?'

Colin put on his favourite air of dignified indifference to opinion.

'I will not let anyone know where I go,' he answered. 'I go to a place I like. Everyone has orders to keep out of the way. I won't be watched and stared at. You know that!'

'You seem to be out all day, but I do not think it has done you harm – I do not think so. The nurse says that you eat much more than you have ever done before.'

'Perhaps,' said Colin, prompted by a sudden inspiration, 'perhaps it is an unnatural appetite.'

'I do not think so, as your food seems to agree with you,' said Dr. Craven. 'You are gaining flesh rapidly and your colour is better.'

'Perhaps – perhaps I am bloated and feverish,' said Colin, assuming a discouraging air of gloom. 'People who are not going to live are often – different.'

Dr. Craven shook his head. He was holding Colin's wrist, and he pushed up his sleeve and felt his arm.

'You are not feverish,' he said thoughtfully, 'and such flesh as you have gained is healthy. If we can keep this up, my boy, we need not talk of dying. Your father will be very happy to hear of this remarkable improvement.'

'I won't have him told!' Colin broke forth fiercely. 'It will only disappoint him if I get worse again – and I may get worse this very night. I might have a raging fever. I feel as if I might be beginning to have one now. I won't have letters written to my father – I won't – I won't! You are making me angry, and you know that is bad for me. I feel hot already. I hate being written about and being talked over as much as I hate being stared at!'

'Hush-h! my boy,' Dr. Craven soothed him. 'Nothing shall be written without your permission. You are too sensitive about things. You must not undo the good which has been done.'

He said no more about writing to Mr. Craven, and when he saw the nurse he privately warned her that such a possibility must not be mentioned to the patient.

'The boy is extraordinarily better,' he said. 'His advance seems almost abnormal. But, of course, he is doing now of his own free will what we could not make him do before. Still, he excites himself very easily and nothing must be said to irritate him.'

Mary and Colin were much alarmed and talked together anxiously. From this time dated their plan of 'play actin'.'

'I may be obliged to have a tantrum,' said Colin regretfully. 'I don't want to have one and I'm not miserable enough now to work myself into a big one. Perhaps I couldn't have one at all. That lump doesn't come in my throat now, and I keep thinking of nice things instead of horrible ones. But if they talk about writing to my father, I shall have to do something.'

He made up his mind to eat less, but unfortunately it was not possible to carry out this brilliant idea when he wakened each morning with an amazing appetite and the table near his sofa was set with a breakfast of home-made bread and fresh butter, snow-white eggs, raspberry jam, and clotted cream. Mary always breakfasted with him, and when they found themselves at the table – particularly if there were delicate slices of sizzling ham sending forth tempting odours from under a hot silver cover – they would look into each other's eyes in desperation.

'I think we shall have to eat it all this morning, Mary,' Colin always ended by saying. 'We can send away some of the lunch and a great deal of the dinner.'

But they never found they could send away anything, and the highly polished condition of the empty plates returned to the pantry awakened much comment.

'I do wish,' Colin would say also, 'I do wish the slices of ham were thicker, and one muffin each is not enough for anyone.'

'It's enough for a person who is going to die,' answered Mary when first she heard this, 'but it's not enough for a person who is going to live. I sometimes feel as if I could eat three when those nice fresh heather and gorse smells from the moor come pouring in at the open window.'

The morning that Dickon – after they had been enjoying themselves in the garden for about two hours – went behind a big rose-bush and brought forth two tin pails and revealed that one was full of rich new milk with cream on the top of it, and that the other held cottage-made currant buns folded in a clean blue and white napkin, buns so carefully tucked in that they were still hot, there was a riot of surprised joyfulness. What a wonderful thing for Mrs. Sowerby to think of! What a kind, clever woman she must be! How good the buns were! And what delicious fresh milk!

'Magic is in her just as it is in Dickon,' said Colin. 'It makes her think of ways to do things – nice things. She is a Magic person. Tell her we are grateful, Dickon – extremely grateful.'

He was given to using rather grown-up phrases at times. He enjoyed them. He liked this so much that he improved upon it.

'Tell her she has been most bounteous and our gratitude is extreme.'

And then forgetting his grandeur he fell to and stuffed himself with buns and drank milk out of the pail in copious draughts in the manner of any hungry little boy who had been taking unusual exercise and breathing in moorland air and whose breakfast was more than two hours behind him.

This was the beginning of many agreeable incidents of the same kind. They actually awoke to the fact that as Mrs. Sowerby had fourteen people to provide food for she might not have enough to satisfy two extra appetites every day. So they asked her to let them send some of their shillings to buy things.

Dickon made the stimulating discovery that in the wood in the park outside the garden where Mary had first found him piping to the wild creatures, there was a deep little hollow where you could build a sort of tiny oven with stones and roast potatoes and eggs in it. Roasted eggs were a previously unknown luxury, and very hot potatoes with salt and fresh butter in them were fit for a woodland king – besides being deliciously satisfying. You could buy both potatoes and eggs and eat as many as you liked without feeling as if you were taking food out of the mouths of fourteen people.

Every beautiful morning the Magic was worked by the mystic circle under the plum-tree which provided a canopy of thickening green leaves after its brief blossom-time was ended. After the ceremony Colin always took his walking exercise, and throughout the day he exercised his newly found power at intervals. Each day he grew stronger and could walk more steadily and cover more ground. And each day his belief in the Magic grew stronger – as well it might. He tried one experiment after another as he felt himself gaining strength, and it was Dickon who showed him the best things of all.

'Yesterday,' he said one morning after an absence, 'I went to Thwaite for Mother, an' near th' Blue Cow Inn I seed Bob Haworth. He's the strongest chap on th' moor. He's the champion wrestler an' he can jump higher than any other chap an' throw th' hammer farther. He's gone all th' way to Scotland for th' sports some years. He's knowed me ever since I was a little 'un an' he's a friendly sort an' I axed him some questions. Th' gentry calls him an athlete and I thought o' thee, Mester Colin, and I says: "How did tha' make tha' muscles stick out that way, Bob? Did tha' do anythin' extra to make thysel' so strong?" An' he says: "Well, yes, lad, I did. A strong man in a show that came to Thwaite once showed me how to exercise my arms an' legs' an' every muscle in my body." An' I says: "Could a delicate chap make himself stronger with 'em, Bob?" an' he laughed an' says, "Art tha' th' delicate chap?" an' I says, "No, but I knows a young gentleman that's gettin' well of a long illness an' I wish I knowed some o' them tricks to tell him about." I didn't say no names an' he didn't ask none. He's friendly same as I said, an' he stood up an' showed me good-natured like, an' I imitated what he did till I knowed it by heart.'

Colin had been listening excitedly.

'Can you show me?' he cried. 'Will you?'

'Aye, to be sure,' Dickon answered, getting up. 'But he says tha' mun do 'em gentle at first an' be careful not to tire thysel'. Rest in between times an' take deep breaths an don't overdo.'

'I'll be careful,' said Colin. 'Show me! Show me! Dickon, you are the most Magic boy in the world!'

Dickon stood up on the grass and slowly went through a carefully practical but simple series of muscle exercises. Colin watched them with widening eyes. He could do a few while he was sitting down. Presently he did a few gently while he stood upon his already steadied feet. Mary began to do them also. Soot, who was watching the performance, became much disturbed and left his branch and hopped about restlessly because he could not do them, too.

From that time the exercises were part of the day's duties as much as the Magic was. It became possible for both Colin and Mary to do more of them each time they tried, and such appetites were the result that but for the basket Dickon put down behind the bush each morning when he arrived, they would have been lost. But the little oven in the hollow and Mrs. Sowerby's bounties were so satisfying that Mrs. Medlock and the nurse and Dr. Craven became mystified again. You can trifle with your breakfast and seem to disdain your dinner if you are full to the brim with roasted eggs and potatoes and richly frothed new milk and oat-cakes and buns and heather honey and clotted cream.

'They are eating next to nothing,' said the nurse. 'They'll die of starvation if they can't be persuaded to take some nourishment. And yet see how they look.'

'Look!' exclaimed Mrs. Medlock indignantly. 'Eh! I'm moithered to death with them. They're a pair of young Satans. Bursting their jackets one day and the next turning up their noses at the best meals Cook can tempt them with. Not a mouthful of that lovely young fowl and bread sauce did they set a fork into yesterday – and the poor woman fair *invented* a pudding for them – and back it's sent. She almost cried. She's afraid she'll be blamed if they starve themselves into their graves.'

Dr. Craven came and looked at Colin long and carefully. He wore an extremely worried expression when the nurse talked with him and showed him the almost untouched tray of breakfast she had saved for him to look at – but it was even more worried when he sat down by Colin's sofa and examined him. He had been called to London on business and had not seen the boy for nearly two weeks. When young things begin to gain health they gain it rapidly. The waxen tinge had left Colin's skin and a warm rose showed through it; his beautiful eyes were clear and the hollows under them and in his cheeks and temples had filled out. His once dark, heavy locks had begun to look as if they sprang healthily from his forehead and were soft and warm with life. His lips were fuller and of a normal colour. In fact, as an imitation of a boy who was a confirmed invalid he was a disgraceful sight. Dr. Craven held his chin in his hand and thought him over.

'I am sorry to hear that you do not eat anything,' he said. 'That will not do. You will lose all you have gained – and you have gained amazingly. You ate so well a short time ago.'

'I told you it was an unnatural appetite,' answered Colin.

Mary was sitting on her stool near by and she suddenly made a very queer sound which she tried so violently to repress that she ended by almost choking.

'What is the matter?' said Dr. Craven, turning to look at her.

Mary became quite severe in her manner.

'It was something between a sneeze and a cough,' she replied, with reproachful dignity, 'and it got into my throat.'

'But,' she said afterwards to Colin, 'I couldn't stop myself. It just burst out because all at once I couldn't help remembering that last big potato you ate and the way your mouth stretched when you bit through that thick, lovely crust with jam and clotted cream on it.'

'Is there any way in which those children can get food secretly?' Dr. Craven inquired of Mrs. Medlock.

'There's no way unless they dig it out of the earth or pick it off the trees,' Mrs. Medlock answered. 'They stay out in the grounds all day and see no one but each other. And if they want anything different to eat from what's sent up to them, they need only ask for it.'

'Well,' said Dr. Craven, 'so long as going without food agrees with them, we need not disturb ourselves. The boy is a new creature.'

'So is the girl,' said Mrs. Medlock. 'She's begun to be downright pretty since she's filled out and lost her ugly little sour look. Her hair's grown thick and healthy looking and she's got a bright colour. The glummest, ill-natured little thing she used to be, and now her and Master Colin laugh together like a pair of crazy young ones. Perhaps they're growing fat on that.'

'Perhaps they are,' said Dr. Craven. 'Let them laugh.'

25 The Curtain

And the secret garden bloomed and bloomed and every morning revealed new miracles. In the robin's nest there were eggs and the robin's mate sat upon them, keeping them warm with her feathery little breast and careful wings. At first she was very nervous, and the robin himself was indignantly watchful. Even Dickon did not go near the close-grown corner in those days, but waited until by the quiet working of some mysterious spell he seemed to have conveyed to the soul of the little pair that in the garden there was nothing which was not quite like themselves – nothing which did not understand the wonderfulness of what was happening to them – the immense, tender, terrible, heart-breaking beauty and solemnity of Eggs. If there had been one person in that garden who had not known through all his or her innermost being that if an Egg were taken away or hurt the whole world would whirl round and crash through space and come to an end – if there had been even one who did not feel it and act accordingly there could have been no happiness even in that golden springtime air. But they all knew it and felt it and the robin and his mate knew they knew it.

At first the robin watched Mary and Colin with sharp anxiety. For some mysterious reason he knew he need not watch Dickon. The first moment he set his dew-bright black eye on Dickon he knew he was not a stranger, but a sort of robin without beak or feathers. He could speak robin (which is quite a distinct language not to be mistaken for any other). To speak robin to a robin is like speaking French to a Frenchman. Dickon always spoke it to the robin himself, so the queer gibberish he used when he spoke to humans did not matter in the least. The robin thought he spoke this gibberish to them because they were not intelligent enough to understand feathered speech. His movements also were robin. They never startled one by being sudden enough to seem dangerous or threatening. Any robin could understand Dickon, so his presence was not even disturbing.

But at the outset it seemed necessary to be on guard against the other two. In the first place the boy creature did not come into the garden on his legs. He was pushed in on a thing with wheels and the skins of wild animals were thrown over him. That in itself was doubtful. Then when he began to stand up and move about he did it in a queer, unaccustomed way, and the others seemed to have to help him. The robin used to secrete himself in a bush and watch this anxiously, his head tilted first to one side and then on the other. He thought that the slow movements might mean that he was preparing to pounce, as cats do. When cats are preparing to pounce they creep over the ground very slowly. The robin talked this over with his mate a great deal for a few days, but after that he decided not to speak of the subject because her terror was so great that he was afraid it might be injurious to the eggs.

When the boy began to walk by himself and even to move more quickly, it was an immense relief. But for a long time – or it seemed a long time to the robin – he was a source of some anxiety. He did not act as the other humans did. He seemed very fond of walking, but he had a way of sitting or lying down for a while and then getting up in a disconcerting manner to begin again.

One day the robin remembered that when he himself had been made to learn to fly by his parents he had done much the same sort of thing. He had taken short flights of a few yards and then had been obliged to rest. So it occurred to him that this boy was learning to fly – or rather to walk. He mentioned this to his mate, and when he told her that the Eggs would probably conduct themselves in the same way after they were fledged, she was quite comforted and even became eagerly interested and derived great pleasure from watching the boy over the edge of her nest – though she always thought that the Eggs would be much cleverer and learn more quickly. But then she said indulgently that humans were always more clumsy and slow than Eggs, and most of them never seemed really to learn to fly at all. You never met them in the air or on tree-tops.

After a while the boy began to move about as the others did, but all three of the children at times did unusual things. They would stand under the trees and move their arms and legs and heads about in a way which was neither walking nor running nor sitting down. They went through these movements at intervals every day, and the robin was never able to explain to his mate what they were doing or trying to do. He could only say that he was sure that the Eggs would never flap about in such a manner, but as the boy who could speak robin fluently was doing the thing with them, birds could be quite sure that the actions were not of a dangerous nature. Of course, neither the robin nor his mate had ever heard of the champion wrestler, Bob Haworth, and his exercises for making the muscle stand out like lumps. Robins are not like human beings; their muscles are always exercised from the first, and so they develop themselves in a natural manner. If you have to fly about to find every meal you eat, your muscles do not become atrophied (atrophied means wasted away through want of use).

When the boy was walking and running about and digging and weeding like the others, the nest in the corner was brooded over by a great peace and content. Fears for the Eggs became things of the past. Knowing that your Eggs were as safe as if they were locked in a bank vault and the fact that you could watch so many curious things going on made sitting a most entertaining occupation. On wet days the Eggs' mother sometimes felt even a little dull because the children did not come into the garden.

But even on wet days it could not be said that Mary and Colin were dull. One morning when the rain streamed down unceasingly and Colin was beginning to feel a little restive, as he was obliged to remain on his sofa because it was not safe to get up and walk about, Mary had an inspiration.

'Now that I am a real boy,' Colin had said, 'my legs and arms and all my body are so full of Magic that I can't keep them still. They want to be doing things all the time. Do you know that when I waken in the morning, Mary, when it's quite early and the birds are just shouting outside and everything seems just shouting for joy – even the trees and things we can't really hear – I feel as if I must jump out of bed and shout myself. And if I did it, just think what would happen!'

Mary giggled inordinately.

'The nurse would come running and Mrs. Medlock would come running and they would be sure you had gone crazy and they'd send for the doctor,' she said.

Colin giggled himself. He could see how they would all look – how horrified by his outbreak and how amazed to see him standing upright.

'I wish my father would come home,' he said. 'I want to tell him myself. I'm always thinking about it – but we couldn't go on like this much longer. I can't stand lying still and pretending, and besides, I look too different. I wish it wasn't raining today.'

It was then Mistress Mary had her inspiration.

'Colin,' she began mysteriously, 'do you know how many rooms there are in this house?'

'About a thousand, I suppose,' he answered.

'There's about a hundred no one ever goes into,' said Mary. 'And one rainy day I went and looked into ever so many of them. No one ever knew, though Mrs. Medlock nearly found me out. I lost my way when I was coming back, and I stopped at the end of your corridor. That was the second time I heard you crying.'

Colin started up on his sofa.

'A hundred rooms no one goes into,' he said. 'It sounds almost like a secret garden. Suppose we go and look at them. You could wheel me in my chair and nobody would know where we went.'

'That's what I was thinking,' said Mary. 'No one would dare to follow us. There are galleries where you could run. We could do our exercises. There is a little Indian room where there is a cabinet full of ivory elephants. There are all sorts of rooms.'

'Ring the bell,' said Colin.

When the nurse came in he gave his orders.

'I want my chair,' he said. 'Miss Mary and I are going to look at the part of the house which is not used. John can push me as far as the picture-gallery because there are some stairs. Then he must go away and leave us alone until I send for him again.'

Rainy days lost their terrors that morning. When the footman had wheeled the chair into the picture-gallery and left the two together in

obedience to orders, Colin and Mary looked at each other delighted.
As soon as Mary had made sure that John was really on his way back to
his own quarters below stairs, Colin got out of his chair.

'I am going to run from one end of the gallery to the other,' he said,
'and then I am going to jump and then we will do Bob Haworth's
exercises.'

And they did all these things and many others. They looked at the
portraits and found the plain little girl dressed in green brocade and
holding the parrot on her finger.

'All these,' said Colin, 'must be my relations. They lived a long
time ago. That parrot one, I believe, is one of my great, great, great
great-aunts. She looks rather like you, Mary – not as you look now, but
as you looked when you came here. Now you are a great deal fatter and
better-looking.'

'So are you,' said Mary, and they both laughed.

They went to the Indian room and amused themselves with the
ivory elephants. They found the rose-coloured brocade boudoir and
the hole in the cushion the mouse had left, but the mice had grown up
and run away and the hole was empty. They saw more rooms and made
more discoveries than Mary had made on her first pilgrimage. They
found new corridors and corners and flights of steps and new old
pictures they liked and weird old things they did not know the use of.
It was a curiously entertaining morning, and the feeling of wandering
about in the same house with other people, but at the same time feeling
as if one were miles away from them was a fascinating thing.

'I'm glad we came,' Colin said. 'I never knew I lived in such a big,
queer old place. I like it. We will ramble about every rainy day. We
shall always be finding new queer corners and things.'

That morning they had found among other things such good
appetites that when they returned to Colin's room it was not possible
to send the luncheon away untouched.

When the nurse carried the tray downstairs she slapped it down on
the kitchen dresser so that Mrs. Loomis, the cook, could see the highly
polished dishes and plates.

'Look at that!' she said. 'This is a house of mystery, and those two
children are the greatest mysteries in it.'

'If they keep that up every day,' said the strong young footman, John, 'there'd be small wonder that he weighs twice as much today as he did a month ago. I should have to give up my place in time, for fear of doing my muscles an injury.'

That afternoon Mary noticed that something new had happened in Colin's room. She had noticed it the day before, but had said nothing because she thought the change might have been made by chance. She said nothing today, but she sat and looked fixedly at the picture over the mantel. She could look at it because the curtain had been drawn aside. That was the change she noticed.

'I know what you want me to tell you,' said Colin, after she had stared a few minutes. 'I always know when you want me to tell you something. You are wondering why the curtain is drawn back. I am going to keep it like that.'

'Why?' asked Mary.

'Because it doesn't make me angry any more to see her laughing. I wakened when it was bright moonlight two nights ago and felt as if the Magic was filling the room and making everything so splendid that I couldn't lie still. I got up and looked out of the window. The room was quite light and there was a patch of moonlight on the curtain, and somehow that made me go and pull the cord. She looked right down at me as if she were laughing because she was glad I was standing there. It made me like to look at her. I want to see her laughing like that all the time. I think she must have been a sort of Magic person perhaps.'

'You are so like her now,' said Mary, 'that sometimes I think perhaps you are her ghost made into a boy.'

That idea seemed to impress Colin. He thought it over and then answered her slowly.

'If I were her ghost – my father would be fond of me,' he said.

'Do you want him to be fond of you?' inquired Mary.

'I used to hate it because he was not fond of me. If he grew fond of me I think I should tell him about the Magic. It might make him more cheerful.'

26 'It's Mother!'

Their belief in the Magic was an abiding thing. After the morning's incantations Colin sometimes gave them Magic lectures.

'I like to do it,' he explained, 'because when I grow up and make great scientific discoveries I shall be obliged to lecture about them, and so this is practice. I can only give short lectures now because I am very young, and, besides, Ben Weatherstaff would feel as if he was in church and he would go to sleep.'

'T' best thing about lecturin',' said Ben, 'is that a chap can get up an' say aught he pleases an' no other chap can answer him back. I wouldn't be agin' lecturin' a bit mysel' sometimes.'

But when Colin held forth under his tree old Ben fixed devouring eyes on him and kept them there. He looked him over with critical affection. It was not so much the lecture which interested him as the legs which looked straighter and stronger each day, the boyish head which held itself up so well, the once sharp chin and hollow cheeks which had filled and rounded out, and the eyes which had begun to hold the light he remembered in another pair. Sometimes when Colin felt Ben's earnest gaze meant that he was much impressed he wondered what he was reflecting on, and once, when he had seemed quite entranced, he questioned him.

'What are you thinking about, Ben Weatherstaff?' he asked.

'I was thinkin',' answered Ben, 'as I'd warrant tha's gone up three or four pound this week. I was lookin' at tha' calves an' tha' shoulders. I'd like to get thee on a pair o' scales.'

'It's the Magic and – and Mrs. Sowerby's buns and milk and things,' said Colin. 'You see, the scientific experiment has succeeded.'

That morning Dickon was too late to hear the lecture. When he came he was ruddy with running and his funny face looked more twinkling than usual. As they had a good deal of weeding to do after the rains, they fell to work. They always had plenty to do after a warm, deep sinking rain. The moisture which was good for the flowers was also good for the weeds, which thrust up tiny blades of grass and points of leaves which must be pulled up before their roots took too firm hold. Colin was as good at weeding as anyone in these days, and he could lecture while he was doing it.

'The Magic works best when you work yourself,' he said this morning. 'You can feel it in your bones and muscles. I am going to read books about bones and muscles, but I am going to write a book about Magic. I am making it up now. I keep finding out things.'

It was not very long after he had said this that he laid down his trowel and stood up on his feet. He had been silent for several minutes, and they had seen he was thinking out lectures, as he often did. When he dropped his trowel and stood upright it seemed to Mary and Dickon as if a sudden strong thought had made him do it. He stretched himself out to his tallest height and he threw out his arms exultantly. Colour glowed in his face and his strange eyes widened with joyfulness. All at once had had realized something to the full.

'Mary! Dickon!' he cried. 'Just look at me!'

They stopped their weeding and looked at him.

'Do you remember that first morning you brought me in here?' he demanded.

Dickon was looking at him very hard. Being an animal-charmer, he could see more things than most people could, and many of them were things he never talked about. He saw some of them now in this boy.

'Aye, that we do,' he answered.

Mary looked hard, too, but she said nothing.

'Just this minute,' said Colin, 'all at once I remembered it myself – when I looked at my hand digging with the trowel – and I had to stand up on my feet to see if it was real. And it *is* real! I'm *well* – I'm *well*!'

'Aye, that tha' art!' said Dickon.

'I'm well! I'm well!' said Colin again, and his face went quite red all over.

He had known it before in a way, he had hoped it and felt it and thought about it, but just at that minute something had rushed all through him – a sort of rapturous belief and realization, and it had been so strong that he could not help calling out.

'I shall live for ever and ever and ever!' he cried grandly. 'I shall find out thousands and thousands of things. I shall find out about people and creatures and everything that grows – like Dickon – and I shall never stop making Magic. I'm well! I'm well! I feel – I feel as if I want to shout out something – something thankful, joyful!'

Ben Weatherstaff, who had been working near a rose-bush, glanced round at him.

'Tha' might sing th' Doxology,' he suggested in his dryest grunt. He had no opinion of the Doxology, and he did not make the suggestion with any particular reverence.

But Colin was of an exploring mind, and he knew nothing about the Doxology.

'What is that?' he inquired.

'Dickon can sing it for thee, I'll warrant,' replied Ben Weatherstaff.

Dickon answered with his all-perceiving animal-charmer's smile.

'They sing it i' church,' he said. 'Mother says she believes th' skylarks sings it when they gets up i' th' morning'.'

'If she says that, it must be a nice song,' Colin answered. 'I've never been in a church myself. I was always too ill. Sing it, Dickon. I want to hear it.'

Dickon was quite simple and unaffected about it. He understood what Colin felt better than Colin did himself. He understood by a sort of instinct so natural that he did not know it was understanding. He pulled off his cap and looked round still smiling.

'Tha' must take off tha' cap,' he said to Colin, 'an' so mun tha', Ben – an' tha' mun stand up, tha' knows.'

Colin took off his cap and the sun shone on and warmed his thick hair as he watched Dickon intently. Ben Weatherstaff scrambled up from his knees and bared his head, too, with a sort of puzzled, half-resentful look on his old face, as if he didn't know exactly why he was doing this remarkable thing.

Dickon stood out among the trees and rose-bushes and began to sing in quite a simple, matter-of-fact way, and in a nice strong boy's voice:

Praise God from whom all blessings flow,
Praise Him all creatures here below,
Praise Him above ye Heavenly Host,
Praise Father, Son, and Holy Ghost. Amen.

When he had finished, Ben Weatherstaff was standing quite still with his jaws set obstinately, but with a disturbed look in his eyes fixed on Colin. Colin's face was thoughtful and appreciative.

'It is a very nice song,' he said. 'I like it. Perhaps it means just what I mean when I want to shout that I am thankful to the Magic.' He stopped and thought in a puzzled way. 'Perhaps they are both the same thing. How can we know the exact names of everything? Sing it again, Dickon. Let us try, Mary. I want to sing it, too. It's my song. How does it begin?' '"Praise God from whom all blessings flow"?'

And they sang it again, and Mary and Colin lifted their voices as musically as they could, and Dickon's swelled quite loud and beautiful – and at the second line Ben Weatherstaff raspingly cleared his throat, and at the third he joined in with such vigour that it seemed almost savage, and when the 'Amen' came to an end, Mary observed that the very same thing had happened to him which had happened when he found out that Colin was not a cripple – his chin was twitching and he was staring and winking, and his leathery old cheeks were wet.

'I never seen no sense in th' Doxology afore,' he said hoarsely, 'but I may change my mind i' time. I should say tha'd gone up five pound this week, Mester Colin – five on 'em!'

Colin was looking across the garden at something attracting his attention, and his expression had become a startled one.

'Who is coming in here?' he said quickly. 'Who is it?'

The door in the ivied wall had been pushed gently open and a woman had entered. She had come in with the last line of their song and she had stood still listening and looking at them. With the ivy behind her, the sunlight drifting through the trees and dappling her long blue cloak, and her nice fresh face smiling across the greenery, she was rather like a softly coloured illustration in one of Colin's books. She had wonderful affectionate eyes which seemed to take everything in – all of them, even Ben Weatherstaff and the 'creatures' and every flower that was in bloom. Unexpectedly as she had appeared, not one of them felt that she was an intruder at all. Dickon's eyes lighted like lamps.

'It's Mother – that's who it is!' he cried, and he went across the grass at a run.

Colin began to move towards her, too, and Mary went with him. They both felt their pulses beat faster.

'It's Mother!' Dickon said again when they met half-way. 'I knowed tha' wanted to see her an' I told her where th' door was hid.'

Colin held out his hand with a sort of flushed royal shyness, but his eyes quite devoured her face.

'Even when I was ill I wanted to see you,' he said, 'you and Dickon and the secret garden. I'd never wanted to see anyone or anything before.'

The sight of his uplifted face brought about a sudden change in her own. She flushed and the corners of her mouth shook and a mist seemed to sweep over her eyes.

'Eh! dear lad!' she broke out tremulously. 'Eh! dear lad!' as if she had not known she were going to say it. She did not say, 'Mester Colin', but just 'dear lad' quite suddenly. She might have said it to Dickon in the same way if she had seen something in his face which touched her. Colin liked it.

'Are you surprised because I am so well?' he asked.

She put her hand on his shoulder and smiled the mist out of her eyes.

'Aye, that I am!' she said; 'but tha'rt so like thy mother tha' made my heart jump.'

'Do you think,' said Colin a little awkwardly, 'that will make my father like me?'

'Aye, for sure, dear lad,' she answered, and she gave his shoulder a soft, quick pat. 'He mun come home – he mun come home.'

'Susan Sowerby,' said Ben Weatherstaff, getting close to her.

'"It's Mother!"'

'Look at th' lad's legs, wilt tha'? They was like drumsticks i' stockin' two months ago – an' I heard folk tell as they was bandy an' knock-kneed both at th' same time. Look at 'em now!'

Susan Sowerby laughed a comfortable laugh.

'They're goin' to be fine strong lad's legs in a bit,' she said. 'Let him go playin', an' workin' in th' garden an' eatin' hearty an' drinkin' plety o' good sweet milk an' there'll not be a finer pair i' Yorkshire, thank God for it.'

She put both hands on Mistress Mary's shoulders and looked her little face over in a motherly fashion.

'An' thee, too!' she said. 'Tha'rt grown near as hearty as our 'Lizabeth Ellen. I'll warrant tha'rt like thy mother, too. Our Martha told me as Mrs. Medlock heard she was a pretty woman. Tha'lt be like a blush-rose when tha' grows up, my little lass, bless thee.'

She did not mention that when Martha came home on her 'day out' and described the plain, sallow child she had said that she had no confidence whatever in what Mrs. Medlock had heard. 'It doesn't stand to reason that a pretty woman could be th' mother o' such a fou' little lass,' she had added obstinately.

Mary had not had time to pay much attention to her changing face. She had only known that she looked 'different' and seemed to have a great deal more hair and that it was growing very fast. But remembering her pleasure in looking at the Memsahib in the past, she was glad to hear that she might some day look like her.

Susan Sowerby went round their garden with them and was told the whole story of it and shown every bush and tree which had come alive. Colin walked on one side of her and Mary on the other. Each of them kept looking up at her comfortable, rosy face, secretly curious about the delightful feeling she gave them – a sort of warm, supported feeling. It seemed as if she understood them as Dickon understood his 'creatures'. She stooped over the flowers and talked about them as if they were children. Soot followed her and once or twice cawed at her and flew upon her shoulder as if it were Dickon's. When they told her about the robin and the first flight of the young ones, she laughed a motherly little mellow laugh in her throat.

'I suppose learnin' 'em to fly is like learnin' children to walk, but

I'm feared I should be all in a worrit if mine had wings instead o' legs,' she said.

It was because she seemed such a wonderful woman in her nice moorland cottage way that at last she was told about the Magic.

'Do you believe in Magic?' asked Colin, after he had explained about Indian fakirs. 'I do hope you do.'

'That I do, lad,' she answered. 'I never knowed it by that name, but what does th' name matter? I warrant they call it a different name i' France an' a different one i' Germany. Th' same thing as set th' seeds swellin' an' th' sun shinin' made thee a well lad an' it's th' Good Thing. It isn't like us poor fools as think it matters if us is called out of our names. Th' Big Good Thing doesn't stop to worrit, bless thee. It goes on makin' worlds by th' million – worlds like us. Never thee stop believin' in th' Big Good Thing an' knowin' th' world's full of it – an' call it what tha' likes. Tha' wert singing' to it when I come into th' garden.'

'I felt so joyful,' said Colin, opening his beautiful, strange eyes at her. 'Suddenly, I felt how different I was – how strong my arms and legs were, you know – and how I could dig and stand – and I jumped up and wanted to shout out something to anything that would listen.'

'Th' Magic listened when tha' sung th' Doxology. It would ha' listened to anything tha'd sung. It was th' joy that mattered. Eh! lad, lad – what's names to th' Joy Maker,' and she gave his shoulders a quick, soft pat again.

She had packed a basket which held a regular feast this morning, and when the hungry hour came and Dickon brought it out from its hiding place, she sat down with them under their tree and watched them devour their food, laughing and quite gloating over their appetites. She was full of fun and made them laugh at all sorts of odd things. She told them stories in broad Yorkshire and taught them new words. She laughed as if she could not help it when they told her of the increasing difficulty there was in pretending that Colin was still a fretful invalid.

'You see we can't help laughing nearly all the time when we are together,' explained Colin. 'And it doesn't sound ill at all. We try to choke it back, but it will burst out and that sounds worse than ever.'

'There's one thing that comes into my mind so often,' said Mary, 'and I can scarcely ever hold in when I think of it suddenly. I keep thinking suppose Colin's face should get to look like a full moon. It isn't like one yet, but he gets a tiny bit fatter every day – and suppose some morning it should look like one – what should we do!'

'Bless us all, I can see tha' has a good bit o' play actin' to do,' said Susan Sowerby. 'But tha' won't have to keep it up much longer. Mester Craven'll come home.'

'Do you think he will?' asked Colin, 'Why?'

Susan Sowerby chuckled softly.

'I suppose it 'ud nigh break thy heart if he found out before tha' told him in tha' own way,' she said. 'Tha's laid awake nights plannin' it.'

'I couldn't bear anyone else to tell him,' said Colin. 'I think about different ways every day. I think now I just want to run into his room.'

'That'd be a fine start for him,' said Susan Sowerby. 'I'd like to see his face, lad. I would that! He mun come back – that he mun.'

One of the things they talked of was the visit they were to make to her cottage. They planned it all. They were to drive over the moor and lunch out of doors among the heather. They would see all the twelve children and Dickon's garden and would not come back until they were tired.

Susan Sowerby got up at last to return to the house and Mrs. Medlock. It was time for Colin to be wheeled back also. But before he got into his chair he stood quite close to Susan and fixed his eyes on her with a kind of bewildered adoration and he suddenly caught hold of the fold of her blue cloak and held it fast.

'You were just what I – what I wanted,' he said. 'I wish you were my mother – as well as Dickon's!'

All at once Susan Sowerby bent down and drew him with her warm arms close against the bosom under the blue cloak – as if he had been Dickon's brother. The quick mist swept over her eyes.

'Eh! dear lad!' she said. 'Thy own mother's in this 'ere very garden, I do believe. She couldna' keep out of it. Thy father mun come back to thee – he mun!'

27 In the Garden

In each century since the beginning of the world wonderful things have been discovered. In the last century more amazing things were found out than in any century before. In this new century hundreds of things still more astounding will be brought to light. At first people refuse to believe that a strange new thing can be done, then they begin to hope it can't be done, then they see it can be done – then it is done and all the world wonders why it was not done centuries ago. One of the new things people began to find out in the last century was that thoughts – just mere thoughts – are as powerful as electric batteries – as good for one as sunlight is, or as bad for one as poison. To let a sad thought or a bad one get into your mind is as dangerous as letting a scarlet fever germ get into your body. If you let it stay there after it has got in you may never get over it as long as you live.

So long as Mistress Mary's mind was full of disagreeable thoughts about her dislikes and sour opinions of people and her determination not to be pleased by or interested in anything, she was a yellow-faced, sickly, bored, and wretched child. Circumstances, however, were very kind to her, though she was not at all aware of it. They began to push her about for her own good. When her mind gradually filled itself with robins, and moorland cottages crowded with children, with queer, crabbed old gardeners and common little Yorkshire housemaids, with springtime and with secret gardens coming alive day by day, and also with a moor boy and his 'creatures', there was no room left for the disagreeable thoughts which affected her liver and her digestion and made her yellow and tired.

So long as Colin shut himself up in his room and thought only of his fears and weakness and his detestation of people who looked at him and reflected hourly on humps and early death, he was a hysterical, half-crazy little hypochondriac who knew nothing of the sunshine and the spring, and also did not know that he could get well and stand upon his feet if he tried to do it. When new, beautiful thoughts began to push out the old, hideous ones, life began to come back to him, his blood ran healthily through his veins, and strength poured into him like a flood. His scientific experiment was quite practical and simple and there was nothing weird about it at all. Much more surprising things can happen to anyone who, when a disagreeable or discouraged thought comes into his mind, just has the sense to remember in time and push it out by putting in an agreeable, determinedly courageous one. Two things cannot be in one place.

> Where you tend a rose, my lad,
> A thistle cannot grow.

While the secret garden was coming alive and two children were coming alive with it, there was a man wandering about certain far-away beautiful places in the Norwegian fjords, and the valleys and mountains of Switzerland, and he was a man who for ten years had kept his mind filled with dark and heartbroken thinking. He had not been courageous; he had never tried to put any other thoughts in the place of the dark ones. He had wandered by blue lakes and thought them; he had lain on mountain sides with sheets of deep-blue gentians blooming all about him and flower breaths filling all the air and he had thought them. A terrible sorrow had fallen upon him when he had been happy and he had let his soul fill itself with blackness and had refused obstinately to allow any rift of light to pierce through. He had forgotten and deserted his home and his duties. When he travelled about, darkness so brooded over him that the sight of him was a wrong done to other people because it was as if he poisoned the air about him with gloom. Most strangers thought he must be either half mad or a man with some hidden crime on his soul. He was a tall man with a drawn face and crooked shoulders, and the name he always entered on hotel registers was 'Archibald Craven, Misselthwaite Manor, Yorkshire, England'.

He had travelled far and wide since the day he saw Mistress Mary in his study and told her she might have her 'bit of earth'. He had been in the most beautiful places in Europe, though he had remained nowhere more than a few days. He had chosen the quietest and remotest spots. He had been on the tops of mountains whose heads were in the clouds and had looked down on other mountains when the sun rose and touched them with such light as made it seem as if the world were just being born.

But the light had never seemed to touch himself until one day when he realized that for the first time in ten years a strange thing had happened. He was in a wonderful valley in the Austrian Tyrol and he had been walking along through such beauty as might have lifted any man's soul out of shadow. He had walked a long way and it had not lifted his. But at last he had felt tired and had thrown himself down to rest on a carpet of moss by a stream. It was a clear little stream which ran quite merrily along on its narrow way through the luscious damp greenness. Sometimes it made a sound rather like very low laughter as it bubbled over and round stones. He saw birds come and dip their heads to drink it in and then flick their wings and fly away. It seemed like a thing alive and yet its tiny voice made the stillness seem deeper. The valley was very, very still.

As he sat gazing into the clear running of the water, Archibald Craven gradually felt his mind and body both grow quiet, as quiet as the valley itself. He wondered if he were going to sleep, but he was not. He sat and gazed at the sunlit water and his eyes began to see things growing at its edge. There was one lovely mass of blue forget-me-nots growing so close to the stream that its leaves were wet and at these he found himself looking as he remembered he had looked at such things years ago. He was actually thinking tenderly how lovely it was and what wonders of blue its hundreds of little blossoms were. He did not know that just that simple thought was slowly filling his mind – filling and filling it until other things were softly pushed aside. It was as if a sweet, clear spring had begun to rise in a stagnant pool and had risen and risen until at last it swept the dark water away. But of course he did not think of this himself. He only knew that the valley seemed to grow quieter and quieter as he sat and stared at the bright, delicate blueness.

He did not know how long he sat there or what was happening to him, but at last he moved as if he were awakening and he got up slowly and stood on the moss carpet, drawing a long, deep, soft breath and wondering at himself. Something seemed to have been unbound and released in him, very quietly.

'What is it?' he said, almost in a whisper, and he passed his hand over his forehead. 'I almost feel as if – I were alive!'

I do not know enough about the wonderfulness of undiscovered things to be able to explain how this had happened to him. Neither does anyone else yet. He did not understand at all himself – but he remembered this strange hour months afterwards when he was at Misselthwaite again and he found out quite by accident that on this very day Colin had cried out as he went into the secret garden:

'I am going to live for ever and ever and ever!'

The singular calmness remained with him the rest of the evening, and he slept a new, reposeful sleep; but it was not with him very long. He did not know that it could be kept. By the next night he had opened the doors wide to his dark thoughts, and they had come trooping and rushing back. He left the valley and went on his wandering way again. But, strange as it seemed to him, there were minutes – sometimes half-hours – when, without his knowing why, the black burden seemed to lift itself again and he knew he was a living man and not a dead one. Slowly – slowly – for no reason that he knew of – he was 'coming alive' with the garden.

As the golden summer changed into the deeper golden autumn he went to the Lake of Como. There he found the loveliness of a dream. He spent his days upon the crystal blueness of the lake or he walked back into the soft, thick verdure of the hills and tramped until he was tired, so that he might sleep. But by this time he had begun to sleep better, he knew, and his dreams had ceased to be a terror to him.

'Perhaps,' he thought, 'my body is growing stronger.'

It was growing stronger but – because of the rare, peaceful hours when his thoughts were changed – his soul was slowly growing stronger, too. He began to think of Misselthwaite and wonder if he should not go home. Now and then he wondered vaguely about his boy and asked himself what he should feel when he went and stood by the carved four-poster bed again and looked down at the sharply chiselled, ivory-white face while it slept and the black lashes rimmed so startlingly the close-shut eyes. He shrank from it.

One marvel of a day he had walked so far that when he returned the moon was high and full and all the world was purple shadow and silver. The stillness of lake and shore and wood was so wonderful that he did not go into the villa he lied in. He walked down to a little bowered terrace at the water's edge and sat upon a seat and breathed in all the heavenly scents of the night. He felt the strange calmness stealing over him and it grew deeper and deeper until he fell asleep.

He did not know when he fell asleep and when he began to dream; his dream was so real that he did not feel as if he were dreaming. He remembered afterwards how intensely wide awake and alert he had thought he was. He thought that as he sat and breathed in the scent of the late roses and listened to the lapping of the water at his feet, he heard a voice calling. It was sweet and clear and happy and far away. It seemed very far, but he heard it as distinctly as if it had been at his very side.

'Archie! Archie! Archie!' it said, and then again, sweeter and clearer than before 'Archie! Archie!'

He thought he sprang to his feet not even startled.

It was such a real voice and it seemed so natural that he should hear it.

'Lilias! Lilias!' he answered. 'Lilias! where are you?'

'In the garden,' it came back like a sound from a golden flute. 'In the garden!'

And then the dream ended. But he did not awaken. He slept soundly and sweetly all through the lovely night. When he did awake at last it was brilliant morning and a servant was standing staring at him. He was an Italian servant and was accustomed, as all the servants of the villa were, to accepting without question any strange thing his foreign master might do. No one ever knew when he would go out or come in or where he would choose to sleep or if he would roam about the garden or lie in the boat on the lake all night. The man held a salver with some letters on it and he waited quietly until Mr. Craven took them. When he had gone away Mr. Craven sat a few moments holding them in his hand and looking at the lake. His strange calm was still upon him and something more – a lightness, as if the cruel thing which had been done had not happened as he thought – as if something had changed. He was remembering the dream – the real – real dream.

'In the garden!' he said, wondering at himself. 'In the garden! But the door is locked and the key is buried deep.'

When he glanced at the letters a few minutes later, he saw that the one lying at the top of the rest was an English letter and came from Yorkshire. It was directed in a plain woman's hand, but it was not a hand he knew. He opened it, scarcely thinking of the writer, but the first words attracted his attention at once.

DEAR SIR,—I am Susan Sowerby that made bold to speak to you once on the moor. It was about Miss Mary I spoke. I will make bold to speak again. Please, sir, I would come home if I was you. I think you would be glad to come and – if you will excuse me, sir – I think your lady would ask you to come if she was here,

Your obedient servant,
SUSAN SOWERBY

Mr. Craven read the letter twice before he put it back in its envelope. He kept thinking about the dream.

'I will go back to Misselthwaite,' he said. 'Yes, I'll go at once.'

And he went through the garden to the villa and ordered Pitcher to prepare for his return to England.

In a few days he was in Yorkshire again, and on his long railroad journey he found himself thinking of his boy as he had never thought in all the ten years past. During those years he had only wished to forget him. Now, though he did not intend to think about him, memories of him constantly drifted into his mind. He remembered the black days when he had raved like a madman because the child was alive and the mother was dead. He had refused to see it, and when he had gone to look at it at last it had been such a weak wretched thing that everyone had been sure it would die in a few days. But to the surprise of those who took care of it the days passed and it lived, and then everyone believed it would be a deformed and crippled creature.

He had not meant to be a bad father, but he had not felt like a father at all. He had supplied doctors and nurses and luxuries, but he had shrunk from the mere thought of the boy and had buried himself in his own misery. The first time after a year's absence he returned to Misselthwaite and the small miserable-looking thing languidly and indifferently lifted to his face the great grey eyes with black lashes round them, so like and yet so horribly unlike the happy eyes he had adored, he could not bear the sight of them and turned away pale as death. After that he scarcely ever saw him except when he was asleep, and all he knew of him was that he was a confirmed invalid, with a vicious, hysterical, half-insane temper. He could only be kept from furies dangerous to himself by being given his own way in every detail.

All this was not an uplifting thing to recall, but as the train whirled him through the mountain passes and golden plains, the man who was 'coming alive' began to think in a new way and he thought long and steadily and deeply.

'Perhaps I have been all wrong for ten years,' he said to himself. 'Ten years is a long time. It may be too late to do anything – quite too late. What have I been thinking of!'

Of course this was the wrong Magic – to begin by saying 'too late'. Even Colin could have told him that. But he knew nothing of Magic – either black or white. This he had yet to learn. He wondered if Susan Sowerby had taken courage and written to him only because the motherly creature had realized that the boy was much worse – was fatally ill. If he had not been under the spell of the curious calmness which had taken possession of him he would have been more wretched than ever. But the calm had brought a sort of courage and hope with it. Instead of giving way to thoughts of the worst he actually found he was trying to believe in better things.

'Could it be possible that she sees that I may be able to do him good and control him?' he thought. 'I will go and see her on my way to Misselthwaite.'

But when on his way across the moor he stopped the carriage at the cottage, seven or eight children who were playing about gathered in a group and bobbing seven or eight friendly and polite curtsies, told him that their mother had gone to the other side of the moor early in the morning to help a woman who had a new baby. 'Our Dickon', they volunteered, was over at the manor working in one of the gardens, where he spent several days each week.

Mr. Craven looked over the collection of sturdy little bodies and round, red-cheeked faces, each one grinning in its own particular way, and he awoke to the fact that they were a healthy, likeable lot. He smiled to their friendly grins, and took a golden sovereign from his pocket and gave it to 'our 'Lizabeth Ellen', who was the oldest.

'If you divide that into eight parts there will be half a crown for each of you,' he said.

Then amid grins and chuckles and bobbing of curtsies, he drove away, leaving ecstasy and nudging elbows and little jumps of joy behind.

The drive across the wonderfulness of the moor was a soothing thing. Why did it seem to give him a sense of homecoming which he had been sure he could never feel again – that sense of the beauty of land and sky and purple bloom of distance, and warming of the heart at drawing nearer to the great old house which had held those of his blood for six hundred years? How he had driven away from it the last time shuddering to think of its closed rooms and the boy living in the four-poster bed with the brocaded hangings. Was it possible that perhaps he might find him changed a little for the better, and that he might overcome his shrinking from him? How real that dream had been – how wonderful and clear the voice which had called back to him, 'In the garden – In the garden!'

'I will try to find the key,' he said. 'I will try to open the door. I must – though I don't know why.'

When he arrived at the Manor the servants who received him with the usual ceremony, noticed that he looked better, and that he did not go to the remote rooms where he usually lived, attended by Pitcher. He went into the library and sent for Mrs. Medlock. She came to him somewhat excited, and curious and flustered.

'How is Master Colin, Medlock?' he inquired.

'Well, sir,' Mrs. Medlock answered, 'he's – he's different, in a manner of speaking.'

'Worse?' he suggested.

Mrs. Medlock really was flushed.

'Well, you see, sir,' she tried to explain, 'neither Dr. Craven, nor the nurse, nor me can exactly make him out.'

'Why is that?'

'To tell the truth, sir, Master Colin might be better and he might be changing for the worse. His appetite, sir, is past understanding – and his ways——'

'Has he become more – more peculiar?' her master asked, knitting his brows anxiously.

'That's it, sir. He's growing very peculiar – when you compare him with what he used to be. He used to eat nothing, and then suddenly he began to eat something enormous – and then he stopped again all at once and the meals were sent back just as they used to be. You never knew, sir, perhaps, that out of doors he never would let himself be taken. The things we've gone through to get him to go out in his chair would leave a body trembling like a leaf. He'd throw himself into such a state that Dr. Craven said he couldn't be responsible for forcing him. Well, sir, just without warning – not long after one of his worst tantrums, he suddenly insisted on being taken out every day by Miss Mary and Susan Sowerby's boy, Dickon, that could push his chair. He took a fancy to both Miss Mary and Dickon, and Dickon brought his tame animals, and, if you'll credit it, sir, out of doors he will stay from morning until night.'

'How does he look?' was the next question.

'If he took his food natural, sir, you'd think he was putting on flesh – but we're afraid it may be a sort of bloat. He laughs sometimes in a queer way when he's alone with Miss Mary. He never used to laugh at all, Dr. Craven is coming to see you at once, if you'll allow him. He never was as puzzled in his life.'

'Where is Master Colin now?' Mr Craven asked.

'In the garden, sir. He's always in the garden – though not a human creature is allowed to go near for fear they'll look at him.'

Mr. Craven scarcely heard her last words.

'In the garden!' he said, and after he had sent Mrs. Medlock away, he stood and repeated it again and again. 'In the garden!'

He had to make an effort to bring himself back to the place he was standing in, and when he felt he was on earth again he turned and went out of the room. He took his way, as Mary had done, through the door in the shrubbery and among the laurels and the fountain beds. The fountain was playing now, and was encircled by beds of brilliant autumn flowers. He crossed the lawn and turned into the Long Walk by the ivied walls. He did not walk quickly, but slowly, and his eyes were on the path. He felt as if he were being drawn back to the place he had so long forsaken, and he did not know why. As he drew near to it his step became still more slow. He knew where the door was, even though the ivy hung over it – but he did not know exactly where it lay – that buried key.

So he stopped and stood still, looking about him, and almost the moment after he had paused he started and listened – asking himself if he were walking in a dream.

The ivy hung thick over the door, the key was buried under the shrubs, no human being had passed that portal for ten lonely years – and yet inside the garden there were sounds. They were the sounds of running, scuffling feet seeming to chase round and round under the trees, they were strange sounds of lowered, suppressed voices – exclamations and smothered, joyous cries. It seemed actually like the laughter of young things, the uncontrollable laughter of children who were trying not to be heard, but who in a moment or so – as their excitement mounted – would burst forth. What in heaven's name was he dreaming of – what in heaven's name did he hear? Was he losing his reason and thinking he heard things which were not for human ears? Was it that the far, clear voice had meant?

And then the moment came, the uncontrollable moment when the sounds forgot to hush themselves. The feet ran faster and faster – they were nearing the garden door – there was quick, strong, young breathing and a wild outbreak of laughing shouts which could not be contained – and the door in the wall was flung wide open, the sheet of ivy swinging back, and a boy burst through it at full speed and, without seeing the outsider, dashed almost into his arms.

Mr. Craven had extended them just in time to save him from falling as a result of his unseeing dash against him, and when he held him away to look at him in amazement at his being there he truly gasped for breath.

He was a tall boy and a handsome one. He was glowing with life, and his running had sent splendid colour leaping to his face. He threw the thick hair back from his forehead and lifted a pair of strange grey eyes – eyes full of boyish laughter and rimmed with black lashes like a fringe. It was the eyes which made Mr. Craven gasp for breath.

'Who – What? Who?' he stammered.

This was not what Colin had expected – this was not what he had planned. He had never thought of such a meeting. And yet to come dashing out – winning a race – perhaps it was even better. He drew himself up to his very tallest. Mary, who had been running with him and had dashed through the door too, believed that he managed to make himself look taller than he had ever looked before – inches taller.

'Father,' he said, 'I'm Colin. You can't believe it. I scarcely can myself, I'm Colin.'

Like Mrs. Medlock, he did not understand what his father meant when he said hurriedly:

'In the garden! In the garden!'

'Yes,' hurried on Colin. 'It was the garden that did it – and Mary and Dickon and the creatures – and the Magic. No one knows. We kept it to tell you when you came. I'm well; I can beat Mary in a race. I'm going to be an athlete.'

He said it all so like a healthy boy – his face flushed, his words tumbling over each other in his eagerness – that Mr. Craven's soul shook with unbelieving joy.

Colin put out his hand and laid it on his father's arm.

'Aren't you glad, Father?' he ended. 'Aren't you glad? I'm going to live for ever and ever and ever!'

Mr. Craven put his hands on both the boy's shoulders and held him still. He knew he dared not even try to speak for a moment.

'Take me into the garden, my boy,' he said at last. 'And tell me all about it.'

And so they led him in.

The place was a wilderness of autumn gold and purple and violet and flaming scarlet, and on every side were sheaves of late lilies standing together – lilies which were white or white and ruby. He remembered well when the first of them had been planted that just at this season of the year their late glories should reveal themselves. Late roses climbed and hung and clustered, and the sunshine deepening the hue of the yellowing trees made one feel that one stood in an embowered temple of gold. The newcomer stood silent just as the children had done when they came into its greyness. He looked round and round.

'I thought it would be dead,' he said.

'Mary thought so at first,' said Colin. 'But it came alive.'

Then they sat down under their tree – all but Colin, who wanted to stand while he told the story.

It was the strangest thing he had ever heard, Archibald Craven thought, as it was poured forth in headlong boy fashion. Mystery and Magic and wild creatures, the weird midnight meeting – the coming of the spring – the passion of insulted pride which had dragged the young rajah to his feet to defy old Ben Weatherstaff to his face. The odd companionship, the play-acting, the great secret so carefully kept. The listener laughed until tears came into his eyes, and sometimes tears came into his eyes when he was not laughing. The Athlete, the Lecturer, the Scientific Discoverer was a laughable, lovable, healthy young human thing.

'Now,' he said at the end of the story, 'it need not be a secret any more. I dare say it will frighten them nearly into fits when they see me – but I am never going to get into the chair again. I shall walk back with you, Father – to the house.'

*

Ben Weatherstaff's duties rarely took him away from the gardens, but on this occasion he made an excuse to carry some vegetables to the kitchen, and being invited into the servants' hall by Mrs. Medlock to drink a glass of beer, he was on the spot – as he had hoped to be – when the most dramatic event Misselthwaite Manor had seen during the present generation actually took place.

One of the windows looking upon the courtyard gave also a glimpse of the lawns. Mrs Medlock, knowing Ben had come from the gardens, hoped that he might have caught sight of his master, and even by chance of his meeting with Master Colin.

'Did you see either of them, Weatherstaff?' she asked.

Ben took his beer-mug from his mouth and wiped his lips with the back of his hand.

'Aye, that I did,' he answered with a shrewdly significant air.

'Both of them?' suggested Mrs. Medlock.

'Both of 'em,' returned Ben Weatherstaff. 'Thank ye kindly, ma'am, I could sup up another mug of it.'

'Together?' said Mrs. Medlock, hastily overfilling his beer-mug in her excitement.

'Together, ma'am,' and Ben gulped down half of his new mug at one gulp.

'Where was Master Colin? How did he look? What did they say to each other?'

'I didna' hear that,' said Ben, 'along o' only bein' on th' step-ladder lookin' over th' wall. But I'll tell thee this. There's been things goin' on outside as you house people knows nowt about. An' what tha'll find out tha'll find out soon.'

And it was not two minutes before he swallowed the last of his beer and waved his mug solemnly towards the window which took in through the shrubbery a piece of the lawn.

'Look here,' he said, 'if tha's curious. Look what's comin' across th' grass.'

When Mrs. Medlock looked she threw up her hands and gave a little shriek, and every man and woman servant within hearing bolted across the servants' hall and stood looking through the window with their eyes almost starting out of their heads.

Across the lawn came the Master of Misselthwaite, and he looked as many of them had never seen him. And by his side, with his head up in the air and his eyes full of laughter, walked as strongly and steadily as any boy in Yorkshire – Master Colin!

A LITTLE PRINCESS

A Little

Princess

Being the whole story of

Sarah Crewe

Frances Hodgson Burnett

Being the Whole Story of Sara Crewe

I do not know whether many people realize how much more than is ever written there really is in a story – how many parts of it are never told – how much more really happened than there is in the book one holds in one's hand and pores over. Stories are something like letters. When a letter is written, how often one remembers things omitted and says: 'Ah, why did I not tell them that?' In writing a book one relates all that one remembers at the time, and if one told all that really happened perhaps the book would never end. Between the lines of every story there is another story, and that is one that is never heard and can only be guessed at by the people who are good at guessing. The person who writes the story may never know all of it, but sometimes he does and wishes he had the chance to begin again.

When I wrote the story of 'Sara Crewe' I guessed that a great deal more had happened at Miss Minchin's than I had had time to find out just then. I knew, of course, that there must have been chapters full of things going on all the time; and when I began to make a play out of the book and called it 'A Little Princess,' I discovered three acts full of things. What interested me most was that I found that there had been girls at the school whose names I had not even known before. There was a little girl whose name was Lottie, who was an amusing little person; there was a hungry scullery-maid who was Sara's adoring friend; Ermengarde was much more entertaining than she had seemed at first; things happened in the garret which had never been hinted at in the book; and a certain gentleman whose name was Melchisedec was an intimate friend of Sara's who should never have been left out of the story if he had only walked into it in time. He and Becky and Lottie lived at Miss Minchin's, and I cannot understand why they did not mention themselves to me at first. They were as real as Sara, and it was careless of them not to come out of the story shadowland and say: 'Here I am – tell about me.' But they did not – which was their fault and not mine. People who live in the story one is writing ought to come forward at the beginning and tap the writing person on the shoulder and say: 'Hallo, what about me?' If they don't, no one can be blamed but themselves and their slouching, idle ways.

After the play of 'A Little Princess' was produced in New York, and so many children went to see it and liked Becky and Lottie and Melchisedec, my publishers asked me if I could not write Sara's story over again and put into it all the things and people who had been left out before, and so I have done it; and when I began I found there were actually pages and pages of things which had happened that had never been put even into the play, so in this new 'Little Princess' I have put all I have been able to discover.

Frances Hodgson Burnett

Contents

List of Illustrations

1 Sara

Once on a dark winter's day, when the yellow fog hung so thick and heavy in the streets of London that the lamps were lighted and the shop windows blazed with gas as they do at night, an odd-looking little girl sat in a cab with her father, and was driven rather slowly through the big thoroughfares.

She sat with her feet tucked under her, and leaned against her father, who held her in his arms, as she stared out of the window at the passing people with a queer old-fashioned thoughtfulness in her big eyes.

She was such a little girl that one did not expect to see such a look on her small face. It would have been an old look for a child of twelve, and Sara Crewe was only seven. The fact was, however, that she was always dreaming and thinking odd things, and could not herself remember any time when she had not been thinking things about grown-up people and the world they belonged to. She felt as if she had lived a long, long time.

At this moment she was remembering the voyage she had just made from Bombay with her father, Captain Crewe. She was thinking of the big ship, of the lascars passing silently to and fro on it, of the children playing about on the hot deck, and of some young officers' wives who used to try to make her talk to them and laugh at the things she said.

Principally, she was thinking of what a queer thing it was that at one time one was in India in the blazing sun, and then in the middle of the ocean, and then driving in a strange vehicle through strange streets where the day was as dark as the night. She found this so puzzling that she moved closer to her father.

'Papa,' she said in a low, mysterious little voice which was almost a whisper, 'papa.'

'What is it, darling?' Captain Crewe answered, holding her closer and looking down into her face. 'What is Sara thinking of?'

'Is this the place?' Sara whispered, cuddling still closer to him. 'Is it, papa?'

'Yes, little Sara, it is. We have reached it at last.' And though she was only seven years old, she knew that he felt sad when he said it.

It seemed to her many years since he had begun to prepare her mind for 'the place', as she always called it. Her mother had died when she was born, so she had never known or missed her. Her young, handsome, rich, petting father seemed to be the only relation she had in the world. They had always played together and been fond of each other. She only knew he was rich because she had heard people say so when they thought she was not listening, and she had also heard them say that when she grew up she would be rich too. She did not know all that being rich meant. She had always lived in a beautiful bungalow, and had been used to seeing many servants who made salaams to her and called her 'Missee Sahib', and gave her her own way in everything. She had had toys and pets and an ayah who worshipped her, and she had gradually learned that people who were rich had these things. That, however, was all she knew about it.

During her short life only one thing had troubled her, and that thing was 'the place' she was to be taken to some day. The climate of India was very bad for children, and as soon as possible they were sent away from it – generally to England and to school. She had seen other children go away, and had heard their fathers and mothers talk about the letters they received from them. She had known that she would be obliged to go also, and though sometimes her father's stories of the voyage and the new country had attracted her, she had been troubled by the thought that he could not stay with her.

'Couldn't you go to that place with me, papa?' she had asked when she was five years old. 'Couldn't you go to school too? I would help you with your lessons.'

'But you will not have to stay for a very long time, little Sara,' he had always said. 'You will go to a nice house where there will be a lot of little girls, and you will play together, and I will send you plenty of books, and you will grow so fast that it will seem scarcely a year before you are big enough and clever enough to come back and take care of papa.'

She had liked to think of that. To keep the house for her father; to ride with him and sit at the head of his table when he had dinner-parties; to talk to him and read his books – that would be what she would like most in the world, and if one must go away to 'the place' in England to attain it, she must make up her mind to go. She did not care very much for other little girls, but if she had plenty of books she could console herself. She liked books more than anything else, and was, in fact, always inventing stories of beautiful things, and telling them to herself. Sometimes she had told them to her father, and he had liked them as much as she did.

'Well, papa,' she said softly, 'if we are here I suppose we must be resigned.'

He laughed at her old-fashioned speech and kissed her. He was really not at all resigned himself, though he knew he must keep that a secret. His quaint little Sara had been a great companion to him, and he felt he should be a lonely fellow when, on his return to India, he went into his bungalow knowing he need not expect to see the small figure in its white frock come forward to meet him. So he held her very closely in his arm as the cab rolled into the big, dull square in which stood the house which was their destination.

It was a big, dull, brick house, exactly like all the others in its row, but that on the front door there shone a brass plate on which was engraved in black letters:

MISS MINCHIN
Select Seminary for Young Ladies

'Here we are, Sara,' said Captain Crewe, making his voice sound as cheerful as possible. Then he lifted her out of the cab and they mounted the steps and rang the bell. Sara often thought afterwards that the house was somehow exactly like Miss Minchin. It was respectable and well-furnished, but everything in it was ugly; and the very arm-chairs seemed to have hard bones in them. In the hall everything was hard and polished – even the red cheeks of the moon face of the tall clock in the corner had a severe varnished look. The drawing-room into which they were ushered was covered by a carpet with a square pattern upon it, the chairs were square, and a heavy marble timepiece stood upon the heavy marble mantel.

As she sat down in one of the stiff mahogany chairs, Sara cast one of her quick looks about her.

'I don't like it, papa,' she said. 'But then I dare say soldiers – even brave ones – don't really *like* going into battle.'

Captain Crewe laughed outright at this. He was young and full of fun, and he never tired of hearing Sara's queer speeches.

'Oh, little Sara,' he said. 'What shall I do when I have no one to say solemn things to me? No one else is quite as solemn as you are.'

'But why do solemn things make you laugh so?' inquired Sara.

Because you are such fun when you say them,' he answered, laughing still more. And then suddenly he swept her into his arms and kissed her very hard, stopping laughing all at once and looking almost as if tears had come into his eyes.

It was just then that Miss Minchin entered the room. She was very like her house, Sara felt: tall and dull, and respectable and ugly. She had large, cold, fishy eyes, and a large, cold, fishy smile. It spread itself into a very large smile when she saw Sara and Captain Crewe. She had heard a great many desirable things of the young soldier from the lady who had recommended her school to him. Among other things, she had heard that he was a rich father who was willing to spend a great deal of money on his little daughter.

'It will be a great privilege to have charge of such a beautiful and promising child, Captain Crewe,' she said, taking Sara's hand and stroking it. 'Lady Meredith has told me of her unusual cleverness. A clever child is a great treasure in an establishment like mine.'

Sara stood quietly, with her eyes fixed upon Miss Minchin's face. She was thinking something odd, as usual.

'Why does she say I am a beautiful child?' she was thinking. 'I am not beautiful at all. Colonel Grange's little girl, Isobel, is beautiful. She has dimples and rose-coloured cheeks, and long hair the colour of gold. I have short black hair and green eyes; besides which, I am a thin child and not fair in the least. I am one of the ugliest children I ever saw. She is beginning by telling a story.'

She was mistaken, however, in thinking she was an ugly child. She was not in the least like Isobel Grange, who had been the beauty of the regiment, but she had an odd charm of her own. She was a slim, supple creature, rather tall for her age, and had an intense, attractive little face. Her hair was heavy and quite black and only curled at the tips; her eyes were greenish grey, it is true, but they were big, wonderful eyes with long, black lashes, and though she herself did not like the colour of them, many other people did. Still she was very firm in her belief that she was an ugly little girl, and she was not at all elated by Miss Minchin's flattery.

'I should be telling a story if I said she was beautiful,' she thought, 'and I should know I was telling a story. I believe I am as ugly as she is – in my way. What did she say that for?'

After she had known Miss Minchin longer she learned why she had said it. She discovered that she said the same thing to each papa and mamma who brought a child to her school.

Sara stood near her father and listened while he and Miss Minchin talked. She had been brought to the seminary because Lady Meredith's two little girls had been educated there, and Captain Crewe had a great respect for Lady Meredith's experience. Sara was to be what was known as 'a parlour-boarder', and she was to enjoy even greater privileges than parlour-boarders usually did. She was to have a pretty bedroom and sitting-room of her own; she was to have a pony and a carriage, and a maid to take the place of the ayah who had been her nurse in India.

'I am not in the least anxious about her education,' Captain Crewe said, with his gay laugh, as he held Sara's hand and patted it. 'The difficulty will be to keep her from learning too fast and too much. She is always sitting with her little nose burrowing into books. She doesn't read them, Miss Minchin; she gobbles them up as if she were a little wolf instead of a little girl. She is always starving for new books to gobble, and she wants grown-up books – great, big, fat ones – French and German as well as English – history and biography and poets, and all sorts of things. Drag her away from her books when she reads too much. Make her ride her pony in the Row or go out and buy a new doll. She ought to play more with dolls.'

'Papa,' said Sara. 'You see, if I went out and bought a new doll every few days I should have more than I could be fond of. Dolls ought to be intimate friends. Emily is going to be my intimate friend.'

Captain Crewe looked at Miss Minchin and Miss Minchin looked at Captain Crewe.

'Who is Emily?' she inquired.

'Tell her, Sara,' Captain Crewe said, smiling.

Sara's green-grey eyes looked very solemn and quite soft as she answered.

'She is a doll I haven't got yet,' she said. 'She is a doll papa is going to buy for me. We are going out together to find her. I have called her Emily. She is going to be my friend when papa is gone. I want her to talk to about him.'

Miss Minchin's large, fishy smile became very flattering indeed.

'What an original child!' she said. 'What a darling little creature!'

'Yes,' said Captain Crewe, drawing Sara close. 'She is a darling little creature. Take great care of her for me, Miss Minchin.'

Sara stayed with her father at his hotel for several days; in fact, she remained with him until he sailed away again to India. They went out and visited many big shops together, and bought a great many things. They bought, indeed, a great many more things than Sara needed; but Captain Crewe was a rash, innocent young man, and wanted his little girl to have everything she admired and everything he admired himself, so between them they collected a wardrobe much too grand for a child of seven. There were velvet dresses trimmed with costly furs, and lace dresses, and embroidered ones, and hats with great, soft ostrich feathers, and ermine coats and muffs, and boxes of tiny gloves and handkerchiefs and silk stockings in such abundant supplies that the polite young women behind the counters whispered to each other that the odd little girl with the big, solemn eyes must be at least some foreign princess – perhaps the little daughter of an Indian rajah.

And at last they found Emily, but they went to a number of toy-shops and looked at a great many dolls before they finally discovered her.

'I want her to look as if she wasn't a doll really,' Sara said. 'I want her to look as if she *listens* when I talk to her. The trouble with dolls, papa' – and she put her head on one side and reflected as she said it – 'the trouble with dolls is that they never seem to *hear*.' So they looked at big ones and little ones – at dolls with black eyes and dolls with blue – at dolls with brown curls and dolls with golden braids, dolls dressed and dolls undressed.

'You see,' Sara said, when they were examining one who had no clothes. 'If, when I find her, she has no frocks, we can take her to a dressmaker and have things made to fit. They will fit better if they are tried on.'

After a number of disappointments they decided to walk and look in at the shop windows and let the cab follow them. They had passed two or three places without even going in, when, as they were approaching a shop which was really not a very large one, Sara suddenly started and clutched her father's arm.

'Oh, papa!' she cried. 'There is Emily!'

A flush had risen to her face, and there was an expression in her green-grey eyes as if she had just recognized some one she was intimate with and fond of.

'She is actually waiting for us!' she said. 'Let us go in to her.'

'Dear me!' said Captain Crewe. 'I feel as if we ought to have some one to introduce us.'

'You must introduce me and I will introduce you,' said Sara. 'But I knew her the minute I saw her – so perhaps she knew me, too.'

Perhaps she had known her. She had certainly a very intelligent expression in her eyes when Sara took her in her arms. She was a large doll, but not too large to carry about easily; she had naturally curling golden-brown hair, which hung like a mantle about her, and her eyes were a deep, clear, grey blue, with soft, thick eyelashes which were real eyelashes and not mere painted lines.

'Of course,' said Sara, looking into her face as she held her on her knee – 'of course, papa, this is Emily.'

So Emily was bought and actually taken to a children's outfitter's shop, and measured for a wardrobe as grand as Sara's own. She had lace frocks, too, and velvet and muslin ones, and hats and coats and

'"*But I knew her the minute I saw her – so perhaps she knew me too*"'

beautiful lace-trimmed underclothes, and gloves and handkerchiefs and furs.

'I should like her always to look as if she was a child with a good mother,' said Sara. 'I'm her mother, though I am going to make a companion of her.'

Captain Crewe would really have enjoyed the shopping tremendously, but that a sad thought kept tugging at his heart. This all meant that he was going to be separated from his beloved, quaint little comrade.

He got out of his bed in the middle of that night and went and stood looking down at Sara, who lay asleep with Emily in her arms. Her black hair was spread out on the pillow and Emily's golden-brown hair mingled with it; both of them had lace-ruffled night-gowns, and both had long eyelashes which lay and curled up on their cheeks. Emily looked so like a real child that Captain Crewe felt glad she was there. He drew a big sigh and pulled his moustache with a boyish expression.

'Heigh-ho, little Sara!' he said to himself. 'I don't believe you know how much your daddy will miss you.'

The next day he took her to Miss Minchin's and left her there. He was to sail away the next morning. He explained to Miss Minchin that his solicitors, Messrs. Barrow & Skipworth, had charge of his affairs in England, and would give her any advice she wanted, and that they would pay the bills she sent in for Sara's expenses. He would write to Sara twice a week, and she was to be given every pleasure she asked for.

'She is a sensible little thing, and she never wants anything it isn't safe to give her,' he said.

Then he went with Sara into her little sitting-room, and they bade each other good-bye. Sara sat on his knee and held the lapels of his coat in her small hands, and looked long and hard at his face.

'Are you learning me by heart, little Sara?' he said, stroking her hair.

'No,' she answered. 'I know you by heart. You are inside my heart.' And they put their arms round each other, and kissed as if they would never let each other go.

When the cab drove away from the door, Sara was sitting on the floor of her sitting-room, with her hands under her chin and her eyes following it until it had turned the corner of the square. Emily was sitting by her, and she looked after it, too. When Miss Minchin sent her sister, Miss Amelia, to see what the child was doing, she found she could not open the door.

'I have locked it,' said a queer, polite little voice from inside. 'I want to be quite by myself, if you please.'

Miss Amelia was fat and dumpy, and stood very much in awe of her sister. She was really the better-natured person of the two, but she never disobeyed Miss Minchin. She went downstairs again, looking almost alarmed.

'I never saw such a funny, old-fashioned child, sister,' she said. 'She has locked herself in, and she is not making the least particle of noise.'

'It is much better than if she kicked and screamed, as some of them do,' Miss Minchin answered. 'I expected that a child as much spoiled as she is would set the whole house in an uproar. If ever a child was given her own way in everything, she is.'

'I've been opening her trunks and putting her things away,' said Miss Amelia. 'I never saw anything like them – sable and ermine on her coats, and real Valenciennes lace on her underclothing. You have seen some of her clothes. What *do* you think of them?'

'I think they are perfectly ridiculous,' replied Miss Minchin sharply, 'but they will look very well at the head of the line when we take the school-children to church on Sunday. She has been provided for as if she were a little princess.'

And upstairs in the locked room Sara and Emily sat on the floor and stared at the corner round which the cab had disappeared, while Captain Crewe looked backward, waving and kissing his hand as if he could not bear to stop.

2 A French Lesson

When Sara entered the schoolroom the next morning everybody
looked at her with wide, interested eyes. By that time every pupil –
from Lavinia Herbert, who was nearly thirteen and felt quite grown
up, to Lottie Legh, who was only just four and the baby of the school –
had heard a great deal about her. They knew very certainly that she
was Miss Minchin's show pupil and was considered a credit to the
establishment. One or two of them had even caught a glimpse of her
French maid, Mariette, who had arrived the evening before. Lavinia
had managed to pass Sara's room when the door was open, and had
seen Mariette opening a box which had arrived late from some shop.

'It was full of petticoats with lace frills on them – frills and frills,'
she whispered to her friend Jessie as she bent over her geography. 'I
saw her shaking them out. I heard Miss Minchin say to Miss Amelia
that her clothes were so grand that they were ridiculous for a child. My
mamma says that children should be dressed simply. She has got one
of those petticoats on now. I saw it when she sat down.'

'She has silk stockings on!' whispered Jessie, bending over her
geography also. 'And what little feet! I never saw such little feet.'

'Oh,' sniffed Lavinia spitefully, 'that is the way her slippers are
made. My mamma says that even big feet can be made to look small if
you have a clever shoemaker. I don't think she is pretty at all. Her eyes
are such a queer colour.'

'She isn't pretty as other pretty people are,' said Jessie, stealing a
glance across the room, 'but she makes you want to look at her again.
She has tremendously long eyelashes, but her eyes are almost green.'

Sara was sitting quietly in her seat, waiting to be told what to do.
She had been placed near Miss Minchin's desk. She was not abashed

at all by the many pairs of eyes watching her. She was interested, and looked back quietly at the children who looked at her. She wondered what they were thinking of, and if they liked Miss Minchin, and if they cared for their lessons, and if any of them had a papa at all like her own. She had had a long talk with Emily about her papa that morning.

'He is on the sea now, Emily,' she had said. 'We must be very great friends to each other and tell each other things. Emily, look at me. You have the nicest eyes I ever saw — but I wish you could speak.'

She was a child full of imaginings and whimsical thoughts, and one of her fancies was that there would be a great deal of comfort in even pretending that Emily was alive and really heard and understood. After Mariette had dressed her in her dark-blue school-room frock and tied her hair with a dark-blue ribbon, she went to Emily who sat in a chair of her own, and gave her a book.

'You can read that while I am downstairs,' she said; and, seeing Mariette looking at her curiously, she spoke to her with a serious little face.

'What I believe about dolls,' she said, 'is that they can do things they will not let us know about. Perhaps, really, Emily can read and talk and walk, but she will only do it when people are out of the room. That is her secret. You see, if people knew that dolls could do things, they would make them work. So, perhaps, they have promised each other to keep it a secret. If you stay in the room, Emily will just sit there and stare; but if you go out, she will begin to read, perhaps, or go and look out of the window. Then if she heard either of us coming, she would just run back and jump into her chair and pretend she had been there all the time.'

'*Comme elle est drôle!*' Mariette said to herself, and when she went downstairs she told the head housemaid about it. But she had already begun to like this odd little girl who had such an intelligent small face and such perfect manners. She had taken care of children before who were not so polite. Sara was a very fine little person, and had a gentle, appreciative way of saying: 'If you please, Mariette,' 'Thank you, Mariette,' which was very charming. Mariette told the head house-maid that she thanked her as if she was thanking a lady.

'*Elle a l'air d'une princesse, cette petite,*' she said. Indeed, she was very much pleased with her new little mistress and liked her place greatly.

After Sara had sat in her seat in the schoolroom for a few minutes, being looked at by the pupils, Miss Minchin rapped in a dignified manner upon her desk.

'Young ladies,' she said, 'I wish to introduce you to your new companion.' All the little girls rose in their places, and Sara rose also. 'I shall expect you all to be very agreeable to Miss Crewe; she has just come to us from a great distance – in fact, from India. As soon as lessons are over you must make each other's acquaintance.'

The pupils bowed ceremoniously, and Sara made a little courtesy, and then they sat down and looked at each other again.

'Sara,' said Miss Minchin in her schoolroom manner, 'come here to me.'

She had taken a book from the desk and was turning over its leaves. Sara went to her politely.

'As your papa has engaged a French maid for you,' she began, 'I conclude that he wishes you to make a special study of the French language.'

Sara felt a little awkward.

'I think he engaged her,' she said, 'because he – he thought I would like her, Miss Minchin.'

'I am afraid,' said Miss Minchin, with a slightly sour smile, 'that you have been a very spoiled little girl and always imagine that things are done because you like them. My impression is that your papa wished you to learn French.'

If Sara had been older or less punctilious about being quite polite to people, she could have explained herself in a very few words. But, as it was, she felt a flush rising on her cheeks. Miss Minchin was a very severe and imposing person, and she seemed so absolutely sure that Sara knew nothing whatever of French that she felt as if it would be almost rude to correct her. The truth was that Sara could not remember the time when she had not seemed to know French. Her father had often spoken it to her when she had been a baby. Her mother had been a Frenchwoman, and Captain Crewe had loved her language, so it happened that Sara had always heard and been familiar with it.

'I – I have never really learned French, but – but—' she began, trying shyly to make herself clear.

One of Miss Minchin's chief secret annoyances was that she did not speak French herself, and was desirous of concealing the irritating fact. She, therefore, had no intention of discussing the matter and laying herself open to innocent questioning by a new little pupil.

'That is enough,' she said with polite tartness. 'If you have not learned, you must begin at once. The French master, Monsieur Dufarge, will be here in a few minutes. Take this book and look at it until he arrives.'

Sara's cheeks felt warm. She went back to her seat and opened the book. She looked at the first page with a grave face. She knew it would be rude to smile, and she was very determined not to rude. But it was very odd to find herself expected to study a page which told her that '*le père*' meant 'the father,' and '*la mère*' meant 'the mother.'

Miss Minchin glanced toward her scrutinizingly.

'You look rather cross, Sara,' she said. 'I am sorry you do not like the idea of learning French.'

'I am very fond of it,' answered Sara, thinking she would try again; 'but——'

'You must not say "but" when you are told to do things,' said Miss Minchin. 'Look at your book again.'

And Sara did so, and did not smile, even when she found that '*le fils*' meant 'the son,' and '*le frère*' meant 'the brother.'

'When Monsieur Dufarge comes,' she thought, 'I can make him understand.'

Monsieur Dufarge arrived very shortly afterward. He was a very nice, intelligent, middle-aged Frenchman, and he looked interested when his eyes fell upon Sara trying politely to seem absorbed in her little book of phrases.

'Is this a new pupil for me, madame?' he said to Miss Minchin. 'I hope that is my good fortune.'

'Her papa – Captain Crewe – is very anxious that she should begin the language. But I am afraid she has a childish prejudice against it. She does not seem to wish to learn,' said Miss Minchin.

'I am sorry of that, mademoiselle,' he said kindly to Sara. 'Perhaps when we begin to study together, I may show you that it is a charming tongue.'

Little Sara rose in her seat. She was beginning to feel rather desperate, as if she were almost in disgrace. She looked up into Monsieur Dufarge's face with her big, green-grey eyes, and they were quite innocently appealing. She knew that he would understand as soon as she spoke. She began to explain quite simply in pretty and fluent French. Madame had not understood. She had not learned French exactly – not out of books – but her papa and other people had always spoken it to her, and she had read it and written it as she had read and written English. Her papa loved it, and she loved it because he did. Her dear mamma, who had died when she was born, had been French. She would be glad to learn anything monsieur would teach her, but what she had tried to explain to madame was that she already knew the words in this book – and she held out the little book of phrases.

When she began to speak Miss Minchin started quite violently and sat staring at her over her eyeglasses, almost indignantly, until she had finished. Monsieur Dufarge began to smile, and his smile was one of great pleasure. To hear this pretty childish voice speaking his own language so simply and charmingly made him feel almost as if he were in his native land – which in dark, foggy days in London sometimes seemed worlds away. When she had finished, he took the phrase-book from her, with a look almost affectionate. But he spoke to Miss Minchin.

'Ah, madame,' he said, 'there is not much I can teach her. She has not *learned* French; she *is* French. Her accent is exquisite.'

'You ought to have told me,' exclaimed Miss Minchin, much mortified, turning on Sara.

'I – I tried,' said Sara. 'I – I suppose I did not begin right.'

Miss Minchin knew she had tried, and that it had not been her fault that she was not allowed to explain. And when she saw that the pupils had been listening, and that Lavinia and Jessie were giggling behind their French grammars, she felt infuriated.

'Silence, young ladies!' she said severely, rapping upon the desk.

'Silence at once!'

And she began from that minute to feel rather a grudge against her show pupil.

3 Ermengarde

On that first morning, when Sara sat at Miss Minchin's side, aware that the whole schoolroom was devoting itself to observing her, she had noticed very soon one little girl, about her own age, who looked at her very hard with a pair of light, rather dull, blue eyes. She was a fat child, who did not look as if she were in the least clever, but she had a good-naturedly pouting mouth. Her flaxen hair was braided in a tight pigtail, tied with a ribbon, and she had pulled this pigtail round her neck, and was biting the end of the ribbon, resting her elbows on the desk, as she stared wonderingly at the new pupil. When Monsieur Dufarge began to speak to Sara, she looked a little frightened; and when Sara stepped forward and, looking at him with the innocent, appealing eyes, answered him, without any warning, in French, the fat little girl gave a startled jump, and grew quite red in her awed amazement. Having wept hopeless tears for weeks in her efforts to remember that '*la mère*' meant 'the mother,' and '*le père*' 'the father' – when one spoke sensible English – it was almost too much for her to suddenly find herself listening to a child her own age who seemed not only quite familiar with these words, but apparently knew any number of others, and could mix them up with verbs as if they were mere trifles.

She stared so hard and bit the ribbon on her pigtail so fast that she attracted the attention of Miss Minchin, who, feeling extremely cross at the moment, immediately pounced upon her.

'Miss St John!' she exclaimed severely. 'What do you mean by such conduct? Remove your elbows! Take your ribbon out of your mouth! Sit up at once!'

Upon which Miss St John gave another jump, and when Lavinia

and Jessie tittered she became redder than ever – so red, indeed, that she almost looked as if tears were coming into her poor, dull, childish eyes; and Sara saw her and was so sorry for her that she began to rather like her and want to be her friend. It was a way of hers always to want to spring into any fray in which some one was made uncomfortable or unhappy.

'If Sara had been a boy and lived a few centuries ago,' her father used to say, 'she would have gone about the country with her sword drawn, rescuing and defending every one in distress. She always wants to fight when she sees people in trouble.'

So she took rather a fancy to fat, slow, little Miss St John, and kept glancing toward her through the morning. She saw that lessons were no easy matter to her, and that there was no danger of her ever being spoiled by being treated as a show pupil. Her French lesson was a pathetic thing. Her pronunciation made even Monsieur Dufarge smile in spite of himself, and Lavinia and Jessie and the more fortunate girls either giggled or looked at her in wondering disdain. But Sara did not laugh. She tried to look as if she did not hear when Miss St John called '*le bon pain*,' '*lee bong pang*.' She had a fine, hot little temper of her own, and it made her feel rather savage when she heard the titters and saw the poor, stupid, distressed child's face.

'It isn't funny, really,' she said, between her teeth, as she bent over her book. 'They ought not to laugh.'

When lessons were over and the pupils gathered together in groups to talk, Sara looked for Miss St John, and finding her bundled rather disconsolately in a window-seat, she walked over to her and spoke. She only said the kind of thing little girls always say to each other by way of beginning an acquaintance, but there was something nice and friendly about Sara, and people always felt it.

'What is your name?' she said.

To explain Miss St John's amazement one must recall that a new pupil is, for a short time, a somewhat uncertain thing; and of this new pupil the entire school had talked the night before until it fell asleep quite exhausted by excitement and contradictory stories. A new pupil with a carriage and a pony and a maid, and a voyage from India to discuss, was not an ordinary acquaintance.

'My name's Ermengarde St John,' she answered.

'Mine is Sara Crewe,' said Sara. 'Yours is very pretty. It sounds like a story-book.'

'Do you like it?' fluttered Ermengarde. 'I – I like yours.'

Miss St John's chief trouble in life was that she had a clever father. Sometimes this seemed to her a dreadful calamity. If you have a father who knows everything, who speaks seven or eight languages, and has thousands of volumes which he has apparently learnt by heart, he frequently expects you to be familiar with the contents of your lesson-books at least; and it is not improbable that he will feel you ought to be able to remember a few incidents of history, and to write a French exercise. Ermengarde was a severe trial to Mr. St John. He could not understand how a child of his could be a notably and unmistakably dull creature who never shone in anything.

'Good heavens!' he had said more than once as he stared at her, 'there are times when I think she is as stupid as her Aunt Eliza!'

If her Aunt Eliza had been slow to learn and quick to forget a thing entirely when she had learned it, Ermengarde was strikingly like her. She was the monumental dunce of the school, and it could not be denied.

'She must be *made* to learn,' her father said to Miss Minchin.

Consequently Ermengarde spent the greater part of her life in disgrace or in tears. She learned things and forgot them; or, if she remembered them, she did not understand them. So it was natural that, having made Sara's acquaintance, she should sit and stare at her with profound admiration.

'You can speak French, can't you?' she said respectfully.

Sara got on to the window-seat, which was a big deep one, and, tucking up her feet, sat with her hands clasped round her knees.

'I can speak it because I have heard it all my life,' she answered. 'You could speak it if you had always heard it.'

'Oh, no, I couldn't,' said Ermengarde. 'I *never* could speak it!'

'Why?' inquired Sara curiously.

Ermengarde shook her head so that the pigtail wabbled.

'You heard me just now,' she said. 'I'm always like that. I can't *say* the words. They're so queer.'

She paused a moment, and then added with a touch of awe in her voice:

'You are *clever*, aren't you?'

Sara looked out of the window into the dingy square, where the sparrows were hopping and twittering on the wet iron railings, and the sooty branches of the trees. She reflected a few moments. She had heard it said very often that she was 'clever,' and she wondered if she was – and *if* she was, how it had happened.

'I don't know,' she said. 'I can't tell.' Then, seeing a mournful look on the round, chubby face, she gave a little laugh and changed the subject.

'Would you like to see Emily?' she inquired.

'Who is Emily?' Ermengarde asked, just as Miss Minchin had done.

'Come up to my room and see,' said Sara, holding out her hand.

They jumped down from the window-seat together, and went upstairs.

'Is it true,' Ermengarde whispered, as they went through the hall – 'is it true that you have a playroom all to yourself?'

'Yes,' Sara answered. 'Papa asked Miss Minchin to let me have one, because – well, it was because when I play I make up stories and tell them to myself, and I don't like people to hear me. It spoils it if I think people listen.'

They had reached the passage leading to Sara's room by this time, and Ermengarde stopped short, staring, and quite losing her breath.

'You *make up* stories!' she gasped. 'Can you do that – as well as speak French? *Can* you?'

Sara looked at her in simple surprise.

'Why, any one can make up things,' she said. 'Have you never tried?'

She put her hand warningly on Ermengarde's.

'Let us go very quietly to the door,' she whispered, 'and then I will open it quite suddenly; perhaps we may catch her.'

She was half laughing, but there was a touch of mysterious hope in her eyes which fascinated Ermengarde, though she had not the remotest idea what it meant, or whom it was she wanted to 'catch', or why she wanted to catch her. Whatsoever she meant, Ermengarde was sure it was something delightfully exciting. So, quite thrilled with expectation, she followed her on tiptoe along the passage. They made not the least noise until they reached the door. Then Sara suddenly turned the handle, and threw it wide open. Its opening revealed the room quite neat and quiet, a fire gently burning in the grate, and a wonderful doll sitting in a chair by it, apparently reading a book.

'Oh, she got back to her seat before we could see her!' Sara exclaimed. 'Of course, they always do. They are as quick as lightning.'

Ermengarde looked from her to the doll and back again.

'Can she – walk?' she asked breathlessly.

'Yes,' answered Sara, 'At least, I believe she can. At least, I *pretend* I believe she can. And that makes it seem as if it were true. Have you never pretended things?'

'No,' said Ermengarde. 'Never. I – tell me about it.'

She was so bewitched by this odd, new companion that she actually stared at Sara instead of at Emily – notwithstanding that Emily was the most attractive doll person she had ever seen.

'Let us sit down,' said Sara, 'and I will tell you. It's so easy that when you begin you can't stop. You just go on and on doing it always. And it's beautiful. Emily, you must listen. This is Ermengarde St John, Emily. Ermengarde, this is Emily. Would you like to hold her?'

'Oh, may I?' said Ermengarde. 'May I, really? She *is* beautiful!' And Emily was put into her arms.

Never in her dull, short life had Miss St John dreamed of such an hour as the one she spent with the queer new pupil before they heard the lunch-bell ring and were obliged to go downstairs.

Sara sat upon the hearth-rug and told her strange things. She sat rather huddled up, and her green eyes shone and her cheeks flushed. She told stories of the voyage, and stories of India; but what fascinated Ermengarde the most was her fancy about the dolls who walked and talked, and who could do anything they chose when the human beings were out of the room, but who must keep their powers a secret and so flew back to their places 'like lightning' when people returned to the room.

'*We* couldn't do it,' said Sara seriously. 'You see, it's a kind of magic.'

Once, when she was relating the story of the search for Emily, Ermengarde saw her face suddenly change. A cloud seemed to pass over it and put out the light in her shining eyes. She drew her breath in so sharply that it made a funny, sad little sound, and then she shut her lips and held them tightly closed, as if she was determined either to do or *not* to do something. Ermengarde had an idea that if she had been like any other little girl, she might have suddenly burst out sobbing and crying. But she did not.

'Have you a – a pain?' Ermengarde ventured.

'Yes,' Sara answered after a moment's silence. 'But it is not in my body.' Then she added something in a low voice which she tried to keep quite steady, and it was this: 'Do you love your father more than anything else in all the whole world?'

Ermengarde's mouth fell open a little. She knew that it would be far from behaving like a respectable child at a select seminary to say that it had never occurred to you that you *could* love your father, that you would do anything desperate to avoid being left alone in his society for ten minutes. She was, indeed, greatly embarrassed.

'I – I scarcely ever see him,' she stammered. 'He is always in the library – reading things.'

'I love mine more than all the world ten times over,' Sara said. 'That is what my pain is. He has gone away.'

She put her head quietly down on her little, huddled-up knees, and sat very still for a few minutes.

'She's going to cry out loud,' thought Ermengarde fearfully.

But she did not. Her short, black locks tumbled about her ears, and she sat still. Then she spoke without lifting her head.

'I promised him I would bear it,' she said. 'And I will. You have to bear things. Think what soldiers bear! Papa is a soldier. If there was a war he would have to bear marching and thirstiness, and, perhaps, deep wounds. And he would never say a word – not one word.'

Ermengarde could only gaze at her, but she felt that she was beginning to adore her. She was so wonderful and different from any one else.

Presently she lifted her face and shook back her black locks, with a queer little smile.

'If I go on talking and talking,' she said, 'and telling you things about pretending, I shall bear it better. You don't forget, but you bear it better.'

Ermengarde did not know why a lump came into her throat and her eyes felt as if tears were in them.

'Lavinia and Jessie are "best friends",' she said rather huskily. 'I wish we could be "best friends". Would you have me for yours? You're clever, and I'm the stupidist child in the school, but I – oh, I do so like you!'

'I'm glad of that,' said Sara. 'It makes you thankful when you are liked. Yes. We will be friends. And I'll tell you what' – a sudden gleam lighting her face – 'I can help you with your French lessons.'

4 Lottie

If Sara had been a different kind of child, the life she led at Miss Minchin's Select Seminary for the next ten years would not have been at all good for her. She was treated more as if she were a distinguished guest at the establishment than as if she were a mere little girl. If she had been a self-opinionated, domineering child, she might have become disagreeable enough to be unbearable through being so much indulged and flattered. If she had been an indolent child, she would have learned nothing. Privately Miss Minchin disliked her, but she was far too worldly a woman to do or say anything which might make such a desirable pupil wish to leave her school. She knew quite well that if Sara wrote to her papa to tell him she was uncomfortable or unhappy, Captain Crewe would remove her at once. Miss Minchin's opinion was that if a child were continually praised and never forbidden to do what she liked, she would be sure to be fond of the place where she was so treated. Accordingly, Sara was praised for her quickness at her lessons, for her good manners, for her amiability to her fellow-pupils, for her generosity if she gave sixpence to a beggar out of her full little purse; the simplest thing she did was treated as if it were a virtue, and if she had not had a disposition and a clever little brain, she might have been a very self-satisfied young person. But the clever little brain told her a great many sensible and true things about herself and her circumstances, and now and then she talked these things over to Ermengarde as time went on.

'Things happen to people by accident,' she used to say. 'A lot of nice accidents have happened to me. It just *happened* that I always liked lessons and books, and could remember things when I learned them. It just happened that I was born with a father who was beautiful and nice and clever, and could give me everything I liked. Perhaps I have not really a good temper at all, but if you have everything you want and every one is kind to you, how can you help but be good-tempered? I don't know' – looking quite serious – 'how I shall ever find out whether I am really a nice child or a horrid one. Perhaps I'm a *hideous* child, and no one will ever know, just because I never have any trials.'

'Lavinia has no trials,' said Ermengarde stolidly, 'and she is horrid enough.'

Sara rubbed the end of her little nose reflectively, as she thought the matter over.

'Well,' she said at last, 'perhaps – perhaps that is because Lavinia is *growing*.'

This was the result of a charitable recollection of having heard Miss Amelia say that Lavinia was growing so fast that she believed it affected her health and temper.

Lavinia, in fact, was spiteful. She was inordinately jealous of Sara. Until the new pupil's arrival, she had felt herself the leader in the school. She had led because she was capable of making herself extremely disagreeable if the others did not follow her. She domineered over the little children, and assumed grand airs with those big enough to be her companions. She was rather pretty, and had been the best-dressed pupil in the procession when the Select Seminary walked out two by two, until Sara's velvet coats and sable muffs appeared, combined with drooping ostrich feathers, and were led by Miss Minchin at the head of the line. This, at the beginning, had been bitter enough; but as time went on it became apparent that Sara was a leader, too, and not because she could make herself disagreeable, but because she never did.

'There's one thing about Sara Crewe,' Jessie had enraged her 'best friend' by saying honestly – 'she's never "grand" about herself the least bit, and you know she might be, Lavvie. I believe I couldn't help being – just a little – if I had so many fine things and was made such a fuss over. It's disgusting, the way Miss Minchin shows her off when parents come.'

' "Dear Sara must come into the drawing-room and talk to Mrs.

Musgrave about India," ' mimicked Lavinia, in her most highly flavoured imitation of Miss Minchin. ' "Dear Sara must speak French to Lady Pitkin. Her accent is so perfect." She didn't learn her French at the Seminary, at any rate. And there's nothing so clever in her knowing it. She says herself she didn't learn it at all. She just picked it up, because she always heard her papa speak it. And, as to her papa, there is nothing so grand in being an Indian officer.'

'Well,' said Jessie slowly, 'he's killed tigers. He killed the one in the skin Sara has in her room. That's why she likes it so. She lies on it and strokes its head, and talks to it as if it was a cat.'

'She's always doing something silly,' snapped Lavinia. 'My mamma says that way of hers of pretending things is silly. She says she will grow up eccentric.'

It was quite true that Sara was never 'grand'. She was a friendly little soul, and shared her privileges and belongings with a free hand. The little ones, who were accustomed to being disdained and ordered out of the way by mature ladies aged ten and twelve, were never made to cry by this most envied of them all. She was a motherly young person, and when people fell down and scraped their knees, she ran and helped them up and patted them, or found in her pocket a bonbon or some other article of a soothing nature. She never pushed them out of her way or alluded to their years as a humiliation and a blot upon their small characters.

'If you are four you are four,' she said severely to Lavinia on an occasion of her having – it must be confessed – slapped Lottie and called her 'a brat'; 'but you will be five next year, and six the year after that. And,' opening large, convicting eyes, 'it only takes sixteen years to make you twenty.'

'Dear me!' said Lavinia, 'how we can calculate!' In fact, it was not to be denied that sixteen and four made twenty – and twenty was an age the most daring was scarcely bold enough to dream of.

So the younger children adored Sara. More than once she had been known to have a tea-party, made up of these despised ones, in her own room. And Emily had been played with, and Emily's own tea-service used – the one with cups which held quite a lot of much-sweetened weak tea and had blue flowers on them. No one had seen such a very real doll's tea-set before. From that afternoon Sara was regarded as a goddess and a queen by the entire alphabet class.

Lottie Legh worshipped her to such an extent that if Sara had not been a motherly person, she would have found her tiresome. Lottie had been sent to school by a rather flighty young papa who could not imagine what else to do with her. Her young mother had died, and as the child had been treated like a favourite doll or a very spoiled pet monkey or lap-dog ever since the first hour of her life, she was a very appalling little creature. When she wanted anything or did not want anything she wept and howled; and, as she always wanted the things she could not have, and did not want the things that were best for her, her shrill little voice was usually to be heard uplifted in wails in one part of the house or another.

Her strongest weapon was that in some mysterious way she had found out that a very small girl who had lost her mother was a person who ought to be pitied and made much of. She had probably heard some grown-up people talking her over in the early days, after her mother's death. So it became her habit to make great use of this knowledge.

The first time Sara took her in charge was one morning when, on passing a sitting-room, she heard both Miss Minchin and Miss Amelia trying to suppress the angry wails of some child who, evidently, refused to be silenced. She refused so strenuously indeed that Miss Minchin was obliged to almost shout – in a stately and severe manner – to make herself heard.

'What *is* she crying for?' she almost yelled.

'Oh – oh – oh!' Sara heard; 'I haven't got any mam – ma-a!'

'Oh, Lottie!' screamed Miss Amelia. 'Do stop, darling! Don't cry! Please don't!'

'Oh! oh! oh!' Lottie howled tempestuously. 'Haven't – got – any – mam – ma-a!'

'She ought to be whipped,' Miss Minchin proclaimed. 'You *shall* be whipped, you naughty child!'

Lottie wailed more loudly than ever. Miss Amelia began to cry. Miss Minchin's voice rose until it almost thundered, then suddenly she sprang up from her chair in impotent indignation and flounced out of the room, leaving Miss Amelia to arrange the matter.

Sara had paused in the hall, wondering if she ought to go into the room, because she had recently begun a friendly acquaintance with Lottie and might be able to quiet her. When Miss Minchin came out and saw her, she looked rather annoyed. She realized that her voice, as heard from inside the room, could not have sounded either dignified or amiable.

'Oh, Sara!' she exclaimed, endeavouring to produce a suitable smile.

'I stopped,' explained Sara, 'because I knew it was Lottie – and I thought, perhaps – just perhaps, I could make her be quiet. May I try, Miss Minchin?'

'If you can. You are a clever child,' answered Miss Minchin, drawing in her mouth sharply. Then, seeing that Sara looked slightly chilled by her asperity, she changed her manner. 'But you are clever in everything,' she said in her approving way. 'I dare say you can manage her. Go in.' And she left her.

When Sara entered the room, Lottie was lying upon the floor, screaming and kicking her small fat legs violently, and Miss Amelia was bending over her in consternation and despair, looking quite red and damp with heat. Lottie had always found, when in her own nursery at home, that kicking and screaming would always be quieted by any means she insisted on. Poor plump Miss Amelia was trying first one method, and then another.

'Poor darling!' she said one moment, 'I know you haven't any mamma, poor——' Then in quite another tone: 'If you don't stop, Lottie, I will shake you. Poor little angel! There – there! You wicked, bad, detestable child, I will smack you! I will!'

Sara went to them quietly. She did not know at all what she was going to do, but she had a vague inward conviction that it would be better not to say such different kinds of things quite so helplessly and excitedly.

'Miss Amelia,' she said in a low voice, 'Miss Minchin says I may try to make her stop – may I?'

Miss Amelia turned and looked at her hopelessly. 'Oh, *do* you think you can?' she gasped.

'I don't know whether I *can*,' answered Sara, still in her half-whisper, but I will try.'

Miss Amelia stumbled up from her knees with a heavy sigh, and Lottie's fat little legs kicked as hard as ever.

'If you will steal out of the room,' said Sara, 'I will stay with her.'

'Oh, Sara!' almost whimpered Miss Amelia. 'We never had such a dreadful child before. I don't believe we *can* keep her.'

But she crept out of the room, and was very much relieved to find an excuse for doing it.

Sara stood by the howling, furious child for a few moments, and looked down at her without saying anything. Then she sat down flat on the floor beside her and waited. Except for Lottie's angry screams, the room was quite quiet. This was a new state of affairs for little Miss Legh, who was accustomed, when she screamed, to hear other people protest and implore and command and coax by turns. To lie and kick and shriek, and find the only person near you not seeming to mind in the least, attracted her attention. She opened her tight-shut streaming eyes to see who this person was. And it was only another little girl. But it was the one who owned Emily and all the nice things. And she was looking at her steadily and as if she was merely thinking. Having paused for a few seconds to find this out, Lottie thought she must begin again, but the quiet of the room and of Sara's odd, interested face made her first howl rather half-hearted.

'I – haven't – any – ma – ma – ma-a!' she announced; but her voice was not so strong.

Sara looked at her still more steadily, but with a sort of understanding in her eyes.

'Neither have I,' she said.

This was so unexpected that it was astounding. Lottie actually dropped her legs, gave a wriggle, and lay and stared. A new idea will stop a crying child when nothing else will. Also it was true that while Lottie disliked Miss Minchin, who was cross, and Miss Amelia, who was foolishly indulgent, she rather liked Sara, little as she knew her. She did not want to give up her grievance, but her thoughts were distracted from it, so she wriggled again, and, after a sulky sob, said:

'Where is she?'

'"I – haven't – any – ma – ma – ma – a!" she announced'

Sara paused a moment. Because she had been told that her mamma was in heaven, she had thought a great deal about the matter, and her thoughts had not been quite like those of other people.

'She went to heaven,' she said. 'But I am sure she comes out sometimes to see me – though I don't see her. So does yours. Perhaps they can both see us now. Perhaps they are both in this room.'

Lottie sat bolt upright, and looked about her. She was a pretty, little, curly-headed creature, and her round eyes were like wet forget-me-nots. If her mamma had seen her during the last half-hour, she might not have thought her the kind of child who ought to be related to an angel.

Sara went on talking. Perhaps some people might think that what she said was rather like a fairy story, but it was all so real to her own imagination that Lottie began to listen in spite of herself. She had been told that her mamma had wings and a crown, and she had been shown pictures of ladies in beautiful white night-gowns, who were said to be angels. But Sara seemed to be telling a real story about a lovely country where real people were.

'There are fields and fields of flowers,' she said, forgetting herself, as usual, when she began, and talking rather as if she were in a dream – 'fields and fields of lilies – and when the soft wind blows over them it wafts the scent of them into the air – and everybody always breathes it, because the soft wind is always blowing. And little children run about in the lily-fields and gather armfuls of them, and laugh and make little wreaths. And the streets are shining. And no one is ever tired, however far they walk. They can float anywhere they like. And there are walls made of pearl and gold all round the city, but they are low enough for the people to go and lean on them, and look down to the earth and smile, and send beautiful messages.'

Whatsoever story she had begun to tell, Lottie would, no doubt, have stopped crying, and been fascinated into listening; but there was no denying that this story was prettier than most others. She dragged herself close to Sara, and drank in every word until the end came – far too soon. When it did come, she was so sorry that she put up her lip ominously.

'I want to go there,' she cried. 'I – haven't any mamma in this school.'

Sara saw the danger-signal, and came out of her dream. She took hold of the chubby hand and pulled her close to her side with a coaxing little laugh.

'I will be your mamma,' she said. 'We will play that you are my little girl. And Emily shall be your sister.'

Lottie's dimples all began to show themselves.

'Shall she?' she said.

'Yes,' answered Sara, jumping to her feet. 'Let us go and tell her. And then I will wash your face and brush your hair.'

To which Lottie agreed quite cheerfully, and trotted out of the room and upstairs with her, without seeming even to remember that the whole of the last hour's tragedy had been caused by the fact that she had refused to be washed and brushed for lunch, and Miss Minchin had been called in to use her majestic authority.

And from that time Sara was an adopted mother.

5 Becky

Of course the greatest power Sara possessed, and the one which gained her even more followers than her luxuries and the fact that she was 'the show pupil,' the power that Lavinia and certain other girls were most envious of, and at the same time most fascinated by in spite of themselves, was her power of telling stories and of making everything she talked about seem like a story, whether it was one or not.

Any one who has been at school with a teller of stories knows what the wonder means – how he or she is followed about and besought in a whisper to relate romances; how groups gather round and hang on the outskirts of the favoured party in the hope of being allowed to join it and listen. Sara not only could tell stories, but she adored telling them. When she sat or stood in the midst of a circle and began to invent wonderful things, her green eyes grew big and shining, her cheeks flushed, and, without knowing that she was doing it, she began to act, and made what she told lovely or alarming by the raising or dropping of her voice, the bend and sway of her slim body, and the dramatic movement of her hands. She forgot that she was talking to listening children; she saw and lived with the fairy folk, or the kings and queens and beautiful ladies, whose adventures she was narrating. Sometimes when she had finished her story, she was quite out of breath with excitement, and would lay her hand on her thin, little, quick-rising chest, and half laugh as if at herself.

'When I am telling it,' she would say, 'it doesn't seem as if it was only made up. It seems more real than you are – more real than the schoolroom. I feel as if I were all the people in the story – one after the other. It *is* queer.'

She had been at Miss Minchin's school about two years when, one foggy winter's afternoon, as she was getting out of her carriage, comfortably wrapped up in her warmest velvets and furs and looking very much grander than she knew, she caught sight, as she crossed the pavement, of a dingy little figure standing on the area steps, and stretching its neck so that its wide-opened eyes might peer at her through the railings. Something in the eagerness and timidity of the smudgy face made her look at it, and when she looked she smiled because it was her way to smile at people.

But the owner of the smudgy face and the wide-open eyes evidently was afraid that she ought not to have been caught looking at pupils of importance. She dodged out of sight like a Jack-in-the-box and scurried back into the kitchen, disappearing so suddenly that if she had not been such a poor, little, forlorn thing, Sara would have laughed in spite of herself. That very evening, as Sara was sitting in the midst of a group of listeners in a corner of the schoolroom telling one of her stories, the very same figure timidly entered the room, carrying a coal-box much too heavy for her, and knelt down upon the hearth-rug to replenish the fire and sweep up the ashes.

She was cleaner than she had been when she peeped through the area railings, but she looked just as frightened. She was evidently afraid to look at the children or seem to be listening. She put on pieces of coal cautiously with her fingers so that she might make no disturbing noise, and she swept about the fire-irons very softly. But Sara saw in two minutes that she was deeply interested in what was going on, and that she was doing her work slowly in the hope of catching a word here and there. And realizing this, she raised her voice and spoke more clearly.

'The Mermaids swam softly about in the crystal-green water, and dragged after them a fishing-net woven of deep-sea pearls,' she said. 'The Princess sat on the white rock and watched them.'

It was a wonderful story about a princess who was loved by a Prince Merman, and went to live with him in shining caves under the sea.

The small drudge before the grate swept the hearth once and then swept it again. Having done it twice, she did it three times; and, as she was doing it the third time, the sound of the story so lured her to listen that she fell under the spell and actually forgot that she had no right to listen at all, and also forgot everything else. She sat down upon her heels as she knelt on the hearth rug, and the brush hung idly in her fingers. The voice of the story-teller went on and drew her with it into winding grottoes under the sea, glowing with soft, clear blue light, and paved with pure golden sands. Strange sea flowers and grasses waved about her, and far away faint singing and music echoed.

The hearth-brush fell from the work-roughened hand, and Lavinia Herbert looked round.

'That girl has been listening,' she said.

The culprit snatched up her brush, and scrambled to her feet. She caught at the coal-box and simply scuttled out of the room like a frightened rabbit.

Sara felt rather hot-tempered.

'I knew she was listening,' she said. 'Why shouldn't she?'

Lavinia tossed her head with great elegance.

'Well,' she remarked, 'I do not know whether your mamma would like you to tell stories to servant girls, but I know *my* mamma wouldn't like *me* to do it.'

'My mamma!' said Sara, looking odd. 'I don't believe she would mind in the least. She knows that stories belong to everybody.'

'I thought,' retorted Lavinia, in severe recollection, 'that your mamma was dead. How can she know things?'

'Do you think she *doesn't* know things?' said Sara, in her stern little voice. Sometimes she had a rather stern little voice.

'Sara's mother knows everything,' piped in Lottie. 'So does my mamma – 'cept Sara is my mamma at Miss Minchin's – my other one knows everything. The streets are shining, and there are fields and fields of lilies, and everybody gathers them. Sara tells me when she puts me to bed.'

'You wicked thing,' said Lavinia, turning on Sara; 'making fairy stories about heaven.'

'There are much more splendid stories in Revelation,' returned Sara. 'Just look and see! How do you know mine are fairy stories? But I can tell you' – with a fine bit of unheavenly temper – 'you will never find out whether they are or not if you're not kinder to people than you are now. Come along, Lottie.' And she marched out of the room, rather hoping that she might see the little servant again somewhere, but she found no trace of her when she got into the hall.

'Who is that little girl who makes the fires?' she asked Mariette that night.

Mariette broke forth into a flow of description.

Ah, indeed, Mademoiselle Sara might well ask. She was a forlorn little thing who had just taken the place of scullery-maid – though, as to being scullery-maid, she was everything else besides. She blacked boots and grates, and carried heavy coal-scuttles up and down stairs, and scrubbed floors and cleaned windows, and was ordered about by everybody. She was fourteen years old, but was so stunted in growth that she looked about twelve. In truth, Mariette was sorry for her. She was so timid that if one chanced to speak to her it appeared as if her poor, frightened eyes would jump out of her head.

'What is her name?' asked Sara, who had sat by the table, with her chin on her hands, as she listened absorbedly to the recital.

Her name was Becky. Mariette heard every one below-stairs calling: 'Becky, do this,' and 'Becky, do that,' every five minutes in the day.

Sara sat and looked into the fire, reflecting on Becky for some time after Mariette left her. She made up a story of which Becky was the ill-used heroine. She thought she looked as if she had never had quite enough to eat. Her very eyes were hungry. She hoped she should see her again, but though she caught sight of her carrying things up or down stairs on several occasions, she always seemed in such a hurry and so afraid of being seen that it was impossible to speak to her.

But a few weeks later on another foggy afternoon, when she entered her sitting-room she found herself confronting a rather pathetic picture. In her own special and pet easy-chair before the bright fire, Becky – with a coal smudge on her nose and several on her apron, with her poor little cap hanging half off her head, and an empty coal-box on the floor near her – sat fast asleep, tired out beyond even the endurance of her hard-working young body. She had been sent up to put the bedrooms in order for the evening. There were a great many of them, and she had been running about all day. Sara's rooms she had saved until the last. They were not like the other rooms, which were plain and bare. Ordinary pupils were expected to be satisfied with mere necessaries. Sara's comfortable sitting-room seemed a bower of luxury to the scullery-maid, though it was, in fact, merely a nice, bright little room. But there were pictures and books in it, and curious things from India; there was a sofa and a low, soft chair; Emily sat in a chair of her own, with the air of a presiding goddess, and there was always a glowing fire and a polished grate. Becky saved it until the end of the afternoon's work, because it rested her to go into it, and she always hoped to snatch a few minutes to sit down in the soft chair and look about her, and think about the wonderful good fortune of the child who owned such surroundings and who went out on the cold days in beautiful hats and coats one tried to catch a glimpse of through the area railing.

On this afternoon, when she had sat down, the sensation of relief to her short, aching legs had been so wonderful and delightful that it had seemed to soothe her whole body, and the glow of warmth and comfort from the fire had crept over her like a spell, until, as she looked at the red coals, a tired, slow smile stole over her smudged face, her head nodded forward without her being aware of it, her eyes drooped, and she fell fast asleep. She had really been only about ten minutes in the room when Sara entered, but she was in as deep a sleep as if she had been, like the Sleeping Beauty, slumbering for a hundred years. But she did not look – poor Becky! – like a Sleeping Beauty at all. She looked only like an ugly, stunted, worn-out little scullery drudge.

Sara seemed as much unlike her as if she were a creature from another world.

On this particular afternoon she had been taking her dancing lesson, and the afternoon on which the dancing-master appeared was rather a grand occasion at the seminary, though it occurred every week. The pupils were attired in their prettiest frocks, and as Sara danced particularly well, she was very much brought forward, and Mariette was requested to make her as diaphanous and fine as possible.

To-day a frock the colour of a rose had been put on her, and Mariette had bought some real buds and made her a wreath to wear on her black locks. She had been learning a new, delightful dance in which she had been skimming and flying about the room, like a large rose-coloured butterfly, and the enjoyment and exercise had brought a brilliant, happy glow into her face.

When she entered the room she floated in with a few of the butterfly steps – and there sat Becky, nodding her cap sideways off her head.

'Oh!' cried Sara softly when she saw her. 'That poor thing!'

It did not occur to her to feel cross at finding her pet chair occupied by the small, dingy figure. To tell the truth, she was quite glad to find it there. When the ill-used heroine of her story wakened, she could talk to her. She crept toward her quietly, and stood looking at her. Becky gave a little snore.

'I wish she'd waken herself,' Sara said. 'I don't like to waken her. But Miss Minchin would be cross if she found out. I'll just wait a few minutes.'

She took a seat on the edge of the table, and sat swinging her slim, rose-coloured legs, and wondering what it would be best to do. Miss Amelia might come in at any moment, and if she did, Becky would be sure to be scolded.

'But she is so tired,' she thought. 'She *is* so tired!'

A piece of flaming coal ended her perplexity for her that very moment. It broke off from a large lump and fell on to the fender. Becky started, and opened her eyes with a frightened gasp. She did not know she had fallen asleep. She had only sat down for one moment and felt the beautiful glow – and here she found herself staring in wild alarm at the wonderful pupil, who sat perched quite near her, like a rose-coloured fairy, with interested eyes.

She sprang up and clutched at her cap. She felt it dangling over her ear, and tried wildly to put it straight. Oh, she had got herself into trouble now with a vengeance! To have impudently fallen asleep on such a young lady's chair! She would be turned out of doors without wages.

She made a sound like a big breathless sob.

'Oh, miss! Oh, miss!' she stuttered. 'I arst yer pardon, miss! Oh, I do, miss!'

Sara jumped down, and came quite close to her.

'Don't be frightened,' she said, quite as if she had been speaking to a little girl like herself. 'It doesn't matter the least bit.'

'I didn't go to do it, miss,' protested Becky. 'It was the warm fire – an' me bein' so tired. It – *wasn't* imperence!'

Sara broke into a friendly little laugh, and put her hand on her shoulder.

'You were tired,' she said; 'you could not help it. You are not really awake yet.'

How poor Becky stared at her! In fact, she had never heard such a nice, friendly sound in any one's voice before. She was used to being ordered about and scolded, and having her ears boxed. And this one – in her rose-coloured dancing afternoon splendour – was looking at her as if she were not a culprit at all – as if she had a right to be tired – even to fall asleep! The touch of the soft, slim little paw on her shoulder was the most amazing thing she had ever known.

'Ain't – ain't yer angry, miss?' she gasped. 'Ain't yer goin' to tell the missus?'

'No,' cried out Sara. 'Of course I'm not.'

The woeful fright in the coal-smutted face made her suddenly so sorry that she could scarcely bear it. One of her queer thoughts rushed into her mind. She put her hand against Becky's cheek.

'Why,' she said, 'we are just the same – I am only a little girl like you. It's just an accident that I am not you, and you are not me!'

Becky did not understand in the least. Her mind could not grasp such amazing thoughts, and 'an accident' meant to her a calamity in which someone was run over or fell off a ladder and was carried to 'the 'orspital'.

'A' accident, miss,' she fluttered respectfully. 'Is it?'

'Yes,' Sara answered, and she looked at her dreamily for a moment. But the next she spoke in a different tone. She realized that Becky did not know what she meant.

'Have you done your work?' she asked. 'Dare you stay here a few minutes?'

Becky lost her breath again.

'Here, miss? Me?'

Sara ran to the door, opened it, and looked out and listened.

'No one is anywhere about,' she explained. 'If your bedrooms are finished, perhaps you might stay a tiny while. I thought – perhaps – you might like a piece of cake.'

The next ten minutes seemed to Becky like a sort of delirium. Sara opened a cupboard, and gave her a thick slice of cake. She seemed to rejoice when it was devoured in hungry bites. She talked and asked questions, and laughed until Becky's fears actually began to calm themselves, and she once or twice gathered boldness enough to ask a question or so herself, daring as she felt it to be.

'Is that——' she ventured, looking longingly at the rose-coloured frock. And she asked it almost in a whisper. 'Is that there your best?'

'It is one of my dancing frocks,' answered Sara. 'I like it; don't you?'

For a few seconds Becky was almost speechless with admiration. Then she said in an awed voice:

'Once I see a princess. I was standin' in the street with the crowd outside Covin' Garden, watchin' the swells go inter the operer. An' there was one every one stared at most. They ses to each other: "That's the princess." She was a growed-up young lady, but she was pink all over – gownd an' cloak, an' flowers an all. I called her to mind the minnit I see you, sittin' there on the table, miss. You looked like her.'

'I've often thought,' said Sara, in her reflecting voice, 'that I should like to be a princess; I wonder what it feels like. I believe I will begin pretending I am one.'

Becky stared at her admiringly, and, as before, did not understand her in the least. She watched her with a sort of adoration. Very soon Sara left her reflections and turned to her with a new question.

'Becky,' she said, 'weren't you listening to that story?'

'Yes, miss,' confessed Becky, a little alarmed again.

'I knowed I hadn't orter, but it was that beautiful I – I couldn't help it.'

'I liked you to listen to it,' said Sara. 'If you tell stories, you like nothing so much as to tell them to people who want to listen. I don't know why it is. Would you like to hear the rest?'

Becky lost her breath again.

'Me hear it?' she cried. 'Like as if I was a pupil, miss! All about the

Prince – and the little white Mer-babies swimming about laughing –
with stars in their hair?'

Sara nodded.

'You haven't time to hear it now, I'm afraid,' she said, 'but if you
will tell me just what time you come to do my rooms, I will try to be
here and tell you a bit of it every day until it is finished. It's a lovely
long one – and I'm always putting new bits to it.'

'Then,' breathed Becky devoutly, 'I wouldn't mind *how* heavy the
coal-boxes was – or *what* the cook done to me, if – if I might have that
to think of.'

'You may,' said Sara, 'I'll tell it *all* to you.'

When Becky went downstairs, she was not the same Becky who
had staggered up, loaded down by the weight of the coal-scuttle. She
had an extra piece of cake in her pocket, and she had been fed and
warmed, but not only by cake and fire. Something else had warmed
and fed her, and the something else was Sara.

When she was gone Sara sat on her favourite perch on the end of
her table. Her feet were on a chair, her elbows on her knees, and her
chin in her hands.

'If I *was* a princess – a real princess,' she murmured, 'I could
scatter largess to the populace. But even if I am only a pretend
princess, I can invent little things to do for people. Things like this.
She was just as happy as if it was largess. I'll pretend that to do things
people like is scattering largess. I've scattered largess.'

6 The Diamond Mines

Not very long after this a very exciting thing happened. Not only Sara, but the entire school, found it exciting, and made it the chief subject of conversation for weeks after it occurred. In one of his letters Captain Crewe told a most interesting story. A friend who had been at school with him when he was a boy had unexpectedly come to see him in India. He was the owner of a large tract of land upon which diamonds had been found, and he was engaged in developing the mines. If all went as was confidently expected, he would become possessed of such wealth as it made one dizzy to think of; and because he was fond of the friend of his school days, he had given him an opportunity to share in the enormous fortune by becoming a partner in his scheme. This, at least, was what Sara gathered from his letters. It is true that any other business scheme, however magnificent, would have had but small attraction for her or for the schoolroom; but 'diamond mines' sounded so like the 'Arabian Nights' that no one could be indifferent. Sara thought them enchanting, and painted pictures, for Ermengarde and Lottie, of labyrinthine passages in the bowels of the earth, where sparkling stones studded the walls and roofs and ceilings, and strange, dark men dug them out with heavy picks. Ermengarde delighted in the story, and Lottie insisted on its being retold to her every evening. Lavinia was very spiteful about it, and told Jessie that she didn't believe such things as diamond mines existed.

'My mamma has a diamond ring which cost forty pounds,' she said. 'And it is not a big one, either. If there were mines full of diamonds, people would be so rich it would be ridiculous.'

'Perhaps Sara will be so rich that she will be ridiculous,' giggled Jessie.

'She's ridiculous without being rich,' Lavinia sniffed.

'I believe you hate her,' said Jessie.

'No, I don't,' snapped Lavinia. 'But I don't believe in mines full of diamonds.'

'Well, people have to get them from somewhere,' said Jessie. 'Lavinia' – with a new giggle – 'what do you think Gertrude says?'

'I don't know, I'm sure; and I don't care if it's something more about that everlasting Sara.'

'Well, it is. One of her "pretends" is that she is a princess. She plays it all the time – even in school. She says it makes her learn her lessons better. She wants Ermengarde to be one, too, but Ermengarde says she is too fat.'

'She *is* too fat,' said Lavinia. 'And Sara is too thin.'

Naturally, Jessie giggled again.

'She says it has nothing to do with what you look like, or what you have. It has only to do with what you *think* of, and what you *do*.'

'I suppose she thinks she could be a princess if she was a beggar,' said Lavinia. 'Let us begin to call her "Your Royal Highness".'

Lessons for the day were over, and they were sitting before the schoolroom fire, enjoying the time they liked best. It was the time when Miss Minchin and Miss Amelia were taking their tea in the sitting-room sacred to themselves. At this hour a great deal of talking was done, and a great many secrets changed hands, particularly if the younger pupils behaved themselves well, and did not squabble or run about noisily, which it must be confessed they usually did. When they made an uproar the older girls usually interfered with scoldings and shakes. They were expected to keep order, and there was danger that, if they did not, Miss Minchin or Miss Amelia would appear and put an end to festivities. Even as Lavinia spoke the door opened and Sara entered with Lottie, whose habit was to trot everywhere after her like a little dog.

'There she is, with that horrid child!' exclaimed Lavinia in a whisper. 'If she's so fond of her, why doesn't she keep her in her own room? She will begin howling about something in five minutes.'

It happened that Lottie had been seized with a sudden desire to play in the schoolroom, and had begged her adopted parent to come with her. She joined a group of little ones who were playing in a corner. Sara curled herself up in the window-seat, opened a book, and began to read. It was a book about the French Revolution, and she was soon lost in a harrowing picture of the prisoners in the Bastille – men who had spent so many years in dungeons that when they were dragged out by those who rescued them, their long, grey hair and beards almost hid their faces, and they had forgotten that an outside world existed at all, and were like beings in a dream.

She was so far away from the schoolroom that it was not agreeable to be dragged back suddenly by a howl from Lottie. Never did she find anything so difficult as to keep herself from losing her temper when she was suddenly disturbed while absorbed in a book. People who are fond of books know the feeling of irritation which sweeps over them at such a moment. The temptation to be unreasonable and snappish is one not easy to manage.

'It makes me feel as if something had hit me,' Sara had told Ermengarde once in confidence. 'And as if I want to hit back. I have to remember things quickly to keep from saying something ill-tempered.'

She had to remember things quickly when she laid her book on the window-seat and jumped down from her comfortable corner.

Lottie had been sliding across the schoolroom floor, and, having first irritated Lavinia and Jessie by making a noise, had ended by falling down and hurting her fat knee. She was screaming and dancing up and down in the midst of a group of friends and enemies, who were alternately coaxing and scolding her.

'Stop this minute, you cry-baby! Stop this minute!' Lavinia commanded.

'I'm not a cry-baby – I'm not!' wailed Lottie. 'Sara, Sa-ra!'

'If she doesn't stop, Miss Minchin will hear her,' cried Jessie. 'Lottie darling, I'll give you a penny!'

'I don't want your penny,' sobbed Lottie; and she looked down at the fat knee, and, seeing a drop of blood on it, burst forth again.

Sara flew across the room and, kneeling down, put her arms round her.

'Now, Lottie,' she said. 'Now, Lottie, you *promised* Sara.'

'She said I was a cry-baby,' wept Lottie.

Sara patted her, but spoke in the steady voice Lottie knew.

'But if you cry, you will be one, Lottie pet. You *promised*.'

Lottie remembered that she had promised, but she preferred to lift up her voice.

'I haven't any mamma,' she proclaimed. 'I haven't – a bit – of mamma.'

'Yes, you have,' said Sara cheerfully. 'Have you forgotten? Don't you know that Sara is your mamma? Don't you want Sara for your mamma?'

Lottie cuddled up to her with a consoled sniff.

'Come and sit in the window-seat with me,' Sara went on, 'and I'll whisper a story to you.'

'Will you?' whimpered Lottie. 'Will you – tell me – about the diamond mines?'

'The diamond mines?' broke out Lavinia. 'Nasty, little spoiled thing, I should like to *slap* her!'

Sara got up quickly on her feet. It must be remembered that she had been very deeply absorbed in the book about the Bastille, and she had had to recall several things rapidly when she realized that she must go and take care of her adopted child. She was not an angel, and she was not fond of Lavinia.

'Well,' she said, with some fire, 'I should like to slap *you* – but I don't want to slap you!' restraining herself. 'At least I both want to slap you – and I should *like* to slap you – but I *won't* slap you. We are not little gutter children. We are both old enough to know better.'

Here was Lavinia's opportunity.

'Ah, yes, your royal highness,' she said. 'We are princesses, I believe. At least one of us is. The school ought to be very fashionable now Miss Minchin has a princess for a pupil.'

Sara started towards her. She looked as if she were going to box her ears. Perhaps she was. Her trick of pretending things was the joy of her life. She never spoke of it to girls she was not fond of. Her new 'pretend' about being a princess was very near to her heart, and she was shy and sensitive about it. She had meant it to be rather a secret, and here was Lavinia deriding it before nearly all the school. She felt the blood rush up into her face and tingle in her ears. She only just saved herself. If you were a princess, you did not fly into rages. Her hand dropped, and she stood quite still a moment. When she spoke it was in a quiet, steady voice; she held her head up, and everybody listened to her.

'It's true,' she said. 'Sometimes I do pretend I am a princess. I pretend I am a princess, so that I can try and behave like one.'

Lavinia could not think of exactly the right thing to say. Several times she had found that she could not think of a satisfactory reply when she was dealing with Sara. The reason of this was that, somehow, the rest always seemed to be vaguely in sympathy with her opponent. She saw now that they were pricking up their ears interestedly. The truth was, they liked princesses, and they all hoped they might hear something more definite about this one, and drew nearer Sara accordingly.

Lavinia could only invent one remark, and it fell rather flat.

'Dear me!' she said, 'I hope, when you ascend the throne, you won't forget us.'

'I won't,' said Sara, and she did not utter another word, but stood quite still, and stared at her steadily as she saw her take Jessie's arm and turn away.

After this, the girls who were jealous of her used to speak of her as 'Princess Sara' whenever they wished to be particularly disdainful, and those who were fond of her gave her the name among themselves as a term of affection. No one called her 'princess' instead of 'Sara', but her adorers were much pleased with the picturesqueness and grandeur of the title, and Miss Minchin, hearing of it, mentioned it more than once to visiting parents, feeling that it rather suggested a sort of royal boarding-school.

To Becky it seemed the most appropriate thing in the world. The acquaintance begun on the foggy afternoon when she had jumped up terrified from her sleep in the comfortable chair, had ripened and grown, though it must be confessed that Miss Minchin and Miss Amelia knew very little about it. They were aware that Sara was 'kind' to the scullery-maid, but they knew nothing of certain delightful moments snatched perilously when, the upstairs rooms being set in order with lightning rapidity, Sara's sitting-room was reached, and the heavy coal-box set down with a sigh of joy. At such times stories were told by instalments, things of a satisfying nature were either produced and eaten or hastily tucked into pockets to be disposed of at night, when Becky went upstairs to her attic to bed.

'But I has to eat 'em careful, miss,' she said once, ' 'cos if I leave the crumbs the rats come out to get 'em.'

'Rats!' exclaimed Sara, in horror. 'Are there *rats* there?'

'Lots of 'em, miss,' Becky answered in quite a matter-of-fact manner. 'There mostly is rats an' mice in attics. You gets used to the noise they makes scuttling about. I've got so I don't mind 'em s' long as they don't run over my piller.'

'Ugh!' said Sara.

'You gets used to anythin' after a bit,' said Becky. 'You have to, miss, if you're born a scullery-maid. I'd rather have rats than cockroaches.'

'So would I,' said Sara 'I suppose you might make friends with a rat in time, but I don't believe I should like to make friends with a cockroach.'

Sometimes Becky did not dare to spend more than a few minutes in the bright, warm room, and when this was the case perhaps only a few words could be exchanged, and a small purchase slipped into the old-fashioned pocket Becky carried under her dress-skirt, tied round her waist with a band of tape. The search for and discovery of satisfying things to eat which could be packed into small compass, added a new interest to Sara's existence. When she drove or walked out, she used to look into shop windows eagerly. The first time it occurred to her to bring home two or three little meat-pies, she felt that she had hit upon a discovery. When she exhibited them, Becky's eyes quite sparkled.

'Oh, miss!' she murmured. 'Them will be nice an' fillin'. It's fillin'ness that's best. Sponge-cake's a 'evingly thing, but it melts away like – if you understand, miss. These'll just *stay* in yer stummick.'

'Well,' hesitated Sara, 'I don't think it would be good if they stayed always, but I do believe they will be satisfying.'

They were satisfying – and so were beef sandwiches, bought at a cook-shop – and so were rolls and Bologna sausage. In time, Becky began to lose her hungry, tired feeling, and the coal-box did not seem so unbearably heavy.

However heavy it was, and whatever the temper of the cook, and the hardness of the work heaped upon her shoulders, she had always the chance of the afternoon to look forward to – the chance that Miss Sara would be able to be in her sitting-room. In fact, the mere seeing of Miss Sara would have been enough without meat-pies. If there was time only for a few words, they were always friendly, merry words that put heart into one; and if there was time for more, then there was an instalment of a story to be told, or some other thing one remembered afterwards and sometimes lay awake in one's bed in the attic to think over. Sara – who was only doing what she unconsciously liked better than anything else, Nature having made her for a giver – had not the least idea what she meant to poor Becky, and how wonderful a benefactor she seemed. If Nature has made you for a giver, your hands are born open, and so is your heart; and though there may be times when your hands are empty, your heart is always full, and you can give things out of that – warm things, kind things, sweet things – help and comfort and laughter – and sometimes gay, kind laughter is the best help of all.

Becky had scarcely known what laughter was through all her poor, little hard-driven life. Sara made her laugh, and laughed with her; and, though neither of them quite knew it, the laughter was as 'fillin'' as the meat-pies.

A few weeks before Sara's eleventh birthday a letter came to her from her father, which did not seem to be written in such boyish high spirits as usual. He was not very well, and was evidently overweighted by the business connected with the diamond mines.

'You see, little Sara,' he wrote, 'your daddy is not a business man at all, and figures and documents bother him. He does not really understand them, and all this seems so enormous. Perhaps, if I was not feverish, I should not be awake, tossing about, one half of the night, and spend the other half in troublesome dreams. If my little missus were here, I dare say she would give me some solemn, good advice. You would, wouldn't you, little missus?'

One of his many jokes had been to call her his 'little missus' because she had such an old-fashioned air.

He had made wonderful preparations for her birthday. Among other things, a new doll had been ordered in Paris, and her wardrobe was to be, indeed, a marvel of splendid perfection. When she had replied to the letter asking her if the doll would be an acceptable present, Sara had been very quaint.

'I am getting very old,' she wrote. 'You see, I shall never live to have another doll given me. This will be my last doll. There is something solemn about it. If I could write poetry, I am sure a poem about 'A Last Doll' would be very nice. But I cannot write poetry. I have tried, and it made me laugh. It did not sound like Watts or Coleridge or Shakespeare at all. No one could ever take Emily's place, but I should respect the Last Doll very much; and I am sure the school would love it. They all like dolls, though some of the big ones – the almost fifteen ones – pretend they are too grown-up.'

Captain Crewe had a splitting headache when he read this letter in his bungalow in India. The table before him was heaped with papers and letters which were alarming him and filling him with anxious dread, but he laughed as he had not laughed for weeks.

'Oh,' he said, 'she's better fun every year she lives. God grant this business may right itself and leave me free to run home and see her. What wouldn't I give to have her little arms round my neck this minute! What *wouldn't* I give!'

The birthday was to be celebrated by great festivities. The schoolroom was to be decorated, and there was to be a party. The boxes containing the presents were to be opened with great ceremony, and there was to be a glittering feast spread in Miss Minchin's sacred room. When the day arrived the whole house was in a whirl of excitement. How the morning passed nobody quite knew, because there seemed such preparations to be made. The schoolroom was being decked with garlands of holly; the desks had been moved away, and red covers had been put on the forms which were arrayed round the room against the wall.

When Sara went into her sitting-room in the morning, she found on the table a small, dumpy package, tied up in a piece of brown paper.

She knew it was a present, and she thought she could guess whom it came from. She opened it quite tenderly. It was a square pin-cushion, made of not quite clean red flannel, and black pins had been stuck carefully into it to form the words, 'Menny hapy returns.'

'Oh!' cried Sara, with a warm feeling in her heart. 'What pains she has taken!' I like it so, it – it makes me feel sorrowful.'

But the next moment she was mystified. On the under-side of the pin-cushion was secured a card bearing in neat letters the name 'Miss Amelia Minchin.'

Sara turned it over and over.

'Miss Amelia!' she said to herself. 'How *can* it be!'

And just at that very moment she heard the door being cautiously pushed open, and saw Becky peeping round it.

There was an affectionate, happy grin on her face, and she shuffled forward and stood nervously pulling at her fingers.

'Do yer like it, Miss Sara?' she said. 'Do yer?'

'Like it?' cried Sara. 'You darling Becky, you made it all yourself.'

Becky gave a hysteric but joyful sniff, and her eyes looked quite moist with delight.

'It ain't nothin' but flannin, an' the flannin ain't new; but I wanted to give yer somethin' an' I made it of nights. I knew yer could *pretend* it was satin with diamond pins in. *I* tried to when I was makin' it. The card, miss,' rather doubtfully, ''t warn't wrong of me to pick it up out o' the dust-bin, was it? Miss 'Meliar had throwed it away. I hadn't no card o' my own, an' I knowed it wouldn't be a proper presink if I didn't pin a card on – so I pinned Miss 'Meliar's.'

Sara flew at her and hugged her. She could not have told herself or any one else why there was a lump in her throat.

'Oh, Becky!' she cried out, with a queer little laugh. 'I love you, Becky – I do, I do!'

'Oh, miss!' breathed Becky. 'Thank yer, miss, kindly; it ain't good enough for that. The – the flannin wasn't new.'

7 The Diamond Mines Again

When Sara entered the holly-hung schoolroom in the afternoon, she did so as the head of a sort of procession. Miss Minchin, in her grandest silk dress, led her by the hand. A manservant followed, carrying the box containing the Last Doll, a housemaid carried a second box, and Becky brought up the rear, carrying a third and wearing a clean apron and a new cap. Sara would have much preferred to enter in the usual way, but Miss Minchin had sent for her, and, after an interview in her private sitting-room, had expressed her wishes.

'This is not an ordinary occasion,' she said. 'I do not desire that it should be treated as one.'

So Sara was led grandly in and felt shy when, on her entry, the big girls stared at her and touched each other's elbows, and the little ones began to squirm joyously in their seats.

'Silence, young ladies!' said Miss Minchin, at the murmur which arose. 'James, place the box on the table and remove the lid. Emma, put yours upon a chair. Becky!' suddenly and severely.

Becky had quite forgotten herself in her excitement, and was grinning at Lottie, who was wriggling with rapturous expectation. She almost dropped her box, the disapproving voice so startled her, and her frightened, bobbing courtesy of apology was so funny that Lavinia and Jessie tittered.

'It is not your place to look at the young ladies,' said Miss Minchin. 'You forget yourself. Put your box down.'

Becky obeyed with alarmed haste and hastily backed toward the door.

'You may leave us,' Miss Minchin announced to the servants with a wave of her hand.

'"Please let her stay – because it is my birthday"'

Becky stepped aside respectfully to allow the superior servants to pass out first. She could not help casting a longing glance at the box on the table. Something made of blue satin was peeping from between the folds of tissue-paper.

'If you please, Miss Minchin,' said Sara suddenly, 'mayn't Becky stay?'

It was a bold thing to do. Miss Minchin was betrayed into something like a slight jump. Then she put her eyeglass up, and gazed at her show pupil disturbedly.

'Becky!' she exclaimed. 'My dearest Sara!'

Sara advanced a step toward her.

'I want her because I know she will like to see the presents,' she explained. 'She is a little girl too, you know.'

Miss Minchin was scandalized. She glanced from one figure to other.

'My dear Sara,' she said, 'Becky is the scullery-maid. Scullery-maids – er – are not little girls.'

It really had not occurred to her to think of them in that light. Scullery-maids were machines who carried coal-scuttles and made fires.

'But Becky is,' said Sara. 'And I know she would enjoy herself. Please let her stay – because it is my birthday.'

Miss Minchin replied with much dignity:

'As you ask it as a birthday favour – she may stay. Rebecca, thank Miss Sara for her great kindness.'

Becky had been backing into the corner, twisting the hem of her apron in delighted suspense. She came forward, bobbing courtesies, but between Sara's eyes and her own there passed a gleam of friendly understanding, while her words tumbled over each other.

'Oh, if you please, miss! I'm that grateful, miss! I did want to see the doll, miss, that I did. Thank you, miss. And thank you, ma'am – turning and making an alarmed bob to Miss Minchin – 'for letting me take the liberty.'

Miss Minchin waved her hand again – this time it was in the direction of the corner near the door.

'Go and stand there,' she commanded. 'Not too near the young ladies.'

Becky went to her place, grinning. She did not care where she was sent, so that she might have the luck of being inside the room, instead of being down-stairs in the scullery, while these delights were going on. She did not even mind when Miss Minchin cleared her throat ominously and spoke again.

'Now, young ladies, I have a few words to say to you,' she announced.

'She's going to make a speech,' whispered one of the girls. 'I wish it was over.'

Sara felt rather uncomfortable. As this was her party, it was probable that the speech was about her. It is not agreeable to stand in a schoolroom and have a speech made about you.

'You are aware, young ladies,' the speech began – for it was a speech – 'that dear Sara is eleven years old to-day.'

'*Dear* Sara!' murmured Lavinia.

'Several of you here have also been eleven years old, but Sara's birthdays are rather different from other little girls' birthdays. When she is older she will be heiress to a large fortune, which it will be her duty to spend in a meritorious manner.'

'The diamond mines,' giggled Jessie, in a whisper.

Sara did not hear her; but as she stood with her green-grey eyes fixed steadily on Miss Minchin, she felt herself growing rather hot. When Miss Minchin talked about money, she felt somehow that she always hated her – and, of course, it was disrespectful to hate grown-up people.

'When her dear papa, Captain Crewe, brought her from India and gave her into my care,' the speech proceeded, 'he said to me, in a jesting way, "I am afraid she will be very rich, Miss Minchin." My reply was, "Her education at my seminary, Captain Crewe, shall be such as will adorn the largest fortune." Sara has become my most accomplished pupil. Her French and her dancing are a credit to the seminary. Her manners – which have caused you to call her Princess Sara – are perfect. Her amiability she exhibits by giving you this afternoon's party. I hope you appreciate her generosity. I wish you to express your appreciation of it by saying aloud all together, "Thank you, Sara!"'

The entire schoolroom rose to its feet as it had done the morning Sara remembered so well.

'Thank you, Sara!' it said, and it must be confessed that Lottie jumped up and down. Sara looked rather shy for a moment. She made a courtesy – and it was a very nice one.

'Thank you,' she said, 'for coming to my party.'

'Very pretty, indeed, Sara,' approved Miss Minchin. 'That is what a real princess does when the populace applauds her. Lavinia' – scathingly – 'the sound you just made was extremely like a snort. If you are jealous of your fellow-pupil, I beg you will express your feelings in some more ladylike manner. Now I will leave you to enjoy yourselves.'

The instant she had swept out of the room the spell her presence always had upon them was broken. The door had scarcely closed before every seat was empty. The little girls jumped or tumbled out of theirs; the older ones wasted no time in deserting theirs. There was a rush toward the boxes. Sara had bent over one of them with a delighted face.

'These are books, I know,' she said.

The little children broke into a rueful murmur, and Ermengarde looked aghast.

'Does your papa send you books for a birthday present?' she exclaimed. 'Why, he's as bad as mine. Don't open them, Sara.'

'I like them,' Sara laughed, but she turned to the biggest box. When she took out the Last Doll it was so magnificent that the children uttered delighted groans of joy, and actually drew back to gaze at in breathless rapture.

'She is almost as big as Lottie,' someone gasped.

Lottie clapped her hands and danced about, giggling.

'She's dressed for the theatre,' said Lavinia. 'Her cloak is lined with ermine.'

'Oh!' cried Ermengarde, darting forward, she has an opera-glass in her hand – a blue-and-gold one.'

'Here is her trunk,' said Sara. 'Let us open it and look at her things.'

She sat down upon the floor and turned the key. The children crowded clamouring around her, as she lifted tray after tray and revealed their contents. Never had the schoolroom been in such an uproar. There were lace collars and silk stockings and handkerchiefs; there was a jewel-case containing a necklace and a tiara which looked quite as if they were made of real diamonds; there was a long sealskin and muff; there were ball dresses and walking dresses and visiting dresses; there were hats and tea-gowns and fans. Even Lavinia and Jessie forgot that they were too elderly to care for dolls, and uttered exclamations of delight and caught up things to look at them.

'Suppose,' Sara said, as she stood by the table, putting a large, black-velvet hat on the impassively-smiling owner of all these splendours – 'suppose she understands human talk and feels proud of being admired.'

'You are always supposing things,' said Lavinia, and her air was very superior.

'I know I am,' said Sara undisturbedly. 'I like it. There is nothing so nice as supposing. It's almost like being a fairy. If you suppose anything hard enough it seems as if it were real.'

'It's all very well to suppose things if you have everything,' said Lavinia. 'Could you suppose and pretend if you were a beggar and lived in a garret?'

Sara stopped arranging the Last Doll's ostrich plumes, and looked thoughtful.

'I *believe* I could,' she said. 'If one was a beggar, one would have to suppose and pretend all the time. But it mightn't be easy.'

She often thought afterward how strange it was that just as she had finished saying this – just at that very moment – Miss Amelia came into the room.

'Sara,' she said, 'your papa's solicitor, Mr. Barrow, has called to see Miss Minchin, and, as she must talk to him alone and the refreshments are laid in her parlour, you had all better come and have your feast now, so that my sister can have her interview here in the schoolroom.'

Refreshments were not likely to be disdained at any hour, and many pairs of eyes gleamed. Miss Amelia arranged the procession into decorum, and then, with Sara at her side heading it, she led it away, leaving the Last Doll sitting upon a chair with the glories of her wardrobe scattered about her; dresses and coats hung upon chair backs, piles of lace-frilled petticoats lying upon their seats.

Becky, who was not expected to partake of refreshments, had the indiscretion to linger a moment to look at these beauties – it really was an indiscretion.

'Go back to your work, Becky,' Miss Amelia had said; but she stopped to reverently pick up first a muff and then a coat, and while she stood looking at them adoringly, she heard Miss Minchin upon the threshold, and, being smitten with terror at the thought of being accused of taking liberties, she rashly darted under the table, which hid her by its tablecloth.

Miss Minchin came into the room, accompanied by a sharp-featured, dry little gentleman, who looked rather disturbed. Miss Minchin herself also looked rather disturbed, it must be admitted, and she gazed at the dry little gentleman with an irritated and puzzled expression.

She sat down with stiff dignity, and waved him to a chair.

'Pray be seated, Mr. Barrow,' she said.

Mr. Barrow did not sit down at once. His attention seemed attracted by the Last Doll and the things which surrounded her. He settled his eyeglasses and looked at them in nervous disapproval. The Last Doll herself did not seem to mind this in the least. She merely sat upright and returned his gaze indifferently.

'A hundred pounds,' Mr. Barrow remarked succinctly. 'All expensive material, and made at a Parisian modiste's. He spent money lavishly enough, that young man.'

Miss Minchin felt offended. This seemed to be a disparagement of her best patron and was a liberty.

Even solicitors had no right to take liberties.

'I beg your pardon, Mr. Barrow,' she said stiffly. 'I do not understand.'

'Birthday presents,' said Mr. Barrow, in the same critical manner, 'to a child eleven years old! Mad extravagance, I call it.'

Miss Minchin drew herself up still more rigidly.

'Captain Crewe is a man of fortune,' she said. 'The diamond mines alone——'

Mr. Barrow wheeled round upon her.

'Diamond mines!' he broke out. 'There are none! Never were!'
Miss Minchin actually got up from her chair.

'What!' she cried. 'What do you mean?'

'At any rate,' answered Mr. Barrow quite snappishly, 'it would
have been much better if there never had been any.'

'Any diamond mines?' ejaculated Miss Minchin, catching at the
back of a chair, and feeling as if a splendid dream was fading away from
her.

'Diamond mines spell ruin oftener than they spell wealth,' said
Mr. Barrow. 'When a man is in the hands of a very dear friend, and is
not a business man himself, he had better steer clear of the dear
friend's diamond mines, or gold mines, or any other kind of mines dear
friends want his money to put into. The late Captain Crewe——'

Here Miss Minchin stopped him with a gasp.

'The *late* Captain Crewe!' she cried out, 'the *late*! You don't come
to tell me that Captain Crewe is——'

'He's dead, ma'am,' Mr. Barrow answered with jerky brusque-
ness. 'Died of jungle fever and business troubles combined. The
jungle fever might not have killed him if he had not been driven mad
by the business troubles, and the business troubles might not have put
an end to him if the jungle fever had not assisted. Captain Crewe is
dead!'

Miss Minchin dropped into her chair again. The words he had
spoken filled her with alarm.

'What *were* his business troubles?' she said. 'What *were* they?'

'Diamond mines,' answered Mr. Barrow, 'and dear friends – and
ruin.'

Miss Minchin lost her breath.

'Ruin!' she gasped out.

'Lost every penny. That young man had too much money. The
dear friend was mad on the subject of the diamond mine. He put all his
own money into it, and all Captain Crewe's. Then the dear friend ran
away – Captain Crewe was already stricken with fever when the news
came. The shock was too much for him. He died delirious, raving
about his little girl – and didn't leave a penny.'

Now Miss Minchin understood, and never had she received such a blow in her life. Her show pupil, her show patron, swept away from the select seminary at one blow. She felt as if she had been outraged and robbed, and that Captain Crewe and Sara and Mr. Barrow were equally to blame.

'Do you mean to tell me,' she cried out, 'that he left *nothing*? That Sara will have no fortune? That the child is a beggar? That she is left on my hands a little pauper instead of an heiress?'

Mr. Barrow was a shrewd business man, and felt it as well to make his own freedom from responsibility quite clear without any delay.

'She is certainly left a beggar,' he replied. 'And she is certainly left on your hands, ma'am, as she hasn't a relation in the world that we know of.'

Miss Minchin started forward. She looked as if she was going to open the door and rush out of the room, to stop the festivities going on joyfully and rather noisily that moment over the refreshments.

'It is monstrous!' she said. 'She's in my sitting-room at this moment, dressed in silk gauze and lace petticoats, giving a party at my expense.'

'She's giving it at your expense, ma'am, if she's giving it,' said Mr. Barrow calmly. 'Barrow and Skipworth are not responsible for anything. There never was a cleaner sweep made of a man's fortune. Captain Crewe died without paying *our* last bill – and it was a big one.'

Miss Minchin turned back from the door in increased indignation. This was worse than any one could have dreamed of its being.

'That is what has happened to me!' she cried. 'I was always so sure of his payments that I went to all sorts of ridiculous expenses for the child. I paid the bills for that ridiculous doll and her ridiculous fantastic wardrobe. The child was to have anything she wanted. She has a carriage and a pony and a maid, and I've paid for all of them since the last cheque came.'

Mr. Barrow evidently did not intend to remain to listen to the story of Miss Minchin's grievances after he had made the position of his firm clear and related the mere dry facts. He did not feel any particular sympathy for irate keepers of boarding-schools.

'You had better not pay for anything more ma'am,' he remarked, 'unless you want to make presents to the young lady. No one will remember you. She hasn't a brass farthing to call her own.'

'But what I am to do?' demanded Miss Minchin as if she felt it entirely his duty to make the matter right. 'What am I to do?'

'There isn't anything to do,' said Mr. Barrow folding up his eyeglasses and slipping them into his pocket. 'Captain Crewe is dead. The child is left a pauper. Nobody is responsible for her but you.'

'I am not responsible for her, and I refuse to be made responsible!' Miss Minchin became quite white with rage.

Mr. Barrow turned to go.

'I have nothing to do with that, madam,' he said uninterestedly. 'Barrow and Skipworth are not responsible. Very sorry the thing has happened, of course.'

'If you think she is to be foisted off on me, you are greatly mistaken,' Miss Minchin gasped. 'I have been robbed and cheated; I will turn her into the street!'

If she had not been so furious, she would have been too discreet to say quite so much. She saw herself burdened with an extravagantly brought-up child whom she had always resented, and she lost all self-control.

Mr. Barrow undisturbedly moved toward the door.

'I wouldn't do that, madam,' he commented, 'it wouldn't look well. Unpleasant story to get about in connection with the establishment. Pupil bundled out penniless and without friends.'

He was a clever business man, and he knew what he was saying. He also knew that Miss Minchin was a business woman, and would be shrewd enough to see the truth. She could not afford to do a thing which would make people speak of her as cruel and hard-hearted.

'Better keep her and make use of her,' he added. 'She's a clever child, I believe. You can get a good deal out of her as she grows older.'

'I will get a good deal out of her before she grows older!' exclaimed Miss Minchin.

'I am sure you will, ma'am,' said Mr. Barrow, with a little sinister smile. 'I am sure you will. Good morning!'

He bowed himself out and closed the door, and it must be confessed that Miss Minchin stood for a few moments and glared at it. What he had said was quite true. She knew it. She had absolutely no redress. Her show pupil had melted into nothingness, leaving only a friendless beggared little girl. Such money as she herself had advanced was lost and could not be regained.

And as she stood there breathless under her sense of injury, there fell upon her ears a burst of gay voices from her own sacred room, which had actually been given up for the feast. She could at least stop this.

But as she started toward the door it was opened by Miss Amelia, who, when she caught sight of the changed, angry face, fell back a step in alarm.

'What *is* the matter, sister?' she ejaculated.

Miss Minchin's voice was almost fierce when she answered:

'Where is Sara Crewe?'

Miss Amelia was bewildered.

'Sara?' she stammered. 'Why, she's with the children in your room, of course.'

'Has she a black frock in her sumptuous wardrobe?' in bitter irony.

'A black frock?' Miss Amelia stammered again. 'A *black* one?'

'She has frocks of every other colour. Has she a black one?'

Miss Amelia began to turn pale.

'No – ye-es!' she said. 'But it is too short for her. She has only the old black velvet, and she has outgrown it.'

'Go and tell her to take off that preposterous pink silk gauze, and put the black one on, whether it is too short or not. She has done with finery!'

Then Miss Amelia began to wring her fat hands and cry.

'Oh, sister!' she sniffed. 'Oh, sister! What *can* have happened?'

Miss Minchin wasted no words.

'Captain Crewe is dead,' she said. 'He has died without a penny. That spoiled, pampered, fanciful child is left a pauper on my hands.'

Miss Amelia sat down quite heavily in the nearest chair.

'Hundreds of pounds have I spent on nonsense for her. And I shall never see a penny of it. Put a stop to this ridiculous party of hers. Go and make her change her frock at once.'

'I?' panted Miss Amelia. 'M-must I go and tell her now?'

'This moment!' was the fierce answer. 'Don't sit staring like a goose. Go!'

Poor Miss Amelia was accustomed to being called a goose. She knew, in fact, that she was rather a goose, and that it was left to geese to do a great many disagreeable things. It was a somewhat embarrassing thing to go into the midst of a room full of delighted children, and tell the giver of the feast that she had suddenly been transformed into a little beggar, and must go upstairs and put on an old black frock which was too small for her. But the thing must be done. This was evidently not the time when questions might be asked.

She rubbed her eyes with her handkerchief until they looked quite red. After which she got up and went out of the room, without venturing to say another word. When her older sister looked and spoke as she had done just now, the wisest course to pursue was to obey orders without any comment. Miss Minchin walked across the room. She spoke to herself aloud without knowing that she was doing it. During the last year the story of the diamond mines had suggested all sorts of possibilities to her. Even proprietors of seminaries might make fortunes in stocks, with the aid of owners of mines. And now, instead of looking forward to gains, she was left to look back upon losses.

'The Princess Sara, indeed!' she said. 'The child has been pampered as if she were a *queen*!'

She was sweeping angrily past the corner table as she said it, and the next moment she started at the sound of a loud, sobbing sniff which issued from under the cover.

'What is that?' she exclaimed angrily. The loud, sobbing sniff was heard again, and she stooped and raised the hanging folds of the table-cover.

'How *dare* you!' she cried out. 'How *dare* you! Come out immediately!'

It was poor Becky who crawled out, and her cap was knocked on one side, and her face was red with repressed crying.

'If you please, 'm – it's me, mum,' she explained. 'I know I hadn't ought to. But I was lookin' at the doll, mum – an' I was frightened when you come in – an' slipped under the table.'

'You have been there all the time, listening,' said Miss Minchin.

'No, mum,' Becky protested, bobbing courtesies. 'Not listenin' – I thought I could slip out without your noticin', but I couldn't an' I had to stay. But I didn't listen, mum – I wouldn't for nothin'. But I couldn't help hearin'.'

Suddenly it seemed almost as if she lost all fear of the awful lady before her. She burst into fresh tears.

'Oh, please, 'm,' she said, 'I daresay you'll give me warnin', mum – but I'm so sorry for poor Miss Sara – I'm so sorry!'

'Leave the room!' ordered Miss Minchin.

Becky courtesied again, the tears openly streaming down her cheeks.

'Yes, 'm; I will, 'm,' she said trembling, 'but oh, I just wanted to arst you: Miss Sara – she's been such a rich young lady, an' she's been waited on, 'and and foot; an' what will she do now, mum, without no maid? If–if, oh please would you let me wait on her after I've done my pots an' kettles? I'd do 'em that quick – if you'd let me wait on her now she's poor. Oh' – breaking out afresh – 'poor little Miss Sara, mum – that was called a princess.'

Somehow, she made Miss Minchin feel more angry than ever. That the very scullery-maid should range herself on the side of this child – whom she realized more fully than ever that she had never liked – was too much. She actually stamped her foot.

'No – certainly not,' she said. 'She will wait on herself, and on other people, too. Leave the room this instant, or you'll leave your place.'

Becky threw her apron over her head and fled. She ran out of the room and down the steps into the scullery, and there she sat down among her pots and kettles, and wept as if her heart would break.

'It's exactly like ones in the stories,' she wailed. 'Them pore princess ones that was drove into the world.'

Miss Minchin had never looked quite so still and hard as she did when Sara came to her, a few hours later, in response to a message she had sent her.

Even by that time it seemed to Sara as if the birthday party had either been a dream or a thing which had happened years ago, and had happened in the life of quite another little girl.

Every sign of the festivities had been swept away; the holly had been removed from the schoolroom walls, and the forms and desks put back into their places. Miss Minchin's sitting-room looked as it always did – all traces of the feast were gone, and Miss Minchin had resumed her usual dress. The pupils had been ordered to lay aside their party frocks; and this having been done, they had returned to the schoolroom and huddled together in groups, whispering and talking excitedly.

'Tell Sara to come to my room,' Miss Minchin had said to her sister. 'And explain to her clearly that I will have no crying or unpleasant scenes.'

'Sister,' replied Miss Amelia, 'she is the strangest child I ever saw. She has actually made no fuss at all. You remember she made none when Captain Crewe went back to India. When I told her what had happened, she just stood quite still and looked at me without making a sound. Her eyes seemed to get bigger and bigger, and she went quite pale. When I had finished, she still stood for a few seconds, and then her chin began to shake, and she turned round and ran out of the room and upstairs. Several of the other children began to cry, but she did not seem to hear them or to be alive to anything but just what I was saying. It made me feel quite queer not to be answered; and when you tell anything sudden and strange, you expect people will say *something* – whatever it is.'

Nobody but Sara herself ever knew what had happened in her room after she had run upstairs and locked her door. In fact, she herself scarcely remembered anything but that she walked up and down, saying over and over again to herself in a voice which did not seem her own:

'My papa is dead! My papa is dead!'

Once she stopped before Emily, who sat watching her from her chair, and cried out wildly:

'Emily! Do you hear? Do you hear – papa is dead! He is dead in India – thousands of miles away.'

When she came into Miss Minchin's sitting-room in answer to her summons, her face was white and her eyes had dark rings around them. Her mouth was set as if she did not wish it to reveal what she had suffered and was suffering. She did not look in the least like the rose-

coloured butterfly child who had flown about from one of her treasures
to the other in the decorated schoolroom. She looked instead a strange,
desolate, almost grotesque little figure.

She had put on, without Mariette's help, the cast-aside black-
velvet frock. It was too short and tight, and her slender legs looked
long and thin, showing themselves from beneath the brief skirt. As she
had not found a piece of black ribbon, her short, thick, black hair
tumbled loosely about her face and contrasted strongly with its pallor.
She held Emily tightly in one arm, and Emily was swathed in a piece of
black material.

'Put down your doll,' said Miss Minchin. 'What do you mean by
bringing her here?'

'No,' Sara answered. 'I will not put her down. She is all I have. My
papa gave her to me.'

She had always made Miss Minchin feel secretly uncomfortable,
and she did so now. She did not speak with rudeness so much as with a
cold steadiness with which Miss Minchin felt it difficult to cope –
perhaps because she knew she was doing a heartless and inhuman
thing.

'You will have no time for dolls in future,' she said. 'You will have
to work and improve yourself and make yourself useful.'

Sara kept her big, strange eyes fixed on her, and said not a word.

'Everything will be very different now,' Miss Minchin went on. 'I
suppose Miss Amelia has explained matters to you.'

'Yes,' answered Sara. 'My papa is dead. He left me no money. I
am quite poor.'

'You are a beggar,' said Miss Minchin, her temper rising at the
recollection of what all this meant. 'It appears that you have no
relations and no home, and no one to take care of you.'

For a moment the thin, pale little face twitched, but Sara again
said nothing.

'What are you staring at?' demanded Miss Minchin sharply. 'Are
you so stupid that you cannot understand? I tell you that you are quite
alone in the world, and have no one to do anything for you, unless I
choose to keep you here out of charity.'

'I understand,' answered Sara, in a low tone; and there was a sound as if she had gulped down something which rose in her throat. 'I understand.'

'That doll,' cried Miss Minchin, pointing to the splendid birthday gift seated near – 'that ridiculous doll, with all her nonsensical extravagant things – I actually paid the bill for her!'

Sara turned her head toward the chair.

'The Last Doll,' she said. 'The Last Doll.' And her little mournful voice had an odd sound.

'The Last Doll, indeed!' said Miss Minchin. 'And she is mine, not yours. Everything you own is mine.'

'Please take it away from me, then,' said Sara. 'I do not want it.'

If she had cried and sobbed and seemed frightened, Miss Minchin might almost have had more patience with her. She was a woman who liked to domineer and feel her power, and as she looked at Sara's pale little steadfast face and heard her proud little voice, she quite felt as if her might was being set at naught.

'Don't put on grand airs,' she said. 'The time for that sort of thing is past. You are not a princess any longer. Your carriage and your pony will be sent away – your maid will be dismissed. You will wear your oldest and plainest clothes – your extravagant ones are no longer suited to your station. You are like Becky – you must work for your living.'

To her surprise, a faint gleam of light came into the child's eyes – a shade of relief.

'Can I work?' she said. 'If I can work it will not matter so much. What can I do?'

'You can do anything you are told,' was the answer. 'You are a sharp child, and pick up things readily. If you make yourself useful I may let you stay here. You speak French well, and you can help with the youngest children.'

'May I?' exclaimed Sara. 'Oh, please, let me! I know I can teach them, I like them and they like me.'

'Don't talk nonsense about people liking you,' said Miss Minchin. 'You will have to do more than teach the little ones. You will run errands and help in the kitchen as well as in the schoolroom. If you don't please me, you will be sent away. Remember that. Now go.'

Sara stood just a moment, looking at her. In her young soul she was thinking deep and strange things. Then she turned to leave the room.

'Stop!' said Miss Minchin. 'Don't you intend to thank me?'

Sara paused, and all the deep, strange thoughts surged up in her breast.

'What for?' she said.

'For my kindness to you,' replied Miss Minchin. 'For my kindness in giving you a home.'

Sara made two or three steps toward her. Her thin little chest heaved up and down, and she spoke in a strange, unchildishly fierce way.

'You are not kind,' she said. 'You are *not* kind, and it is *not* a home.' And she had turned and run out of the room before Miss Minchin could stop her or do anything but stare after her with stony anger.

She went up the stairs slowly, but panting for breath, and she held Emily tightly against her side.

'I wish she could talk,' she said to herself. 'If she could speak – if she could speak!'

She meant to go to her room and lie down on the tiger-skin, with her cheek upon the great cat's head, and look into the fire and think and think and think. But just before she reached the landing Miss Amelia came out of the door and closed it behind her, and stood before it, looking nervous and awkward. The truth was that she felt secretly ashamed of the thing she had been ordered to do.

'You – you are not to go in there,' she said.

'Not go in?' exclaimed Sara, and she fell back a pace.

'That is not your room now,' Miss Amelia answered, reddening a little.

Somehow, all at once, Sara understood. She realized that this was the beginning of the change Miss Minchin had spoken of.

'Where is my room?' she asked, hoping very much that her voice did not shake.

'You are to sleep in the attic next to Becky.'

Sara knew where it was. Becky had told her about it. She turned, and mounted up two flights of stairs. The last one was narrow, and covered with shabby strips of old carpet. She felt as if she were walking away and leaving far behind her the world in which that other child, who no longer seemed herself, had lived. This child, in her short, tight old frock, climbing the stairs to the attic, was quite a different creature.

When she reached the attic door and opened it, her heart gave a dreary little thump. Then she shut the door and stood against it and looked about her.

Yes, this was another world. The room had a slanting roof and was whitewashed. The whitewash was dingy and had fallen off in places. There was a rusty grate, an old iron bedstead, and a hard bed covered with a faded coverlet. Some pieces of furniture too much worn to be used downstairs had been sent up. Under the skylight in the roof, which showed nothing but an oblong piece of dull grey sky, there stood an old battered red footstool. Sara went to it and sat down. She seldom cried. She did not cry now. She laid Emily across her knees and put her face down upon her and her arms around her, and sat there, her little black head resting on the black draperies not saying one word, not making one sound.

And as she sat in this silence there came a low tap at the door — such a low, humble one that she did not at first hear it, and, indeed, was not roused until the door was timidly pushed open and a poor tear-smeared face appeared peeping round it. It was Becky's face, and Becky had been crying furtively for hours and rubbing her eyes with her kitchen apron until she looked strange indeed.

'Oh, miss,' she said under her breath. 'Might I — would you allow me — jest to come in?'

Sara lifted her head and looked at her. She tried to begin to smile, and somehow she could not. Suddenly — and it was all through the loving mournfulness of Becky's streaming eyes — her face looked more like a child's not so much too old for her years. She held out her hand and gave a little sob.

'Oh, Becky,' she said. 'I told you we were just the same — only two little girls — just two little girls. You see how true it is. There's no difference now. I'm not a princess any more.'

Becky ran to her and caught her hand, and hugged it to her breast, kneeling beside her and sobbing with love and pain.

'Yes, miss, you are,' she cried, and her words were all broken. 'Whats'ever 'appens to you – whats'ever – you'd be a princess all the same – an' nothin' couldn't make you nothin' different.'

8 In The Attic

The first night she spent in her attic was a thing Sara never forgot. Durings its passing, she lived through a wild, unchildlike woe of which she never spoke to any one about her. There was no one who would have understood. It was, indeed, well for her that as she lay awake in the darkness her mind was forcibly distracted, now and then, by the strangeness of her surroundings. It was, perhaps, well for her that she was reminded by her small body of material things. If this had not been so, the anguish of her young mind might have been too great for a child to bear. But, really, while the night was passing she scarcely knew that she had a body at all, or remembered any other thing than one.

'My papa is dead!' she kept whispering to herself. 'My papa is dead!'

It was not until long afterward that she realized that her bed had been so hard that she turned over and over in it to find a place to rest, that the darkness seemed more intense than any she had ever known, and that the wind howled over the roof among the chimneys like something which wailed aloud. Then there was something worse. This was certain scufflings and scratches and squeakings in the walls and behind the skirting boards. She knew what they meant, because Becky had described them. They meant rats and mice who were either fighting with each other or playing together. Once or twice she even heard sharp-toed feet scurrying across the floor, and she remembered in those after days, when she recalled things, that when first she heard them she started up in bed and sat trembling, and when she lay down again covered her head with the bedclothes.

The change in her life did not come about gradually, but was made all at once.

'She must begin as she is to go on,' Miss Minchin said to Miss Amelia. 'She must be taught at once what she is to expect.'

Mariette had left the house the next morning. The glimpse Sara caught of her sitting-room, as she passed its open door, showed her that everything had been changed. Her ornaments and luxuries had been removed, and a bed had been placed in a corner to transform it into a new pupil's bedroom.

When she went down to breakfast she saw that her seat at Miss Minchin's side was occupied by Lavinia, and Miss Minchin spoke to her coldly.

'You will begin your new duties, Sara,' she said, 'by taking your seat with the younger children at a smaller table. You must keep them quiet, and see that they behave well and do not waste their food. You ought to have been down earlier. Lottie has already upset her tea.'

That was the beginning, and from day to day the duties given to her were added to. She taught the younger children French and heard their other lessons, and these were the least of her labours. It was found that she could be made use of in numberless directions. She could be sent on errands at any time and in all weathers. She could be told to do things other people neglected. The cook and the housemaids took their tone from Miss Minchin, and rather enjoyed ordering about the 'young one' who had been made so much fuss over for so long. They were not servants of the best class, and had neither good manners nor good tempers, and it was frequently convenient to have at hand some one on whom blame could be laid.

During the first month or two, Sara thought that her willingness to do things as well as she could, and her silence under reproof, might soften those who drove her so hard. In her proud little heart she wanted them to see that she was trying to earn her living and not accepting charity. But the time time came when she saw that no one was softened at all; and the more willing she was to do as she was told, the more domineering and exacting careless housemaids became, and the more ready a scolding cook was to blame her.

If she had been older, Miss Minchin would have given her the bigger girls to teach and saved money by dismissing an instructress; but while she remained and looked like a child, she could be made more useful as a sort of little superior errand girl and maid-of-all-work. An ordinary errand boy would not have been so clever and reliable. Sara could be trusted with difficult commissions and complicated messages. She could even go and pay bills, and she combined with this the ability to dust a room well and to set things in order.

Her own lessons became things of the past. She was taught nothing, and only after long and busy days spent in running here and there at everybody's orders was she grudgingly allowed to go into the deserted schoolroom, with a pile of old books, and study alone at night.

'If I do not remind myself of the things I have learned, perhaps I may forget them,' she said to herself. 'I am almost a scullery-maid, and if I am a scullery-maid who knows nothing, I shall be like poor Becky. I wonder if I could *quite* forget, and begin to drop my *h*'s and not remember that Henry the Eighth had six wives.'

One of the most curious things in her new existence was her changed position among the pupils. Instead of being a sort of small royal personage among them, she no longer seemed to be one of their number at all. She was kept so constantly at work that she scarcely ever had an opportunity of speaking to any of them, and she could not avoid seeing that Miss Minchin preferred that she should live a life apart from that of the occupants of the schoolroom.

'I will not have her forming intimacies and talking to the other children,' that lady said. 'Girls like a grievance, and if she begins to tell romantic stories about herself, she will become an ill-used heroine, and parents will be given a wrong impression. It is better that she should live a separate life – one suited to her circumstances. I am giving her a home, and that is more than she has any right to expect from me.'

Sara did not expect much, and was far too proud to try to continue to be intimate with girls who evidently felt rather awkward and uncertain about her. The fact was that Miss Minchin's pupils were a set of dull, matter-of-fact young people. They were accustomed to being rich and comfortable, and as Sara's frocks grew shorter and shabbier and queerer-looking, and it became an established fact that she wore shoes with holes in them and was sent out to buy groceries and carry them through the streets in a basket on her arm when the cook wanted them in a hurry, they felt rather as if, when they spoke to her, they were addressing an under-servant.

'To think that she was the girl with the diamond mines,' Lavinia commented. 'She does look an object. And she's queerer than ever. I never liked her much, but I can't bear that way she has now of looking at people without speaking – just as if she was finding them out.'

'I am,' said Sara promptly, when she heard of this. 'That's what I look at some people for. I like to know about them. I think them over afterward.'

The truth was that she had saved herself annoyance several times by keeping her eye on Lavinia, who was quite ready to make mischief, and would have been rather pleased to have made it for the ex-show pupil.

Sara never made any mischief herself, or interfered with any one. She worked like a drudge; she tramped through the wet streets, carrying parcels and baskets; she laboured with the childish in-attention of the little ones' French lessons; as she became shabbier and more forlorn-looking, she was told that she had better take her meals down-stairs; she was treated as if she was nobody's concern, and her heart grew proud and sore, but she never told any one what she felt.

'Soldiers don't complain,' she would say between her small, shut teeth. 'I am not going to do it; I will pretend this is part of a war.'

But there were hours when her child heart might almost have broken with loneliness but for three people.

The first, it must be owned, was Becky – just Becky. Throughout all that first night spent in the garret, she had felt a vague comfort in knowing that on the other side of the wall in which the rats scuffled and squeaked there was another young human creature. And during the nights that followed the sense of comfort grew. They had little chance to speak to each other during the day. Each had her own tasks to perform, and any attempt at conversation would have been regarded as a tendency to loiter and lose time.

'Don't mind me, miss,' Becky whispered during the first morning, 'if I don't say nothin' polite. Some un 'd be down on us if I did. I *means* "please" an' "thank you" an' "beg pardon," but I dassn't to take time to say it.'

But before daybreak she used to slip into Sara's attic and button her dress and give her such help as she required before she went downstairs to light the kitchen fire. And when night came Sara always heard the humble knock at her door which meant that her handmaid was ready to help her again if she was needed. During the first weeks of her grief Sara felt as if she were too stupefied to talk, so it happened that some time passed before they saw each other much or exchanged visits. Becky's heart told her that it was best that people in trouble be left alone.

The second of the trio of comforters was Ermengarde, but odd things happened before Ermengarde found her place.

When Sara's mind seemed to awaken again to the life about her, she realized that she had forgotten that an Ermengarde lived in the world. The two had always been friends, but Sara had felt as if she were years the older. It could not be contested that Ermengarde was as dull as she was affectionate. She clung to Sara in a simple, helpless way; she brought her lessons to her that she might be helped; she listened to her every word and besieged her with requests for stories. But she had nothing interesting to say herself, and she loathed books of every description. She was, in fact, not a person one would remember when one was caught in the storm of a great trouble, and Sara forgot her.

It had been all the easier to forget her because she had been suddenly called home for a few weeks. When she came back she did not see Sara for a day or two, and when she met her for the first time she encountered her coming down a corridor with her arms full of garments which were to be taken downstairs to be mended. Sara herself had already been taught to mend them. She looked pale and unlike herself, and she was attired in the queer, outgrown frock whose shortness showed so much thin black leg.

Ermengarde was too slow a girl to be equal to such a situation. She could not think of anything to say. She knew what had happened, but, somehow, she had never imagined Sara could look like this – so odd and poor and almost like a servant. It made her quite miserable, and she could do nothing but break into a short hysterical laugh and exclaim – aimlessly and as if without any meaning:

'Oh, Sara! is that you?'

'Yes,' answered Sara, and suddenly a strange thought passed through her mind and made her face flush.

She held the pile of garments in her arms, and her chin rested upon the top of it to keep it steady. Something in the look of her straight-gazing eyes made Ermengarde lose her wits still more. She felt as if Sara had changed into a new kind of girl, and she had never known her before. Perhaps it was because she had suddenly grown poor, and had to mend things and work like Becky.

'Oh,' she stammered. 'How – how are you?'

'I don't know,' Sara replied. 'How are you?'

'I'm – I'm quite well,' said Ermengarde, overwhelmed with shyness. Then spasmodically she thought of something to say which seemed more intimate. 'Are you – are you very unhappy?' she said in a rush.

Then Sara was guilty of an injustice. Just at that moment her torn heart swelled within her, and she felt that if any one was as stupid as that, one had better get away from her.

'What do you think?' she said. 'Do you think I am very happy?' and she marched past her without another word.

In course of time she realized that if her wretchedness had not made her forget things, she would have known that poor, dull Ermengarde was not to be blamed for her unready, awkward ways. She was always awkward, and the more she felt, the more stupid she was given to being.

But the sudden thought which had flashed upon her had made her over-sensitive.

'She is like the others,' she had thought. 'She does not really want to talk to me. She knows no one does.'

So for several weeks a barrier stood between them. When they met by chance Sara looked the other way, and Ermengarde felt too stiff and embarrassed to speak. Sometimes they nodded to each other in passing, but there were times when they did not even exchange a greeting.

'If she would rather not talk to me,' Sara thought, 'I will keep out of her way. Miss Minchin makes that easy enough.'

Miss Minchin made it so easy that at last they scarcely saw each other at all. At that time it was noticed that Ermengarde was more stupid than ever, and that she looked listless and unhappy. She used to sit in the window-seat, huddled in a heap, and stare out of the window without speaking. Once Jessie, who was passing, stopped to look at her curiously.

'What are you crying for, Ermengarde?' she asked.

'I'm not crying,' answered Ermengarde in a muffled, unsteady voice.

'You are,' said Jessie. 'A great big tear just rolled down the bridge of your nose and dropped off at the end of it. And there goes another.'

'Well,' said Ermengarde, 'I'm miserable – and no one need interfere.' And she turned her plump back and took out her handkerchief and boldly hid her face in it.

That night, when Sara went to her attic, she was later than usual. She had been kept at work until after the hour at which the pupils went to bed, and after she had gone to her lessons in the lonely schoolroom. When she reached the top of the stairs, she was surprised to see a glimmer of light coming from under the attic door.

'Nobody goes there but myself,' she thought quickly, 'but someone has lighted a candle.'

Someone had, indeed, lighted a candle, and it was not burning in the kitchen candlestick she was expected to use, but in one of those belonging to the pupils' bedrooms. The someone was sitting upon the battered footstool, and was dressed in her nightgown and wrapped up in a red shawl. It was Ermengarde.

'Ermengarde!' cried Sara. She was so startled that she was almost frightened. 'You will get into trouble.'

Ermengarde stumbled up from her footstool. She shuffled across the attic in her bedroom slippers, which were too large for her. Her eyes and nose were pink with crying.

'I know I shall – if I'm found out,' she said. 'But I don't care – I don't care a bit. Oh, Sara, please tell me. What *is* the matter? Why don't you like me any more?'

Something in her voice made the familiar lump rise in Sara's throat. It was so affectionate and simple – so like the old Ermengarde who had asked her to be 'best friends'. It sounded as if she had not meant what she had seemed to mean during these past weeks.

'I do like you,' Sara answered. 'I thought'– you see, everything is different now. I thought you – were different.'

Ermengarde opened her wet eyes wide.

'Why, it was you who were different!' she cried. 'You didn't want to talk to me. I didn't know what to do. It was you who were different after I came back.'

Sara thought a moment. She saw she had made a mistake.

'I *am* different,' she explained, 'though not in the way you think. Miss Minchin does not want me to talk to the girls. Most of them don't want to talk to me. I thought – perhaps – you didn't. So I tried to keep out of your way.'

'Oh, Sara,' Ermengarde almost wailed in her reproachful dismay. And then after one more look they rushed into each other's arms. It must be confessed that Sara's small black head lay for some minutes on the shoulder covered by the red shawl. When Ermengarde had seemed to desert her, she had felt horribly lonely.

Afterward they sat down upon the floor together, Sara clasping her knees with her arms, and Ermengarde rolled up in her shawl. Ermengarde looked at the odd, big-eyed little face adoringly.

'I couldn't bear it any more,' she said. 'I daresay you could live without me, Sara; but I couldn't live without you. I was nearly *dead*. So to-night, when I was crying under the bedclothes, I thought all at once of creeping up here and just begging you to let us be friends again.'

'You are nicer than I am,' said Sara. 'I was too proud to try and make friends. You see, now that trials have come, they have shown that I am *not* a nice child. I was afraid they would. Perhaps' – wrinkling her forehead wisely – 'that is what they were sent for.'

'I don't see any good in them,' said Ermengarde stoutly.

'Neither do I – to speak the truth,' admitted Sara frankly. 'But I suppose there *might* be good in things, even if we don't see it. There *might*' – doubtfully – 'be good in Miss Minchin.'

Ermengarde looked round the attic with a rather fearsome curiosity.

'Sara,' she said, 'do you think you can bear living here?'

Sara looked around also.

'If I pretend it's quite different, I can,' she answered. 'Or if I pretend it is a place in a story.'

She spoke slowly. Her imagination was beginning to work for her. It had not worked for her at all since her troubles had come upon her. She had felt as if it had been stunned.

'Other people have lived in worse places. Think of the Count of Monte Cristo in the dungeons of the Château d'If. And think of the people in the Bastille!'

'The Bastille,' half whispered Ermengarde, watching her and beginning to be fascinated. She remembered stories of the French Revolution which Sara had been able to fix in her mind by her dramatic relation of them. None but Sara could have done it.

A well-known glow came into Sara's eyes.

'Yes,' she said, hugging her knees. 'That will be a good place to pretend about. I am a prisoner in the Bastille. I have been here for years and years – and years; and everybody has forgotten about me. Miss Minchin is the jailer – and Becky' – a sudden light adding itself to the glow in her eyes – 'Becky is the prisoner in the next cell.'

She turned to Ermengarde, looking quite like the old Sara.

'I shall pretend that,' she said 'and it will be a great comfort.'

Ermengarde was at once enraptured and awed.

'And will you tell me all about it?' she said. 'May I creep up here at night, whenever it is safe, and hear the things you have made up in the day? It will seem as if we were more "best friends" than ever.'

'Yes,' answered Sara, nodding. 'Adversity tries people, and mine has tried you and proved how nice you are.'

9 Melchisedec

The third person in the trio was Lottie. She was a small thing and did not know what adversity meant, and was much bewildered by the alteration she saw in her young adopted mother. She had heard it rumoured that strange things had happened to Sara, but she could not understand why she looked different – why she wore an old black frock and came into the schoolroom only to teach instead of to sit in her place of honour and learn lessons herself. There had been much whispering among the little ones when it had been discovered that Sara no longer lived in the rooms in which Emily had so long sat in state. Lottie's chief difficulty was that Sara said so little when one asked her questions. At seven mysteries must be made very clear if one is to understand them.

'Are you very poor now, Sara?' she had asked confidentially the first morning her friend took charge of the small French class. 'Are you as poor as a beggar?' She thrust a fat hand into the slim one and opened round, tearful eyes. 'I don't want you to be as poor as a beggar.'

She looked as if she was going to cry, and Sara hurriedly consoled her.

'Beggars have nowhere to live,' she said courageously. 'I have a place to live in.'

'Where do you live?' persisted Lottie. 'The new girl sleeps in your room, and it isn't pretty any more.'

'I live in another room,' said Sara.

'Is it a nice one?' inquired Lottie. 'I want to go and see it.'

'You must not talk,' said Sara. 'Miss Minchin is looking at us. She will be angry with me for letting you whisper.'

She had found out already that she was to be held accountable for everything which was objected to. If the children were not attentive, if they talked, if they were restless, it was she who would be reproved.

But Lottie was a determined little person. If Sara would not tell her where she lived, she would find out in some other way. She talked to her small companions and hung about the elder girls and listened when they were gossiping; and acting upon certain information they had unconsciously let drop, she started late one afternoon on a voyage of discovery, climbing stairs she had never known the existence of, until she reached the attic floor. There she found two doors near each other, and opening one, she saw her beloved Sara standing upon an old table and looking out of the window.

'Sara!' she cried aghast. 'Mamma Sara!' She was aghast because the attic was so bare and ugly, and seemed so far away from all the world. Her short legs had seemed to have been mounting hundreds of stairs.

Sara turned round at the sound of her voice. It was her turn to be aghast. What would happen now? If Lottie began to cry and any one chanced to hear, they were both lost. She jumped down from her table and ran to the child.

'Don't cry and make a noise,' she implored. 'I shall be scolded if you do, and I have been scolded all day. It's – it's not such a bad room, Lottie.'

'Isn't it?' gasped Lottie, and as she looked round it she bit her lip. She was a spoiled child yet, but she was fond enough of her adopted parent to make an effort to control herself for her sake. Then, somehow, it was quite possible that any place in which Sara lived might turn out to be nice. 'Why isn't it, Sara?' she almost whispered.

Sara hugged her close and tried to laugh. There was a sort of comfort in the warmth of the plump, childish body. She had had a hard day, and had been staring out of the windows with hot eyes.

'You can see all sorts of things you can't see downstairs,' she said.

'What sort of things?' demanded Lottie, with that curiosity Sara could always awaken even in bigger girls.

'Chimneys – quite close to us – with smoke curling up in wreaths and clouds and going up into the sky – and sparrows hopping about and talking to each other just as if they were people – and other attic windows where heads may pop out any minute and you can wonder who they belong to. And it all feels as high up – as if it was another world.'

'Oh, let me see it!' cried Lottie. 'Lift me up!' Sara lifted her up, and they stood on the old table together and leaned on the edge of the flat window in the roof, and looked out.

Any one who has not done this does not know what a different world they saw. The slates spread out on either side of them and slanted down into the rain gutter-pipes. The sparrows, being at home there, twittered and hopped about quite without fear. Two of them perched on the chimney-top nearest, and quarrelled with each other fiercely until one pecked the other and drove him away. The garret window next to theirs was shut because the house next door was empty.

'I wish someone lived there,' Sara said. 'It is so close that if there was a little girl in the attic, we could talk to each other through the windows and climb over to see each other, if we were not afraid of falling.'

The sky seemed so much nearer than when one saw it from the street, that Lottie was enchanted. From the attic window, among the chimney-pots, the things which were happening in the world below seemed almost unreal. One scarcely believed in the existence of Miss Minchin and Miss Amelia and the schoolroom, and the roll of wheels in the square seemed a sound belonging to another existence.

'Oh, Sara!' cried Lottie, cuddling in her guarding arm. 'I like this attic – I like it! It is nicer than downstairs!'

'Look at that sparrow,' whispered Sara, 'I wish I had some crumbs to throw to him.'

'I have some!' came in a little shriek from Lottie. 'I have part of a bun in my pocket; I bought it with my penny yesterday, and I saved a bit.'

When they threw out a few crumbs the sparrow jumped and flew away to an adjacent chimney-top. He was evidently not accustomed to intimates in attics, and unexpected crumbs startled him. But when Lottie remained quite still and Sara chirped very softly – almost as if she were a sparrow herself – he saw that the thing which had alarmed him represented hospitality, after all. He put his head on one side, and from his perch on the chimney looked down at the crumbs with twinkling eyes. Lottie could scarcely keep still.

'Will he come? Will he come?' she whispered.

'His eyes look as if he would,' Sara whispered back. 'He is thinking and thinking whether he dare. Yes, he will! Yes, he is coming!'

He flew down and hopped towards the crumbs, but stopped a few inches away from them, putting his head on one side again, as if reflecting on the chances that Sara and Lottie might turn out to be big cats and jump on him. At last his heart told him they were really nicer than they looked, and he hopped nearer and nearer, darted at the biggest crumb with a lightning peck, seized it, and carried it away to the other side of his chimney.

'Now he *knows*,' said Sara. 'And he will come back for the others.'

He did come back, and even brought a friend, and the friend went away and brought a relative, and among them they made a hearty meal over which they twittered and chattered and exclaimed, stopping every now and then to put their heads on one side and examine Lottie and Sara. Lottie was so delighted that she quite forgot her first shocked impression of the attic. In fact, when she was lifted down from the table and returned to earthly things, as it were, Sara was able to point out to her many beauties in the room which she herself would not have suspected the existence of.

'It is so little and so high above everything,' she said, 'that it is almost like a nest in a tree. The slanting ceiling is so funny. See, you can scarcely stand up at this end of the room; and when the morning begins to come I can lie in bed and look right up into the sky through that flat window in the roof. It is like a square patch of light. If the sun is going to shine, little pink clouds float about, and I feel as if I could touch them. And if it rains, the drops patter and patter as if they were saying something nice. Then if there are stars, you can lie and try to count how many go into the patch. It takes such a lot. And just look at that tiny, rusty grate in the corner. It it was polished and there was a fire in it, just think how nice it would be. You see, it's really a beautiful little room.'

She was walking round the small place, holding Lottie's hand and making gestures which described all the beauties she was making herself see. She quite made Lottie see them, too. Lottie could always believe in the things Sara made pictures of.

'You see,' she said, 'there could be a thick, soft blue Indian rug on the floor; and in that corner there could be a soft little sofa, with cushions to curl up on; and just over it could be a shelf full of books so that one could reach them easily; and there could be a fur rug before the fire, and hangings on the wall to cover up the whitewash, and pictures. They would have to be little ones, but they could be beautiful; and there could be a lamp with a deep rose-coloured shade; and a table in the middle, with things to have tea with; and a little fat copper kettle singing on the hob; and the bed could be quite different. It could be made soft and covered with a lovely silk coverlet. It could be beautiful. And perhaps we could coax the sparrows until we made such friends with them that they would come and peck at the window and ask to be let in.'

'Oh, Sara!' cried Lottie, 'I should like to live here!'

When Sara had persuaded her to go downstairs again, and, after setting her in her way, had come back to her attic, she stood in the middle of it and looked about her. The enchantment of her imaginings for Lottie had died away. The bed was hard and covered with its dingy quilt. The whitewashed wall showed its broken patches, the floor was cold and bare, the grate was broken and rusty, and the battered footstool, tilted sideways on its injured leg, the only seat in the room. She sat down on it for a few minutes and let her head drop in her hands. The mere fact that Lottie had come and gone away again made things seem a little worse – just as perhaps prisoners feel a little more desolate after visitors come and go, leaving them behind.

'It's a lonely place,' she said. 'Sometimes it's the loneliest place in the world.'

She was sitting in this way when her attention was attracted by a slight sound near her. She lifted her head to see where it came from, and if she had been a nervous child she would have left her seat on the battered footstool in a great hurry. A large rat was sitting up on his hind-quarters and sniffing the air in an interested manner. Some of Lottie's crumbs had dropped upon the floor and their scent had drawn him out of his hole.

He looked so queer and so like a grey-whiskered dwarf or gnome that Sara was rather fascinated. He looked at her with his bright eyes, as if she were asking a question. He was evidently so doubtful that one of the child's queer thoughts came into her mind.

'I dare say it's rather hard to be a rat,' she mused. 'Nobody likes you. People jump and run away and scream out: "Oh, a horrid rat!" I shouldn't like people to scream and jump and say: "Oh, a horrid Sara!" the moment they saw me, and set traps for me, and pretend they were dinner. It's so different to be a sparrow. But nobody asked this rat if he wanted to be a rat when he was made. Nobody said: "Wouldn't you rather be a sparrow?"'

She had sat so quietly that the rat had begun to take courage. He was very much afraid of her, but perhaps he had a heart like the sparrow and it told him that she was not a thing which pounced. He was very hungry. He had a wife and a large family in the wall, and they had had frightfully bad luck for several days. He had left the children crying bitterly, and felt he would risk a good deal for a few crumbs, so he cautiously dropped upon his feet.

'Come on,' said Sara, 'I'm not a trap. You can have them, poor thing! Prisoners in the Bastille used to make friends with rats. Suppose I make friends with you.'

How it is that animals understand things I do not know, but it is certain that they do understand. Perhaps there is a language which is not made of words and everything in the world understands it. Perhaps there is a soul hidden in everything and it can always speak, without even making a sound, to another soul. But whatsoever was the reason, the rat knew from that moment that he was safe – even though he was a rat. He knew that this young human being sitting on the red footstool would not jump up and terrify him with wild, sharp noises, or throw heavy objects at him which, if they did not fall and crush him, would send him limping in his scurry back to his hole. He was really a very nice rat, and did not mean the least harm. When he had stood on his hind-legs and sniffed the air, with his bright eyes fixed on Sara, he had hoped that she would understand this, and would not begin by hating him as an enemy. When the mysterious thing which speaks without saying any words told him that she would not, he went softly toward the crumbs and began to eat them. As he did it he glanced every now and then at Sara, just as the sparrows had done, and his expression was so very apologetic that it touched her heart.

She sat and watched him without making any movement. One crumb was very much larger than the others – in fact, it could scarcely be called a crumb. It was evident that he wanted that piece very much, but it lay quite near the footstool and he was still rather timid.

'I believe he wants it to carry to his family in the wall,' Sara thought. 'If I do not stir at all, perhaps he will come and get it.'

She scarcely allowed herself to breathe, she was so deeply interested. The rat shuffled a little nearer and ate a few more crumbs, then he stopped and sniffed delicately, giving a side glance at the occupant of the footstool; then he darted at the piece of bun with something very like the sudden boldness of the sparrow, and the instant he had possession of it fled back to the wall, slipped down a crack in the skirting board, and was gone.

'I knew he wanted it for his children,' said Sara. 'I do believe I could make friends with him.'

A week or so afterward, on one of the rare nights when Ermengarde found it safe to steal up to the attic, when she tapped on the door with the tips of her fingers Sara did not come to her for two or three minutes. There was, indeed, such a silence in the room at first that Ermengarde wondered if she could have fallen asleep. Then, to her surprise, she heard her utter a little, low laugh and speak coaxingly to someone.

'There!' Ermengarde heard her say. 'Take it and go home, Melchisedec! Go home to your wife!'

Almost immediately Sara opened the door, and when she did so she found Ermengarde standing with alarmed eyes upon the threshold.

'Who – who *are* you talking to, Sara?' she gasped out.

Sara drew her in cautiously, but she looked as if something pleased and amused her.

'You must promise not to be frightened – not to scream the least bit, or I can't tell you,' she answered.

'*The rat shuffled a little nearer and ate a few more crumbs*'

Ermengarde felt almost inclined to scream on the spot, but managed to control herself. She looked all round the attic and saw no one. And yet Sara had certainly been speaking *to* someone. She thought of ghosts.

'Is it – something that will frighten me?' she asked timorously.

'Some people are afraid of them,' said Sara. 'I was at first – but I am not now.'

'Was it – a ghost?' quaked Ermengarde.

'No,' said Sara, laughing. 'It was my rat.'

Ermengarde made one bound, and landed in the middle of the little dingy bed. She tucked her feet under her night-gown and the red shawl. She did not scream, but she gasped with fright.

'Oh! oh!' she cried, under her breath. 'A rat! A rat!'

'I was afraid you would be frightened,' said Sara. 'But you needn't be. I am making him tame. He actually knows me and comes out when I call him. Are you too frightened to want to see him?'

The truth was that, as the days had gone on, and with the aid of scraps brought up from the kitchen, her curious friendship had developed, she had gradually forgotten that the timid creature she was becoming familiar with was a mere rat.

At first Ermengarde was too much alarmed to do anything but huddle in a heap upon the bed and tuck up her feet, but the sight of Sara's composed little countenance and the story of Melchisedec's first appearance began at last to rouse her curiosity, and she leaned forward over the edge of the bed and watched Sara go and kneel down by the hole in the skirting board.

'He – he won't run out quickly and jump on the bed, will he?' she said.

'No,' answered Sara, 'He's as polite as we are. He is just like a person. Now watch!'

She began to make a low, whistling sound – so low and coaxing that it could only have been heard in entire stillness. She did it several times, looking entirely absorbed in it. Ermengarde thought she looked as if she were working a spell. And at last, evidently in response to it, a grey-whiskered, bright-eyed head peeped out of the hole. Sara had some crumbs in her hand. She dropped them, and Melchisedec came quietly forth and ate them. A piece of larger size than the rest he took and carried in the most businesslike manner back to his home.

'You see,' said Sara, 'that is for his wife and children. He is very nice. He only eats the little bits. After he goes back I can always hear his family squeaking for joy. There are three kinds of squeaks. One kind is the children's, and one is Mrs. Melchisedec's, and one is Melchisedec's own.'

Ermengarde began to laugh.

'Oh, Sara!' she said. 'You *are* queer – but you are nice.'

'I know I am queer,' admitted Sara cheerfully, 'and I *try* to be nice.' She rubbed her forehead with her little brown paw, and a puzzled, tender look came into her face. 'Papa always laughed at me,' she said, 'but I liked it. He thought I was queer, but he liked me to make up things. I – I can't help making up things. If I didn't, I don't believe I could live.' She paused and glanced round the attic. 'I'm sure I couldn't live here,' she added in a low voice.

Ermengarde was interested, as she always was. 'When you talk about things,' she said, 'they seem as if they grew real. You talk about Melchisedec as if he was a person.'

'He *is* a person,' said Sarah. 'He gets hungry and frightened, just as we do; and he is married and has children. How do we know he doesn't think things, just as we do? His eyes look as if he was a person. That was why I gave him a name.'

She sat down on the floor in her favourite attitude, holding her knees.

'Besides,' she said, 'he is a Bastille rat sent to be my friend. I can always get a bit of bread the cook has thrown away, and it is quite enough to support him.'

'Is it the Bastille yet?' asked Ermengarde eagerly. 'Do you always pretend it is the Bastille?'

'Nearly always,' answered Sara. 'Sometimes I try to pretend it is another kind of place; but the Bastille is generally easiest – particularly when it is cold.'

Just at that moment Ermengarde almost jumped off the bed, she was so startled by a sound she heard. It was like two distinct knocks on the wall.

'What is that?' she exclaimed.

Sara got up from the floor and answered quite dramatically:

'It is the prisoner in the next cell.'

'Becky!' cried Ermengarde enraptured.

'Yes,' said Sara. 'Listen; the two knocks meant, "Prisoner, are you there?"'

She knocked three times on the wall herself, as if in answer.

'That means, "Yes, I am here, and all is well."' Four knocks came from Becky's side of the wall.

'That means,' explained Sara. '"Then, fellow-sufferer, we will sleep in peace. Good night."'

Ermengarde quite beamed with delight.

'Oh, Sara!' she whispered joyfully, 'it is like a story!'

'It *is* a story,' said Sara. '*Everything's* a story. You are a story – I am a story. Miss Minchin is a story.'

And she sat down again and talked until Ermengarde forgot that she was a sort of escaped prisoner herself, and had to be reminded by Sara that she could not remain in the Bastille all night, but must steal noiselessly downstairs again and creep back into her deserted bed.

10 The Indian Gentleman

But it was a perilous thing for Ermengarde and Lottie to make pilgrimages to the attic. They could never be quite sure when Sara would be there, and they could scarcely ever be certain that Miss Amelia would not make a tour of inspection through the bedrooms after the pupils were supposed to be asleep. So their visits were rare ones, and Sara lived a strange and lonely life. It was a lonelier life when she was downstairs than when she was in her attic. She had no one to talk to; and when she was sent out on errands and walked through the streets, a forlorn little figure carrying a basket or a parcel, trying to hold her hat on when the wind was blowing, and feeling the water soak through her shoes when it was raining, she felt as if the crowds hurrying past her made her loneliness greater. When she had been the Princess Sara, driving through the streets in her brougham, or walking, attended by Mariette, the sight of her bright, eager little face and picturesque coats and hats had often caused people to look after her. A happy, beautifully cared for little girl naturally atttracts attention. Shabby, poorly dressed children are not rare enough and pretty enough to make people turn around to look at them and smile. No one looked at Sara in these days, and no one seemed to see her as she hurried along the crowded pavements. She had begun to grow very fast, and, as she was dressed only in such clothes as the plainer remnants of her wardrobe would supply, she knew she looked very queer indeed. All her valuable garments had been disposed of, and such as had been left for her use was expected to wear so long as she could put them on at all. Sometimes, when she passed a shop window with a mirror in it, she almost laughed outright on catching a glimpse of herself, and sometimes her face went red and she bit her lip and turned away.

In the evening, when she passed houses whose windows were lighted up, she used to look into the warm rooms and amuse herself by imagining things about the people she saw sitting before the fires or about the tables. It always interested her to catch glimpses of rooms before the shutters were closed. There were several families in the square in which Miss Minchin lived, with which she had become quite familiar in a way of her own. The one she liked best she called the Large Family. She called it the Large Family not because the members of it were big – for, indeed, most of them were little – but because there were so many of them. There were eight children in the Large Family, and a stout, rosy mother, and a stout, rosy father, and a stout, rosy grandmother, and any number of servants. The eight children were always either being taken out to walk or to ride in perambulators by comfortable nurses, or they were going to drive with their mamma, or they were flying to the door in the evening to meet their papa and kiss him and dance around him and drag off his overcoat and look in the pockets for packages, or they were crowding about the nursery windows and looking out and pushing each other and laughing – in fact, they were always doing something enjoyable and suited to the tastes of a large family. Sara was quite fond of them, and had given them names out of books – quite romantic names. She called them the Montmorencys when she did not call them the Large Family. The fat, fair baby with the lace cap was Ethelberta Beauchamp Montmorency; the next baby was Violet Cholmondeley Montmorency; the little boy who could just stagger and who had such round legs was Sydney Cecil Vivian Montmorency; and then came Lilian Evangeline Maud Marion, Rosalind Gladys, Guy Clarence, Veronica Eustacia, and Claude Harold Hector.

One evening a very funny thing happened – though, perhaps, in one sense it was not a funny thing at all.

Several of the Montmorencys were evidently going to a children's party, and just as Sara was about to pass the door they were crossing the pavement to get into the carriage which was waiting for them. Veronica Eustacia and Rosalind Gladys, in white lace frocks and lovely sashes, had just got in, and Guy Clarence aged five, was following them. He was such a pretty fellow and had such rosy cheeks and blue eyes, and such a darling little round head covered with curls, that Sara forgot her basket and shabby cloak altogether – in fact, forgot everything but that she wanted to look at him for a moment. So she paused and looked.

It was Christmas time, and the Large Family had been hearing many stories about children who were poor and had no mammas and papas to fill their stockings and take them to the pantomime – children who were, in fact, cold and thinly clad and hungry. In the stories, kind people – sometimes little boys and girls with tender hearts – invariably saw the poor children and gave them money or rich gifts, or took them home to beautiful dinners. Guy Clarence had been affected to tears that very afternoon by the reading of such a story, and he had burned with a desire to find such a poor child and give her a certain sixpence he possessed, and thus provide for her for life. An entire sixpence, he was sure, would mean affluence for evermore. As he crossed the strip of red carpet laid across the pavement from the door to the carriage, he had this very sixpence in the pocket of his very short man-o'-war trousers. And just as Rosalind Gladys got into the vehicle and jumped onto the seat in order to feel the cushions spring under her, he saw Sara standing on the wet pavement in her shabby frock and hat, with her old basket on her arm, looking at him hungrily.

He thought that her eyes looked hungry because she had perhaps had nothing to eat for a long time. He did not know that they looked so because she was hungry for the warm, merry life his home held and his rosy face spoke of, and that she had a hungry wish to snatch him in her arms and kiss him. He only knew that she had big eyes and a thin face and thin legs, and a common basket and poor clothes. So he put his hand in his pocket and found his sixpence, and walked up to her benignly.

'Here, poor little girl,' he said. 'Here is a sixpence. I will give it to you.'

Sara started, and all at once realized that she looked exactly like poor children she had seen, in her better days, waiting on the pavements to watch her as she got out of her brougham. And she had given them pennies many a time. Her face went red and then it went pale, and for a second she felt as if she could not take the dear little sixpence.

'Oh, no!' she said. 'Oh no, thank you; I mustn't take it, indeed!'

Her voice was so unlike an ordinary street child's voice, and her manner was so like the manner of a well-bred little person that Veronica Eustacia (whose real name was Janet) and Rosalind Gladys (who was really called Nora) leaned forward to listen.

But Guy Clarence was not to be thwarted in his benevolence. He thrust the sixpence into her hand.

'Yes, you must take it, poor girl!' he insisted stoutly. 'You can buy things to eat with it. It is a whole sixpence!'

There was something so honest and kind in his face, and he looked so likely to be heartbrokenly disappointed if she did not take it, that Sara knew she must not refuse him. To be as proud as that would be a cruel thing. So she actually put her pride in her pocket, though it must be admitted her cheeks burned.

'Thank you,' she said. 'You are a kind, kind little darling thing.' And as he scrambled joyfully into the carriage she went away, trying to smile, though she caught her breath quickly and her eyes were shining through a mist. She had known that she looked odd and shabby, but until now she had not known that she might be taken for a beggar.

As the Large Family's carriage drove away, the children inside it were talking with interested excitement.

'Oh, Donald' (this was Guy Clarence's name), Janet exclaimed alarmedly, 'why did you offer that little girl your sixpence? I'm sure she is not a beggar!'

'She didn't speak like a beggar!' cried Nora, 'and her face didn't really look like a beggar's face!'

'Besides, she didn't beg,' said Janet. 'I was so afraid she might be angry with you. You know, it makes people angry to be taken for beggars when they are not beggars.'

'She wasn't angry,' said Donald, a trifle dismayed, but still firm. 'She laughed a little, and she said I was a kind, kind little darling thing. And I was!' – stoutly. 'It was my whole sixpence.'

Janet and Nora exchanged glances.

'A beggar girl would never have said that,' decided Janet. 'She would have said: "Thank yer kindly, little gentleman – thank yer, sir," and perhaps she would have bobbed a courtesy.'

Sara knew nothing about the fact, but from that time the Large Family was as profoundly interested in her as she was in it. Faces used to appear at the nursery windows when she passed, and many discussions concerning her were held round the fire.

'She is a kind of servant at the seminary,' Janet said. 'I don't believe she belongs to anybody. I believe she is an orphan. But she is not a beggar, however shabby she looks.'

And afterward she was called by all of them, 'The-little-girl-who-is-not-a-beggar,' which was, of course, rather a long name, and sounded very funny sometimes when the youngest ones said it in a hurry.

Sara managed to bore a hole in the sixpence, and hung it on an old bit of narrow ribbon round her neck. Her affection for the Large Family increased – as, indeed, her affection for everything she could love increased. She grew fonder and fonder of Becky, and she used to look forward to the two mornings a week when she went into the schoolroom to give the little ones their French lesson. Her small pupils loved her, and strove with each other for the privilege of standing close to her and insinuating their small hands into hers. It fed her hungry heart to feel them nestling up to her. She made such friends with the sparrows that when she stood upon the table, put her head and shoulders out of the attic window, and chirped, she heard almost immediately a flutter of wings and answering twitters and a little flock of dingy town birds appeared and alighted on the slates to talk to her and make much of the crumbs she scattered. With Melchisedec she had become so intimate that he actually brought Mrs. Melchisedec with him sometimes, and now and then one or two of his children. She used to talk to him, and somehow, he looked quite as if he understood.

There had grown in her mind rather a strange feeling about Emily, who always sat and looked on at everything. It arose in one of her moments of great desolateness. She would have liked to believe or pretend to believe that Emily understood and sympathized with her. She did not like to own to herself that her only companion could feel and hear nothing. She used to put her in a chair sometimes and sit opposite to her on the old red footstool, and stare and pretend about her until her own eyes would grow large with something which was almost like fear – particularly at night when everything was so still, when the only sound in the attic was the occasional sudden scurry and squeak of Melchisedec's family in the wall. One of her 'pretends' was that Emily was a kind of good witch who could protect her. Sometimes, after she had stared at her until she was wrought up to the highest pitch of fancifulness, she would ask her questions and find herself *almost* feeling as if she would presently answer. But she never did.

'As to answering, though,' said Sara, trying to console herself, 'I don't answer very often. I never answer when I can help it. When people are insulting you, there is nothing so good for them as not to say a word – just to look at them and *think*. Miss Minchin turns pale with rage when I do it, Miss Amelia looks frightened, and so do the girls. When you will not fly into a passion people know you are stronger than they are, because you are strong enough to hold in your rage, and they are not, and they say stupid things they wish they hadn't said afterward. There's nothing so strong as rage, except what makes you hold it in – that's stronger. It's a good thing not to answer your enemies. I scarcely ever do. Perhaps Emily is more like me than I am like myself. Perhaps she would rather not answer her friends, even. She keeps it all in her heart.'

But though she tried to satisfy herself with these arguments, she did not find it easy. When, after a long, hard day, in which she had been sent here and there, sometimes on long errands through wind and cold and rain, she came in wet and hungry, and was sent out again because nobody chose to remember that she was only a child, and that her slim legs might be tired and her small body might be chilled; when she had been given only harsh words and cold, slighting looks for thanks; when the cook had been vulgar and insolent; when Miss Minchin had been in her worst mood, and when she had seen the girls sneering among themselves at her shabbiness – then she was not always able to comfort her sore, proud, desolate heart with fancies when Emily merely sat upright in her old chair and stared.

One of these nights, when she came up to the attic cold and hungry, with a tempest raging in her young breast, Emily's stare seemed so vacant, her sawdust legs and arms so inexpressive, that Sara lost all control over herself. There was nobody but Emily – no one in the world. And there she sat.

'I shall die presently,' she said at first.

Emily simply stared.

'I can't bear this,' said the poor child, trembling. 'I know I shall die. I'm cold; I'm wet; I'm starving to death. I've walked a thousand miles today, and they have done nothing but scold me from morning until night. And because I could not find that last thing the cook sent me for, they would not give me any supper. Some men laughed at me because my old shoes made me slip down in the mud. I'm covered with mud now. And they laughed. Do you hear?'

She looked at the staring glass eyes and complacent face, and suddenly a sort of heartbroken rage seized her. She lifted her little savage hand and knocked Emily off the chair, bursting into a passion of sobbing – Sara who never cried.

'You are nothing but a *doll*!' she cried. 'Nothing but a doll – doll – doll! You care for nothing. You are stuffed with sawdust. You never had a heart. Nothing could ever make you feel. You are a *doll*!'

Emily lay on the floor, with her legs ignominiously doubled up over her head, and a new flat place on the end of her nose; but she was calm, even dignified. Sara hid her face in her arms. The rats in the wall began to fight and bite each other and squeak and scramble. Melchisedec was chastising some of his family.

Sara's sobs gradually quietened themselves. It was so unlike her to break down that she was surprised at herself. After a while she raised her face and looked at Emily, who seemed to be gazing at her round the side of one angle, and somehow, by this time actually with a kind of glassy-eyed sympathy. Sara bent and picked her up. Remorse overtook her. She even smiled at herself a very little smile.

'You can't help being a doll,' she said with a resigned sigh, 'any more than Lavinia and Jessie can help not having any sense. We are not all made alike. Perhaps you do your sawdust best.' And she kissed her and shook her clothes straight, and put her back upon her chair.

She had wished very much that someone would take the empty house next door. She wished it because of the attic window which was so near her. It seemed as if it would be so nice to see it propped open some day and a head and shoulders rising out of the square aperture.

'If it looked a nice head,' she thought, 'I might begin by saying: "Good morning," and all sorts of things might happen. But, of course, it's not really likely that any one but under-servants would sleep there.'

One morning, on turning the corner of the square after a visit to the grocer's, the butcher's, and the baker's, she saw, to her great delight, that during her rather prolonged absence, a van full of furniture had stopped before the next house, the front doors were thrown open, and men in shirt-sleeves were going in and out carrying heavy packages and pieces of furniture.

'It's taken!' she said. 'It really *is* taken! Oh, I do hope a nice head will look out of the attic window!'

She would almost have liked to join the group of loiterers who had stopped on the pavement to watch the things carried in. She had an idea that if she could see some of the furniture she could guess something about the people it belonged to.

'Miss Minchin's tables and chairs are just like her,' she thought. 'I remember thinking that the first minute I saw her, even though I was so little. I told papa afterward, and he laughed and said it was true. I am sure the Large Family have fat, comfortable arm-chairs and sofas, and I can see that their red-flowery wall-paper is exactly like them. It's warm and cheerful and kind-looking and happy.'

She was sent out for parsley to the greengrocer's later in the day, and when she came up the area steps her heart gave a quick beat of recognition. Several pieces of furniture had been set out of the van upon the pavement. There was a beautiful table of elaborately wrought teakwood, and some chairs, and a screen covered with rich Oriental embroidery. The sight of them gave her a weird, homesick feeling. She had seen things so like them in India. One of the things Miss Minchin had taken from her was a carved teak-wood desk her father had sent her.

'They are beautiful things,' she said. 'They look as if they ought to belong to a nice person. All the things look rather grand. I suppose it is a rich family.'

The vans of furniture came and were unloaded and gave place to others all day. Several times it so happened that Sara had an opportunity of seeing things carried in. It became plain that she had been right in guessing that the new-comers were people of large means. All the furniture was rich and beautiful, and a great deal of it was Oriental. Wonderful rugs and draperies and ornaments were taken from the vans, many pictures, and books enough for a library. Among other things there was a superb god Buddha in a splendid shrine.

'Someone in the family *must* have been in India,' Sara thought. 'They have got used to Indian things and like them. I *am* glad. I shall feel as if they were friends, even if a head never looks out of the attic window.'

When she was taking in the evening's milk for the cook (there was really no odd job she was not called upon to do), she saw something occur which made the situation more interesting than ever. The handsome, rosy man who was the father of the Large Family walked across the square in the most matter-of-fact manner, and ran up the steps of the next-door house. He ran up them as if he felt quite at home and expected to run up and down them many a time in the future. He stayed inside quite a long time, and several times came out and gave directions to the workmen, as if he had a right to do so. It was quite certain that he was in some intimate way connected with the new-comers and was acting for them.

'If the new people have children,' Sara speculated, 'the Large Family children will be sure to come and play with them, and they *might* come up into the attic just for fun.'

At night, after her work was done, Becky came in to see her fellow-prisoner and bring her news.

'It's a Nindian gentleman that's comin' to live next door, miss,' she said. 'I don't know whether he's a black gentleman or not, but he's a Nindian one. He's very rich, an' he's ill, an' the gentleman of the Large Family is his lawyer. He's had a lot of trouble, an' it's made him ill an' low in his mind. He worships idols, miss. He's an 'eathen an' bows down to wood an' stone. I seen a' idol bein' carried in for him to worship. Somebody had oughter send him a trac'. You can get a trac' for a penny.'

Sara laughed a little.

'I don't believe he worships that idol,' she said. 'Some people like to keep them to look at because they are interesting. My papa had a beautiful one, and he did not worship it.'

But Becky was rather inclined to prefer to believe that the new neighbour was 'an 'eathen'. It sounded so much more romantic than that he should merely be the ordinary kind of gentleman who went to church with a prayer-book. She sat and talked long that night of what he would be like, of what his wife would be like if he had one, and of what his children would be like if they had children. Sara saw that privately she could not help hoping very much that they would all be black and would wear turbans, and, above all, that – like their parent – they would all be ' 'eathens'.

'I never lived next door to no 'eathens, miss,' she said. 'I should like to see what sort o' ways they'd have.'

It was several weeks before her curiosity was satisfied, and then it was revealed that the new occupant had neither wife nor children. He was a solitary man with no family at all, and it was evident that he was shattered in health and unhappy in mind.

A carriage drove up one day and stopped before the house. When the footman dismounted from the box and opened the door the gentleman who was the father of the Large Family got out first. After him there descended a nurse in uniform, then came down the steps two menservants. They came to assist their master, who, when he was helped out of the carriage, proved to be a man with a haggard, distressed face, and a skeleton body wrapped in furs. He was carried up the steps, and the Large Family went with him, looking very anxious. Shortly afterward a doctor's carriage arrived, and the doctor went in – plainly to take care of him.

'There is such a yellow gentleman next door, Sara,' Lottie whispered at the French class afterward. 'Do you think he is a Chinese? The geography says the Chinese men are yellow.'

'No, he is not Chinese,' Sara whispered back. 'He is very ill. Go on with your exercise, Lottie. "*Non, monsieur. Je n'ai pas le canif de mon oncle*".'

That was the beginning of the story of the Indian gentleman.

11 Ram Dass

There were fine sunsets even in the square, sometimes. One would only see parts of them, however, between the chimneys and over the roofs. From the kitchen windows one could not see them at all, and could only guess that they were going on because the bricks looked warm and the air rosy or yellow for a while, or perhaps one saw a blazing glow strike a particular pane of glass somewhere. There was, however, one place from which one could see all the splendour of them: the piles of red or gold clouds in the west; or the purple ones edged with dazzling brightness; or the little fleecy, floating ones, tinged with rose-colour and looking like flights of pink doves scurrying across the blue in a great hurry if there was a wind. The place where one could see all this, and seem at the same time to breathe a purer air, was of course, the attic window. When the square suddenly seemed to begin to glow in an enchanted way and look wonderful in spite of its sooty trees and railings, Sara knew something was going on in the sky; and when it was at all possible to leave the kitchen without being missed or called back, she invariably stole away and crept up the flights of stairs, and, climbing on the old table, got her head and body as far out of the window as possible. When she had accomplished this, she always drew a long breath and looked all round her. It used to seem as if she had all the sky and the world to herself. No one else ever looked out of the other attics. Generally the skylights were closed; but even if they were propped open to admit air, no one seemed to come near them. And there Sara would stand, sometimes turning her face upward to the blue which seemed so friendly and near – just like a lovely vaulted ceiling – sometimes watching the west and all the wonderful things that happened there: the clouds melting or drifting or waiting softly to be changed pink or crimson or snow-white or purple or pale dove-grey. Sometimes they made islands or great mountains enclosing lakes of deep turquoise-blue, or liquid amber, or chrysoprase-green; sometimes dark headlands jutted into strange, lost seas; sometimes slender strips of wonderful lands joined other wonderful lands together. There were places where it seemed that one could run or climb or stand and wait to see what next was coming – until, perhaps, as it all melted, one could float away. At least it seemed so to Sara, and nothing had ever been quite so beautiful to her as the things she saw as she stood on the table – her body half out of the skylight – the sparrows twittering with sunset softness on the slates. The sparrows always seemed to her to twitter with a sort of subdued softness just when these marvels were going on.

There was such a sunset as this a few days after the Indian gentleman was brought to his new home; and, as it fortunately happened that the afternoon's work was done in the kitchen and nobody had ordered her to go anywhere or perform any task, Sara found it easier than usual to slip away and go upstairs.

She mounted her table and stood looking out. It was a wonderful moment. There were floods of molten gold covering the west, as if a glorious tide was sweeping over the world. A deep, rich yellow light filled the air; the birds flying across the tops of the houses showed quite black against it.

'It's a Splendid one,' said Sara softly to herself. 'It makes me feel almost afraid – as if something strange was just going to happen. The Splendid ones always make me feel like that.'

She suddenly turned her head because she heard a sound a few yards away from her. It was an odd sound, like a queer little squeaky chattering. It came from the window of the next attic. Some one had come to look at the sunset as she had. There was a head and part of a body emerging from the skylight, but it was not the head or body of a little girl or a housemaid; it was a picturesque white-swathed form and dark-faced, gleaming-eyed, white-turbaned head of a native Indian – 'a lascar,' Sara said to herself quickly – and the sound she had heard came from a small monkey he held in his arms as if he were fond of it, and which was snuggling and chattering against his breast.

As Sara looked toward him he looked toward her. The first thing she thought was that his dark face looked sorrowful and homesick. She felt absolutely sure he had come up to look at the sun, because he had seen it so seldom in England that he longed for a sight of it. She looked at him interestedly for a second, and then smiled across the slates. She had learned to know how comforting a smile, even from a stranger, may be.

Hers was evidently a pleasure to him. His whole expression altered, and he showed such gleaming white teeth as he smiled back that it was as if a light had been illuminated in his dusky face. The friendly look in Sara's eyes was always very effective when people felt tired or dull.

It was perhaps in making his salute to her that he loosened his hold on the monkey. He was an impish monkey and always ready for adventure, and it is probable that the sight of a little girl excited him. He suddenly broke loose, jumped on to the slates, ran across them chattering, and actually leaped on to Sara's shoulder, and from there down into her attic room. It made her laugh and delighted her; but she knew he must be restored to his master – if the lascar was his master – and she wondered how this was to be done. Would he let her catch him, or would he be naughty and refuse to be caught, and perhaps get away and run off over the roofs and be lost? That would not do at all. Perhaps he belonged to the Indian gentleman, and the poor man was fond of him.

She turned to the lascar, feeling glad that she remembered still some of the Hindustani she had learned when she lived with her father. She could make the man understand. She spoke to him in the language he knew.

'Will he let me catch him?' she asked.

She thought she had never seen more surprise and delight than the dark face expressed when she spoke in the familiar tongue. The truth was that the poor fellow felt as if his gods had intervened, and the kind little voice came from heaven itself. At once Sara saw that he had been accustomed to European children. He poured forth a flood of respectful thanks. He was the servant of Missee Sahib. The monkey was a good monkey and would not bite; but, unfortunately, he was difficult to catch. He would flee from one spot to another, like the lightning. He was disobedient, though not evil. Ram Dass knew him as if he were his child, and Ram Dass he would sometimes obey, but not always. If Missee Sahib would permit Ram Dass, he himself could cross the roof to her room, enter the window, and regain the unworthy little animal. But he was evidently afraid Sara might think he was taking a great liberty and ·perhaps would not let him come.

But Sara gave him leave at once.

'Can you get across?' she inquired.

'In a moment,' he answered her.

'Then come,' she said, 'he is flying from side to side of the room as if he was frightened.'

Ram Dass slipped through his attic window and crossed to hers as steadily and lightly as if he had walked on roofs all his life. He slipped through the skylight and dropped upon his feet without a sound. Then he turned to Sara and salaamed again. The monkey saw him and uttered a little scream. Ram Dass hastily took the precaution of shutting the skylight, and then went in chase of him. It was not a very long chase. The monkey prolonged it a few minutes evidently for the more fun of it, but presently he sprang chattering on to Ram Dass's shoulder and sat there chattering and clinging to his neck with a weird little skinny arm.

Ram Dass thanked Sara profoundly. She had seen that his quick native eyes had taken in at a glance all the bare shabbiness of the room, but he spoke to her as if he were speaking to the little daughter of a rajah, and pretended that he observed nothing. He did not presume to remain more than a few moments after he had caught the monkey, and those moments were given to further deep and grateful obeisance to her in return for her indulgence. This little evil one, he said, stroking the monkey, was, in truth, not so evil as he seemed, and his master, who was ill, was sometimes amused by him. He would have been made sad if his favourite had run away and been lost. Then he salaamed once more, and got through the skylight and across the slates again with as much agility as the monkey himself had displayed.

When he had gone Sara stood in the middle of her attic and thought of many things his face and his manner had brought back to her. The sight of his native costume and the profound reverence of his manner stirred all her past memories. It seemed a strange thing to remember that she – the drudge whom the cook had said insulting things to an hour ago – had only a few years ago been surrounded by people who all treated her as Ram Dass had treated her; who salaamed when she went by, whose foreheads almost touched the ground when she spoke to them, who were her servants and her slaves. It was like a sort of dream. It was all over, and it could never come back. It certainly seemed that there was no way in which any change could take place. She knew what Miss Minchin intended that her future should be. So long as she was too young to be used as a regular teacher, she would be used as an errand girl and servant, and yet expected to remember what she had learned and in some mysterious way to learn more. The greater number of her evenings she was supposed to spend at study, and at various indefinite intervals she was examined, and knew she would have been severely admonished if she had not advanced as was expected of her. The truth, indeed was that Miss Minchin knew that she was too anxious to learn to require teachers. Give her books, and she would devour them and end by knowing them by heart. She might be trusted to be equal to teaching a good deal in the course of a few years. This was what would happen; when she was older she would be expected to drudge in the schoolroom as she drudged now in various parts of the house; they would be obliged to give her respectable clothes, but they would be sure to be plain and ugly, and to make her look somehow like a servant. That was all there seemed to be to look forward to, and Sara stood quite still for several minutes and thought it over.

Then a thought came back to her which made the colour rise in her cheek and a spark light itself in her eyes. She straightened her thin little body and lifted her head.

'Whatever comes,' she said, 'cannot alter one thing. If I am a princess in rags and tatters, I can be a princess inside. It would be easy to be a princess if I were dressed in cloth of gold, but it is a great deal more of a triumph to be one all the time when one knows it. There was Marie Antoinette when she was in prison and her throne was gone and she had only a black gown on, and her hair was white, and they insulted her and called her Widow Capet. She was a great deal more like a queen then than when she was so gay and everything was so grand. I like her best then. Those howling mobs of people did not frighten her. She was stronger than they were, even when they cut her head off.'

This was not a new thought, but quite an old one, by this time. It had consoled her through many a bitter day, and she had gone about the house with an expression in her face which Miss Minchin could not understand and which was a source of great annoyance to her, as it seemed as if the child were mentally living a life which held her above the rest of the world. It was as if she scarcely heard the rude and acid things said to her; or, if she heard them, did not care for them at all. Sometimes, when she was in the midst of some harsh, domineering speech, Miss Minchin would find the still, unchildish eyes fixed upon her with something like a proud smile in them. At such times she did not know that Sara was saying to herself:

'You don't know that you are saying things to a princess, and that if I chose I could wave my hand and order you to execution. I only spare you because I *am* a princess, and you are a poor, stupid, unkind, vulgar old thing, and don't know any better.'

This used to interest and amuse her more than anything else; and queer and fanciful as it was, she found comfort in it and it was a good thing for her. While the thought held possession of her, she could not be made rude and malicious by the rudeness and malice of those about her.

'A princess must be polite,' she said to herself.

And so when the servants, taking their tone from their mistress, were insolent and ordered her about, she would hold her head erect and reply to them with a quaint civility which often made them stare at her.

'She's got more airs and graces than if she come from Buckingham Palace, that young one,' said the cook, chuckling a little sometimes. 'I lose my temper with her often enough, but I will say she never forgets her manners. "If you please, cook"; "Will you be so kind, cook?"; "I beg your pardon, cook"; "May I trouble you, cook?" She drops 'em about the kitchen as if they was nothing.'

'Miss Minchin. . . . was so enraged that she actually flew
at her and boxed her ears'

The morning after the interview with Ram Dass and his monkey, Sara was in the schoolroom with her small pupils. Having finished giving them their lessons, she was putting the French exercise books together and thinking, as she did it, of the various things royal personages in disguise were called upon to do: Alfred the Great, for instance, burning the cakes and getting his ears boxed by the wife of the neatherd. How frightened she must have been when she found out what she had done. If Miss Minchin should find out that she – Sara, whose toes were almost sticking out of her boots – was a princess – a real one! The look in her eyes was exactly the look which Miss Minchin most disliked. She would not have it; she was quite near her, and was so enraged that she actually flew at her and boxed her ears – exactly as the neatherd's wife had boxed King Alfred's. It made Sara start. She wakened from her dream at the shock, and, catching her breath, stood still a second. Then, not knowing she was going to do it, she broke into a little laugh.

'What are you laughing at, you bold, impudent child?' Miss Minchin exclaimed.

It took Sara a few seconds to control herself sufficiently to remember that she was a princess. Her cheeks were red and smarting from the blows she had received.

'I was thinking,' she answered.

'Beg my pardon immediately,' said Miss Minchin.

Sara hesitated a second before she replied.

'I will beg your pardon for laughing, if it was rude,' she said then, 'but I won't beg your pardon for thinking.'

'What were you thinking?' demanded Miss Minchin. 'How dare you think? What were you thinking?'

Jessie tittered, and she and Lavinia nudged each other in unison. All the girls looked up from their books to listen. Really, it always interested them a little when Miss Minchin attacked Sara. Sara always said something queer, and never seemed the least bit frightened. She was not in the least frightened now, though her boxed ears were scarlet and her eyes were as bright as stars.

'I was thinking,' she answered grandly and politely, 'that you did not know what you were doing.'

'That I did not know what I was doing?' Miss Minchin fairly gasped.

'Yes,' said Sara. 'And I was thinking what would happen if I were a princess and you boxed my ears – what I should do to you. And I was thinking that if I were one, you would never dare to do it, whatever I said or did. And I was thinking how surprised and frightened you would be if you suddenly found out——'

She had the imagined future so clearly before her eyes that she spoke in a manner which had an effect even upon Miss Minchin. It almost seemed for the moment to her narrow, unimaginative mind that there must be some real power hidden behind this candid daring.

'What?' she exclaimed. 'Found out what?'

'That I really was a princess,' said Sara, 'and could do anything – anything I liked.'

Every pair of eyes in the room widened to its full limit. Lavinia leaned forward on her seat to look.

'Go to your room,' cried Miss Minchin breathlessly, 'this instant! Leave the schoolroom! Attend to your lessons, young ladies!'

Sara made a little bow.

'Excuse me for laughing if it was impolite,' she said, and walked out of the room, leaving Miss Minchin struggling with her rage, and the girls whispering over their books.

'Did you see her? Did you see how queer she looked?' Jessie broke out. 'I shouldn't be at all surprised if she did turn out to be something. Suppose she should!'

12 The Other Side of The Wall

When one lives in a row of houses, it is interesting to think of the things which are being done and said on the other side of the wall of the very rooms one is living in. Sara was fond of amusing herself by trying to imagine the things hidden by the wall which divided the Select Seminary from the Indian gentleman's house. She knew that the schoolroom was next to the Indian gentleman's study, and she hoped that the wall was thick, so that the noise made sometimes after lesson hours would not disturb him.

'I am growing quite fond of him,' she said to Ermengarde. 'I should not like him to be disturbed. I have adopted him for a friend. You can do that with people you never speak to at all. You can just watch them, and think about them and be sorry for them, until they seem almost like relations. I'm quite anxious sometimes when I see the doctor call twice a day.'

'I have very few relations,' said Ermengarde reflectively, 'and I'm very glad of it. I don't like those I have. My two aunts are always saying: "Dear me, Ermengarde! You are very fat. You shouldn't eat sweets", and my uncle is always asking me things like: "When did Edward the Third ascend the throne?" and "Who died of a surfeit of lampreys?"'

Sara laughed.

'People you never speak to can't ask you questions like that,' she said, 'and I'm sure the Indian gentleman wouldn't, even if he was quite intimate with you. I am fond of him.'

She had become fond of the Large Family because they looked happy; but she had become fond of the Indian gentleman because he looked unhappy. He had evidently not fully recovered from some very severe illness. In the kitchen – where, of course, the servants, through some mysterious means, knew everything – there was much discussion of his case. He was not an Indian gentleman really, but an Englishman who had lived in India. He had met with great misfortunes which had for a time so imperilled his whole fortune that he had thought himself ruined and disgraced for ever. The shock had been so great that he had almost died of brain-fever; and ever since he had been shattered in health, though his fortunes had changed and all his possessions had been restored to him. His trouble and peril had been connected with mines.

'And mines with diamonds in 'em!' said the cook. 'No savin's of mine never goes into no mines – particular diamond ones' – with a side glance at Sara. 'We all know somethin' of *them*.'

'He felt as my papa felt,' Sara thought. 'He was ill as my papa was; but he did not die.'

So her heart was more drawn to him than before. When she was sent out at night she used sometimes to feel quite glad, because there was always a chance that the curtains of the house next door might not yet be closed, and she could look into the warm room and see her adopted friend. When no one was about she used sometimes to stop, and, holding the iron railings, wish him good night as if he could hear her.

'Perhaps you can *feel* if you can't hear,' was her fancy. 'Perhaps kind thoughts reach people somehow, even through windows and doors and walls. Perhaps you feel a little warm and comforted, and don't know why, when I am standing here in the cold and hoping you will get well and happy again. I am so sorry for you,' she would whisper in an intense little voice. 'I wish you had a "Little Missus" who could pet you as I used to pet papa when he had a headache. I should like to be your "Little Missus" myself, poor dear! Good night – good night. God bless you!'

She would go away, feeling quite comforted and a little warmer herself. Her sympathy was so strong that it seemed as if it *must* reach him somehow as he sat alone in his armchair by the fire, nearly always in a great dressing-gown, and nearly always with his forehead resting in his hand as he gazed hopelessly into the fire. He looked to Sara like a man who had a trouble on his mind still, not merely like one whose troubles lay all in the past.

'He always seems as if he were thinking of something that hurts him *now*,' she said to herself, 'but he has got his money back and he will get over his brain-fever in time, so he ought not to look like that. I wonder if there is something else.'

If there was something else – something even servants did not hear of – she could not help believing that the father of the Large Family knew it – the gentleman she called Mr. Montmorency. Mr. Montmorency went to see him often, and Mrs. Montmorency and all the little Montmorencys went, too, though less often. He seemed particularly fond of the two elder little girls – the Janet and Nora who had been so alarmed when their small brother Donald had given Sara his sixpence. He had, in fact, a very tender place in his heart for all children, and particularly for little girls. Janet and Nora were as fond of him as he was of them, and looked forward with the greatest pleasure to the afternoons when they were allowed to cross the square and make their well-behaved little visits to him. They were extremely decorous little visits, because he was an invalid.

'He is a poor thing,' said Janet, 'and he says we cheer him up. We try to cheer him up very quietly.'

Janet was the head of the family, and kept the rest of it in order. It was she who decided it was discreet to ask the Indian gentleman to tell stories about India, and it was she who saw when he was tired, and it was time to steal quietly away and tell Ram Dass to go to him. They were very fond of Ram Dass. He could have told any number of stories if he had been able to speak anything but Hindustani. The Indian gentleman's real name was Mr. Carrisford, and Janet told Mr. Carrisford about the encounter with the little-girl-who-was-not-a-beggar. He was very much interested, and all the more so when he heard from Ram Dass of the adventure of the monkey on the roof. Ram Dass made for him a very clear picture of the attic and its desolateness – of the bare floor and broken plaster, the rusty, empty grate, and the hard, narrow bed.

'Carmichael,' he said to the father of the Large Family, after he had heard this description, 'I wonder how many of the attics in this square are like that one, and how many wretched little servant-girls sleep on such beds, while I toss on my down pillows, loaded and harassed by wealth that is, most of it – not mine.'

'My dear fellow,' Mr. Carmichael answered cheerily, 'the sooner you cease tormenting yourself the better it will be for you. If you possessed all the wealth of all the Indies, you could not set right all the discomforts in the world, and if you began to refurnish all the attics in this square, there would still remain all the attics in all the other squares and streets to put in order. And there you are!'

Mr. Carrisford sat and bit his nails as he looked into the glowing bed of coals in the grate.

'Do you suppose,' he said slowly, after a pause, 'do you think it is possible that the other child – the child I never cease thinking of, I believe – could be – could *possibly* be reduced to any such condition as the poor little soul next door?'

Mr. Carmichael looked at him uneasily. He knew that the worst thing the man could do for himself, for his reason and his health, was to begin to think in this particular way of this particular subject.

'If the child at Madame Pascal's school in Paris was the one you are in search of,' he answered soothingly, 'she would seem to be in the hands of people who can afford to take care of her. They adopted her because she had been the favourite companion of their little daughter who died. They had no other children, and Madame Pascal said that they were extremely well-to-do Russians.'

'And the wretched woman actually did not know where they had taken her!' exclaimed Mr. Carrisford.

Mr. Carmichael shrugged his shoulders.

'She was a shrewd, worldly Frenchwoman, and was evidently only too glad to get the child so comfortably off her hands when the father's death left her totally unprovided for. Women of her type do not trouble themselves about the futures of children who might prove burdens. The adopted parents apparently disappeared and left no trace.'

'But you say "*if*" the child was the one I am in search of. You say "if". We are not sure. There was a difference in the name.'

'Madame Pascal pronounced it as if it were Carew instead of

Crewe – but that might be merely a matter of pronunciation. The circumstances were curiously similar. An English officer in India had placed his motherless little girl at the school. He had died suddenly after losing his fortune.' Mr. Carmichael paused a moment, as if a new thought had occurred to him. 'Are you *sure* the child was left at a school in Paris? Are you sure it was Paris?'

'My dear fellow,' broke forth Carrisford, with restless bitterness, 'I am *sure* of nothing. I never saw either the child or her mother. Ralph Crewe and I loved each other as boys, but we had not met since our school-days, until we met in India. I was absorbed in the magnificent promise of the mines. He became absorbed, too. The whole thing was so huge and glittering that we half lost our heads. When we met we scarcely spoke of anything else. I only knew that the child had been sent to school somewhere. I do not even remember, now, *how* I knew it.'

He was beginning to be excited. He always became excited when his still weakened brain was stirred by memories of the catastrophes of the past.

Mr. Carmichael watched him anxiously. It was necessary to ask some questions but they must be put quietly and with caution.

'But you had reason to think the school *was* in Paris?'

'Yes,' was the answer, 'because her mother was a Frenchwoman, and I had heard that she wished her child to be educated in Paris. It seemed only likely that she would be there.'

'Yes,' Mr. Carmichael said, 'it seems more than probable.'

The Indian gentleman leaned forward and struck the table with a long, wasted hand.

'Carmichael,' he said, 'I *must* find her. If she is alive, she is somewhere. If she is friendless and penniless, it is through my fault. How is a man to get back his nerve with a thing like that on his mind? This sudden change of luck at the mines has made realities of all our most fantastic dreams, and poor Crewe's child may be begging in the street!'

'No, no,' said Carmichael. 'Try to be calm. Console yourself with the fact that when she is found you have a fortune to hand over to her.'

'Why was I not man enough to stand my ground when things

looked black?' Carrisford groaned in petulant misery. 'I believe I should have stood my ground if I had not been responsible for other people's money as well as my own. Poor Crewe had put into the scheme every penny that he owned. He trusted me – he *loved* me. And he died thinking I had ruined him – I – Tom Carrisford, who played cricket at Eton with him. What a villain he must have thought me!'

'Don't reproach yourself so bitterly.'

'I don't reproach myself because the speculation threatened to fail – I reproach myself for losing my courage. I ran away like a swindler and a thief because I could not face my best friend and tell him I had ruined him and his child.'

The good-hearted father of the Large Family put his hand on his shoulder comfortingly.

'You ran away because your brain had given way under the strain of mental torture,' he said. 'You were half delirious already. If you had not been you would have stayed and fought it out. You were in a hospital, strapped down in bed, raving with brain-fever, two days after you left the place. Remember that.'

Carrisford dropped his forehead in his hands.

'Good God! Yes,' he said. 'I was driven mad with dread and horror. I had not slept for weeks. The night I staggered out of my house all the air seemed full of hideous things mocking and mouthing at me.'

'That is explanation enough in itself,' said Mr. Carmichael. 'How could a man on the verge of brain-fever judge sanely!'

Carrisford shook his drooping head.

'And when I returned to consciousness poor Crewe was dead – and buried. And I seemed to remember nothing. I did not remember the child for months and months. Even when I began to recall her existence everything seemed in a sort of a haze.'

He stopped a moment and rubbed his forehead. 'It sometimes seems so now when I try to remember. Surely I must some time have heard Crewe speak of the school she was sent to. Don't you think so?'

'He might not have spoken of it definitely. You never seem even to have heard her real name.'

'He used to call her by an odd pet name he had invented. He called her his "Little Missus". But the wretched mines drove everything else out of our heads. We talked of nothing else. If he spoke of the school, I forgot – I forgot. And now I shall never remember.'

'Come, come,' said Carmichael. 'We shall find her yet. We will continue to search for Madame Pascal's good-natured Russians. She seemed to have a vague idea that they lived in Moscow. We will take that as a clue. I will go to Moscow.'

'If I were able to travel, I would go with you,' said Carrisford, 'but I can only sit here wrapped in furs and stare at the fire. And when I look into it I seem to see Crewe's gay young face gazing back at me. He looks as if he were asking me a question. Sometimes I dream of him at night, and he always stands before me and asks the same question in words. Can you guess what he says, Carmichael?'

Mr. Carmichael answered him in a rather low voice.

'Not exactly,' he said.

'He always says: "Tom, old man – Tom – where is the Little Missus?"' He caught at Carmichael's hand and clung to it. 'I must be able to answer him – I must!' he said. 'Help me to find her. Help me.'

On the other side of the wall Sara was sitting in her garret talking to Melchisedec, who had come out for his evening meal.

'It has been hard to be a princess to-day, Melchisedec,' she said. 'It has been harder than usual. It gets harder as the weather grows colder and the streets get more sloppy. When Lavinia laughed at my muddy skirt as I passed her in the hall, I thought of something to say all in a flash – and I only just stopped myself in time. You can't sneer back at people like that – if you are a princess. But you have to bite your tongue to hold yourself in. I bit mine. It was a cold afternoon, Melchisedec. And it's a cold night.'

Quite suddenly she put her black head down in her arms, as she often did when she was alone.

'Oh, papa,' she whispered, 'what a long time it seems since I was your "Little Missus"!'

This was what happened that day on both sides of the wall.

13 One of the Populace

The winter was a wretched one. There were days on which Sara tramped through snow when she went on her errands; there were worse days when the snow melted and combined itself with mud to form slush; there were others when the fog was so thick that the lamps in the streets were lighted all day and London looked as it had looked the afternoon, several years ago, when the cab had driven through the thoroughfares with Sara tucked up on its seat, leaning against her father's shoulder. On such days the windows of the house of the Large Family always looked delightfully cosy and alluring, and the study in which the Indian gentleman sat glowed with warmth and rich colour. But the attic was dismal beyond words. There were no longer sunsets or sunrises to look at, and scarcely ever any stars, it seemed to Sara. The clouds hung low over the skylight, and were either grey or mud-colour, or dropping heavy rain. At four o'clock in the afternoon, even when there was no special fog, the daylight was at an end. If it was necessary to go to her attic for anything, Sara was obliged to light a candle. The women in the kitchen were depressed, and that made them more ill-tempered than ever. Becky was driven like a little slave.

' ''Twarn't for you, miss,' she said hoarsely to Sara one night when she had crept into the attic— ' 'twarn't for you, an' the Bastille, an' bein' the prisoner in the next cell, I should die. That there does seem real now, doesn't it? The missus is more like the head jailer every day she lives. I can jest see them big keys you say she carries. The cook, she's like one of the under-jailers. Tell me some more, please, miss – tell me about the subt'ranean passage we've dug under the walls.'

'I'll tell you something warmer,' shivered Sara. 'Get your coverlet and wrap it round you, and I'll get mine, and we will huddle it close together on the bed, and I'll tell you about the tropical forest where the Indian gentleman's monkey used to live. When I see him sitting on the table near the window and looking out into the street with that mournful expression, I always feel sure he is thinking about the tropical forest where he used to swing by his tail from cocoanut-trees. I wonder who caught him, and if he left a family behind who had depended on him for cocoanuts.'

'That is warmer, miss,' said Becky gratefully, 'but, someways, even the Bastille is sort of heatin' when you gets to tellin' about it.'

'That is because it makes you think of something else,' said Sara, wrapping the coverlet round her until only her small dark face was to be seen looking out of it. 'I've noticed this. What you have to do with your mind, when your body is miserable, is to make it think of something else.'

'Can you do it, miss?' faltered Becky, regarding her with admiring eyes.

Sara knitted her brows a moment.

'Sometimes I can and sometimes I can't,' she said stoutly. 'But when I *can* I'm all right. And what I believe is that we always could – if we practised enough. I've been practising a good deal lately, and it's beginning to be easier than it used to be. When things are horrible – just horrible – I think as hard as ever I can of being a princess. I say to myself: "I am a princess, and I am a fairy one, and because I am a fairy nothing can hurt me or make me uncomfortable," You don't know how it makes you forget' – with a laugh.

She had many opportunities of making her mind think of something else, and many opportunities of proving to herself whether or not she was a princess. But one of the strongest tests she was ever put to came on a certain dreadful day which, she often thought afterward, would never quite fade out of her memory even in the years to come.

For several days it had rained continuously; the streets were chilly and sloppy and full of dreary, cold mist; there was mud everywhere – sticky London mud – and over everything the pall of drizzle and fog. Of course there were several long and tiresome errands to be done – there always were on days like this – and Sara was sent out again and again, until her shabby clothes were damp through. The absurd old feathers on her forlorn hat were more draggled and absurd than ever, and her down-trodden shoes were so wet that they could not hold any more water. Added to this, she had been deprived of her dinner, because Miss Minchin had chosen to punish her. She was so cold and hungry and tired that her face began to have a pinched look, and now and then some kindhearted person passing her in the street glanced at her with sudden sympathy. But she did not know that. She hurried on, trying to make her mind think of something else. It was really very necessary. Her way of doing it was to 'pretend' and 'suppose' with all the strength that was left in her. But really this time it was harder than she had ever found it, and once or twice she thought it almost made her more cold and hungry instead of less so. But she persevered obstinately, and as the muddy water squelched through her broken shoes and the wind seemed trying to drag her thin jacket from her, she talked to herself as she walked, though she did not speak aloud or even move her lips.

'Suppose I had dry clothes on,' she thought. 'Suppose I had good shoes and a long, thick coat and merino stockings and a whole umbrella. And suppose – suppose – just when I was near a baker's where they sold hot buns, I should find sixpence – which belonged to nobody. *Suppose*, if I should go into the shop and buy six of the hottest buns and eat them all without stopping.'

Some very odd things happened in this world sometimes.

It certainly was an odd thing that happened to Sara. She had to cross the street just when she was saying this to herself. The mud was dreadful – she almost had to wade. She picked her way as carefully as she could, but she could not save herself much; only, in picking her way, she had to look down at her feet and the mud, and in looking down – just as she reached the pavement – she saw something shining in the gutter. It was actually a piece of silver – a tiny piece trodden upon by many feet, but still with spirit enough left to shine a little. Not quite a sixpence, but the next thing to it – a fourpenny piece.

In one second it was in her cold little red-and-blue hand.

'Oh,' she gasped, 'it is true! It is true!'

And then, if you will believe me, she looked straight at the shop directly facing her. And it was a baker's shop, and a cheerful stout, motherly woman with rosy cheeks was putting into the window a tray of delicious new baked hot buns, fresh from the oven – large, plump, shiny buns, with currants in them.

It almost made Sara feel faint for a few seconds – the shock, and the sight of the buns, and the delightful odours of warm bread floating up through the baker's cellar window.

She knew she need not hesitate to use the little piece of money. It had evidently been lying in the mud for some time, and its owner was completely lost in the stream of passing people who crowded and jostled each other all day long.

'But I'll go and ask the baker woman if she has lost anything,' she said to herself, rather faintly. So she crossed the pavement and put her wet foot on the step. As she did so she saw something that made her stop.

It was a little figure more forlorn even than herself – a little figure which was not much more than a bundle of rags, from which small, bare, red, muddy feet peeped out, only because the rags with which their owner was trying to cover them were not long enough. Above the rags appeared a shock head of tangled hair, and a dirty face with big, hollow, hungry eyes.

Sara knew they were hungry eyes the moment she saw them, and she felt a sudden sympathy.

'This,' she said to herself, with a little sigh, 'is one of the populace – and she is hungrier than I am.'

The child – this 'one of the populace' – stared up at Sara, and shuffled herself aside a little, so as to give her room to pass. She was used to being made to give room to everybody. She knew that if a policeman chanced to see her he would tell her to 'move on'.

Sara clutched her little fourpenny piece and hesitated a few seconds. Then she spoke to her.

'Are you hungry?' she asked.

The child shuffled herself and her rags a little more.

'Ain't I jist?' she said in a hoarse voice. 'Jist ain't I?'

'Haven't you had any dinner?' said Sara,

'No dinner' – more hoarsely still and with more shuffling. 'Nor yet no bre'fast – nor yet no supper. No nothin'.'

'Since when?' asked Sara.

'Dunno. Never got nothin' to-day – nowhere. I've axed an' axed.'

Just to look at her made Sara more hungry and faint. But those queer little thoughts were at work in her brain, and she was talking to herself, though she was sick at heart.

'If I'm a princess,' she was saying – 'if I'm a princess – when they were poor and driven from their thrones – they always shared – with the populace – if they met one poorer and hungrier than themselves. They always shared. Buns are a penny each. If it had been sixpence I could have eaten six. It won't be enough for either of us. But it will be better than nothing.'

'Wait a minute,' she said to the beggar child.

She went into the shop. It was warm and smelled deliciously. The woman was just going to put some more hot buns into the window.

'If you please,' said Sara, 'have you lost fourpence – a silver fourpence?' And she held the forlorn little piece of money out to her.

The woman looked at it and then at her – at her intense little face and draggled, once fine clothes.

'Bless us, no!' she answered. 'Did you find it?'

'Yes,' said Sara. 'In the gutter.'

'Keep it then,' said the woman. 'It may have been there for a week, and goodness knows who lost it. *You* could never find out.'

'I know that,' said Sara, 'but I thought I would ask you.'

'Not many would,' said the woman, looking puzzled and interested and good-natured all at once.

'Do you want to buy something?' she added, as she saw Sara glance at the buns.

'Four buns, if you please,' said Sara. 'Those at a penny each.'

The woman went to the window and put some in a paper bag.

Sara noticed that she put in six.

'I said four, if you please,' she explained. 'I have only fourpence.'

'I'll throw in two for makeweight,' said the woman, with her good-natured look. 'I dare say you can eat them some time. Aren't you hungry?'

A mist rose before Sara's eyes.

'Yes,' she answered. 'I am very hungry, and I am much obliged to you for your kindness; and' – she was going to add – 'there is a child outside who is hungrier than I am.' But just at that moment two or three customers came in at once, and each one seemed in a hurry, so she could only thank the woman again and go out.

The beggar girl was still huddled up in the corner of the step. She looked frightful in her wet and dirty rags. She was staring straight before her with a stupid look of suffering, and Sara saw her suddenly draw the back of her roughened black hand across her eyes to rub away the tears which seemed to have surprised her by forcing their way from under the lids. She was muttering to herself.

Sara opened the paper bag and took out one of the hot buns, which had already warmed her own cold hands a little.

'See,' she said, putting the bun in the ragged lap, 'this is nice and hot. Eat it, and you will not feel so hungry.'

The child started and stared up at her, as if such sudden, amazing good luck almost frightened her; then she snatched up the bun and began to cram it into her mouth with great wolfish bites.

'Oh, my! Oh, my!' Sara heard her say hoarsely, in wild delight. '*Oh, my!*'

Sara took out three more buns and put them down.

The sound in the hoarse, ravenous voice was awful.

'She is hungrier than I am,' she said to herself. 'She's starving.' But her hand trembled when she put down the fourth bun. I'm not starving,' she said – and she put down the fifth.

The little ravenous London savage was still snatching and devouring when she turned away. She was too ravenous to give any thanks, even if she had ever been taught politeness – which she had not. She was only a poor little wild animal.

'Good–bye,' said Sara.

When she reached the other side of the street she looked back. The child had a bun in each hand, and had stopped in the middle of a bite to watch her. Sara gave her a little nod, and the child, after another stare – a curious lingering stare – jerked her shaggy head in response, and until Sara was out of sight she did not take another bite or even finish the one she had begun.

At that moment the baker-woman looked out of her shop window.

'Well, I never!' she exclaimed. 'If that young 'un hasn't given her buns to a beggar child! It wasn't because she didn't want them, either. Well, well, she looked hungry enough. I'd give something to know what she did it for.'

She stood behind her window for a few moments and pondered. Then her curiosity got the better of her. She went to the door and spoke to the beggar child.

'Who gave you those buns?' she asked her.

The child nodded her head towards Sara's vanishing figure.

'What did she say?' inquired the woman.

'Axed me if I was 'ungry,' replied the hoarse voice.

'What did you say?'

'Said I was jist.'

'And then she came in and got the buns, and gave them to you, did she?'

The child nodded.

'How many?'

'Five.'

The woman thought it over.

'Left just one for herself,' she said in a low voice. 'And she could have eaten the whole six – I saw it in her eyes.'

She looked after the little draggled far-away figure, and felt more disturbed in her usually comfortable mind than she had felt for many a day.

'I wish she hadn't gone so quick,' she said. 'I'm blest if she shouldn't have had a dozen.' Then she turned to the child.

'Are you hungry yet?' she said.

'I'm allus hungry,' was the answer, 'but 't ain't as bad as it was.'

'Come in here,' said the woman, and she held open the shop door.

The child got up and shuffled in. To be invited into a warm place full of bread seemed an incredible thing. She did not know what was going to happen. She did not care, even.

'Get yourself warm,' said the woman, pointing to a fire in the tiny back-room. 'And look here; when you are hard up for a bit of bread, you can come in here and ask for it. I'm blest if I won't give it to you for that young one's sake.'

Sara found some comfort in her remaining bun. At all events, it was very hot, and it was better than nothing. As she walked along she broke off small pieces and ate them slowly to make them last longer.

'Suppose it was a magic bun,' she said, 'and a bite was as much as a whole dinner. I should be over-eating myself if I went on like this.'

It was dark when she reached the square where the Select Seminary was situated. The lights in the houses were all lighted. The blinds were not yet drawn in the windows of the room where she nearly always caught glimpses of members of the Large Family. Frequently at this hour she could see the gentleman she called Mr. Montmorency sitting in a big chair, with a small swarm round him, talking, laughing, perching on the arms of his seat or on his knees or leaning against them. This evening the swarm was about him, but he was not seated. On the contrary, there was a good deal of excitement going on. It was evident that a journey was to be taken, and it was Mr. Montmorency who was to take it. A brougham stood before the door, and a big portmanteau had been strapped upon it. The children were dancing about, chattering and hanging on to their father. The pretty rosy mother was standing near him, talking as if she was asking final questions. Sara paused a moment to see the little ones lifted up and kissed and the bigger ones bent over and kissed also.

'I wonder if he will stay away long,' she thought. 'The portmanteau is rather big. Oh, dear, how they will miss him! I shall miss him myself – even though he doesn't know I am alive.'

When the door opened she moved away – remembering the sixpence – but she saw the traveller come out and stand against the background of the warmly lighted hall, the older children still hovering about him.

'Will Moscow be covered with snow?' said the little girl Janet. 'Will there be ice everywhere?'

'Shall you drive in a droshky?' cried another. 'Shall you see the Czar?'

'I will write and tell you all about it,' he answered, laughing. 'And I will send you pictures of mujiks and things. Run into the house. It is a hideous damp night. I would rather stay with you than go to Moscow. Good night! Good night, duckies! God bless you!' And he ran down the steps and jumped into the brougham.

'If you find the little girl, give her our love,' shouted Guy Clarence, jumping up and down on the doormat.

Then they went in and shut the door.

'Did you see,' said Janet to Nora, as they went back to the room – 'the little-girl-who-is-not-a-beggar was passing? She looked all cold and wet, and I saw her turn her head over her shoulder and look at us. Mamma says her clothes always look as if they had been given her by some one who was quite rich – some one who only let her have them because they were too shabby to wear. The people at the school always send her out on errands on the horridest days and nights there are.'

Sara crossed the square to Miss Minchin's area steps, feeling faint and shaky.

'I wonder who the girl is,' she thought – 'the little girl he is going to look for.'

And she went down the area steps, hugging her basket and finding it very heavy indeed, as the father of the Large Family drove quickly on his way to the station to take the train which was to carry him to Moscow, where he was to make his best efforts to search for the lost little daughter of Captain Crewe.

14 What Melchisedec Heard and Saw

On this very afternoon, while Sara was out, a strange thing happened in the attic. Only Melchisedec saw and heard it; and he was so much alarmed and mystified that he scuttled back to his hole and hid there, and really quaked and trembled as he peeped out furtively and with great caution to watch what was going on.

The attic had been very still all the day after Sara had left it in the early morning. The stillness had only been broken by the pattering of the rain upon the slates and the skylight. Melchisedec had, in fact, found it rather dull; and when the rain ceased to patter and perfect silence reigned, he decided to come out and reconnoitre, though experience taught him that Sara would not return for some time. He had been rambling and sniffing about, and had just found a totally unexpected and unexplained crumb left from his last meal, when his attention was attracted by a sound on the roof. He stopped to listen with a palpitating heart. The sound suggested that something was moving on the roof. It was approaching the skylight; it reached the skylight. The skylight was being mysteriously opened. A dark face peered into the attic; then another face appeared behind it, and both looked in with signs of caution and interest. Two men were outside on the roof, and were making silent preparations to enter through the skylight itself. One was Ram Dass, and the other was a young man who was the Indian gentleman's secretary; but of course Melchisedec did not know this. He only knew that the men were invading the silence and privacy of the attic; and as the one with the dark face let himself down through the aperture with such lightness and dexterity that he did not make the slightest sound, Melchisedec turned tail and fled precipitately back to his hole. He was frightened to death. He had ceased to be timid with Sara, and knew she would never throw anything but crumbs, and would never make any sound other than the soft, low, coaxing whistling; but strange men were dangerous things to remain near. He lay close and flat near the entrance of his home, just managing to peep through the crack with a bright, alarmed eye. How much he understood of the talk he heard I am not in the least able to say; but, even if he had understood it all, he would probably have remained greatly mystified.

The secretary who was light and young, slipped through the skylight as noiselessly as Ram Dass had done; and he caught a last glimpse of Melchisedec's vanishing tail.

'Was that a rat?' he asked Ram Dass, in a whisper.

'Yes; a rat, Sahib,' answered Ram Dass, also whispering. 'There are many in the walls.'

'Ugh!' exclaimed the young man, 'it is a wonder the child is not terrified by them.'

Ram Dass made a gesture with his hands. He also smiled respectfully. He was in this place as the intimate exponent of Sara, though she had only spoken to him once.

'The child is the little friend of all things, Sahib,' he answered. 'She is not as other children. I see her when she does not see me. I slip across the slates and look at her many nights to see that she is safe. I watch her from my window when she does not know I am near. She stands on the table there and looks out at the sky as if it spoke to her. The sparrows come at her call. The rat she has fed and tamed in her loneliness. The poor slave of the house comes to her for comfort. There is a little child who comes to her in secret; there is one older who worships her and would listen to her for ever if she might. This I have seen when I have crept across the roof. By the mistress of the house – who is an evil woman – she is treated like a pariah; but she has the bearing of a child who is of the blood of kings!'

'You seem to know a great deal about her,' the secretary said.

'All her life each day I know,' answered Ram Dass. 'Her going out I know, and her coming in; her sadness and her poor joys; her coldness and her hunger. I know when she sits alone until midnight, learning from her books; I know when her secret friends steal to her and she is happier – as children can be, even in the midst of poverty – because they come and she may laugh and talk with them in whispers. If she were ill I should know, and I would come and serve her if it might be done.'

'You are sure no one comes near this place but herself, and that she will not return and surprise us. She would be frightened if she found us here, and the Sahib Carrisford's plan would be spoiled.'

Ram Dass crossed noiselessly to the door and stood close to it.

'None mount here but herself, Sahib,' he said. 'She has gone out with her basket and may be gone for hours. If I stand here I can hear any step before it reaches the last flight of the stairs.'

The secretary took a pencil and a tablet from his breast pocket.

'Keep your ears open,' he said; and he began to walk slowly and softly round the miserable little room, making rapid notes on his tablet as he looked at things.

First he went to the narrow bed. He pressed his hand upon the mattress and uttered an exclamation.

'As hard as a stone,' he said. 'That will have to be altered some day when she is out. A special journey can be made to bring it across. It cannot be done to-night.' He lifted the covering and examined the one thin pillow.

'Coverlet dingy and worn, blanket thin, sheets patched and ragged,' he said. 'What a bed for a child to sleep in – and in a house which calls itself respectable! There has not been a fire in that grate for many a day,' glancing at the rusty fireplace.

'Never since I have seen it,' said Ram Dass. 'The mistress of the house is not one who remembers that another than herself may be cold.'

The secretary was writing quickly on his tablet. He looked up from it as he tore off a leaf and slipped it into his breast pocket.

'It is a strange way of doing the thing,' he said. 'Who planned it?'

Ram Dass made a modestly apologetic obeisance.

'It is true that the first thought was mine, Sahib,' he said, 'though it was naught but a fancy. I am fond of this child; we are both lonely. It is her way to relate her visions to her secret friends. Being sad one night. I lay close to the open skylight and listened. The vision she related told what this miserable room might be if it had comforts in it. She seemed to see it as she talked, and she grew cheered and warmed as she spoke. Then she came to this fancy; and the next day, the Sahib being ill and wretched, I told him of the thing to amuse him. It seemed then but a dream, but it pleased the Sahib. To hear of the child's doings gave him entertainment. He became interested in her and asked questions. At last he began to please himself with the thought of making her visions real things.'

'You think that it can be done while she sleeps? Suppose she awakened,' suggested the secretary; and it was evident that whatsoever the plan referred to was, it had caught and pleased his fancy as well as the Sahib Carrisford's.

'I can move as if my feet were of velvet,' Ram Dass replied, 'and children sleep soundly – even the unhappy ones. I could have entered this room in the night many times, and without causing her to turn upon her pillow. If the other bearer passes to me the things through the window, I can do all and she will not stir. When she awakens she will think a magician has been there.'

He smiled as if his heart warmed under his white robe, and the secretary smiled back at him.

'It will be like a story from the "Arabian Nights",' he said. 'Only an Oriental could have planned it. It does not belong to London fogs.'

They did not remain very long, to the great relief of Melchisedec, who, as he probably did not comprehend their conversation, felt their movements and whispers ominous. The young secretary seemed interested in everything. He wrote down things about the floor, the fire-place, the broken footstool, the old table, the walls – which last he touched with his hand again and again, seeming much pleased when he found that a number of old nails had been driven in various places.

'You can hang things on them,' he said.

Ram Dass smiled mysteriously.

'Yesterday, when she was out,' he said, 'I entered, bringing with me small, sharp nails which can be pressed into the wall without blows from a hammer. I placed many in the plaster where I may need them. They are ready.'

The Indian gentleman's secretary stood still and looked round him as he thrust his tablets back into his pocket.

'I think I have made notes enough; we can go now,' he said. 'The Sahib Carrisford has a warm heart. It is a thousand pities that he has not found the lost child.'

'If he should find her his strength would be restored to him,' said Ram Dass. 'His God may lead to him yet.'

Then they slipped through the skylight as noiselessly as they had entered it. And, after he was quite sure they had gone, Melchisedec was greatly relieved, and in the course of a few minutes felt it safe to emerge from his hole again and scuffle about in the hope that even such alarming human beings as these might have chanced to carry crumbs in their pockets and drop one or two of them.

15 The Magic

When Sara had passed the house next door she had seen Ram Dass closing the shutters, and caught her glimpse of this room also.

'It is a long time since I saw a nice place from the inside,' was the thought which crossed her mind.

There was the usual bright fire glowing in the grate, and the Indian gentleman was sitting before it. His head was resting in his hand, and he looked as lonely and unhappy as ever.

'Poor man!' said Sara. 'I wonder what *you* are supposing.'

And this was what he was 'supposing' at that very moment.

'Suppose,' he was thinking, 'suppose – even if Carmichael traces the people to Moscow – the little girl they took from Madame Pascal's school in Paris is *not* the one we are in search of. Suppose she proves to be quite a different child. What steps shall I take next?'

When Sara went into the house she met Miss Minchin, who had come downstairs to scold the cook.

'Where have you wasted your time?' she demanded. 'You have been out for hours.'

'It was so wet and muddy,' Sara answered, 'it was hard to walk, because my shoes were so bad and slipped about.'

'Make no excuses,' said Miss Minchin, 'and tell no falsehoods.'

Sara went into the cook. The cook had received a severe lecture, and was in a fearful temper as a result. She was only too rejoiced to have some one to vent her rage on, and Sara was a convenience, as usual.

'Why didn't you stay all night?' she snapped.

Sara laid her purchases on the table.

'Here are the things,' she said.

The cook looked them over, grumbling. She was in a very savage humour indeed.

'May I have something to eat?' Sara asked rather faintly.

'Tea's over and done with,' was the answer. 'Did you expect me to keep it hot for you?'

Sara stood silent for a second.

'I had no dinner,' she said next, and her voice was quite low. She made it low because she was afraid it would tremble.

'There's some bread in the pantry,' said the cook. 'That's all you'll get at this time of day.'

Sara went and found the bread. It was old and hard and dry. The cook was in too vicious a humour to give her anything to eat with it. It was always safe and easy to vent her spite on Sara. Really, it was hard for the child to climb the three long flights of stairs leading to her attic. She often found them long and steep when she was tired; but to-night it seemed as if she would never reach the top. Several times she was obliged to stop to rest. When she reached the top landing she was glad to see the glimmer of a light coming from under the door. That meant that Ermengarde had managed to creep up to pay her a visit. There was some comfort in that. It was better than to go into the room alone and find it empty and desolate. There presence of plump, comfortable Ermengarde, wrapped in her red shawl, would warm it a little.

Yes; there Ermengarde was when she opened the door. She was sitting in the middle of the bed, with her feet tucked safely under her. She had never become intimate with Melchisedec and his family, though they rather fascinated her. When she found herself alone in the attic she always preferred to sit on the bed until Sara arrived. She had, in fact, on this occasion had time to become rather nervous, because Melchisedec had appeared and sniffed about a good deal, and once had made her utter a repressed squeal by sitting up on his hind-legs, and, while he looked at her, sniffing pointedly in her direction.

'Oh, Sara,' she cried out, 'I *am* glad you have come. Melchy *would* sniff about so. I tried to coax him to go back, but he wouldn't for such a long time. I like him, you know; but it does frighten me when he sniffs right at me. Do you think he ever *would* jump?'

'No,' answered Sara.

'"I'm very sorry," Sara said, "I haven't one crumb left"'

Ermengarde crawled forward on the bed to look at her.

'You *do* look tired, Sara,' she said. 'You are quite pale.'

'I *am* tired,' said Sara, dropping on to the lopsided footstool. 'Oh, there's Melchisedec, poor thing. He's come to ask for his supper.'

Melchisedec had come out of his hole as if he had been listening for her footstep. Sara was quite sure he knew it. He came forward with an affectionate, expectant expression as Sara put her hand in her pocket and turned it inside out, shaking her head.

'I'm very sorry,' she said. 'I haven't one crumb left. Go home, Melchisedec, and tell your wife there was nothing in my pocket. I'm afraid I forgot because the cook and Miss Minchin were so cross.'

Melchisedec seemed to understand. He shuffled resignedly, if not contentedly, back to his home.

'I did not expect to see you to-night, Ermie,' Sara said.

Ermengarde hugged herself in the red shawl.

'Miss Amelia has gone out to spend the night with her old aunt,' she explained. 'No one else ever comes and looks into the bedrooms after we are in bed. I could stay here until morning if I wanted to.'

She pointed toward the table under the skylight. Sara had not looked toward it as she came in. A number of books were piled upon it. Ermengarde's gesture was a dejected one.

'Papa has sent me some more books, Sara,' she said. 'There they are.'

Sara looked round and got up at once. She ran to the table, and picking up the top volume, turned over its leaves quickly. For the moment she forgot her discomforts.

'Ah,' she cried out, 'how beautiful! Carlyle's "French Revolution"'. I have *so* wanted to read that!'

'I haven't,' said Ermengarde. 'And papa will be so cross if I don't. He'll expect me to know all about it when I go home for the holidays. What *shall* I do?'

Sara stopped turning over the leaves and looked at her with an excited flush on her cheeks.

'Look here,' she cried, 'if you'll lend me these books, *I'll* read them – and tell you everything that's in them afterwards – and I'll tell it so that you will remember it, too.'

'Oh goodness!' exclaimed Ermengarde. 'Do you think you can?'

'I know I can,' Sara answered. 'The little ones always remember what I tell them.'

'Sara,' said Ermengarde, hope gleaming in her round face, 'if you'll do that, and make me remember. I'll – I'll give you anything.'

'I don't want you to give me anything,' said Sara. I want your books – I want them!' And her eyes grew big, and her chest heaved.

'Take them, then,' said Ermengarde. 'I wish I wanted them – but I don't. I'm not clever, and my father is, and he thinks I ought to be.'

Sara was opening one book after the other. 'What are you going to tell your father?' she asked, a slight doubt dawning in her mind.

'Oh, he needn't know,' answered Ermengarde. 'He'll think I've read them.'

Sara put down her book and shook her head slowly. 'That's almost like telling lies,' she said. 'And lies – well, you see, they are not only wicked – they're *vulgar*. Sometimes' – reflectively – 'I've thought perhaps I might do something wicked – might suddenly fly into a rage and kill Miss Minchin, you know, when she was ill-treating me – but I *couldn't* be vulgar. Why can't you tell your father *I* read them?'

'He wants me to read them,' said Ermengarde, a little discouraged by this unexpected turn of affairs.

'He wants you to know what is in them,' said Sara. 'And if I can tell it to you in an easy way and make you remember it, I should think he would like that.'

'He'll like it if I learn anything in *any* way,' said rueful Ermengarde. 'You would if you were my father.'

'It's not your fault that——' began Sara. She pulled herself up and stopped rather suddenly. She had been going to say: 'It's not your fault that you are stupid.'

'That what?' Ermengarde asked.

'That you can't learn things quickly,' amended Sara. 'If you can't, you can't. If I can – why, I can; that's all.'

She always felt very tender of Ermengarde, and tried not to let her feel too strongly the difference between being able to learn anything at once, and not being able to learn anything at all. As she looked at her plump face, one of her wise, old-fashioned thoughts came to her.

'Perhaps,' she said, 'to be able to learn things quickly isn't everything. To be kind is worth a great deal to other people. If Miss Minchin knew everything on earth and was like what she is now, she'd still be a detestable thing, and everybody would hate her. Lots of clever people have done harm and have been wicked. Look at Robespierre——'

She stopped and examined Ermengarde's countenance, which was beginning to look bewildered. 'Don't you remember?' she demanded. 'I told you about him not long ago. I believe you've forgotten.'

'Well, I don't remember *all* of it,' admitted Ermengarde.

'Well, you wait a minute,' said Sara, 'and I'll take off my wet things and wrap myself in the coverlet and tell you over again.'

She took off her hat and coat and hung them on a nail against the wall, and she changed her wet shoes for an old pair of slippers. Then she jumped on the bed, and drawing the coverlet about her shoulders, sat with her arms round her knees.

'Now, listen,' she said.

She plunged into the gory records of the French Revolution, and told such stories of it that Ermengarde's eyes grew round with alarm and she held her breath. But though she was rather terrified, there was a delightful thrill in listening, and she was not likely to forget Robespierre again, or to have any doubts about the Princess de Lamballe.

'You know they put her head on a pike and danced round it,' Sara exclaimed. 'And she had beautiful floating blonde hair; and when I think of her, I never see her head on her body, but always on a pike, with those furious people dancing and howling.'

It was agreed that Mr. St John was to be told the plan they had made, and for the present the books were to be left in the attic.

'Now let's tell each other things,' said Sara. 'How are you getting on with your French lessons?'

'Ever so much better since the last time I came up here and you explained the conjugations. Miss Minchin could not understand why I did my exercises so well that first morning.'

Sara laughed a little and hugged her knees.

'She doesn't understand why Lottie is doing her sums so well,' she said, 'but it is because she creeps up here, too, and I help her.' She glanced round the room. 'The attic would be rather nice – if it wasn't so dreadful,' she said, laughing again. 'It's a good place to pretend in.'

The truth was that Ermengarde did not know anything of the sometimes almost unbearable side of life in the attic, and she had not a sufficiently vivid imagination to depict it for herself. On the rare occasions that she could reach Sara's room she only saw that side of it which was made exciting by things which were 'pretended' and stories which were told. Her visits partook of the character of adventures; and though sometimes Sara looked rather pale, and it was not to be denied that she had grown very thin, her proud little spirit would not admit of complaints. She had never confessed that at times she was almost ravenous with hunger, as she was to-night. She was growing rapidly, and her constant walking and running about would have given her a keen appetite even if she had had abundant and regular meals of a much more nourishing nature than the unappetizing, inferior food snatched at such odd times as suited the kitchen convenience. She was growing used to a certain gnawing feeling in her young stomach.

'I suppose soldiers feel like this when they are on a long and weary march,' she often said to herself. She liked the sound of the phrase, 'long and weary march.' It made her feel rather like a soldier. She had also a quaint sense of being a hostess in the attic.

'If I lived in a castle,' she argued, 'and Ermengarde was the lady of another castle, and came to see me, with knights and squires and vassals riding with her, and pennons flying; when I heard the clarions sounding outside the drawbridge I should go down to receive her, and I should spread feasts in the banquet-hall and call in minstrels to sing and play and relate romances. When she comes into the attic I can't spread feasts, but I can tell stories, and not let her know disagreeable things. I dare say poor chatelaines had to do that in times of famine, when their lands had been pillaged.' She was a proud, brave little chatelaine, and dispensed generously the one hospitality she could offer – the dreams she dreamed – the visions she saw – the imaginings which were her joy and comfort.

So, as they sat together, Ermengarde did not know that she was faint as well as ravenous, and that while she talked she now and then wondered if her hunger would let her sleep when she was left alone. She felt as if she had never been quite so hungry before.

'I wish I was as thin as you, Sara,' Ermengarde said suddenly. 'I believe you are thinner than you used to be. Your eyes look so big, and look at the sharp little bones sticking out of your elbow!'

Sara pulled down her sleeve, which had pushed itself up.

'I always was a thin child,' she said bravely, 'and I always had big green eyes.'

'I love your queer eyes,' said Ermengarde, looking into them with affectionate admiration. 'They always look as if they saw such a long way. I love them, and I love them to be green – though they look black generally.'

'They are cat's eyes,' laughed Sara, 'but I can't see in the dark with them – because I have tried, and I couldn't – I wish I could.'

It was just at this minute that something happened at the skylight which neither of them saw. If either of them had chanced to turn and look, she would have been startled by the sight of a dark face which peered cautiously into the room and disappeared as quickly and almost as silently as it had appeared. Not *quite* as silently, however. Sara, who had keen ears, suddenly turned a little and looked up at the roof.

'That didn't sound like Melchisedec,' she said. 'It wasn't scratchy enough.'

'What?' said Ermengarde, a little startled.

'Didn't you think you heard something?' asked Sara.

'N-no,' Ermengarde faltered. 'Did you?'

'Perhaps I didn't,' said Sara, 'but I thought I did. It sounded as if something was on the slates – something that dragged softly.'

'What could it be?' said Ermengarde. 'Could it be – robbers?'

'No,' Sara began cheerfully. 'There is nothing to steal——'

She broke off in the middle of her words. They both heard the sound that checked her. It was not on the slates, but on the stairs below, and it was Miss Minchin's angry voice. Sara sprang off the bed, and put out the candle.

'She is scolding Becky,' she whispered, as she stood in the

darkness. 'She is making her cry.'

'Will she come in here?' Ermengarde whispered back, panic-stricken.

'No. She will think I am in bed. Don't stir.'

It was very seldom that Miss Minchin mounted the last flight of stairs. Sara could only remember that she had done it once before. But now she was angry enough to be coming at least part of the way up, and it sounded as if she was driving Becky before her.

'You impudent, dishonest child!' they heard her say. 'Cook tells me she has missed things repeatedly.'

''Twarn't me, mum,' said Becky, sobbing. 'I was 'ungry enough, but 'twarn't me – never!'

'You deserve to be sent to prison,' said Miss Minchin's voice. 'Picking and stealing! Half a meat-pie, indeed!'

''Twarn't me,' wept Becky. 'I could 'ave eat a whole 'un – but I never laid a finger on it.'

Miss Minchin was out of breath between temper and mounting the stairs. The meat-pie had been intended for her special late supper. It became apparent that she boxed Becky's ears.

'Don't tell falsehoods' she said. 'Go to your room this instant.'

Both Sara and Ermengarde heard the slap, and then heard Becky run in her slipshod shoes up the stairs and into her attic. They heard her door shut, and knew that she threw herself upon her bed.

'I could 'ave e't two of 'em,' they heard her cry into her pillow. 'An' I never took a bite. 'Twas cook give it to her policeman.'

Sara stood in the middle of the room in the darkness. She was clenching her little teeth and opening and shutting fiercely her outstretched hands. She could scarcely stand still, but she dared not move until Miss Minchin had gone down the stairs and all was still.

'The wicked, cruel thing!' she burst forth. 'The cook takes things herself and then says Becky steals them. She *doesn't*! She *doesn't*! She's so hungry sometimes that she eats crusts out of the ash-barrel!' She pressed her hands hard against her face and burst into passionate little sobs, and Ermengarde, hearing this unusual thing, was overawed by it. Sara was crying! The unconquerable Sara! It seemed to denote something new – some mood she had never known. Suppose——!

Suppose! A new dread possibility presented itself to her kind, slow, little mind all at once. She crept off the bed in the dark and found her way to the table where the candle stood. She struck a match and lit the candle. When she had lighted it, she bent forward and looked at Sara, with her new thought growing to a defnite fear in her eyes.

'Sara,' she said in a timid, almost awe-stricken voice, 'are – are – you never told me – I don't want to be rude, but – are *you* ever hungry?'

It was too much just at that moment. The barrier broke down. Sara lifted her face from her hands.

'Yes,' she said in a new passionate way. 'Yes, I am. I'm so hungry now that I could almost eat *you*. And it makes it worse to hear poor Becky. She's hungrier than I am.'

Ermengarde gasped.

'Oh! Oh!' she cried woefully, 'and I never knew!'

'I didn't want you to know,' Sara said. 'It would have made me feel like a street beggar. I know I look like a street beggar.'

'No, you don't – you don't!' Ermengarde broke in. 'Your clothes are a little queer – but you *couldn't* look like a street beggar. You haven't a street beggar face.'

'A little boy once gave me a sixpence for charity,' said Sara, with a short little laugh in spite of herself. 'Here it is.' And she pulled out the thin ribbon from her neck. 'He wouldn't have given me his Christmas sixpence if I hadn't looked as if I needed it.'

Somehow the sight of the dear little sixpence was good for both of them. It made them laugh a little, though they both had tears in their eyes.

'Who was he?' asked Ermengarde, looking at it quite as if it had not been a mere ordinary silver sixpence.

'He was a darling little thing going to a party,' said Sara. 'He was one of the Large Family, the little one with the round legs – the one I call Guy Clarence. I suppose his nursery was crammed with Christmas presents and hampers full of cakes and things, and he could see I had had nothing.'

Ermengarde gave a little jump backward. The last sentences had recalled something to her troubled mind and given her a sudden inspiration.

'Oh, Sara!' she cried. 'What a silly thing I am not to have thought of it!'

'Of what?'

'Something splendid!' said Ermengarde, in an excited hurry. 'This very afternoon my nicest aunt sent me a box. It is full of good things. I never touched it, I had so much pudding at dinner, and I was so bothered about papa's books.' Her words began to tumble over each other. 'It's got cake in it, and little meat-pies, and jam-tarts and buns, and oranges and red-currant wine, and figs and chocolate. I'll creep back to my room and get it this minute, and we'll eat it now.'

Sara almost reeled. When one is faint with hunger the mention of food has sometimes a curious effect. She clutched Ermengarde's arm.

'Do you think – you *could*?' she ejaculated.

'I know I could,' answered Ermengarde, and she ran to the door – opened it softly – put her head out into the darkness, and listened. Then she went back to Sara. 'The lights are out. Everybody's in bed. I can creep – and creep – and no one will hear.'

It was so delightful that they caught each other's hands and a sudden light sprang into Sara's eyes.

'Ermie!' she said. 'Let us *pretend*! Let us pretend it's a party! And oh, won't you invite the prisoner in the next cell?'

'Yes! Yes! Let us knock on the wall now. The jailer won't hear.'

Sara went to the wall. Through it she could hear poor Becky crying more softly. She knocked four times.

'That means: "Come to me through the secret passage under the wall",' she explained. '"I have something to communicate".'

Five quick knocks answered her.

'She is coming,' she said.

Almost immediately the door of the attic opened and Becky appeared. Her eyes were red and her cap was sliding off, and when she caught sight of Ermengarde she began to rub her face nervously with her apron.

'Don't mind me a bit, Becky!' cried Ermengarde.

'Miss Ermengarde has asked you to come in,' said Sara, 'because she is going to bring a box of good things up here to us.'

Becky's cap almost fell off entirely, she broke in with such excitement.

'To eat, miss?' she said. 'Things that's good to eat?'

'Yes,' answered Sara, 'and we are going to pretend a party.'

'And you shall have as much as you *want* to eat,' put in Ermengarde. 'I'll go this minute!'

She was in such a haste that as she tiptoed out of the attic she dropped her red shawl and did not know it had fallen. No one saw it for a minute or so. Becky was too much overpowered by the good luck which had befallen her.

'Oh, miss! oh, miss!' she gasped. 'I know it was you that asked her to let me come. It – it makes me cry to think of it.' And she went to Sara's side and stood and looked at her worshippingly.

But in Sara's hungry eyes the old light had begun to glow and transform her world for her. Here in the attic – with the cold night outside – with the afternoon in the sloppy streets barely passed – with the memory of the awful unfed look in the beggar child's eyes not yet faded – this simple, cheerful thing had happened like a thing of magic.

She caught her breath.

'Somehow, something always happens,' she cried, 'just before things get to the very worst. It is as if the Magic did it. If I could only just remember that always. The worst thing never *quite* comes.'

She gave Becky a little cheerful shake.

'No, no! You mustn't cry!' she said. 'We must make haste and set the table.'

'Set the table, miss?' said Becky, gazing round the room. 'What'll we set it with?'

Sara looked round the attic too.

'There doesn't seem to be much,' she answered half laughing.

That moment she saw something and pounced upon it. It was Ermengarde's red shawl which lay upon the floor.

'Here's the shawl,' she cried. 'I know she won't mind it. It will make such a nice red tablecloth.'

They pulled the old table forward, and threw the shawl over it. Red is a wonderfully kind and comfortable colour. It began to make the room look furnished directly.

'How nice a red rug would look on the floor!' exclaimed Sara. 'We must pretend there is one!'

Her eyes swept the bare boards with a swift glance of admiration. The rug was laid down already.

'How soft and thick it is!' she said, with the little laugh which Becky knew the meaning of; and she raised and set her foot down again delicately as if she felt something under it.

'Yes, miss,' answered Becky, watching her with serious rapture. She was always quite serious.

'What next, now?' said Sara, and she stood still and put her hands over her eyes. 'Something will come if I think and wait a little' – in a soft, expectant voice. 'The Magic will tell me.'

One of her favourite fancies was that on 'the outside', as she called it, thoughts were waiting for people to call them. Becky had seen her stand and wait many a time before, and knew that in a few seconds she would uncover an enlightened laughing face.

In a moment she did.

'There!' she cried. 'It has come! I know now! I must look among the things in the old trunk I had when I was a princess.'

She flew to its corner and kneeled down. It had not been put in the attic for her benefit, but because there was no room for it elsewhere. Nothing had been left in it but rubbish. But she knew she should find something. The Magic always arranged that kind of thing in one way or another.

In a corner lay a package, so insignificant-looking that it had been overlooked, and when she herself had found it she had kept it as a relic. It contained a dozen small white handkerchiefs. She seized them joyfully and ran to the table. She began to arrange them upon the red table-cover, patting and coaxing them into shape with the narrow lace edge curling outward, her Magic working its spells for her as she did it.

'These are the plates,' she said. 'They are golden plates. These are the richly embroidered napkins. Nuns worked them in convents in Spain.'

'Did they, miss?' breathed Becky, her very soul uplifted by the information.

'You must pretend it,' said Sara. 'If you pretend it enough, you will see them.'

'Yes, miss,' said Becky; and as Sara returned to the trunk she devoted herself to the effort of accomplishing an end so much to be desired.

Sara turned suddenly to find her standing by the table, looking very queer indeed. She had shut her eyes, and was twisting her face in strange, convulsive contortions, her hands hanging stiffly clenched at her sides. She looked as if she was trying to lift some enormous weight.

'What is the matter, Becky?' Sara cried. 'What are you doing?'

Becky opened her eyes with a start.

'I was a-"pretendin'," miss,' she answered a little sheepishly. 'I was tryin' to see it like you do. I almost did,' with a hopeful grin. 'But it takes a lot o' stren'th.'

'Perhaps it does if you are not used to it,' said Sara, with friendly sympathy, 'but you don't know how easy it is when you've done it often. I wouldn't try so hard just at first. It will come to you after a while. I'll just tell you what things are. Look at these.'

She held an old summer hat in her hand which she had fished out of the bottom of the trunk. There was a wreath of flowers on it. She pulled the wreath off.

'These are garlands for the feast,' she said grandly. 'They fill all the air with perfume. There's a mug on the wash-stand, Becky. Oh – and bring the soap-dish for a centre-piece.'

Becky handed them to her reverently.

'What are they now, miss?' she inquired. 'You'd think they was made of crockery – but I know they ain't.'

'This is a carven flagon,' said Sara, arranging tendrils of the wreath about the mug. 'And this' – bending tenderly over the soap-dish and heaping it with roses – 'is purest alabaster encrusted with gems.'

She touched the things gently, a happy smile hovering about her lips which made her look as if she were a creature in a dream.

'My ain't it lovely!' whispered Becky.

'If we just had something for bonbon dishes,' Sara murmured. 'There!' – darting to the trunk again. 'I remember I saw something this minute.'

It was only a bundle of wool wrapped in red and white tissue-paper, but the tissue-paper was soon twisted into the form of little dishes, and was combined with the remaining flowers to ornament the candlestick which was to light the feast. Only the Magic could have made it more than an old table covered with a red shawl and set with rubbish from a long-unopened trunk. But Sara drew back and gazed at it, seeing wonders; and Becky, after staring in delight, spoke with bated breath.

'This 'ere,' she suggested, with a glance round the attic – 'is it the Bastille now – or has it turned into somethin' different?'

'Oh, yes, yes!' said Sara, 'quite different. It is a banquet-hall!'

'My eye, miss!' ejaculated Becky. 'A blanket-'all!' and she turned to view the splendours about her with awed bewilderment.

'A banquet-hall,' said Sara. 'A vast chamber where feasts are given. It has a vaulted roof, and a minstrels' gallery, and a huge chimney filled with blazing oaken logs, and it is brilliant with waxen tapers twinkling on every side.'

'My eye, Miss Sara!' gasped Becky again.

Then the door opened, and Ermengarde came in, rather staggering under the weight of her hamper. She started back with an exclamation of joy. To enter from the chill darkness outside, and find one's self confronted by a totally un-anticipated festal board, draped with red, adorned with white napery, and wreathed with flowers, was to feel that the preparations were brilliant indeed.

'Oh, Sara!' she cried out. 'You are the cleverest girl I ever saw!'

Isn't it nice?' said Sara. 'They are things out of my old trunk. I asked my Magic, and it told me to go and look.'

'But oh, miss,' cried Becky, 'wait till she's told you what they are! They ain't just – oh, miss, please tell her,' appealing to Sara.

So Sara told her, and because her Magic helped her she made her *almost* see it all: the golden platters – the vaulted spaces – the blazing logs – the twinkling waxed tapers. As the things were taken out of the hamper – the frosted cakes – the fruits – the bonbons and the wine – the feast became a splendid thing.

'It's like a real party!' cried Ermengarde.

'It's like a queen's table,' sighed Becky.

Then Ermengarde had a sudden brilliant thought.

'I'll tell you what, Sara,' she said. 'Pretend you are a princess now and this is a royal feast.'

'But it's your feast,' said Sara, 'you must be the princess, and we will be your maids of honour.'

'Oh, I can't,' said Ermengarde. 'I'm too fat, and I don't know how. *You* be her.'

'Well, if you want me to,' said Sara.

But suddenly she thought of something else and ran to the rusty grate.

'There is a lot of paper and rubbish stuffed in here!' she exclaimed.

'If we light it, there will be a bright blaze for a few minutes, and we shall feel as if it was a real fire.' She struck a match and lighted it up with a great specious glow which illuminated the room.

'By the time it stops blazing,' Sara said, 'we shall forget about its not being real.'

She stood in the dancing glow and smiled.

'Doesn't it *look* real?' she said. 'Now we will begin the party.'

She led the way to the table. She waved her hand graciously to Ermengarde and Becky. She was in the midst of her dream.

'Advance, fair damsels,' she said in her happy dream-voice, 'and be seated at the banquet-table. My noble father, the king who is absent on a long journey, has commanded me to feast you.' She turned her head slightly toward the corner of the room. 'What, ho! there, minstrels! Strike up with your viols and bassoons. Princesses,' she explained rapidly to Ermengarde and Becky, 'always had minstrels to play at their feasts. Pretend there is a minstrel gallery up there in the corner. Now we will begin.'

They had barely had time to take their pieces of cake into their hands – not one of them had time to do more, when – they all three sprang to their feet and turned pale faces toward the door – listening – listening.

Some one was coming up the stairs. There was no mistake about it. Each of them recognized the angry, mounting tread, and knew that the end of all things had come.

'It's – the missus!' choked Becky, and dropped her piece of cake upon the floor.

'Yes,' said Sara, her eyes growing shocked and large in her small white face. 'Miss Minchin has found us out.'

Miss Minchin struck the door open with a blow of her hand. She was pale herself, but it was with rage. She looked from the frightened faces to the banquet-table, and from the banquet-table to the last flicker of the burnt paper in the grate.

'I have been suspecting something of this sort,' she exclaimed, 'but I did not dream of such audacity. Lavinia was telling the truth.'

So they knew that it was Lavinia who had somehow guessed their secret and had betrayed them. Miss Minchin strode over to Becky and boxed her ears for a second time.

'You impudent creature!' she said. 'You leave the house in the morning!'

Sara stood still, her eyes growing larger, her face paler. Ermengarde burst into tears.

'Oh, don't send her away,' she sobbed. 'My aunt sent me the hamper. We're – only – having a party.'

'So I see,' said Miss Minchin witheringly. 'With the Princess Sara at the head of the table.' She turned fiercely on Sara. 'It is your doing, I know,' she cried. 'Ermengarde would never have thought of such a thing. You decorated the table, I suppose – with this rubbish,' She stamped her foot at Becky. 'Go to your attic!' she commanded, and Becky stole away, her face hidden in her apron, her shoulders shaking.

Then it was Sara's turn again.

'I will attend to you to-morrow. You shall have neither breakfast, dinner, nor supper!'

'I have not had either dinner or supper to-day, Miss Minchin,' said Sara, rather faintly.

'Then all the better. You will have something to remember. Don't stand there. Put those things into the hamper again.'

She began to sweep them off the table into the hamper herself, and caught sight of Ermengarde's new books.

'And you' – to Ermengarde – 'have brought your beautiful new books into this dirty attic. Take them up and go back to bed. You will stay there all day to-morrow, and I shall write to your papa. What would *he* say if he knew where you are to-night?'

Something she saw in Sara's grave, fixed gaze at this moment made her turn on her fiercely.

'What are you thinking of?' she demanded. 'Why do you look at me like that?'

'I was wondering,' answered Sara, as she had answered that notable day in the schoolroom.

'What were you wondering?'

It was very like the scene in the schoolroom. There was no pertness in Sara's manner. It was only sad and quiet.

'I was wondering,' she said in a low voice, 'what *my* papa would say if he knew where I am to-night.'

Miss Minchin was infuriated just as she had been before, and her anger expressed itself, as before, in an intemperate fashion. She flew at her and shook her.

'You insolent, unmanageable child!' she cried. 'How dare you! How dare you!'

She picked up the books, swept the rest of the feast back into the hamper in a jumbled heap, thrust it into Ermengarde's arms, and pushed her before her toward the door.

'I will leave you to wonder,' she said. 'Go to bed this instant.' And she shut the door behind herself and poor stumbling Ermengarde, and left Sara standing quite alone.

The dream was quite at an end. The last spark had died out of the paper in the grate and left only black tinder; the table was left bare, the golden plates and richly embroidered napkins, and the garlands, were transformed again into old handkerchiefs, scraps of red and white paper, and discarded artificial flowers all scattered on the floor; the minstrels in the minstrel gallery had stolen away, and the viols and bassoons were still. Emily was sitting with her back against the wall, staring very hard. Sara saw her, and went and picked her up with trembling hands.

'There isn't any banquet left, Emily,' she said. 'And there isn't any princess. There is nothing left but the prisoners in the Bastille.' And she sat down and hid her face.

What would have happened if she had not hidden it just then, and if she had chanced to look up at the skylight at the wrong moment, I do not know – perhaps the end of this chapter might have been quite different – because if she had glanced at the skylight she would certainly have been startled by what she would have seen. She would have seen exactly the same face pressed against the glass and peering in at her as it had peered in earlier in the evening when she had been talking to Ermengarde.

But she did not look up. She sat with her little black head in her arms for some time. She always sat like that when she was trying to bear something in silence. Then she got up and went slowly to the bed.

'I can't pretend anything else – while I am awake,' she said. 'There wouldn't be any use in trying. If I go to sleep, perhaps a dream will come and pretend for me.'

She suddenly felt so tired – perhaps through want of food – that she sat down on the edge of the bed quite weakly.

'Suppose there was a bright fire in the grate, with lots of little dancing flames,' she murmured. 'Suppose there was a comfortable chair before it – and suppose there was a small table near, with a little hot – hot supper on it. And suppose' – as she drew the thin coverings over her – 'suppose this was a beautiful soft bed, with fleecy blankets and large downy pillows. Suppose – suppose——' And her very weariness was good to her, for her eyes closed and she fell fast asleep.

She did not know how long she slept. But she had been tired enough to sleep deeply and profoundly – too deeply and soundly to be disturbed by anything, even by the squeaks and scamperings of Melchisedec's entire family, if all his sons and daughters had chosen to come out of their hole to fight and tumble and play.

When she awakened it was rather suddenly, and she did not know that any particular thing had called her out of her sleep. The truth was, however, that it was a sound which had called her back – a real sound – the click of the skylight as it fell in closing after a lithe white figure which slipped through it and crouched down close by upon the slates of the roof – just near enough to see what happened in the attic, but not near enough to be seen.

At first she did not open her eyes. She felt too sleepy and – curiously enough – too warm and comfortable. She was so warm and comfortable, indeed, that she did not believe she was really awake. She never was as warm and cosy as this except in some lovely vision.

'What a nice dream!' she murmured. 'I feel quite warm. I – don't – want – to – wake – up.'

Of course it was a dream. She felt as if warm, delightful bedclothes were heaped upon her. She could actually *feel* blankets, and when she put out her hand it touched something exactly like a satin-covered eider-down quilt. She must not awaken from this delight – she must be quite still and make it last.

But she could not – even though she kept her eyes closed tightly, she could not. Something was forcing her to awaken – something in the room. It was a sense of light, and a sound – the sound of a crackling, roaring little fire.

'Oh, I am awakening,' she said mournfully. 'I can't help it – I can't.'

Her eyes opened in spite of herself. And then she actually smiled – for what she saw she had never seen in the attic before, and knew she never should see.

'Oh, I *haven't* awakened,' she whispered, daring to rise on her elbow and look all about her. 'I am dreaming yet.' She knew it *must* be a dream, for if she were awake such things could not – could not be.

Do you wonder that she felt sure she had not come back to earth? This is what she saw. In the grate there was a glowing, blazing fire; on the hob was a little brass kettle hissing and boiling; spread upon the floor was a thick, warm crimson rug; before the fire a folding-chair, unfolded, and with cushions on it; by the chair a small folding-table, unfolded, covered with a white cloth, and upon it spread small covered dishes, a cup, a saucer, a teapot; on the bed were new warm coverings and a satin-covered down quilt; at the foot a curious wadded silk robe, a pair of quilted slippers, and some books. The room of her dream seemed changed into fairyland – and it was flooded with warm light, for a bright lamp stood on the table covered with a rosy shade.

She sat up, resting on her elbow, and her breathing came short and fast.

'It does not – melt away,' she panted. 'Oh, I never had such a dream before.' She scarcely dared to stir; but at last she pushed the bedclothes aside, and put her feet on the floor with a rapturous smile.

'I am dreaming – I am getting out of bed.' she heard her own voice say; and then, and she stood up in the midst of it all, turning slowly from side to side – 'I am dreaming it stays – real! I'm dreaming it *feels* real. It's bewitched – or I'm bewitched. I only *think* I see it all.' Her words began to hurry themselves. 'If I can only keep on thinking it,' she cried. 'I don't care! I don't care!'

She stood panting a moment longer, and then cried out again.

'Oh, it isn't true!' she said. 'It *can't* be true! But oh, how true it seems!'

The blazing fire drew her to it, and she knelt down and held out her hands close to it – so close that the heat made her start back.

'A fire I only dreamed wouldn't be *hot*,' she cried.

She sprang up, touched the table, the dishes, the rug; she went to the bed and touched the blankets. She took up the soft wadded dressing-gown, and suddenly clutched it to her breast and held it to her cheek.

'It's warm. It's soft!' she almost sobbed. 'It's real. It must be!'

She threw it over her shoulders, and put her feet into the slippers.

'They are real, too. It's all real!' she cried. 'I am *not* – I am *not* dreaming!'

She almost staggered to the books and opened the one which lay upon the top. Something was written on the flyleaf – just a few words, and they were these:

'To the little girl in the attic. From a friend.'

When she saw that – wasn't it a strange thing for her to do? – she put her face down upon the page and burst into tears.

'I don't know who it is,' she said, 'but somebody cares for me a little. I have a friend.'

She took her candle and stole out of her own room and into Becky's and stood by her bedside.

'Becky, Becky!' she whispered as loudly as she dared. 'Wake up!'

When Becky wakened, and she sat upright staring aghast, her face still smudged with traces of tears, beside her stood a little figure in a luxurious wadded robe of crimson silk. The face she saw was a shining,

'"It's true! It's true!" she cried'

wonderful thing. The Princess Sara – as she remembered her – stood at her very bedside, holding a candle in her hand.

'Come,' she said. 'Oh, Becky, come!'

Becky was too frightened to speak. She simply got up and followed her, with her mouth and eyes open, and without a word.

And when they crossed the threshold, Sara shut the door gently and drew her into the warm, glowing midst of things which made her brain reel and her hungry senses faint.

'It's true! It's true!' she cried. 'I've touched them all. They are as real as we are. The Magic has come and done it, Becky, while we were asleep – the Magic that won't let those worst things *ever* quite happen.'

16 The Visitor

Imagine, if you can, what the rest of the evening was like. How they crouched by the fire, which blazed and leaped and made so much of itself in the little grate. How they removed the covers of the dishes and found rich, hot, savoury soup, which was a meal in itself, and sandwiches, and muffins enough for both of them. The mug from the washstand was used as Becky's teacup, and the tea was so delicious that it was not necessary to pretend that it was anything else but tea. They were warm and full-fed and happy, and it was just like Sara, having found her strange good fortune real, she should give herself up to the enjoyment of it to the utmost. She had lived such a life of imaginings that she was quite equal to accepting any wonderful thing that happened, and almost to cease, in a short time, to find it bewildering.

'I don't know anyone in the world who could have done it,' she said, 'but there has been someone. And here we are sitting by their fire – and – and – it's *true*! And whoever it is – wherever they are – I have a friend, Becky – someone is my friend.'

It cannot be denied that as they sat before the blazing fire and ate the nourishing, comfortable food, they felt a kind of rapturous awe, and looked into each other's eyes with something like doubt.

'Do you think,' Becky faltered once, in a whisper – 'do you think it could melt away, miss? Hadn't we better be quick?' And she hastily crammed her sandwich into her mouth. If it was only a dream, kitchen manners would be overlooked.

'No, it won't melt away,' said Sara. 'I am *eating* this muffin, and I can taste it. You never really eat things in dreams. You only think you are going to eat them. Besides, I keep giving myself pinches; and I touched a hot piece of coal just now, on purpose.'

The sleepy comfort which at length almost overpowered them was a heavenly thing. it was the drowsiness of happy, well-fed childhood, and they sat in the fire-glow and luxuriated in it until Sara found herself turning to look at her transformed bed.

There were even blankets enough to share with Becky. The narrow couch in the next attic was more comfortable that night than its occupant had ever dreamed that it could be.

As she went out of the room, Becky turned upon the threshold and looked about her with devouring eyes.

'If it ain't here in the mornin', miss,' she said 'it's been here to-night, anyways, an' I shan't never forget it.' She looked at each particular thing, as if to commit it to memory. 'The fire was *there*,' pointing with her finger, 'an' the table was before it; an' the lamp was there, an' the light looked rosy red; an' there was a satin cover on your bed, an' a warm rug on the floor, an' everythin' looked beautiful; an'' – she paused a second, and laid her hand on her stomach tenderly – 'there *was* soup an' sandwiches an' muffins – there *was*.' And, with this conviction a reality at least, she went away.

Through the mysterious agency which works in schools and among servants, it was quite well known in the morning that Sara Crewe was in horrible disgrace, that Ermengarde was under punishment, and that Becky would have been packed out of the house before breakfast, but that a scullery-maid could not be dispensed with at once. The servants knew that she was allowed to stay because Miss Minchin could not easily find another creature helpless and humble enough to work like a bounden slave for so few shillings a week. The elder girls in the schoolroom knew that if Miss Minchin did not send Sara away it was for practical reasons of her own.

'She's growing so fast and learning such a lot, somehow,' said Jessie to Lavinia, 'that she will be given classes soon, and Miss Minchin knows she will have to work for nothing. It was rather nasty of you, Lavvy, to tell about her having fun in the garret. How did you find it out?'

'I got it out of Lottie. She's such a baby she didn't know she was telling me. There was nothing nasty at all in speaking to Miss Minchin. I felt it my duty' – priggishly. 'She was being deceitful. And it's ridiculous that she should look so grand, and be made so much of, in her rags and tatters!'

'What were they doing when Miss Minchin caught them?'

'Pretending some silly thing. Ermengarde had taken up her hamper to share with Sara and Becky. She never invites us to share things. Not that I care, but it's rather vulgar of her to share with servant-girls in attics. I wonder Miss Minchin didn't turn Sara out – even if she does want her for a teacher.'

'If she was turned out where would she go?' inquired Jessie, a trifle anxiously.

'How do I know?' snapped Lavinia. 'She'll look rather queer when she comes into the schoolroom this morning, I should think – after what's happened. She had no dinner yesterday, and she's not to have any to-day.'

Jessie was not as ill-natured as she was silly. She picked up her book with a little jerk.

'Well, I think it's horrid,' she said. 'They've no right to starve her to death.'

When Sara went into the kitchen that morning the cook looked askance at her, and so did the housemaids; but she passed them hurriedly. She had, in fact, overslept herself a little, and as Becky had done the same, neither had had time to see the other, and each had come downstairs in haste.

Sara went into the scullery. Becky was violently scrubbing a kettle, and was actually gurgling a little song in her throat. She looked up with a wildly elated face.

'It was there when I wakened, miss – the blanket,' she whispered excitedly. 'It was as real as it was last night.'

'So was mine,' said Sara. 'It is all there now – all of it. While I was dressing I ate some of the cold things we left.'

'Oh, laws! oh, laws!' Becky uttered the exclamation in a sort of rapturous groan, and ducked her head over the kettle just in time, as the cook came in from the kitchen.

Miss Minchin had expected to see in Sara, when she appeared in the schoolroom, very much what Lavinia had expected to see. Sara had always been an annoying puzzle to her, because severity never made her cry or look frightened. When she was scolded she stood still and listened politely with a grave face; when she was punished she performed her extra tasks or went without her meals, making no complaint or outward sign of rebellion. The very fact that she never made an impudent answer seemed to Miss Minchin a kind of impudence in itself. But after yesterday's deprivation of meals, the violent scene of last night, the prospect of hunger to-day, she must surely have broken down. It would be strange indeed if she did not come downstairs with pale cheeks and red eyes and an unhappy, humbled face.

Miss Minchin saw her for the first time when she entered the schoolroom to hear the little French class its lessons and superintend its exercises. And she came in with a springing step, colour in her cheeks, and a smile hovering about the corners of her mouth. It was the most astonishing thing Miss Minchin had ever known. It gave her quite a shock. What was the child made of? What could such a thing mean? She called her at once to her desk.

'You do not look as if you realize that you are in disgrace,' she said. 'Are you absolutely hardened?'

The truth is that when one is still a child – or even if one is grown up – and has been well fed, and has slept long and softly and warm; when one has gone to sleep in the midst of a fairy story, and has wakened to find it real, one cannot be unhappy or even look as if one were; and one could not, if one tried, keep a glow of joy out of one's eyes. Miss Minchin was almost struck dumb by the look of Sara's eyes when she lifted them and made her perfectly respectful answer.

'I beg your pardon, Miss Minchin,' she said. 'I know that I am in disgrace.'

'Be good enough not to forget it and look as if you had come into a fortune. It is an impertinence. And remember you are to have no food to-day.'

'Yes, Miss Minchin,' Sara answered; but as she turned away her heart leaped with the memory of what yesterday had been, 'If the Magic had not saved me just in time,' she thought, 'how horrible it would have been!'

'She can't be very hungry,' whispered Lavinia. 'Just look at her.

Perhaps she is pretending she has had a good breakfast' – with a spiteful laugh.

'She's different from other people,' said Jessie, watching Sara with her class. 'Sometimes I'm a bit frightened of her.'

'Ridiculous thing!' ejaculated Lavinia.

All through the day the light was in Sara's face, and the colour in her cheek. The servants cast puzzled glances at her, and whispered to each other, and Miss Amelia's small blue eyes wore an expression of bewilderment. What such an audacious look of well-being, under august displeasure, could mean she could not understand. It was, however, just like Sara's singular obstinate way. She was probably determined to brave the matter out.

One thing Sara had resolved upon, as she thought things over. The wonders which had happened must be kept a secret, if such a thing were possible. If Miss Minchin should choose to mount to the attic again, of course all would be discovered. But it did not seem likely that she would do so for some time at least, unless she was led by suspicion. Ermengarde and Lottie would be watched with such strictness that they would not dare to steal out of their beds again. Ermengarde could be told the story and trusted to keep it secret. If Lottie made any discoveries, she could be bound to secrecy also. Perhaps the Magic itself would help to hide its own marvels.

'But whatever happens,' Sara kept saying to herself all day – '*whatever* happens, somewhere in the world there is a heavenly kind person who is my friend – my friend. If I never know who it is – if I never can even thank him – I shall never feel quite so lonely. Oh, the Magic was *good* to me!'

If it was possible for weather to be worse than it had been the day before, it was worse this day – wetter, muddier, colder. There were more errands to be done, the cook was more irritable, and, knowing that Sara was in disgrace, she was more savage. But what does anything matter when one's Magic has just proved itself one's friend. Sara's supper of the night before had given her strength, she knew that she should sleep well and warmly, and, even though she had naturally begun to be hungry again before evening, she felt that she could bear it until breakfast-time on the following day, when her meals would surely be given to her again. It was quite late when she was at last allowed to go upstairs. She had been told to go into the schoolroom and study until ten o'clock, and she had become interested in her work, and remained over her books later.

When she reached the top flight of stairs and stood before the attic door, it must be confessed that her heart beat rather fast.

'Of course it *might* all have been taken away,' she whispered, trying to be brave. 'It might only have been lent to me for just that one awful night. But it *was* lent to me – I had it. It was real.'

She pushed the door open and went in. Once inside, she gasped slightly, shut the door, and stood with her back against it, looking from side to side.

The Magic had been there again. It actually had, and it had done even more than before. The fire was blazing, in lovely leaping flames, more merrily than ever. A number of new things had been brought into the attic which so altered the look of it that if she had not been past doubting, she would have rubbed her eyes. Upon the low table another supper stood – this time with cups and plates for Becky as well as herself; a piece of bright, heavy, strange embroidery covered the battered mantel, and on it some ornaments had been placed. All the bare, ugly things which could be covered with draperies had been concealed and made to look pretty. Some odd materials of rich colours had been fastened against the wall with fine, sharp tacks – so sharp that they could be pressed into the wood and plaster without hammering. Some brilliant fans were pinned up, and there were several large cushions, big and substantial enough to use as seats. A wooden box was covered with a rug, and some cushions lay on it, so that it wore quite the air of a sofa.

Sara slowly moved away from the door and simply sat down and looked and looked again.

'It is exactly like something fairy come true,' she said. 'There isn't the least difference. I feel as if I might wish for anything – diamonds or bags of gold – and they would appear! *That* wouldn't be any stranger than this. Is this my garret? Am I the same cold, ragged, damp Sara? And to think I used to pretend and pretend and wish there were fairies! The one thing I always wanted was to see a fairy story come true. I am *living* in a fairy story. I feel as if I might be a fairy myself, and able to turn things into anything else.'

She rose and knocked upon the wall for the prisoner in the next cell, and the prisoner came.

When she entered she almost dropped in a heap upon the floor. For a few seconds she quite lost her breath.

'Oh, laws!' she gasped. 'Oh, laws, miss!' – just as she had done in the scullery.

'You see,' said Sara.

On this night Becky sat on a cushion upon the hearth-rug and had a cup and saucer of her own.

When Sara went to bed she found that she had a new thick mattress and big downy pillows. Her old mattress and pillow had been removed to Becky's bedstead, and, consequently, with these additions Becky had been supplied with unheard-of comfort.

'Where does it all come from?' Becky broke forth once. 'Laws! who does it, miss?'

'Don't let us even *ask*,' said Sara. 'If it were not that I want to say: "Oh, thank you," I would rather not know. It makes it more beautiful.'

From that time life became more wonderful day by day. The fairy story continued. Almost every day something new was done. Some new comfort or ornament appeared each time Sara opened the door at night, until in a short time the attic was a beautiful little room full of all sorts of odd and luxurious things. The ugly walls were gradually entirely covered with pictures and draperies, ingenious pieces of folding furniture appeared, a bookshelf was hung up and filled with books, new comforts and conveniences appeared one by one, until there seemed nothing left to be desired. When Sara went downstairs in the morning, the remains of the supper were on the table; and when she returned to the attic in the evening, the magician had removed them and left another nice little meal. Miss Minchin was as harsh and insulting as ever, Miss Amelia as peevish, and the servants were as vulgar and rude. Sara was sent on errands in all weathers, and scolded and driven hither and thither; she was scarcely allowed to speak to Ermengarde and Lottie; Lavinia sneered at the increasing shabbiness of her clothes; and the other girls stared curiously at her when she appeared in the schoolroom. But what did it all matter while she was living in this wonderful mysterious story? It was more romantic and delightful than anything she had ever invented to comfort her starved young soul and save herself from despair. Sometimes, when she was scolded, she could scarcely keep from smiling.

'If you only knew!' she was saying to herself. 'If you only knew!'

The comfort and happiness she enjoyed were making her stronger, and she had them always to look forward to. If she came home from her errands wet and tired and hungry, she knew she would soon be warm and well fed after she had climbed the stairs. During the hardest day she could occupy herself blissfully by thinking of what she should see when she opened the attic door, and wondering what new delight had been prepared for her. In a very short time she began to look less thin. Colour came into her cheeks, and her eyes did not seem so much too big for her face.

'Sara Crewe looks wonderfully well,' Miss Minchin remarked disapprovingly to her sister.

'Yes,' answered poor, silly Miss Amelia. 'She is absolutely fattening. She was beginning to look like a little starved crow.'

'Starved!' exclaimed Miss Minchin angrily. 'There was no reason why she should look starved. She always had plenty to eat!'

'Of – of course,' agreed Miss Amelia humbly, alarmed to find that she had, as usual, said the wrong thing.

'There is something very disagreeable in seeing that sort of thing in a child of her age,' said Miss Minchin, with haughty vagueness.

'What – sort of thing?' Miss Amelia ventured.

'It might almost be called defiance,' answered Miss Minchin, feeling annoyed because she knew the thing she resented was nothing like defiance, and she did not know what other unpleasant term to use. 'The spirit and will of any other child would have been entirely humbled and broken by – by the changes she has had to submit to. But, upon my word, she seems as little subdued as if – as if she were a princess.'

'Do you remember,' put in the unwise Miss Amelia, 'what she said to you that day in the schoolroom about what you would do if you found out that she was——'

'No, I don't,' said Miss Minchin. 'Don't talk nonsense.' But she remembered very clearly indeed.

Very naturally, even Becky was beginning to look plumper and less frightened. She could not help it. She had her share in the secret fairy story too. She had two mattresses, two pillows, plenty of bed-covering, and every night a hot supper and a seat on the cushions by the fire. The Bastille had melted away, the prisoners no longer existed. Two comforted children sat in the midst of delights. Sometimes Sara read aloud from her books, sometimes she learned her own lessons, sometimes she sat and looked into the fire and tried to imagine who her friend could be, and wished she could say to him some of the things in her heart.

Then it came about that another wonderful thing happened. A man came to the door and left several parcels. All were addressed in large letters: 'To the Little Girl in the right-hand attic.'

Sara herself was sent to open the door, and took them in. She laid the two largest parcels on the hall table, and was looking at the address, when Miss Minchin came down the stairs and saw her.

'Take the things to the young lady to whom they belong,' she said severely. 'Don't stand there staring at them.'

'They belong to me,' answered Sara quietly.

'To you?' exclaimed Miss Minchin. 'What do you mean?'

'I don't know where they come from,' said Sara, 'but they are addressed to me. I sleep in the right-hand attic. Becky has the other one.'

Miss Minchin came to her side and looked at the parcels with an excited expression.

'What is in them?' she demanded.

'I don't know,' replied Sara.

'Open them,' she ordered.

Sara did as she was told. When the packages were unfolded Miss Minchin's countenance wore suddenly a singular expression. What she saw was pretty and comfortable clothing – clothing of different kinds: shoes, stockings, and gloves, and a warm and beautiful coat. There were even a nice hat and an umbrella. They were all good and expensive things, and on the pocket of the coat was pinned a paper, on which were written these words: 'To be worn every day. – Will be replaced by others when necessary.'

Miss Minchin was quite agitated. This was an incident which suggested strange things to her sordid mind. Could it be that she had made a mistake, after all, and that the neglected child had some powerful though eccentric friend in the background – perhaps some previously unknown relation, who had suddenly traced her whereabouts, and chose to provide for her in this mysterious and fantastic way? Relations were sometimes very odd – particularly rich old bachelor uncles, who did not care for having children near them. A man of that sort might prefer to overlook his young relation's welfare at a distance. Such a person, however, would be sure to be crotchety and hot-tempered enough to be easily offended. It would not be very pleasant if there were such a one, and he should learn all the truth about the thin, shabby clothes, the scant food, and the hard work. She felt very queer indeed, and very uncertain, and she gave a side glance at Sara.

'Well,' she said, in a voice such as she had never used since the little girl lost her father, 'someone is very kind to you. As the things have been sent, and you are to have new ones when they are worn out, you may as well go and put them on and look respectable. After you are dressed you may come downstairs and learn your lessons in the schoolroom. You need not go out on any more errands to-day.'

About half an hour afterward, when the schoolroom door opened and Sara walked in, the entire seminary was struck dumb with amazement.

'My word!' ejaculated Jessie, jogging Lavinia's elbow. 'Look at the Princess Sara!'

Everybody was looking, and when Lavinia looked she turned quite red.

It was the Princess Sara indeed. At least, since the days when she had been a princess, Sara had never looked as she did now. She did not seem the Sara they had seen come down the back stairs a few hours ago. She was dressed in the kind of frock Lavinia had been used to envying her the possession of. It was deep and warm in colour, and beautifully made. Her slender feet looked as they had done when Jessie had admired them, and the hair, whose heavy locks had made her look rather like a Shetland pony when it fell loose about her small, odd face, was tied back with a ribbon.

'Perhaps someone has left her a fortune,' Jessie whispered. 'I always thought something would happen to her. She is so queer.'

'Perhaps the diamond mines have suddenly appeared again,' said Lavinia scathingly. 'Don't please her by staring at her in that way, you silly thing.'

'Sara,' broke in Miss Minchin's deep voice, 'come and sit here.'

And while the whole schoolroom stared and pushed with elbows, and scarcely made any effort to conceal its excited curiosity, Sara went to her old seat of honour, and bent her head over her books.

That night, when she went to her room, after she and Becky had eaten their supper she sat and looked at the fire seriously for a long time.

'Are you making something up in your head, miss?' Becky inquired with respectful softness. When Sara sat in silence and looked into the coals with dreaming eyes it generally meant that she was making a new story. But this time she was not, and she shook her head.

'No,' she answered. 'I am wondering what I ought to do.'

Becky stared – still respectfully. She was filled with something approaching reverence for everything Sara did and said.

'I can't help thinking about my friend,' Sara explained. 'If he wants to keep himself a secret, it would be rude to try and find out who he is. But I do so want him to know how thankful I am to him – and how happy he has made me. Any one who is kind wants to know when people have been made happy. They care for that more than for being thanked. I wish – I do wish——'

She stopped short, because her eyes at that instant fell upon something standing on a table in a corner. It was something she had found in the room when she came up to it only two days before. It was a little writing-case fitted with paper and envelopes and pens and ink.

'Oh,' she exclaimed, 'why did I not think of that before?'

She rose and went to the corner and brought the case back to the fire.

'I can write to him,' she said joyfully, 'and leave it on the table.

Then perhaps the person who takes the things away will take it, too. I won't ask him anything. He won't mind my thanking him, I feel sure.'

So she wrote a note. This is what she said:

I hope you will not think it is impolite that I should write this note to you when you wish to keep yourself a secret. Please believe I do not mean to be impolite or try to find out anything at all; only I want to thank you for being so kind to me – so heavenly kind – and making everything like a fairy story. I am so grateful to you, and I am so happy – and so is Becky. Becky feels just as thankful as I do – it is all just as beautiful and wonderful to her as it is to me. We used to be so lonely and cold and hungry, and now – oh, just think what you have done for us! Please let me say just these words. It seems as if I *ought* to say them. *Thank* you – *thank* you – *thank* you!

'THE LITTLE GIRL IN THE ATTIC.'

The next morning she left this on the little table, and in the evening it had been taken away with the other things; so she knew the Magician had received it, and she was happier for the thought. She was reading one of her new books to Becky just before they went to their respective beds, when her attention was attracted by a sound at the skylight. When she looked up from her page she saw that Becky had heard the sound also, as she had turned her head to look and was listening rather nervously.

'Something's there, miss,' she whispered.

'Yes,' said Sara slowly. 'It sounds – rather like a cat – trying to get in.'

She left her chair and went to the skylight. It was a queer little sound she heard – like a soft scratching. She suddenly remembered something and laughed. She remembered a quaint little intruder who had made his way into the attic once before. She had seen him that very afternoon, sitting disconsolately on a table before a window in the Indian gentleman's house.

'Suppose,' she whispered in pleased excitement – 'just suppose it was the monkey who had got away again. Oh, I wish it was!'

She climbed on a chair, very cautiously raised the skylight, and peeped out. It had been snowing all day, and on the snow, quite near her, crouched a tiny, shivering figure, whose small black face wrinkled itself piteously at sight of her.

'It *is* the monkey,' she cried out. 'He has crept out of the Lascar's attic, and he saw the light.'

Becky ran to her side.

'Are you going to let him in, miss?' she said.

'Yes,' Sara answered joyfully. 'It's too cold for monkeys to be out. They're delicate. I'll coax him in.'

She put a hand out delicately, speaking in a coaxing voice – as she spoke to the sparrows and to Melchisedec – as if she were some friendly little animal herself and lovingly understood their timid wildness.

'Come along, monkey darling,' she said. 'I won't hurt you.'

He knew she would not hurt him. He knew it before she laid her soft, caressing little paw on him and drew him toward her. He had felt human love in the slim brown hands of Ram Dass, and he felt it in hers. He let her lift him through the skylight, and when he found himself in her arms he cuddled up to her breast and took friendly hold of a piece of her hair, looking up into her face.

'Nice monkey! Nice monkey!' she crooned, kissing his funny head. 'Oh, I do love little animal things.'

He was evidently glad to get to the fire, and when she sat down and held him on her knee he looked from her to Becky with mingled interest and appreciation.

'He *is* plain-looking, miss, ain't he?' said Becky.

'He looks like a very ugly baby,' laughed Sara. 'I beg your pardon, monkey; but I'm glad you are not a baby. Your mother *couldn't* be proud of you, and no one would dare to say you looked like any of your relations. Oh, I do like you!'

She leaned back in her chair and reflected.

'Perhaps he's sorry he's so ugly,' she said, 'and it's always on his mind. I wonder if he *has* a mind. Monkey, my love, have you a mind?'

But the monkey only put up a tiny paw and scratched his head.

'What shall you do with him?' Becky asked.

'I shall let him sleep with me to-night, and then take him back to the Indian gentleman to-morrow. I am sorry to take you back, monkey; but you must go. You ought to be fondest of your own family; and I'm not a *real* relation.'

And when she went to bed she made him a nest at her feet, and he curled and slept there as if he were a baby and much pleased with his quarters.

17 'It Is The Child'

The next afternoon three members of the Large Family sat in the Indian gentleman's library, doing their best to cheer him up. They had been allowed to come into perform this office because he had specially invited them. He had been living in a state of suspense for some time, and to-day he was waiting for a certain event very anxiously. This event was the return of Mr. Carmichael from Moscow. His stay there had been prolonged from week to week. On his first arrival there, he had not been able satisfactorily to trace the family he had gone in search of. When he felt at last sure that he had found them and had gone to their house, he had been told that they were absent on a journey. His efforts to reach them had been unavailing, so he had decided to remain in Moscow until their return. Mr. Carrisford sat in his reclining-chair, and Janet sat on the floor beside him. He was very fond of Janet. Nora had found a footstool, and Donald was astride the tiger's head which ornamented the rug made of the animal's skin. It must be owned that he was riding it rather violently.

'Don't chirrup so loud, Donald,' Janet said. 'When you come to cheer an ill person up you don't cheer him up at the top of your voice. Perhaps cheering up is too loud, Mr. Carrisford?' – turning to the Indian gentleman.

But he only patted her shoulder.

'No, it isn't,' he answered. 'And it keeps me from thinking too much.'

'I'm going to be quiet,' Donald shouted. 'We'll all be as quiet as mice.'

'Mice don't make a noise like that,' said Janet.

Donald made a bridle of his handkerchief and bounced up and

down on the tiger's head.

'A whole lot of mice might,' he said cheerfully. 'A thousand mice might.'

'I don't believe fifty thousand mice would,' said Janet severely, 'and we have to be as quiet as *one* mouse.'

Mr. Carrisford laughed and patted her shoulder again.

'Papa won't be very long now,' she said. 'May we talk about the lost little girl?'

'I don't think I could talk much about anything else just now,' the Indian gentleman answered, knitting his forehead with a tired look.

'We like her so much,' said Nora. 'We call her the little *un*-fairy princess.'

'Why?' the Indian gentleman inquired, because the fancies of the Large Family always made him forget things a little.

It was Janet who answered.

'It is because, though she is not exactly a fairy, she will be so rich when she is found that she will be like a princess in a fairy tale. We called her the fairy princess at first, but it didn't quite suit.'

'Is it true,' said Nora, 'that her papa gave all his money to a friend to put in a mine that had diamonds in it, and then the friend thought he had lost it all and ran away because he felt as if he was a robber?'

'But he wasn't really, you know,' put in Janet hastily.

The Indian gentleman took hold of her hand quickly.

'No, he wasn't really,' he said.

'I am sorry for the friend,' Janet said, 'I can't help it. He didn't mean to do it, and it would break his heart. I am sure it would break his heart.'

'You are an understanding little woman, Janet,' the Indian gentleman said, and he held her hand close.

'Did you tell Mr. Carrisford,' Donald shouted again, 'about the little-girl-who-isn't-a-beggar? Did you tell him she has new nice clothes? P'r'aps she's been found by somebody when she was lost.'

'There's a cab!' exclaimed Janet. 'It's stopping before the door. It is papa!'

They all ran to the windows to look out.

'Yes, it's papa,' Donald proclaimed. 'But there is no little girl.'

All three of them incontinently fled from the room and tumbled into the hall. It was in this way they always welcomed their father. They were to be heard jumping up and down, clapping their hands, and being caught up and kissed.

Mr. Carrisford made an effort to rise, and sank back again into his chair.

'It is no use,' he said. 'What a wreck I am!'

Mr. Carmichael's voice approached the door.

'No, children,' he was saying, 'you may come in after I have talked to Mr. Carrisford. Go and play with Ram Dass.'

Then the door opened and he came in. He looked rosier than ever, and brought an atmosphere of freshness and health with him; but his eyes were disappointed and anxious as they met the invalid's look of eager question even as they grasped each other's hands.

'What news?' Mr. Carrisford asked. 'The child the Russian people adopted?'

'She is not the child we are looking for,' was Mr. Carmichael's answer. 'She is much younger than Captain Crewe's little girl. Her name is Emily Carew. I have seen and talked to her. The Russians were able to give me every detail.'

How wearied and miserable the Indian gentleman looked! His hand dropped from Mr. Carmichael's.

'Then the search has to be begun over again,' he said. 'That is all. Please sit down.'

Mr. Carmichael took a seat. Somehow, he had gradually grown fond of this unhappy man. He was himself so well and happy, and so surrounded by cheerfulness and love, that desolation and broken health seemed pitifully unbearable things. If there had been the sound of just one gay little high-pitched voice in the house, it would have been so much less forlorn. And that a man should be compelled to carry about in his breast the thought that he had seemed to wrong and desert a child was not a thing one could face.

'Come, come,' he said in his cheery voice, 'we'll find her yet.'

'We must begin at once. No time must be lost,' Mr. Carrisford fretted. 'Have you any new suggestion to make – any whatsoever?'

Mr. Carmichael felt rather restless, and he rose and began to pace the room with a thoughtful, though uncertain face.

'Well, perhaps,' he said. 'I don't know what it may be worth. The fact is, an idea occurred to me as I was thinking the thing over in the train on the journey from Dover.'

'What was it? If she is alive, she is somewhere.'

'Yes; she is *somewhere*. We have searched the schools in Paris. Let us give up Paris and begin in London. That was my idea – to search London.'

'There are schools enough in London,' said Mr. Carrisford. Then he slightly started, roused by a recollection. 'By the way, there is one next door.'

'Then we will begin there. We cannot begin nearer than next door.'

'No,' said Carrisford. 'There is a child there who interests me; but she is not a pupil. And she is a little dark, forlorn creature, as unlike poor Crewe as a child could be.'

Perhaps the Magic was at work again at that very moment – the beautiful Magic. It really seemed as if it might be so. What was it that brought Ram Dass into the room – even as his master spoke – salaaming respectfully, but with a scarcely concealed touch of excitement in his dark, flashing eyes?

'Sahib,' he said, 'the child herself has come – the child the sahib felt pity for. She brings back the monkey, who had again run away to her attic under the roof. I have asked that she remain. It was my thought that it would please the sahib to see and speak with her.'

'Who is she?' inquired Mr. Carmichael.

'God knows,' Mr. Carrisford answered. 'She is the child I spoke of. A little drudge at the school.' He waved his hand to Ram Dass, and addressed him. 'Yes, I should like to see her. Go and bring her in.' Then he turned to Mr. Carmichael. 'While you have been away,' he explained, 'I have been desperate. The days were so dark and long. Ram Dass told me of this child's miseries, and together we invented a romantic plan to help her. I suppose it was a childish thing to do; but it gave me something to plan and think of. Without the help of an agile, soft-footed Oriental like Ram Dass, however, it could not have been done.'

Then Sara came into the room. She carried the monkey in her
arms, and he evidently did not intend to part from her, if it could be
helped. He was clinging to her and chattering, and the interesting
excitement of finding herself in the Indian gentleman's room had
brought a flush to Sara's cheeks.

'Your monkey ran away again,' she said, in her pretty voice. 'He
came to my garret window last night, and I took him in because it was
so cold. I would have brought him back if it had not been so late. I
knew you were ill and might not like to be disturbed.'

The Indian gentleman's hollow eyes dwelt on her with curious
interest.

'That was very thoughtful of you,' he said.

Sara looked towards Ram Dass, who stood near the door.

'Shall I give him to the lascar?' she asked.

'How do you know he is a lascar?' said the Indian gentleman,
smiling a little.

'Oh, I know lascars,' Sara said, handing over the reluctant
monkey. 'I was born in India.'

The Indian gentleman sat upright so suddenly, and with such a
change of expression, that she was for a moment quite startled.

'You were born in India,' he exclaimed, 'were you? Come here.'
And he held out his hand.

Sara went to him and laid her hand in his, as he seemed to want to
take it. She stood still, and her green-grey eyes met his wonderingly.
Something seemed to be the matter with him.

'You live next door?' he demanded.

'Yes; I live at Miss Minchin's seminary.'

'But you are not one of her pupils?'

A strange little smile hovered about Sara's mouth. She hesitated a
moment.

'I don't think I know exactly *what* I am,' she replied.

'Why not?'

'At first I was a pupil, and a parlour-boarder; but now——'

'You were a pupil! What are you now?'

The queer little sad smile was on Sara's lips again.

'I sleep in the attic, next to the scullery-maid,' she said. 'I run errands for the cook – I do anything she tells me; and I teach the little ones their lessons.'

'Question her, Carmichael,' said Mr. Carrisford, sinking back as if he had lost his strength. 'Question her; I cannot.'

The big, kind father of the Large Family knew how to question little girls. Sara realized how much practice he had had when he spoke to her in his nice, encouraging voice.

'What do you mean by "At first," my child?' he inquired.

'When I was first taken there by my papa.'

'Where is your papa?'

'He died,' said Sara, very quietly. 'He lost all his money and there was none left for me. There was no one to take care of me or to pay Miss Minchin.'

'Carmichael!' the Indian gentleman cried out loudly. 'Carmichael!'

'We must not frighten her,' Mr. Carmichael said aside to him in a quick, low voice; and he added aloud to Sara: 'So you were sent up into the attic, and made into a little drudge. That was about it, wasn't it?'

'There was no one to take care of me,' said Sara. 'There was no money; I belong to nobody.'

'How did your father lose his money?' the Indian gentleman broke in breathlessly.

'He did not lose it himself,' Sara answered, wondering still more each moment. 'He had a friend he was very fond of – he was *very* fond of him. It was his friend who took his money. He trusted his friend too much.'

The Indian gentleman's breath came more quickly.

'The friend might have *meant* to do no harm,' he said. 'It might have happened through a mistake.'

Sara did not know how unrelenting her quiet young voice sounded as she answered. If she had known, she would surely have tried to soften it for the Indian gentleman's sake.

'The suffering was just as bad for my papa,' she said. 'It killed him.'

'What was your father's name?' the Indian gentleman said. 'Tell me.'

'His name was Ralph Crewe,' Sara answered, feeling startled. 'Captain Crewe. He died in India.'

The haggard face contracted, and Ram Dass sprang to his master's side.

'Carmichael,' the invalid gasped, 'it is the child – the child!'

For a moment Sara thought he was going to die. Ram Dass poured out drops from a bottle, and held them to his lips. Sara stood near, trembling a little. She looked in a bewildered way at Mr. Carmichael.

'What child am I?' she faltered.

'He was your father's friend,' Mr. Carmichael answered her. 'Don't be frightened. We have been looking for you for two years.'

Sara put her hand up to her forehead, and her mouth trembled. She spoke as if she were in a dream.

'And I was at Miss Minchin's all the while,' she half whispered. 'Just on the other side of the wall.'

18 'I Tried Not to Be'

It was pretty, comfortable Mrs. Carmichael who explained every-thing. She was sent for at once, and came across the square to take Sara into her warm arms and make clear to her all that had happened. The excitement of the totally unexpected discovery had been temporarily almost overpowering to Mr. Carrisford in his weak condition.

'Upon my word,' he said faintly to Mr. Carmichael, when it was suggested that the little girl should go into another room, 'I feel as if I do not want to lose sight of her.'

'I will take care of her,' Janet said, 'and mamma will come in a few minutes.' And it was Janet who led her away.

'We're so glad you are found,' she said. 'You don't know how glad we are that you are found.'

Donald stood with his hands in his pockets, and gazed at Sara with reflecting and self-reproachful eyes.

'If I'd just asked what your name was when I gave you my sixpence,' he said, 'you would have told me it was Sara Crewe, and then you would have been found in a minute.'

Then Mrs. Carmichael came in. She looked very much moved, and suddenly took Sara in her arms and kissed her.

'You look bewildered, poor child,' she said. 'And it is not to be wondered at.'

Sara could only think of one thing.

'Was he,' she said, with a glance toward the closed door of the library – 'was *he* the wicked friend? Oh, do tell me!'

Mrs. Carmichael was crying as she kissed her again. She felt as if she ought to be kissed very often because she had not been kissed for so long.

'He was not wicked, my dear,' she answered. 'He did not really lose your papa's money. He only thought he had lost it; and because he loved him so much his grief made him so ill that for a time he was not in his right mind. He almost died of brain-fever, and long before he began to recover your papa was dead.'

'And he did not know where to find me,' murmured Sara. 'And I was so near.' Somehow, she could not forget that she had been so near.

'He believed you were in school in France,' Mrs. Carmichael explained. 'And he was continually misled by false clues. He has looked for you everywhere. When he saw you pass by, looking so sad and neglected, he did not dream that you were his friend's poor child; but because you were a little girl, too, he was sorry for you, and wanted to make you happier. And he told Ram Dass to climb into your attic window and try to make you comfortable.'

Sara gave a start of joy; her whole look changed.

'Did Ram Dass bring the things?' she cried out. 'Did he tell Ram Dass to do it? Did he make the dream that came true?'

'Yes, my dear – yes! He is kind and good, and he was sorry for you, for little lost Sara Crewe's sake.'

The library door opened and Mr. Carmichael appeared, calling Sara to him with a gesture.

'Mr. Carrisford is better already,' he said. 'He wants you to come to him.'

Sara did not wait. When the Indian gentleman looked at her as she entered, he saw that her face was all alight.

She went and stood before his chair, with her hands clasped together against her breast.

'You sent the things to me,' she said, in a joyful, emotional little voice – 'the beautiful, beautiful things? *You* sent them!'

'Yes, poor dear child, I did,' he answered her. He was weak and broken with long illness and trouble, but he looked at her with the look she remembered in her father's eyes – that look of loving her and wanting to take her in his arms. It made her kneel down by him, just as she used to kneel by her father when they were the dearest friends and lovers in the world.

'Then it is you who are my friend,' she said. 'It is you who are my friend!' And she dropped her face on his thin hand and kissed it again and again.

'The man will be himself again in three weeks,' Mr. Carmichael said aside to his wife. 'Look at his face already.'

In fact, he did look changed. Here was the 'Little Missus', and he had new things to think of and plan for already. In the first place, there was Miss Minchin. She must be interviewed and told of the change which had taken place in the fortunes of her pupil.

Sara was not to return to the seminary at all. The Indian gentleman was very determined upon that point. She must remain where she was, and Mr. Carmichael should go and see Miss Minchin himself.

'I am glad I need not go back,' said Sara. 'She will be very angry. She does not like me; though perhaps it is my fault, because I do not like her.'

But, oddly enough, Miss Minchin made it unnecessary for Mr. Carmichael to go to her, by actually coming in search of her pupil herself. She had wanted Sara for something, and on inquiry had heard an astonishing thing. One of the housemaids had seen her steal out of the area with something hidden under her cloak, and had also seen her go up the steps of the next door and enter the house.

'What does she mean?' cried Miss Minchin to Miss Amelia.

'I don't know, I'm sure, sister,' answered Miss Amelia. 'Unless she has made friends with him because he has lived in India.'

'It would be just like her to thrust herself upon him and try to gain his sympathies in some such impertinent fashion,' said Miss Minchin. 'She must have been in the house two hours. I will not allow such presumption. I shall go and inquire into the matter, and apologize for her intrusion.'

Sara was sitting on a footstool close to Mr. Carrisford's knee, and listening to some of the many things he felt it necessary to try to explain to her, when Ram Dass announced the visitor's arrival.

Sara rose involuntarily, and became rather pale; but Mr. Carrisford saw that she stood quietly, and showed none of the ordinary signs of child terror.

Miss Minchin entered the room with a sternly dignified manner.

She was correctly and well dressed, and rigidly polite.

'I am sorry to disturb Mr. Carrisford,' she said, 'but I have explanations to make. I am Miss Minchin, the proprietress of the Young Ladies' Seminary next door.'

The Indian gentleman looked at her for a moment in silent scrutiny. He was a man who had naturally a rather hot temper, and he did not wish it to get too much the better of him.

'So you are Miss Minchin?' he said.

'I am, sir.'

'In that case,' the Indian gentleman replied, 'you have arrived at the right time. My solicitor, Mr. Carmichael, was just on the point of going to see you.'

Mr. Carmichael bowed slightly, and Miss Minchin looked from him to Mr. Carrisford in amazement.

'Your solicitor!' she said. 'I do not understand. I have come here as a matter of duty. I have just discovered that you have been intruded upon through the forwardness of one of my pupils – a charity pupil. I came to explain that she intruded without my knowledge.' She turned upon Sara. 'Go home at once,' she commanded indignantly. 'You shall be severely punished. Go home at once.'

The Indian gentleman drew Sara to his side and patted her hand.

'She is not going.'

Miss Minchin felt rather as if she must be losing her senses.

'Not going!' she repeated.

'No,' said Mr. Carrisford. 'She is not going *home* – if you give your house that name. Her home for the future will be with me.'

Miss Minchin fell back in amazed indignation.

'With *you* ! With *you*, sir! What does this mean?'

'Kindly explain the matter, Carmichael,' said the Indian gentleman, 'and get it over as quickly as possible.' And he made Sara sit down again, and held her hands in his – which was another trick of her papa's.

Then Mr. Carmichael explained – in the quiet, level-toned, steady manner of a man who knew his subject, and all its legal significance, which was a thing Miss Minchin understood as a business woman, and did not enjoy.

'"Go home at once," she commanded indignantly'

'Mr. Carrisford, madam,' he said, 'was an intimate friend of the late Captain Crewe. He was his partner in certain large investments. The fortune which Captain Crewe supposed he had lost has been recovered, and is now in Mr. Carrisford's hands.'

'The fortune!' cried Miss Minchin; and she really lost colour as she uttered the exclamation. 'Sara's fortune!'

'It *will* be Sara's fortune,' replied Mr. Carmichael, rather coldly. 'It *is* Sara's fortune now, in fact. Certain events have increased it enormously. The diamond mines have retrieved themselves.'

'The diamond mines!' Miss Minchin gasped out. If this was true, nothing so horrible, she felt, had ever happened to her since she was born.

'The diamond mines,' Mr. Carmichael repeated, and he could not help adding, with a rather sly, unlawyer-like smile: 'There are not many princesses, Miss Minchin, who are richer than your little charity pupil, Sara Crewe, will be. Carrisford has been searching for her for nearly two years; he has found her at last, and he will keep her.'

After which he asked Miss Minchin to sit down while he explained matters to her fully, and went into such detail as was necessary to make it quite clear to her that Sara's future was an assured one, and that what had seemed to be lost was to be restored to her tenfold; also, that she had in Mr. Carrisford a guardian as well as a friend.

Miss Minchin was not a clever woman, and in her excitement she was silly enough to make one desperate effort to regain what she could not help seeing she had lost through her own worldly folly.

'He found her under my care,' she protested. 'I have done everything for her. But for me she would have starved in the streets.'

Here the Indian gentleman lost his temper.

'As to starving in the streets,' he said, 'she might have starved more comfortably there than in your attic.'

'Captain Crewe left her in my charge,' Miss Minchin argued. 'She must return to it until she is of age. She can be a parlour-boarder again. She must finish her education. The law will interfere in my behalf.'

'Come, come, Miss Minchin,' Mr. Carmichael interposed, 'the law will do nothing of the sort. If Sara herself wishes to return to you, I dare say Mr. Carrisford might not refuse to allow it. But that rests with Sara.'

'Then,' said Miss Minchin, 'I appeal to Sara. I have not spoiled you, perhaps,' she said awkwardly to the little girl, 'but you know that your papa was pleased with your progress. And – ahem! – I have always been fond of you.'

Sara's green-grey eyes fixed themselves on her with the quiet, clear look Miss Minchin particularly disliked.

'Have *you*, Miss Minchin?' she said. 'I did not know that.'

Miss Minchin reddened and drew herself up.

'You ought to have known it,' said she, 'but children, unfortunately, never know what is best for them. Amelia and I always said you were the cleverest child in the school. Will you not do your duty to your poor papa and come home with me?'

Sara took a step toward her and stood still. She was thinking of the day when she had been told that she belonged to nobody, and was in danger of being turned into the street; she was thinking of the cold, hungry hours she had spent alone with Emily and Melchisedec in the attic. She looked Miss Minchin steadily in the face.

'You know why I will not go home with you, Miss Minchin,' she said. 'You know quite well.'

A hot flush showed itself on Miss Minchin's hard angry face.

'You will never see your companions again,' she began. 'I will see that Ermengarde and Lottie are kept away——'

Mr. Carmichael stopped her with polite firmness.

'Excuse me,' he said, 'she will see any one she wishes to see. The parents of Miss Crewe's fellow-pupils are not likely to refuse her invitations to visit her at her guardian's house. Mr. Carrisford will attend to that.'

It must be confessed that even Miss Minchin flinched. This was worse than the eccentric bachelor uncle who might have a peppery temper and be easily offended at the treatment of his niece. A woman of sordid mind could easily believe that most people would not refuse to allow their children to remain friends with a little heiress of diamond mines. And if Mr. Carrisford chose to tell certain of her patrons how unhappy Sara Crewe had been made, many unpleasant things might happen.

'You have not undertaken an easy charge,' she said to the Indian gentleman, as she turned to leave the room. 'You will discover that very soon. The child is neither truthful nor grateful. I suppose' – to Sara – 'that you feel now that you are a princess again.'

Sara looked down and flushed a little, because she thought her pet fancy might not be easy for strangers – even nice ones – to understand at first.

'I – tried not to be anything else,' she answered in a low voice – 'even when I was coldest and hungriest – I *tried* not to be.'

'Now it will not be necessary to try,' said Miss Minchin acidly, as Ram Dass salaamed her out of the room.

She returned home, and, going to her sitting-room, sent at once for Miss Amelia. She sat closeted with her all the rest of the afternoon, and it must be admitted that poor Miss Amelia passed through more than one bad quarter of an hour. She shed a good many tears, and mopped her eyes a good deal. One of her unfortunate remarks almost caused her sister to snap her head entirely off, but it resulted in an unusual manner.

'I'm not as clever as you, sister,' she said, 'and I am always afraid to say things to you for fear of making you angry. Perhaps if I were not so timid it would be better for the school and for both of us. I must say I've often thought it would have been better if you had been less severe on Sara Crewe, and had seen that she was decently dressed and more comfortable. I *know* she was worked too hard for a child of her age, and I know she was only half fed——'

'How dare you say such a thing!' exclaimed Miss Minchin.

'I don't know how I dare,' Miss Amelia answered, with a kind of reckless courage, 'but now I've begun I may as well finish, whatever happens to me. The child was a clever child and a good child – and she would have paid you for any kindness you had shown her. But you didn't show her any. The fact was, she was too clever for you, and you always disliked her for that reason. She used to see through us both——'

'Amelia!' gasped her infuriated elder, looking as if she would box her ears and knock her cap off, as she had often done to Becky.

But Miss Amelia's disappointment had made her hysterical enough not to care what occurred next.

'She did! She did!' she cried. 'She saw through us both. She saw that you were a hard-hearted, worldly woman, and that I was a weak fool, and that we were both of us vulgar and mean enough to grovel on our knees before her money, and behave ill to her because it was taken from her – though she behaved herself like a princess even when she was a beggar. She did – she did – like a little princess!' and her hysterics got the better of the poor woman, and she began to laugh and cry both at once, and rock herself backward and forward in such a way as made Miss Minchin stare aghast.

'And now you've lost her,' she cried wildly, 'and some other school will get her and her money, and if she were like any other child she'd tell how she's been treated, and all our pupils would be taken away and we should be ruined. And it serves us right; but it serves you right more than it does me, for you are a hard woman, Maria Minchin – you're a hard, selfish, worldly woman!'

And she was in danger of making so much noise with her hysterical chokes and gurgles that her sister was obliged to go to her and apply salts and sal volatile to quiet her, instead of pouring forth her indignation at her audacity.

And from that time forward, it may be mentioned, the elder Miss Minchin actually began to stand a little in awe of a sister who, while she looked so foolish, was evidently not quite so foolish as she looked, and might consequently, break out and speak truths people did not want to hear.

That evening, when the pupils were gathered together before the fire in the schoolroom, as was their custom before going to bed, Ermengarde came in with a letter in her hand and a queer expression on her round face. It was queer because, while it was an expression of delighted excitement, it was combined with such amazement as seemed to belong to a kind of shock just received.

'What *is* the matter?' cried two or three voices at once.

'Is it anything to do with the row that has been going on?' said Lavinia eagerly. 'There has been such a row in Miss Minchin's room;

Miss Amelia has had something like hysterics and has had to go to bed.'

Ermengarde answered them slowly, as if she were half stunned.

'I have just had this letter from Sara,' she said, holding it out to let them see what a long letter it was.

'From Sara!' Every voice joined in that exclamation.

'Where is she?' almost shrieked Jessie.

'Next door,' said Ermengarde, still slowly, 'with the Indian gentleman.'

'Where? Where? Has she been sent away? Does Miss Minchin know? Was the row about that? Why did she write? Tell us! Tell us!'

There was a perfect babel, and Lottie began to cry plaintively.

Ermengarde answered them slowly, as if she were half plunged out into what, at the moment, seemed the most important and self-explaining thing.

'There *were* diamond mines,' she said stoutly. 'There *were*!'

Open mouths and open eyes confronted her.

'They were real,' she hurried on. 'It was all a mistake about them. Something happened for a time, and Mr. Carrisford thought they were ruined——'

'Who is Mr. Carrisford?' shouted Jessie.

'The Indian gentleman. And Captain Crewe thought so, too – and he died; and Mr. Carrisford had brain-fever and ran away, and *he* almost died. And he did not know where Sara was. And it turned out that there were millions and millions of diamonds in the mines; and half of them belong to Sara; and they belonged to her when she was living in the attic with no one but Melchisedec for a friend, and the cook ordering her about. And Mr. Carrisford found her this afternoon, and he has got her in his home – and she will never come back – and she will be more a princess than she ever was – a hundred and fifty thousand times more. And I am going to see her to-morrow afternoon. There!'

Even Miss Minchin herself could scarcely have controlled the uproar after this; and though she heard the noise, she did not try. She was not in the mood to face anything more than she was facing in her room, while Miss Amelia was weeping in bed. She knew that the news hád penetrated the walls in some mysterious manner, and that every servant and every child would go to bed talking about it.

So until almost midnight the entire seminary, realizing somehow that all rules were laid aside, crowded round Ermengarde in the schoolroom and heard read and re-read the letter containing a story which was quite as wonderful as any Sara herself had ever invented, and which had the amazing charm of having happened to Sara herself and the mystic Indian gentleman in the very next house.

Becky, who had heard it also, managed to creep upstairs earlier than usual. She wanted to get away from people and go and look at the little magic room once more. She did not know what would happen to it. It was not likely that it would be left to Miss Minchin. It would be taken away, and the attic would be bare and empty again. Glad as she was for Sara's sake, she went up the last flight of stairs with a lump in her throat and tears blurring her sight. There would be no fire to-night, and no rosy lamp; no supper, and no princess sitting in the glow reading or telling stories – no princess!

She choked down a sob as she pushed the attic door open, and then she broke into a low cry.

The lamp was flushing the room, the fire was blazing, the supper was waiting; and Ram Dass was standing smiling into her startled face.

'Missee sahib remembered,' he said. 'She told the sahib all. She wished you to know the good fortune which was befallen her. Behold a letter on the tray. She has written. She did not wish that you should go to sleep unhappy. The sahib commands you to come to him to-morrow. You are to be the attendant of missee sahib. To-night I take these things back over the roof.'

And having said this with a beaming face, he made a little salaam and slipped through the skylight with an agile silentness of movement which showed Becky how easily he had done it before.

19 'Anne'

Never had such joy reigned in the nursery of the Large Family. Never had they dreamed of such delights as resulted from an intimate acquaintance with the little-girl-who-was-not-a-beggar. The mere fact of her sufferings and adventures made her a priceless possession. Everybody wanted to be told over and over again the things which had happened to her. When one was sitting by a warm fire in a big, glowing room, it was quite delightful to hear how cold it could be in an attic. It must be admitted that the attic was rather delighted in, and that its coldness and bareness quite sank into insignificance when Melchisedec was remembered, and one heard about the sparrows and things one could see if one climbed on the table and stuck one's head and shoulders out of the skylight.

Of course the thing loved best was the story of the banquet and the dream which was true. Sara told it for the first time the day after she had been found. Several members of the Large Family came to take tea with her, and as they sat or curled up on the hearth-rug she told the story in her own way, and the Indian gentleman listened and watched her. When she had finished she looked up at him and put her hand on his knee.

'That is my part,' she said. 'Now won't you tell your part of it, Uncle Tom?' He had asked her to call him always 'Uncle Tom'. 'I don't know your part yet, and it must be beautiful.'

So he told them how, when he sat alone, ill and dull and irritable, Ram Dass had tried to distract him by describing the passers-by, and there was one child who passed oftener than any one else; he had begun to be interested in her – partly perhaps because he was thinking a great deal of a little girl, and partly because Ram Dass had been able to relate the incident of his visit to the attic in chase of the monkey. He had described its cheerless look, and the bearing of the child, who seemed as if she was not of the class of those who were treated as drudges and servants. Bit by bit, Ram Dass had made discoveries concerning the wretchedness of her life. He had found out how easy a matter it was to climb across the few yards of roof to the skylight, and this fact had been the beginning of all that followed.

'Sahib,' he had said one day, 'I could cross the slates and make the child a fire when she is out on some errand. When she returned, wet and cold, to find it blazing, she would think a magician had done it.'

The idea had been so fanciful that Mr. Carrisford's sad face had lighted with a smile, and Ram Dass had been so filled with rapture that he had enlarged upon it and explained to his master how simple it would be to accomplish numbers of other things. He had shown a childlike pleasure and invention, and the preparations for the carrying out of the plan had filled many a day with interest which would otherwise have dragged wearily. On the night of the frustrated banquet Ram Dass had kept watch, all his packages being in readiness in the attic which was his own; and the person who was to help him had waited with him, as interested as himself in the odd adventure. Ram Dass had been lying flat upon the slates, looking in at the skylight, when the banquet had come to its disastrous conclusion; he had been sure of the profoundness of Sara's wearied sleep; and then, with a dark lantern, he had crept into the room, while his companion had remained outside and handed the things to him. When Sara had stirred ever so faintly, Ram Dass had closed the lantern-slide and lain flat upon the floor. These and many other exciting things the children found out by asking a thousand questions.

'I am so glad,' Sara said. 'I am so *glad* it was you who were my friend!'

There never were such friends as these two became. Somehow, they seemed to suit each other in a wonderful way. The Indian gentleman had never had a companion he liked quite as much as he liked Sara. In a month's time he was, as Mr. Carmichael had prophesied he would be, a new man. He was always amused and interested, and he began to find an actual pleasure in the possession of the wealth he had imagined that he loathed the burden of. There were so many charming things to plan for Sara. There was a little joke between them that he was a magician, and it was one if his pleasures to invent things to surprise her. She found beautiful new flowers growing in her room, whimsical little gifts tucked under pillows, and once, as they sat together in the evening, they heard the scratch of a heavy paw on the door, and when Sara went to find out what it was, there stood a great dog – a splendid boarhound – with a grand silver and gold collar bearing an inscription in raised letters. 'I am Boris,' it read, 'I serve the Princess Sara.'

There was nothing the Indian gentleman loved more than the recollection of the little princess in rags and tatters. The afternoons in which the Large Family, or Ermengarde and Lottie, gathered to rejoice together were very delightful. But the hours when Sara and the Indian gentleman sat alone and read or talked had a special charm of their own. During their passing many interesting things occurred.

One evening, Mr. Carrisford, looking up from his book, noticed that his companion had not stirred for some time, but sat gazing into the fire.

'What are you "supposing", Sara?' he asked.

Sara looked up, with a bright colour on her cheek.

'I *was* supposing,' she said, 'I was remembering that hungry day, and a child I saw.'

'But there were a great many hungry days,' said the Indian gentleman, with a rather sad tone in his voice. 'Which hungry day was it?'

'I forgot you didn't know,' said Sara. 'It was the day the dream came true.'

Then she told him the story of the bun-shop, and the fourpence she picked up out of the sloppy mud, and the child who was hungrier than herself. She told it quite simply, and in as few words as possible; but somehow the Indian gentleman found it necessary to shade his eyes with his hand and look down at the carpet.

'And I was supposing a kind of plan,' she said, when she had finished. 'I was thinking I should like to do something.'

'What was it?' said Mr. Carrisford, in a low tone. 'You may do anything you like to do, princess.'

'I was wondering,' rather hesitated Sara – 'you know, you say I have so much money – I was wondering if I could go to see the bun-woman, and tell her that if, when hungry children – particularly on those dreadful days – come and sit on the steps, or look in at the window, she would just call them in and give them something to eat, and she might send the bills to me. Could I do that?'

'You shall do it to-morrow morning,' said the Indian gentleman.

'Thank you,' said Sara. 'You see, I know what it is to be hungry, and it is very hard when one cannot even *pretend* it away.'

'Yes, yes, my dear,' said the Indian gentleman. 'Yes, yes, it must be. Try to forget it. Come and sit on this footstool near my knee, and only remember you are a princess.'

'Yes,' said Sara, smiling, 'and I can give buns and bread to the populace.' And she went and sat on the stool, and the Indian gentleman (he used to like her to call him that, too, sometimes) drew her small dark head down upon his knee and stroked her hair.

The next morning, Miss Minchin, in looking out of her window, saw the thing she perhaps least enjoyed seeing. The Indian gentleman's carriage, with its tall horses, drew up before the door of the next house, and its owner and a little figure, warm with soft, rich furs, descended the steps to get into it. The little figure was a familiar one, and reminded Miss Minchin of days in the past. It was followed by another as familiar – the sight of which she found very irritating. It was Becky, who, in the character of delighted attendant, always accompanied her young mistress to her carriage, carrying wraps and belongings. Already Becky had a pink, round face.

A little later the carriage drew up before the door of the baker's shop, and its occupants got out, oddly enough, just as the bun-woman was putting a tray of smoking hot buns into the window.

When Sara entered the shop the woman turned and looked at her, and, leaving the buns, came and stood behind the counter. For a moment she looked at Sara very hard indeed, and then her good-natured face lighted up.

'I'm sure that I remember you, miss,' she said. 'And yet——'

'Yes,' said Sara, 'once you gave me six buns for fourpence, and——'

'And you gave five of 'em to a beggar child,' the woman broke in on her. 'I've always remembered it. I couldn't make it out at first.' She turned round to the Indian gentleman and spoke her next words to him. 'I beg your pardon, sir, but there's not many young people that notices a hungry face in that way; and I've thought of it many a time. Excuse the liberty, miss' – to Sara – 'but you look rosier and – well, better than you did that – that——'

'I am better, thank you,' said Sara. 'And – I am much happier – and I have come to ask you to do something for me.'

'Me, miss!' exclaimed the bun-woman, smiling cheerfully. 'Why, bless you! yes, miss. What can I do?'

And then Sara, leaning on the counter, made her little proposal concerning the dreadful days and the hungry waifs and the hot buns.

The woman watched her, and listened with an astonished face.

'Why bless me!' she said again when she had heard it all, 'it'll be a pleasure to me to do it. I am a working-woman myself and cannot afford to do much on my own account, and there's sights of trouble on every side; but, if you'll excuse me, I'm bound to say I've given away many a bit of bread since that wet afternoon, just along o' thinking of you – an' how wet an' cold you was, an' how hungry you looked an' yet you gave away your hot buns as if you was a princess.'

The Indian gentleman smiled involuntarily at this and Sara smiled a little, too, remembering what she had said to herself when she put the buns down on the ravenous child's ragged lap.

'She looked so hungry,' she said. 'She was even hungrier than I was.'

'She was starving,' said the woman. 'Many's the time she's told me of it since – how she sat there in the wet, and felt as if a wolf was a-tearing at her poor young insides.'

'Oh, have you seen her since then?' exclaimed Sara. 'Do you know where she is?'

'Yes, I do,' answered the woman, smiling more good-naturedly than ever. 'Why, she's in that there back-room, miss, an' has been for a month; an' a decent, well-meanin' girl she's goin' to turn out, an' such a help to me in the shop an' in the kitchen as you'd scarce believe, knowin' how she's lived.'

She stepped to the door of the little back-parlour and spoke; and the next minute a girl came out and followed her behind the counter. And actually it was the beggar-child, clean and neatly clothed, and looking as if she had not been hungry for a long time. She looked shy, but she had a nice face, now that she was no longer a savage, and the wild look had gone from her eyes. She knew Sara in an instant, and stood and looked at her as if she could never look enough.

'You see,' said the woman, 'I told her to come when she was hungry, and when she'd come I'd give her odd jobs to do; an' I found she was willing, and somehow I got to like her; and the end of it was, I've given her a place an' a home, and she helps me, an' behaves well, an' is as thankful as a girl can be. Her name's Anne. She has no other.'

The children stood and looked at each other for a few minutes; and than Sara took her hand out of her muff and held it out across the counter, and Anne took it, and they looked straight into each other's eyes.

'I am so glad,' Sara said. 'And I have just thought of something. Perhaps Mrs. Brown will let you be the one to give the buns and bread to the children. Perhaps you would like to do it because you know what it is to be hungry, too.'

'Yes, miss,' said the girl.

And, somehow, Sara felt as if she understood her, though she said so little, and only stood still and looked and looked after her as she went out of the shop with the Indian gentleman, and they got into the carriage and drove away.

LITTLE LORD FAUNTLEROY

LITTLE LORD FAUNTLEROY

Frances Hodgson Burnett

Contents

List of Illustrations

1 A Great Surprise

Cedric himself knew nothing whatever about it. It had never been even mentioned to him. He knew that his papa had been an Englishman, because his mamma had told him so; but then his papa had died when he was so little a boy that he could not remember very much about him, except that he was big, and had blue eyes and a long moustache, and that it was a splendid thing to be carried around the room on his shoulder. Since his papa's death, Cedric had found out that it was best not to talk to his mamma about him. When his father was ill, Cedric had been sent away, and when he had returned, everything was over; and his mother, who had been very ill too, was only just beginning to sit in her chair by the window. She was pale and thin, and all the dimples had gone from her pretty face and her eyes looked large and mournful, and she was dressed in black.

'Dearest,' said Cedric (his papa had called her that always, and so the little boy had learned to say it), 'Dearest, is my papa better?'

He felt her arms tremble, and so he turned his curly head, and looked in her face. There was something in it that made him feel that he was going to cry.

'Dearest,' he said, 'is he well?'

Then suddenly his loving little heart told him that he'd better put both his arms around her neck and kiss her again and again, and keep his soft cheek close to hers; and he did so, and she laid her face on his shoulder and cried bitterly, holding him as if she could never let him go again.

'Yes, he is well,' she sobbed; 'he is quite, quite well, but we – we have no one left but each other. No one at all.'

Then, little as he was, he understood that his big, handsome young papa would not come back any more; that he was dead, as he had heard of other people being, although he could not comprehend exactly what strange thing had brought all this sadness about. It was because his mamma always cried when he spoke of his papa that he secretly made up his mind it was better not to speak of him very often to her, and he found out, too, that it was better not to let her sit still and look into the fire or out of the window without moving or talking. He and his mamma knew very few people, and lived what might have been thought very lonely lives, although Cedric did not know it was lonely until he grew older and heard why it was they had no visitors. Then he was told that his mamma was an orphan, and quite alone in the world when his papa had married her. She was very pretty, and had been living as companion to a rich old lady who was not kind to her, and one day Captain Cedric Errol, who was calling at the house, saw her run up the stairs with tears on her eyelashes; and she looked so sweet and innocent and sorrowful that the Captain could not forget her. And after many strange things had happened, they knew each other well and loved each other dearly, and were married, although their marriage brought them the ill will of several persons. The one who was most angry of all, however, was the Captain's father, who lived in England, and was a very rich and important old nobleman, with a very bad temper, and a very violent dislike to America and Americans. He had two sons older than Captain Cedric; and it was the law that the elder of these sons should inherit the family title and estates, which were very rich and splendid; if the eldest son died the next one would be heir; so though he was a member of such a great family, there was little chance that Captain Cedric would be very rich himself.

But it so happened that Nature had given to the younger son gifts which she had not bestowed upon his elder brothers. He had a beautiful face and a fine, strong, graceful figure; he had a bright smile and a sweet, gay voice; he was brave and generous, and had the kindest heart in the world, and seemed to have the power to make everyone love him. But it was not so with his elder brothers; neither of them was handsome, or very kind or clever. When they were boys at Eton, they were not popular; when they were at college, they cared nothing for study, and wasted both time and money, and made few real friends.

The old Earl, their father, was constantly disappointed and humiliated by them; his heir was no honour to his noble name, and did not promise to end in being anything but a selfish, wasteful, insignificant man, with no manly or noble qualities. It was very bitter, the old Earl thought, that the son who was only third, and would have only a very small fortune, should be the one who had all the gifts, and all the charms, and all the strength and beauty. Sometimes he almost hated the handsome young man because he seemed to have the good things which should have gone with the stately title and the magnificent estates; and yet, in the depths of his proud, stubborn old heart, he could not help caring very much for his youngest son. It was in one of his fits of petulance that he sent him off to travel in America; he thought he would send him away for a while, so that he should not be made angry by constantly contrasting him with his brothers, who were at that time giving him a great deal of trouble by their wild ways.

But after about six months, he began to feel lonely, and longed in secret to see his son again, so he wrote to Captain Cedric and ordered him home. The letter he wrote crossed on its way a letter the Captain had just written to his father telling of his love for the pretty American girl, and of his intended marriage; and when the Earl received that letter, he was furiously angry. Bad as his temper was, he had never given way to it in his life as he gave way to it when he read the Captain's letter. His valet, who was in the room when it came, thought his lordship would have a fit of apoplexy, he was so wild with anger. For an hour he raged like a tiger, and then he sat down and wrote to his son, and ordered him never to come near his old home, nor to write to his father or brothers again. He told him he might live as he pleased, and die where he pleased, that he should be cut off from his family for ever, and that he need never expect help from his father as long as he lived.

The Captain was very sad when he read the letter; he was very fond of England, and he dearly loved the beautiful home where he had been born; he had even loved his ill-tempered old father, and had sympathized with him in his disappointments; but he knew he need expect no kindness from him in the future. At first he scarcely knew what to do; he had not been brought up to work, and had no business experience, but he had courage and plenty of determination. So he sold his commission in the English army, and after some trouble found a situation in New York, and married. The change from his old life in England was very great, but he was young and happy and he hoped that hard work would do great things for him in the future. He had a small house in a quiet street, and his little boy was born there, and everything was so gay and cheerful, in a simple way, that he was never sorry for a moment that he had married the rich old lady's pretty companion just because she was so sweet and he loved her and she loved him. She was very sweet indeed, and her little boy was like both her and his father. Though he was born in so quiet and cheap a little home, it seemed as if there never had been a more fortunate baby. In the first place he was always well, and so he never gave anyone trouble; in the second place he had so sweet a temper and ways so charming that he was a pleasure to everyone; and in the third place he was so beautiful to look at that he was quite a picture. Instead of being a bald-headed baby, he started in life with a quantity of soft, fine, gold-coloured hair, which curled up at the ends, and went into loose rings by the time he was six months old; he had big brown eyes and long eyelashes and a darling little face; he had so strong a back and splendid sturdy legs that at nine months he learned suddenly to walk, his manners were so good, for a baby, that it was delightful to make his acquaintance. He seemed to feel that everyone was his friend, and when anyone spoke to him, when he was in his carriage in the street, he would give the stranger one sweet serious look with the brown eyes, and then follow in with a lovely, friendly smile; and the consequence was, that there was not a person in the neighbourhood of the quiet street where he lived – even to the groceryman at the corner, who was considered the crossest creature alive – who was not pleased to see him, and speak to him. And every month of his life he grew handsomer and more interesting.

When he was old enough to walk out with his nurse, dragging a small wagon and wearing a short white kilt skirt, and a big white hat set back on his curly yellow hair, he was so handsome and strong and rosy that he attracted everyone's attention, and his nurse would come home and tell his mamma stories of the ladies who had stopped their carriages to look at and speak to him, and of how pleased they were when he talked to them in his cheerful little way, as if he had known them always. His greatest charm was this cheerful, fearless, quaint little way of making friends with people. I think it arose from his having a very confiding nature, and a kind little heart that sympathized with everyone, and wished to make everyone as comfortable as he liked to be himself. It made him very quick to understand the feelings of those about him. Perhaps this had grown on him too, because he had lived so much with his father and mother, who were always loving and considerate and tender and well bred. He had never heard an unkind or uncourteous word spoken at home; he had always been loved and caressed and treated tenderly, and so his childish soul was full of kindness and innocent warm feeling. He had always heard his mamma called by pretty, loving names, and so he used them himself when he spoke to her; he had always seen that his papa watched over her and took great care of her, and so he learned too to be careful of her.

So when he knew his papa would come back no more and saw how very sad his mamma was, there gradually came into his kind little heart the thought that he must do what he could to make her happy. He was not much more than a baby, but that thought was in his mind whenever he climbed upon her knee and kissed her, and put his curly head on her neck, and when he brought his toys and picture books to show her, and when he curled up quietly by her side as she used to lie on the sofa. He was not old enough to know of anything else to do, so he did what he could, and was more of a comfort to her than he could have understood.

'Oh, Mary,' he heard her say once to her old servant, 'I am sure he is trying to help me in his innocent way – I know he is. He looks at me sometimes with a loving, wondering little look, as if he were sorry for me, and then he will come and pet me or show me something. He is such a little man, I really think he knows.'

As he grew older he had a great many quaint little ways which amused and interested people greatly. He was so much of a companion for his mother that she scarcely cared for any other. They used to walk together and talk together and play together. When he was quite a little fellow he learned to read; and after that he used to lie on the hearth-rug, in the evening, and read aloud – sometimes stories, and sometimes big books such as older people read, and sometimes even the newspaper; and often at such times Mary, in the kitchen, would hear Mrs. Errol laughing with delight at the quaint things he said.

'And, indade,' said Mary to the groceryman, 'nobody cud help laughin' at the quare little ways of him – and his ould-fashioned sayin's! Didn't he come into my kitchen the noight the new prisident was nominated and shtand afore the fire, lookin' loike a pictur', wid his hands in his shmall pockets, an' his innocent bit of a face as sayrious as a jedge? An' sez he to me: "Mary," sez he, "I'm very much int'rusted in the 'lection," sez he. "I'm a 'publican, an' so is Dearest. Are you a 'publican, Mary?" "Sorra a bit," sez I; "I'm the bist o' dimmycrats!" An' he looks up at me wid a look that ud go to yer heart, and sez he: "Mary," sez he, "the country will go to ruin." An' nivver a day since thin has he let go by widout argyin' wid me to change me polytics.'

Mary was very fond of him, and very proud of him too. She had been with his mother ever since he was born; and after his father's death, had been cook and housemaid and nurse and everything else. She was proud of his graceful, strong little body and his pretty manners, especially proud of the bright curly hair which waved over his forehead and fell in charming love-locks on his shoulders. She was willing to work early and late to help his mamma to make his small suits and keep them in order.

''Ristycratic, is it?' she would say. 'Faith and I'd loike to see the choild on Fifth Avey-*noo* as he looks loike him an' shteps out as handsome as himself. An' ivvery man, woman and choild lookin' afther him in his bit of a black velvet skirt made out of the misthress's ould gownd; an' his little head up an' his curly hair flyin' an' shinin'. It's like a young lord he looks.'

Cedric did not know that he looked like a young lord; he did not know what a lord was. His greatest friend was the groceryman at the corner – the cross groceryman, who was never cross to him. His name was Mr. Hobbs, and Cedric admired and respected him very much. He thought him a very rich and powerful person, he had so many things in his store – prunes and figs and oranges and biscuits – and he had a horse and wagon. Cedric was fond of the milkman and the baker and the apple-woman, but he liked Mr. Hobbs best of all, and was on terms of such intimacy with him that he went to see him every day, and often sat with him quite a long time discussing the topics of the hour. It was quite surprising how many things they found to talk about – the Fourth of July, for instance. When they began to talk about the Fourth of July there really seemed no end to it. Mr. Hobbs had a very bad opinion of 'the British', and he told the whole story of the Revolution, relating very wonderful and patriotic stories about the villainy of the enemy and the bravery of the revolutionary heroes, and he even generously repeated part of the Declaration of Independence. Cedric was so excited that his eyes shone and his cheeks were red and his curls were all rubbed and tumbled into a yellow mop. He could hardly wait to eat his dinner after he went home, he was so anxious to tell his mamma. It was perhaps Mr. Hobbs who gave him his first interest in politics. Mr. Hobbs was fond of reading the newspapers, and so Cedric heard a great deal about what was going on in Washington; and Mr. Hobbs would tell him whether the President was doing his duty or not. And once, when there was an election, he found it all quite grand, and probably but for Mr. Hobbs and Cedric the country might have been wrecked. Mr. Hobbs took him to see a great torchlight procession, and many of the men who carried torches remembered afterwards a stout man who stood near a lamp-post and held on his shoulder a handsome little shouting boy, who waved his cap in the air.

It was not long after this election, when Cedric was between seven and eight years old, that the very strange thing happened which made so wonderful a change in his life. It was quite curious, too, that the day it happened he had been talking to Mr. Hobbs about England and the Queen, and Mr. Hobbs had said some very severe things about the aristocracy, being specially indignant against earls and marquises. It had been a hot morning; and after playing soldiers with some friends of his, Cedric had gone into the store to rest, and had found Mr. Hobbs looking very fierce over a piece of the *Illustrated London News*, which contained a picture of some court ceremony.

'Ah,' he said, 'That's the way they go on now; but they'll get enough of it some day, when those they've trod on rise and blow 'em up sky-high – earls and marquises and all! It's coming, and they may look out for it!'

Cedric had perched himself as usual on the high stool and pushed his hat back, and put his hands in his pockets in delicate compliment to Mr. Hobbs.

'Did you ever know many marquises, Mr. Hobbs?' Cedric inquired; 'or earls?'

'No,' answered Mr. Hobbs with indignation; 'I guess not. I'd like to catch one of 'em inside here; that's all! I'll have no grasping tyrants sittin' 'round on my biscuit barrels!'

And he was so proud of the sentiment that he looked around proudly and mopped his forehead.

'Perhaps they wouldn't be earls if they knew any better,' said Cedric, feeling some vague sympathy for their unhappy condition.

'Wouldn't they!' said Mr. Hobbs. 'They just glory in it! It's in 'em. They're a bad lot.'

They were in the midst of their conversation when Mary appeared. Cedric thought she had come to buy some sugar, perhaps, but she had not. She looked almost pale as if she were excited about something.

'Come home, darlint,' she said; 'the misthress is wantin' yez.'

Cedric slipped down from his stool. 'Does she want me to go out with her, Mary?' he asked. 'Good morning,·Mr. Hobbs. I'll see you again.'

He was surprised to see Mary staring at him in a dumbfounded fashion, and he wondered why she kept shaking her head. 'What's the matter, Mary?' he said. 'Is it the hot weather?'

'No,' said Mary, 'but there's strange things happenin' to us.'

'Has the sun given Dearest a headache?' he inquired anxiously.

But it was not that. When he reached his own house there was a coupé standing before the door, and someone was in the little parlour talking to his mamma. Mary hurried him upstairs and put on his best summer suit of cream-coloured flannel with the red scarf around the waist, and combed out his curly locks.

'Lords, is it?' he heard her say. 'An' the nobility an' gintry. Och! bad cess to them! Lords indade – worse luck.'

It was really very puzzling, but he felt sure his mamma would tell him what all the excitement meant, so he allowed Mary to bemoan herself without asking many questions. When he was dressed, he ran downstairs and went into the parlour. A tall, thin old gentleman with a sharp face was sitting in an armchair. His mother was standing near by with a pale face, and he saw that there were tears in her eyes.

'Oh, Ceddie!' she cried out, and ran to her little boy and caught him in her arms and kissed him in a little frightened, troubled way. 'Oh, Ceddie darling!'

The tall old gentleman rose from his chair and looked at Cedric with his sharp eyes. He rubbed his thin chin with his bony hand as he looked. He seemed not at all displeased.

'And so,' he said at last slowly, 'and so this is little Lord Fauntleroy.'

2 Cedric's Friends

There was never a more amazed little boy than Cedric during the week that followed; there was never so strange or so unreal a week. In the first place, the story his mamma told him was a very curious one. He was obliged to hear it two or three times before he could understand it. He could not imagine what Mr. Hobbs would think of it. It began with earls; his grandpapa, whom he had never seen, was an earl; and his eldest uncle, if he had not been killed by a fall from his horse, would have been an earl too in time; and after his death, his other uncle would have been an earl, if he had not died suddenly, in Rome, of fever. After that, his own papa, if he had lived, would have been an earl; but since they had all died and only Cedric was left, it appeared that *he* was to be an earl after his grandpapa's death – and for the present he was Lord Fauntleroy.

He turned quite pale when he was first told of it.

'Oh, Dearest,' he said, 'I should rather not be an earl. None of the boys are earls. Can't I *not* be one?'

But it seemed to be unavoidable. And when, that evening, they sat together by the open window looking out into the shabby street, he and his mother had a long talk about it. Cedric sat on his footstool, clasping one knee in his favourite attitude and wearing a bewildered little face rather red from the exertion of thinking. His grandfather had sent for him to come to England and his mamma thought he must go.

'Because', she said, looking out of the window with sorrowful eyes, 'I know your papa would wish it to be so, Ceddie. He loved his home very much; and there are many things to be thought of that a little boy can't quite understand. I should be a selfish little mother if I did not send you. When you are a man you will see why.'

Ceddie shook his head mournfully. 'I shall be very sorry to leave Mr. Hobbs,' he said. 'I'm afraid he'll miss me, and I shall miss him. And I shall miss them all.'

When Mr. Havisham – who was the family lawyer of the Earl of Dorincourt, and who had been sent by him to bring Lord Fauntleroy to England – came the next day, Cedric heard many things. But somehow it did not console him to hear that he was to be a very rich man when he grew up, and that he would have castles here and castles there, and great parks and deep mines and grand estates and tenantry. He was troubled about his friend, Mr. Hobbs, and he went to see him at the store soon after breakfast in great anxiety of mind.

He found him reading the morning paper, and he approached him with a grave demeanour. He really felt it would be a great shock to Mr. Hobbs to hear what had befallen him, and on his way to the store he had been thinking how it would be best to break the news.

'Hallo!' said Mr. Hobbs. 'Mornin'!'

'Good morning,' said Cedric.

He did not climb up on the high stool as usual but sat down on a biscuit box and clasped his knee, and was so silent for a few moments that Mr. Hobbs finally looked up inquiringly over the top of his newspaper.

'Hallo!' he said again.

Cedric gathered all his strength of mind together.

'Mr. Hobbs,' he said, 'do you remember what we were talking about yesterday morning?'

'Well,' replied Mr. Hobbs, 'seems to me it was England.'

'Yes,' said Cedric; 'but just when Mary came for me, you know?'

Mr. Hobbs rubbed the back of his head.

'We *was* mentioning Queen Victoria and the aristocracy.'

'Yes,' said Cedric rather hesitatingly, 'and – and earls; don't you know?'

'Why, yes,' returned Mr. Hobbs; 'we *did* touch 'em up a little; that's so!'

Cedric flushed up to the curly hair on his forehead. Nothing so embarrassing as this had ever happened to him in his life. He was a little afraid that it might be a trifle embarrassing to Mr. Hobbs too.

'Mr. Hobbs looked up enquiringly over the top of his newspaper'

'You said', he proceeded, 'that you wouldn't have them sitting 'round on your biscuit barrels.'

'So I did!' returned Mr. Hobbs stoutly. 'And I meant it. Let 'em try it – that's all!'

'Mr. Hobbs,' said Cedric, 'one is sitting on this box now!'

Mr. Hobbs almost jumped out of his chair.

'What!' he exclaimed.

'Yes,' Cedric announced with due modesty; '*I* am one – or I am going to be. I shan't deceive you.'

Mr. Hobbs looked agitated. He rose up suddenly and went to look at the thermometer.

'The mercury's got into your head!' he exclaimed, turning back to examine his young friend's countenance. 'It *is* a hot day! How do you feel? Got any pain? When did you begin to feel that way?'

He put his big hand on the little boy's hair. This was more embarrassing than ever.

'Thank you,' said Ceddie; 'I'm all right. There is nothing the matter with my head. I'm sorry to say it's true, Mr. Hobbs. That was what Mary came to take me home for. Mr. Havisham was telling my mamma, and he is a lawyer.'

Mr. Hobbs sank into his chair and mopped his forehead with his handkerchief.

'*One* of us has got a sunstroke!' he exclaimed.

'No,' returned Cedric, 'we have not. We shall have to make the best of it, Mr. Hobbs. Mr. Havisham came all the way from England to tell us about it. My grandpapa sent him.'

Mr. Hobbs stared wildly at the innocent, serious little face before him.

'Who is your grandfather?' he asked.

Cedric put his hand in his pocket and carefully drew out a piece of paper, on which something was written in his own round, irregular hand.

'I couldn't easily remember it, so I wrote it down on this,' he said. And he read aloud slowly: '"John Arthur Molyneux Errol, Earl of Dorincourt," That is his name, and he lives in a castle – in two or three castles, I think. And my papa, who died, was his youngest son; and I shouldn't have been a lord or an earl if my papa hadn't died; and my papa wouldn't have been an earl if his two brothers hadn't died. But they all died, and there is no one but me – no boy – and so I have to be one; and my grandpapa has sent for me to come to England.'

Mr. Hobbs seemed to grow hotter and hotter. He mopped his forehead and his bald spot and breathed hard. He began to see that something very remarkable had happened; but when he looked at the little boy sitting on the biscuit box with the innocent, anxious expression in his childish eyes, and saw that he was not changed at all, but was simply as he had been the day before, just a handsome, cheerful, brave little fellow in a black cloth suit and red neck-ribbon, all this information about the nobility bewildered him. He was all the more bewildered because Cedric gave it with such ingenuous simplicity and plainly without realizing himself how stupendous it was.

'Wha—what did you say your name was?' Mr. Hobbs inquired.

'It's Cedric Errol, Lord Fauntleroy,' answered Cedric. 'That was what Mr. Havisham called me. He said when I went into the room: "And so this is little Lord Fauntleroy!"'

'Well,' said Mr Hobbs, 'I'll be – jiggered!'

This was an exclamation he always used when he was very much astonished or excited. He could think of nothing else to say just as that puzzling moment.

Cedric felt it to be quite a proper and suitable ejaculation. His respect and affection for Mr. Hobbs were so great that he admired and approved of all his remarks. He had not seen enough of society as yet to make him realize that sometimes Mr. Hobbs was not quite conventional. He knew, of course, that he was different from his mamma, but then his mamma was a lady, and he had an idea that ladies were always different from gentlemen.

He looked at Mr. Hobbs wistfully.

'England is a long way off, isn't it?' he asked.

'It's across the Atlantic Ocean,' Mr. Hobbs answered.

'That's the worst of it,' said Cedric. 'Perhaps I shall not see you again for a long time. I don't like to think of that, Mr. Hobbs.'

'The best of friends must part,' said Mr. Hobbs.

'Well,' said Cedric, 'we have been friends for a great many years, haven't we?'

'Ever since you was born,' Mr. Hobbs answered. 'You was about six weeks old when you were first walked out on this street.'

'Ah,' remarked Cedric with a sigh, 'I never thought I should have to be an earl then!'

'You think', said Mr. Hobbs, 'there's no getting out of it?'

'I'm afraid not,' answered Cedric. 'My mamma says that my papa would wish me to do it. But if I have to be an earl, there's one thing I can do: I can try to be a good one. I'm not going to be a tyrant. And if there is ever to be another war with America I shall try to stop it.'

His conversation with Mr. Hobbs was a long and serious one. Once having got over the first shock, Mr. Hobbs was not so rancorous as might have been expected; he endeavoured to resign himself to the situation, and before the interview was at an end he had asked a great many questions. As Cedric could answer but few of them he endeavoured to answer them himself, and being fairly launched on the subject of earls and marquises and lordly estates, explained many things in a way which would probably have astonished Mr. Havisham, could that gentleman have heard it.

But then there were many things which astonished Mr. Havisham. He had spent all his life in England, and was not accustomed to American people and American habits. He had been connected professionally with the family of the Earl of Dorincourt for nearly forty years, and he knew all about its grand estates and its great wealth and importance; and, in a cold business-like way, he felt an interest in this little boy who, in the future, was to be the master and owner of them all – the future Earl of Dorincourt. He had known all about the old Earl's disappointment in his elder sons and all about his fierce rage at Captain Cedric's American marriage, and he knew how he still hated the gentle little widow and would not speak of her except with bitter and cruel words. He insisted that she was only a common American girl who had entrapped his son into marrying her because she knew he was an earl's son. The old lawyer himself had more than half believed this was all true. He had seen a great many selfish, mercenary people in his life, and he had not a good opinion of

Americans. When he had been driven into the cheap street, and his coupé had stopped before the cheap small house, he had felt actually shocked. It seemed really quite dreadful to think that the future owner of Dorincourt Castle and Wyndham Towers and Chorlworth, and all the other stately splendours, should have been born and brought up in an insignificant house in a street with a sort of greengrocery at the corner. He wondered what kind of a child he would be, and what kind of a mother he had. He rather shrank from seeing them both. He had a sort of pride in the noble family whose legal affairs he had conducted so long, and it would have annoyed him very much to have found himself obliged to manage a woman who would seem to him a vulgar, money-loving person, with no respect for her dead husband's country and the dignity of his name. It was a very old name and a very splendid one, and Mr. Havisham had a great respect for it himself, though he was only a cold, keen, business-like old lawyer.

When Mary handed him into the small parlour he looked around it critically. It was plainly furnished, but it had a home-like look; there were no cheap, common ornaments, and no cheap, gaudy pictures; the few adornments on the walls were in good taste, and about the room were many pretty things which a woman's hand might have made.

'Not at all bad so far,' he had said to himself; 'but perhaps the Captain's taste predominated.' But when Mrs. Errol came into the room, he began to think she herself might have had something to do with it. If he had not been quite a self-contained and stiff old gentleman, he would probably have started when he saw her. She looked in the simple black dress, fitting closely to her slender figure, more like a young girl than the mother of a boy of seven. She had a pretty, sorrowful young face, and a very tender, innocent look in her large brown eyes – the sorrowful look that had never quite left her face since her husband had died. Cedric was used to seeing it there; the only times he had ever seen it fade out had been when he was playing with her or talking to her, and had said some old-fashioned thing, or used some long word he had picked up out of the newspapers or in his conversations with Mr. Hobbs. He was fond of using long words, and he was always pleased when they made her laugh, though he could not understand why they were laughable; they were quite serious matters with him. The lawyer's experience taught him to read people's characters very shrewdly, and as soon as he saw Cedric's mother he knew that the old Earl had made a great mistake in thinking her a vulgar, mercenary woman. Mr. Havisham had never been married, he had never even been in love, but he divined that this pretty young creature with the sweet voice and sad eyes had married Captain Errol only because she loved him with all her affectionate heart, and that she had never once thought it an advantage that he was an earl's son. And he saw he should have no trouble with her, and he began to feel that perhaps little Lord Fauntleroy might not be such a trial to his noble family after all. The Captain had been a handsome fellow, and the young mother was very pretty, and perhaps the boy might be well enough to look at.

When he first told Mrs. Errol what he had come for, she turned very pale.

'Oh,' she said, 'will he have to be taken away from me? We love each other so much! He is such a happiness to me! He is all I have. I have tried to be a good mother to him.' And her sweet young voice trembled, and the tears rushed into her eyes. You do not know what he has been to me!' she said.

The lawyer cleared his throat.

'I am obliged to tell you', he said, 'that the Earl of Dorincourt is not – is not very friendly towards you. He is an old man, and his prejudices are very strong. He has always especially disliked America and Americans, and was very much enraged by his son's marriage. I am sorry to be the bearer of so unpleasant a communication, but he is very fixed in his determination not to see you. His plan is that Lord Fauntleroy shall be educated under his own supervision; that he shall live with him. The Earl is attached to Dorincourt Castle, and spends a great deal of time there. He is a victim to inflammatory gout, and is not fond of London. Lord Fauntleroy will, therefore, be likely to live chiefly at Dorincourt. The Earl offers to you as a home Court Lodge, which is situated pleasantly, and is not very far from the Castle. He also offers you a suitable income. Lord Fauntleroy will be permitted to visit you; the only stipulation is, that you shall not visit him or enter the park gates. You see you will not be really separated from your son, and I assure you, madam, the terms are not so harsh as – as they might have been. The advantage of such surroundings and education as Lord Fauntleroy will have, I am sure you must see, will be very great.'

He felt a little uneasy less she should begin to cry or make a scene, as he knew some women would have done. It embarrassed and annoyed him to see women cry.

But she did not. She went to the window and stood with her face turned away for a few moments, and he saw she was trying to steady herself.

'Captain Errol was very fond of Dorincourt,' she said at last. 'He loved England, and everything English. It was always a grief to him that he was parted from his home. He was proud of his home, and of his name. He would wish – I know he would wish – that his son should know the beautiful old places, and be brought up in such a way as would be suitable to his future position.'

Then she came back to the table and stood looking up at Mr. Havisham very gently.

'My husband would wish it,' she said. 'It will be best for my little boy. I know – I am sure the Earl would not be so unkind as to try to teach him not to love me; and I know – even if he tried – that my little boy is too much like his father to be harmed. He has a warm, faithful nature, and a true heart. He would love me even if he did not see me; and so long as we may see each other I ought not to suffer very much.'

'She thinks very little of herself,' the lawyer thought. 'She does not make any terms for herself.'

'Madam,' he said aloud, 'I respect your consideration for your son. He will thank you for it when he is a man. I assure you Lord Fauntleroy will be most carefully guarded, and every effort will be used to ensure his happiness. The Earl of Dorincourt will be as anxious for his comfort and well-being as you yourself could be.'

'I hope', said the tender little mother, in a rather broken voice, 'that his grandfather will love Ceddie. The little boy has a very affectionate nature; and he has always been loved.'

Mr. Havisham cleared his throat again. He could not quite imagine the gouty, fiery-tempered old Earl loving anyone very much; but he knew it would be to his interest to be kind, in his irritable way, to the child who was to be his heir. He knew too that if Ceddie were at all a credit to his name, his grandfather would be proud of him.

'Lord Fauntleroy will be comfortable, I am sure,' he replied. 'It was with a view to his happiness that the Earl desired that you should be near enough to him to see him frequently.'

He did not think it would be discreet to repeat the exact words the Earl had used, which were in fact neither polite nor amiable.

Mr. Havisham preferred to express his noble patron's offer in smoother and more courteous language.

He had another slight shock when Mrs. Errol asked Mary to find her little boy and bring him to her, and Mary told her where he was.

'Sure I'll foind him aisy enough, ma'am,' she said; 'for it's wid Mr. Hobbs he is this minnit, settin' on his high shtool by the counther an' talkin' pollytics, most loikely, or enj'yin' hisself among the soap an' candles an' pertaties, as sinsible an' shwate as ye plase.'

'Mr. Hobbs has known him all his life,' Mrs. Errol said to the lawyer. 'He is very kind to Ceddie, and there is a great friendship between them.'

Remembering the glimpse he had caught of the store as he passed it, and having a recollection of the barrels of potatoes and apples and the various odds and ends, Mr. Havisham felt his doubts arise again. In England gentlemen's sons did not make friends of grocerymen, and it seemed to him a rather singular proceeding. It would be very awkward if the child had bad manners and a disposition to like low company. One of the bitterest humiliations of the old Earl's life had been that his two elder sons had been fond of low company. Could it be, he thought, that this boy shared their bad qualities instead of his father's good qualities.

He was thinking uneasily about this as he talked to Mrs. Errol until the child came into the room. When the door opened he actually hesitated a moment before looking at Cedric. It would perhaps have seemed very queer to a great many people who knew him, if they could have known the curious sensations that passed through Mr. Havisham when he looked down at the boy, who ran into his mother's arms. He experienced a revulsion of feeling which was quite exciting. He recognized in an instant that here was one of the finest and handsomest little fellows he had ever seen. His beauty was something unusual. He had a strong, lithe, graceful little body and a manly little face; he held his childish head up, and carried himself with quite a brave little air; he was so like his father that it was really startling; he had his father's golden hair and his mother's brown eyes, but there was nothing sorrowful or timid in them. They were innocently fearless eyes; he looked as if he had never feared or doubted anything in his life.

'He is the best-bred-looking and handsomest little fellow I ever saw,' was what Mr. Havisham thought. What he said aloud was simply: 'And so this is little Lord Fauntleroy.'

And after this the more he saw of little Lord Fauntleroy the more of a surprise he found him. He knew very little about children, though he had seen plenty of them in England – fine, handsome, rosy girls and boys, who were strictly taken care of by their tutors and governesses, and who were sometimes shy, and sometimes a trifle boisterous, but never very interesting to a ceremonious, rigid old lawyer. Perhaps his personal interest in little Lord Fauntleroy's fortunes made him notice Ceddie more than he had noticed other children; but, however that was, he certainly found himself noticing him a great deal.

Cedric did not know he was being observed, and he only behaved himself in his ordinary manner. He shook hands with Mr. Havisham in his friendly way when they were introduced to each other, and he answered all his questions with the unhesitating readiness with which he answered Mr. Hobbs. He was neither shy nor bold, and when Mr. Havisham was talking to his mother, the lawyer noticed that he listened to the conversation with as much interest as if he had been quite grown up.

'He seems to be a very mature little fellow,' Mr. Havisham said to the mother.

'I think he is, in some things,' she answered. 'He has always been very quick to learn, and he has lived a great deal with grown-up people. He has a funny little habit of using long words and expressions he has read in books, or has heard others use, but he is very fond of childish play. I think he is rather clever, but he is a very boyish little boy sometimes.'

The next time Mr. Havisham met him he saw that this last was quite true. As his coupé turned the corner he caught sight of a small group of small boys, who were evidently much excited. Two of them were about to run a race, and one of them was his young lordship, and he was shouting and making as much noise as the noisiest of his companions. He stood side by side with another boy, one little red leg advanced a step.

'One to make ready!' yelled the starter. 'Two to be steady. Three – and away!'

Mr. Havisham found himself leaning out of the window of his coupé with a curious feeling of interest. He really never remembered having seen anything quite like the way in which his lordship's lordly little red legs flew up behind his knickerbockers and tore over the ground as he shot out in the race at the signal word. He shut his small hands and set his face against the wind; his bright hair streamed out behind.

'Hooray, Ced Errol!' all the boys shouted, dancing and shrieking with excitement. 'Hooray, Billy Williams! Hooray, Ceddie! Hooray, Billy! Hooray! 'Ray! 'Ray!'

'I really believe he is going to win,' said Mr. Havisham. The way in which the red legs flew and flashed up and down, the shrieks of the boys, the wild efforts of Billy Williams whose brown legs were not to be despised as they followed closely in the rear of the red legs, made him feel some excitement. 'I really – I really can't help hoping he will win!' he said, with an apologetic sort of cough.

At that moment the wildest yell of all went up from the dancing, hopping boys. With one last frantic leap the future Earl of Dorincourt had reached the lamp-post at the end of the block and touched it, just two seconds before Billy Williams flung himself at it panting.

'Three cheers for Ceddie Errol!' yelled the little boys. 'Hooray for Ceddie Errol!'

Mr. Havisham drew his head in at the window of his coupé and leaned back with a dry smile.

'Bravo, Lord Fauntleroy!' he said.

As his carriage stopped before the door of Mrs. Errol's house, the victor and the vanquished were coming towards it, attended by the clamouring crew. Cedric walked by Billy Williams and was speaking to him. His elated little face was very red, his curls clung to his hot, moist forehead, his hands were in his pockets.

'You see,' he was saying, evidently with the intention of making defeat easy for his unsuccessful rival, 'I guess I won because my legs are a little longer than yours. I guess that was it. You see, I'm three days older than you, and that gives me a 'vantage. I'm three days older.'

And this view of the case seemed to cheer Billy Williams so much that he began to smile on the world again, and felt able to swagger a little, almost as if he had won the race instead of losing it. Somehow Ceddie Errol had a way of making people feel comfortable. Even in the first flush of his triumphs, he remembered that the person who was beaten might not feel so gay as he did, and might like to think that he *might* have been the winner under different circumstances.

That morning Mr. Havisham had quite a long conversation with the winner of the race – a conversation which made him smile his dry smile, and rub his chin with his bony hand several times.

Mrs. Errol had been called out of the parlour, and the lawyer and Cedric were left together. At first Mr. Havisham wondered what he should say to his small companion. He had an idea that perhaps it would be best to say several things which might prepare Cedric for meeting his grandfather, and perhaps for the great change that was to come to him. He could see that Cedric had not the least idea of the sort of thing he was to see when he reached England, or of the sort of home that waited for him there. He did not even know yet that his mother was not to live in the same house with him. They had thought it best to let him get over the first shock before telling him.

Mr. Havisham sat in an armchair on one side of the open window; on the other side was another still larger chair, and Cedric sat in that and looked at Mr. Havisham. He sat well back in the depths of his big seat, his curly head against the cushioned back, his legs crossed and his hands thrust deep into his pockets, in a quite Mr. Hobbs–like way. He had been watching Mr. Havisham very steadily when his mamma had been in the room, and after she was gone he still looked at him in respectful thoughtfulness. There was a short silence after Mrs. Errol went out, and Cedric seemed to be studying Mr. Havisham, and Mr.

Havisham was certainly studying Cedric. He could not make up his mind as to what an elderly gentleman should say to a little boy who won races, and wore short knickerbockers and red stockings on legs which were not long enough to hang over a big chair when he sat well back in it.

But Cedric relieved him by suddenly beginning the conversation himself.

'Do you know,' he said, 'I don't know what an earl is?'

'Don't you?' said Mr. Havisham.

'No,' replied Ceddie. 'And I think when a boy is going to be one he ought to know. Don't you?'

'Well – yes,' answered Mr. Havisham.

'Would you mind,' said Ceddie respectfully, 'would you mind 'splaining it to me?' (Sometimes when he used his long words he did not pronounce them quite correctly.) 'What made him an earl?'

'A king or queen in the first place,' said Mr. Havisham. 'Generally he is made an earl because he has done some service to his sovereign, or some great deed.'

'Oh,' said Cedric; 'that's like the President.'

'Is it?' said Mr. Havisham. 'Is that why your presidents are elected?'

'Yes,' answered Ceddie cheerfully. 'When a man is very good and knows a great deal, he is elected president. They have torch-light processions and bands, and everybody makes speeches. I used to think I might perhaps be a president, but I never thought of being an earl. I didn't know about earls,' he said rather hastily, lest Mr. Havisham might feel it impolite in him not to have wished to be one. 'If I'd known about them, I dare say I should have thought I should like to be one.'

'It is rather different from being a president,' said Mr. Havisham.

'Is it?' asked Cedric. 'How? Are there no torch-light processions?'

Mr. Havisham crossed his own legs and put the tips of his fingers carefully together. He thought perhaps the time had come to explain matters rather more clearly.

'An earl is – is a very important person,' he began.

'So is a president!' put in Ceddie. 'The torch-light processions are five miles long, and they shoot up rockets, and the band plays! Mr. Hobbs took me to see them.'

'An earl', Mr. Havisham went on, feeling rather uncertain of his ground, 'is frequently of very ancient lineage——'

'What's that?' asked Ceddie.

'Of very old family – extremely old.'

'Ah,' said Cedric, thrusting his hands deeper into his pockets. 'I suppose that is the way with the apple-woman near the park. I dare say she is of ancient lin-lenage. She is so old it would surprise you how she can stand up. She's a hundred, I should think, and yet she is out there when it rains even. I'm sorry for her, and so are the other boys. Billy Williams once had nearly a dollar, and I asked him to buy five cents' worth of apples from her every day until he had spent it all. That made twenty days, and he grew tired of apples after a week; but then – it was quite fortunate – a gentleman gave me fifty cents and I bought apples from her instead. You feel sorry for anyone that's so poor and has such ancient lin-lenage. She says hers has gone into her bones and the rain makes it worse.'

Mr. Havisham felt rather at a loss as he looked at his companion's innocent, serious little face.

'I am afraid you did not quite understand me,' he explained. 'When I said "ancient lineage" I did not mean old age; I meant that the name of such a family has been known in the world a long time; perhaps for hundreds of years persons bearing that name have been known and spoken of in the history of their country.'

'Like George Washington,' said Ceddie. 'I've heard of him ever since I was born, and he was known about long before that. Mr. Hobbs says he will never be forgotten. That's because of the Declaration of Independence, you know, and the Fourth of July. You see, he was a very brave man.'

'The first Earl of Dorincourt', said Mr. Havisham solemnly, 'was created an earl four hundred years ago.'

'Well, well!' said Ceddie. 'That was a long time ago! Did you tell Dearest that? It would in'trust her very much. We'll tell her when she comes in. She always likes to hear cur'us things. What else does an earl do besides being created?'

'A great many of them have helped to govern England. Some of them have been brave men and have fought in great battles in the old days.'

'I should like to do that myself,' said Cedric. 'My papa was a soldier, and he was a very brave man – as brave as George Washington. Perhaps that was because he would have been an earl if he hadn't died. I am glad earls are brave. That's a great 'vantage – to be a brave man. Once I used to be rather afraid of things – in the dark, you know; but when I thought about the soldiers in the Revolution and George Washington – it cured me.'

'There is another advantage in being an earl sometimes,' said Mr. Havisham slowly, and he fixed his shrewd eyes on the little boy with a rather curious expression. 'Some earls have a great deal of money.'

He was curious because he wondered if his young friend knew what the power of money was.

'That's a good thing to have,' said Ceddie innocently. 'I wish I had a great deal of money.'

'Do you?' said Mr. Havisham. 'And why?'

'Well,' explained Cedric, 'there are so many things a person can do with money. You see, there's the apple-woman. If I were very rich I should buy her a little tent to put her stall in, and a little stove, and then I should give her a dollar every morning it rained, so that she could afford to stay at home. And then – oh! I'd give her a shawl. And, you see, her bones wouldn't feel so badly. Her bones are not like our bones; they hurt her when she moves. It's very painful when your bones hurt you. If I were rich enough to do all those things for her I guess her bones would be all right.'

'Ahem!' said Mr. Havisham. 'And what else would you do if you were rich?'

'Oh, I'd do a great many things. Of course I should buy Dearest all sorts of beautiful things, needle-books and fans and gold thimbles and rings, and an encyclopaedia, and a carriage, so that she needn't have to wait for the street-cars. If she liked pink silk dresses, I should buy her some, but she likes black best. But I'd take her to the big stores, and tell her to look round and choose for herself. And then Dick——'

'Who is Dick?' asked Mr. Havisham.

'Dick is a boot-black,' said his young lordship, quite warming up in his interest in plans so exciting. 'He is one of the nicest boot-blacks you ever knew. He stands at the corner of a street down town. I've known him for years. Once when I was very little I was walking out with Dearest and she bought me a beautiful ball that bounced, and I was carrying it and it bounced into the middle of the street where the carriages and horses were, and I was so disappointed I began to cry – I was very little. I had kilts on, and Dick was blacking a man's shoes, and he said "Hallo!" and he ran in between the horses and caught the ball for me and wiped it off with his coat and gave it to me and said: "It's all right, young 'un." So Dearest admired him very much, and so did I, and ever since then, when we go down town, we talk to him. He says "Hallo!" and I say "Hallo!" and then we talk a little, and he tells me how trade is. It's been bad lately.'

'And what would you like to do for him?' inquired the lawyer, rubbing his chin and smiling a queer smile.

'Well,' said Lord Fauntleroy, settling himself in his chair with a business air, 'I'd buy Jake out.'

'And who is Jake?' Mr. Havisham asked.

'He's Dick's partner, and he is the worst partner a fellow could have! Dick says so. He isn't a credit to the business, and he isn't square. He cheats, and that makes Dick mad. It would make you mad, you know, if you were blacking boots as hard as you could, and being square all the time, and your partner wasn't square at all. People like Dick, but they don't like Jake, and so sometimes they don't come twice. So if I were rich, I'd buy Jake out and get Dick a "boss" sign – he says a "boss" sign goes a long way; and I'd get him some new clothes and new brushes, and start him out fair. He says all he wants is to start out fair.'

There could have been nothing more confiding and innocent than the way in which his small lordship told his little story, quoting his friend Dick's bits of slang in the most candid good faith. He seemed to feel not a shade of a doubt that his elderly companion would be just as interested as he was himself. And in truth Mr. Havisham was beginning to be greatly interested; but perhaps not quite so much in

Dick and the apple-woman as in this kind little lordling, whose curly head was so busy, under its yellow thatch, with good-natured plans for his friends, and who seemed somehow to have forgotten himself altogether.

'Is there anything——' he began. 'What would you get for yourself if you were rich?'

'Lots of things!' answered Lord Fauntleroy briskly; 'but first I'd give Mary some money for Bridget – that's her sister, with twelve children and a husband out of work. She comes here and cries, and Dearest gives her things in a basket, and then she cries again, and says: "Blessin's be on yez, for a beautiful lady." And I think Mr. Hobbs would like a gold watch and chain to remember me by, and a meerschaum pipe. And then I'd like to get up a company.'

'A company!' exclaimed Mr. Havisham.

'Like a Republican rally,' explained Cedric, becoming quite excited. 'I'd have torches and uniforms and things for all the boys, and myself too. And we'd march, you know, and drill. That's what I'd like for myself, if I were rich.'

The door opened and Mrs. Errol came in.

'I am sorry to have been obliged to leave you so long,' she said to Mr. Havisham; 'but a poor woman, who is in great trouble, came to see me.'

'This young gentleman', said Mr. Havisham, 'has been telling me about some of his friends, and what he would do for them if he were rich.'

'Bridget is one of his friends,' said Mrs. Errol; 'and it is Bridget to whom I have been talking in the kitchen. She is in great trouble now because her husband has rheumatic fever.'

Cedric slipped down out of his big chair.

'I think I'll go and see her,' he said, 'and ask her how he is. He's a nice man when he is well. I'm obliged to him because he once made me a sword out of wood. He's a very talented man.'

'He ran out of the room, and Mr. Havisham rose from his chair. He seemed to have something in his mind which he wished to speak of. He hesitated a moment, and then said, looking down at Mrs. Errol:

'Before I left Dorincourt Castle I had an interview with the

Earl, in which he gave me some instructions. He is desirous that his grandson should look forward with some pleasure to his future life in England, and also to his acquaintance with himself. He said that I must let his lordship know that the change in his life would bring him money and the pleasures children enjoy; if he expressed any wishes I was to gratify them, and to tell him that his grandfather had given him what he wished. I am aware that the Earl did not expect anything quite like this; but if it would give Lord Fauntleroy pleasure to assist this poor woman, I should feel that the Earl would be displeased if he were not gratified.'

For the second time he did not repeat the Earl's exact words. His lordship had indeed said:

'Make the lad understand that I can give him anything he wants. Let him know what it is to be the grandson of the Earl of Dorincourt. Buy him everything he takes a fancy to: let him have money in his pockets, and tell him his grandfather put it there.'

His motives were far from being good, and if he had been dealing with a nature less affectionate and warm-hearted than little Lord Fauntleroy's, great harm might have been done. And Cedric's mother was too gentle to suspect any harm. She thought that perhaps this meant that a lonely, unhappy old man, whose children were dead, wished to be kind to her little boy, and win his love and confidence. And it pleased her very much to think that Ceddie would be able to help Bridget. It made her happier to know that the very first result of the strange fortune which had befallen her little boy was that he could do kind things for those who needed kindness. Quite a warm colour bloomed on her pretty young face.

'Oh,' she said, 'that was very kind of the Earl; Cedric will be so glad! He has always been fond of Bridget and Michael. They are quite deserving. I have often wished I had been able to help them more. Michael is a hard-working man when he is well, but he has been ill a long time and needs expensive medicines and warm clothing and nourishing food. He and Bridget will not be wasteful of what is given them.'

Mr. Havisham put his thin hand in his breast pocket and drew forth a large pocket-book. There was a queer look in his keen face. The truth was he was wondering what the Earl of Dorincourt would say when he was told what was the first wish of his grandson that had been granted. He wondered what the cross, worldly, selfish old nobleman would think of it.

'I do not know that you have realized', he said, 'that the Earl of Dorincourt is an exceedingly rich man. He can afford to gratify any caprice. I think it would please him to know that Lord Fauntleroy had been indulged in any fancy. If you will call him back and allow me, I shall give him five pounds for these people.'

'That would be twenty-five dollars!' exclaimed Mrs. Errol. 'It will seem like wealth to them. I can scarcely believe that it is true.'

'It is quite true,' said Mr. Havisham with his dry smile. 'A great change has taken place in your son's life, a great deal of power will lie in his hands.'

'Oh,' cried his mother. 'And he is such a little boy – a very little boy. How can I teach him to use it well? It makes me half afraid. My pretty little Ceddie!'

The lawyer slightly cleared his throat. It touched his worldly, hard old heart to see the tender, timid look in her brown eyes.

'I think, madam,' he said, 'that if I may judge from my interview with Lord Fauntleroy this morning, the next Earl of Dorincourt will think for others as well as for his noble self. He is only a child yet, but I think he may be trusted.'

Then his mother went for Cedric and brought him back into the parlour. Mr. Havisham heard him talking before he entered the room.

'It's infam-natory rheumatism,' he was saying, 'and that's a kind of rheumatism that's dreadful. And he thinks about the rent not being paid, and Bridget says that makes the inf'ammation worse. And Pat could get a place in a store if he had some clothes.'

His little face looked quite anxious when he came in. He was very sorry for Bridget.

'Dearest said you wanted me,' he said to Mr. Havisham. 'I've been talking to Bridget.'

Mr. Havisham looked down at him a moment. He felt a little awkward and undecided. As Cedric's mother had said, he was a very little boy.

'*Mr. Havisham handed him the money*'

'The Earl of Dorincourt———' he began, and then he glanced involuntarily at Mrs. Errol.

Little Lord Fauntleroy's mother suddenly kneeled down by him and put her tender arms around his childish body.

'Ceddie,' she said, 'the Earl is your grandpapa, your own papa's father. He is very, very kind, and he loves you and wishes you to love him, because the sons who were his little boys are dead. He wishes you to be happy and to make other people happy. He is very rich, and he wishes you to have everything you would like to have. He told Mr. Havisham so, and gave him a great deal of money for you. You can give some to Bridget now; enough to pay her rent and buy Michael everything. Isn't that fine, Ceddie? Isn't he good?' And she kissed the child on his round cheek, where the bright colour suddenly flashed up in his excited amazement.

He looked from his mother to Mr. Havisham.

'Can I have it now?' he cried. 'Can I give it to her this minute? She's just going.'

Mr. Havisham handed him the money. It was in fresh clean greenbacks and made a neat roll.

Ceddie flew out of the room.

'Bridget!' they heard him shout, as he tore into the kitchen. 'Bridget, wait a minute! Here's some money. It's for you, and you can pay the rent. My grandpapa gave it to me. It's for you and Michael!'

'Oh, Master Ceddie!' cried Bridget, in an awe-stricken voice. 'It's twenty-foive dollars is here. Where be's the misthress?'

'I think I shall have to go and explain it to her,' Mrs. Errol said.

So she too went out of the room, and Mr. Havisham was left alone for a while. He went to the window and stood looking out into the street reflectively. He was thinking of the old Earl of Dorincourt, sitting in his great, splendid gloomy library at the castle, gouty and lonely, surrounded by grandeur and luxury, but not really loved by anyone, because in all his long life he had never really loved anyone but himself; he had been selfish and self-indulgent, and arrogant and passionate; he had cared so much for the Earl of Dorincourt and his pleasures that there had been no time for him to think of other people; all his wealth and power, all the benefits from his noble name and high rank, had seemed to him to be things only to be used to amuse and give pleasure to the Earl of Dorincourt; and now that he was an old man, all this excitement and self-indulgence had only brought him ill-health and irritability and a dislike of the world, which certainly disliked him. In spite of all his splendour, there was never a more unpopular old nobleman than the Earl of Dorincourt, and there could scarcely have been a more lonely one. He could fill his castle with guests if he chose. He could give great dinners and splendid hunting parties; but he knew that in secret the people who would accept his invitations were afraid of his frowning old face and sarcastic, biting speeches. He had a cruel tongue and a bitter nature, and he took pleasure in sneering at people and making them feel uncomfortable, when he had the power to do so, because they were sensitive or proud or timid.

Mr. Havisham knew his hard, fierce ways by heart, and he was thinking of him as he looked out of the window into the quiet, narrow street. And there rose in his mind, in sharp contrast, the picture of the cheery, handsome little fellow sitting in the big chair and telling his story of his friends, Dick and the apple-woman, in his generous, innocent, honest way. And he thought of the immense income, the beautiful, majestic estates, the wealth, and power for good or evil, which in the course of time would lie in the small, chubby hands little Lord Fauntleroy thrust so deep into his pockets.

'It will make a great difference,' he said to himself. 'It will make a great difference.'

Cedric and his mother came back soon after. Cedric was in high spirits. He sat down in his own chair, between his mother and the lawyer, and fell into one of his quaint attitudes, with his hands on his knees. He was glowing with enjoyment of Bridget's relief and rapture.

'She cried!' he said. 'She said she was crying for joy. I never saw anyone cry for joy before. My grandpapa must be a very good man. I didn't know he was so good a man. It's more – more agreeabler to be an earl than I thought it was. I'm almost glad – I'm almost *quite* glad I'm going to be one.'

3 Leaving Home

Cedric's good opinion of the advantages of being an earl increased greatly during the next week. It seemed almost impossible for him to realize that there was scarcely anything he might wish to do which he could not do easily; in fact I think it may be said that he did not fully realize it at all. But at least he understood, after a few conversations with Mr. Havisham, that he could gratify all his nearest wishes, and he proceeded to gratify them with a simplicity and delight which caused Mr. Havisham much diversion. In the week before they sailed for England he did many curious things. The lawyer long after remembered the morning they went down together to pay a visit to Dick, and the afternoon they so amazed the apple-woman of ancient lineage by stopping before her stall and telling her she was to have a tent and a stove and a shawl and a sum of money, which seemed to her quite wonderful.

'For I have to go to England and be a lord,' explained Cedric sweet-temperedly. 'And I shouldn't like to have your bones on my mind every time it rained. My own bones never hurt, so I think I don't know how painful a person's bones can be, but I've sympathized with you a great deal, and I hope you'll be better.'

'She a very good apple-woman,' he said to Mr. Havisham as they walked away, leaving the proprietress of the stall almost gasping for breath, and not at all believing in her great fortune. 'Once, when I fell down and cut my knee, she gave me an apple for nothing. I've always remembered her for it. You know you always remember people who are kind to you.'

It had never occurred to his honest, simple, little mind that there were people who could forget kindnesses.

The interview with Dick was quite exciting. Dick had just been having a great deal of trouble with Jake, and was in low spirits when they saw him. His amazement when Cedric calmly announced that they had come to give him what seemed a very great thing to him, and would set all his troubles right, almost struck him dumb. Lord Fauntleroy's manner of announcing the object of his visit was very simple and unceremonious. Mr. Havisham was much impressed by its directness as he stood by and listened. The statement that his old friend had become a lord, and was in danger of being an earl if he lived long enough, caused Dick to so open his eyes and mouth, and start, that his cap fell off. When he picked it up he uttered a rather singular exclamation. Mr. Havisham thought it singular, but Cedric had heard it before.

'I soy!' he said, 'what 're yer givin' us?' This plainly embarrassed his lordship a little, but he bore himself bravely.

'Everybody thinks it not true at first,' he said. 'Mr. Hobbs thought I'd had a sunstroke. I didn't think I was going to like it myself, but I like it better now I'm used to it. The one who is the earl now – he's my grandpapa; and he wants me to do anything I like. He's very kind, if he *is* an earl; and he sent me a lot of money by Mr. Havisham, and I've brought some to you to buy Jake out.'

And the end of the matter was that Dick actually bought Jake out, and found himself the possessor of the business, and some new brushes and a most astonishing sign and outfit. He could not believe in his good luck any more easily than the apple-woman of ancient lineage could believe in hers; he walked about like a boot-black in a dream; he stared at his young benefactor and felt as if he might wake up at any moment. He scarcely seemed to realize anything until Cedric put out his hand to shake hands with him before going away.

'Well, goodbye,' he said; and though he tried to speak steadily, there was a little tremble in his voice and he winked his big brown eyes. 'And I hope trade'll be good. I'm sorry I'm going away to leave you, but perhaps I shall come back again when I'm an earl. And I wish you'd write to me, because we were always good friends. And if you write to me, here's where you must send your letter.' And he gave him a slip of paper. 'And my name isn't Cedric Errol any more; it's Lord

Fauntleroy and – and goodbye, Dick.'

Dick winked his eyes also, and yet they looked rather moist about the lashes. He was not an educated boot-black, and he would have felt it difficult to tell what he felt just then, if he had tried; perhaps that was why he didn't try, and only winked his eyes and swallowed a lump in his throat.

'I wish ye wasn't goin' away,' he said in a husky voice. Then he winked his eyes again. Then he looked at Mr. Havisham and touched his cap. 'Thanky, sir, fur bringin' him down here an' fur wot ye've done. He's – he's a queer little feller,' he added. 'I've allers thort a heap of him. He's such a game little feller, an' – an' such a queer little 'un.'

And when they turned away he stood and looked after them in a dazed kind of way, and there was still a mist in his eyes and a lump in his throat, as he watched the gallant little figure marching gaily along by the side of its tall, rigid escort.

Until the day of his departure his lordship spent as much time as possible with Mr. Hobbs in the store. Gloom had settled upon Mr. Hobbs; he was much depressed in spirits. When his young friend brought to him in triumph the parting gift of a gold watch and chain, Mr. Hobbs found it difficult to acknowledge it properly. He laid the case on his stout knee, and blew his nose violently several times.

'There's something written on it,' said Cedric, 'inside the case. I told the man myself what to say. "From his oldest friend, Lord Fauntleroy, to Mr. Hobbs. When this you see, remember me." I don't want you to forget me.'

Mr. Hobbs blew his nose very loudly again.

'I shan't forget you,' he said, speaking a trifle huskily, as Dick had spoken; 'nor don't you go and forget me when you get among the British arrystocracy.'

'I shouldn't forget you whoever I was among,' answered his lordship. 'I've spent my happiest hours with you; at least, some of my happiest hours. I hope you'll come to see me some time. I'm sure my grandpapa would be very much pleased. Perhaps he'll write and ask you when I tell him about you? You – you wouldn't mind his being an earl, would you? I mean you wouldn't stay away just because he was one, if he invited you to come?'

'I'd come to see you,' replied Mr. Hobbs graciously.

So it seemed to be agreed that if he received a pressing invitation from the Earl to come and spend a few months at Dorincourt Castle, he was to lay aside his republican prejudices and pack his valise at once.

At last the preparations were complete; the day came when the trunks were taken to the steamer, and the hour arrived when the carriage stood at the door. Then a curious feeling of loneliness came upon the little boy. His mamma had been shut up in her room for some time; when she came down the stairs her eyes looked large and wet, and her sweet mouth was trembling. Cedric went to her, and she bent down to him, and he put his arms around her, and they kissed each other. He knew something made them both sorry, though he scarcely knew what it was; but one tender little thought rose to his lips.

'We liked this little house, Dearest, didn't we?' he said. 'We always will like it, won't we?'

'Yes – yes,' she answered in a low, sweet voice. 'Yes, darling.'

And then they went into the carriage and Cedric sat very close to her, and as she looked back out of the window he looked at her, and stroked her hand and held it close.

And then, it seemed almost directly, they were on the steamer in the midst of the wildest bustle and confusion; carriages were driving down and leaving passengers; passengers were getting into a state of excitement about baggage which had not arrived and threatened to be too late; big trunks and cases were being bumped down and dragged about; sailors were uncoiling ropes and hurrying to and fro; officers were giving orders; ladies and gentlemen and children and nurses were coming on board – some were laughing and looked gay, some were silent and sad, here and there two or three were crying and touching their eyes with their handkerchiefs. Cedric found something to interest him on every side; he looked at the piles of rope, at the furled sails, at the tall, tall masts which seemed almost to touch the hot blue sky; he began to make plans for conversing with the sailors and gaining some information on the subject of pirates.

It was just at the very last, when he was standing leaning on the railing of the upper deck and watching the final preparations, enjoying the excitement and the shouts of the sailors and wharfmen, that his attention was called to a slight bustle in one of the groups not far from him. Someone was hurriedly forcing his way through this group and coming towards him. It was a boy, with something red in his hand. It was Dick. He came up to Cedric quite breathless.

'I've run all the way,' he said. 'I've come down to see ye off. Trade's been prime! I bought this for ye out o' what I made yesterday. Ye kin wear it when ye get among the swells. I lost the paper when I was tryin' to get through them fellers downstairs. They didn't want to let me up. It's a handkercher.'

He poured it all forth as if in one sentence. A bell rang and he made a leap away before Cedric had time to speak.

'Goodbye!' he panted. 'Wear it when ye get among the swells.' And he darted off and was gone.

A few seconds later they saw him struggle through the crowd on the lower deck, and rush on shore just before the gang-plank was drawn in. He stood on the wharf and waved his cap.

Cedric held the handkerchief in his hand. It was of bright red silk, ornamented with purple horseshoes and horses' heads.

There was a great straining and creaking and confusion. The people on the wharf began to shout to their friends, and the people on the steamer shouted back:

'Goodbye! Goodbye! Goodbye, old fellow!' Everyone seemed to be saying: 'Don't forget us. Write when you get to Liverpool. Goodbye! Goodbye!'

Little Lord Fauntleroy leaned forward and waved the red handkerchief.

'Goodbye, Dick!' he shouted lustily. 'Thank you! Goodbye, Dick!'

And the big steamer moved away, and the people cheered again, and Cedric's mother drew the veil over her eyes, and on the shore there was left great confusion; but Dick saw nothing save the bright, childish face and the bright hair that the sun shone on and the breeze lifted, and he heard nothing but the hearty childish voice calling 'Goodbye, Dick!' as little Lord Fauntleroy steamed slowly away from the home of his birth to the unknown land of his ancestors.

4 In England

It was during the voyage that Cedric's mother told him that his home was not to be hers; and when he first understood it his grief was so great that Mr. Havisham saw that the Earl had been wise in making the arrangements that his mother should be quite near him, and see him often; for it was very plain he could not have borne the separation otherwise. But his mother managed the little fellow so sweetly and lovingly, and made him feel that she would be so near him, that after a while he ceased to be oppressed by the feat of any real parting.

'My house is not far from the Castle, Ceddie,' she repeated each time the subject was referred to – 'a very little way from yours, and you can always run in and see me every day, and you will have so many things to tell me, and we shall be so happy together! It is a beautiful place. Your papa has often told me about it. He loved it very much; and you will love it too.'

'I should love it better if you were there,' his small lordship said with a heavy little sigh.

He could not but feel puzzled by so strange a state of affairs, which could put his 'Dearest' in one house and himself in another.

The fact was that Mrs. Errol had thought it better not to tell him why this plan had been made.

'I should prefer he should not be told,' she said to Mr. Havisham. 'He would not really understand; he would only be shocked and hurt; and I feel sure that his feeling for the Earl will be a more natural and affectionate one if he does not know that his grandfather dislikes me so bitterly. He has never seen hatred or hardness, and it would be a great blow to him to find out that anyone could hate me. He is so loving himself, and I am so dear to him! It is better for him that he should not be told until he is much older, and it is far better for the Earl. It would make a barrier between them, even though Ceddie is such a child.'

So Cedric only knew that there was some mysterious reason for the arrangement, some reason which he was not old enough to understand, but which would be explained when he was older. He was puzzled; but after all it was not the reason he cared about so much; and after many talks with his mother, in which she comforted him and placed before him the bright side of the picture, the dark side of it gradually began to fade out, though now and then Mr. Havisham saw him sitting in some queer little old-fashioned attitude, watching the sea, with a very grave face, and more than once he heard an unchildish sigh rise to his lips.

'I don't like it,' he said once as he was having one of his almost venerable talks with the lawyer. 'You don't know how much I don't like it; but there are a great many troubles in this world, and you have to bear them. Mary says so, and I've heard Mr. Hobbs say it too. And Dearest wants me to like to live with my grandpapa, because, you see, all his children are dead, and that's very mournful. It makes you sorry for a man when all his children have died – and one was killed suddenly.'

One of the things which always delighted the people who made the acquaintance of his young lordship was the sage little air he wore at times when he gave himself up to conversation; combined with his occasionally elderly remarks and the extreme innocence and serious-ness of his round childish face, it was irresistible. He was such a handsome, blooming, curly headed little fellow, that, when he sat down and nursed his knee with his chubby hands, and conversed with much gravity, he was a source of great entertainment to his hearers. Gradually Mr. Havisham had begun to derive a great deal of private pleasure and amusement from his society.

'And so you are going to try to like the Earl?' he said.

'Yes,' answered his lordship. 'He's my relation, and of course you have to like your relations: and besides, he's been very kind to me. When a person does so many things for you and wants you to have everything you wish for, of course you'd like him if he wasn't your relation; but when he's your relation and does that, why you're very ' fond of him.'

'Do you think', suggested Mr. Havisham, 'that he will be fond of you?'

'Well,' said Cedric, 'I think he will, because, you see, I'm his relation too, and I'm his boy's little boy besides, and, well, don't you see – of course he must be fond of me now, or he wouldn't want me to have everything that I like, and he wouldn't have sent you for me.'

'Oh,' remarked the lawyer, 'that's it, is it?'

'Yes,' said Cedric, 'that's it. Don't you think that's it too? Of course a man would be fond of his grandson.'

The people who had been seasick had no sooner recovered from their seasickness, and come on deck to recline in their steamer chairs and enjoy themselves, than everyone seemed to know the romantic story of little Lord Fauntleroy, and everyone took an interest in the little fellow, who ran about the ship or walked with his mother or the tall, thin old lawyer, or talked to the sailors. Everyone liked him; he made friends everywhere. He was ever ready to make friends. When the gentlemen walked up and down the deck, and let him walk with them, he stepped out with a manly, sturdy little tramp, and answered all their jokes with much gay enjoyment; when the ladies talked to him there was always laughter in the group of which he was the centre; when he played with the children there was always magnificent fun on hand. Among the sailors he had the heartiest friends; he heard miraculous stories about pirates and shipwrecks and desert islands; he learned to splice ropes and rig toy ships, and gained an amount of information concerning 'tops'les' and 'mains'les,' quite surprising. His conversations had indeed quite a nautical flavour at times, and on one occasion he raised a shout of laughter in a group of ladies and gentlemen who were sitting on deck, wrapped in shawls and overcoats, by saying sweetly, and with a very engaging expression:

'Shiver my timbers, but it's a cold day!'

It surprised him when they laughed. He had picked up this seafaring remark from an 'elderly naval man' of the name of Jerry, who told him stories in which it occurred frequently. To judge from his stories of his own adventures, Jerry had made some two or three thousand voyages, and had been invariably shipwrecked on each occasion on an island densely populated with bloodthirsty cannibals. Judging also by these same exciting adventures, he had been partially roasted and eaten frequently and had been scalped some fifteen or twenty times.

'That is why he is so bald,' explained Lord Fauntleroy to his mamma. 'After you have been scalped several times the hair never grows again. Jerry's never grew after the last time, when the King of the Parromachaweekins did it with the knife made out of the skull of the Chief of the Wopslemumpkies. He says it was one of the most serious times he ever had. He was so frightened that his hair stood right straight up when the king flourished his knife, and it never would lie down, and the king wears it that way now, and it looks something like a hairbrush. I never heard anything like the asperiences Jerry has had! I should so like to tell Mr. Hobbs about them!'

Sometimes, when the weather was very disagreeable and people were kept below decks in the saloon, a party of his grown-up friends would persuade him to tell them some of these 'asperiences' of Jerry's, and, as he sat relating them with great delight and fervour, there was certainly no more popular voyager on any ocean steamer crossing the Atlantic than little Lord Fauntleroy. He was always innocently and good-naturedly ready to do his small best to add to the general entertainment, and there was a charm in the very unconsciousness of his own childish importance.

'Jerry's stories int'rust them very much,' he said to his mamma. 'For my part – you must excuse me, Dearest – but sometimes I should have thought they couldn't be all quite true, if they hadn't happened to Jerry himself; but as they all happened to Jerry – well, it's very strange, you know, and perhaps sometimes he may forget and be a little mistaken, as he's been scalped so often. Being scalped a great many times might make a person forgetful.'

It was eleven days after he had said goodbye to his friend Dick before he reached Liverpool; and it was on the night of the twelfth day that the carriage, in which he and his mother and Mr. Havisham had driven from the station, stopped before the gates of Court Lodge. They could not see much of the house in the darkness. Cedric only saw that there was a carriage drive under great arching trees, and after the carriage had rolled down this carriage drive a short distance, he saw an open door and a stream of bright light coming through it.

Mary had come with them to attend her mistress, and she had reached the house before them. When Cedric jumped out of the carriage he saw one or two servants standing in the wide bright hall, and Mary stood in the doorway.

Lord Fauntleroy sprang at her with a gay little shout.

'Did you get here, Mary?' he said. 'Here's Mary, Dearest,' and he kissed the maid on her rough red cheek.

'I am glad you are here, Mary,' Mrs. Errol said to her in a low voice. 'It is such a comfort to me to see you. It takes the strangeness away.' And she held out her little hand, which Mary squeezed encouragingly. She knew how this first 'strangeness' must feel to this little mother who had left her own land and was about to give up her child.

The English servants looked with curiosity at both the boy and his mother. They had heard all sorts of rumours about them both; they knew how angry the old Earl had been, and why Mrs. Errol was to live at the Lodge and her little boy at the Castle; they knew all about the great fortune he was to inherit and about the savage old grandfather and his gout and his tempers.

'He'll have no easy time of it, poor little chap,' they had said among themselves.

But they did not know what sort of a little lord had come among them; they did not quite understand the character of the next Earl of Dorincourt.

He pulled off his overcoat quite as if he were used to doing things for himself, and began to look about him. He looked about the broad hall, at the pictures and stags' antlers and curious things that ornamented it. They seemed curious to him because he had never seen such things before in a private house.

'Dearest,' he said, 'this is a very pretty house, isn't it? I am glad you are going to live here. It's quite a large house.'

It was quite a large house compared to the one in the shabby New York street, and it was very pretty and cheerful. Mary led them upstairs to a bright chintz-hung bedroom where a fire was burning, and a large snow-white Persian cat was sleeping luxuriously on the white fur hearthrug.

'It was the housekaper up at the Castle, ma'am, sint her to yez,' explained Mary. 'It's herself is a kind-hearted lady an' has had iverything done to prepar' fur yez. I seem her meself a few minnits, an' she was fond av the Capt'in, ma'am, an' graivs fur him; and she said to say the big cat slapin' on the rug moight make the room same homeloike to yez. She knowed Capt'in Errol whin he was a bye – an' a foine handsum' bye she ses he was, an' a foine young man wid a plisint word fur everyone, great an' shmall. An' ses I to her, ses I, "He's lift a bye that's loike him, ma'am, fur a foiner little felly niver sthipped in shoe-leather".'

When they were ready they went downstairs into another big bright room; its ceiling was low, and the furniture was heavy and beautifully carved, the chairs were deep and had high massive backs, and there were queer shelves and cabinets with strange, pretty ornaments on them. There was a great tiger-skin before the fire, and an armchair on each side of it. The stately white cat had responded to Lord Fauntleroy's stroking and followed him downstairs, and when he threw himself down upon the rug she curled herself up grandly beside him as if she intended to make friends. Cedric was so pleased that he put his head down by hers, and lay stroking her, not noticing what his mother and Mr. Havisham were saying.

They were indeed speaking in a rather low tone. Mrs. Errol looked a little pale and agitated.

'He need not go tonight?' she said. 'He will stay with me tonight?'

'Yes,' answered Mr. Havisham in the same low tone; 'it will not be necessary for him to go tonight. I myself will go to the Castle as soon as we have dined, and inform the Earl of our arrival.'

Mrs. Errol glanced down at Cedric. He was lying in a graceful, careless attitude upon the black-and-yellow skin; the fire shone on his handsome, flushed little face, and on the tumbled, curly hair spread out on the rug; the big cat was purring in drowsy content; she liked the caressing touch of the kind little hand on her fur.

Mrs. Errol smiled faintly.

'His lordship does not know all that he is taking from me,' she said rather sadly. Then she looked at the lawyer. 'Will you tell him, if you please,' she said, 'that I should rather not have the money?'

'The money!' Mr. Havisham exclaimed. 'You cannot mean the income he proposed to settle upon you?'

'Yes,' she answered quite simply; 'I think I should rather not have it. I am obliged to accept the house, and I thank him for it, because it makes it possible for me to be near my child; but I have a little money of my own – enough to live simply upon – and I should rather not take the other, as he dislikes me so much I should feel a little as if I were selling Cedric to him. I am giving him up only because I love him enough to forget myself for his good, and because his father would wish it to be so.'

Mr. Havisham rubbed his chin.

'This is very strange,' he said. 'He will be very angry. He won't understand it.'

'I think he will understand it after he thinks it over,' she said. 'I do not really need the money, and why should I accept luxuries from the man who hates me so much that he takes my little boy from me – his son's child?'

Mr. Havisham looked reflective for a few moments.

'I will deliver your message,' he said afterwards.

And then the dinner was brought in and they sat down together, the big cat taking a seat on a chair near Cedric's and purring majestically throughout the meal.

When, later in the evening, Mr. Havisham presented himself at the Castle, he was taken at once to the Earl. He found him sitting by the fire in a luxurious easy chair, his foot on a gout-stool. He looked at the lawyer sharply from under his shaggy eyebrows, but Mr. Havisham could see that, in spite of his pretence at calmness, he was nervous and secretly excited.

'Well,' he said; 'well, Havisham, come back, have you? What's the news?'

'Lord Fauntleroy and his mother are at Court Lodge,' replied Mr. Havisham. 'They bore the voyage very well and are in excellent health.'

The Earl made a half-impatient sound and moved his hand restlessly.

'Glad to hear it,' he said brusquely. 'So far, so good. Make yourself comfortable. Have a glass of wine and settle down. What else?'

'His lordship remains with his mother tonight. Tomorrow I will bring him to the Castle.'

The Earl's elbow was resting on the arm of his chair; he put his hand up and shielded his eyes with it.

'Well?' he said; 'go on. You know I told you not to write to me about the matter, and I know nothing whatever about it. What kind of a lad is he? I don't care about the mother; what sort of lad is he?'

Mr. Havisham drank a little of the glass of port he had poured out for himself, and sat holding it in his hand.

'It is rather difficult to judge of the character of a child of seven,' he said cautiously.

The Earl's prejudices were very intense. He looked up quickly and uttered a rough word.

'A fool, is he?' he exclaimed. 'Or a clumsy cub? His American blood tells, does it?'

'I do not think it has injured him, my lord,' replied the lawyer in his dry, deliberate fashion. 'I don't know much about children, but I thought him rather a fine lad.'

His manner of speech was always deliberate and unenthusiastic, but he made it a trifle more so than usual. He had a shrewd fancy that it would be better that the Earl should judge for himself, and be quite unprepared for his first interview with his grandson.

'Healthy and well grown?' asked my lord.

'Apparently very healthy, and quite well grown,' replied the lawyer.

'Straight-limbed and well enough to look at?' demanded the Earl.

A very slight smile touched Mr. Havisham's thin lips. There rose up before his mind's eye the picture he had left at Court Lodge – the beautiful, graceful child's body lying upon the tiger-skin in careless comfort – the bright, tumbled hair spread on the rug – the bright, rosy boy's face.

'Rather a handsome boy, I think, my lord, as boys go,' he said, 'though I am scarcely a judge perhaps. But you will find him somewhat different to most English children, I dare say.'

'I haven't a doubt of that,' snarled the Earl, a twinge of gout seizing him 'A lot of impudent little beggars, those American children; I've heard that often enough.'

'It is not exactly impudence in his case,' said Mr. Havisham. 'I can scarcely describe what the difference is. He has lived more with older people than with children, and the difference seems to be a mixture of maturity and childishness.'

'American impudence!' protested the Earl. 'I've heard of it before. They call it precocity and freedom. Beastly, impudent, bad manners; that's what it is!'

Mr. Havisham drank some more port. He seldom argued with his lordly patron – never when his lordly patron's noble leg was inflamed by gout. At such times it was always better to leave him alone. So there was a silence of a few moments, it was Mr. Havisham who broke it.

'I have a message to deliver from Mrs. Errol,' he remarked.

'I don't want any of her messages!' growled his lordship; 'the less I hear of her the better.'

'This is a rather important one,' explained the lawyer. 'She prefers not to accept the income you proposed to settle on her.'

The Earl started visibly.

'What's that?' he cried out. 'What's that?'

Mr. Havisham repeated his words.

'She says it is not necessary, and that as the relations between you are not friendly——'

'Not friendly!' ejaculated my lord savagely; 'I should say they were not friendly! I hate to think of her! A mercenary, sharp-voiced American! I don't wish to see her!'

'My lord,' said Mr. Havisham, 'you can scarcely call her mercenary. She has asked for nothing. She does not accept the money you offer her.'

'All done for effect!' snapped his noble lordship. 'She wants to wheedle me into seeing her. She thinks I shall admire her spirit. I don't admire it! It's only American independence! I won't have her living like a beggar at my park gates. As she's the boy's mother she has a position to keep up, and she shall keep it up. She shall have the money, whether she likes it or not!'

'She won't spend it,' said Mr. Havisham.

'I don't care whether she spends it or not!' blustered my lord. 'She shall have it sent to her. She shan't tell people that she has to live like a pauper because I have done nothing for her! She wants to give the boy a bad opinion of me! I suppose she has poisoned his mind against me already!'

'No,' said Mr. Havisham. 'I have another message, which will prove to you that she has not done that.'

'I don't want to hear it!' panted the Earl, out of breath with anger and excitement and gout.

But Mr. Havisham delivered it.

'She asks you not to let Lord Fauntleroy hear anything which would lead him to understand that you separate him from her because of your prejudice against her. He is very fond of her, and she is convinced that it would cause a barrier to exist between you. She says he would not comprehend it and it might make him fear you in some measure, or at least cause him to feel less affection for you. She has told him that he is too young to understand the reason, but shall hear it when he is older. She wishes that there should be no shadow on your first meeting.'

The Earl sank back into his chair. His deepest fierce old eyes gleamed under his beetling brows.

'Come, now!' he said, still breathlessly. 'Come now! You don't mean the mother hasn't told him?'

'Not one word, my lord,' replied the lawyer coolly. 'That I can assure you. The child is prepared to believe you the most amiable and affectionate of grandparents. Nothing – absolutely nothing – has been said to him to give him the slightest doubt of your perfection. And as I carried out your commands in every detail, while in New York, he certainly regards you as a wonder of generosity.'

'He does, eh?' said the Earl.

'I give you my word of honour', said Mr. Havisham, 'that Lord Fauntleroy's impressions of you will depend entirely upon yourself. And if you will pardon the liberty I take in making the suggestion, I think you will succeed better with him if you take the precaution not to speak slightingly of his mother.'

'Pooh, pooh!' said the Earl. 'The youngster's only seven years old!'

'He has spent those seven years at his mother's side,' returned Mr. Havisham; 'and she has all his affection.'

5 At the Castle

It was late in the afternoon when the carriage containing little Lord
Fauntleroy and Mr. Havisham drove up the long avenue which led to
the Castle. The Earl had given orders that his grandson should arrive
in time to dine with him, and for some reason best known to himself he
had also ordered that the child should be sent alone into the room in
which he intended to receive him. As the carriage rolled up the avenue,
Lord Fauntleroy sat leaning comfortably against the luxurious
cushions, and regarded the prospect with great interest. He was, in
fact, interested in everything he saw. He had been interested in the
carriage, with its large, splendid horses and their glittering harness; he
had been interested in the tall coachman and footman, with their
resplendent livery; and he had been especially interested in the coronet
on the panels, and had struck up an acquaintance with the footman for
the purpose of inquiring what it meant.

When the carriage reached the great gates of the park, he looked
out of the window to get a good view of the huge stone lions
ornamenting the entrance. The gates were opened by a motherly,
rosy-looking woman, who came out of a pretty ivy-covered lodge. Two
children ran out of the house and stood looking with round wide-open
eyes at the little boy in the carriage, who looked at them also. Their
mother stood curtsying and smiling, and the children, on receiving a
sign from her, made bobbing little curtsies too.

'Does she know me?' asked Lord Fauntleroy. 'I think she must
think she knows me.' And he took off his his black velvet cap to her and
smiled.

'How do you do?' he said brightly. 'Good afternoon!'

The woman seemed pleased, he thought. The smile broadened on her rosy face and a kind look came into her blue eyes.

'God bless your lordship!' she said. 'God bless your pretty face! Good luck and happiness to your lordship! Welcome to you!'

Lord Fauntleroy waved his cap and nodded to her again as the carriage rolled by her.

'I like that woman,' he said. 'She looks as if she liked boys. I should like to come here and play with her children. I wonder if she has enough to make up a company?'

Mr. Havisham did not tell him that he would scarcely be allowed to make playmates of the gate-keeper's children. The lawyer thought there was time enough for giving him that information.

The carriage rolled on and on between the great beautiful trees which grew on each side of the avenue and stretched their broad swaying branches in an arch across it. Cedric had never seen such trees, they were so grand and stately, and their branches grew so low down on their huge trunks. He did not then know that Dorincourt Castle was one of the most beautiful in all England; that its park was one of the broadest and finest, and its trees and avenue almost without rivals. But he did know that it was all very beautiful. He liked the big, broad-branched trees, with the late afternoon sunlight striking golden lances through them. He liked the perfect stillness which rested on everything. He felt a great, strange pleasure in the beauty of which he caught glimpses under and between the sweeping boughs – the great, beautiful spaces of the park, with still other trees, standing sometimes stately and alone, and sometimes in groups. Now and then they passed places where tall ferns grew in masses, and again and again the ground was azure with the bluebells swaying in the soft breeze. Several times he started up with a laugh of delight as a rabbit leaped up from under the greenery and scudded away with a twinkle of short white tail behind it. Once a covey of partridges rose with a sudden whir and flew away, and then he shouted and clapped his hands.

'It's a beautiful place, isn't it?' he said to Mr. Havisham. 'I never saw such a beautiful place. It's prettier even than Central Park.'

He was rather puzzled by the length of time they were on their way.

'How far is it', he said at length, 'from the gate to the front door?'

'It is between three and four miles,' answered the lawyer.

That's a long way for a person to live from his gate,' remarked his lordship.

Every few moments he saw something new to wonder at and admire. When he caught sight of the deer, some couched in the grass, some standing with their pretty antlered heads turned with a half-startled air towards the avenue as the carriage wheels disturbed them, he was enchanted.

'Has there been a circus', he cried, 'or do they live here always? Whose are they?'

'They live here,' Mr. Havisham told him. 'They belong to the Earl, your grandfather.'

It was not long after this that they saw the Castle. It rose up before them stately and beautiful and grey, the last rays of the sun casting dazzling lights on its many windows. It had turrets and battlements and towers; a great deal of ivy grew upon its walls; all the broad open space about it was laid out in terraces and lawns and beds of brilliant flowers.

'It's the most beautiful place I ever saw!' said Cedric, his round face flushing with pleasure. 'It reminds anyone of a king's palace. I saw a picture of one once in a fairy-book.'

He saw the great entrance door thrown open and many servants standing in two lines looking at him. He wondered why they were standing there, and admired their liveries very much. He did not know that they were there to do honour to the little boy to whom all this splendour would one day belong – the beautiful Castle like the fairy king's palace, the magnificent park, the grand old trees, the dells full of ferns and bluebells where the hares and rabbits played, the dappled, large-eyed deer couching in the deep grass. It was only a couple of weeks since he had sat with Mr. Hobbs among the potatoes and canned peaches, with his legs dangling from the high stool; it would not have been possible for him to realize that he had very much to do with all this grandeur. At the head of the line of servants there stood an elderly woman in a rich, plain, black silk gown; she had grey hair and wore a cap. As he entered the hall she stood nearer than the rest, and the child thought from the look in her eyes that she was going to speak to him.

Mr. Havisham, who held his hand, paused a moment.

'This is Lord Fauntleroy, Mrs. Mellon,' he said. 'Lord Fauntleroy, this is Mrs. Mellon, who is the housekeeper.'

Cedric gave her his hand, his eyes lighting up.

'Was it you who sent the cat?' he said. 'I'm much obliged to you, ma'am.'

Mrs. Mellon's handsome old face looked as pleased as the face of the lodge-keeper's wife had done.

'I should know his lordship anywhere,' she said to Mr. Havisham. 'He has the Captain's face and way. It's a great day, this, sir.'

Cedric wondered why it was a great day. He looked at Mrs. Mellon curiously. It seemed to him for a moment as if there were tears in her eyes, and yet it was evident she was not unhappy. She smiled down at him.

'The cat left two beautiful kittens here,' she said: 'they shall be sent up to your lordship's nursery.'

Mr. Havisham said a few words to her in a low voice.

'In the library, sir,' Mrs. Mellon replied. 'His lordship is to be taken there alone.'

A few minutes later the very tall footman in livery, who had escorted Cedric to the library door, opened it and announced: 'Lord Fauntleroy, my lord,' in quite a majestic tone. If he was only a footman, he felt it was rather a grand occasion when the heir came home to his own land and possessions, and was ushered into the presence of the old Earl, whose place and title he was to take.

Cedric crossed the threshold into the room. It was a very large and splendid room, with massive carven furniture in it, and shelves upon shelves of books; the furniture was so dark, and the draperies so heavy, the diamond-paned windows were so deep, and it seemed such a distance from one end of it to the other, that, since the sun had gone down, the effect of it all was rather gloomy. For a moment Cedric thought there was nobody in the room, but soon he saw that by the fire burning on the wide hearth there was a large easy chair, and that in that chair someone was sitting – someone who did not at first turn to look at him.

But he had attracted attention in one quarter at least. On the floor, by the armchair, lay a dog, a huge tawny mastiff with body and limbs almost as big as a lion's; and this great creature rose majestically and slowly, and marched towards the little fellow with a heavy step.

Then the person in the chair spoke. 'Dougal,' he called, 'come back, sir.'

But there was no more fear in little Lord Fauntleroy's heart than there was unkindness – he had been a brave little fellow all his life. He put his hand on the big dog's collar in the most natural way in the world, and they strayed forward together, Dougal sniffing as he went.

And then the Earl looked up. What Cedric saw was a large old man with shaggy white hair and eyebrows, and a nose like an eagle's beak between his deep fierce eyes. What the Earl saw was a graceful childish figure in a black velvet suit, with a lace collar, and with lovelocks waving about the handsome, manly little face, whose eyes met his with a look of innocent good-fellowship. If the Castle was like the palace in a fairy story, it must be owned that little Lord Fauntleroy was himself rather like a small copy of the fairy prince, though he was not at all aware of the fact, and perhaps was rather a sturdy young model of a fairy. But there was a sudden glow of triumph and exultation in the fiery old Earl's heart as he saw what a strong beautiful boy this grandson was, and how unhesitatingly he looked up as he stood with his hand on the big dog's neck. It pleased the grim old nobleman that the child should show no shyness or fear, either of the dog or of himself.

Cedric looked at him just as he had looked at the woman at the lodge and at the housekeeper, and came quite close to him.

'Are you the Earl?' he said. 'I'm your grandson, you know, that Mr. Havisham brought. I'm Lord Fauntleroy.'

He held out his hand because he thought it must be the polite and proper thing to do even with earls. 'I hope you are very well,' he continued, with the utmost friendliness. 'I'm very glad to see you.'

The Earl shook hands with him, with a curious gleam in his eyes; just at first he was so astonished that he scarcely knew what to say. He stared at the picturesque little apparition from under his shaggy brows, and took it all in from head to foot.

'They strayed forward together, Dougal sniffing as he went'

'Glad to see me, are you?' he said.

'Yes,' answered Lord Fauntleroy, 'very.'

There was a chair near him, and he sat down on it; it was a high-backed, rather tall chair, and his feet did not touch the floor when he had settled himself in it, but he seemed to be quite comfortable as he sat there and regarded his august relative intently and modestly.

'I've kept wondering what you would look like,' he remarked. 'I used to lie in my berth in the ship and wonder if you would be anything like my father.'

'Am I?' asked the Earl.

'Well,' Cedric replied, 'I was very young when he died, and I may not remember exactly how he looked, but I don't think you are like him.'

'You are disappointed, I suppose?' suggested his grandfather.

'Oh no!' responded Cedric politely. 'Of course you would like anyone to look like your father; but of course you would enjoy the way your grandfather looked, even if he wasn't like your father. You know how it is yourself about admiring your relations.'

The Earl leaned back in his chair and stared. He could not be said to know how it was about admiring his relations. He had employed most of his noble leisure in quarrelling violently with them, in turning them out of his house, and applying abusive epithets to them; and they all hated him cordially.

'Any boy would love his grandfather,' continued Lord Fauntleroy, 'especially one that had been as kind to him as you have been.'

Another queer gleam came into the old nobleman's eyes.

'Oh,' he said, 'I have been kind to you, have I?'

'Yes,' answered Lord Fauntleroy brightly; 'I'm ever so much obliged to you about Bridget and the apple-woman and Dick!'

'Bridget!' exclaimed the Earl. 'Dick! The apple-woman!'

'Yes,' explained Cedric; 'the ones you gave me all that money for – the money you told Mr. Havisham to give me if I wanted it.'

'Ha!' ejaculated his lordship. 'That's it, is it! The money you were to spend as you liked. What did you buy with it? I should like to hear something about that.'

He drew his shaggy eyebrows together and looked at the child sharply. He was secretly curious to know in what way the lad had indulged himself.

'Oh,' said Lord Fauntleroy, 'perhaps you didn't know about Dick and the apple-woman and Bridget. I forgot you lived such a long way off from them. They were particular friends of mine. And you see Michael had the fever——'

'Who's Michael?' asked the Earl.

'Michael is Bridget's husband, and they were in great trouble. When a man is sick and can't work and has twelve children you know how it is. And Michael had always been a sober man. And Bridget used to come to our house and cry. And the evening Mr. Havisham was there, she was in the kitchen crying because they had almost nothing to eat and couldn't pay the rent; and I went in to see her, and Mr. Havisham sent for me and he said you had given him some money for me. And I ran as fast as I could into the kitchen and gave it to Bridget; and that made it all right; and Bridget could scarcely believe her eyes. That's why I'm so obliged to you.'

'Oh,' said the Earl in his deep voice, 'that was one of the things you did for yourself, was it? What else?'

Dougal had been sitting by the tall chair; the great dog had taken its place there when Cedric sat down. Several times it had turned and looked up at the boy as if interested in the conversation. Dougal was a solemn dog, who seemed to feel altogether too big to take life's responsibilities lightly. The old Earl, who knew the dog well, had watched it with secret interest. Dougal was not a dog whose habit it was to make acquaintances rashly, and the Earl wondered somewhat to see how quietly the brute sat under the touch of the childish hand. And, just at this moment, the big dog gave little Lord Fauntleroy one more look of dignified scrutiny, and deliberately laid its huge, lion-like head on the boy's black-velvet knee.

The small hand went on stroking this new friend as Cedric answered:

'Well, there was Dick,' he said. 'You'd like Dick, he's so square.'

This was an Americanism the Earl was not prepared for.

'What does that mean?' he inquired.

Lord Fauntleroy paused a moment to reflect. He was not very sure himself what it meant. He had taken it for granted as meaning something very creditable because Dick had been fond of using it.

'I think it means that he wouldn't cheat anyone,' he exclaimed, 'or hit a boy who was under his size, and that he blacks people's boots very well and makes them shine as much as he can. He's a professional boot-black.'

'And he's one of your acquaintances, is he?' said the Earl.

'He's an old friend of mine,' replied his grandson. 'Not quite as old as Mr. Hobbs, but quite old. He gave me a present before the ship sailed.'

He put his hand into his pocket and drew forth a neatly folded red object and opened it with an air of affectionate pride. It was the red silk handkerchief with the large purple horseshoes and heads on it.

'He gave me this,' said his young lordship. 'I shall keep it always. You can wear it round your neck or keep it in your pocket. He bought it with the first money he earned after I bought Jake out and gave him the new brushes. It's a keepsake. I put some poetry in Mr. Hobbs's watch. It was, "When this you see, remember me." When this I see I shall always remember Dick.'

The sensations of the Right Honourable the Earl of Dorincourt could scarcely be described. He was not an old nobleman who was very easily bewildered, because he had seen a great deal of the world; but here was something he found so novel that it almost took his lordly breath away, and caused him some singular emotions. He had never cared for children; he had been so occupied with his own pleasures that he had never had time to care for them. His own sons had not interested him when they were very young – though sometimes he remembered having thought Cedric's father a handsome and strong little fellow. He had been so selfish himself that he had missed the pleasure of seeing unselfishness in others, and he had not known how tender and faithful and affectionate a kind-hearted little child can be, and how innocent and unconscious are its simple, generous impulses. A boy had always seemed to him a most objectionable little animal, selfish and greedy and boisterous when not under strict restraint; his own two eldest sons had given their tutors constant trouble and annoyance, and of the younger one he fancied he had heard few complaints because the boy was of no particular importance. It had never once occurred to him that he should like his grandson; he had sent for the little Cedric because his pride impelled him to do so. If the boy was to take his place in the future, he did not wish his name to be ridiculous by descending to an uneducated boor. He had been convinced the boy would be a clownish fellow if he were brought up in America. He had no feeling of affection for the lad, his only hope was that he should find him decently well featured and with a respectable share of sense; he had been so disappointed in his other sons, and had been made so furious by Captain Errol's American marriage, that he had never once thought that anything creditable could come of it. When the footman had announced Lord Fauntleroy he had almost dreaded to look at the boy lest he should find him all he had feared. It was because of this feeling that he had ordered that the child should be sent to him alone. His pride could not endure that others should see his disappointment if he was to be disappointed. His proud, stubborn old heart therefore had leaped within him when the boy came forward with his graceful easy carriage, his fearless hand on the big dog's neck. Even in the moments when he had hoped the most, the Earl had never hoped that his grandson would look like that. It seemed almost too good to be true that this should be the boy he had dreaded to see – the child of the woman he so disliked – this little fellow with so much beauty and such a brave, childish grace! The Earl's stern composure was quite shaken by this startling surprise.

And then their talk began; and he was still more curiously moved and more and more puzzled. In the first place he was so used to seeing people rather afraid and embarrassed before him, that he had expected nothing else but that his grandson would be timid or shy. But Cedric was no more afraid of the Earl than he had been of Dougal. He was not bold; he was only innocently friendly, and he was not conscious that there should be any reason why he should be awkward or afraid. The Earl could not help seeing that the little boy took him for a friend and treated him as one, without having any doubt of him at all. It was quite plain as the little fellow sat there in his tall chair and talked in his friendly way that it had never occurred to him that this large, fierce-looking old man could be anything but kind to him, and rather pleased to see him there. And it was plain, too, that in his childish way he wished to please and interest his grandfather. Cross and hard-hearted and worldly as the old Earl was, he could not help feeling a secret and novel pleasure in this very confidence. After all, it was not disagreeable to meet someone who did not distrust or shrink from him, or seem to detect the ugly part of his nature; someone who looked at him with clear, unsuspecting eyes – if it was only a little boy in a black-velvet suit.

So the old man leaned back in his chair, and led his young companion on to telling him still more of himself, and with that odd gleam in his eyes watched the little fellow as he talked. Lord Fauntleroy was quite willing to answer all his questions and chatted on in his genial little way quite composedly. He told him all about Dick and Jerry and the apple-woman and Mr. Hobbs; he described the Republican Rally in all the glory of its banners and transparencies, torches and rockets. In the course of the conversation he reached the Fourth of July and the Revolution, and was just becoming enthusiastic, when he suddenly remembered something and stopped very abruptly.

'What is the matter?' demanded his grandfather. 'Why don't you go on?'

Lord Fauntleroy moved rather uneasily in his chair. It was evident to the Earl that Lord Fauntleroy was embarrassed by the thought which had just occurred to him.

'I was just thinking that perhaps you mightn't like it,' he replied. 'Perhaps someone belonging to you might have been there. I forgot you were an Englishman.'

'You can go on,' said my lord. 'No one belonging to me was there. You forgot you were an Englishman too.'

'Oh no,' said Cedric quickly. 'I'm an American!'

'You are an Englishman,' said the Earl grimly. 'Your father was an Englishman.'

It amused him a little to say this, but it did not amuse Cedric. The lad had never thought of such a development as this. He felt himself grow quite hot up to the roots of his hair.

'I was born in America,' he protested. 'You have to be an American if you are born in America. I beg your pardon', with serious politeness and delicacy, 'for contradicting you. Mr. Hobbs told me, if there was another war, you know, I should have to – to be an American.'

The Earl gave a grim half-laugh – it was short and grim, but it was a laugh.

'You would, would you?' he said.

He hated America and Americans, but it amused him to see how serious and interested this small patriot was. He thought that so good an American might make a rather good Englishman when he was a man.

They had not time to go very deep into the Revolution again – and indeed Lord Fauntleroy felt some delicacy about returning to the subject – before dinner was announced.

Cedric left his chair and went to his noble kinsman. He looked down at his gouty foot.

'Would you like me to help you?' he said politely. 'You could lean on me, you know. Once when Mr. Hobbs hurt his foot with a potato barrel rolling on it, he used to lean on me.'

The big footman almost perilled his reputation and his situation by smiling. He was an aristocratic footman who had always lived in the best of noble families, and he had never smiled, indeed he would have felt himself a disgraced and vulgar footman if he had allowed himself to be led by any circumstance whatever into such an indiscretion as a smile. But he had a very narrow escape. He only just saved himself by staring straight over the Earl's head at a very ugly picture.

The Earl looked his valiant young relative over from head to foot.

'Do you think you could do it?' he asked gruffly.

'I *think* I could,' said Cedric. 'I'm strong. I'm seven, you know. You could lean on your stick on one side, and on me on the other. Dick says I've a good deal of muscle for a boy that's only seven.'

He shut his hand and moved it upwards to his shoulder, so that the Earl might see the muscle Dick had kindly approved of, and his face was so grave and earnest that the footman found it necessary to look very hard indeed at the ugly picture.

'Well,' said the Earl, 'you may try.'

Cedric gave him his stick, and began to assist him to rise. Usually the footman did this, and was violently sworn at when his lordship had an extra twinge of gout. The Earl was not a very polite person as a rule, and many a time the huge footmen about him quaked inside their imposing liveries.

But this evening he did not swear, though his gouty foot gave him more twinges than one. He chose to try an experiment. He got up slowly and put his hand on the small shoulder presented to him with so much courage. Little Lord Fauntleroy made a careful step forward, looking down at the gouty foot.

'Just lean on me,' he said with encouraging good cheer. 'I'll walk very slowly.'

If the Earl had been supported by the footman he would have rested less on his stick and more on his assistant's arm. And yet it was part of his experiment to let his grandson feel his burden as no light weight. It was quite a heavy weight indeed, and after a few steps his young lordship's face grew quite hot, and his heart beat rather fast, but he braced himself sturdily, remembering his muscle and Dick's approval of it.

'Don't be afraid of leaning on me,' he panted. 'I'm all right – if – if it isn't a very long way.'

It was not really very far to the dining-room, but it seemed rather a long way to Cedric before they reached the chair at the head of the table. The hand on his shoulder seemed to grow heavier at every step, and his face grew redder and hotter, and his breath shorter, but he never thought of giving up; he stiffened his childish muscles, held his head erect and encouraged the Earl as he limped along.

'Does your foot hurt very much when you stand on it?' he asked. 'Did you ever put it in hot water and mustard? Mr. Hobbs used to put his in hot water. Arnica is a very nice thing, they tell me.'

The big dog stalked slowly beside them, and the big footman followed; several times he looked very queer as he watched the little figure making the very most of all its strength, and bearing its burden with such goodwill. The Earl too looked rather queer, once, as he glanced sideways down at the flushed little face.

When they entered the room where they were to dine, Cedric saw it was a very large and imposing one, and that the footman who stood behind the chair at the head of the table stared very hard as they came in.

But they reached the chair at last. The hand was removed from his shoulder and the Earl was fairly seated.

Cedric took out Dick's handkerchief and wiped his forehead.

'It's a warm night, isn't it?' he said. 'Perhaps you need a fire because – because of your foot, but it seems just a little warm to me.'

His delicate consideration for his noble relative's feelings was such that he did not wish to seem to intimate that any of his surroundings were unnecessary'

'You have been doing some rather hard work,' said the Earl.

'Oh no!' said Lord Fauntleroy, 'It wasn't exactly hard, but I got a little warm. A person will get warm in summer time.'

And he rubbed his damp curls rather vigorously with the gorgeous handkerchief. His own chair was placed at the other end of the table, opposite his grandfather's. It was a chair with arms, and intended for a much larger individual than himself; indeed everything he had seen so far – the great rooms, with their high ceilings, the massive furniture, the big footman, the big dog, the Earl himself – were all of proportions calculated to make this little lad feel that he was very small indeed. But that did not trouble him; he had never thought himself very large or important, and he was quite willing to accommodate himself even to circumstances which rather overpowered him.

Perhaps he had never looked so little a fellow as when seated now in his great chair, at the end of the table. Notwithstanding his solitary existence, the Earl chose to live in considerable state. He was fond of his dinner, and he dined in a formal style. Cedric looked at him across a glitter of splendid glass and plate, which to his unaccustomed eyes seemed quite dazzling. A stranger looking on might well have smiled at the picture – the great stately room, the big liveried servants, the bright lights, the glittering silver and glass, the fierce-looking old nobleman at the head of the table and the very small boy at the foot. Dinner was usually a very serious matter with the Earl – and it was a very serious matter with the cook, if his lordship was not pleased or had an indifferent appetite. Today, however, his appetite seemed a

trifle better than usual, perhaps because he had something to think of
besides the flavour of the *entrées* and the management of the gravies.
His grandson gave him something to think of. He kept looking at him
across the table. He did not say very much himself, but he managed to
make the boy talk. He had never imagined that he could be entertained
by hearing a child talk, but Lord Fauntleroy at once puzzled and
amused him, and he kept remembering how he had let the childish
shoulder feel his weight just for the sake of trying how far the boy's
courage and endurance would go, and it pleased him to know that his
grandson had not quailed and had not seemed to think even for a
moment of giving up what he had undertaken to do.

'You don't wear your coronet all the time?' remarked Lord
Fauntleroy respectfully.

'No,' replied the Earl with his grim smile; 'it is not becoming to
me.'

'Mr. Hobbs said you always wore it,' said Cedric; 'but after he
thought it over, he said he supposed you must sometimes take it off to
put yout hat on.'

'Yes,' said the Earl, 'I take it off occasionally.'

And one of the footmen suddenly turned aside and gave a singular
little cough behind his hand.

Cedric finished his dinner first, and then he leaned back in his
chair and took a survey of the room.

'You must be very proud of your house,' he said, 'it's such a
beautiful house. I never saw anything so beautiful; but of course as I'm
only seven, I haven't seen much.'

'And you think I must be proud of it, do you?' said the Earl.

'I should think anyone would be proud of it,' replied Lord
Fauntleroy. 'I should be proud of it if it were my house. Everything
about it is beautiful. And the park, and those trees, how beautiful they
are and how the leaves rustle!'

Then he paused an instant and looked across the table rather
wistfully.

'It's a very big house for just two people to live in, isn't it?' he said.

'It is quite large enough for two,' answered the Earl. 'Do you find
it too large?'

His little lordship hesitated a moment.

'I was only thinking', he said, 'that if two people lived in it who were not very good companions, they might feel lonely sometimes.'

'Do you think I shall make a good companion?' inquired the Earl.

'Yes,' replied Cedric, 'I think you will. Mr. Hobbs and I were great friends. He was the best friend I had except Dearest.'

The Earl made a quick movement of his bushy eyebrows.

'Who is Dearest?'

'She is my mother,' said Lord Fauntleroy in a rather low, quiet little voice.

Perhaps he was a trifle tired, as his bedtime was nearing, and perhaps after the excitement of the last few days it was natural he should be tired, so perhaps too the feeling of weariness brought to him a vague sense of loneliness in the remembrance that tonight he was not to sleep at home, watched over by the loving eyes of that 'best friend' of his. They had always been 'best friends', this boy and his young mother. He could not help thinking of her, and the more he thought of her the less he was inclined to talk, and by the time the dinner was at an end the Earl saw that there was a faint shadow on his face. But Cedric bore himself with excellent courage, and when they went back to the library, though the tall footman walked on one side of his master, the Earl's hand rested on his grandson's shoulder, though not so as before.

When the footman left them alone, Cedric sat down upon the hearthrug near Dougal. For a few minutes he stroked the dog's ears in silence and looked at the fire.

The Earl watched him. The boy's eyes looked wistful and thoughtful, and once or twice he gave a little sigh. The Earl sat still, and kept his eyes fixed on his grandson.

'Fauntleroy,' he said at last, 'what are you thinking of?'

Fauntleroy looked up with a manful effort at a smile.

'I was thinking about Dearest,' he said; 'and – and I think I'd better get up and walk up and down the room.'

He rose up, and put his hands in his small pockets, and began to walk to and fro. His eyes were very bright and his lips were pressed together, but he kept his head up and walked firmly. Dougal moved lazily and looked at him, and then stood up. He walked over to the child, and began to follow him uneasily. Fauntleroy drew one hand from his pocket and laid it on the dog's head.

'He's a very nice dog,' he said. 'He's my friend. He knows how I feel.'

'How do you feel?' asked the Earl.

It disturbed him to see the struggle the little fellow was having with his first feeling of homesickness, but it pleased him to see that he was making so brave an effort to bear it well. He liked this childish courage.

'Come here,' he said.

Fauntleroy went to him.

'I never was away from my own house before,' said the boy, with a troubled look in his brown eyes. 'It makes a person feel a strange feeling when he has to stay all night in another person's castle instead of in his own house. But Dearest is not very far away from me. She told me to remember that – and – and I'm seven – and I can look at the picture she gave me.'

He put his hand in his pocket, and brought out a small violet velvet-covered case.

'This is it,' he said. 'You see, you press this spring and it opens, and she is in there!'

He had come close to the Earl's chair, and, as he drew forth the little case, he leaned against the arm of it, and against the old man's arm too, as confidingly as if children had always leaned there.

'There she is,' he said, as the case opened; and he looked up with a smile.

The Earl knitted his brows; he did not wish to see the picture, but he looked at it in spite of himself; and there looked up at him from it such a pretty young face – a face so like the child's at his side – that it quite startled him.

'I suppose you think you are very fond of her?' he said.

'Yes,' answered Lord Fauntleroy, in a gentle tone, and with simple directness; 'I do think so, and I think it's true. You see Mr. Hobbs was my friend, and Dick and Bridget and Mary and Michael, they were my friends too; but Dearest – well, she is my *close* friend, and we always tell each other everything. My father left her to me to take care of, and when I am a man I am going to work and earn money for her.'

'What do you think of doing?' inquired his grandfather.

His young lordship slipped down upon the hearthrug, and sat there with the picture still in his hand. He seemed to be reflecting seriously before he answered.

'I did think perhaps I might go into business with Mr. Hobbs,' he said; 'but I should *like* to be a president.'

'We'll send you to the House of Lords instead,' said his grandfather.

'Well,' remarked Lord Fauntleroy, 'if I *couldn't* be a president, and if that is a good business, I shouldn't mind. The grocery business is dull sometimes.'

Perhaps he was weighing the matter in his mind, for he sat very quiet after this, and looked at the fire for some time.

The Earl did not speak again. He leaned back in his chair and watched him. A great many strange new thoughts passed through the old nobleman's mind. Dougal had stretched himself out and gone to sleep with his head on his huge paws. There was a long silence.

In about half an hour's time Mr. Havisham was ushered in. The great room was very still when he entered. The Earl was still leaning back in his chair. He moved as Mr. Havisham approached and held up his hand in a gesture of warning – it seemed as if he had scarcely intended to make the gesture – as if it were almost involuntary. Dougal was still asleep, and close beside the great dog, sleeping also, with his curly head upon his arm, lay little Lord Fauntleroy.

6 The Earl and His Grandson

When Lord Fauntleroy wakened in the morning – he had not wakened at all when he had been carried to bed the night before – the first sounds he was conscious of were the crackling of a wood fire and the murmur of voices.

'You will be careful, Dawson, not to say anything about it,' he heard someone say. 'He does not know why she is not to be with him, and the reason is to be kept from him.'

'If them's his lordship's orders, mem,' another voice answered, 'they'll have to be kep', I suppose. But, if you'll excuse the liberty, mem, as it's between ourselves, servant or no servant, all I have to say is, it's a cruel thing – parting that poor, pretty, young widdered cre'tur from her own flesh and blood, and him such a little beauty and a nobleman born. James and Thomas, mem, last night in the servants' hall, they both of 'em say as they never see anythink in their two lives – nor yet no other gentleman in livery – like that little fellow's ways, as innercent an' polite an' interested as if he'd been sitting there dining with his best friend – and the temper of a' angel, instead of one (if you'll excuse me, mem), as it's well known is enough to curdle your blood in your veins at times. And as to looks, mem, when we was rung for, James and me, to go into the library and bring him upstairs, and James lifted him up in his arms, what with his little innercent face all red and rosy, and his little head on James's shoulder and his hair hanging down, all curly an' shinin', a prettier, takiner sight you'd never wish to see. An' it's my opinion, my lord wasn't to it neither, for he looked at him, and he says to James, "See you don't wake him!" he says.'

Cedric moved on his pillow, and turned over, opening his eyes.

There were two women in the room. Everything was bright and cheerful with gay-flowered chintz. There was a fire on the hearth, and the sunshine was streaming in through the ivy-entwined windows. Both women came towards him, and he saw that one of them was Mrs. Mellon, the housekeeper, and the other a comfortable, middle-aged woman, with a face as kind and good-humoured as a face could be.

'Good morning, my lord,' said Mrs. Mellon. 'Did you sleep well?'

His lordship rubbed his eyes and smiled.

'Good morning,' he said. 'I didn't know I was here.'

'You were carried upstairs when you were asleep,' said the housekeeper. 'This is your bedroom, and this is Dawson, who is to take care of you.'

Fauntleroy sat up in bed and held out his hand to Dawson as he had held it out to the Earl.

'How do you do, ma'am?' he said. 'I'm much obliged to you for coming to take care of me.'

'You can call her Dawson, my lord,' said the housekeeper with a smile. 'She is used to being called Dawson.'

'*Miss* Dawson or *Mrs.* Dawson?' inquired his lordship.

'Just Dawson, my lord,' said Dawson herself, beaming all over. 'Neither Miss nor Missis, bless your little heart! Will you get up now, and let Dawson dress you, and then have your breakfast in the nursery?'

'I learned to dress myself many years ago, thank you,' answered Fauntleroy. 'Dearest taught me. "Dearest" is my mamma. We had only Mary to do all the work – washing and all – and so of course it wouldn't do to give her so much trouble. I can take my bath, too, pretty well, if you'll just be kind enough to 'zamine the corners after I'm done.'

Dawson and the housekeeper exchanged glances.

'Dawson will do anything you ask her to,' said Mrs. Mellon.

'That I will, bless him,' said Dawson, in her comforting, good-humoured voice. 'He shall dress himself if he likes, and I'll stand by, ready to help him if he wants me.'

'Thank you,' responded Lord Fauntleroy; 'it's a little hard sometimes about the buttons, you know, and then I have to ask somebody.'

He thought Dawson a very kind woman, and before the bath and the dressing were finished they were excellent friends, and he had found out a great deal about her. He had discovered that her husband had been a soldier and had been killed in a real battle, and that her son was a sailor, and was away on a long cruise, and that he had seen pirates and cannibals and Chinese people and Turks, and that he brought home strange shells, and pieces of coral which Dawson was ready to show at any moment, some of them being in her trunk. All this was very interesting. He also found out that she had taken care of little children all her life, and that she had just come from a great house in another part of England, where she had been taking care of a beautiful little girl whose name was Lady Gwyneth Vaughan.

'And she is a sort of relation of your lordship's,' said Dawson. 'And perhaps some time you may see her.'

'Do you think I shall?' said Fauntleroy. 'I should like that. I never knew any little girls, but I always like to look at them.'

When he went into the adjoining room to take his breakfast and saw what a great room it was, and found there was another adjoining it, which Dawson told him was his also, the feeling that he was very small indeed came over him again so strongly that he confided it to Dawson, as he sat down to the table on which the pretty breakfast service was arranged.

'I am a very little boy', he said rather wistfully, 'to live in such a large castle, and have so many big rooms – don't you think so?'

'Oh, come,' said Dawson, 'you feel just a little strange at first, that's all; but you'll get over that very soon, and then you'll like it here. It's such a beautiful place, you know.'

'It's a very beautiful place of course,' said Fauntleroy with a little sigh, 'but I should like it better if I didn't miss Dearest so. I always had my breakfast with her in the morning, and put the sugar and cream in her tea for her, and handed her the toast. That made it very sociable of course.'

'Oh well,' answered Dawson comfortably, 'you know you can see her every day, and there's no knowing how much you'll have to tell her. Bless you, wait till you've walked about a bit and seen things – the dogs, and the stables with all the horses in them. There's one of them I know you'll like to see——'

'Is there?' exclaimed Fauntleroy. 'I'm very fond of horses. I was very fond of Jim. He was the horse that belonged to Mr. Hobbs's grocery wagon. He was a beautiful horse when he wasn't balky.'

'Well,' said Dawson, 'you just wait till you've seen what's in the stables. And, deary me, you haven't looked even into the very next room yet!'

'What is there?' asked Fauntleroy.

'Wait until you've had your breakfast, and then you shall see,' said Dawson.

At this he naturally began to grow curious, and he applied himself assiduously to his breakfast. It seemed to him that there must be something worth looking at in the next room; Dawson had such a consequential, mysterious air.

'Now then,' he said, slipping off his seat a few minutes later; 'I've had enough. Can I go and look at it?'

Dawson nodded and led the way, looking more mysterious and important than ever. He began to be very much interested indeed.

When she opened the door of the room, he stood upon the threshold and looked about him in amazement. He did not speak; he only put his hands in his pockets and stood there flushing up to his forehead and looking in.

He flushed up because he was so surprised and, for the moment, excited. To see such a place was enough to surprise any ordinary boy.

The room was a large one too, as all the rooms seemed to be, and it appeared to him more beautiful than the rest, only in a different way. The furniture was not so massive and antique as was that in the rooms he had seen downstairs; the draperies and rugs and walls were brighter; there were shelves full of books, and on the tables were numbers of toys – beautiful, ingenious things – such as he had looked at with wonder and delight through the shop windows in New York.

'It looks like a boy's room,' he said at last, catching his breath a little. 'Who do they belong to?'

'Go and look at them,' said Dawson. 'They belong to you!'

'To me!' he cried. 'To me! Why do they belong to me? Who gave them to me?' And he sprang forward with a gay little shout. It seemed almost too much to be believed. 'It was Grandpapa!' he said, with his eyes as bright as stars. 'I know it was Grandpapa!'

'Yes, it was his lordship,' said Dawson; 'and if you will be a nice little gentleman, and not fret about things, and will enjoy yourself, and be happy all the day, he will give you anything you ask for.'

It was a tremendously exciting morning. There were so many things to be examined, so many experiments to be tried; each novelty was so absorbing that he could scarcely turn from it to look at the next. And it was so curious to know that all this had been prepared for himself alone; that, even before he had left New York, people had come down from London to arrange the rooms he was to occupy, and had provided the books and playthings most likely to interest him.

'Did you ever know anyone', he said to Dawson, 'who had such a kind grandfather?'

Dawson's face wore an uncertain expression for a moment. She had not a very high opinion of his lordship the Earl. She had not been in the house many days, but she had been there long enough to hear the old nobleman's peculiarities discussed very freely in the servants' hall.

'An' of all the wicious, savage, hill-tempered hold fellows it was ever my hill-luck to wear livery hunder,' the tallest footman had said, 'he's the wiolentest and wust by a long shot.'

And this particular footman, whose name was Thomas, had also repeated to his companions below stairs some of the Earl's remarks to Mr. Havisham, when they had been discussing these very preparations.

'Give him his own way and fill his rooms with toys,' my lord had said. 'Give him what will amuse him, and he'll forget about his mother quickly enough. Amuse him, and fill his mind with other things, and we shall have no trouble. That's boy nature.'

So perhaps, having had this truly amiable object in view, it did not please him so very much to find it did not seem to be exactly this particular boy's nature. The Earl had passed a bad night and had spent the morning in his room; but at noon, after he had lunched, he sent for his grandson.

Fauntleroy answered the summons at once. He came down the broad staircase with a bounding step; the Earl heard him run across the hall, and then the door opened and he came in with red cheeks and sparkling eyes.

'I was waiting for you to send for me,' he said. 'I was ready a long time ago. I'm *ever* so much obliged to you for all those things! I'm *ever* so much obliged to you! I have been playing with them all the morning.'

'Oh,' said the Earl, 'you like them, do you?'

'I like them so much – well, I couldn't tell you how much!' said Fauntleroy, his face glowing with delight. 'There's one that's like baseball, only you play it on a board with black and white pegs, and you keep your score with some counters on a wire. I tried to teach Dawson, but she couldn't quite understand it just at first – you see she never played baseball, being a lady; and I'm afraid I wasn't very good at explaining it to her. But you know all about it, don't you?'

'I'm afraid I don't,' replied the Earl. 'It's an American game, isn't it? Is it something like cricket?'

'I never saw cricket,' said Fauntleroy; 'but Mr. Hobbs took me several times to see baseball. It's a splendid game. You get so excited! Would you like me to go and get my game and show it to you? Perhaps it would amuse you and make you forget about your foot. Does your foot hurt you very much this morning?'

'More than I enjoy,' was the answer.

'Then perhaps you couldn't forget it,' said the little fellow anxiously. 'Perhaps it would bother you to be told about the game. Do you think it would amuse you, or do you think it would bother you?'

'Go and get it,' said the Earl.

It certainly was a novel entertainment this – making a companion of a child who offered to teach him to play games, but the very novelty of it amused him. There was a smile lurking about the Earl's mouth when Cedric came back with the box containing the game in his arms, and an expression of the most eager interest on his face.

'May I pull that little table over here to your chair?' he asked.

'Ring for Thomas,' said the Earl. 'He will place it for you.'

'Oh, I can do it myself,' answered Fauntleroy. 'It's not very heavy.'

'Very well,' replied his grandfather. The lurking smile deepened on the old man's face as he watched the little fellow's preparations; there was such an absorbed interest in them. The small table was dragged forward and placed by his chair, and the game taken from its box and arranged upon it.

'It's very interesting when you once begin,' said Fauntleroy. 'You see, the black pegs can be your side and the white ones mine. They're men, you know, and once round the field is a home run and counts one – and these are the outs – and here is the first base and that's the second and that's the third and that's the home-base.'

He entered into the details of explanation with the greatest animation. He showed all the attitudes of pitcher and catcher and batter in the real game, and gave a dramatic description of a wonderful 'hot ball' he had seen caught on the glorious occasion on which he had witnessed a match in company with Mr. Hobbs. His vigorous, graceful little body, his eager gestures, his simple enjoyment of it all were pleasant to behold.

When at last the explanations and illustrations were at an end and the game began in good earnest, the Earl still found himself entertained. His young companion was wholly absorbed; he played with all his childish heart; his gay little laughs when he made a good throw, his enthusiasm over a 'home run', his impartial delight over his own good luck or his opponent's, would have given a flavour to any game.

If a week before anyone had told the Earl of Dorincourt that on that particular morning he would be forgetting his gout and his bad temper in a child's game, played with black and white wooden pegs, on a gaily painted board, with a curly headed small boy for a companion, he would without doubt have made himself very unpleasant; and yet he certainly had forgotten himself when the door opened and Thomas announced a visitor.

The visitor in question, who was an elderly gentleman in black, and no less a person than the clergyman of the parish, was so startled by the amazing scene which met his eye that he almost fell back a pace, and ran some risk of colliding with Thomas.

There was in fact no part of his duty that the Reverend Mr. Mordaunt found so decidedly unpleasant as that part which compelled

'"It's very interesting when you once begin", said Fauntleroy'

him to call upon his noble patron at the Castle. His noble patron
indeed usually made these visits as disagreeable as it lay in his lordly
power to make them. He abhorred churches and charities, and flew
into violent rages when any of his tenantry took the liberty of being
poor and ill and needed assistance. When his gout was at its worst, he
did not hesitate to announce that he would not be bored and irritated
by being told stories of their miserable fortunes; when his gout
troubled him less and he was in a somewhat more humane frame of
mind, he would perhaps give the rector some money, after having
bullied him in the most painful manner, and berated the whole parish
for its shiftlessness and imbecility. But, whatsoever his mood, he never
failed to make as many sarcastic and embarrassing speeches as
possible, and to cause the Reverend Mr. Mordaunt to wish it were
proper and Christian-like to throw something heavy at him. During all
the years in which Mr. Mordaunt had been in charge of Dorincourt
parish, the rector certainly did not remember having seen his lordship,
of his own free will, do anyone a kindness, or, under any circumstances
whatever, show that he thought of anyone but himself.

He had called today to speak to him of a specially pressing case,
and as he had walked up the avenue, he had, for two reasons, dreaded
his visit more than usual. In the first place, he knew that his lordship
had for several days been suffering from the gout, and had been in so
villainous a humour that rumours of it had even reached the village –
carried there by one of the young women servants to her sister, who
kept a little shop and retailed darning-needles and cotton and
peppermints and gossip, as a means of earning an honest living. What
Mrs. Dibble did not know about the Castle and its inmates, and the
farmhouses and their inmates, and the village and its population, was
really not worth being talked about. And of course she knew
everything about the Castle, because her sister Jane Shorts was one of
the upper housemaids, and was very friendly and intimate with
Thomas.

'And the way his lordship do go on!' said Mrs. Dibble, over the
counter, 'and the way he do use language, Mr. Thomas told Jane
herself, no flesh or blood as is in livery could stand – for throw a plate
of toast at Mr. Thomas hisself, he did, not more than two days since,

and if it weren't for other things being agreeable and the society below stairs most genteel, warning would have been gave within a' hour!'

And the rector heard all this, for somehow the Earl was a favourite black sheep in the cottages and farmhouses, and his bad behaviour gave many a good woman something to talk about when she had company to tea.

And the second reason was even worse, because it was a new one and had been talked about with the most excited interest.

Who did not know of the old nobleman's fury when his handsome son the Captain had married the American lady? Who did not know how cruelly he had treated the Captain, and how the big, gay, sweet-smiling young man, who was the only member of the grand family anyone liked, had died in a foreign land, poor and unforgiven? Who did not know how fiercely his lordship had hated the poor young creature who had been this son's wife, and how he had hated the thought of her child and never meant to see the boy – until his two sons died and left him without an heir? And then, who did not know that he had looked forward without any affection or pleasure to his grandson's coming, and that he had made up his mind that he should find the boy a vulgar, awkward, pert American lad, more likely to disgrace his noble name than to honour it?

The proud, angry old man thought he had kept all his thoughts secret. He did not suppose anyone had dared to guess at, even less talk over what he felt, and dreaded; but his servants watched him, and read his face and his ill-humours and fits of gloom, and discussed them in the servants' hall. And while he thought himself quite secure from the common herd, Thomas was telling Jane and the cook and the butler and the housemaids and the other footmen that it was his opinion that 'the hold man was wuss than usual a-thinkin' hover the Captin's boy, an' hanticipatin' as he won't be no credit to the fambly. An' serve him right,' added Thomas; 'hit's 'is hown fault. Wot can he iggspect from a child brought up in pore circumstances in that there low Hamerica?'

And as the Reverend Mr. Mordaunt walked under the great trees he remembered that this questionable little boy had arrived at the Castle only the evening before, and that there were nine chances to one that his lordship's worst fears were realized, and twenty-two chances to one that if the poor little fellow had disappointed him, the Earl was even now in a tearing rage, and ready to vent all his rancour on the first person who called – which it appeared probable would be his reverend self.

Judge then of his amazement when, as Thomas opened the library door, his ears were greeted by a delightful ring of childish laughter.

'That's two out!' almost shouted an excited, clear little voice. 'You see it's two out!'

And there was the Earl's chair, and the gout-stool, and his foot on it; and by him a small table and a game on it; and quite close to him, actually leaning against his arm and his ungouty knee, was a little boy with face glowing, and eyes dancing with excitement. 'It's two out!' the little stranger cried. 'You hadn't any luck that time, had you?' And then they both recognized at once that someone had come in.

The Earl glanced around, knitted his shaggy eyebrows as he had a trick of doing, and when he saw who it was, Mr. Mordaunt was still more surprised to see that he looked even less disagreeable than usual instead of more so. In fact, he looked almost as if he had forgotten for the moment how disagreeable he was, and how unpleasant he really could make himself when he tried.

'Ah,' he said in his harsh voice, but giving his hand rather graciously, 'good morning, Mordaunt. I've found a new employment, you see.'

He put his other hand on Cedric's shoulder – perhaps deep down in his heart there was a stir of gratified pride that it was such an heir he had to present; there was a spark of something like pleasure in his eyes as he moved the boy slightly forward.

'This is the new Lord Fauntleroy,' he said, 'Fauntleroy, this is Mr. Mordaunt, the rector of the parish.'

Fauntleroy looked up at the gentleman in the clerical garments, and gave him his hand.

'I am very glad to make your acquaintance, sir,' he said, remembering the words he had heard Mr. Hobbs use on one or two occasions when he had been greeting a new customer with ceremony. Cedric felt quite sure that one ought to be more than usually polite to a minister.

Mr. Mordaunt held the small hand in his a moment as he looked down at the child's face, smiling involuntarily. He liked the little fellow from that instant – as in fact people always did like him. And it was not the boy's beauty and grace which most appealed to him; it was the simple, natural kindliness in the little lad which made any words he uttered, however quaint and unexpected, sound pleasant and sincere. As the rector looked at Cedric, he forgot to think of the Earl at all. Nothing in the world is so strong as a kind heart, and somehow this kind little heart, though it was only the heart of a child, seemed to clear all the atmosphere of the big gloomy room and make it brighter.

'I am delighted to make your acquaintance, Lord Fauntleroy,' said the rector. 'You made a long journey to come to us. A great many people will be glad to know you made it safely.'

'It *was* a long way,' answered Fauntleroy; 'but Dearest, my mother, was with me, and I wasn't lonely. Of course you are never lonely if your mother is with you; and the ship was beautiful.'

'Take a chair, Mordaunt,' said the Earl. Mr. Mordaunt sat down. He glanced from Fauntleroy to the Earl.

'Your lordship is greatly to be congratulated,' he said warmly. But the Earl plainly had no intention of showing his feelings on the subject.

'He is like his father,' he said rather gruffly. 'Let us hope he'll conduct himself more creditably.' And then he added: 'Well, what is it this morning, Mordaunt? Who is in trouble now?'

This was not as bad as Mr. Mordaunt had expected, but he hesitated a second before he began.

'It is Higgins,' he said; 'Higgins of Edge Farm. He has been very unfortunate. He was ill himself last autumn, and his children had scarlet fever. I can't say that he is a very good manager, but he has had ill-luck, and of course he is behindhand in many ways. He is in trouble about his rent now. Newick tells him if he doesn't pay it he must leave the place; and of course that would be a very serious matter. His wife is ill, and he came to me yesterday to beg me to see you about it, and ask you for time. He thinks if you would give him time he could catch up again.'

'They all think that,' said the Earl, looking rather black.

Fauntleroy made a movement forward. He had been standing

between his grandfather and the visitor, listening with all his might. He had begun to be interested in Higgins at once. He wondered how many children there were, and if the scarlet fever had hurt them very much. His eyes were wide open and were fixed upon Mr. Mordaunt with intense interest as that gentleman went on with the conversation.

'Higgins is a well-meaning man,' said the rector, making an effort to strengthen his plea.

'He is a bad enough tenant,' replied his lordship. 'And he is always behindhand, Newick tells me.'

'He is in great trouble now,' said the rector. 'He is very fond of his wife and children, and if the farm is taken from him they may literally starve. He cannot give them the nourishing things they need. Two of the children were left very low after the fever, and the doctor orders for them wine and luxuries that Higgins cannot afford.'

At this Fauntleroy moved a step nearer.

'That was the way with Michael,' he said.

The Earl slightly started. 'I forgot *you*!' he said, 'I forgot we had a philanthropist in the room. Who was Michael?' And the gleam of queer amusement came back into the old man's deep-set eyes.

'He was Bridget's husband, who had the fever,' answered Fauntleroy; 'and he couldn't pay the rent or buy wine and things. And you gave me that money to help him.'

The Earl drew his brows together into a curious frown, which somehow was scarcely grim at all. He glanced across at Mr. Mordaunt.

'I don't know what sort of a landed proprietor he will make,' he said. 'I told Havisham the boy was to have what he wanted – and what he wanted, it seems, was money to give to beggars.'

'Oh, but they weren't beggars,' said Fauntleroy eagerly. 'Michael was a splendid bricklayer! They all worked.'

'Oh,' said the Earl, 'they were not beggars. They were splendid bricklayers and boot-blacks and apple-women.'

He bent his gaze on the boy for a few seconds in silence. The fact was that a new thought was coming to him, and though perhaps it was not promoted by the noblest emotions, it was not a bad thought. 'Come here,' he said at last.

Fauntleroy went and stood as near to him as possible without encroaching on the gouty foot.

'What would *you* do in this case?' his lordship asked.

It must be confessed that Mr. Mordaunt experienced for the moment a curious sensation. Being a man of great thoughtfulness, and having spent so many years on the estate of Dorincourt, knowing the tenantry, rich and poor, the people of the village, honest and industrious, dishonest and lazy, he realized very strongly what power for good or evil would be given in the future to this one small boy standing there, his brown eyes wide open, his hands deep in his pockets; and the thought came to him also that a great deal of power might perhaps, through the caprice of a proud, self-indulgent old man, be given to him now, and that if his young nature were not a simple and generous one, it might be the worst thing that could happen, not only for others, but for himself.

'And what would *you* do in such a case?' demanded the Earl.

Fauntleroy drew a little nearer, and laid one hand on his knee, with the most confiding air of good comradeship.

'If I were very rich,' he said, 'and not only just a little boy, I should let him stay, and give him the things for his children; but then, I am only a boy.' Then, after a second's pause, in which his face brightened visibly: '*You* can do anything, can't you?' he said.

'Humph!' said my lord, staring at him. 'That's your opinion, is it?' And he was not displeased either.

'I mean you can give anyone anything,' said Fauntleroy. 'Who's Newick?'

'He is my agent,' answered the Earl, 'and some of my tenants are not overfond of him.'

'Are you going to write him a letter now?' inquired Fauntleroy. 'Shall I bring you the pen and ink? I can take the game off this table.'

It plainly had not for an instant occurred to him that Newick would be allowed to do his worst.

The Earl paused a moment, still looking at him. 'Can you write?' he asked.

'Yes,' answered Cedric, 'but not very well.'

'Move the things from the table,' commanded my lord, 'and bring the pen and ink, and a sheet of paper from my desk.'

Mr. Mordaunt's interest began to increase. Fauntleroy did as he was told very deftly. In a few moments the sheet of paper, the big inkstand and the pen were ready.

'There,' he said gaily, 'now you can write it.'

'You are to write it,' said the Earl.

'I!' exclaimed Fauntleroy, and a flush overspread his forehead. 'Will it do if I write it? I don't always spell quite right when I haven't a dictionary and nobody tells me.'

'It will do,' answered the Earl. 'Higgins will not complain of the spelling. I'm not the philanthropist; you are. Dip your pen in the ink.'

Fauntleroy took up the pen and dipped it in the ink-bottle, then he arranged himself in position, leaning on the table.

'Now,' he inquired, 'what must I say?'

'You may say, "Higgins is not to be interfered with for the present", and sign it "Fauntleroy",' said the Earl.

Fauntleroy dipped his pen in the ink again, and, resting his arm, began to write. It was rather a slow and serious process, but he gave his whole soul to it. After a while, however, the manuscript was complete, and he handed it to his grandfather with a smile slightly tinged with anxiety.

'Do you think it will do?' he asked.

The Earl looked at it, and the corners of his mouth twitched a little.

'Yes,' he answered; 'Higgins will find it entirely satisfactory.' And he handed it to Mr. Mordaunt.

What Mr. Mordaunt found written was this:

Dear mr Newik if you pleas mr higins is not to be inturfeared with for the present and oblige

Yours rispecferly

FAUNTLEROY.

'Mr. Hobbs always signed his letters that way,' said Fauntleroy; 'and I thought I'd better say "please". Is that exactly the right way to spell "interfered"?'

'It's not exactly the way it is spelled in the dictionary,' answered the Earl.

'I was afraid of that,' said Fauntleroy. 'I ought to have asked. You see that's the way with words of more than one syllable; you have to look in the dictionary. It's always safest. I'll write it over again.'

And write it over again he did, making quite an imposing copy, and taking precautions in the matter of spelling by consulting the Earl himself.

'Spelling is a curious thing,' he said. 'It's so often different from what you expect it to be. I used to think "please" was spelled p-l-e-e-s, but it isn't, you know; and you'd think "dear" was spelled d-e-r-e, if you didn't inquire. Sometimes it almost discourages you.'

When Mr. Mordaunt went away he took the letter with him, and he took something else with him also – namely, a pleasanter feeling and a more hopeful one than he had ever carried home with him down that avenue or any previous visit he had made at Dorincourt Castle.

When he was gone Fauntleroy, who had accompanied him to the door, went back to his grandfather.

'May I go to Dearest now?' he said. 'I think she will be waiting for me.'

The Earl was silent for a moment.

'There is something in the stable for you to see first,' he said. 'Ring the bell.'

'If you please,' said Fauntleroy, with his quick little flush, 'I'm very much obliged; but I think I'd better see it tomorrow. She will be expecting me all the time.'

'Very well,' answered the Earl. 'We will order the carriage.' Then he added dryly: 'It's a pony.'

Fauntleroy drew a long breath.

'A pony!' he exclaimed. 'Whose pony is it?'

'Yours,' replied the Earl.

'Mine?' cried the little fellow. 'Mine – like the things upstairs?'

'Yes,' said his grandfather. 'Would you like to see it? Shall I order it to be brought round?'

Fauntleroy's cheeks grew redder and redder.

'I never thought I should have a pony!' he said. 'I never thought that! How glad Dearest will be. You give me *everything*, don't you?'

'Do you wish to see it?' inquired the Earl.

Fauntleroy drew a long breath. 'I *want* to see it,' he said. 'I want to see it so much I can hardly wait. But I'm afraid there isn't time.'

'You *must* go and see your mother this afternoon?' asked the Earl. 'You think you can't put it off?'

'Why,' said Fauntleroy, 'she has been thinking about me all the morning, and I have been thinking about her?'

'Oh,' said the Earl, 'you have, have you? Ring the bell.'

As they drove down the avenue, under the arching trees, he was rather silent. But Fauntleroy was not. He talked about the pony. What colour was it? How big was it? What was its name? What did it like to eat best? How old was it? How early in the morning might he get up and see it?

'Dearest will be so glad!' he kept saying. 'She will be so much obliged to you for being so kind to me! She knows I always liked ponies so much, but we never thought I should have one. There was a little boy on Fifth Avenue who had one, and he used to ride out every morning and we used to take a walk past his house to see him.'

He leaned back against the cushions and regarded the Earl with rapt interest for a few minutes and in entire silence.

'I think you must be the best person in the world,' he burst forth at last. 'You are always doing good, aren't you? – and thinking about other people. Dearest says that is the best kind of goodness; not to think about yourself, but to think about other people. That is just the way you are, isn't it?'

His lordship was so dumbfounded to find himself presented in such agreeable colours that he did not know exactly what to say. He felt that he needed time for reflection. To see each of his ugly, selfish motives changed into a good and generous one by the simplicity of a child was a singular experience.

Fauntleroy went on, still regarding him with admiring eyes – those great, clear, innocent eyes!

'You make so many people happy,' he said. 'There's Michael and Bridget and their twelve children, and the apple-woman and Dick and Mr. Hobbs, and Mr. Higgins and Mrs. Higgins and their children, and Mr. Mordaunt – because of course he was glad – and Dearest and me, about the pony and all the other things. Do you know, I've counted it up on my fingers and in my mind, and it's twenty-seven people you've been kind to. That's a good many – twenty-seven!'

'And I was the person who was kind to them, was I?' said the Earl.

'Why, yes, you know,' answered Fauntleroy. 'You made them all happy. Do you know', with some delicate hesitation, 'that people are sometimes mistaken about earls when they don't know them. Mr. Hobbs was. I am going to write to him and tell him about it.'

'What was Mr. Hobbs's opinion of earls?' asked his lordship.

'Well, you see, the difficulty was', replied his young companion, 'that he didn't know any, and he'd only read about them in books. He thought – you mustn't mind it – that they were gory tyrants; and he said he wouldn't have them hanging around his store. But if he'd known *you*, I'm sure he would have felt quite different. I shall tell him about you.'

'What shall you tell him?'

'I shall tell him,' said Fauntleroy, glowing with enthusiasm, 'that you are the kindest man I ever heard of. And you are always thinking of other people, and making them happy, and – and I hope when I grow up I shall be just like you.'

'Just like me!' repeated his lordship, looking at the little kindling face. And a dull red crept up under his withered skin, and he suddenly turned his eyes away and looked out of the carriage window at the great beech trees, with the sun shining on their glossy, red-brown leaves.

'*Just* like you,' said Fauntleroy, adding modestly: 'If I can. Perhaps I'm not good enough, but I'm going to try.'

The carriage rolled on down the stately avenue under the beautiful, broad-branched trees, through the spaces of green shade and lanes of golden sunlight. Fauntleroy saw again the lovely places where the ferns grew high and the bluebells swayed in the breeze; he saw the deer, standing or lying in the deep grass, turn their large startled eyes as the carriage passed, and caught glimpses of the brown rabbits as they scurried away. He heard the whir of the partridges and the calls and songs of the birds, and it all seemed even more beautiful to him than before. All his heart was filled with pleasure and happiness in the beauty that was on every side. But the old Earl saw and heard very different things, though he was apparently looking out too. He saw a long life, in which there had been neither generous deeds nor kind thoughts; he saw years in which a man who had been young and strong and rich and powerful had used his youth and strength and wealth and power only to please himself and kill time as the days and years succeeded each other; he saw this man, when the time had been killed and old age had come, solitary and without real friends in the midst of all his splendid wealth; he saw people who disliked or feared him, and people who would flatter and cringe to him, but no one who really cared whether he lived or died, unless they had something to gain or lose by it. He looked out on the broad acres which belonged to him, and he knew what Fauntleroy did not – how far they extended, what wealth they represented and how many people had homes on their soil. And he knew too – another thing Fauntleroy did not – that in all those homes, humble or well to do, there was probably not one person, however much he envied the wealth and stately name and power, and however willing he would have been to possess them, who would for an instant have thought of calling the noble owner 'good', or wishing, as this simple-souled little boy had, to be like him.

And it was not exactly pleasant to reflect upon, even for a cynical, worldly old man, who had been sufficient unto himself for seventy years and who had never deigned to care what opinion the world held of him so long as it did not interfere with his comfort or entertainment. And the fact was, indeed, that he had never before condescended to reflect upon it at all, and he only did so now because a child had believed him better than he was and by wishing to follow in his illustrious footsteps and imitate his example, had suggested to him the curious question whether he was exactly the person to take as a model.

Fauntleroy thought the Earl's foot must be hurting him, his brows knitted themselves together so, as he looked out at the park; and thinking this, the considerate little fellow tried not to disturb him, and enjoyed the trees and the ferns and the deer in silence. But at last the carriage, having passed the gates and bowled through the green lanes for a short distance, stopped. They had reached Court Lodge; and Fauntleroy was out upon the ground almost before the big footman had time to open the carriage door.

The Earl wakened from his reverie with a start.

'What!' he said. 'Are we here?'

'Yes,' said Fauntleroy. 'Let me give you your stick. Just lean on me when you get out.'

'I am not going to get out,' replied his lordship brusquely.

'Not — not to see Dearest?' exclaimed Fauntleroy with astonished face.

'"Dearest" will excuse me,' said the Earl dryly. 'Go to her and tell her that not even a new pony would keep you away.'

'She will be disappointed,' said Fauntleroy. 'She will want to see you very much.'

'I am afraid not,' was the answer. 'The carriage will call for you as we come back. Tell Jefferies to drive on, Thomas.'

Thomas closed the carriage door: and, after a puzzled look, Fauntleroy ran up the drive. The Earl had the opportunity – as Mr. Havisham once had – of seeing a pair of handsome, strong little legs flash over the ground with astonishing rapidity. Evidently their owner had no intention of losing any time. The carriage rolled slowly away, but his lordship did not at once lean back; he still looked out. Through a space in the trees he could see the house door; it was wide open. The little figure dashed up the steps; another figure – a little figure too, slender and young, in its black gown – ran to meet it. It seemed as if they flew together, as Fauntleroy leaped into his mother's arms, hanging about her neck and covering her sweet young face with kisses.

7 At Church

On the following Sunday morning Mr. Mordaunt had a large congregation. Indeed he could scarcely remember any Sunday on which the church had been so crowded. People appeared upon the scene who seldom did him the honour of coming to hear his sermons. There were even people from Hazelton, which was the next parish. There were hearty, sunburned farmers; stout, comfortable, apple-cheeked wives in their best bonnets and most gorgeous shawls, and half a dozen children or so to each family. The doctor's wife was there, with her four daughters. Mrs. Kimsey and Mr. Kimsey, who kept the druggist's shop, and made pills, and did up powders for everybody within ten miles, sat in their pew; Mrs. Dibble in hers, Miss Smiff, the village dressmaker, and her friend Miss Perkins, the milliner, sat in theirs; the doctor's young man was present, and the druggist's apprentice; in fact, almost every family on the countryside was represented in one way or another.

In the course of the preceding week, many wonderful stories had been told of little Lord Fauntleroy. Mrs. Dibble had been kept so busy attending to customers who came in to buy a pennyworth of needles or a ha'p'orth of tape and to hear what she had to relate, that the little shop bell over the door had nearly twinkled itself to death over the coming and going. Mrs. Dibble knew exactly how his small lordship's rooms had been furnished for him, what expensive toys had been bought, how there was a beautiful brown pony awaiting him and a small groom to attend it, and a little dog-cart, with silver-mounted harness. And she could tell, too, what all the servants had said when they had caught glimpses of the child on the night of his arrival; and how every female below stairs had said it was a shame, so it was, to part the poor pretty dear from his mother; and had all declared their hearts came into their mouths when he went alone into the library to see his grandfather, for 'there was no knowing how he'd be treated, and his lordship's temper was enough to fluster them with old heads on their shoulders, let alone a child'.

'But if you'll believe me, Mrs. Jennifer, mum,' Mrs. Dibble had said, 'fear that child does not know – so Mr. Thomas hisself says; an' set an' smile he did, an' talked to his lordship as if they'd been friends ever since his first hour. An' the Earl so took aback, Mr. Thomas says, that he couldn't do nothing but listen and stare from under his eyebrows. An' it's Mr. Thomas's opinion, Mrs. Bates, mum, that bad as he is, he was pleased in his secret soul, an' proud too; for a handsomer little fellow, or with better manners, though so old-fashioned, Mr. Thomas says, he'd never wish to see.'

And then there had come the story of Higgins. the Reverend Mr. Mordaunt had told it at his own dinner table, and the servant who had heard it had told it in the kitchen, and from there it had spread like wildfire.

And on market-day, when Higgins had appeared in town, he had been questioned on every side, and Newick had been questioned too, and in response had shown to two or three people the note signed 'Fauntleroy'.

And so the farmers' wives had found plenty to talk of over their tea and their shopping, and they had done the subject full justice and made the most of it. And on Sunday they had either walked to church or had been driven in their gigs by their husbands, who were perhaps a trifle curious themselves about the new little lord who was to be in time the owner of the soil.

It was by no means the Earl's habit to attend church, but he chose to appear on this first Sunday – it was his whim to present himself in the huge family pew, with Fauntleroy at his side.

There were many loiterers in the churchyard and many lingerers in the lane that morning. There were groups at the gates and in the porch, and there had been much discussion as to whether my lord would really appear or not. When this discussion was at its height, one good woman suddenly uttered an exclamation.

'Eh,' she said, 'that must be the mother, pretty young thing.'

All who had heard turned and looked at the slender figure in black coming up the path. The veil was thrown back from her face and they could see how fair and sweet it was, and how the bright hair curled as softly as a child's under the little widow's cap.

She was not thinking of the people about; she was thinking of Cedric, and of his visits to her, and his joy over his new pony, on which he had actually ridden to her door the day before, sitting very straight and looking very proud and happy. But soon she could not help being attracted by the fact that she was being looked at and that her arrival had created some sort of sensation. She first noticed it because an old woman in a red cloak made a bobbing curtsy to her, and then another did the same thing and said, 'God bless you, my lady!' and one man after another took off his hat as she passed. For a moment she did not understand, and then she realized that it was because she was little Lord Fauntleroy's mother that they did so, and she flushed rather shyly, and smiled and bowed too, and said, 'Thank you,' in a gentle voice to the old woman who had blessed her. To a person who had always lived in a bustling, crowded American city this simple deference was very novel, and at first just a little embarrassing; but after all, she could not help liking and being touched by the friendly warmheartedness of which it seemed to speak. She had scarcely passed through the stone porch into the church before the great event of the day happened. The carriage from the Castle with its handsome horses and tall, liveried servants, bowled round the corner and down the green lane.

'Here they come!' went from one looker-on to another.

And then the carriage drew up, and Thomas stepped down and opened the door, and a little boy, dressed in black velvet, and with a splendid mop of bright waving hair jumped out.

Every man, woman and child looked curiously upon him.

'He's the Captain over again!' said those of the onlookers who remembered his father. 'He's the Captain's self to the life!'

He stood there in the sunlight looking up at the Earl, as Thomas helped that nobleman out, with the most affectionate interest that could be imagined. The instant he could help, he put out his hand and

*'All who heard turned and looked at the slender figure
in black coming up the path'*

offered his shoulder as if he had been seven feet high. It was plain enough to everyone that however it might be with other people, the Earl of Dorincourt struck no terror into the breast of his grandson.

'Just lean on me,' they heard him say. 'How glad the people are to see you, and how well they all seem to know you!'

'Take off your cap, Fauntleroy,' said the Earl. 'They are bowing to you.'

'To me!' cried Fauntleroy, whipping off his cap in a moment, baring his bright head to the crowd and turning shining, puzzled eyes on them as he tried to bow to everyone at once.

'God bless your lordship!' said the curtsying, red-cloaked old woman who had spoken to his mother; 'long life to you!'

'Thank you, ma'am,' said Fauntleroy. And then they went into the church, and were looked at there, on their way up the aisle to the square red-cushioned and curtained pew. When Fauntleroy was fairly seated he made two discoveries which pleased him: the first was that, across the church, where he could look at her, his mother sat and smiled at him; the second, that at one end of the pew against the wall knelt two quaint figures, carven in stone, facing each other as they kneeled on either side of a pillar supporting two stone missals, their pointed hands folded as if in prayer, their dress very antique and strange. On the tablet by them was written something of which he could only read the curious words:

Here lyeth ye bodye of Gregorye Arthure Fyrst Earle of Dorincort allsoe of Alisone Hildegarde hys wyfe.

'May I whisper?' inquired his lordship, devoured by curiosity.

'What is it?' said his grandfather.

'Who are they?'

'Some of your ancestors', answered the Earl, 'who lived a few hundred years ago.'

'Perhaps,' said Lord Fauntleroy, regarding them with respect, 'perhaps I got my spelling from them.' And then he proceeded to find his place in the church service. When the music began he stood up and looked across at his mother, smiling. He was very fond of music, and his mother and he often sang together, so he joined in with the rest, his pure, sweet, high voice rising as clear as the song of a bird. He quite forgot himself in his pleasure in it. The Earl forgot himself a little too, as he sat in his curtain-shielded corner of the pew and watched the boy. Cedric stood with the big psalter open in his hands, singing with all his childish might, his face a little uplifted, happily; and as he sang a long ray of sunshine crept in and slanting through a golden pane of a stained-glass window brightened the falling hair about his young head. His mother, as she looked at him across the church, felt a thrill pass through her heart, and a prayer rose in it too; a prayer that the pure, simple happiness of his childish soul might last, and that the strange, great fortune which had fallen to him might bring no wrong or evil with it. There were many soft anxious thoughts in her tender heart in those new days.

'Oh, Ceddie,' she had said to him the evening before, as she hung over him in saying goodnight before he went away, 'oh, Ceddie dear, I wish for your sake I was very clever and could say a great many wise things! But only be good, dear, only be brave, only be kind and true always, and then you will never hurt anyone so long as you live, and you may help many, and the big world may be better because my little child was born. And that is best of all, Ceddie – it is better than everything else, that the world should be a little better because a man has lived – even ever so little better, dearest.'

And on his return to the Castle Fauntleroy had repeated her words to his grandfather.

'And I thought about you when she said that,' he ended; 'and I told her that was the way the world was because you had lived, and I was going to try if I could be like you.'

'And what did she say to that?' asked his lordship a trifle uneasily.

'She said that was right, and we must always look for good in people and try to be like it.'

Perhaps it was this the old man remembered as he glanced through the divided folds of the red curtain of his pew. Many times he looked over the people's heads to where his son's wife sat alone, and he saw the fair face the unforgiven dead had loved, and the eyes which were so like those of the child at his side; but what his thoughts were, and whether they were hard and bitter, or softened a little, it would have been hard to discover.

As they came out of the church, many of those who had attended the service stood waiting to see them pass. As they neared the gate a man who stood with his hat in his hand made a step forward and then hesitated. He was a middle-aged farmer, with a careworn face.

'Well, Higgins,' said the Earl.

Fauntleroy turned quickly to look at him.

'Oh,' he exclaimed, 'is it Mr. Higgins?'

'Yes,' answered the Earl dryly; 'and I suppose he came to take a look at his new landlord.'

'Yes, my lord,' said the man, his sunburned face reddening. 'Mr. Newick told me his young lordship was kind enough to speak for me, and I thought I'd like to say a word of thanks, if I might be allowed.'

Perhaps he felt some wonder when he saw what a little fellow it was who had innocently done so much for him, and who stood there looking up just as one of his own less fortunate children might have done – apparently not realizing his own importance in the least.

'I've a great deal to thank your lordship for,' he said; 'a great deal. I——'

'Oh,' said Fauntleroy, 'I only wrote the letter. It was my grandfather who did it. But you know how he is about always being good to everybody. Is Mrs. Higgins well now?'

Higgins looked a trifle taken aback. He also was somewhat startled at hearing his noble landlord presented in the character of a benevolent being, full of engaging qualities.

'I – well, yes, your lordship,' he stammered; 'the missus is better since the trouble was took off her mind. It was worrying broke her down.'

'I'm glad of that,' said Fauntleroy. 'My grandfather was very sorry about your children having the scarlet fever, and so was I. He has had children himself. I'm his son's little boy, you know.'

Higgins was on the verge of being panic-stricken. he felt it would be the safer and more discreet plan not to look at the Earl, as it had been well known that his fatherly affection for his sons had been such that he had seen them about twice a year, and that when they had been ill he had promptly departed for London, because he would not be bored with doctors and nurses. It was a little trying therefore to his lordship's nerves to be told, while he looked on, his eyes gleaming from under his shaggy eyebrows, that he felt an interest in scarlet fever.

'You see, Higgins,' broke in the Earl with a fine grim smile, 'you people have been mistaken in me. Lord Fauntleroy understands me. When you want reliable information on the subject of my character, apply to him. Get into the carriage, Fauntleroy.'

And Fauntleroy jumped in, and the carriage rolled away down the green lane, and even when it turned the corner into the high road the Earl was still grimly smiling.

8 Learning to Ride

Lord Dorincourt had occasion to wear his grim smile many a time as the days passed by. Indeed, as his acquaintance with his grandson progressed, he wore the smile so often that there were moments when it almost losts its grimness. There is no denying that before Lord Fauntleroy had appeared on the scene the old man had been growing very tired of his loneliness and his gout and his seventy years. After so long a life of excitement and amusement, it was not agreeable to sit alone even in the most splendid room, with one foot on a gout-stool, and with no other diversion than flying into a rage, and shouting at a frightened footman who hated the sight of him. The old Earl was too clever a man not to know perfectly well that his servants detested him, and that even if he had visitors, they did not come for love of him – though some found a sort of amusement in his sharp, sarcastic talk, which spared no one. So long as he had been strong and well, he had gone from one place to another, pretending to amuse himself, though he had not really enjoyed it; and when his health began to fail, he felt tired of everything and shut himself up at Dorincourt with his gout and his newspapers and his books. But he could not read all the time, and he became more and more 'bored', as he called it. He hated the long nights and days, and he grew more and more savage and irritable. And then Fauntleroy came; and when the Earl saw the lad, fortunately for the little fellow, the secret pride of the grandfather was gratified at the outset. If Cedric had been a less handsome little fellow the old man might have taken so strong a dislike to the boy that he would not have given himself the chance to see his grandson's finer qualities. But he chose to think that Cedric's beauty and fearless spirit were the results of Dorincourt blood and a credit to the Dorincourt rank. And then when he heard the lad talk, and saw what a well-bred little fellow he was, notwithstanding his boyish ignorance of all that his new position meant, the old Earl liked his grandson more, and actually began to find himself rather entertained. It had amused him to give into those childish hands the power to bestow a benefit on poor Higgins. My lord cared nothing for poor Higgins, but it pleased him a little that his grandson would be talked about by the country people and would begin to be popular with the tenantry, even in his childhood. Then it had gratified him to drive to church with Cedric and to see excitement and interest caused by the arrival. He knew how the people would speak of the beauty of the little lad; of his fine, strong, straight little body; of his erect bearing, his handsome face and his bright hair, and how they would say (as the Earl had heard one woman exclaim to another) that the boy was 'every inch a lord'. My lord of Dorincourt was an arrogant old man, proud of his name, proud of his rank, and therefore proud to show the world that at last the House of Dorincourt had an heir who was worthy of the position he was to fill.

The morning the new pony had been tried the Earl had been so pleased that he had almost forgotten his gout. When the groom had brought out the pretty creature, which arched its brown glossy neck and tossed its fine head in the sun, the Earl had sat at the open window of the library and had looked on while Fauntleroy took his first riding lesson. He wondered if the boy would show signs of timidity. It was not a very small pony, and he had often seen children lose courage in making their first essay at riding.

Fauntleroy mounted in great delight. He had never been on a pony before, and he was in the highest spirits. Wilkins, the groom, led the animal by the bridle up and down before the library window.

'He's a well plucked 'un, he is,' Wilkins remarked in the stable afterwards with many grins, 'It weren't no trouble to put *him* up. An a old 'un wouldn't ha' sat any straighter when he *were* up. He ses – ses he to me, "Wilkins," he ses, "am I sitting up straight? They sit up straight at the circus," ses he. And I ses, "As straight as a arrer, your lordship!" – an' he laughs, as pleased as could be, an' he ses "That's right," he ses, "you tell me if I don't sit up straight, Wilkins."'

But sitting up straight and being led at a walk were not altogether and completely satisfactory. After a few minutes Fauntleroy spoke to his grandfather – watching him from the window.

'Can't I go by myself?' he asked. 'And can't I go faster? The boy on Fifth Avenue used to trot and canter!'

'Do you think you could trot and canter?' said the Earl.

'I should like to try,' answered Fauntleroy.

His lordship made a sign to Wilkins, who at the signal brought up his own horse and mounted it and took Fauntleroy's pony by the leading-rein.

'Now,' said the Earl, 'let him trot.'

The next few minutes were rather exciting to the small equestrian. He found that trotting was not so easy as walking, and the faster the pony trotted, the less easy it was.

'It j-jolts a g-goo-good deal – do-doesn't it?' he said to Wilkins. 'D-does it j-jolt y-you?'

'No, my lord,' answered Wilkins. 'You'll get used to it in time. Rise in your stirrups.'

'I'm ri-rising all the t-time,' said Fauntleroy.

He was both rising and falling rather uncomfortably and with many shakes and bounces. He was out of breath and his face grew red, but he held on with all his might, and sat as straight as he could. The Earl could see that from his window. When the riders came back within speaking distance, after they had been hidden by the trees a few minutes. Fauntleroy's hat was off, his cheeks were like poppics, and his lips were set, but he was still trotting manfully.

'Stop a minute!' said his grandfather. 'Where's your hat?'

Wilkins touched his. 'It fell off, your lordship,' he said with evident enjoyment. 'Wouldn't let me stop to pick it up, my lord.'

'Not much afraid, is he?' asked the Earl dryly.

'Him, your lordship!' exclaimed Wilkins, 'I shouldn't say as he knowed what it meant. I've taught young gen'lemen to ride afore, an' I never see one stick on more determiner.'

'Tired?' said the Earl to Fauntleroy. 'Want to get off?'

'It jolts you more than you think it will,' admitted his young lordship frankly. 'And it tires you a little too; but I don't want to get off. I want to learn how. As soon as I've got my breath I want to go back for the hat.'

The cleverest person in the world, if he had undertaken to teach Fauntleroy how to please the old man who watched him, could not have taught him anything which would have succeeded better. As the pony trotted off again towards the avenue, a faint colour crept up in the fierce old face, and the eyes, under the shaggy brows, gleamed with a pleasure such as his lordship had scarcely expected to know again. And he sat and watched quite eagerly until the sound of the horses' hoofs returned. When they did come, which was after some time, they came at a faster pace. Fauntleroy's hat was still off, Wilkins was carrying it for him; his cheeks were redder than before, and his hair was flying about his ears, but he came at quite a brisk canter.

'There,' he panted as they drew up, 'I c-cantered. I didn't do it as well as the boy on Fifth Avenue, but I did it, and I stayed on!'

He and Wilkins and the pony were close friends after that. Scarcely a day passed on which the country people did not see them out together, cantering gaily on the high road or through the green lanes. The children in the cottages would run to the door to look at the proud little brown pony with the gallant little figure sitting so straight in the saddle, and the young lord would snatch off his cap and swing it at them, and shout, 'Hallo! Good morning!' in a very unlordly manner, though with great heartiness. Sometimes he would stop and talk with the children, and once Wilkins came back to the Castle with a story of how Fauntleroy had insisted on dismounting near the village school, so that a boy who was lame and tired might ride home on his pony.

'An' I'm blessed,' said Wilkins, in telling the story at the stables, 'I'm blessed if he'd hear of anything else! He wouldn't let me get down, because he said the boy mightn't feel comfortable on a big horse. An' ses he, "Wilkins," ses he, "that boy's lame and I'm not, and I want to talk to him too." And up the lad has to get, and my lord trudges alongside of him with his hands in his pockets, and his cap on the back of his head, a-whistling and talking as easy as you please! And when we come to the cottage, an' the boy's mother come out all in a taking to see what's up, he whips off his cap an' ses he, "I've brought your son home, ma'am," ses he, "because his leg hurt him, and I don't think that stick is enough for him to lean on; and I'm going to ask my grandfather to have a pair of crutches made for him." An' I'm blest if the woman wasn't struck all of a heap, as well she might be! I thought I should 'a' hex-plodid, myself!'

When the Earl heard the story he was not angry, as Wilkins had been half afraid that he would be; on the contrary, he laughed outright, and called Fauntleroy up to him, and made him tell all about the matter from beginning to end, and then he laughed again. And actually, a few days later, the Dorincourt carriage stopped in the green lane before the cottage where the lame boy lived, and Fauntleroy jumped out and walked up to the door, carrying a pair of strong, light, new crutches, shouldered like a gun, and presented them to Mrs. Hartle (the lame boy's name was Hartle) with these words: 'My grandfather's compliments, and if you please, these are for your boy, and we hope he will get better.'

'I said your compliments,' he explained to the Earl when he returned to the carriage. 'You didn't tell me to, but I thought perhaps you forgot. That was right, wasn't it?'

And the Earl laughed again, and did not say it was not. In fact, the two were becoming more intimate every day, and every day Fauntleroy's faith in his lordship's benevolence and virtue increased. He had no doubt whatever that his grandfather was the most amiable and generous of elderly gentlemen. Certainly he himself found his wishes gratified almost before they were uttered; and such gifts and pleasures were lavished upon him, that he was sometimes almost bewildered by his own possessions. Apparently he was to have everything he wanted, and to do everything he wished to do. And though this would certainly not have been a very wise plan to pursue with all small boys, his young lordship bore it amazingly well. Perhaps, notwithstanding his sweet nature, he might have been somewhat spoiled by it, if it had not been for the hours he spent with his mother at Court Lodge. That 'best friend' of his watched over him very closely and tenderly. The two had many long talks together, and he never went back to the Castle with her kisses on his cheeks without carrying in his heart some simple, pure words worth remembering.

There was one thing, it is true, which puzzled the little fellow very much. He thought over the mystery of it much oftener than anyone supposed; even his mother did not know how often he pondered on it; the Earl for a long time never suspected that he did so at all. But being quick to observe, the little boy could not help wondering why it was that his mother and grandfather never seemed to meet. He had noticed that they never did meet. When the Dorincourt carriage stopped at Court Lodge the Earl never alighted, and on the rare occasions of his lordship's going to church, Fauntleroy was always left to speak to his mother in the porch alone, or perhaps to go home with her. And yet, every day, fruit and flowers were sent to Court Lodge from the hothouses at the Castle. But the one virtuous action of the Earl's which had set him upon the pinnacle of perfection in Cedric's eyes, was what he had done soon after that first Sunday when Mrs. Errol had walked home from church unattended. About a week later, when Cedric was going one day to visit his mother, he found at the door, instead of the large carriage and prancing pair, a pretty little brougham and a handsome bay horse.

'That is a present from you to your mother,' the Earl said abruptly. 'She cannot go walking about the country. She needs a carriage. The man who drives will take charge of it. It is a present from *you*.'

Fauntleroy's delight could but feebly express itself. He could scarcely contain himself until he reached the lodge. His mother was gathering roses in the garden. He flung himself out of the little brougham and flew to her.

'Dearest!' he cried. 'Could you believe it? This is yours! He says it is a present from me. It is your own carriage to drive everywhere in!'

He was so happy that she did not know what to say. She could not have borne to spoil his pleasure by refusing to accept the gift, even though it came from the man who chose to consider himself her enemy. She was obliged to step into the carriage, roses and all, and let herself be taken for a drive, while Fauntleroy told her stories of his grandfather's goodness and amiability. They were such innocent stories that sometimes she could not help laughing a little, and then she would draw her little boy closer to her side and kiss him, feeling glad that he could see only good in the old man who had so few friends.

The very next day after that, Fauntleroy wrote to Mr. Hobbs. He wrote quite a long letter, and after the first copy was written, he brought it to his grandfather to be inspected.

'Because', he said, 'it's so uncertain about the spelling. And if you'll tell me the mistakes, I'll write it out again.'

This was what he had written:

My dear mr hobbs i want to tell you about my granfarther he is the best earl you ever new it is a mistake about earls being tirents he is not a tirent at all i wish you new him you would be good friends i am sure you would he has the gout in his foot and is a grate sufrer but he is so pashent i love him more every day becaus no one could help loving an earl that who is kind to every one in this world i wish you could talk to him he knows everything in the world you can ask him any question but he has never plaid base ball he has given me a pony and cart and my mamma a bewtifle carige and i have three rooms and toys of all kinds it would serprise you you would like the castle and the park it is such a large castle you could lose yourself wilkins tells me wilkins is my groom he says there is a dungon under the castle it is so pretty every thing in the park would serprise you there are such big trees and there are deers and rabbits and games flying about in the cover my grandfarther is very rich but he is not proud and orty as you thought earls always were i like to be with him the people are so polite and kind they take of their hats to you and the women make curtsies and sometimes say god bless you i can ride now but at first it shook me when i troted my grandfarther let a poor man stay on his farm when he could not pay his rent and mrs mellon went to take wine and things to his sick children i should like to see you and i wish dearest could live at the castle but i am very happy when i don't miss her too much and i love my granfarther every one does plees write soon.

your afechshnet old friend

CEDRIC ERROL

p s no one is in the dungon my granfarther never had any one langwishin in there

p s he is such a good earl he reminds me of you he is a unerversle favrit

'Do you miss your mother very much?' asked the Earl when he had finished reading this.

'Yes,' said Fauntleroy, 'I miss her all the time.'

He went and stood before the Earl and put his hand on his knee looking up at him.

'*You* don't miss her, do you?' he said.

'I don't know her,' answered his lordship rather crustily.

'I know that,' said Fauntleroy, 'and that's what makes me wonder. She told me not to ask you any questions, and – and I won't, but sometimes I can't help thinking, you know, and it makes me all puzzled. But I'm not going to ask any questions. And when I miss her very much, I go and look out of my window to where I see her light shine for me every night through an open place in the trees. It is a long way off, but she puts it in her window as soon as it is dark and I can see it twinkle far away, and I know what it says.'

'What does it say?' asked my lord.

'It says, "Good night, God keep you all the night!" – just what she used to say when we were together. Every night she used to say that to me, and every morning she said, "God bless you all the day!" So you see I am quite safe all the time——'

'Quite, I have no doubt,' said his lordship dryly. And he drew down his beetling eyebrows and looked at the little boy so fixedly and so long that Fauntleroy wondered what he could be thinking of.

9 The Poor Cottages

The fact was, his lordship the Earl of Dorincourt thought in those days of many things of which he had never thought before, and all his thoughts were in one way or another connected with his grandson. His pride was the strongest part of his nature, and the boy gratified it at every point. Through this pride he began to find a new interest in life. He began to take pleasure in showing his heir to the world. The world had known of his disappointment in his sons; so there was an agreeable touch of triumph in exhibiting this new Lord Fauntleroy, who could disappoint no one. He wished the child to appreciate his own power and to understand the splendour of his position; he wished that others should realize it too. He made plans for his future. Sometimes in secret he actually found himself wishing that his own past life had been a better one, and that there had been less in it than this pure, childish heart would shrink from if it knew the truth. It was not agreeable to think how the beautiful innocent face would look if its owner should be made by any chance to understand that his grandfather had been called for many a year 'the wicked Earl of Dorincourt'. The thought even made him feel a trifle nervous. He did not wish the boy to find it out. Sometimes in this new interest he forgot his gout, and after a while his doctor was surprised to find his noble patient's health growing better than he had expected it ever would be again. Perhaps the Earl grew better because the time did not pass so slowly for him, and he had something to think of besides his pains and infirmities.

One fine morning people were amazed to see little Lord Fauntleroy riding his pony with another companion than Wilkins. This new companion rode a tall, powerful, grey horse, and was no other than the Earl himself. It was in fact Fauntleroy who had suggested this plan. As he had been on the point of mounting his pony he had said rather wistfully to his grandfather:

'I wish you were going with me. When I go away I feel lonely because you are left all by yourself in such a big castle. I wish you could ride too.'

And the greatest excitement had been aroused in the stables a few minutes later by the arrival of an order that Selim was to be saddled for the Earl. After that Selim was saddled almost every day; and the people became accustomed to the sight of the tall grey horse carrying the tall grey old man with his handsome, fierce, eagle face, by the side of the brown pony which bore little Lord Fauntleroy. And in their rides together through the green lanes and pretty country roads, the two riders became more intimate than ever. And gradually the old man heard a great deal about 'Dearest' and her life. As Fauntleroy trotted by the big horse he chatted gaily. There could not well have been a brighter little comrade, his nature was so happy. It was he who talked the most. The Earl often was silent, listening and watching the joyous, glowing face. Sometimes he would tell his young companion to set the pony off at a gallop, and when the little fellow dashed off, sitting so straight and fearless, he would watch the boy with a gleam of pride and pleasure in his eyes; and Fauntleroy when, after such a dash, he came back waving his cap with a laughing shout, always felt that he and his grandfather were very good friends indeed.

One thing that the Earl discovered was that his son's wife did not lead an idle life. It was not long before he learned that the poor people knew her very well indeed. When there was sickness or sorrow or poverty in any house, the little brougham often stood before the door.

'Do you know,' said Fauntleroy once, 'they all say, "God bless you!" when they see her, and the children are glad. There are some who go to her house to be taught to sew. She says she feels so rich now that she wants to help the poor ones.'

It had not displeased the Earl to find that the mother of his heir had a beautiful young face and looked as much like a lady as if she had been a duchess, and in one way it did not displease him to know that she was popular and beloved by the poor. And yet he was often conscious of a hard, jealous pang when he saw how she filled her child's heart and how the boy clung to her as his best beloved. The old man would have desired to stand first himself and have no rival.

That same morning he drew up his horse on an elevated point of the moor over which they rode, and made a gesture with his whip, over the broad, beautiful landscape spread before them.

'Do you know that all that land belongs to me?' he said to Fauntleroy.

'Does it?' answered Fauntleroy. 'How much it is to belong to one person, and how beautiful!'

'Do you know that some day it will all belong to you – that and a great deal more?'

'To me!' exclaimed Fauntleroy in rather an awestricken voice. 'When?'

'When I am dead,' his grandfather answered.

'Then I don't want it,' said Fauntleroy; 'I want you to live always.'

'That's kind,' answered the Earl in his dry way; 'nevertheless some day it will all be yours – some day you will be the Earl of Dorincourt.'

Little Lord Fauntleroy sat very still in his saddle for a few moments. He looked over the broad moors, the green farms, the beautiful copses, the cottages in the lanes, the pretty villages, and over the trees to where the turrets of the great castle rose, grey and stately. Then he gave a queer little sigh.

'What are you thinking of?' asked the Earl.

'I am thinking', replied Fauntleroy, 'what a little boy I am, and of what Dearest said to me.'

'What was it?' inquired the Earl.

'She said that perhaps it was not so easy to be very rich; that if anyone had so many things always, one might sometimes forget that everyone else was not so fortunate, and that one who is rich should always be careful and try to remember. I was talking to her about how good you were, and she said that was such a good thing, because an earl had so much power, and if he cared only about his own pleasure and never thought about the people who lived on his lands, they might have trouble that he could help – and there were so many people, and it would be such a hard thing. And I was just looking at all those houses,

552   Little Lord Fauntleroy

and thinking how I should have to find out about the people when I was an earl. How did you find out about them?'

As his lordship's knowledge of his tenantry consisted in finding out which of them paid their rent promptly, and in turning out those who did not, this was rather a hard question. 'Newick finds out for me,' he said, and he pulled his great grey moustache, and looked at his small questioner rather uneasily.

'We will go home now,' he added; 'and when you are an earl, see to it that you are a better one than I have been!'

He was very silent as they rode home. He felt it to be almost incredible that he, who had never really loved anyone in his life, should find himself growing so fond of this little fellow – as without doubt he was. At first he had only been pleased and proud of Cedric's beauty and bravery, but there was something more than pride in his feeling now. He laughed a grim, dry laugh all to himself sometimes, when he thought how he liked to have the boy near him, how he liked to hear his voice, and how in secret he really wished to be liked and thought well of by his small grandson.

'I'm an old fellow in my dotage, and I have nothing else to think of,' he would say to himself; and yet he knew it was not that altogether. And if he allowed himself to admit the truth, he would perhaps have found himself obliged to own that the very things which attracted him, in spite of himself, were the qualities he had never possessed – the frank, true, kindly nature, the affectionate trustfulness which could never think evil.

It was only about a week after that ride when, after a visit to his mother, Fauntleroy came into the library with a troubled, thoughtful face. He sat down in that high-backed chair in which he had sat on the evening of his arrival, and for a while he looked at the embers on the hearth. The Earl watched him in silence, wondering what was coming. It was evident that Cedric had something on his mind. At last he looked up, 'Does Newick know all about the people?' he asked.

'It is his business to know about them,' said his lordship. 'Been neglecting it – has he?'

Contradictory as it may seem, there was nothing which entertained and edified him more than the little fellow's interest in his tenantry. He had never taken any interest in them himself, but it pleased him well enough that, with all his childish habits of thought and in the midst of all his childish amusements and high spirits, there should be such a quaint seriousness working in the curly head.

'There is a place,' said Fauntleroy, looking up at him with wide-open, horror-stricken eyes. 'Dearest has seen it; it is at the other end of the village. The houses are close together, and almost falling down; you can scarcely breathe; and the people are so poor, and everything is dreadful! Often they have fever and the children die; and it makes them wicked to live like that, and be so poor and miserable! It is worse than Michael and Bridget! The rain comes in at the roof! Dearest went to see a poor woman who lived there. She would not let me come near her until she had changed all her things. The tears ran down her cheeks when she told me about it!'

The tears had come into his own eyes, but he smiled through them.

'I told her you didn't know, and I would tell you,' he said. He jumped down and came and leaned against the Earl's chair. 'You can make it all right,' he said, 'just as you made it all right for Higgins. You always make it all right for everybody. I told her you would, and that Newick must have forgotten to tell you.'

The Earl looked down at the hand on his knee. Newick had not forgotten to tell him; in fact, Newick had spoken to him more than once of the desperate condition of the end of the village known as Earl's Court. He knew all about the tumbledown, miserable cottages, and the bad drainage, and the damp walls and broken windows and leaking roofs, and all about the poverty, the fever and the misery. Mr. Mordaunt had painted it all to him in the strongest words he could use, and his lordship had used violent language in response; and, when his gout had been at the worst, he had said that the sooner the people of Earl's Court died and were buried by the parish the better it would be – and there was an end of the matter. And yet, as he looked at the small hand on his knee, and from the small hand to the honest, earnest, frank-eyed face, he was actually a little ashamed both of Earl's Court and of himself.

'What!' he said. 'You want to make a builder of model cottages of me, do you?' And he positively put his own hand upon the childish one and stroked it.

'Those must be pulled down,' said Fauntleroy with great eagerness. 'Dearest says so. Let us – let us go and have them pulled down tomorrow. The people will be so glad when they see you! They'll know you have come to help them!' And his eyes shone like stars in his glowing face.

The Earl rose from his chair and put his hand on the child's shoulder. 'Let us go out and take our walk on the terrace,' he said with a short laugh, 'and we can talk it over.'

And though he laughed two or three times again, as they walked to and fro on the broad stone terrace, where they walked together almost every fine evening, he seemed to be thinking of something which did not displease him, and still he kept his hand on his small companion's shoulder.

10 The Earl Alarmed

The truth was that Mrs. Errol had found a great many sad things in the course of her work among the poor of the little village that appeared so picturesque when it was seen from the moor-sides. Everything was not as picturesque when seen near by, as it looked from a distance. She had found idleness and poverty and ignorance where there should have been comfort and industry. And she had discovered after a while that Erleboro was considered to be the worst village in that part of the country. Mr. Mordaunt had told her a great many of his difficulties and discouragements, and she had found out a great deal by herself. The agents who had managed the property had always been chosen to please the Earl, and had cared nothing for the degradation and wretchedness of the poor tenants. Many things, therefore, had been neglected which should have been attended to, and matters had gone from bad to worse.

As to Earl's Court, it was a disgrace, with its dilapidated houses and miserable, careless, sickly people. When first Mrs. Errol went to the place, it made her shudder. Such ugliness and slovenliness and want seemed worse in a country place than in a city. It seemed as if there it might be helped. And as she looked at the squalid, uncared-for children growing up in the midst of vice and brutal indifference, she thought of her own little boy spending his days in the great, splendid castle, guarded and served like a young prince, having no wish ungratified, and knowing nothing but luxury and ease and beauty. And a bold thought came into her wise little mother-heart. Gradually she had begun to see, as had others, that it had been her boy's good fortune to please the Earl very much, and that he would scarcely be likely to be denied anything for which he expressed a desire.

'The Earl would give him everything,' she said to Mr. Mordaunt. 'He would indulge his every whim. Why should not that indulgence be used for the good of others? It is for me to see that this shall come to pass.'

She knew she could trust the kind, childish heart; so she told the little fellow the story of Earl's Court, feeling sure that he would speak of it to his grandfather, and hoping that some good results would follow.

And strange as it appeared to everyone, good results did follow. The fact was that the strongest power to influence the Earl was his grandson's perfect confidence in him – the fact that Cedric always believed that his grandfather was going to do what was right and generous. He could not quite make up his mind to let him discover that he had no inclination to be generous at all, and that he wanted his own way on all occasions, whether it was right or wrong. It was such a novelty to be regarded with admiration as a benefactor of the entire human race and the soul of nobility, that he did not enjoy the idea of looking into the affectionate brown eyes and saying 'I am a violent, selfish old rascal; I never did a generous thing in my life, and I don't care about Earl's Court or the poor people' – or something which would amount to the same thing. He actually had learned to be fond enough of that small boy with the mop of yellow love-locks, to feel that he himself would prefer to be guilty of an amiable action now and then. And so – though he laughed at himself – after some reflection, he sent for Newick, and had quite a long interview with him on the subject of the Court, and it was decided that the wretched hovels should be pulled down and new houses should be built.

'It is Lord Fauntleroy who insists on it,' he said dryly; 'he thinks it will improve the property. You can tell the tenants that it's his idea.' And he looked down at his small lordship, who was lying on the hearthrug playing with Dougal. The great dog was the lad's constant companion, and followed him about everywhere, stalking solemnly after him when he walked, and trotting majestically behind when he rode or drove.

Of course both the country people and the town people heard of the proposed improvement. At first many of them would not believe it;

but when a small army of workmen arrived and commenced pulling down the crazy, squalid cottages, people began to understand that little Lord Fauntleroy had done them a good turn again, and that through his innocent interference the scandal of Earl's Court had at last been removed. If he had only known how they talked about him and praised him everywhere, and prophesied great things for him when he grew up, how astonished he would have been! But he never suspected it. He lived his simple, happy child life, frolicking about in the park; chasing the rabbits to their burrows; lying under the trees on the grass, or on the rug in the library, reading wonderful books and talking to the Earl about them, and then telling the stories again to his mother; writing long letters to Dick and Mr. Hobbs, who responded in characteristic fashion; riding out at his grandfather's side, or with Wilkins as escort. As they rode through the market town he used to see the people turn and look, and he noticed that as they lifted their hats their faces often brightened very much, but he thought it was all because his grandfather was with him.

'They are so fond of you,' he once said, looking up at his lordship with a bright smile. 'Do you see how glad they are when they see you? I hope they will some day be as fond of me. It must be nice to have *every*body like you.'

And he felt quite proud to be the grandson of so greatly admired and beloved an individual.

When the cottages were being built, the lad and his grandfather used to ride over to Earl's Court together to look at them, and Fauntleroy was full of interest. He would dismount from his pony and go and make acquaintance with the workmen, asking them questions about building and bricklaying, and telling them things about America. After two or three such conversations, he was able to enlighten the Earl on the subject of brickmaking as they rode home.

'I always like to know about things like those,' he said, 'because you never know what you are coming to.'

When he left them the workmen used to talk him over among themselves, and laugh at his odd, innocent speeches; but they liked him and liked to see him stand among them, talking away, with his hands in his pockets, his hat pushed back on his curls, and his small

'*The lad and his grandfather used to ride over to
Earl's Court together to look at the cottages*'

face full of eagerness. 'He's a rare 'un,' they used to say. 'An' a noice little outspoken chap too. Not much o' th' bad stock in him.' And they would go home and tell their wives about him, and the women would tell each other, and so it came about that almost everyone talked of, or knew some story of, little Lord Fauntleroy; and gradually almost everyone knew that the 'wicked Earl' had found something he cared for at last – something which had touched and even warmed his hard, bitter old heart.

But no one knew quite how much it had been warmed, and how day by day the old man found himself caring more and more for the child, who was the only creature that had ever trusted him. He found himself looking forward to the time when Cedric would be a young man, strong and beautiful, with life all before him, but having still that kind heart and the power to make friends everywhere; and the Earl wondered what the lad would do, and how he would use his gifts. Often as he watched the little fellow lying upon the hearth, conning some big book, the light shining on the bright young head, his old eyes would gleam and his cheek would flush.

'The boy can do anything,' he would say to himself, 'anything!'

He never spoke to anyone else of his feeling for Cedric; when he spoke of him to others it was always with the same grim smile. But Fauntleroy soon knew that his grandfather loved him and always liked him to be near – near to his chair if they were in the library, opposite to him at table or by his side when he rode or drove or took his evening walk on the broad terrace.

'Do you remember,' Cedric said once, looking up from his book as he lay on the rug, 'do you remember what I said to you that first night about our being good companions? I don't think any people could be better friends than we are, do you?'

'We are pretty good companions, I should say,' replied his lordship. 'Come here.'

Fauntleroy scrambled up and went to him.

'Is there anything you want?' the Earl asked. 'Anything you have not?'

The little fellow's brown eyes fixed themselves on his grandfather with a rather wistful look.

'Only one thing,' he answered.

'What is that?' inquired the Earl.

Fauntleroy was silent a second. He had not thought matters over to himself so long for nothing.

'What is it?' my lord repeated.

Fauntleroy answered.

'It is Dearest,' he said.

The old Earl winced a little.

'But you see her almost every day,' he said. 'Is not that enough?'

'I used to see her all the time,' said Fauntleroy. 'She used to kiss me when I went to sleep at night, and in the morning she was always there, and we could tell each other things without waiting.'

The old eyes and young ones looked into each other through a moment of silence. Then the Earl knitted his brows.

'Do you *never* forget about your mother?' he said.

'No,' answered Fauntleroy, 'never; and she never forgets about me. I shouldn't forget about *you* you know, if I didn't live with you. I should think about you all the more.'

'Upon my word,' said the Earl, after looking at him a moment longer, 'I believe you would!'

The jealous pang that came when the boy spoke so of his mother seemed even stronger than it had been before – it was stronger because of this old man's increasing affection for the boy.

But it was not long before he had other pangs, so much harder to face that he almost forgot, for the time, he had ever hated his son's wife at all. And in a strange and startling way it happened. One evening, just before the Earl's Court cottages were completed, there was a grand dinner party at Dorincourt. There had not been such a party at the Castle for a long time. A few days before it took place, Sir Harry Lorridaile and Lady Lorridaile, who was the Earl's only sister, actually came for a visit – a thing which caused the greatest excitement in the village and set Mrs. Dibble's shop-bell tinkling madly again, because it was well known that Lady Lorridaile had only been to Dorincourt once since her marriage, thirty-five years before. She was a handsome old lady with white curls and dimpled, peachy cheeks, and she was as good as gold, but she had never approved of her brother any more than did the rest of the world, and having a strong will of her own and not being at all afraid to speak her mind frankly, she had, after several lively quarrels with his lordship, seen very little of him since her young days.

She had heard a great deal of him that was not pleasant through the years in which they had been separated. She had heard about his neglect of his wife, and of the poor lady's death; and of his indifference to his children; and of the two weak, vicious, unprepossessing elder boys who had been no credit to him or to anyone else. Those two elder sons, Bevis and Maurice, she had never seen; but once there had come to Lorridaile Park a tall, stalwart, beautiful young fellow about eighteen years old who had told her that he was her nephew Cedric Errol, and that he had come to see her because he was passing near the place and wished to look at his Aunt Constantia, of whom he had heard his mother speak. Lady Lorridaile's kind heart had warmed through and through at the sight of the young man, and she had made him stay with her a week, and petted him and made much of him and admired him immensely. He was so sweet-tempered, light-hearted, spirited a lad, that when he went away she had hoped to see him often again; but she never did, because the Earl had been in a bad humour when he went back to Dorincourt, and had forbidden him ever to go to Lorridaile Park again. But Lady Lorridaile had always remembered him tenderly, and though she feared he had made a rash marriage in America, she had been very angry when she heard how he had been cast off by his father and that no one really knew where or how he lived. At last there came a rumour of his death, and then Bevis had been thrown from his horse and killed, and Maurice had died in Rome of the fever; and soon after came the story of the American child who was to be found and brought home as Lord Fauntleroy.

'Probably to be ruined as the others were,' she said to her husband, 'unless his mother is good enough and has a will of her own to help her to take care of him.'

But when she heard that Cedric's mother had been parted from him she was almost too indignant for words.

'It is disgraceful, Harry!' she said. 'Fancy a child of that age being taken from his mother, and made the companion of a man like my brother! The old Earl will either be brutal to the boy or indulge him until he is a little monster. If I thought it would do any good to write——'

'It wouldn't, Constantia,' said Sir Harry.

'I know it wouldn't,' she answered. 'I know his lordship the Earl of Dorincourt too well; but it is outrageous.'

Not only the poor people and farmers heard about little Lord Fauntleroy; others knew of him. He was talked about so much and there were so many stories of him – of his beauty, his sweet temper, his popularity and his growing influence over the Earl his grandfather – that rumours of him reached the gentry at their country places and he was heard of in more than one county of England. People talked about him at the dinner-tables, ladies pitied his young mother, and wondered if the boy were as handsome as he was said to be, and men who knew the Earl and his habits laughed heartily at the stories of the little fellow's belief in his lordship's amiability. Sir Thomas Asshe of Asshaine Hall, being in Erleboro one day, met the Earl and his grandson riding together and stopped to shake hands with my lord and congratulate him on his change of looks and on his recovery from the gout. 'And d'ye know,' he said, when he spoke of the incident afterwards, 'the old man looked as proud as a turkey-cock; and upon my word I don't wonder, for a handsomer, finer lad than his grandson I never saw! As straight as a dart, and sat his pony like a young trooper!'

And so by degrees Lady Lorridaile, too, heard of the child; she heard about Higgins, and the lame boy, and the cottages at Earl's Court, and a score of other things – and she began to wish to see the little fellow. And just as she was wondering how it might be brought about, to her utter astonishment, she received a letter from her brother inviting her to come with her husband to Dorincourt.

'It seems incredible!' she exclaimed. 'I have heard it said that the child has worked miracles, and I begin to believe it. They say my brother adores the boy and can scarcely endure to have him out of sight. And he is so proud of him! Actually I believe he wants to show him to us.' And she accepted the invitation at once.

When she reached Dorincourt Castle with Sir Harry, it was late in the afternoon, and she went to her room at once before seeing her brother. Having dressed for dinner she entered the drawing-room. The Earl was there standing near the fire and looking very tall and imposing; and at his side stood a little boy in black velvet, and a large Vandyke collar of rich lace – a little fellow whose round bright face was so handsome, and who turned upon her such beautiful, candid brown eyes, that she almost uttered an exclamation of pleasure and surprise at the sight.

As she shook hands with the Earl, she called him by the name she had not used since her girlhood.

'What, Molyneux,' she said, 'is this the child?'

'Yes, Constantia,' answered the Earl, 'this is the boy. Fauntleroy, this is your grand-aunt, Lady Constantia Lorridaile.'

'How do you do, grand-aunt?' said Fauntleroy.

Lady Lorridaile put her hand on his shoulder, and after looking down into his upraised face a few seconds, kissed him warmly.

'I am your Aunt Constantia,' she said, 'and I loved your poor papa, and you are very like him.'

'It makes me glad when I am told I am like him,' answered Fauntleroy, 'because it seems as if everyone liked him – just like Dearest, eszackly – Aunt Constantia' (adding the two words after a second's pause).

Lady Lorridaile was delighted. She bent and kissed him again, and from that moment they were warm friends.

'Well, Molyneux,' she said aside to the Earl afterwards, 'it could not possibly be better than this!'

'I think not,' answered his lordship dryly. 'He is a fine little fellow. We are great friends. He believes me to be the most charming and sweet-tempered of philanthropists. I will confess to you, Constantia – as you would find it out if I did not – that I am in some slight danger of becoming rather an old fool about him.'

'What does his mother think of you?' asked Lady Lorridaile, with her usual straightforwardness.

'I have not asked her,' answered the Earl, slightly scowling.

'Well,' said Lady Lorridaile, 'I will be frank with you at the outset, Molyneux, and tell you I don't approve of your course, and that it is my intention to call on Mrs. Errol as soon as possible; so if you wish to quarrel with me you had better mention it at once. What I hear of the young creature makes me quite sure that the child owes her everything. We were told even at Lorridaile Park that your poorer tenants adore her already.'

'They adore *him*,' said the Earl, nodding towards Fauntleroy. 'As to Mrs. Errol, you'll find her a pretty little woman. I'm rather in debt to her for giving some of her beauty to the boy, and you can go to see her if you like. All I ask is that she will remain at Court Lodge, and that you will not ask me to go and see her,' and he scowled a little again.

'But he doesn't hate her as much as he used to, that is plain enough to me,' her ladyship said to Sir Harry afterwards. 'And he is a changed man in a measure, and, incredible as it may seem, Harry, it is my opinion that he is being made into a human being, through nothing more or less than his affection for that innocent, affectionate little fellow. Why, the child actually loves him – leans on his chair and against his knees. My lord's own children would as soon have thought of nestling up to a tiger.'

The very next day she went to call upon Mrs. Errol. When she returned she said to her brother:

'Molyneux, she is the loveliest little woman I ever saw! She has a voice like a silver bell, and you may thank her for making the boy what he is. She has given him more than her beauty, and you make a great mistake in not persuading her to come and take charge of you. I shall invite her to Lorridaile.'

'She'll not leave the boy,' replied the Earl.

'I must have the boy too,' said Lady Lorridaile, laughing.

But she knew Fauntleroy would not be given up to her, and each day she saw more clearly how closely those two had grown to each other, and how all the proud, grim old man's ambition and hope and love centred themselves in the child, and how the warm, innocent nature returned his affection with most perfect trust and faith.

She knew too that the prime reason for the great dinner party was the Earl's secret desire to show the world his grandson and heir; and to let people see that the boy who had been so much spoken of and described was even a finer little specimen of boyhood than rumour had made him.

'Bevis and Maurice were such a bitter humiliation to him,' she said to her husband. 'Everyone knew it. He actually hated them. His pride has full sway here.' Perhaps there was not one person who accepted the invitation without feeling some curiosity about little Lord Fauntleroy, and wondering if he would be on view.

And when the time came he was on view.

'The lad has good manners,' said the Earl. 'He will be in no one's way. Children are usually idiots or bores – mine were both – but he can actually answer when he's spoken to, and be silent when he is not. He is never offensive.'

But he was not allowed to be silent very long. Everyone had something to say to him. The fact was they wished to make him talk. The ladies petted him and asked him questions and the men asked him questions too, and joked with him, as the men on the steamer had done when he crossed the Atlantic. Fauntleroy did not quite understand why they laughed so sometimes when he answered them, but he was so used to seeing people amused when he was quite serious, that he did not mind. He thought the whole evening delightful. The magnificent rooms were so brilliant with lights, there were so many flowers, the gentlemen seemed so gay, and the ladies wore such beautiful, wonderful dresses, and such sparkling ornaments in their hair and on their necks. There was one young lady who, he heard them say, had just come down from London, where she had spent 'the season'; and she was so charming that he could not keep his eyes from her. She was a rather tall young lady, with a proud little head and very soft hair, and large eyes the colour of purple pansies, and the colour of her cheeks and lips was like that of a rose. She was dressed in a beautiful white dress, and had pearls around her throat. There was one strange thing about this young lady. So many gentlemen stood near her, and seemed anxious to please her, that Fauntleroy thought she must be something like a princess. He was so much interested in her that without knowing it he drew nearer and nearer to her and at last she turned and spoke to him.

'Come here, Lord Fauntleroy,' she said, smiling; 'and tell me why you look at me so.'

'I was thinking how beautiful you are,' his young lordship replied.

Then all the gentlemen laughed outright, and the young lady laughed a little too, and the rose colour in her cheeks brightened.

'Ah, Fauntleroy,' said one of the gentlemen who had laughed most heartily, 'make the most of your time! When you are older you will not have the courage to say that.'

'But nobody could help saying it,' said Fauntleroy sweetly. 'Could you help it? Don't *you* think she is pretty too?'

'We are not allowed to say what we think,' said the gentleman, while the rest laughed more than ever.

But the beautiful young lady – her name was Miss Vivian Herbert – put out her hand and drew Cedric to her side, looking prettier than before, if possible.

'Lord Fauntleroy shall say what he thinks,' she said; 'and I am much obliged to him. I am sure he thinks what he says.' And she kissed him on his cheek.

'I think you are prettier than anyone I ever saw,' said Fauntleroy, looking at her with innocent, admiring eyes, 'except Dearest. Of course, I couldn't think anyone *quite* as pretty as Dearest. I think she is the prettiest person in the world.'

'I am sure she is,' said Miss Vivian Herbert. And she laughed and kissed his cheek again.

She kept him by her side a great part of the evening, and the group of which they were the centre was very gay. He did not know how it happened, but before long he was telling them all about America, and the Republican Rally, and Mr. Hobbs and Dick, and in the end he proudly produced from his pocket Dick's parting gift – the red silk handkerchief.

'I put it in my pocket tonight because it was a party,' he said. 'I thought Dick would like me to wear it at a party.'

And queer as the big, flaming, spotted thing was, there was a serious, affectionate look in his eyes, which prevented his audience from laughing very much.

'You see I like it,' he said, 'because Dick is my friend.'

But though he was talked to so much, as the Earl had said, he was in no one's way. He could be quiet and listen when others talked, and so no one found him tiresome. A slight smile crossed more than one face when several times he went and stood near his grandfather's chair, or sat on a stool close to him, watching him and absorbing every word he uttered with the most charmed interest. Once he stood so near the chair's arm that his cheek touched the Earl's shoulder, and his lordship, detecting the general smile, smiled a little himself. He knew what the lookers-on were thinking, and he felt some secret amusement in their seeing what a good friend he was to this youngster, who might have been expected to share the popular opinion of him.

Mr. Havisham had been expected to arrive in the afternoon, but, strange to say, he was late. Such a thing had really never been known to happen before during all the years in which he had been a visitor at Dorincourt Castle. He was so late that the guests were on the point of rising to go in to dinner when he arrived. When he approached his host the Earl regarded him with amazement. He looked as if he had been hurried or agitated; his dry, keen old face was actually pale.

'I was detained', he said, in a low voice to the Earl, 'by – an extraordinary event.'

It was as unlike the methodic old lawyer to be agitated by anything as it was to be late, but it was evident that he had been disturbed. At dinner he ate scarcely anything, and two or three times, when he was spoken to, he started as if his thoughts were far away. At dessert, when Fauntleroy came in, he looked at him more than once, nervously and uneasily. Fauntleroy noted the look and wondered at it. He and Mr. Havisham were on friendly terms, and they usually exchanged smiles.

The lawyer seemed to have forgotten to smile that evening.

The fact was he forgot everything but the strange and painful news he knew he must tell the Earl before the night was over – the strange news which he knew would be so terrible a shock, and which would change the face of everything. As he looked about at the splendid rooms and the brilliant company – at the people gathered together, he knew, more that they might see the bright-haired little fellow near the Earl's chair than for any other reason – as he looked at the proud old man and at little Lord Fauntleroy smiling at his side, he really felt quite shaken, notwithstanding that he was a hardened old lawyer. What a blow it was that he must deal them!

He did not exactly know how the long superb dinner ended. He sat through it as if he were in a dream, and several times he saw the Earl glance at him in surprise.

But it was over at last, and the gentlemen joined the ladies in the drawing-room. They found Fauntleroy sitting on a sofa with Miss Vivian Herbert – the great beauty of the last London season; they had been looking at some pictures, and he was thanking his companion, as the door opened.

'I'm ever so much obliged to you for being so kind to me!' he was saying; 'I never was at a party before, and I've enjoyed myself so much!'

He had enjoyed himself so much that when the gentlemen gathered about Miss Herbert again and began to talk to her, as he listened and tried to understand their laughing speeches his eyelids began to droop. They drooped until they covered his eyes two or three times, and then the sound of Miss Herbert's low, pretty laugh would bring him back, and he would open them again for about two seconds. He was quite sure he was not going to sleep, but there was a large, yellow satin cushion behind him and his head sank against it, and after a while his eyelids drooped for the last time. They did not even quite open when, as it seemed a long time after, someone kissed him lightly on the cheek. It was Miss Vivian Herbert, who was going away, and she spoke to him softly.

'Good night, little Lord Fauntleroy,' she said. 'Sleep well.'

And in the morning he did not know that he had tried to open his eyes and had murmured sleepily:

'Good night – I'm so – glad – I saw you – you are so – pretty——'

He only had a very faint recollection of hearing the gentlemen laugh again and of wondering why they did it.

No sooner had the last guest left the room than Mr. Havisham turned from his place by the fire, and stepped nearer the sofa, where he stood looking down at the sleeping occupant. Little Lord Fauntleroy was taking his ease luxuriously. One leg crossed the other and swung over the edge of the sofa; one arm was flung easily above his head; the warm flush of healthy, happy, childish sleep was on his quiet face; his waving tangle of bright hair strayed over the yellow satin cushion. He made a picture well worth looking at.

As Mr. Havisham looked at it, he put his hand up and rubbed his shaven chin, with a harassed countenance.

'Well, Havisham,' said the Earl's harsh voice behind him. 'What is it? It is evident something has happened. What was the extraordinary event, if I may ask?'

Mr. Havisham turned from the sofa, still rubbing his chin.

'It was bad news,' he answered, 'distressing news, my lord – the worst of news. I am sorry to be the bearer of it.'

The Earl had been uneasy for some time during the evening, as he glanced at Mr. Havisham, and when he was uneasy he was always ill-tempered.

'Why do you look so at the boy!' he exclaimed irritably. 'You have been looking at him all the evening as if—— See here now, why should you look at the boy, Havisham, and hang over him like some bird of ill-omen! What has your news to do with Lord Fauntleroy?'

'My lord,' said Mr. Havisham, 'I will waste no words. My news has everything to do with Lord Fauntleroy. And if we are to believe it – it is not Lord Fauntleroy who lies sleeping before us, but only the son of Captain Errol. And the present Lord Fauntleroy is the son of your son Bevis, and is at this moment in a lodging-house in London.'

The Earl clutched the arms of his chair with both his hands until the veins stood out upon them; the veins stood out of his forehead too; his fierce old face was almost livid.

'What do you mean!' he cried out. 'You are mad! Whose lie is this?'

'If it is a lie', answered Mr. Havisham, 'it is painfully like the truth. A woman came to my chambers this morning. She said your son Bevis married her six years ago in London. She showed me her marriage certificate. They quarrelled a year after the marriage, and he paid her to keep away from him. She has a son five years old. She is an American of the lower classes – an ignorant person – and until lately she did not fully understand what her son could claim. She consulted a lawyer, and found out that the boy was really Lord Fauntleroy and the heir to the earldom of Dorincourt; and she, of course, insists on his claims being acknowledged.'

There was a movement of the curly head on the yellow satin cushion. A soft, long, sleepy sigh came from the parted lips, and the little boy stirred in his sleep, but not at all restlessly or uneasily. Not at all as if his slumber were disturbed by the fact that he was being proved a small impostor and that he was not Lord Fauntleroy at all and never would be the Earl of Dorincourt. He only turned his rosy face more on its side as if to enable the old man who stared at it so solemnly to see it better.

The handsome, grim old face was ghastly. A bitter smile fixed itself upon it.

'I should refuse to believe a word of it,' he said, 'if it were not such a low, scoundrelly piece of business that it becomes quite possible in connection with the name of my son Bevis. It is quite like Bevis. He was always a disgrace to us. Always a weak, untruthful, vicious young brute with low tastes – my son and heir, Bevis, Lord Fauntleroy. The woman is an ignorant, vulgar person, you say?'

'I am obliged to admit that she can scarcely spell her own name,' answered the lawyer. 'She is absolutely uneducated and openly mercenary. She cares for nothing but the money. She is very handsome in a coarse way, but——'

The fastidious old lawyer ceased speaking and gave a sort of shudder.

The veins on the old Earl's forehead stood out like purple cords. Something else stood out upon it too – cold drops of moisture. He took out his handkerchief and swept them away. His smile grew even more bitter.

'And I,' he said, 'I objected to – to the other woman, the mother of this child' – pointing to the sleepy form on the sofa – 'I refused to recognize her. And yet she could spell her own name. I suppose this is retribution.'

Suddenly he sprang up from his chair and began to walk up and down the room. Fierce and terrible words poured forth from his lips. His rage and hatred and cruel disappointment shook him as a storm shakes a tree. His violence was something dreadful to see, and yet Mr. Havisham noticed that at the very worst of his wrath he never seemed to forget the little sleeping figure on the yellow satin cushions, and that he never once spoke loud enough to awaken it.

'I might have known it,' he said. 'They were a disgrace to me from their first hour! I hated them both; and they hated me! Bevis was the worst of the two. I will not believe this yet though! I will contend against it to the last. But it is like Bevis – it is like him!'

And then he raged again and asked questions about the woman, about her proofs, and pacing the room, turned first white and then purple in his repressed fury.

When at last he had learned all there was to be told, and knew the worst, Mr. Havisham looked at him with a feeling of anxiety. He looked broken and haggard and changed. His rages had always been bad for him, but this one had been worse than the rest because there had been something more than rage in it.

He came slowly back to the sofa, at last, and stood near it.

'If anyone had told me I could be fond of a child,' he said, his harsh voice low and unsteady, 'I should not have believed them. I always detested children – my own more than the rest. I am fond of this one; he is fond of me' (with a bitter smile). 'I am not popular; I never was. But he is fond of me. He never was afraid of me – he always trusted me. He would have filled my place better than I have filled it. I know that. He would have been an honour to the name.'

He bent down and stood a minute or so looking at the happy, sleeping face. His shaggy eyebrows were knitted fiercely, and yet somehow he did not seem fierce at all. He put up his hand, pushed the bright hair back from the forehead, and then turned away and rang the bell.

When the largest footman appeared, he pointed to the sofa.

'Take,' he said, and then his voice changed a little, 'take Lord Fauntleroy to his room.'

11 Anxiety in America

When Mr. Hobbs's young friend left him to go to Dorincourt Castle and become Lord Fauntleroy, and the groceryman had time to realize that the Atlantic Ocean lay between himself and the small companion who had spent so many agreeable hours in his society, he really began to feel very lonely indeed. The fact was, Mr. Hobbs was not a clever man, nor even a bright one; he was indeed rather a slow and heavy person, and he had never made many acquaintances. He was not mentally energetic enough to know how to amuse himself, and in truth he never did anything of an entertaining nature but read the newspapers and add up his accounts. It was not very easy for him to add up his accounts, and sometimes it took him a long time to bring them out right; and in the old days little Lord Fauntleroy, who had learned how to add up quite nicely with his fingers and a slate and pencil, had sometimes even gone to the length of trying to help him; and then too he had been so good a listener and had taken such an interest in what the newspaper said, and he and Mr. Hobbs had held such long conversations about the Revolution and the British and the elections and the Republican party, that it was no wonder his going left a blank in the grocery store. At first it seemed to Mr. Hobbs that Cedric was not really far away, and would come back again; that some day he would look up from his paper and see the lad standing in the doorway, in his white suit and red stockings, and with his straw hat on the back of his head, and would hear him say in his cheerful little voice: 'Hallo, Mr. Hobbs! This is a hot day – isn't it?' But as the days passed on and this did not happen, Mr. Hobbs felt very dull and uneasy. He did not even enjoy his newspaper as much as he used to. He would put the paper down on his knee after reading it, and sit and stare at the high stool for a long time. There were some marks on the long legs which made him feel quite dejected and melancholy. They were marks made by the heels of the next Earl of Dorincourt, when he kicked and talked at the same time. It seems that even youthful earls kick the legs of things they sit on; noble blood and lofty lineage do not prevent it. After looking at those marks Mr. Hobbs would take out his gold watch and open it and stare at the inscription: 'From his oldest friend, Lord Fauntleroy, to Mr. Hobbs. When this you see, remember me.' And after staring at it awhile he would shut it up with a loud snap, and sigh and get up and go and stand in the doorway – between the box of potatoes and the barrel of apples – and look up the street. At night, when the store was closed, he would light his pipe and walk slowly along the pavement until he reached the house where Cedric had lived, on which there was a sign that read, 'This House to Let'; and he would stop near it and look up and shake his head, and puff at his pipe very hard, and after a while walk mournfully back again.

This went on for two or three weeks before any new idea came to him. Being slow and ponderous, it always took him a long time to reach a new idea. As a rule he did not like new ideas, but preferred old ones. After two or three weeks, however, during which, instead of getting better, matters really grew worse, a novel plan slowly and deliberately dawned upon him. He would go to see Dick. He smoked a great many pipes before he arrived at the conclusion, but finally he did arrive at it. He would go to see Dick. He knew all about Dick. Cedric had told him, and his idea was that perhaps Dick might be some comfort to him in the way of talking things over.

So one day when Dick was very hard at work blacking a customer's boots, a short stout man with a heavy face and a bald head stopped on the pavement and stared for two or three minutes at the boot-black's sign, which read:

PROFESOR DICK TIPTON
CAN'T BE BEAT.

He stared at it so long that Dick began to take a lively interest in him, and when he had put the finishing touch to his customer's boots he said:

'"Why boss!" he exclaimed, "d'ye know him yerself?"

'Want a shine, sir?'

The stout man came forward deliberately and put his foot on the rest.

'Yes,' he said.

Then, when Dick fell to work, the stout man looked from Dick to the sign and from the sign to Dick.

'Where did you get that?' he asked.

'From a friend o' mine,' says Dick, 'a little feller. He guv' me the whole outfit. He was the best little feller ye ever saw. He's in England now. Gone to be one o' those lords.'

'Lord – Lord,' asked Mr. Hobbs, with ponderous slowness, 'Lord Fauntleroy – goin' to be Earl of Dorincourt?'

Dick almost dropped his brush.

'Why, boss,' he exclaimed, 'd'ye know him yerself?'

'I've known him', answered Mr. Hobbs, wiping his warm forehead, 'ever since he was born. We were lifetime acquaintances – that's what *we* were.'

It really made him feel quite agitated to speak of it. He pulled the splendid gold watch out of his pocket and opened it, and showed the inside of the case to Dick.

'"When this you see, remember me",' he read. 'That was his parting keepsake to me. "I don't want you to forget me" – those were his words – I'd ha' remembered him', he went on, shaking his head, 'if he hadn't given me a thing, an' I hadn't seen hide nor hair on him again. He was a companion as *any* man would remember.'

'He was the nicest little feller I ever see,' said Dick. 'An' as to sand – I never ha' seen so much sand to a little feller. I thought a heap o' him, I did – an' we was friends too – we was sort o' chums frum the fust, that little 'un an' me. I grabbed his ball from under a stage fur him, an' he never forgot it; an' he'd come down here, he would, with his mother or his nuss, an' he'd holler: "Hallo, Dick!" at me, as friendly as if he was six feet high, when he warn't knee high to a grasshopper, and was dressed in gal's clo'es. He was a gay little chap, and when you was down on your luck it did you good to talk to him.'

'That's so,' said Mr. Hobbs. 'It was a pity to make an earl out of him. He would have *shone* in the grocery business – or dry goods either; he would have *shone*!' And he shook his head with deeper regret than ever.

It proved that they had so much to say to each other that it was not possible to say it all at one time, and so it was agreed that the next night Dick should make a visit to the store and keep Mr. Hobbs company. The plan pleased Dick well enough. He had been a street waif nearly all his life, but he had never been a bad boy, and he had always had a private yearning for a more respectable kind of existence. Since he had been in business for himself, he had made enough money to enable him to sleep under a roof instead of out in the streets, and he had begun to hope he might reach even a higher plane in time. So, to be invited to call on a stout, respectable man who owned a corner store, and even had a horse and wagon, seemed to him quite an event.

'Do you know anything about earls and castles?' Mr. Hobbs inquired. 'I'd like to know more of the particulars.'

'There's a story some on 'em in the *Penny Story Gazette*,' said Dick. 'It's called the "Crime of a Coronet; or, the Revenge of the Countess May". It's a boss thing too. Some of us boys 're takin' it to read.'

'Bring it up when you come,' said Mr. Hobbs, 'an' I'll pay for it. Bring all you can find that have any earls in 'em. If there aren't earls, markises 'll do, or dooks – though *he* never made mention of any dooks or markises. We did go over coronets a little, but I never happened to see any. I guess they don't keep 'em 'round here.'

'Tiffany 'd have 'em if anybody did,' said Dick, 'but I don't know as I'd know one if I saw it.'

Mr. Hobbs did not explain that he would not have known one if he saw it. He merely shook his head ponderously.

'I s'pose there is very little call for 'em,' he said, and that ended the matter.

This was the beginning of quite a substantial friendship. When Dick went up to the store Mr. Hobbs received him with great hospitality. He gave him a chair tilted against the door, near a barrel of apples, and after his young visitor was seated, he made a jerk at them with the hand in which he held his pipe, saying:

'Help yerself.'

Then he looked at the story papers, and after that they read and discussed the British aristocracy; and Mr. Hobbs smoked his pipe very hard and shook his head a great deal. He shook it most when he pointed out the high stool with the marks on its legs.

'There's his very kicks,' he said impressively; 'his very kicks. I sit and look at 'em by the hour. This is a world of ups an' it's a world of downs. Why, he'd set there, and eat biscuits out of a box, an' apples out of a barrel, an' pitch his cores into the street; an' now he's a lord a-livin' in a castle. Those are a lord's kicks; they'll be an earl's kicks some day. Sometimes I says to myself, says I, "Well, I'll be jiggered!"'

He seemed to derive a great deal of comfort from his reflections and Dick's visit. Before Dick went home they had a supper in the small back room; they had biscuits and cheese and sardines, and other canned things out of the store, and Mr. Hobbs solemnly opened two bottles of ginger ale, and pouring out two glasses, proposed a toast.

'Here's to *him*!' he said, lifting his glass, 'an' may he teach 'em a lesson – earls an' markises an' dooks an' all!'

After that night the two saw each other often, and Mr. Hobbs was much more comfortable and less desolate. They read the *Penny Story Gazette* and many other interesting things, and gained a knowledge of the habits of the nobility and gentry which would have surprised those despised classes if they had realized it. One day Mr. Hobbs made a pilgrimage to a bookstore down town for the express purpose of adding to their library. He went to a clerk and leaned over the counter to speak to him.

'I want', he said, 'a book about earls.'

'What!' exclaimed the clerk.

'A book', repeated the groceryman, 'about earls.'

'I'm afraid', said the clerk, looking rather queer, 'that we haven't what you want.'

'Haven't?' said Mr. Hobbs anxiously. 'Well, say markises then – or dooks.'

'I know of no such book,' answered the clerk.

Mr. Hobbs was much disturbed. He looked down at the floor, then he looked up.

'None about female earls?' he inquired.

'I'm afraid not,' said the clerk with a smile.

'Well,' exclaimed Mr. Hobbs, 'I'll be jiggered!'

He was just going out of the store, when the clerk called him back and asked him if a story in which the nobility were chief characters would do. Mr. Hobbs waid it would – if he could not get an entire volume devoted to earls. So the clerk sold him a book called *The Tower of London*, written by Mr. Harrison Ainsworth, and he carried it home.

When Dick came they began to read it. It was a very wonderful and exciting book, and the scene was laid in the reign of the famous English queen who is called by some people Bloody Mary. And as Mr. Hobbs heard of Queen Mary's deeds and the habit she had of chopping people's heads off, putting them to the torture and burning them alive he became very much excited. He took his pipe out of his mouth and stared at Dick, and at last he was obliged to mop the perspiration from his brow with his red pocket-handkerchief.

'Why, he ain't safe!' he said. 'He ain't safe! If the women folks can sit up on their thrones an' give the word for things like that to be done, who's to know what's happening to him this very minute? He's no more safe than nothing! Just let a woman like that get mad, an' no one's safe!'

'Well,' said Dick, though he looked rather anxious himself, 'ye see this 'ere 'un isn't the one that's bossin' things now. I know her name's Victohry, an' this 'un here in the book – her name's Mary.'

'So it is,' said Mr. Hobbs, still mopping his forehead, 'so it is. An' the newspapers are not sayin' anything about any racks, thumbscrews or stake-burnin's – but still it doesn't seem as if 'twas safe for him over there with those queer folks. Why, they tell me they don't keep the Fourth o' July!'

He was privately uneasy for several days; and it was not until he received Fauntleroy's letter and had read it several times, both to himself and to Dick, and had also read the letter Dick got about the same time, that he became composed again.

But they both found great pleasure in their letters. They read and reread them, and talked them over and enjoyed every word of them. And they spent days over the answers they sent, and read them over almost as often as the letters they had received.

It was rather a labour for Dick to write his. All his knowledge of reading and writing he had gained during a few months when he had lived with his elder brother, and had gone to a night school; but, being a sharp boy, he had made the most of that brief education, and had spelled out things in newspapers since then, and practised writing with bits of chalk on pavements or walls or fences. He told Mr. Hobbs all about his life and about his elder brother, who had been rather good to him after their mother died, when Dick was quite a little fellow. Their father had died some time before. The brother's name was Ben, and he had taken care of Dick as well as he could, until the boy was old enough to sell newspapers and run errands. They had lived together, and as he grew older Ben had managed to get along until he had quite a decent place in a store.

'And then,' exclaimed Dick with disgust, 'blest if he didn't go an' marry a gal! Just went and got spoony, an' hadn't any more sense left! Married her, an' set up house-keepin' in two back rooms. An' a hefty 'un she was, a regular tiger-cat. She'd tear things to pieces when she got mad – and she was mad *all* the time. Had a baby just like her – yell day 'n' night! An' if I didn't have to 'tend it, an' when it screamed, she'd fire things at me. She fired a plate at me one day an' hit the baby – cut its chin. Doctor said he'd carry the mark till he died. A nice mother she was! Crackey! but didn't we have a time – Ben 'n' mehself 'n' the young 'un. She was mad at Ben because he didn't make money faster; 'n' at last he went out West with a man to set up a cattle ranch. An' he hadn't been gone a week 'fore, one night, I got home from sellin' my papers, 'n' the rooms wus locked up 'n' empty, 'n' the woman o' the house, she told me Minna 'd gone – shown a clean pair o' heels. Some 'un else said she'd gone across the water to be nuss to a lady as had a little baby too. Never heard a word of her since – nuther has Ben. If I'd ha bin him, I wouldn't ha' fretted a bit – 'n' I guess he didn't. But he thought a heap o' her at the start. Tell you, he was spoons on her. She was a daisy-lookin' gal, too, when she was dressed up 'n' not mad. She'd big black eyes 'n' black hair down to her knees; she'd make it into a rope as big as your arm, and twist it 'round 'n' round her head; 'n' I tell you her eyes 'd snap! Folks used to say she was part *I*tali-un – said her mother or father 'd come from there, 'n' it made her queer. I tell ye she was one of 'em – she was!'

He often told Mr. Hobbs stories of her and of his brother Ben, who, since his going out West, had written once or twice to Dick. Ben's luck had not been good, and he had wandered from place to place; but at last he had settled on a ranch in California, where he was at work at the time when Dick became acquainted with Mr. Hobbs.

'That gal,' said Dick one day, 'she took all the grit out o' him. I couldn't help feeling sorry for him sometimes.'

They were sitting in the store doorway together, and Mr. Hobbs was filling his pipe.

'He oughtn't to 'ave married,' he said solemnly as he rose to get a match. 'Women – I never could see any use in 'em myself.'

As he took the match from its box, he stopped and looked down on the counter.

'Why,' he said, 'if here isn't a letter! I didn't see it afore. The postman must have laid it down when I wasn't noticin', or the newspaper slipped over it.'

He picked it up and looked at it carefully.

'It's from *him*!' he exclaimed. 'That's the very one it's from!'

He forgot his pipe altogether. He went back to his chair quite excited, and took his pocket-knife and opened the envelope.

'I wonder what news there is this time,' he said.

And then he unfolded the letter and read as follows:

DORINCOURT CASTLE.

MY DEAR MR HOBBS,—i write this in a great hury becaus i have something curous to tell you i know you will be very much suprised my dear frend when i tel you. It is all a mistake and i am not a lord and I shall not have to be an earl there is a lady whitch was marid to my uncle bevis who is dead and she has a little boy and he is lord fauntleroy because that is the way it is in England the earls eldest sons little boy is the earl if every body else is dead i mean if his farther and grandfarther are dead my grandfarther is not dead but my uncle bevis is and so his boy is lord Fauntleroy and i am not becaus my papa was the youngest son and my name is Cedric Errol like it was when I was in New York and all the things will belong to the other boy i thought at first i should have to give him my pony and cart but my grandfarther says i need not my grandfarther is very sorry and i think he does not like the lady but preaps he thinks dearest and i are sorry becaus i shall not be an earl i would like to be an earl now better than i thout i would at first becaus this is a beautifle castle and i like every body so and when you arc rich you can do so many things i am not rich now becaus when your papa is only the youngest son he is not very rich i am going to learn to work so that I can take care of dearest i have been asking Wilkins about grooming horses preaps i might be a groom or a coachman, the lady brought her little boy to the castle and my grandfarther and Mr. Havisham talked to her i think she was angry she talked loud and my grandfarther was angry too i never saw him angry before i wish it did not make them all mad i thort i would tell you and Dick right away becaus you would be intrusted so no more at present with love from

your old frend

CEDRIC ERROL (Not lord Fauntleroy).

Mr. Hobbs fell back in his chair, the letter dropped on his knee, his penknife slipped to the floor and so did the envelope.

'Well', he ejaculated, 'I am jiggered!'

He was dumbfounded that he actually changed his exclamation. It had always been his habit to say, 'I *will* be jiggered,' but this time he said, 'I *am* jiggered.' Perhaps he really *was* jiggered. There is no knowing.

'Well,' said Dick, 'the whole thing's bust up, hasn't it?'

'Bust!' said Mr. Hobbs. 'It's my opinion it's all a put-up job o' the British 'ristycrats to rob him of his rights because he's an American. They've had a spite agin us ever since the Revolution, an' they're takin' it out on him. I told you he wasn't safe, an' see what's happened! Like as not, the whole government's got together to rob him of his lawful ownin's.'

He was very much agitated. He had not approved of the change in his young friend's circumstances at first, but lately he had become more reconciled to it, and after the receipt of Cedric's letter he had perhaps even felt some secret pride in his young friend's magnificence. He might not have a good opinion of earls, but he knew that even in

America money was considered rather an agreeable thing, and if all the wealth and grandeur were to go with the title, it must be rather hard to lose it.

'They're trying to rob him,' he said, 'that's what they're doing, and folks that have money ought to look after him.'

And he kept Dick with him until quite a late hour to talk it over, and when that young man left he went with him to the corner of the street; and on his way back he stopped opposite the empty house for some time, staring at the 'To Let', and smoking his pipe in much disturbance of mind.

12 The Rival Claimants

A very few days after the dinner-party at the Castle, almost everybody
in England who read the newspapers at all knew the romantic story of
what had happened at Dorincourt. It made a very interesting story
when it was told with all the details. There was the little American boy
who had been brought to England to be Lord Fauntleroy, and who was
said to be so fine and handsome a little fellow, and to have already
made people fond of him; there was the old Earl, his grandfather, who
was so proud of his heir; there was the pretty young mother who had
never been forgiven for marrying Captain Errol; and there was the
strange marriage of Bevis, the dead Lord Fauntleroy, and the strange
wife, of whom no one knew anything, suddenly appearing with her
son, and saying that he was the real Lord Fauntleroy and must have his
rights. All these things were talked about and written about, and
caused a tremendous sensation. And then there came the rumour that
the Earl of Dorincourt was not satisfied with the turn affairs had taken,
and would perhaps contest the claim by law, and the matter might end
with a wonderful trial.

There never had been such excitement before in the county in
which Erlesboro was situated. On market-days people stood in groups
and talked and wondered what would be done; the farmers' wives
invited one another to tea that they might tell one another all they had
heard and all they thought and all they thought other people thought.
They related wonderful anecdotes about the Earl's rage and his
determination not to acknowledge the new Lord Fauntleroy, and his
hatred of the woman who was the claimant's mother. But of course it
was Mrs. Dibble who could tell the most, and who was more in
demand than ever.

'An' a bad look-out it is,' she said. 'An' if you were to ask me, ma'am, I should say as it was a judgment on him for the way he's treated that sweet young cre'tur' as he parted from her child – for he's got that fond of him an, that set on him an' that proud on him as he's a'most drove mad by what's happened. An' what's more, this new one's no lady, as his little lordship's ma is. She's a bold-faced, black-eyed thing, as Mr. Thomas says no gentleman in livery 'u'd bemean hisself to be guv orders by; an' let her come into the house, he says, an' he goes out of it. An' the boy don't no more compare with the other one than nothin' you could mention. An' mercy knows what's goin' to come of it all, an' where it's to end, an' you might have knocked me down with a feather when Jane brought the news.'

In fact there was excitement everywhere; at the Castle, in the library, where the Earl and Mr. Havisham sat and talked; in the servant's hall, where Mr. Thomas and the butler and the other men and women servants gossiped and exclaimed at all times of the day; and in the stables, where Wilkins went about his work in a quite depressed state of mind, and groomed the brown pony more beautifully than ever, and said mournfully to the coachman that he 'never taught a young gen'leman to ride as took to it more nat'ral or was a better-plucked one than he was. He was a one as it were some pleasure to ride behind'.

But in the midst of all this disturbance there was one person who was quite calm and untroubled. That person was the little Lord Fauntleroy who was said not to be Lord Fauntleroy at all. When first the state of affairs had been explained to him, he had felt some little anxiousness and perplexity, it is true, but its foundation was not in baffled ambition.

While the Earl told him what had happened, he had sat on a stool holding on to his knee, as he so often did when he was listening to anything interesting; and by the time the story was finished he looked quite sober.

'It makes me feel very queer,' he said; 'it makes me feel – queer!'

The Earl looked at the boy in silence. It made him feel queer too – queerer than he had ever felt in his whole life. And he felt more queer still when he saw that there was a troubled expression on the small face which was usually so happy.

'Will they take Dearest's house away from her – and her carriage?' Cedric asked in a rather unsteady, anxious little voice.

'*No!*' said the Earl decidedly – in quite a loud voice in fact. 'They can take nothing from her.'

'Ah,' said Cedric with evident relief. 'Can't they?'

Then he looked up at his grandfather, and there was a wistful shade in his eyes, and they looked very big and soft.

'That other boy,' he said rather tremulously, 'he will have to – to be your boy now – as I was – won't he?'

'*No!*' answered the Earl – and he said it so fiercely and loudly that Cedric jumped.

'No?' he exclaimed in wonderment. 'Won't he? I thought——'

He stood up from his stool quite suddenly.

'Shall I be your boy, even if I'm not going to be an earl?' he said. 'Shall I be your boy, just as I was before?' And his flushed little face was all alight with eagerness.

How the old Earl did look at him from his head to foot, to be sure! How his great shaggy brows did draw themselves together, and how queerly his deep eyes shone under them – how very queerly!

'My boy!' he said – and, if you'll believe it, his very voice was queer, almost shaky and a little broken and hoarse, not at all what you would expect an earl's voice to be, though he spoke more decidedly and peremptorily even than before. 'Yes, you'll be my boy as long as I live; and by George, sometimes I feel as if you were the only boy I had ever had.'

Cedric's face turned red to the roots of his hair; it turned red with relief and pleasure. He put both his hands deep into his pockets and looked squarely into his noble relative's eyes.

'Do you?' he said. 'Well then, I don't care about the earl part at all. I don't care whether I'm an earl or not. I thought – you see, I thought the one that was going to be the earl would have to be your boy too, and – and I couldn't be. That was what made me feel so queer.'

The Earl put his hand on his shoulder and drew him nearer.

'They shall take nothing from you that I can hold for you,' he said, drawing his breath hard. 'I won't believe yet that they can take anything from you. You were made for the place, and – well, you may fill it still. But whatever comes, you shall have all that I can give you – all!'

It scarcely seemed as if he were speaking to a child, there was such determination in his face and voice; it was more as if he were making a promise to himself – and perhaps he was.

He had never before known how deep a hold upon him his fondness for the boy and his pride in him had taken. He had never seen his strength and good qualities and beauty as he seemed to see them now. To his obstinate nature it seemed impossible – more than impossible – to give up what he had so set his heart upon. And he had determined that he would not give it up without a fierce struggle.

Within a few days after she had seen Mr. Havisham, the woman who claimed to be Lady Fauntleroy presented herself at the Castle, and brought her child with her. She was sent away. The Earl would not see her, she was told by the footman at the door; his lawyer would attend to her case. It was Thomas who gave the message, and who expressed his opinion of her freely afterward, in the servants' hall. He 'hoped' he said, ''as he had wore livery in 'igh famblies long enough to know a lady when he see one, an' if that was a lady he was no judge of females'.

'The one at the Lodge,' added Thomas loftily, ''Merican or no 'Merican, she's one o' the right sort, as any gentleman u'd reckinize with 'alf a heye. I remarked it myself to Henery when fust we called there.'

The woman drove away; the look on her handsome common face half frightened, half fierce. Mr. Havisham had noticed, during his interviews with her, that though she had a passionate temper and a coarse, insolent manner, she was neither so clever nor so bold as she meant to be; she seemed sometimes to be almost overwhelmed by the position in which she had placed herself. It was as if she had not expected to meet with such opposition.

'She is evidently', the lawyer said to Mrs. Errol, 'a person from the lower walks of life. She is uneducated and untrained in everything, and quite unused to meeting people like ourselves on any terms of equality. She does not know what to do. Her visit to the Castle quite cowed her.

She was infuriated, but she was cowed. The Earl would not receive her, but I advised him to go with me to the Dorincourt Arms, where she is staying. When she saw him enter the room, she turned white, though she flew into a rage at once, and threatened and demanded in one breath.'

The fact was that the Earl had stalked into the room and stood, looking like a venerable aristocratic giant, staring at the woman from under his beetling brows, and not condescending a word. He simply stared at her, taking her in from head to foot as if she were some repulsive curiosity. He let her talk and demand until she was tired without himself uttering a word, and then he said:

'You say you are my eldest son's wife. If that is true, and if the proof you offer is too much for us, the law is on your side. In that case your boy is Lord Fauntleroy. The matter will be sifted to the bottom, you may rest assured. If your claims are proved, you will be provided for. I want to see nothing either of you or the child as long as I live. The place will unfortunately have enough of you after my death. You are exactly the kind of person I should have expected my son Bevis to choose.'

And then he turned his back upon her and stalked out of the room as he had stalked into it.

Not many days after that a visitor was announced to Mrs. Errol, who was writing in her little morning-room. The maid who brought the message looked rather excited; her eyes were quite round with amazement in fact, and being young and inexperienced, she regarded her mistress with nervous sympathy.

'It's the Earl hisself, ma'am!' she said in tremulous awe.

When Mrs. Errol entered the drawing-room a very tall, majestic-looking old man was standing on the tiger-skin rug. He had a handsome, grim old face, with an aquiline profile, a long white moustache and an obstinate look.

'Mrs. Errol, I believe?' he said.

'Mrs. Errol,' she answered.

'I am the Earl of Dorincourt,' he said.

He paused a moment, almost unconsciously, to look into her uplifted eyes. They were so like the big, affectionate, childish eyes he had seen uplifted to his own so often every day during the last few months, that they gave him a quite curious sensation.

'The boy is very like you,' he said abruptly.

'It has been often said so, my lord,' she replied, 'but I have been glad to think him like his father also.'

As Lady Lorridaile had told him, her voice was very sweet, and her manner was very simple and dignified. She did not seem in the least troubled by his sudden coming.

'Yes,' said the Earl, 'he is like – my son – too.' He put his hand up to his big white moustache and pulled it fiercely. 'Do you know', he said, 'why I have come here?'

'I have seen Mr. Havisham,' Mrs. Errol began, 'and he has told me of the claims which have beeen made——'

'I have come to tell you', said the Earl, 'that they will be investigated and contested, if a contest can be made. I have come to tell you that the boy shall be defended with all the power of the law. His rights——'

The soft voice interrupted him.

'He must have nothing that is *not* his by right, even if the law can give it to him,' she said.

'Unfortunately the law cannot,' said the Earl. 'If it could it should. This outrageous woman and her child——'

'Perhaps she cares for him as much as I care for Cedric, my lord,' said little Mrs. Errol. 'And if she was your eldest son's wife, her son is Lord Fauntleroy, and mine is not.'

She was no more afraid of him than Cedric had been, and she looked at him just as Cedric would have looked, and he, having been an old tyrant all his life, was privately pleased by it. People so seldom dared to differ from him that there was an entertaining novelty in it.

'I suppose', he said, scowling slightly, 'that you would much prefer that he should not be the Earl of Dorincourt?'

Her fair young face flushed.

'It is a very magnificent thing to be the Earl of Dorincourt, my lord,' she said. 'I know that, but I care most that he should be what his father was – brave and just and true always.

'In striking contrast to what his grandfather was, eh?' said his lordship sardonically.

'I have not had the pleasure of knowing his grandfather,' replied Mrs. Errol, 'but I know my little boy believes——' She stopped short a moment, looking quietly into his face, and then she added: 'I know that Cedric loves you.'

'Would he have loved me', said the Earl dryly, 'if you had told him why I did not receive you at the Castle?'

'No,' answered Mrs. Errol; 'I think not. That was why I did not wish him to know.'

'Well,' said my lord brusquely, 'there are few women who would not have told him.'

He suddenly began to walk up and down the room, pulling his great moustache more violently than ever.

'Yes, he is fond of me,' he said, 'and I am fond of him. I can't say I ever was fond of anything before. I am fond of him. He pleased me from the first. I am an old man, and was tired of my life. He has given me something to live for, I am proud of him. I was satisfied to think of his taking his place some day as the head of the family.'

He came back and stood before Mrs. Errol.

'I am miserable,' he said. 'Miserable!'

He looked as if he was. Even his pride could not keep his voice steady or his hands from shaking. For a moment it almost seemed as if his deep, fierce eyes had tears in them. 'Perhaps it is because I am miserable that I have come to you,' he said, quite glaring down at her. 'I used to hate you; I have been jealous of you. This wretched, disgraceful business has changed that. After seeing that repulsive woman who calls herself the wife of my son Bevis, I actually felt it would be a relief to look at you. I have been an obstinate old fool, and I suppose I have treated you badly. You are like the boy, and the boy is the first object in my life. I am miserable, and I came to you merely because you are like the boy, and he cares for you, and I care for him. Treat me as well as you can, for the boy's sake.'

He said it all in his harsh voice, and almost roughly, but somehow he seemed so broken down for the time that Mrs. Errol was touched to the heart. She got up and moved an armchair a little forward.

'I wish you would sit down,' she said in a soft, pretty, sympathetic way. 'You have been so much troubled that you are very tired, and you need all your strength.'

It was just as new to him to be spoken to and cared for in that gentle, simple way as it was to be contradicted. He was reminded of 'the boy' again, and he actually did as she asked him. Perhaps his disappointment and wretchedness were good discipline for him; if he had not been wretched he might have continued to hate her, but just at present he found her a little soothing. Almost anything would have seemed pleasant by contrast with Lady Fauntleroy; and this one had so sweet a face and voice, and a pretty dignity when she spoke or moved. Very soon, by the quiet magic of these influences, he began to feel less gloomy, and then he talked still more.

'Whatever happens', he said, 'the boy shall be provided for. He shall be taken care of, now and in the future.'

Before he went away he glanced around the room.

'Do you like the house?' he demanded.

'Very much,' she answered.

'This is a cheerful room,' he said. 'May I come here again and talk this matter over?'

'As often as you wish, my lord,' she replied.

And then he went out to his carriage and drove away, Thomas and Henry almost stricken dumb upon the box at the turn affairs had taken.

13 Dick to the Rescue

Of course as soon as the story of Lord Fauntleroy and the difficulties of the Earl of Dorincourt were discussed in the English newspapers, they were discussed in the American newspapers. The story was too interesting to be passed over lightly, and it was talked of a great deal. There were so many versions of it that it would have been an edifying thing to buy all the papers and compare them. Mr. Hobbs read so much about it that he became quite bewildered. One paper described his young friend Cedric as an infant in arms – another as a young man at Oxford, winning all the honours, and distinguishing himself by writing Greek poems; one said he was engaged to a young lady of great beauty, who was the daughter of a duke; another said he had just been married; the only thing, in fact, which was *not* said was that he was a little boy between seven and eight, with handsome legs and curly hair. One said he was no relation to the Earl of Dorincourt at all, but was a small impostor who had sold newspapers and slept in the streets of New York before his mother imposed upon the family lawyer, who came to America to look for the Earl's heir. Then came the descriptions of the new Lord Fauntleroy and his mother. Sometimes she was a gipsy, sometimes an actress, sometimes a beautiful Spaniard; but it was always agreed that the Earl of Dorincourt was her deadly enemy, and would not acknowledge her son as his heir if he could help it; and as there seemed to be some slight flaw in the papers she had produced, it was expected that there would be a long trial, which would be far more interesting than anything ever carried into court before. Mr. Hobbs used to read the papers until his head was in a whirl, and in the evening he and Dick would talk it all over. They found out what an important personage an Earl of Dorincourt was, and what a magnificent income he possessed, and how many estates he owned, and how stately and beautiful was the Castle in which he lived; and the more they learned the more excited they became.

'Seems like somethin' orter be done,' said Mr. Hobbs. 'Things like them orter be held on to – earls or no earls.'

But there really was nothing they could do but each write a letter to Cedric, containing assurances of their friendship and sympathy. They wrote those letters as soon as they could after receiving the news; and after having written them, they handed them over to each other to be read.

This is what Mr. Hobbs read in Dick's letter:

DERE FREND,—i got ure letter an Mr Hobbs got his an we are sory u are down on ure luck an we say hold on as longs u kin and dont let no one git ahed of u. There is a lot of ole theves wil make al they kin of u ef u dont kepe ure i skinned. But this is mosly to say that ive not forgot wot u did for me an if there aint no better way cum over here and go in pardners with me. Biznes is fine and ile see no harm cums to u. Enny big feler that trise to cum it over u wil hafter setle it fust with Perfessor Dick Tipton. So no more at present

DICK.

And this was what Dick read in Mr. Hobbs's letter:

DEAR SIR,—Yrs received and wd say things looks bad. I believe its a put up job and them thats done it ought to be looked after sharp. And what I write to say is two things. Im going to look this thing up. Keep quiet and I'll see a lawyer and do all I can. And if the worst happens and them earls is too many for us theres a partnership in the grocery business ready for you when yure old enough and a home and a friend in

Yrs truly,

SILAS HOBBS.

'Well,' said Mr. Hobbs, 'he's pervided for between us, if he aint a earl.'

'So he is,' said Dick. 'I'd ha' stood by him. Blest if I didn't like that little feller fust rate.'

The very next morning one of Dick's customers was rather surprised. He was a young lawyer just beginning practice; as poor as a very young lawyer can possibly be, but a bright, energetic young fellow, with a sharp wit and a good temper. He had a shabby office near Dick's stand, and every morning Dick blacked his boots for him, and quite often they were not exactly watertight, but he always had a friendly word or a joke for Dick.

That particular morning, when he put his foot on the rest, he had an illustrated paper in his hand – an enterprising paper, with pictures in it of conspicuous people and things. He had just finished looking it over, and when the last boot was polished, he handed it to the boy.

'Here's a paper for you, Dick,' he said; 'you can look it over when you drop in at Delmonico's for your breakfast. Picture of an English castle in it, and an English earl's daughter-in-law. Fine young woman too – lots of hair – though she seems to be raising rather a row. You ought to become familiar with the nobility and gentry, Dick. Begin on the Right Honourable the Earl of Dorincourt and Lady Fauntleroy. Hallo! I say, what's the matter?'

The pictures he spoke of were on the front page, and Dick was staring at one of them with his eyes and mouth open, and his sharp face almost pale with excitement.

'What's to pay, Dick?' said the young man. 'What has paralysed you?'

Dick really did look as if something tremendous had happened. He pointed to the picture, under which was written: 'Mother of Claimant (Lady Fauntleroy).'

It was the picture of a handsome woman, with large eyes and heavy braids of black hair wound around her head.

'Her!' said Dick 'My, I know her better'n I know you!'

The young man began to laugh.

'Where did you meet her, Dick?' he said. 'At Newport? Or when you ran over to Paris the last time?'

Dick actually forgot to grin. He began to gather his brushes and things together, as if he had something to do which would put an end to his business for the present.

'Never mind,' he said. 'I know her! An' I've struck work for this morning.'

And in less than five minutes from that time he was tearing through the streets on his way to Mr. Hobbs and the corner store. Mr. Hobbs could scarcely believe the evidence of his senses when he looked across the counter and saw Dick rush in with the paper in his hand. The boy was out of breath with running; so much out of breath, in fact, that he could scarcely speak as he threw the paper down on the counter.

'Hallo!' exclaimed Mr. Hobbs. 'Hallo! What you got there?'

'Look at it!' panted Dick. 'Look at that woman in the picture! That's what you look at! *She* ain't no 'ristocrat, *she* ain't!' with withering scorn. 'She's no lord's wife. You may eat me, if it ain't Minna – *Minna*! I'd know her anywhere, an' so'd Ben. Jest ax him.'

Mr. Hobbs dropped into his seat.

'I knowed it was a put-up job,' he said. 'I knowed it; and they done it on account o' him bein' a 'Merican!'

'Done it!' cried Dick with disgust. '*She* done it, that's who done it. She was allers up to her tricks; an' I'll tell yer wot come to me, the minnit I saw her pictur'. There was one o' them papers we saw had a letter in it that said somethin' 'bout her boy, an' it said he had a scar on his chin. Put 'em together – her 'n' that there scar! Why that there boy o' hers ain't no more a lord than I am! It's *Ben*'s boy – the little chap she hit when she let fly that plate at me.'

Professor Dick Tipton had always been a sharp boy, and earning his living in the streets of a big city had made him still sharper. He had learned to keep his eyes open and his wits about him, and it must be confessed he enjoyed immensely the excitement and impatience of the moment. If little Lord Fauntleroy could only have looked into the store that morning he would certainly have been interested, even if all the discussion and plans had been intended to decide the fate of some other boy than himself.

Mr. Hobbs was almost overwhelmed by his sense of responsibility, and Dick was all alive and full of energy. He began to write a letter to Ben, and he cut out the picture and enclosed it to him, and Mr. Hobbs wrote a letter to Cedric and one to the Earl. They were in the midst of this letter-writing when a new idea came to Dick.

'Say,' he said, 'the feller that give me the paper, he's a lawyer. Let's ax him what we'd better do. Lawyers knows it all.'

Mr. Hobbs was immensely impressed by this suggestion and Dick's business capacity.

'That's so!' he replied. 'This here calls for lawyers.'

And leaving the store in care of a substitute, he struggled into his coat and marched down town with Dick, and the two presented themselves with their romantic story in Mr. Harrison's office, much to that young man's astonishment.

If he had not been a very young lawyer, with a very enterprising mind and a great deal of spare time on his hands, he might not have been so readily interested in what they had to say, for it all certainly sounded very wild and queer; but he chanced to want something to do very much, and he chanced to know Dick, and Dick chanced to say his say in a very sharp, telling sort of way.

'And', said Mr. Hobbs, 'say what your time's worth a' hour and look into this thing thorough, and I'll pay the damage – Silas Hobbs, corner of Blank Street, Vegetables and Fancy Groceries.'

'Well,' said Mr. Harrison, 'it will be a big thing if it turns out all right, and it will be almost as big a thing for me as for Lord Fauntleroy; and at any rate, no harm can be done by investigating. It appears there has been some dubiousness about the child. The woman contradicted herself in some of her statements about his age, and aroused suspicion. The first persons to be written to are Dick's brother and the Earl of Dorincourt's family lawyer.'

And actually before the sun went down, two letters had been written and sent in two different directions – one speeding out of New York harbour on a mail steamer on its way to England, and the other on a train carrying letters and passengers bound for California. And the first was addressed to 'T. Havisham Esq.', and the second to 'Benjamin Tipton'.

And after the store was closed that evening, Mr. Hobbs and Dick sat in the back room and talked together until midnight.

14 The Exposure

It is astonishing how short a time it takes for very wonderful things to happen. It had taken only a few minutes, apparently, to change all the fortunes of the little boy dangling his red legs from the high stool in Mr. Hobbs's store, and to transform him from a small boy, living the simplest life in a quiet street, into an English nobleman, the heir to an earldom and magnificent wealth. It had taken only a few minutes, apparently, to change him from an English nobleman into a penniless little impostor, with no right to any of the splendours he had been enjoying. And surprising as it may appear, it did not take nearly so long a time as one might have expected to alter the face of everything again and to give back to him all that he had been in danger of losing.

It took the less time because, after all, the woman who had called herself Lady Fauntleroy was not nearly so clever as she was wicked; and when she had been closely pressed by Mr. Havisham's questions about her marriage and her boy, she had made one or two blunders which had caused suspicion to be awakened; and then she had lost her presence of mind and her temper, and in her excitement and anger had betrayed herself still further. All the mistakes she made were about her child. There seemed no doubt that she had been married to Bevis, Lord Fauntleroy, and had quarrelled with him and had been paid to keep away from him; but Mr. Havisham found out that her story of the boy's being born in a certain part of London was false; and just when they all were in the midst of the commotion caused by this discovery, there came the letter from the young lawyer in New York, and Mr. Hobbs's letters also.

What an evening it was when those letters arrived, and when Mr. Havisham and the Earl sat and talked their plans over in the library!

'After my first three meetings with her', said Mr. Havisham, 'I began to suspect her strongly. It appeared to me that the child was older than she said he was, and she made a slip in speaking of the date of his birth and then tried to patch the matter up. The story these letters bring fits in with several of my suspicions. Our best plan will be to cable at once for these two Tiptons, say nothing about them to her, and suddenly confront her with them when she is not expecting it. She is only a very clumsy plotter after all. My opinion is that she will be frightened out of her wits, and will betray herself on the spot.'

And that was what actually happened. She was told nothing, and Mr. Havisham kept her from suspecting anything by continuing to have interviews with her, in which he assured her he was investigating her statements; and she really began to feel so secure that her spirits rose immensely and she began to be as insolent as might have been expected.

But one fine morning, as she sat in her sitting-room at the inn called the Dorincourt Arms, making some very fine plans for herself, Mr. Havisham was announced; and when he entered he was followed by no less than three persons – one was a sharp-faced boy and one was a big young man, and the third was the Earl of Dorincourt.

She sprang to her feet and actually uttered a cry of terror. It broke from her before she had time to check it. She had thought of these newcomers as being thousands of miles away, when she had ever thought of them at all, which she had scarcely done for years. She had never expected to see them again. It must be confessed that Dick grinned a little when he saw her.

'Hallo, Minna!' he said.

The big young man – who was Ben – stood still a minute and looked at her.

'Do you know her?' Mr. Havisham asked, glancing from one to the other.

'Yes,' said Ben. 'I know her and she knows me.' And he turned his back on her and went and stood looking out of the window as if the sight of her was hateful to him, as indeed it was. Then the woman, seeing herself so baffled and exposed, lost all control over herself and flew into such a rage as Ben and Dick had often seen her in before.

Dick grinned a trifle more as he watched her and heard the names she called them all and the violent threats she made, but Ben did not turn to look at her.

'I can swear to her in any court,' he said to Mr. Havisham, 'and I can bring a dozen others who will. Her father is a respectable sort of man, though he's low down in the world. Her mother was just like herself. She's dead, but he's alive, and he's honest enough to be ashamed of her. He'll tell you who she is, and whether she married me or not.'

Then he clenched his hand suddenly and turned on her.

'Where's the child?' he demanded. 'He's going with me! He is done with you and so am I!'

And just as he finished saying the words, the door leading into the bedroom opened a little, and the boy, probably attracted by the sound of the loud voices, looked in. He was not a handsome boy, but he had rather a nice face, and he was quite like Ben, his father, as anyone could see, and there was the three-cornered scar on his chin.

Ben walked up to him and took his hand, and his own was trembling.

'Yes,' he said, 'I could swear to him too. Tom,' he said to the little fellow, 'I'm your father, I've come to take you away. Where's your hat?'

The boy pointed to where it lay on a chair. It evidently rather pleased him to hear he was going away. He had been so accustomed to queer experiences that it did not surprise him to be told by a stranger that he was his father. He objected so much to the woman who had come a few months before to the place where he had lived since his babyhood, and who had suddenly announced that she was his mother, that he was quite ready for a change. Ben took up the hat and marched to the door.

'If you want me again', he said to Mr. Havisham, 'you know where to find me.'

He walked out of the room, holding the child's hand and not looking at the woman once. She was fairly raving with fury, and the Earl was calmly gazing at her through his eye-glasses, which he had quietly placed upon his aristocratic eagle nose.

'Come, come, my young woman,' said Mr. Havisham. 'This won't do at all. If you don't want to be locked up, you really must behave yourself.'

And there was something so very business-like in his tones that, probably feeling that the safest thing she could do would be to get out of the way, she gave him one savage look and dashed past him into the next room and slammed the door.

'We shall have no more trouble with her,' said Mr. Havisham.

And he was right; for that very night she left the Dorincourt Arms and took the train to London, and was seen no more.

When the Earl left the room after the interview he went at once to his carriage.

'To Court Lodge,' he said to Thomas.

'To Court Lodge,' said Thomas to the coachman as he mounted the box, 'an' you may depend on it, things is taking a uniggspected turn.'

When the carriage stopped at Court Lodge, Cedric was in the drawing-room with his mother.

The Earl came in without being announced. He looked an inch or so taller and a great many years younger. His deep eyes flashed.

'Where', he said, 'is Lord Fauntleroy?'

Mrs. Errol came forward, a flush rising to her cheek. 'Is it Lord Fauntleroy?' she asked. 'Is it indeed?' The Earl put out his hand and grasped hers.

'Yes,' he answered, 'it is.'

Then he put his other hand on Cedric's shoulder.

'Fauntleroy,' he said in his unceremonious, authoritative way, 'ask your mother when she will come to us at the Castle.'

Fauntleroy flung his arms around his mother's neck.

'To live with us!' he cried. 'To live with us always!'

The Earl looked at Mrs. Errol, and Mrs. Errol looked at the Earl. His lordship was entirely in earnest. He had made up his mind to waste no time in arranging this matter. He had begun to think it would suit him to make friends with his heir's mother.

'"*Fauntleroy, ask your mother when she will come
to us at the castle.*"'

'Are you quite sure you want me?' said Mrs. Errol with her soft, pretty smile.

'Quite sure,' he said bluntly. 'We have always wanted you, but we were not exactly aware of it. We hope you will come.'

15 His Eighth Birthday

Ben took his boy and went back to his cattle ranch in California, and he returned under very comfortable circumstances. Just before his going Mr. Havisham had an interview with him in which the lawyer told him that the Earl of Dorincourt wished to do something for the boy who might have turned out to be Lord Fauntleroy, and so he had decided that it would be a good plan to invest in a cattle ranch of his own, and put Ben in charge of it on terms which would make it pay him very well, and which would lay a foundation for his son's future. And so when Ben went away he went as the prospective master of a ranch which would be almost as good as his own, and might easily become his own in time, as indeed it did in the course of a few years; and Tom, the boy, grew up on it into a fine young man and was devotedly fond of his father; and they were so successful and happy that Ben used to say that Tom made up to him for all the troubles he had ever had.

But Dick and Mr. Hobbs – who had actually come over with the others to see that things were properly looked after – did not return for some time. It had been decided at the outset that the Earl would provide for Dick, and would see that he received a solid education; and Mr. Hobbs had decided that as he himself had left a reliable substitute in charge of his store, he could afford to wait to see the festivities which were to celebrate Lord Fauntleroy's eighth birthday. All the tenantry were invited, and there were to be feasting and dancing and games in the park, and bonfires and fireworks in the evening.

'Just like the Fourth of July!' said Lord Fauntleroy. 'It seems a pity my birthday wasn't on the Fourth, doesn't it? For then we could keep them both together.'

It must be confessed that at first the Earl and Mr. Hobbs were not as intimate as it might have been hoped they would become, in the interests of the British Aristocracy. The fact was that the Earl had known very few grocery men and Mr. Hobbs had not had many close acquaintances who were earls; and so in their rare interviews conversation did not flourish. It must also be owned that Mr. Hobbs had been rather overwhelmed by the splendours Fauntleroy felt it his duty to show him.

The entrance gate and the stone lions and the avenue impressed Mr. Hobbs somewhat at the beginning, and when he saw the Castle and the flower gardens and the hothouses and the terraces and the peacocks and the dungeon and the armour and the great staircase and the stables and the liveried servants, he really was quite bewildered. But it was the picture gallery which seemed to be the finishing stroke.

'Somethin' in the manner of a museum?' he said to Fauntleroy, when he was led into the great beautiful room.

'N-no——!' said Fauntleroy rather doubtfully. 'I don't *think* it's a museum. My grandfather says these are my ancestors.'

'Your aunt's sisters!' ejaculated Mr. Hobbs. '*All* of 'em. Your great-uncle, he *must* have had a family! Did he raise 'em all?'

And he sank into a seat and looked around him with an agitated countenance, until with the greatest difficulty Lord Fauntleroy managed to explain that the walls were not lined entirely with the protraits of the progeny of his great-uncle.

He found it necessary, in fact, to call in the assistance of Mrs. Mellon, who knew all about the pictures, and could tell who painted them and when, and who added romantic stories of the lords and ladies who were the originals. When Mr. Hobbs once understood, and had heard some of these stories, he was very much fascinated and liked the picture gallery almost better than anything else; and he would often walk over from the village where he stayed at the Dorincourt Arms, and would spend half an hour or so wandering about the gallery, staring at the painted ladies and gentlemen who also stared at him, and shaking his head nearly all the time.

'And they was all earls,' he would say, 'or pretty nigh it! An' *he*'s goin' to be one of 'em, an' own it all!'

Privately he was not nearly so much disgusted with earls and their mode of life as he had expected to be, and it is to be doubted whether his strictly Republican principles were not shaken a little by a closer acquaintance with castles and ancestors and all the rest of it. At any rate, one day he uttered a very remarkable and unexpected sentiment.

'I wouldn't have minded bein' one of 'em myself!' he said – which was really a great concession.

What a grand day it was when little Lord Fauntleroy's birthday arrived, and how his young lordship enjoyed. it! How beautiful the park looked, filled with the thronging people dressed in their gayest and best, and with the flags flying from the tents and the top of the Castle! Nobody had stayed away who could possibly come, because everybody was really glad that little Lord Fauntleroy was to be little Lord Fauntleroy still, and some day was to be the master of everything. Everyone wanted to have a look at him, and at his pretty, kind mother, who had made so many friends. And positively everyone liked the Earl rather better, and felt more amiably towards him because the little boy loved and trusted him so, and because, also, he had now made friends with and behaved respectfully to his heir's mother. It was said that he was even beginning to be fond of her too, and that between his young lordship and his young lordship's mother, the Earl might be changed in time into quite a well-behaved old nobleman, and everybody might be happier and better off.

What scores and scores of people there were under the trees, and in the tents, and on the lawns! Farmers and farmers' wives in their Sunday suits and bonnets and shawls; girls and their sweethearts; children frolicking and chasing about; and old dames in red cloaks gossiping together. At the Castle there were ladies and gentlemen who had come to see the fun, and to congratulate the Earl, and to meet Mrs. Errol. Lady Lorridaile and Sir Harry were there, and Sir Thomas Asshe and his daughters, and Mr. Havisham of course; and then beautiful Miss Vivian Herbert, with the loveliest white gown and lace parasol, and a circle of gentlemen to take care of her – though she evidently liked Fauntleroy better than all of them put together. And when he saw her and ran to her and put his arms around her neck, she put her arms around him too, and kissed him as warmly as if he had been her own favourite little brother, and she said:

'Dear little Lord Fauntleroy! Dear little boy! I am so glad! I am so glad!'

And afterwards she walked about the grounds with him, and let him show her everything. And when he took her to where Mr. Hobbs and Dick were, and said to her, 'This is my old, old friend Mr. Hobbs, Miss Herbert, and this is my other old friend Dick. I told them how pretty you were, and I told them they should see you if you came to my birthday' – she shook hands with them both, and stood and talked to them in her prettiest way, asking them about America and their voyage and their life since they had been in England; while Fauntleroy stood by, looking up at her with adoring eyes, and his cheeks quite flushed with delight because he saw that Mr. Hobbs and Dick liked her so much.

'Well,' said Dick solemnly afterwards, 'she's the daisiest gal I ever saw! She's – well, she's just a daisy, that's what she is, 'n' no mistake!'

Everybody looked after her as she passed, and everyone looked after little Lord Fauntleroy. And the sun shone and the flags fluttered and the games were played and the dances danced, and as the gaieties went on and the joyous afternoon passed, his little lordship was simply radiantly happy.

The whole world seemed beautiful to him.

There was someone else who was happy too – an old man, who, though he had been rich and noble all his life, had not often been very honestly happy. Perhaps indeed I shall tell you that I think it was because he was rather better than he had been that he was rather happier. He had not indeed suddenly become as good as Fauntleroy thought him; but at least he had begun to love something, and he had several times found a sort of pleasure in doing the kind things which the innocent, kind little heart of a child had suggested – and that was a beginning. And every day he had been more pleased with his son's wife. It was true, as the people said, that he was beginning to like her too. He liked to hear her sweet voice and to see her sweet face; and as he sat in his armchair, he used to watch her and listen as she talked to her boy; and he heard loving, gentle words which were new to him, and he began to see why the little fellow who had lived in a New York side street, and known grocery men and made friends with boot-blacks, was still so well bred and manly a little fellow that he made no one ashamed of him, even when fortune changed him into the heir to an English earldom, living in an English castle.

It was really a very simple thing after all – it was only that he had lived near a kind and gentle heart, and had been taught to think kind thoughts always and to care for others. It is a very little thing, perhaps, but it is the best thing of all. He knew nothing of earls and castles; he was quite ignorant of all grand and splendid things; but he was always lovable because he was simple and loving. To be so is like being born a king.

As the old Earl of Dorincourt looked at him that day, moving about the park among the people, talking to those he knew and making his ready little bow when anyone greeted him, entertaining his friends Dick and Mr. Hobbs, or standing near his mother or Miss Herbert listening to their conversation, the old nobleman was very well satisfied with him. And he had never been better satisfied than he was when they went down to the biggest tent, where the more important tenants of the Dorincourt estate were sitting down to the grand collation of the day.

They were drinking toasts; and, after they had drunk the health of the Earl with much more enthusiasm than his name had ever been greeted with before, they proposed the health of 'Little Lord Fauntleroy'. And if there had ever been any doubt at all as to whether his lordship was popular or not, it would have been settled that instant. Such a clamour of voices and such a rattle of glasses and applause! They had begun to like him so much, those warm-hearted people, that they forgot to feel any restraint before the ladies and gentlemen from the Castle, who had come to see them. They made quite a decent uproar, and one or two motherly women looked tenderly at the little fellow where he stood, with his mother on one side and the Earl on the other, and grew quite moist about the eyes, and said to one another:

'God bless him, the pretty little dear!'

Little Lord Fauntleroy was delighted. He stood and smiled, and made bows, and flushed rosy red with pleasure up to the roots of his bright hair.

'Is it because they like me, Dearest?' he said to his mother. 'Is it,

Dearest? I'm so glad!'

And then the Earl put his hand on the child's shoulder and said to him:

'Fauntleroy, say to them that you thank them for their kindness.'

Fauntleroy gave a glance up at him and then at his mother.

'Must I?' he asked just a trifle shyly, and she smiled, and so did Miss Herbert, and they both nodded. And so he made a little step forward, and everybody looked at him – such a beautiful, innocent little fellow he was, too, with his brave, trustful face! – and he spoke as loudly as he could, his childish voice ringing out quite clear and strong.

'I'm ever so much obliged to you!' he said, 'and – I hope you'll enjoy my birthday – because I've enjoyed it so much – and – I'm very glad I'm going to be an earl – I didn't think at first I should like it, but now I do – and I love this place so, and I think it is beautiful – and – and – and when I am an earl, I am going to try to be as good as my grandfather.'

And amid the shouts and clamour of applause, he stepped back with a little sigh of relief, and put his hand into the Earl's and stood close to him, smiling and leaning against his side.

And that would be the very end of my story; but I must add one curious piece of information, which is that Mr. Hobbs became so fascinated with high life and was so reluctant to leave his young friend that he actually sold his corner store in New York, and settled in the English village of Erlesboro, where he opened a shop which was patronized by the Castle and consequently was a great success. And though he and the Earl never became very intimate, if you will believe me, that man Hobbs became in time more aristocratic than his lordship himself, and he read the Court news every morning, and followed all the doings of the House of Lords! And about ten years after, when Dick who had finished his education and was going to visit his brother in California, asked the good grocer if he did not wish to return to America, he shook his head seriously.

'Not to live there,' he said 'Not to live there; I want to be near *him*, an' sort o' look after him. It's a good enough country for them that's young an' stirrin' – but there's faults in it. There's not an aunt-sister among 'em – nor a earl!'